D0037310

ISLAND IN THE SEA OF TIME

S. M. Stirling

A ROC BOOK

ROC
Published by New American Library, a division of
Penguin Group (USA) Inc., 375 Hudson Street,
New York, New York 10014, USA
Penguin Group (Canada), 90 Eglinton Avenue East, Suite 700, Toronto,
Ontario M4P 2Y3, Canada (a division of Pearson Penguin Canada Inc.)
Penguin Books Ltd., 80 Strand, London WC2R 0RL, England
Penguin Ireland, 25 St. Stephen's Green, Dublin 2,
Ireland (a division of Penguin Books Ltd.)
Penguin Group (Australia), 250 Camberwell Road, Camberwell, Victoria 3124,
Australia (a division of Pearson Australia Group Pty. Ltd.)
Penguin Books India Pvt. Ltd., 11 Community Centre, Panchsheel Park,
New Delhi - 110 017, India
Penguin Group (NZ), 67 Apollo Drive, Mairangi Bay,
Auckland 1311, New Zealand (a division of Pearson New Zealand Ltd.)
Penguin Books (South Africa) (Pty.) Ltd., 24 Sturdee Avenue,
Rosebank, Johannesburg 2196, South Africa

Penguin Books Ltd., Registered Offices:
80 Strand, London WC2R 0RL, England

First published by Roc, an imprint of New American Library,
a division of Penguin Group (USA) Inc.

First Printing, March 1998
20 19 18

Copyright © Stephen M. Stirling, 1998
All rights reserved

Lyrics to "A Girl Needs a Knife" by Neil Gaiman are copyright © Neil
Gaiman, 1995, and used by his kind permission. They are taken from the
Flash Girls CD *Maurice and I*.

Cover art by Mike Wimmer

ROC REGISTERED TRADEMARK—MARCA REGISTRADA

Printed in the United States of America

To Jan, as always, forever.
And to Harry—
for setting a good example.

ACKNOWLEDGMENTS

Many thanks to the people of Nantucket, and *none* of the characters in this book are intended to represent any individuals living or dead! Thanks also to the United States Coast Guard, which responded nobly to the ignorant inquisitiveness of the author. All errors, mistakes, lapses of taste, and infelicities of expression are purely mine. Admiration and thanks also to the archaeologists and historians who piece together the past of our species from shards and the equivalent of landfill.

Particular thanks on-island to Tracy and Swede Plaut; to Randy Lee of Windshadow Engineering; to Wendy and Randy Hudson of Cisco Brewers (who make a *great* pale ale); to Harvey Young, the friendly (common) native Nantucketer (less common) at Young's Bicycles; to the Bartletts of Ocean View Farm; to Mimi Beman of Mitchell's Book Corner; and to many, many others.

Thanks also to Chief Petty Officer James for the tour and answering an afternoon of questions on his lovely ship!

And to John Barnes for dialectical (in both senses of the word) help; to Poul Anderson for catching a couple of embarrassing errors; to Heather Alexander for the use of her beautiful *Harvest Season;* to Laura Anne Gilman, for really *editing*; and to Walter John Williams for the manuals.

CHAPTER ONE

March, 1998 A.D.

Ian Arnstein stepped off the ferry gangway and hefted his bags. Nantucket on a foggy March evening was chilly enough to make him thankful he'd worn the heavier overcoat; Southern Californian habits could betray you, here on the coast of New England. Thirty-odd miles *off* the coast. The summer houses built out over the water were still shuttered, and most of the shops were closed—tourist season wouldn't really start until Daffodil Weekend in late April, when the population began to climb from seven thousand to sixty. He was a tourist of sorts himself, even though he came here regularly; to the locals he was still a "coof," of course, or "from away," to use a less old-fashioned term. *Everybody* whose ancestors hadn't arrived in the seventeenth century was a coof, to the core of old-time inhabitants, a "wash-ashore" even if he'd lived here for years. This was the sort of place where they talked about "going to America" when they took the ferry to the mainland.

He trudged past Easy Street, which wasn't, and turned onto Broad, which wasn't either, up to the whaling magnate's mansion that he stayed in every year. It had been converted to an inn back in the 1850s, when the magnate's wife insisted on moving to Boston for the social life. Few buildings downtown were much more recent than that. The collapse of the whaling industry during the Civil War era had frozen Nantucket in time, down to the huge American elms along Main Street and the cobblestone alleys. The British travel writer Jan Morris had called it the most beautiful small town in the world, mellow brick and shingle in Federal or neoclassical style. A ferociously restrictive building code kept it that way, a place where Longfellow and

Whittier would have felt at home and Melville would have taken a few minutes to notice the differences.

Mind you, it probably smells a lot better these days. Must have reeked something fierce when the harborfront was lined with whale-oil renderies. It had its own memories for him, now. Still painful, but life was like that. People died, marriages too, and you went on.

He hurried up Broad Street and hefted his bags up the brick stairs to the white neoclassical doors with their overhead fanlights flanked by white wooden pillars. The desk was just within, but the tantalizing smells came from downstairs. The whalers were long gone, but they still served a mean seafood dinner in the basement restaurant at the John Cofflin House.

Doreen Rosenthal pecked at her computer and sneezed; there was a dry tickle in her throat she was dolorously certain was another spring cold. Behind her the motors whined, turning the telescope toward the sky. It wasn't a very big reflector, just above the amateur level, but it *was* an instrument of sorts, and you could massage information out of the results. *Sort of like 0.01 percent of Mount Palomar.* Astronomy posts weren't that easy to find for student interns, and the Margaret Milson Association had given her this one. It meant living on Nantucket, but that wasn't so bad; she was the quiet sort even at U. Mass. She'd finally managed to lose some weight, having nothing better to do with her spare time than exercise. *Well, a little weight, and it's going to be more.* Even in winter, the island was a good place to bike, or you could find somewhere private to do *kata*. When it wasn't storming, of course; and there was a wild excitement to that, when the waves came crashing into the docks, spray flying higher than the roofs of the houses.

And always, there were the stars. The rooms below the observatory held decades of observation, all stored in digital form now. Endless fascination.

She took a bite out of a shrimp salad sandwich and frowned as the computer screen flickered. Not another glitch! She leaned forward, fingers unconsciously twisting a lock of her long black hair. No, the digital CCD camera was running continuous exposures. . . .

Stargazers didn't actually look at the stars through an

eyepiece anymore. It was ten minutes before she realized what was happening in the sky.

Jared Cofflin sighed and leaned back in his office chair. There really wasn't much for a police chief to do on Nantucket in the winter. An occasional drunk-and-disorderly, maybe some kids going on a joyride, now and then a domestic dispute; they'd gone seven straight years without a homicide. But April came 'round again, and pretty soon the summer people would be flooding in. Summer was busy. Coofs were a rowdy lot. Not that the island could do without them, although sometimes he very much wished it could. Once it had been Nantucketers who traveled, from Greenland to Tahiti.

With a wry grin, he thought of a slogan someone had suggested to the Chamber of Commerce once as a joke: *We used to kill a lot of whales. Come to Nantucket!*

The little police station was in a building that had once housed the fire department, and across a narrow road from a restaurant-cum-nightspot. The buildings on both sides were two stories of gray shingle with white trim, like virtually everything on the island that wasn't red brick with white trim. *About time for supper,* he thought. No point in going home; he hadn't gotten any better at serious cooking since Betty passed on five years ago. Better to step over and get a burger.

He sighed, stood, hitched at his gunbelt, and reached for his hat, looking around at the white-painted concrete blocks, the boxes of documents piled in corners and bursting out of their cardboard prisons. *Hell of a life.* And he'd had to let the belt out another notch recently; it seemed unfair, when the rest of him was the same lanky beanpole it'd been when he graduated from high school back around LBJ's inauguration.

The lights flickered. Nantucket was just about to switch over to mainland power, via an underwater cable. For the next few months they had to soldier along on the old diesel generators, though.

"Christ," he said. "Not *another* power-out."

He walked out into the street and stopped, jarred as if he'd walked into a wall. Stock-still, he stood for a full four minutes staring upward. It was the screams from people around him that brought him back to himself.

*   *   *

Nor'easter at twenty knots. Just what we needed, Captain Marian Alston thought with satisfaction. She kept a critical eye and ear on the mast captains' work as the royals and topgallants were doused and struck.

"Clew up! Rise tacks and sheets!"

"Ease the royal sheets!"

The pinrail supervisor bellowed into the wind: "Haul around on the clewlines, buntlines, and bunt-leechlines!"

The upper sails thuttered and cracked as the clewlines hauled them up to the yards, spilling wind and letting the ship come a little more upright, although the deck still sloped like the roof of a house.

"Lay them to aloft," Alston said to the sailing master. "Sea furl."

The crew swarmed up the ratlines and out along the yards that bore the sails, hauling up armfuls of canvas as they bent over the yards; doll-tiny shapes a hundred feet and more above her head as they fought the mad flailing of the wet Dacron.

No sense in leaving that much sail up, on a night as dirty as this looks to be. Too easy for the ship to be knocked down or taken aback by a sudden shift of wind. The chill bit through the thick yellow waterproof fabric of her foul-weather gear like cold damp fingers poking and prodding.

She stood with legs braced against the roll and hands locked behind her back by the ship's triple wheel, a tall slim woman from the Sea Islands of South Carolina, ebony-black, close-cropped wiry hair a little gray at the temples; her face was handsome in a high-cheeked fashion like a Benin bronze. Spray came over the quarterdeck railing like drops of salt rain, cold on her face and down her neck. The sun was setting westward over a heaving landscape of gray-black water streaked with foam, and the ship plunged across the wind with the yards sharp-braced. Her prow threw rooster tails every time the sharp cutwater plowed into a swell, twin spouts jetting up over the forecastle from the hawseholes where the anchor chains ran down through the deck. Then the ship would heave free as if shrugging her shoulders, water foaming across the forecastle deck and swirling out the scuppers.

Alston smiled behind the expressionless mask of her face. *Now this, this is real sailing,* she thought.

The Coast Guard training ship *Eagle* was a three-masted steel-hulled windjammer. It had been built in 1936, and the original incarnation was called the *Horst Wessel* before the United States took it as war reparations. There were still embarrassing swastikas buried under the layers of paint here and there, but it was sound engineering, solid work from Blohm & Voss, the firm that built the *Bismarck*. Three hundred feet from prow to stern, a hundred and fifty to the tops of the main and foremasts, eighteen hundred tons of splendid, lovely anachronism. Good for another fifty years hard sailing, if the Powers That Be didn't decide to scrap her.

"Secure the forward lookout," she said. It was getting a little dangerous for someone to perch up in the bows.

"Come about, ma'am?" the sailing master asked.

"In a minute or two, Mr. Hiller," she said.

Nantucket was off to the northeast, fairly close, and it paid to be careful in the dark; the sea between the island and Hyannis on the mainland was shoal water, full of sandbars, and southeast was worse. She'd been tacking into the teeth of the wind for practice's sake; fairly soon she'd turn and let the *Eagle* run southwestward. Cadets and crewpeople were swarming up the rigging; more stood by on deck, poised to haul on ropes. Archaic, but the best training for sea duty there was—the Coast Guard still taught stellar navigation, too, despite the fact that you could push a button on a GPS unit and get your exact location from the satellites. Lieutenant William Walker was taking a sight on Arcturus from the edge of the quarterdeck, and Victor Ortiz was running one of his pupils through the same procedure. Usually they did the first cruise of the season without cadets, but this year the Powers in their ineffable wisdom had changed the schedules a little. Completely rearranged them, in fact, causing everybody endless bother and inconvenience. It was a considerable relief to get out to sea, where a captain was her own master.

"The wind's southing, ma'am," Thomas Hiller, the sailing master, hinted.

"Brace them sharp, then."

The centuries-old litany of repeated orders echoed across the deck; *Eagle* had been built to operate the old-fashioned way, no high-geared winches or powered haulage. It ended with a boatswain's mate bellowing: "Ease starboard, haul port, lively port!"

"Heave!" shouted the line leader in a trained scream that cut through the moan of the wind.

"Ho!" chorused the twenty young men and women on the line, surging back in unison.

"Heave!"

"Ho!"

"Ma'am." Alston looked up. Hiller looked a little lost, which was a first. He'd been on the *Eagle* for eight years. "Ma'am . . . there's something odd about the compass reading."

An old-fashioned magnetic card compass binnacle stood before the wheels. She took a step and looked down into it; the card was *whirling,* spinning in complete circles. Captain Alston blinked in surprise. What on earth could cause that? The sky was clear to the horizon, only a little high cloud boiling in on the wind—unusually good weather for this time of year and these latitudes, although there might be a storm riding in on the nor'easter. No lightning, certainly. Then she noticed that the gyro repeater compass was quivering too.

Marian Alston had been in the Coast Guard much of her thirty-eight years, commanded the *Eagle* for four, and served on search-and-rescue craft and armed cutters before that; she'd joined up the year sea duty was opened to women. You learned to trust your gut. And never, never to trust the sea.

"Finish up and get them down," she said.

Cadets and crew poured down the ratlines, the latter sometimes helping the former along; for the first few weeks out, there would always be the odd officer cadet who froze a hundred and fifty feet up on a swaying rope.

A fat blue spark jumped from her hand to the metal housing between the ship's three wheels. Alston bit back a startled obscenity—you had to set an example—and shook her hand. Something white-hot stretched for an instant from sky to sea off to her left. More sparks flew; people were leaping and cursing all across the deck. Not the four hands standing on the benchlike platforms either side of the wheels, she noted with satisfaction. They flinched, their eyes went wide, but they kept her steady on the heading they'd been given.

Light flickered from left to right behind her, curving ahead of the ship in a line only a few hundred yards away—curving from east to west, in a line her navigator's eye could see was the arc of a huge circle. St. Elmo's fire ran along the *Eagle*'s rigging, blue witch-flame. The curses were turning to screams as the lightning reared up into a crawling dome of orange and white overhead. *Like being under the biggest, gaudiest salad bowl in the world,* ran through her mind as she stood paralyzed for a moment. Then the noise on deck penetrated.

Easily. The roaring wind had dropped away to nothing in the space of a few seconds, and the drumhead-taut sails slackened and thuttered limp. The motion of the ship lost its purposeful rolling plunge, changed to a shuddering as the waves turned into a formless chop, and then to a slow sway as they subsided. Shouts and screams echoed through an eerie silence as the rigging's moaning song of cloven air died.

"Silence there!" she snapped, quiet but carrying. "Mr. Roysins, let's get some order here. Whatever's happening, panic won't help."

But it would feel so good, part of her mind gibbered, looking up at the dome of lights that turned night into shadowless day.

"On with engines," she said. Max the diesel hammered into life and steerageway came on the ship. "Strike all sails. Give me a depth-finder reading."

She clenched her hands behind her back and rose slightly on her toes, ignoring the blasting arch of fire. "We've got a ship to sail."

"Got the stores covered?" Chief Cofflin asked, as he pushed through the crowd on Main Street.

"Right, liquor, grocery, and jewelry—just in case. We're stretched pretty thin."

His assistant hesitated; he was a short thin young man named George Swain, and a fourth cousin. *Everyone* on the island was a cousin, except wash-ashores. It made for a certain lack of formality. So did the fact that there were only twenty-five officers on the force.

"Some of our own people are a mite shaky, Chief."

"Ayup. Don't blame 'em, George. Still, we've got a job to do." He stopped to think for a moment, running through a list of names in his head. "Get everyone who's off-duty back on. And call Ed Geary, Dave Smith, Johnnie Scott, and Sean Mahoney. Tell them to each pick six friends they can trust and come down to the station. Deputize 'em."

George missed a step. "Chief, we can't do that on our own say-so!"

"I can and I just did," Cofflin said. "Ed's a good man and he knows an emergency when he sees one, and so are the rest. You call them and get them posted. Meanwhile, let's see if I can talk some sense into these people here." The selectmen or somebody should be doing it; he was a policeman, not a politician. But they were probably out there running around with the rest of the crowd.

He mounted the steps of the bank at the head of Main Street and looked down the cobbles toward the big planter at the foot of the street. The lights on the cast-iron lamp-posts shone on a sea of faces, on a street that should be mostly clear this time of night. Overhead the ghastly, garish lights still crawled and sparked, adding a weird touch to the upturned faces; all it needed was torches and pitchforks to be something out of a movie. He raised a battery-powered megaphone to his lips.

"Now, let's have some sense here," he said.

"What the fuck's going on?" someone yelled, and the crowd roared with him.

"QUIET, DAMMIT!"

The bullhorn cut through the gathering madness, stopped it feeding on itself.

"If I knew what was going on, I'd tell you," Cofflin said bluntly, in the silence that followed. "I can tell you going hog-wild won't help any. That—" he pointed upward toward the shimmering dome of light—"hasn't hurt anyone yet. But we've had a dozen accidents, a suicide, and two assaults-with-intent tonight. That *has* hurt people."

It wasn't real easy to have a riot in a town of four thousand people; particularly not when most of them were old-stock Yankees and phlegmatic by inclination and raising . . . but everyone was coming real close about now. He looked up. If he thought it'd do any *good,* he'd be inclined to start screaming himself. The dome of fire had been there all night, hanging over the town, over the whole island, like the face of an angry God. Every church on the island was jam-packed, but at least those people weren't causing any harm and might be doing some good.

"The phone to the mainland's out," he went on. "Radio and TV are nothing but static; the airport can't get through either. The last planes from Hyannis and Boston didn't arrive. Now why don't you all go home and get some sleep. If things aren't back to normal in the morning, we'll—"

A collective shout that was half gasp went up from the crowd. The stars were back. There was no transition this time; one minute the dome of lights was there, and the next it wasn't. He suddenly realized that a sound had accompanied it, like very faint frying bacon, noticeable only when it was gone.

The crowd's gasp turned to a long moan of relief.

"—we'll take further measures," he went on. "And we'll all try not to do anything that will make us feel damned silly in the morning, won't we?"

He could feel the tension in the crowd ease, like a wave easing back from the beach. People were laughing, talking to their neighbors, slapping each other on the back, even hugging—though he'd bet that those were coofs. A few were crying in sheer reaction. Cofflin himself breathed a silent prayer of thanks to a God he didn't believe should be bothered with trivialities. *Everything's all right,* he thought, looking up at the infinitely welcome stars. His gaze sharpened. *Mebbe so. Mebbe not.*

"So why don't you all go home now?" he went on to the people. "It's—" he looked at his wrist—"two-thirty and I'm plenty tired."

The crowd began to break up. George came up, holding his cell phone. "Geary wants to know if we still need help," he said.

"Ayup," Cofflin said. The assistant blinked surprise. "Son," Cofflin went on, "don't say a word to anyone else, but take a gander up there."

He nodded skyward. The younger man looked up. "Nothing but stars, Chief," he said. "And I'm glad to see them, I'll tell you that."

"Ayup. But take a look at the *moon,* George."

The other policeman's face went slack, then white. The moon was a crescent a few days past new; and it ought to be right out there now, getting ready to set. Instead it was nearly full. . . .

"And the North Star should be just about there. T'ain't. Just be glad nobody else's noticed yet," Cofflin said grimly. "Now let's see if the phones to the mainland are working again."

Doreen Rosenthal looked at the image on her screen and blinked again. One hand raised close-chewed nails toward her mouth, and she forced it down with an effort of will. The other twisted itself into her hair. She'd felt like weeping with relief when that weird . . . *phenomenon. Let's not get emotional here* . . . had gone away. Now she was feeling sick again, with a griping pain below her breastbone.

"Let's look for the polestar," she said. One had to be systematic. She split the screen and called up an exposure from last night's sequence beside the latest one for comparison. Her fingers flew over the keyboard. "This doesn't make any sense at all," she complained. Nothing was where it should be!

A thought struck her. *Now you're going completely nuts,* she thought. Still, it couldn't hurt. It wouldn't take a minute to call up the program and get the data fed.

More keystrokes. Nothing. *Well, there's one crazy idea junked.* Lucky nobody would ever know she'd tried. Then she paused. "Well, it can't hurt to be absolutely sure."

"Search . . . for . . . all . . . correlations," she typed. Now the program would run a back-and-forth search until it found a stellar pattern corresponding to the one on the latest CCG exposure.

Dawn was turning the eastern horizon pale pink before she was sure.

Gevalt, she thought. It seemed appropriate. Tears trickled down her face to drop and blotch on the keyboard.

This can't be happening to me! I'm an overweight Jewish grad student from Hoboken, New Jersey! Things like this didn't happen to anyone, and if they did it was to some blonde in a movie, meeting Bruce Willis or something. Her arms hugged her middle, feeling a cramping like a bad period.

Mother, help! That calmed her a little. Mother would have panicked even worse, if she had been here. "You're a scientist, act like one," she chided herself, blowing her nose and wiping the keyboard. "Let's firm this up and get a little precision here."

    * * *

"Ma'am, still nothing," the radio operator said.

Captain Alston had been staring up at the infinitely welcome stars. A new unease was eating at the first relief as she checked and rechecked. Either her memory had deserted her, or . . .

She shook her head and stepped into the small rectangular deckhouse behind the wheels, rather grandly called the Combat Information Center. She preferred to think of it as the radio shack. "Still gettin' static?" she asked.

"No, ma'am. It's clear since those lights went away. There just isn't anything to *receive*, not on any of the frequencies."

She bit back *that's impossible*. Obviously everything that had happened since sundown was impossible; nevertheless, it was happening. A thought occurred to her.

"Try a GPS reading," she said.

That should read the ship's location off to within a few feet. "Nothing, ma'am. Nothing. Maybe the storm scrambled all our electronics."

Not unless it was EMP like a fusion bomb's, Alston thought. Or maybe the elves had carried them off to fairyland and Br'er Fox would be by any minute, riding on Willy the Orca; right now one hypothesis looked about as good as another. The crewman's voice was taking on a shrill note.

"Steady, sailor." She paused. "Lieutenant, you have a pocket receiver, don't you?"

The young man nodded. It was a camper's model, accurate to within a few hundred yards, looking much like a hand calculator. William Walker pulled it out and punched at the keys.

"No reading, ma'am." His Montana twang was as expressionless as if this was a training exercise. "As far as this unit's concerned, the satellites just aren't there t'all."

"Ma'am! I've got someone on the radiophone."

Alston carefully did *not* lunge for the receiver. "Who?"

"Nantucket, ma'am." That made sense; they were only a few miles away. As much as anything made sense this night. "It's the harbor. They're sort of babbling, ma'am."

"Ms. Rosenthal, I'm really rather busy."

Cofflin's long bony face was set in implacable politeness; he ran a hand through his thinning blond hair as he spoke, his blue eyes bloodshot with sleeplessness. Most of Nantucket had gone home and gone to sleep, but the ones still awake were slowly realizing that the island was still cut off from all communication with the outside world. Pretty soon the rest would wake up, and try to turn on the TV and find out what CNN had to say. *Then we will be well and truly fucked.* Normally he wasn't much of a swearing man, hadn't been since the Navy, but now . . .

"Chief Cofflin, *I know what happened.*"

That brought him up. Doreen Rosenthal was a coof, but she wasn't one of the flake-and-nut brigade, the artists and artisans and neo-hippies who were much of the island's permanent population. She was a student of astronomy, good enough to get an internship at the MM, and Cofflin had a solid Yankee respect for learning.

"What?" he said sharply.

"I was . . . I was taking observations. When it happened. I kept the, well, I kept the video going. I got a good shot when the . . . whatever it was stopped."

Cofflin looked at her.

"I got a good shot of the *stars,* Chief Cofflin," she went on, pushing her thick-lensed glasses back up her nose.

Cofflin took her elbow. "Look, we've all had a rough night—" he began.

She pulled away. "The stars are *wrong.*"

Her voice was shrill but not hysterical. Not by tonight's standards, at least.

"How are the stars wrong?" he prompted.

"They're in the wrong places." She fumbled in the big canvas carrying bag beside her chair, one with *University of Mass. Amherst* on it, and pulled out a printout. Spreading it on the desk, she pointed out circles and lines drawn around the white dots of stars. "See, the polar orientations—"

Cofflin swallowed. "Give me the gist, please, Ms. Rosenthal."

She looked up at him, white around the lips. "I ran a comparison—I've got a stellar progressions program on my computer. This is not the sky of March 1998."

"Why haven't the morning planes arrived?" someone said plaintively. "We *still* can't raise the mainland. We've had to ground everything because we can't file flight plans, and there are people waiting for their planes!"

Cofflin held on to the tightly controlled fear that made him want to snap at the hapless airport employee, or at Rosenthal for blowing her nose behind him. The airport was a little stretch of double pavement off in the middle of the island's moor and scrubland not far from the south coast. Twin-engine prop puddle jumpers flew in from the mainland, and private planes. Right now it looked a little forlorn in the light of earliest dawn, the sky blue but bleak and cold with mare's tails of high cloud. The buildings were shingle-covered, like most stuff on the island; a bunch of mainlanders were waiting, with their children and carry-on luggage. Waiting to go to an America he suspected they'd never see again.

"Sorry, Mary," he said. "That's what I'm trying to find out. Andy Toffler here yet?"

"You called?" a voice said. "Jared. Mornin', ma'am."

Cofflin turned; there was Andy, in a battered old leather flying jacket, holding a paper cup of coffee and one of the *Emergency Town Meeting—1:00 P.M. Today* flyers the police chief had ordered spread around.

"Andy. I need an emergency flight to the mainland."

"I hate to take her up so soon," the pilot said. "God alone knows what all that whatever-it-was did to the electronics. I still can't get my radio to pick up anything but stations here on Nantucket."

"It's the only seaplane on the island," Chief Cofflin said.

Andy looked at him. "Something wrong, Jared?" he said. "I mean, beyond what we know's wrong. Why do you need a floatplane to hop over to Boston?" His eyes narrowed as he looked at Rosenthal and saw the carrying case over Cofflin's shoulder. "Why the scattergun?"

"Andy, you wouldn't believe me if I told you. Look, I don't often ask for favors, but—"

"Okay, okay," the pilot said, spreading his hands in a placating gesture. He'd been a fighter jock once, but the bravado had mellowed with the years that left him bald on top. Not all the Kentucky was out of his voice, though. "No problem. We're tanked up. Y'all come on aboard."

Cofflin handed the astronomer in through the door and followed himself, folding his lanky frame into the copilot's seat. The little floatplane shuddered as the prop spun and then settled down to a steady vibrating roar behind the silver circle. He reached for the headphones.

"Mind if I make a call?"

"Go right ahead," Toffler said, running through his flight check. "Hope you have better luck than I did."

As the airplane taxied out on the little wheels built into the floats, Cofflin turned to the frequency the Coast Guard ship used. "*Eagle, Eagle,* this is Cofflin, over," he said. "Do you read?"

"Cofflin, this is *Eagle.* Captain Alston heah." The Coast Guard officer's voice was accented like gumbo, but it carried a sense of crisp confidence that the policeman was glad to hear. "Anythin' new since we spoke?"

Alston had taken Rosenthal's news with a long silence, then calmly said that her own observations of the night sky were "compatible." It was nice to have someone else who wasn't inclined to gibber.

"I'm taking a floatplane and doing some reconnaissance on the mainland," Cofflin replied. "We need . . . ah, confirmation of Rosenthal's theory."

There was a pause on the other end of the line. Then: "Could you stop off here and pick someone up? I'd like to have one of my people go along, if you don't mind."

"Captain, I'd appreciate it. There's room for one more— just me, the pilot, and Ms. Rosenthal at present."

And the astronomer was there because he'd been afraid she'd crack up if he left her behind; crack up, and/or start babbling her findings all over town. Behind him her face was crumpled and blotched, and she was going through Kleenex at a ferocious rate. He really didn't blame her much. It must be even worse for a scientist, used to an orderly and predictable world.

"That's fine, Chief Cofflin," Alston said. "You have our location?"

"Roger that."

"We'll heave to, and anchor after you pick up my officer."

"Roger. Cofflin out." He looked at the pilot. "You got that?"

"Hop, skip, and a jump."

The Coast Guard officer turned out to be a fresh-faced young lieutenant with an M-16 over his shoulder, plus webbing with ammunition. He hopped nimbly from the ship's boat to the right float of the seaplane, and offered a hand all around as he slid into the other rear seat, putting the assault rifle between his knees. He had a camera, too, something better than the Polaroid Cofflin had brought.

"Lieutenant William Walker," he said; there was a Western twang to his voice, and he looked like a younger version of the Marlboro Man, square-jawed and handsome in a boyish way.

No, Cofflin thought. *He looks like . . . what's that guy's name . . . Redford, yeah.*

"Happy to meet you."

"Can't say as I'm too happy about anything, at the moment," Cofflin said with a dry smile, shaking his hand. It was hard and felt extremely strong. "But welcome aboard." He nodded at the assault rifle. "See you came prepared."

Walker chuckled. "The sum total of the *Eagle*'s armament, if you don't count the flare pistol," he said. "I notice . . ." He nodded at the shotgun in turn.

Conversation died away as they accelerated, throwing up spray from the floats. "Water looks odd," Toffler commented as they lifted and circled the windjammer, then headed for the mainland. "And what the hell's that?" He indicated a silvery patch below.

"Take a look," Cofflin said.

The plane banked and slid down, swooping; not all Toffler's fighter-pilot reflexes had gone the way of his hair. They leveled out and made a pass with the floats nearly touching the water, the heavy salt smell filling the cabin. And not only salt.

"It's fish," Cofflin said, wrinkling his nose. "Dead fish. Damn, but there's a lot of 'em." Seagulls swarmed around the massive shoal, diving and pecking.

"Cod," Lieutenant Walker said, peering out through binoculars. "Thousands and thousands of cod, big cod."

Cofflin grunted skeptically. There hadn't been concentrations of codfish like that around New England waters for . . . then he remembered what Rosenthal had told him, and shivered.

"What killed them?" he said, trying to lose awe in practicality.

"There's a curving mark in the water," the astronomer behind him said suddenly. He started a little; she hadn't spoken much since the airport. "See, you can follow it." Different shades of blue, and a crosshatching of waves.

The Coast Guard lieutenant used his binoculars. "The

lady's right. It's the edge of a circle, a very big circle, or at least some geometric figure. Like the effect you get with a river estuary emptying into the sea, or two very distinct currents . . . I've never seen anything quite like it, though. Like two different bodies of water just starting to merge."

"Never seen anything like it. That's something we're all getting used to saying," Cofflin said dryly. He clicked on the radiophone and relayed the information to the *Eagle*.

"Could you fly along the edge of the phenomenon for a few miles?" Alston said. "I'd like to get a radius."

"Good idea." He handed the radiophone to Walker, who called the data to his commander.

A few minutes later she answered: "Got that. Just a second. . . . Not a circle. It's pretty well a precise ellipse, centered somewhere on the island. Not an exact distance in miles or kilometers, though—something like twenty-three point four miles across and five in height. We were *just* inside the edge of it, then."

Cofflin grinned humorlessly at the tinge of bitterness and took the radiophone. "Bad luck for you, Captain—but good for the rest of us, I think. We're heading in to the coast now."

"You folks know something that I don't?" Toffler said. Sweat shone on his forehead and the high dome of his head, and the Kentucky accent was stronger.

"Fill him in, Ms. Rosenthal," Cofflin said wearily.

The fact of what had happened was beginning to sink in now, and it left silence in the wake of the astronomer's hesitant voice.

"The . . . the *transition event* must have included a body of water around the island," she finished. "That's what we're seeing here. There would be differences in temperature, salinity, and so forth. Perhaps the fish were caught at the, um, interface. It looked electrical and it affected our electronic apparatus. Where it met the water, I think it electrocuted some of the sea life."

The floatplane flew low, a few hundred feet up, over intensely blue ocean just rough enough to show whitecaps; the sky was clear but a little hazy with high cloud. After a few minutes, Toffler tipped one wing and spoke:

"Thar she blows."

Cofflin shaped a silent whistle. Thar she did, in twin-tailed spouts. He'd never in his life seen that many whales;

the spouts and glistening backs stretched for miles. "Big pod," he said expressionlessly. "Right whales. Blackfish."

Which had been virtually extinct in these waters since the eighteenth century.

By the time they overflew a Cape Cod empty of roads and houses and reached Boston, he was almost unsurprised at what they found. There was still a bay and islands, but only roughly like the maps. Dense forest grew almost to the water's edge, huge broadleaf trees towering hundreds of feet into the air, and birds rose in their tens of thousands from salt marsh and creekmouth, enough to make the pilot swerve. Toffler circled for a few minutes, aimlessly. What clear spots there were on dry land looked to be the result of old forest fires. Under his numbness Cofflin thought how beautiful it was, with an unhuman comeliness that made Yosemite look like a cultivated garden.

"Well," he said, "I think you were right, miss." Rosenthal nodded and sneezed into her Kleenex.

Walker pointed. "There."

A stretch of shingle beach edged a seaside clearing where a creek ran into the sea. In it were a score or so of shelters made by bending saplings into U-shapes, and then covering the sides with bark and brush, like Stone Age versions of Quonset huts. Fires trickled smoke, and human figures pointed upward. When the plane came lower overhead they scattered like drops of mercury on dry ice; a few pushed big log canoes into the water and paddled frantically away along the shore. Lower, and they could see a woman turn back, scoop up a crying infant, and scuttle for the edge of the woods with the child in her arms.

"Can you take us down there, Andy?"

"Sure," the pilot said. "Water's calm, and that looks like a sloping surface—I should be able to ground the floats."

The seaplane turned into the wind and sank. There was a skip . . . skip . . . skip sensation as the floats touched; the airplane surged forward, then sank back to a slightly nose-up position as Toffler turned it toward the shore. Cofflin cracked the door and looked down.

"Sand and gravel . . . getting shallow, any minute now . . ."

Toffler killed the engine and the plane coasted forward. The aluminum of the floats touched bottom; they slewed about slightly and stopped. Cofflin picked up his shotgun and stepped down, onto the float and then into knee-deep water. He wiped his brow.

"Hot for March," he said, looking inland.

Walker followed him, using his binoculars again. "Can't see any of the . . . Indians, I suppose. Looks like they've cleared out."

"Wouldn't you?" Toffler asked. "Let's get the plane secured. We need to stake down some lines."

The men occupied themselves. Rosenthal took some items from her backpack and fiddled with them. "You're right, Chief Cofflin. It's eighty Fahrenheit." That was unusual for Massachusetts in early spring. "And look at the trees, the other vegetation."

Cofflin straightened up and did. "Season's pretty far along," he said. "But how do we know it's March?"

"I worked on my calculations," she said. "It's March, all right. Early spring, at least, but I'm morally certain it's the same day, down to the hour, that it, ah, would have been. Sunrise was at exactly the right time." She paused. "The climate may well be in a warmer phase."

Cofflin nodded, feeling his stomach twist with a sensation that was becoming unpleasantly familiar; sheer whirling disorientation, as if the ground kept vanishing from beneath his feet. He clicked off half a dozen pictures of the shore, then handed the camera to the astronomer.

"Let's take a look. Andy, you take the left; Lieutenant Walker, you're right; I'm point; and Ms. Rosenthal, you keep behind me, and get plenty of pictures."

"Why?" she said, with a flicker of spirit, and a sneeze.

"Because you're not armed," he replied, glad to see the stunned depression leaving her face.

The air was not only warm, it was fresh like nothing he'd ever smelled. Closer to the huts it wasn't as pleasant; evidently whoever lived there had never heard of latrines. From the look of it they kept dogs, too. The primitive wickiups were even cruder than they'd looked at a distance; inside were hides and furs, bedding made of spruce branches and grass. All around was a scattering of tools made of bone, stone, horn, and wood, and shallow lug-handled soapstone dishes. Hide stretchers, fire-carved bowls, wooden racks lashed together with thongs that held drying fish . . . He picked up a flint scraper somebody had abandoned beside a raw deerhide. Not a museum piece, he

realized suddenly. It was still warm from the hand of whoever had left it.

"Incoming!"

Cofflin hit the deck with old reflex, and something went
shunk into the ground ahead of him. *A spear,* he thought.
It seemed pretty slender for that, though, more like a huge
arrow. His hands racked the slide of the shotgun automatically. *Five rounds, mixed rifled slugs and deershot,* he
thought.

Then he saw the men. Six, maybe ten of them running
forward in dashes from cover to cover, short brown men
with queues of shoulder-length black hair, naked except for
hide breechclouts looped through belts around their waists.
One of them fitted another of the slender javelins into a
wooden holder with a curved end piece to hold a shaft in
position and a butterfly-shaped stone weight on its end. He
ran a few steps, half-skipping sideways, and swept his arm
forward. The spear came forward, pivoting out on the end
of the flexing stick.

Spear-thrower, Cofflin realized. *Atlatl.* He'd read about it
in a *National Geographic* article. The stick extended the
length of the thrower's arm, giving enormous leverage. The
spear blurred through the air and someone shouted with
pain—Andy, he realized with a sudden stab of panic. Their
pilot. The surge of adrenaline cut through the glassy barrier
insulating him from the world. Suddenly everything became
real again, and he knew that he could die here.

"Over their heads!" he shouted, and let a round off.
Walker followed suit, the M-16 giving its light spiteful crack
over the dull thump of his shotgun.

One of the Indians screamed and threw away his spears,
pelting back toward the woods. The others dropped to the
ground. Cofflin twisted to look over his shoulder; Rosenthal was next to Andy, working on his leg. A spear was
through the pilot's calf, but from the way he was swearing
it wasn't immediately fatal.

"How's he look?" he asked.

"I'm not sure," the astronomer said. "There isn't much
bleeding."

"Hurts like hell, but it's through the muscle," the pilot
said, his voice tight with control. "Miss, get my knife out
and cut it off here—that's right. Now let's pull . . . *Christ,
woman* . . . sorry. Okay, okay, now pack it with the hand-

kerchief." He looked up at Cofflin. "I've got a first-aid kit in the plane. Should be all right, but I'm not going to be runnin' any marathons soon."

"I doubt they hold 'em here," Cofflin said, voice tight with relief.

"Heads up," the young Coast Guard officer said.

The Indians were getting up . . . and moving forward, fitting more javelins to their spear-throwers. Their voices sounded, a shrill yipping broken with howls like wolves. Deliberately like wolves, he realized.

"Damn, but they've got guts," Cofflin said. *Thinking straight, too. Saw that the noise didn't hurt anyone, and now they're coming to clear the strangers out of their homes. Probably their families're waiting back in the woods.*

Maybe in their stories the hero always beat the evil magician in the end. It still took guts to attack outlandish men who climbed out of a great metal bird.

"I hate to hurt them," Toffler said, echoing his thought. "It's their home."

"Them or us. That Mighty Mattel is more accurate than my scattergun, lieutenant. Try to wound."

Walker set himself, exhaled, and squeezed his trigger. This time one of the Indians fell, screaming and clutching at his leg. The others wavered. Walker fired again, and dirt spurted up at another's feet. That was enough for most of them; they followed the first and ran yelling into the woods. The last man threw down his javelins and spear-thrower and charged, a longer stabbing spear in one hand and a flint hatchet in the other, dodging and jinking like a broken-field runner. His face was a contorted mass of glaring eyes and bared teeth.

"Damn, he's not stopping for shit," Cofflin said, Navy reflexes taking over from peacetime habit. "Take him down, lieutenant." *Poor brave bastard.*

Crack. The Indian fell.

The islanders waited tensely, but there was no sound save the birds and insects. Nothing moved. At last Cofflin stood. "Let's take a look at them," he said. "Ms. Rosenthal, could you get the aid kit from the plane, please?"

The wounded Indians were short men, neither over five-six; they wore a long roach of hair on top of their heads, braided at the back, but the sides of their heads were shaved and painted vermilion. Their skin was a light copper brown, their features sharper than Cofflin would have expected. The first one to fall had a gouge over the big muscle of his thigh; he stopped trying to squeeze it shut with his hands and started crawling when they approached, naked terror on his face. He pulled a stone knife from a birchbark sheath at his waist and swiped at them; he was chanting, something high-pitched and rhythmic.

Death song, Cofflin guessed, dredging at bits of old knowledge. *Okay, let's see if we can communicate.*

He put down his shotgun and spread his open hands. The Indian waited, tense and wary. His eyes widened as Rosenthal came up beside the other man. Cofflin glanced aside at her. *Oh,* he thought. The astronomer was wearing a T-shirt under an open jean jacket, and her gender was entirely obvious.

"I think the fact that you're a woman makes him less frightened, Ms. Rosenthal," he said. "Wait a minute. Get out one of the rolls of bandage."

Slowly, Cofflin mimed a wound on his leg, and binding it up, then pointed to his companion. After a moment, the Indian made an odd circular motion of his head that seemed to correspond to a nod. His bloody hand began to return the flint knife to its sheath. Cofflin shook his head, then made a waving motion with his hands. He took the scraper from his own belt, tossed it aside, and pointed to the Indian as he recovered it.

Reluctantly, the Indian did the same with his own weapon. "All right, doctor," Cofflin said. "Move slowly, and be careful. I've got you covered. Put some of the antiseptic powder on it, then bandage it up."

He held the shotgun ready. Rosenthal licked her lips and moved in, motions slow and careful. The narrow black eyes of the wounded man went wide for an instant as the astringent powder struck the wound, but he moved the leg to let the woman finish bandaging it. She sat back, sneezed, and looked helplessly at her blood-covered hands.

"All right, back off again," Cofflin said. Maybe the gesture of goodwill would help. "Lieutenant, what about the other one?"

"He's bad," the Coast Guardsman said. "Sorry. Thighbone's broken, compound fracture. I've stopped the bleeding and put him out, but without a good doctor and antibiotics, he's a dead man."

Cofflin watched the other wounded Indian drag himself backward toward the woods. *If we leave him, he'll die. On the other hand, if we take him away, they'll think God knows what. On the third hand, we can patch him up, maybe teach him a little English, and he can interpret. Give him some presents, knives, pots and pans, costume jewelry. Squanto R Us.*

"All right, then," he said. "Let's get out of this screwup."

The limp weight of the unconscious man brought back other, unpleasant memories for Cofflin. He thrust them aside; manhandling the dead weight into the airplane was hard enough as it was. As an afterthought, he taped the man's wrists and ankles together. Having him wake up and freak in midair was not something he wanted to experience. Then they returned for the pilot; with an arm over each man's shoulder he made a slow hopping way back to the airplane.

"Goddam," he sighed, settling into the pilot's seat. "You know, I was feeling pretty lousy coming here. As if nothing was real, you know. But this, this feels *damned* real. Shot in the leg by an Indian. Goddam."

Cofflin nodded. So did Walker, and Rosenthal sneezed agreement. He picked up the radiophone.

"Might as well have an ambulance waiting," he said, looking down at the wounded man lying unconscious at his feet. The bandage around his thigh was glistening red. "And then there's that Town Meeting."

"Captain, it's the XO. I think you should come at once, ma'am."

Marian Alston cursed silently and tore herself away from the radiophone. "Take down anything they say," she said to the operator.

The cadet who'd brought the news looked scared green. Lieutenant Commander Roysins, her executive officer, had excused himself half an hour ago, when Walker reported the news from . . . where Boston ought to have been but wasn't. No way to keep it secret, not on shipboard; the rumor was running through the hull like a fire, and she'd have to do something—say something to the crew—soon.

"Ma'am."

The wind on the quarterdeck was fairly stiff, and the *Eagle* pitched at her anchors, bows into the whitecaps.

"Captain on deck!"

"As you were."

She returned the officer of the deck's salute and went down the companionway behind the radio shack. The officers' cabins were tiny cubicles on the deck directly below. The largest was the flag cabin at the rear, usually empty except for important visitors. Hers was just ahead of it to the left, little more than a glorified closet, something she'd often thought confirmed her conviction that God was an ironist. The rest of Officers' Country stretched ahead and to the wardroom on the other side.

The XO's cabin door was shut. "He won't answer, ma'am. I tried."

"Stand easy," she said, and pounded on the metal with her own fist. "Mr. Roysins, open this door! That's an order!"

Silence. Fear dried her mouth. She slammed at the door again. "Roysins!"

Still nothing. She licked her lips. "Beauchamp," she said to the cadet. "My regards to the officer on watch in the engine room, and someone with a toolkit to this cabin, on the double."

"Ma'am!" The cadet bolted, glad of an order.

Alston waited, expressionless, until he returned. With him was a bald man in stained blues with a toolbox and a squared-away baseball cap with EAGLE across its front in gold letters.

"Ma'am?" he said.

"Let's have this open, Chief," she said. Baker, a CPO and a reliable man.

He nodded phlegmatically and went to work. Thirty seconds later the door swung open. There wasn't any of the smell she'd feared, the sort that happened when a man hung or shot himself. Roysins was lying on his back in the bunk, staring open-eyed at the low ceiling of the cabin. One arm trailed down, moving with the motion of the ship, and an empty glass rolled beside an equally empty plastic pill container. The other arm clutched something to his chest. Alston ducked in and put her fingers to the man's neck, just to be sure. The skin was already cooling. She gently pulled the framed picture of Roysins's wife and children free, then crossed the man's arms on his chest and closed the eyes, holding them shut for a moment to make sure they'd stay that way. A coverlet went over his face.

God damn you, Roysins, she thought sadly. *I* needed *you, dammit.* She was going to need all the officers, to keep things going. This was no time to bug out. Roysins wouldn't have suicided if a car crash or a tornado had lost him his family, she felt fairly sure. It was the feeling of absolute separation. *But that's an illusion. Nobody's died, they just got . . . unavailable.* Still, she was beginning to realize why the old buccaneers had used marooning as a punishment, instead of just knocking someone on the head and pitching him overboard.

"My compliments to the operations officer, and I'll see her in my cabin," she said. "Chief, get a sailmaker and some cloth in here."

She looked at her watch. 1000 hours. Christ.

CHAPTER TWO

March, 1250 B.C.

March, Year 1 After the Event

Ian Arnstein wandered down the street, pushing the bicycle he'd just bought with his last two-hundred-dollar traveler's check; he always felt ridiculous riding one of the things—another of the drawbacks of being several inches over six feet. *And I never even liked basketball.* It was a cruelly pretty day, blue sky and wisps of cloud, warm enough that he was comfortable in a long-sleeved shirt and no jacket. There were daffodils set out in pots, and the whole town had the scrubbed, fresh-painted air that it always did . . . and nothing was the same. He wheeled the bicycle into the guesthouse where he was staying and up the stairs into his room, and stood looking at the fireplace.

"Still functional, I suppose," he said to himself, stroking his bushy reddish-brown beard; it had stayed luxuriant while the hair vanished from the top of his head. Except for that he might have been a face off an Assyrian bas-relief, heavy hooked nose and strong features, apart from the mild scholar's eyes.

When winter came, a working fireplace . . .

The bags and boxes from the grocery store nearly hid it—nearly hid the whole wall, come to that. Spare clothing, canned food, dried peas, everything he could think of. There hadn't been many people in the stores, and he'd still been able to write traveler's checks, which proved that nobody had thought through the implications of the rumors. He looked at his watch. Nearly noon. Unbelievable rumors, but they accounted for what had happened better than anything else.

Time for the Town Meeting. *That* was going to be

crowded. It was also probably going to determine whether or not he met a long, nasty death in the coming months. Possibly whether he was killed for the meat on his bones. He shivered. That was the problem with the sort of reading he did for recreation. History undermined certain comfortable assumptions about how human beings acted. . . .

He sat at the desk, slumped with his head in his hands. At this point in the type of novel that was his favorite reading the hero would be brimming with ideas, getting people moving, organizing things, providing some leadership.

"The problem is," he said to himself, "I couldn't lead three sailors into a whorehouse. Somebody else will have to do it."

"The moderator's not . . . available," the town clerk said.

"What do you mean, *not available*?" Jared Cofflin answered, frantic. "Look, Joseph, we've *got* to get this Town Meeting under way."

The old man nodded somberly. "But Alan Scinters isn't going to moderate it," he said.

The sound from the crowd out in the auditorium of the high school was growing louder, more insistent. To Cofflin's ears it was beginning to sound uncomfortably like the mob on Main Street last night.

There was supposed to be room for seven hundred and fifty, plus another hundred and fifty in the little annex where nonvoters sat. From the noise, there were more than a thousand heads crammed in, and more milling around in the corridors outside. The auditorium was named after a former principal of the old Nantucket High School; it was big, a broad blunt wedge with concrete steps that were upholstered in blue where people sat and left bare in the strips they were supposed to use for stairs. The whole idea had been sold to the Town Meeting as a civic center and place for amateur theatricals as well as a school facility.

The principal had been a fearsome old biddy, by all accounts, and she'd ruled with an iron hand for the best part of two generations. He tried to imagine how she'd have handled this.

"Why *isn't* Scinters going to do it?"

"Because he and the chairman of the board of selectmen have been in Boston since Friday last!" Joseph Starbuck snapped. "Of the other four selectmen, Vida . . . Dr. Coleman has her under sedation." The town clerk's mouth shut like a steel trap. "Along with about a hundred others right now. Four suicides, he says, and a dozen attempted. Jane's babbling, and that leaves Tom and Clarice."

Cofflin blinked: those two weren't the brightest of the lot. "Well, somebody's got to do it. Listen to them out there! They *need* someone who sounds like he knows what he's doing. You're the town clerk."

"I'm not up to it. Too old, getting set in m'ways. Afraid you'll have to do it, Cofflin."

"*Me?* I'm the police chief, not an elected official!"

"You're also the only one who seems to be doing anything much. You know what's going on. Get out there, man, or we'll have a riot on our hands."

For a moment Jared Cofflin felt his mind stutter. *I wanted someone to take over!* The reality of what he'd found on the mainland still sat in his mind like a lump of stodgy food, refusing to split up and move through the rest of his brain. If he couldn't come to terms with this . . . *event*, how on earth was he going to help everyone else do it? *They* all *want someone to take over, and they want it now.*

Jared Cofflin took a deep breath and walked out onto the stage. The acoustics were superb, enough to bring across the rasp of fear and building rage in the crowd's undertone. These people were in fear of their lives, and if the man who spoke didn't give them something to calm their terror they might well rip him into quite literal pieces. And then go on to destroy the town and any chance of saving their lives in a surge of blind ferocity.

He walked out to the podium and stood in front of the meeting, shoulders slightly hunched as if he was facing into a winter storm. "All right," he began. "You know we're still not in contact with anyone on the mainland. Some of you have probably heard why. Now I'll tell you all. The whole—" he suppressed the word that came to mind— "damned island is back in, well, in the past."

The noise burst over him like surf. He quieted it—somehow, eventually—and went on: "Over at the observatory, Ms. Rosenthal—" he nodded to where she sat not far from him—"used the computer and telescope there to figure it out."

"What if they're wrong? Computers—" someone shouted.

"You may not have noticed," Cofflin said, stung into heavy sarcasm, "but we're still cut off from the mainland. Because there isn't any mainland, at least, no buildings or roads. Just wilderness. I went and took a look personally. Nothing but trees and Indians with spears.

"Quiet! We're not going to get anything done by shouting!" Cofflin bellowed, angry at last and somehow no longer in the least afraid. "George, Matt, Susan, get those people there out of here!"

Most of those who'd broken down let themselves be led away quietly. One had to be put in a hammerlock and handcuffed. "Put him in the cells—he can cool off overnight," Cofflin said. Unfortunately, that was one of the town selectmen. *There goes half of what's left of our elected government.*

The babble subsided. "All right, now you know. Andy Toffler and me and Ms. Rosenthal here, and Lieutenant Walker from the *Eagle,* flew over to the mainland this morning. There's no Hyannis, and there's no Boston, no roads and no buildings. The Indians threw spears at us. We took some pictures—Andy, could you get that projector working?"

The wounded pilot wheeled his chair about on the dais, slipping the pictures they'd taken under an overhead projector that threw them enlarged onto a pull-down screen.

The pictures flicked on, sharp close-ups of the Indian camp. Then a blurred one as Doreen dove for cover, and then another series done with steady clarity. *She may have been on the verge of a breakdown, but she kept doing her share of the work,* he thought with respect. Good pictures too: an Indian winding up, running forward, the streak of the spear, then the weapon standing in the ground. At last two of each of the wounded Indians, close-ups of their faces and gear.

"Captain Alston of the Coast Guard ship *Eagle*—the *Eagle* was just offshore last night and ended up here with us, for those of you who didn't know—has something to say. Let's let Captain Alston talk, people," he said.

His own voice was hoarse, his head ringing with too little sleep and too much coffee. Captain Alston cleared her throat. Hard weathered hands turned the uniform cap as she stood, then stopped as if she was forcing herself not to fidget. Otherwise she stood calm as a statue, a welcome contrast to how most people were acting.

"We were near the edge of the, ah, phenomenon," she said.

Her Southern accent made her voice soft, but the diction was oddly precise, almost finicky, as if every word was carefully chosen. The voice of an autodidact, self-educated.

"It evidently, ah, transposed an ellipse of ocean as well as the island, reachin' several miles offshore; we've seen evidence of that—dead fish caught at the rim, and so fo'th. The only thing we could tell about it was that it was electrical in nature—there were static discharges and effects on our electronic equipment. My observations of the stars confirm Ms. Rosenthal's. The stars have moved, and the shift's . . . the same sort that would be produced by bein' . . . thrown back in time. How long did you say, Ms. Rosenthal?" She pronounced the title *miz*.

"The spring of 1250 B.C.," Rosenthal said. "Three thousand two hundred and forty-eight years before the present. Before what was . . . before the . . . transition event."

"All right, now," Cofflin said when order had been restored. "Doc Coleman?"

Coleman, a lean, bony man in his sixties who headed the island's hospital-clinic, stood up. "I'm treating the . . . Indian. His leg wound's stabilized. He's never been vaccinated, he's got no fillings or other dental work on his teeth—remarkably good teeth, by the way—and from the X-rays, he's had several broken bones that healed without benefit of casts."

"All right," Cofflin said. "We've obviously got an emergency here. We're . . . " It was hard to go on. "We're back in the past, somehow—the whole island is. The question is, what are we going to do about it?"

Someone raised his hand. Cofflin recognized him vaguely, as much because of the way he looked as for a few brief exchanges of words; some sort of professor who spent part of his summers here. A Californian; tall, balding, with a brown bush of beard and beak-nosed. He looked a lot calmer than most of the people here. Maybe he'd keep people paying attention until things quieted down.

"You, sir."

"Ian Arnstein—Dr. Ian Arnstein. I'm a professor of classical history at the University of San Diego. I was wondering if anyone had considered the implications of what's happened to us."

The Westerner looked around. "Look, either . . . whatever happened will reverse itself, or it won't. If it goes into reverse, we don't have to worry. We *do* have to worry if it doesn't. We're all in danger of death if it doesn't."

"How so, professor?" Cofflin asked. *We're in danger of complete chaos, sure enough.* That had been his main worry.

"Chief Cofflin, there's no United States out there. There are no oil refineries, no farms to ship us produce, no A&P to deliver vegetables and canned food. No factories. Once we use anything up, it's *gone* unless we replace it ourselves. What are we going to eat? Winter's coming in another seven months; what are we going to heat houses with? Banks, money—it's all worthless now."

That brought complete silence. The sheer weirdness of what had happened had overwhelmed most, to the exclusion of practical matters. Cofflin was impressed. *This one is a thinker,* he decided. Then the thought struck home.

"You have any ideas, Professor Arnstein?" he said calmly, while he scribbled a note: *Get the guards back on the stores SOONEST.* He handed the note to his assistant. The man nodded and hurried out.

"Well, yes. I've, ah, I've read a lot of speculative fiction about things like this, and I'm a historian. We need to get organized. Supplies will have to be rationed. We have to get working on inventory so we know what it is we've got, and then we have to conserve everything that can't be replaced. We need to start building up our food supplies. It ought to be possible to fish—the fishing grounds around here should be fantastically rich—and we should see what can be grown. There will be whales. We could get firewood and so forth from the mainland—and maybe we could trade, as well."

"Indians!" someone shouted. "We could get corn from the Indians, like the Pilgrims."

"If you hadn't *shot* at them," Pamela Lisketter said.

Cofflin recognized her too, a member of the flake-and-nut contingent, a weaver who sold fantastically expensive handmade blankets to support a "simple" lifestyle. She was a tall thin woman, her only noticeable features large green-gold eyes and an air of intense conviction; she was involved in every good cause, and a great many marginal ones as well.

"Ms. Lisketter," Cofflin said, "I assure you we acted strictly in self-defense. Now please let Professor Arnstein finish."

Arnstein shook his head. "We can trade for hides and game, maybe, but not corn. If this is the thirteenth century B.C., the local paleo-Indians will still be pure hunter-gatherers. Maize hasn't gotten far out of Mexico yet. There were farming villages . . . ah, there *are* farming villages away down in Mexico and Central America, but even the Olmecs haven't happened yet, or maybe they're just starting. I'd have to look it up."

A hand went up, and Cofflin nodded. The chief librarian of the Athenaeum rose, Martha Stoddard, a spinster lady of about forty, dry and spare; archaeology was her hobby.

"The Olmecs built . . . are building . . ." For a moment uncharacteristic puzzlement showed on her slightly horse-like Yankee face. "Well, the first Olmec ceremonial centers were started about the thirteenth century B.C. at San Lorenzo, yes, and the first Chavin temples in Peru. Dr. Arnstein is right about the local Indians, I'm afraid. Not paleo-Indians, late Archaic phase. No farming to speak of. Possibly some gardens with squash and gourds, but no corn. You said that there was forest down to the water's edge near Boston?"

"Ayup, Ms. Stoddard."

"There you are, then. When the Puritans arrived, that was all open land around there—cleared by Indians for cornfields and fuel. That hasn't happened yet."

She sat down again, and Arnstein continued: "Europe, though, Europe is in the Bronze Age. We could get grain there. We *do* have a ship."

Everyone looked at Captain Alston. "I'm willing to help," she said. "But Dr. Arnstein is right—we need to get organized."

Arnstein nodded vigorously. "We need an executive—a president, a coordinator, something like that. And a council. I don't exactly know the procedures for your Town Meetings, but I'd like to propose—"

"Hey, he's not a registered voter in this town!" Lisketter exclaimed. "He's an off-islander!"

You're one to talk, Pamela Lisketter, Cofflin thought.

Granted she'd been on the island ten years, and was quite popular with her own crowd, but she was a coof nonetheless.

Cofflin knocked his empty water glass on the podium as a makeshift gavel. "We're *all* locals now," he said sharply. "Think about it for a moment, people."

Arnstein had stopped, uncertain. He cleared his throat and went on: "I'd like to propose Chief Cofflin as . . . ah, as chief executive officer for the duration of the emergency or until we come up with something better."

The town clerk shot to his feet. "Seconded!"

"Now, wait a—" Cofflin began. Hands shot up all over the room.

"Carried by acclamation," the man said.

You're going to regret this, Joseph Starbuck, Cofflin thought with a glower.

Arnstein spoke again. "I'd also like to propose that the chief executive officer appoint a council to propose measures to get us through this emergency. We can elect a . . . a legislature later, but we need to do things *right now* if we're going to pull through."

"Seconded!" Joseph Starbuck said again.

The hands shot up again. Cofflin's neck bristled slightly; he could feel the mood of the meeting shifting, turning from unfocused rage to an equally unbalanced hope. It could turn again as quickly, if he disappointed it.

"All right," Cofflin said. "And you're one, Joseph. Captain Alston, you're another; Professor Arnstein, Ms. Rosenthal, Ms. Lisketter, Ms. Brand"—who owned Brand Farms, the island's main nursery and truck-garden operation—"and the rest of the selectmen."

"Chief," Dr. Coleman said, touching his sleeve as the last of the townsfolk straggled out. "A word."

"Mmm-hmm?"

"The Indian's dying," he said.

Cofflin blinked surprise. "You said his leg was stable?" he said mildly.

"It is," Coleman nodded. "That's not it. As far as I can tell, he's dying of the common cold. Possibly the flu, but it looks more like a monster cold on steroids, and that's what Ms. Rosenthal has. I thought it might be better to tell you quietly."

"Nobody *dies* of a cold, Doc."

"I know that, but he's managing it somehow. Progressive congestion of the nasal and bronchial passages, faster than I can drain, fever over a hundred and seven. Nothing I've got works." He shook his head. "It came on like wildfire. It's as if his immune system had no resistance at all, as if he were a petri dish full of a growth solution."

Arnstein had come up while they were speaking. "Virgin field," he murmured.

Cofflin's eyes flew open. He remembered Rosenthal sneezing. Coleman was nodding somberly.

"It's what they call it when a disease hits a population with no previous exposure," he said quietly. "The results can be . . . unpleasant. Minor diseases, childhood diseases, they become killers."

Arnstein bobbed his head; he was six-six, and seemed accustomed to directing his body language downward. "Ninety percent of the Indians in the Americas died within a century of Columbus," he said. "Never been exposed to the Afro-Eurasian disease environment. It might be even worse here."

"Why?" Cofflin whispered.

"Well, we don't have smallpox, thank God, but these Indians—they're a lot more thinly scattered, less numerous than the ones the European discoverers met, would have met, three thousand years from now. There probably aren't any epidemic diseases at all, and not many endemic ones. But now . . ." he shrugged. "Measles . . . I wonder if anyone here has measles? We'd better check. That could be very bad. Even in Europe and Asia, it didn't arrive in the Roman Empire until the second century, but when it did a quarter of the population died of it. Hmmm . . ." He trailed off, mumbling.

"Jesus," Cofflin said.

Coleman's face had turned pale. "I'll . . . we'll have to be very careful, *very* careful, with anyone who touches shore off this island. I'm going to start checking to see if anyone has measles."

"Measles, syphilis, anything like that," Arnstein said. "Otherwise, we could exterminate whole groups just by breathing on them."

"Jesus." Cofflin kneaded his eyes in a vain attempt to dislodge what felt like hot sand.

"I should test," Coleman said. "For everything. AIDS, too . . . of course, I can't test the entire . . ." Suddenly a grim smile lit his face. "Wait a minute. I *can* do that. Can't I?"

"Doctor, you can do anything you please for the public good right now. Anything you can get past me and the Town Meeting, that is."

"And that's the situation, people," Captain Alston said.

She was speaking from the quarterdeck bridge above the pilothouse, with the ship's officers around her. The crew covered the main deck, standing by divisions as if for an inspection at Quarters, all within easy hearing distance. They murmured, the sound growing louder and louder, until the petty officers and boatswain shouted for quiet.

Easier to deal with than civilians, she thought. The town meeting ashore had been the next thing to a riot, and it had lasted most of the day. At least you could tell people in uniform to shut up and listen. She glanced over at Nantucket; they'd dropped anchor in the dredged channel that led to the steamer dock, there being no room to tie up with the big ferry at its moorings. For the moment she was just as glad not to be at quayside. The situation on board would be easier to handle if it could be kept isolated from the rest of the island for a little while.

This anchorage is going to be a bitch in rough weather, she thought, her mind distracted for a moment. *Sheltered enough for ordinary storms, but in a really stiff norther . . .*

When full quiet had been restored, she went on:

"Ladies and gentlemen, we're in an . . . unprecedented situation. There is no United States Coast Guard. There is no United States. We're marooned, adrift in time."

She pointed. "A little more than seven thousand of us altogether, and the rest of the planet in a state of savagery. However, we still need discipline and organization. Accordingly, anyone who wants to take his or her chance ashore may do so now. Those who wish to remain with the ship will be under orders as before, and I'm placing the ship at the disposal of Chief Cofflin and the Council in Nantucket. There may be no United States, but these people are still Americans—and helping them is what we're in this uniform for."

"What about our families?" someone called.

Alston clamped her hands behind her back. "There's nothing to be done about that. Everyone and everythin' we knew is *gone*. People, either this . . . whatever it was will reverse itself, or it won't," she said. "If it does, everything is back to normal—except that y'all make your fortunes on the talk-show circuit."

That brought a shaky laugh. She went on: "But we have to operate on the assumption that it won't. Because if it doesn't, and we sit down and wait for a return that doesn't happen, we're all going to die. If we work, we may pull through. As for our people ashore . . . they'll have to assume we were lost, somehow. Nobody knows what happened back up in the . . . future." It was still a little hard to say it. "At a guess, the year 1998 got the Nantucket that should be here, in which case they'll have some inkling of what happened to us. Grief is natural, but we've no time to sit down and cry."

Not if I have any say in the matter, she added mentally.

Keeping people too busy to think was an ancient military tradition, and for very good reason. She hadn't asked to be stuck in this situation, but things weren't going to fall apart if she had anything to do with it. The United States Coast Guard, or the Lord God Almighty, or fate, or whatever, had left them in her hands.

The uproar began as she finished speaking. It lasted far into the night, and ended with half a dozen cadets and a couple members of her crew sedated or under restraint.

"But nobody," she said in the officers' wardroom, "wants to jump ship."

"I think it may have struck them that at least they get rations here," Hiller said.

Like her, the sailing master didn't have any ties ashore. Well, she had two children, but they'd gone with their father in the divorce and that was going on fifteen years ago. Wouldn't have done any good to fight for custody, not in South Carolina with what John knew and threatened to reveal if she contested, and it would have wrecked her career when things came out. At least John had warned her first, not just blabbed to the wind.

Some of the other officers still looked as if they'd been hit behind the ear with a sandbag. Most of them did have people back when. Walker, now, Walker looked *excited*. She had her doubts about him, anyway. Intelligent, hardworking, and they even shared a hobby in the martial arts, but there was something . . .

"Speaking of rations, how are we found?" she asked.

The fuel-oil tanks were full—they'd topped up in New London before they left. Thank God for small mercies. The *Eagle*'s auxiliary was a fairly recent thousand-horsepower Caterpillar diesel named Max, practically immortal given that the ship's own machine shop could make most replacement parts; the generators and freshwater plant ran off the same fuel system. Oil would be the weak point. *Wind only from now on,* she thought. *We use the auxiliary in nothing but* real *emergencies.*

"Ma'am," the quartermaster said. "We'll be out of fresh vegetables and the like shortly. Flour, canned and dried goods, and so forth, maybe four weeks. But ma'am, two hundred people take a lot of feeding."

"Reduced rations immediately then. Use the perishables first, and I'll talk to Chief Cofflin and see what they can spare from shore. From what Lieutenant Walker says, the fishing and so forth will be very good. We can lend a hand with that right away. We'll also probably be making a run to England—well, to the British Isles, whatever they're called here-and-now—to trade for grain. I'd like your ideas on that ASAP, by tomorrow morning, if you please."

Officers needed to be kept busy too. "Also on how we can convert the ship for operations in a low-tech environment. More fuel's out of the question, and so are electronics or most machine parts except those we can make in the shop on board or get from the island. We'll be lucky to get cordage and sails."

"Captain Alston." That was the former operations officer, Sandy Rapczewicz, now acting XO. She was a competent-looking woman in her thirties with a weathered, pug-nosed Slavic face; her eyes were red, but she seemed calm enough. A teenaged son ashore, Alston remembered, and a husband. "I was just thinking. We're in the past, right?"

She nodded. Rapczewicz went on: "But if we, um, do things—make contact with the locals, that sort of thing—won't we, um, sort of change the way things happened? It isn't in the history books, thousands of people and a ship appearing in Moses' time."

Silence fell around the table. Alston nodded. "Sandy,

you're right." Some of the officers were beginning to look frightened. "On shore, I talked about that to some of Cofflin's Council, a history professor and an astronomer, and the town librarian, who's an amateur archaeologist." Odd what types ended up on Nantucket, but it wasn't your average island. "One thing they agreed on—even if we all dropped dead tomorrow morning, we've *already* changed history."

"How's that, Captain? We haven't done anything yet."

"We're here. A lot of buildings and so forth are here, including brick and concrete and stone that'll last. When Europeans arrived, they'd find the ruins. More important, the islanders already sent some people ashore, they had contact with the Indians—and according to the doctor in charge of the local clinic, the one they brought back is dying of the common cold."

That brought everyone up. "The person with the cold sneezed on one of the others on shore, too, which means their whole tribe probably has it by now. You think *that* isn't going to change history? They'll pass it on, since not all of them will keel over at once. And as a practical matter, everyone on the island isn't going to drop dead tomorrow. People will try to survive. Even if everything goes wrong, hundreds will be around for years, and everything they do will change things."

Rapczewicz crossed herself. "Then we could be destroying the future—everyone we know, the whole country."

"If we have, we've *already* done it. Think it through. We're still here, so the history that produced us is too, somewhere, probably. Arnstein—the history professor— thinks that what'll happen is that there will be two futures, the one we came from, and the one that happens because we landed here. Rosenthal, the scientist, says that that could be—something to do with quantum mechanics."

"Yeah, the Many Worlds interpretation. We studied it in physics," Lieutenant Walker said thoughtfully.

Alston cleared her throat. "In any case, it's irrelevant. We can't do anything about it. Even mass suicide, which is not going to happen, wouldn't change the fact that we're here and the consequences that follow. But we *do* have to eat, y'all will recollect. So, ladies and gentlemen, let's get down to some serious plannin'."

The meeting went on for hours. As the officers left for

their bunks, Alston signaled to Walker to stay. "Lieutenant, I think you've had an idea that you're not sharing."

"Ma'am," the young man said. He hesitated. "It's just that there are so many *possibilities* here."

"Including death by starvation, unfortunately. That has to be our maximum priority for the present."

"Yes, ma'am."

The younger officer had a boyishly open face, green eyes, and a mop of reddish-brown hair; he looked like an overgrown Huck Finn. *And I can believe that as much as I want to,* she thought.

"Thank you, ma'am."

Alston sighed and sat alone, cradling her coffee and wishing for a drink. Coast Guard ships were dry, though, just like the Navy's. Like the Navy's had been . . . would be . . . whatever.

She poured another cup. Thinking about what had happened made her head hurt even worse. She'd considered drawing a trank herself, she needed the sleep, but no. She also needed her wits if something happened. Lucky for her she'd never been able to strike any deep roots, anywhere. At least she was used to disadvantages.

What more can the Supreme Ironist do? Let's see, you're a woman. A black woman. A black woman who came up through the ranks. A black, ex-ranker, divorced woman. A black, ex-ranker, divorced, gay woman. A black, ex-ranker, divorced, gay woman in charge of a ship. A black, ex-ranker, divorced, gay woman in command of a ship thrown back three thousand years in time with a crew getting more hysterical by the moment. What else could happen?

She had an uneasy feeling she'd find out.

The Nantucket Council was meeting around an office table in the Town Building, on Broad Street down by the Whaling Museum. The building was eighteenth-century brick Georgian on the outside, late-twentieth Institutional Bland inside. Voices sounded through open windows as outside, slippery mounds of fish were manhandled into boxes, garbage bags, and the backs of pickups and the island's ubiquitous Jeep Cherokees for distribution. The smell was already fairly powerful.

Coffin rapped his knuckles on the table and spoke: "All right, people, we've toted it up, and with strict rationing we've got enough food for about two to three weeks from our reserves. Thank God not many of the summer people had arrived, but we're still up against it. Captain Alston? What's the fishing situation?"

Marian Alston had been sitting quietly, making notes now and then. Occasionally she would change a small ball of hard rubber from one hand to another, squeezing steadily.

"There are two real trawlers operating out of Nantucket, and another that was here from Mattapoisett, sheltering from rough weather. As long as the fuel lasts, they can pull in enough to give everyone on the island a pound or more of fish a day—the schools of cod and herring and flounder and whatnot out there have to be seen to be believed. The main problem is breaking nets because the yields are so heavy."

"Thank God for that," Cofflin said. "Both Nantucket trawlers were slated to be junked next year," he went on. He'd been a commercial fisherman himself for a while, between getting out of high school and joining the Navy; he'd gone into police work after that. Like most trades that were really essential, working the nets had paid squat and had zero prospects. Back up in the twentieth, at least. Here the priorities were different.

Alston nodded. "As long as the fuel lasts, they'll be very useful. When it's gone, which will be fairly soon, they're useless. We can adapt the scallop boats to long-line hand fishing—there's an old man on the island we found who knows the technique, and we've got him giving lessons to yachtsmen and they're teaching others. We can use the sailing yachts too. They won't be what you'd call efficient, but they'll do for seine netting. Without fuel to spare, the motorboats are worthless—unless we cut them down and convert them to dories. I've got some parties workin' on that, too, but we're short of beams, planks, wood of all kinds."

"No problem there." Cofflin pushed a pile of papers across the table. "Here's a list of surplus buildings. Use the materials. Lord knows the island's got plenty of house carpenters—they're yours for this. Get in touch with Sam Macy. He's about the best housebuilder, and everyone knows him." He paused. "Bottom line, what are the fishing prospects?"

"Good. We're landing several tons a day already. Even

shore fishing is yielding significant amounts. The hand techniques should be coming online about the time we run out of motor fuel for the trawlers, giving us our daily needs and about a quarter or more over for reserves. The problem is preservation. We need salt, and lots of it. Even more when we start bringing in whalemeat."

"Whales! You can't kill *whales*!" Pamela Lisketter gasped.

The other members of the Council looked down the table at her. "Why not?" Rosenthal snapped.

"They're an *endangered species*!"

"Not here they're not," Captain Alston said. "They're a navigation hazard. You can't sail five miles out there without bumping into the damned things. We need the meat, and we need oil for lighting and cooking, and the rest of them we can grind up and use on the crops."

She turned to the farm owner. "Ms. Brand, we'll also be producing a lot of fish offal, by-products. Good fertilizer, I understand."

Dr. Coleman cut in. "Save the livers of the cod. We're going to have problems with vitamin deficiencies, too. I've rounded up all the supplements and pills on the island, but with the shortage of fresh greens and fruits you're projecting, we may have actual scurvy by winter."

Cofflin nodded. "Right now, we'll eat fresh fish and whale meat, plus perishables, and save all the canned goods and other keepers for the winter to eke out what we salt down and preserve and what we can grow. Doc, we should be able to get wild fruits and berries. Would cranberries and blueberries help? We've got a couple of hundred acres of cranberry bog, right enough."

"If they're properly preserved, yes, they'll help with the vitamin problem."

Martha Stoddard tapped the table in her turn, with one finger. "There are a lot of wild plants that have useful quantities of vitamins, and edible seaweed too. My Girl Scout troop was doing a project on them. Some of the seaweed can be dried, as well. Dulse, for example—health food stores sell dried dulse as a snack. High in vitamin C."

"Good," Cofflin said. "Why don't you and the doctor get together on that?"

"Medicinal herbs too," Coleman said. "I'm experimenting with producing simple antibiotics, but we're going to be short of a good deal else."

"Good. Now that we know we're not going to starve to death right away, what about the next few months to a year?" Cofflin said. He looked over at Angelica Brand.

"I'm sorry, Chief, but my operation is basically for flowers and luxury vegetables," she said. "There's only the greenhouses, and about a hundred acres under vegetables every summer, and that's a drop in the bucket."

Cofflin restrained an impulse to run his hands through his hair. Brand Farms was the only real agricultural enterprise on the island. There were a few hobby farms, an herb grower, private vegetable gardens, people who kept a cow or a horse or something, a lone vineyard, and that was it. It had been a long, *long* time since Nantucket fed itself. Even back in the Revolutionary War there had been famine here when the British blockaded the island, and they'd already been trading whale oil and fish for grain. The manager of the A&P had been invaluable in tracking down all the food reserves, but there just wasn't much. Deliveries from the mainland came three times a week even in winter.

Then Brand struck the palm of her hand to her forehead. "Wait a minute—my off-season cover crop is winter rye. If I don't plow that up for vegetables, we can harvest it, by hand if we have to. Call it a hundred acres at twenty or so bushels . . . say two thousand bushels of grain. Not until late August, though. That's about . . ." She punched her calculator. "About one-fifth of our needs for a year, not counting what I'd have to hold back as seed."

"Potatoes," Ian Arnstein said. The others looked at him; he flushed slightly and went on: "Potatoes are a pretty complete diet, they grow well in a sandy soil, and an acre will support two people. They keep well, too. The Irish used to live off potatoes and skim milk. We could live on potatoes and salt fish over the winter, probably."

Angelica Brand went into a huddle with the A&P manager and her secretary and pecked at her calculator. At last she said:

"It's pretty elementary farming, and we've got our usual shipment of seed potatoes on hand at my place. We could plant a couple of hundred acres, although that will cut down on the period for living off stored food," she said. "Plus I can put in a few hundred acres of corn and vegetables, drawing on my own stocks and the stuff from the gardening and supply shops. But I don't have the equipment to cultivate that much, even counting the relics used as lawn ornaments and such I've been tracking down. There isn't that much cleared land on the island, in fact, even if we use lawns and flowerbeds. Incidentally, we should use some of the lawns for fodder, grazing and hay, if we can."

Chief Cofflin closed his eyes, then opened them in decision. "People are going crazy sitting around with nothing to do, anyways." Most of the island's economy depended on tourists. The demand for real estate agents, store clerks, waiters, and cooks had taken an abrupt nosedive. "We'll do the clearing and planting by hand if we have to." He went on, "We'll divide them into teams. Ms. Brand, you use your tractors to do the heavy clearing, plus what earthmoving equipment we can dig up. Then we'll have the teams move in and get ready to plant with hand tools. Anything else you've got seed for, too. Carrots, beets, turnips, you name it. Find the best land and we'll worry about compensation for the owners later, if we live."

"How are we going to pay people to work? It's just sinking in that money isn't worth much anymore," the town clerk said.

That *was* a good question. "Any ideas?"

Starbuck nodded. "Food. I say anyone who wants to eat, works. We can run a sort of chit system, so many hours drawing so much, and then juggle it. Of course, we'll have to figure out something different for people who *can't* work, and eventually we'll need a money of our own. But that's going to have to wait."

Martha Stoddard cleared her throat. "The older people, we've got a lot of retirees, they can do things like childminding. We'll need a day-care system with everybody able-bodied working."

"Good idea, Martha. Yours too, Joseph: work if you want to eat. Damn, you know, that sounds pretty good. . . . Any objections?" Cofflin didn't see any. "Speaking of money, we'll have to make a register of houses, land, and cars and suchlike owned by coo . . . by people who weren't here when the Event happened. We'll have to commandeer property owned by residents, too, but let's make it clear from the beginning that there'll be compensation eventually."

Everyone nodded. Angelica Brand returned to her specialty:

"Chief, this island is just a big sand dune out in the ocean. There's not much in the way of nutrients in this soil, and I don't have much fertilizer, either. What's more, the best land has the thickest scrub cover."

"Plant everything you can, and you've got the stuff from the composting sewage works." He silently thanked God they'd managed to keep that going, for a few crucial hours a day at least. Without it they might have had plague already. "We can use sludge from septic tanks too, if it's treated—find out how. I'm putting you in charge of food production. Levy the people you need. From now on we're farmers, like it or not."

"Brush," Arnstein said. The others looked at him, and he hurried on: "We have to clear the brush anyway, so we burn it and turn under the ashes. Slash-and-burn farming. The ashes should enrich the soil for a year or two."

Brand nodded and began to make notes. "We'll be short of hand tools. I'll get on to the machine shop. Seahaven Engineering ought to be able to handle what we'll need, them and the plumbers. And seed's going to be a problem next year—these hybrids don't breed true. . . . And I suppose we'll have to keep all the livestock for breeding."

"Everything that *can* breed," Cofflin agreed.

Martha Stoddard spoke again: "You might try locating wild Jerusalem artichokes, here and on the mainland. They're a native plant. Yield and methods are about like potatoes, and they like a poor sandy soil. They keep well right in the soil overwinter, too."

Cofflin looked at her with respect. "Now, that's an excellent idea, Martha. Perhaps your scout troop could start in on that as well."

"And this being March, the stores would be full of packets of garden seed," Martha went on thoughtfully. "The feed stores might have whole unmilled oats, too. Some of them might sprout."

She paused for a moment. "And get on to Paul Hillwater, the botanist—he's been doing a study of Nantucket's historical ecology for years now. He can advise us on what *not* to clear, to keep wind erosion down and block salt spray. That used to be quite a problem here when the island was mostly bare."

Angelica Brand nodded and started to speak; Cofflin held up a hand. "Hold off on that for a moment, Angelica. The Professor suggested something. Ron, you heard anything yet you can't handle in the way of toolmaking?"

Ron Leaton, the owner of Seahaven Engineering, was a slender man in early middle age, with long-fingered hands like a violinist. "Oh, I can work up anything you want," he said. "Give me power and bar stock or sheet steel. The problem is there's only one of me. I can do *any*thing, but not *every*thing."

That *was* a problem. Nantucket simply didn't have much industry. Seahaven was a one-man quasi-hobby; most of Leaton's living had come from his computer dealership, with the machine shop in his basement. At that, it was the sole and singular metalworking facility on the island, unless you counted the high school shop classes and the *Eagle*'s onboard machine shop.

Cofflin pressed his fingers to his forehead. "Let's look at it this way. What have you got, what can it do, and what can you do to do more of it?"

"Ah . . ." Leaton frowned. "Well, I've got a 1956-type Bridgeport milling machine, with digital controls added on, an old Atlas twelve-by-thirty-six engine lathe, an Atlas horizontal milling machine, a seven-inch Ammco shaper, and I just got in a Schaublin eight-by-eighteen precision toolmaking lathe, a real beauty—Swiss. All light-to-medium stuff. There may be more on-island. I'll start looking."

The head of the Nantucket Electric Company cut in: "You made those flanges for us, and some other fairly heavy work. The turbocharger, for instance."

"Yup, but I sort of cheated—used the Bridgeport as a vertical lathe with a rotary table." He looked around. "Forty-eight inches by twenty-nine, machined out of solid five-eighths plate—"

Cofflin cleared his throat. Leaton flushed and continued:

"Bottom line, Chief, is that I *could* make just about anything, including more tools; a lathe is one of the few tools that can make a copy of itself. It'll be a little awkward without a foundry, but I could make a round bar bed lathe, the Unimat type; it'll work perfectly well, just not as durable as a cast or forged bed. I'm making a tool cutter of my own right now, or was before this all happened."

"Excuse me," Arnstein cut in. "You're saying that eventually you could duplicate your operation, and then duplicate it again, and so forth? And that you can do pretty well any metal shape?"

"Yup," Leaton said, obviously puzzled. "Give me the metal, and yes. Wasn't that what I was saying?"

"You could make, for example, a steam engine?"

"Well, I do that all the time—little ones, and they're working scale models. I've got machinery that can work to ten-thousandths of an inch, and Watt did it with tolerances of an *eighth* of an inch. I've got a nice set of Weber measuring-gauge blocks, after all. I could turn out, say, a twenty-five-horsepower model in a week, maybe convert an old VW flat-type engine. Need a welder to help me with the boiler . . . maybe use a propane tank . . . but hell, we've got half a dozen top-notch welders and some heavy bending rolls. Bit difficult to make really *big* cylinders without a foundry or casting plant, but I could if you gave me a month or two to tool up. Up to a couple of hundred horsepower. But we don't have the fuel for many of those. Hell, we can't keep the town power plant running for more than six months, no matter how we ration, right, Fred?"

The head of the Electric Company nodded, abstracted; he was making frantic notes.

Cofflin let out a long sigh. "Well, you'll need more space than that basement, and more people. Look up anyone with experience, and, hmm, you and Joseph here scout for a building that'll give you room to expand."

He noticed Lisketter scowling. "Ms. Lisketter, what about your artisans?"

She tapped the edges of the papers in front of her. *What are we going to do when we run out of paper?* he thought.

"There are dozens of weavers," she said. "And . . ."

Cofflin was surprised at the cogent, well-organized list that followed. He nodded at the end of it. "Good work, Ms. Lisketter. So we'll be well enough off for clothing when our current stores run out?"

They'd also have a large surplus of silversmiths and graphic artists. And, thank God, a number of metalworkers, farriers, three genuine blacksmiths; one who specialized in blades, a visitor caught here. Plenty of pottery makers, and there was even a glassblower who'd just moved his studio to the island last year.

She shook her head. "We don't have the raw materials.

We need flax and wool—cotton if you can get it. I know it's not our top priority, but . . ."

Arnstein cleared his throat. "Cotton might be available in the Caribbean or Mexico," he said. "Flax and wool certainly from Europe."

"We could grow flax here—the climate's right. It's a useful oilseed as well. We could get the flax seed along with grain from Europe," Brand said thoughtfully. "Grinding grain might be a problem—"

"Ayup," Cofflin said. "Remember the Old Mill? We'll finally get some use out of the damned tourist trap."

There was a chuckle around the table, particularly from the native islanders. The Old Mill was a shingled windmill, kept functional for the tourist trade.

Brand spoke: "Chief, get me seed and tools and people and I can produce grain. But I'd have to have the seed *soon*, for spring planting—it looks like the growing season's longer here, but even so, it'll be tight. We could use more animal breeding stock as well. There's some poultry, and those will reproduce fast. It's the larger stock that are the problem. We have a small herd of sheep, good dual-purpose Corriedales; and four stallions, forty-two mares, twenty-one geldings; and some cows, several of them in calf, thank God, so we should get a bull calf or two, but not a pig on the island. Pigs would be ideal—they breed so quickly and eat anything—and we could use ewes, mares and cows as well. They're the limiting factor."

Cofflin looked at Alston. She spread her hands. "I can take the *Eagle* across the Atlantic easily enough," she said. "Assumin' the winds and currents are basically similar, in about two weeks on the northern route, with a little more to get back. Plus whatever time it takes to dicker with the locals and to load. The *Eagle* wasn't designed to carry cargo. My only real problem is the stars, now that we're back to celestial navigation as our only means of finding where we are. Everything's slightly off. We can compensate, but it'll take time to figure out how."

Rosenthal spoke: "I can get you a new set of data, complete tables. I'll have the printout to you in a couple of days."

The chief gnawed at his lip, wishing he'd been able to get more sleep. Risking the *Eagle* was not something he wanted to do, not at all. It was a priceless asset . . . but an asset had to be *used*.

"Let's see if we can get some figures here," he said.

They consulted, punched calculators—*oh, those are going to be missed when the batteries run out*—argued. In the end the results showed that there *might* be enough to keep them through winter from what they could grow and catch with the resources already on the island . . . if their assumptions weren't wrong, and everyone pitched in.

"No margin," he said. "That settles it, we need more food." He turned to the Coast Guard officer. "When were you planning on going whaling?" he said.

"We're rigging for it now, and Mr. Leaton has done a fine job, a harpoon gun that ought to work. Tomorrow we start, and we don't think it'll take more than a few days to get all the dead whales you can handle, using a plane for spotting. Some of your people are getting the rending tubs and whatever out of the Whaling Museum right now. Lookin' like they'll be functional."

Cofflin nodded. "Where can we get bulk salt? Anyone know?"

Arnstein cleared his throat. "The Bahamas—Inagua island, down at the southern tip. There are big salt lagoons there, or at least there were in our time. You can scoop it up around the edges with shovels."

Cofflin chuckled. "Damn, but that education of yours is turning out useful."

"Actually I honeymooned there with my late wife. The tour guide told me."

Alston spoke: "That's shoal water. I'd hate to take the *Eagle* in close there."

Cofflin nodded. "What's that two-master sailing yacht called . . ."

"The *Yare*," Alston said. "Wooden-hulled topmast schooner, about a hundred tons burden, Canadian-built, old but still sound. Small auxiliary engine. It's a replica—the original design was a revenue cutter. There's another tied up, the *Bentley,* seventy-foot schooner, about three-quarters her displacement, but the masts and rigging need work. The *Yare* can leave anytime. I'll put one of my officers in command."

"All right, we'll send the *Yare* to Inagua. We send the *Eagle* east for grain. Everyone draw up your wish lists of things to get that might be there." He paused and thought. "Professor, what should we take for trade goods?"

"Almost anything," Arnstein said. "Cloth, ornaments—with the number of jewelry stores on the island, that should be no problem—metal tools, anything like that. Bits of glass would probably do, wire . . ."

"I'm putting you in charge of it," Cofflin said. "Incidentally, you're going." Arnstein yelped. "You're the closest thing to an expert on dealing with primitives we have."

"But I won't even be able to *talk* to them!" Arnstein protested.

"I thought you knew ancient languages?"

"I know Latin, which isn't spoken yet, and *Greek,* classical Greek, and I've read Homer and looked at the Linear B stuff. But even the classical period's seven hundred years in the future! Homeric Greek is to classical what Shakespeare's English is to ours, and Mycenaean is five hundred years before *that*, call it Chaucerian. And they won't be speaking Greek on the shores of the English Channel, anyway."

"Neither will anyone else be able to talk to the locals, will they?" Cofflin said.

"Not unless we have a Lithuanian," Arnstein admitted. The others looked at him. "Lithuanian is a very conservative language," he said. "About like Sanskrit, which is being spoken in northwestern India at this date. Indo-European languages should be spreading through western Europe about now, defining *now* as being the last millennium and a half or so, unless you believe Colin Renfrew's nonsense . . . sorry, academic squabble. But someone who spoke it would probably be able to pick up any of the early versions of Indo-European fairly quickly, other things being equal." He shrugged. "But how likely are we to find—"

Doreen Rosenthal cleared her throat, twisting a lock of hair around a finger. "My mother came from Vilnus. I speak it," she said.

Martha Stoddard looked up from her notepad. "There's a fairly good languages section at the Athenaeum," she noted. "And I know at least one retired linguist on island. Speaking of which, Jared, we're going to be doing a fair bit of research on one thing and t'other. Old-style ways of doing, and such." She frowned. "Plus we ought to print out some things on CD-ROM, right now, while we can."

"Good idea, Martha. You're in charge of research projects, of course." Cofflin turned his head to the manager of the Nantucket Electric Company. "Fred, how are we fixed for energy?"

"I've got about one month's fuel," he said. "Fuel barge was tied up at the . . . Event, topping up to take us through to the switchover to the mainland cable. According to the gas stations and boating people, there's enough gasoline for, say, two weeks at normal usage. After that, well, we might be able to get those windmills going again. Remember that wind-farm idea?" Everyone nodded. The tall frames of the wind generators still stuck up out of fields around the town. "That would give us, oh, five, eight percent of our usual output indefinitely."

Cofflin nodded. "We're closing down all private autos as of now," he said. "Official use, ambulances, fire engines, and Angelica's tractors only. The trawlers have first priority. How many bicycles do we have?"

"About thirty-five hundred, counting private, in the rental places, and in the stores."

"Good, that'll help." One advantage of being a tourist trap. "Fred, you get together with Doc Coleman, and we'll arrange an essential-uses-only electricity schedule. That ought to stretch the fuel oil. The rest of us will have to go to bed with the sun until we get whale-oil lanterns. Next . . ."

It was a relief to be finally *doing* something.

"We're working like *slaves!*" the man complained.

He was thirty-something, and from the look of his jeans and plaid shirt, wealthy. Certainly coof—that New York accent was a dead giveaway. Not liking the work much, from the way he straightened and rubbed at his back and threw down his billhook.

I can't blame him, Angelica Brand thought. *This is something out of a made-for-TV special.* She was a farmer from twelve generations of farmers, but *her* generation used tractors and genetic engineering.

Pictures of Nantucket from back in her great-grandfather's day showed a landscape that looked like North Dakota, hardly a bush over knee-high, but most of the island was overgrown now with a thick head-high spiny growth of scrub oak, bayberry, beach plum, red cedar, honeysuckle, pitch pine, and God knew what, all laced together with wild grapevines and *Rosa rugosa*.

The tractors, bulldozers, and earthmoving equipment from construction sites had knocked down much of the aboveground brush.The machines left the scrub still chest-high to head-high, many of the main stems still unbroken. The clumsy untrained labor of hundreds was scarcely sufficient to cut the brush loose and drag it into windrows for burning, especially when most of them had never lifted anything heavier than a computer mouse or a squash racket in their lives. The smell of it was acrid in her nostrils, but the ash would be useful. Clumps of men and women were scattered through the scraggly-looking wreckage she was supposed to turn into a field, hacking and levering and dragging at the roots. Tools were in short supply, too.

Other squads were slumped resting near the truck with the water, hardly even bothering to lie in its shade despite the unseasonable heat. A few were putting a better edge on their tools at the portable grindstone someone had dug out of an attic. It was the foot-powered type, and worth its weight in gold.

The man thrust his hands under her nose. "*Look* at this!"

Shreds of skin hung down from broken blisters, and bits of the cloth he'd used to wrap his hands clung, sticky with the lymph. Angelica Brand nodded sympathetically. "We've got a tub of ointment back at the house," she said. "When your shift's off, come on up. There's some cider, too."

"I'm a certified public accountant!" the man half screamed. Spittle flung from his lips. "I'm *finished* with this!"

He'd picked up the billhook again. It had a wooden shaft five feet long, with a steel blade socketed onto the end, like an arm-long single-edged knife with an inward-curving tip at the end.

"You can take this fucking thing and ram it up your *ass*, bitch!"

Angelica planted her hands on her hips and glared back. "Don't you use language like that to me, mister!" she snapped, fatigue and irritation flaring. "I don't care if you were a rocket scientist. We have to *eat* this winter. Or do you think somebody's going to dock with a ship full of bananas and Big Macs?"

"I'm an accountant, not a farmer!"

"We don't *need* accountants right now. And if you don't work, you don't get any rations. No exceptions for the able-bodied."

A woman's voice shouted: *"Don! No!"*

The accountant ignored it. Brand's anger turned to a yell of fear as the man swung at her with the billhook. If he hadn't been staggering with exhaustion he might have hit her. A root caught at her boot and she went over backward, staring at the sunlight breaking off the edge of the heavy tool as he swung it upward.

Thunk. The butt end of another billhook drove into the berserker's back. He screamed and whirled, but a third tripped him. Men and women piled on, wrestling him to the ground and holding him despite his thrashings.

"Obliged, Ted," Angelica said shakily, getting to her feet and dusting herself off. The man nodded silently, which was like Theodore Corby; she'd known him since she was a girl, and he never used a word where an economical movement of the chin would do. "Much obliged."

She looked around. "Well, nobody said to stop working!" she called. "Come on, everyone, there's a job to be done!"

"What'll we do with this guy?"

The man had stopped roaring and heaving. Now he was lying prone in the dirt and ash, crying noisily.

"I . . ." She hesitated. *I run a vegetable farm!* she thought. Five to fifty people worked on it, according to season, and this had *never* happened before. "Bring him along. We'd better call the Chief."

"Ooooh, gross. Totally, totally *gross.*"

Ned Shaw turned. The girl was looking at the yard-long cod she'd just pulled in; the lines were arranged over a rollbar around the boat, to make hauling easier. The big fish swayed, flapping, thirty-odd pounds of bad temper on the end of a heavy hook and line.

"Tie it off, tie it off!" he barked, pushing down the crowded deck. He'd been a scalloper most of his life, done some other fishing, but he'd never seen anything like that fish.

The girl made a face, but she swung the line inboard and paid out, letting the cod drop to the boards of the deck. It flopped and jumped, and she skittered backward.

"Like this," Shaw said.

He put a boot on the fish—it must weigh thirty-five pounds and it wasn't happy at all—and swung a length of stick with a heavy steel nut on the end. Two crunching blows and the fish was still.

"That's good eating, that cod," the fisherman said, heaving it into the well in the center of the boat with a grunt of effort. *Mebbe forty, forty-five.*

His crew—clerks, salesgirls, high school students, shopkeepers, computer operators—looked at the fish and swallowed. They were all hungry, but . . .

Then the lines began to jerk all around him. "Get to it!" he yelled.

Lines whirred. Cod came up them; sometimes two or three of the crew would have to pull on a single line, and once a six-foot monster came over the side with people yelling and dancing to get out of its way. That one Shaw pinned to the deck with a boathook, and it took half a dozen two-handed blows of the club to kill it. He looked up, panting. The well in the center of the twenty-foot boat was full of fish, a slippery blue-gray mound of them. The deck was slimy underfoot, covered in scales; the crew were equally smeared, the hair of the women hanging in rattails. They grinned back at him.

"Good day's work," he said. "Get the tarpaulin over them and we'll head in. Lucky we don't have to clean them."

The girl who'd caught the first fish of the day daubed at herself. "Gross," she muttered.

CHAPTER THREE

March, Year 1 A.E.

"Closer. Slow, slow."

Lieutenant Walker squatted in the prow of the longboat and broke open the harpoon gun. It was shaped like an outsized shotgun. He slid the long steel harpoon down the barrel, cushioned in its wooden sabot. Its mechanism gave a smooth oiled *snick* as he closed it and swung the simple post-and-groove sights onto the side of the whale, aiming six feet behind the eye. His helper leaned forward and clipped the end of the line to a ring welded onto the shaft just behind the folding barbs and the bulge that held a charge of bursting powder.

Whoever ran this up knew his way around a machine shop, Walker thought. He'd always liked hunting, and a good weapon doubled the pleasure.

Spray lapped into his face like the tongue of a salty dog. Behind him the crew of sailors and cadets stroked at their oars again. The day was an enormous bowl of blue, only the tiny dot of the *Eagle* to break the watery horizon, and scarcely a cloud in the sky. It was hot enough to make him sweat, despite the droplets of seawater striking cold on his T-shirt. Ahead the whale lay basking like a flexible black reef; a right whale, with a huge head that made up a third of its sixty feet. Blackfish, the type that had been the staple of inshore whaling in New England before they were hunted out and the big whalers began to sail to Hawaii and Kamchatka. A white patch of barnacles marked its snout; when it raised a flipper he could see white skin beneath, vivid in contrast to the dark-blue water and the coal color of the animal. Close enough to see the eyes, like golf balls set into the sides of a submarine. It blew, a tall double plume that turned into a mist of spray falling across them.

Whales were spouting all around, hundreds of them, pod after pod.

"Feels like murder," one of the cadets muttered. The whales had never been hunted, evidently not even by Indians in canoes. You could get within touching distance sometimes.

"Looks like dinner," Walker said cheerfully. "Ready for it . . . *now*." He squeezed the trigger.

Tump. The harpoon blasted out of the barrel, blurring through the air. Line whipped out from the improvised tub beside the harpoon gun. It began to smoke with friction, and Cadet Simpson tossed seawater from her bucket on it. *Whack*. A flat, wet sound as the steel hit the whale's side.

"Hang on!" Walker yelled.

The whale dove with a smash of its tail that left Walker drenched and dripping, grinning as he clung to the harpoon gun's mount. The longboat lurched forward, and the crew fell over one another in a tangle of oars punctuated by yells. Water fountained up from either side of the bows as the line jerked forward and down, pulling them along like an outboard motor gone berserk. The Nantucket sleigh ride, they'd called it in the old days. The Coast Guard officer counted the seconds:

. . . *five . . . six . . . hope the fucking fuse works this time . . . seven . . .* He wouldn't be able to hear the blast underwater, but the whale would surely feel it.

The line went slack as the whale broached, half its length out of the water. Blood streamed from the hole gouged by the grenade, but the four barbs held fast. The great animal lay on the surface and threshed in its death agony, nearly swamping the boat that had killed it. All around, other whales were fleeing the sound of its distress, blowing and diving. At last it slumped into stillness, floating quietly as the crew of the longboat bailed out the water.

"Thank God this type floats when it's dead," Walker said. "Let's make her fast."

The *Eagle* was making sail in their direction; there were lookouts up at the mastheads with binoculars. Cadet Simpson slipped out of her pants and jacket and went overboard with a line to make fast around the whale's flukes. Walker watched with interest; someday they'd have to admit that the old fraternization rules didn't make much sense. Or maybe there would be opportunities when they went east, next week. . . .

The ship was looming larger, moving fairly quickly despite the four whales secured to her sides. This one towed astern, and they'd have enough for starters.

He looked east. Who knew what waited there? *Upon a peak in Darien . . .*

"We'll take hundreds of these," Ian Arnstein said.

The spearhead was seven inches long, and three wide at the broadest, cut and ground out of a straightened section of automobile leaf spring. The edge was razor-sharp, tapering to a murderous point. The tang was socketed onto a smooth eight-foot wooden shaft; the whole ensemblage felt heavy and solid and well balanced. Deadly. Ian hefted it and tried to imagine using it. *Damn. I'd rather have read about this than had to do it,* he thought.

Seahaven Engineering had moved into a big former boathouse, out east of town near the head of the harbor. The machine shop was noisy, clangs and thumps and shrill screaming sounds as somebody pushed a piece of metal against a grindstone; it smelled of iron and ozone.

Ronald Leaton nodded; he was looking as tired as everyone else, and was dressed in a grease-stained baseball cap and overalls that looked like they'd been on for days. "Here's some of the other stuff you ordered."

Big knives ground out of bar stock, and short Roman-style swords. Those had smoothed wooden hilts, brass pommels, and an S-shaped guard made of rebar and welded on. Ian picked one up and hefted it, prodding the point into the battered wooden table it rested on.

"These are probably better steel than the originals," he said.

"Yup. That long fancy one you wanted will take another day or two. Got a book from one of the stores, *The Complete Bladesmith,* had a lot of useful hints. John Martins is setting up a forge—he's that blacksmith who was here visiting Barbara Allis. He made things like that for hobbyists. And here's our masterpiece."

This time Ronald had used a whole leaf from a spring for the crossbow. It was set at the front of a rifle-type stock.

"How does it cock?" Ian asked. There was a steel claw arrangement hooked to the center of the wire string stretched across the shallow cord of the bow. He pulled at the string with a tentative hand. It was like a solid bar, immovable.

"That's a *stiff* draw," he said.

"Over three hundred and fifty pounds," the machinist said. "Brace the stock against your hip and hold the grip. Now put your other hand on the forestock, through that oval metal loop that sticks out beyond the wood. Feel that catch under your thumb? Press it down."

Ian obeyed. A steel lever came out of its slot in the forestock, hinged at the rear a few inches ahead of the trigger guard.

"Pump it back and forth, like the lever on a car jack."

There was a soft heavy resistance with every stroke, and the crossbow's string inched backward. At the sixth it clicked home near the trigger action and the rear sight, the heavy steel bow bent and ready.

Ian whistled. Not even the windlass-wound monsters the crossbowmen of medieval Genoa and Venice used were more powerful, and it had taken far less time to cock, barely ten seconds, probably less with practice. *Almost as fast as a bow,* he thought. And it took years to make a good archer; this you could learn to use in a couple of days. *Well, we understand mechanical advantage better than they did back then in medieval times . . . in the future.* The confusion of tenses made it difficult even to *talk* about time travel.

"We'd better go out back to test this," Ronald said.

The paved space was full of people sorting car parts, putting aside ones to keep in stock for the limited number of vehicles that were being kept running; a crew of car mechanics and enthusiastic amateurs were working on a four-wheeled horse cart made out of tubing and two-by-fours and the wheels and axles from a Saab. A hundred paces away a wooden target was propped up against the wall of an unoccupied summer cottage.

"Just a front and back sight on the bow," Ronald said. "Here's something to shoot."

He handed Ian a bolt, eighteen inches of heavy wooden dowel with a three-bladed steel head at one end and a trio of plastic flight feathers at the other. Ian dropped it into the slot and snuggled the butt against his shoulder. Squeeze the trigger . . .

Whunnng. The cord whipped forward, and the bolt flashed in a snapping blurr. *Whunk!* It struck in one corner of the target, sunk half its length and quivering like a malignant bee. Ian pushed his glasses up his nose and whistled.

"Not bad," he said. "Not bad at all."

He looked at how the bolt had plowed itself a foot deep through solid wood. *Logical. These things used to pierce armor.*

They certainly weren't going to be making smokeless powder and metal cartridges anytime soon. They *might* be able to make black powder and muskets in a few years. In the meantime these would save a lot of utterly irreplaceable ammunition.

"Lunch," Ronald said, as someone hammered on a triangle back at Seahaven Engineering. "If you don't mind fish."

"Fortunately, I don't," Ian said. People on the island who were allergic to it were in deep trouble.

"Or there's steak," Ronald went on, grinning.

"What?"

"Whale steak. Sort of like beef, only fishy. We made the harpoon gun, so we get dibs."

"Morning, Chief."

"Morning, Fred."

Fred Roberts was up the frame of the wind generator, head and hands inside the opened housing. "You wouldn't believe how things corrode in this sea air."

"Oh, I guess I would," Cofflin said dryly, leaning his bicycle against the steel of the support. "Always thought these eggbeaters were a boondoggle. Your tax dollars at waste."

More of the Nantucket Electric Company people and teams from the general population were running up sheds around the base. He recognized four or five men who'd worked as house carpenters before the Event, with dozens of the unskilled doing fetch-and-carry. Cofflin looked inside the long shed; electricians were setting up row after row of car batteries in parallel, on bookshelf-style supports that filled the inside. He nodded at their greetings. The batteries would help even out the flow of power from the windmills, taking up the slack when the air was calm or giving extra at peak demand. Luckily, it was a rare day on the island without a breeze. He ducked back out; Fred was answering his last remark:

"They were a boondoggle, but we're lucky to have them. . . . *There*." He pulled his head out of the machine and wiped his face on the sleeve of his overall. "Got it, I think. We should be able to get most of these things running, for a while at least. Robbing Peter to pay Paul, and it'll get harder and harder to replace lost parts. I suppose we could rewind the coils by hand with telephone wire . . ."

His voice died off into a preoccupied mumble, an expert talking with himself. Cofflin nodded and looked out over the landscape of the island that had been his ancestors' home for fifteen generations. More, if you counted the very faint trace of Indian blood.

Not far away, one of Brand's tractors was dragging an improvised harrow over half-cleared land. People were walking behind it in long rows stretched across the turned gray-brown soil. The first row were making holes with shovels, hoes, billhooks, and sticks. The second row had sacks slung from their shoulders, and they were dropping in quartered potatoes, each piece with two eyes for sprouting. The third were carrying buckets, dropping in a dollop of fertilizer—better not to ask where it came from—and filling in the holes, tamping them down with their hands. It came to him that he'd never seen that many people working in a field, not even when he spent a few summers picking tobacco in the Connecticut Valley. Not that many . . . not in America, at least. In Asia, yes. Though most of his traveling there had been behind the splinter shield of a 20mm.

Fred was climbing down the ladder built into the support leg. "It's amazing," he said. "Here we're doing just a few things, and everyone on the island is working dawn to dusk."

Cofflin took a Tupperware container of fish sticks from the carryall at the rear of the bike. He opened the top and offered some to the other man. Fred sighed, then brightened slightly at the taste.

"S'good," he said.

"Ayup. Martha made 'em up. Not looking forward to the day the spices run out," he said. "Reason I came was we need more ice. Until we can salt down the fish, that is. Loads are coming in pretty fast."

"Well, I suppose we could switch on the A&P again, and put buckets of water in the freezers. . . ."

Marian Alston strolled toward the point where the streets met, hands in her pockets. It was very dark without the streetlights, but heaven was frosted with stars and the moon was full. She walked quietly; nobody was about at this hour, and the houses around were dark and shuttered, waiting for summer dwellers who would never arrive. Trees overarched brick sidewalks crumpled into unevenness by thrusting roots; she took the middle of the road, where a little cool white light filtered through the leaves of the elms. The night was quiet enough that an occasional voice from the distant center of town sounded clear. The crickets in the small marsh up the street were louder. Both seemed to enhance the silence.

Tempting to leave it all. Sail away from the problem, go see the strangeness she'd been landed in, lose herself in wandering and adventure. *Not really an option, of course.* Yet it was *Eagle* she loved, and the sea. This island was too new to her to hold her heart.

Different, she thought. She'd liked to walk out at night sometimes when she was a girl in her father's house. The sky looked cooler here; life was colored in shades of blue and fog-gray, without the yeasty aliveness of the Low Country. She wondered what it would be like to visit there now, so long and long before the first small wooden ships dropped anchor before rivers not yet named Ashley or Cooper. No crumbled tabby ruins to find among the trees, overgrown remains of Great House and slave quarters. No weathered wooden shacks; no clipped green golf courses amid the palmettos either. Just water, reeds, stars . . . her lips quirked. Indians, of course. The mosquitoes would be there too.

She shook her head ruefully and returned to the present. The monument in the center of the crossroads was small and unassuming. No statue, just a round millstone base and above a granite plinth with the names of the island's Union dead. Very many names, for so small a town; men who could have stayed home in comfort, and the way the war turned out wouldn't have affected their lives one bit. Men who ended lying on bloodstained tables down from Cemetery Ridge, with their bones shattered into splinters by minié balls and the surgeon's saw ready; men shivering and puking out their lives with yellow fever in the swamps along the Chickahominy; men drowned in the blackness of Farragut's ironclad in Mobile Bay; men down in the red clay while ants marched over their tongues toward sightless eyes. They had gone a long way from home, to die among angry strangers.

The captain of the *Eagle* took two steps backward and came to attention. Her salute was slow, with a precise quivering snap at the end. Then she turned and walked homeward.

"Still working, Ms. Rosenthal?" Ian Arnstein asked.

Doreen Rosenthal started and looked up from her books.

The *Eagle* had electric light still, which was one reason why she'd moved aboard a little early. He didn't intend to move his bag of essentials and crates of references into the little cubbyhole they'd assigned him until tomorrow, the day of their departure. He sat down across from her; the officers' wardroom was empty, although there was coffee in the corner for the night watch.

"Studying, not working," she said, holding up the cover of the book. It was a physics text; the title made very little sense to him. "Trying to figure out what happened to us. That's Doreen, by the way. No sense in being formal if we're going on a cruise." She smiled shyly.

He smiled back. "Well, it beats bush-clearing detail, Doreen." Everyone on the Council was supposed to put in at least a few hours. It made sense in a political sort of way, he supposed, but his back hurt. "Most people call me Ian."

"Funny, you don't *look* Scottish."

They shared a laugh. "My parents were extremely assimilated. Any luck with the search for the causes of the Event?"

He went over to the urn and poured them both a cup; no more coffee soon, so make the best of it. No more cream or sugar, either—the output of the few dozen cows on the island was reserved for the sick and children. Cows could breed, but he didn't even know if sugarcane had been domesticated yet, and they certainly weren't going to be sending any expeditions to India to find out for a while. *I wonder if we could get honeybees in England?* he thought.

One more thing to look up. He remembered that there hadn't been any in the Americas when the settlers arrived, but not whether anyone was raising them at this early date in the Old World. Or there might be some hives on Nantucket.

"No luck," Doreen said, sticking a piece of paper in the book and closing it.

"How do you take it?"

"Black."

Paper . . . Ian shoved the thought into the enormous to-do file. "Do you favor the Act of God hypothesis, or the Saucer People theory?" he asked with a grin, setting down the cups. "Those are the two main schools of thought on the island, and apart from food and blisters, people don't talk about much else. Then there are the dissenting minority churches; the Satan-did-it, and the Government Secret Project slash Conspiracy. And a new eclectic faith, the Saucer People Are Part of the Conspiracy."

"I'm in the minority," she said ruefully. "I comprehend the vastness of my own ignorance. I'm morally certain that whatever caused the Event was deliberate, at least in the sense that a chemical plant blowing up is deliberate. The whole thing was too . . . too artificial not to be the result of intent, even if it was an accident, some machine somewhen going off half cocked, or whatever, somewhere and somewhen. The precise ellipse around the island, for instance. But apart from that I've got no earthly inkling what happened. I did have a wild idea . . ."

"What?" he said eagerly. "Tell me."

She rubbed a hand across the cover of the book. "I thought . . . well, how do we know this is the same universe, exactly, as the one we left? I decided to try to remeasure the physical constants, to see if anything had changed."

"And?"

"And everything's exactly the same, as far as I can determine—I don't have much in the way of equipment, you understand. Gravity, electrical resistance, they're all the same. For that matter, solid-state electronics wouldn't work here if the constants were *very* different." She sighed. "As I said, I'm beginning to comprehend how much I don't know."

"Socrates thought that was the beginning of wisdom," Ian said.

Doreen's mouth twisted wryly. "It's the beginning of use-lessness," she said. "I mean, *you* know a lot of things that *are* useful. History's your specialty. What earthly use is my degree here?" She propped her head on a palm. "I suppose I could teach school, or something of that nature. Maybe a self-defense course, if I can get back in the swing—I used to do that sort of thing. The only really useful thing I've done since the Event is figure out exactly when we were."

"You've come up with a number of good ideas," Ian said stoutly, patting her hand. "Which is more than most of the selectmen. The only thing they did was manage to acquire some popularity before the Event, totally irrelevant now. You helped with the navigation tables and saved invalu-able time."

"What *is* relevant?" Doreen said moodily, sipping at her coffee. "Certainly not my plans for an academic career. Did you know, I wanted to be a ballet dancer once?" She looked down at herself and sighed. "When I was six. But even then it was obvious I'd never have legs up to my armpits."

Ian shrugged. "I've had an academic career," he said. "Not the same field, of course. At least you don't have to worry about cutbacks now."

She looked up at him. "You don't seem as . . . disori-ented as most of us."

"Cofflin and the captain aren't, much," Ian said. "Which is fortunate, because it's keeping us alive. As for me, well, I'm a historian, and here we are in capital-H History. I didn't have any close ties at home, so . . ."

He stirred the coffee and looked at the rear of the spoon. *Made in Japan.* Nothing much made in Japan right now except pots . . . Jomon? No, that was thousands of years before *this*. He shivered slightly. It could awe you, the sense of years before years, lives before lives, the sheer *depth* of history, even at the best of times. Right now . . .

He cast off the feeling. "I wanted to be a science fiction writer myself," he said. "I even wrote a few books—fantasy really, under a pen name. Then there was this car accident, my wife was killed . . ."

"I'm sorry," Doreen said. It seemed to be genuine. She patted his hand.

"Frankly, we were about to get divorced. Then I got a teaching position, which was an incredible stroke of luck when you consider the market for classical-era historians, and never had time for the writing. Not fiction, at least. But I always kept up reading it. Time travel's a fairly common theme in science fiction, and some of it's surprisingly well thought out." He shrugged. "Could have been worse; at one point, I was thinking of specializing in the Byzantine period, and *there's* something recondite for you."

"Ian . . ." she paused. "What do you think's going to happen to us?"

He spread his hands, palms out. "How should I know? We might all be turned into turnips tomorrow or carried off to Alpha Centauri, or thrown back into the Jurassic and eaten by velociraptors, or . . . hell, my sense of the orderly and predictable course of nature has taken a severe knock! If we're left here? We might make it. I'm more hopeful than I was right after the Event. But it'll be close. This voyage is important."

Doreen nodded thoughtfully, one hand touching the smooth oak staff beside her. "I'll do my best."

"If you don't mind me saying so, you're doing better than a lot of people too. Adjusting, that is," Arnstein said.

"My father's dead, I'm an only child, and my mother . . . well, we're not close," she said. "I could *almost* wish to see her face when she gets the news. No husband, no kids, no time for it yet. There are friends I'm going to miss, but it's not like they're dead. They're just not here."

Of course, we could have wiped them all out by landing here, Ian thought. He kept that firmly to himself. Nobody wanted to think about that hypothesis. Better to believe the more comforting one, that they had simply started another branch on the tree of time.

"It's fortunate that it's Nantucket, in a way," he said. "Most of the islanders were born here, and they're pretty clannish anyway."

"Yeah, I get the idea some of them have hardly noticed the outside world vanishing," Doreen laughed.

"Why don't we take a turn on deck?" he said. "The stars may be different, but they're pretty."

The shy smile returned. "Don't mind if I do."

"There's a certain irony involved here," Captain Alston said next morning, looking over the bales and boxes that her ship would be taking east.

Most of the cargo was from the boutiques and souvenir shops of the town—costume jewelry and colored beads, packed in green plastic garbage bags. Ditto for the cloth, the more colorful the better. There was a fair sampling of liquor, some tools, knives, the spears . . .

Booze, beads, and trinkets for the bare-arsed spear-chuckers of England, she thought.

Her father would have loved this. For a moment she smiled at the memory of a big soft-spoken figure with a workingman's hard hands, swinging her up toward the ceiling. Later he'd encouraged the reading habit in a girl, and that in a dirt-poor rural setting where it was unusual for anyone. The only time he'd ever really lost his temper with her was when her marks fell off. *White man wants a dumb nigger,* he'd shouted. *Smart black folk scare 'em. You scare 'em, girl, you scare the* shit *out of every one, or you'll feel my hand.*

The smile died. Her family had been farmers on Prince Island since slavery days. After emancipation that had meant owning their own land, not sharecropping; her great-great-grandfather had used his back pay to buy the farm when he mustered out of the Union Army's black regiments in 1865. Not much of a farm, but it had fed them and paid their tax for generations, and they'd hung on to it through Reconstruction, Jim Crow, and the Depression. Through times when being too prosperous or too independent could get a black man hung from a tree, doused in kerosene, and burned alive while he was still kicking. When the real-estate taxes went through the roof, her father had lost the land to a consortium building a resort. Nothing much had gone right for him after that, until the cancer came and ended it.

But he *would* have enjoyed seeing this.

Ian Arnstein nodded. "I wish we had a specialist in the European Bronze Age," he said, rubbing at his reddish-brown beard. "I wish anyone *knew* anything useful about the European Bronze Age."

"You've been doing a lot of research," Alston said. She liked seeing someone who took their work seriously. "You and Ms. Rosenthal and the librarian."

"Ms. Stoddard, yes. And not finding out much. I can tell you that Stonehenge has been up for a long time, and I can tell you that the Wessex Culture buried its chieftains with gold and amber and worked bronze. I can't tell you what language they spoke, or how they were organized, or whether they were peaceful or the equivalent of Comanches."

"You're a hell of a lot better than nothing," Alston said.

They were standing on the docks, as townsfolk-turned-stevedores carried bundles up the gangways and nets full of bales and boxes swung by on pulleys rigged from a cargo boom pivoting on the mainmast. The captain of the *Eagle* looked eastward and smiled.

"We'll go see."

Words welled up, from a poet who'd touched something in her; she stood looking out to sea and let them roll through her mind:

> What shall we tell you? Tales, marvelous tales
> Of ships and stars and isles where good men rest,
> Where nevermore the rose of sunset pales,
> And winds and shadows fall towards the West . . .

Martha Stoddard stood and watched the departure. Last night's fog had lifted, leaving only a few patches drifting silver-gray against the darker wolf-gray of the ocean. Engines throbbed, sacrificing precious fuel to take the ship through the narrow channel, around Brant Point and its lighthouse, past the breakwaters and into the open sea. She supposed that next time it would be boats with human beings sweating at the oars. . . .

Orders rang out, faint across the waters. The figures of the crew were ant-tiny on the yards, their feet resting on the rope rests below. Canvas dropped, fluttered, filled out in graceful curves. The yards braced around, and slowly, slowly, the great ship moved; water rippled smoothly back from either side of her sharp cutwater. Then she seemed to bow, rose again in a burst of spray, gathered speed toward the rising sun, and left a wake creamy white across the long blue swells. The crowd on the docks cheered themselves hoarse, then gradually fell silent and began to disperse, off to the work that awaited. A few lingered until the hull of the ship disappeared behind the curve of the world.

That's that, she thought.

Oh, the ship would be in radio contact, but she was getting a new appreciation of what distance meant. Martha

Stoddard had lived on Nantucket most of her life, nearly all of it except for her university days. You could feel very isolated here, especially in the winter when a storm closed down the ferry and airport and sent waves crashing up to the base of Main Street. Loneliness had never been a problem with her; she was content enough with her books and music—and oh, how she missed the music, there at a touch—and unwilling to tolerate much of the compromise that having other people in your life meant. It was only now that she realized what *isolated* really meant.

Jared Cofflin was among the last to turn away from the dock. Martha had a nodding acquaintance with him for many years, but they'd never really talked much before the . . . Event. He looked a little lost in civilian clothes, but he'd insisted that if they wanted to call him chief executive officer of the island instead of police chief, he wasn't going to wear a badge and gun. Another facet of the man revealed by the Event.

Odd that we're calling it that, she thought. Although she supposed they had to have some name for whatever it was that had happened. *And don't think too much about it, don't wonder how or why or who as you lie waiting for sleep, or it will drive you mad and Doc Coleman will have to come with the needle and the soothing words. . . .*

"Wish you were off with them, then, Jared?" she said.

He started, taken out of his brown study. A rueful smile lit his bony middle-aged face, and he smoothed a hand over the thinning blond hair on his scalp. "Ayup. Looks to be interesting over there."

"You're working too hard," she said suddenly.

"Everyone's working too hard," he answered. "We have to."

"You're doing the type that keeps you from sleeping, too. Not a good thing. What did you have planned?"

"Spending the morning doing paperwork, and the afternoon going 'round and seeing how things are developing."

"Going to and fro in the world, eh?"

He smiled, a chuckle of genuine humor this time. "Well, Pastor Deubel has been hinting that I'm inspired from that direction," he said.

"Man's a fool," she snorted. *And attracting more attention than is healthy.*

"A natural-born damned fool," he said, nodding agreement.

"Well, if you're going to be inspecting this afternoon, come inspect my Girl Scout troop. They're doing good work—"

"They are at that."

"—and they deserve to get a word for it."

He nodded, relaxing a little. "I think I'll do that, Martha."

"They're also making a picnic lunch of the edible greens," she said. "You're welcome to share it."

He smiled. "Bribery?" Fresh vegetables were already running out, the frozen were tightly rationed, and the canned were being saved for winter.

"Consider it research."

They stood on the dock, acknowledging the greetings of the crews of the fishing boats; the first loads would be coming in soon, to add to the malodorous vats of fish offal that stood waiting to be dragged out to the fields.

"Be seeing you, then," Jared said, hitching at his belt and settling his shoulders like a man contemplating a hard day's work.

She stood for a moment more, looking eastward. History and archaeology were her hobby; one thing that had always impressed her was how thin the record of the past was, a thing assembled out of rubbish and broken pots and the chance survival of a few words. Whatever they found east over the sea, it would be surprising.

Martha smiled to herself. Life had ceased to be dull, at any rate. On the other hand, there was that old Chinese saying. . . .

"Interesting times," she murmured to herself, drawing the jacket closer around herself against the chill spring morning. "Extremely interesting."

CHAPTER FOUR

March, Year 1 A.E.

Daurthunnicar son of Ubrotarix hid his relief as the last of the ponies swam ashore from where they'd been pushed off the decks; that was safer for their legs than scrambling over the sides of a beached ship. The stocky hammerheaded beasts shook themselves, snapping and kicking as their masters led them up the beach, whinnying at the pair hitched to the chariot in which he stood. Transporting horses across open sea was like a dream sent by the Night Ones, endless toil and danger. He made a sign with the bronze-headed tomahawk thonged to his wrist to avert ill luck at the thought. But they'd lost few of the chariot ponies that were the wealth and strength of the tribe. Lost hardly anything, in truth. One boat swept away and gone when the weather turned bad, no more. He'd feared worse, for his people were not sailors, although they'd dwelt near the shores of the sea a hand and half a hand of generations. Before that they came from the east, from the hills and great rivers and endless forests, and in the distant times of the heroes and gods-among-us they'd lived on the sea of grass where the sun rose.

The two great ships drawn up on the shore were another sign that his luck was good once more, his luck and the luck of his clan and tribe; he'd bargained for weeks to gain the help of the southron traders, offering goods and trading rights. Without them it would have taken a long time to get the whole of his people across the waters to the White Island, if it could have been done at all. As it was, most of the folk and their goods had come in canoes and rafts and coracles of tanned, tarred bullhide. A few now camped in the round wattle huts of the Earth Folk village that had been here before the Iraiina came; the rest up and down the shore in hide tents and boothies made of branches and turf, more than enough in these warm spring days. The traders had their own tents, near the beached ships—a sensible precaution, Daurthunnicar thought, although their leaders had drunk mead with him from a single cup where their blood had mingled, and sworn oaths to his gods and theirs. He put more trust in their need of him, and of the price he'd promised for their aid.

Their leader came toward him, a slight dark man in a tunic of fine Southland linen stained by the sea, with a cloak over his shoulder held by a golden brooch. A short bronze sword hung from his studded belt, and a knife; the men who followed him carried shield and spear, or bows. The traders traded where the local folk were strong, but they were ready enough to raid if the pickings looked good. The chariot chieftain had seen their men fight; they were well armed and well ordered, and their ships were wonders—sixty feet long, with a score of oars on either side and a square sail. Daurthunnicar raised his ax again, in salute, but he kept the advantage of height that the chariot gave him. The young nephew who held the reins kept the restive ponies motionless.

"*Diawas Pithair* give you strength," he said politely, invoking the Sky Father who was the overgod of the Iraiina. "And the Horned Man ward the Night Ones from the paths of your dreams."

Isketerol of Tartessos inclined his head. "And the Lady of the Horses be gracious to you, chieftain, and make your herds fertile," he said with equal courtesy.

He spoke the tongue of the Iraiina people well, but with an accent and choice of words unlike anything Daurthunnicar had ever heard. He'd said that he'd learned it not far from the shores of the Middle Sea, where kindred tribes had come to make their camps long before.

"We have fulfilled our oath," the merchant went on. "All your people are here, safe and hale."

Daurthunnicar grinned. "Hale when they stop puking," he said. "And I and the vanguard have begun to make good our word, as well. Come."

The Tartessian stepped up into the car; the wicker floor gave slightly under his weight, but the framework of light wood beneath was strong, and a chariot could hold three at a pinch. The driver chucked his tongue and leaned for-

ward, and the shaggy ponies broke into a walk, then a trot.
Daurthunnicar stood effortlessly erect despite the bumping
of the unsprung wheels over rut and clod and root, knees
and balance keeping him so with a skill learned since he
was barely able to toddle. Isketerol did well enough for a
sailor, only needing to lay one steadying hand lightly on
the leather bucket that held javelins when the war-car was
rigged for battle. The merchant's men trotted after, along
with a half-dozen of Daurthunnicar's own war band,
younger sons and such who had sworn themselves to his
personal service. Men hailed the chief as he passed through
the encampment, through the smoke of fires and the smells
of cooking, sweat and horse dung and damp wool. It didn't
stink too badly, despite the sprawling disorder; the chief
and his clan leaders and the heads of household saw to
that, and they wouldn't be here much longer anyway.
Women and *diasas*—slaves—bowed low as the chariot went
by, sun winking on ornaments of bronze and gold studding
the wicker sides and the harness of the horses.

His driver drew rein before a rough pen of woven saplings. Inside were a score of captives; Earth Folk, natives
of the island, taken prisoner in the month since the vanguard came ashore. Some of them bore wounds, but the
invaders hadn't bothered to gather in any of the severely
injured. Guards lifted their spears and cried Daurthunnicar
hail as he leapt down.

"Good strong ones," he said to his ally. "The women are
comely—I've had a few myself. They and the men will work
hard if they're beaten well, and the children can be raised
to any useful task. We've taken gold and copper, as well;
hides, furs, grain. Your ships will not go empty from our
new land."

Isketerol nodded, appraising the captives carefully
through the bruises and dirt that were their only clothing.
"The mines at home can always use more hands," he said.

Daurthunnicar smiled. It wasn't safe to keep too many
unfree males about, even of the rabbit-hearted Earth Folk.
*Hmm. When we've beaten them thoroughly, we'll leave the
villages that submit standing. They can pay tribute.* Thus had
his ancestors done with the Earth Folk on the mainland,
and over generations remade them in their own image.

"A fine beginning," Isketerol went on.

"And only a beginning," Daurthunnicar agreed.

He looked north and west where the wildwood fenced in sight. Inland were open downs his scouts had traveled, and farther west still were the larger kingdoms of the Earth Folk. There they had once built their circles of standing stones, bigger even than the ones on the mainland. There they had gold, copper, tin, herds. True, they were many, but once he'd won some initial victories to show that luck and Sky Father and the *Mirutha* were with him, he could summon more warriors from across the narrow sea. The tribes were on the move there, pressed by their own growing numbers and by new migrants from the eastern lands; the *Keruthinii* were distant kinfolk, but no less fierce and greedy for that.

Young men would come to pledge their axes to him, and perhaps households and clans after them. His folk would grow strong and spread over the land, and it would be theirs and their sons', and their sons' sons'.

The High Chief of the Iraiina smiled at his tomorrows.

"Reveille, reveille; heave out, trice up, lash and stow, lash and stow!"

The whistling pipes and the orders echoed through the *Eagle*. On the quarterdeck the officer of the watch nodded and the brass bell was struck, its clear metallic tones echoing across the deck.

"Sir!" the master-at-arms barked. "Crew turned out!"

Marian Alston smiled and cocked an ear at the sounds from the deck above, familiar as heartbeat. Now the mops began flogging the deck; scrub down weather decks, sweep down compartments, wipe down deckhouses. The harsh rasp of holystones on wet teak sounded. She finished her morning routine of stretching and chin-ups on the bar in the corner of her cabin and did a few *kata*—the sort you could do with barely arm's length on either side—before padding into the bathroom to brush her teeth. 0630 hours, and she was actually looking forward to the fried fish of breakfast; she left the last of the cornflakes to those who really needed them. Seasickness had never been one of her problems, even in the sort of blow they'd had last week south of Iceland: hundred-foot seas and freezing sleet.

And today . . .

"Today we ought to sight land," she said ten minutes later, sliding into her place at the wardroom table; the com-

manding officer usually ate breakfast and lunch in the officers' wardroom and dinner in the flag cabin aft. There was
a buzz of speculation among the morning watch. Next the
night-watch reports, the ship's situation-and-condition sum-
mary; freshwater consumption, distance to nearest point of
land . . . Everything routine, or as routine as it could be
under the circumstances.

"I still say Bristol would be a better bet, ma'am," Lieutenant Hendriksson said.

Alston shook her head, neatly filleting her cod while
compensating for the roll of the ship and grabbing a sliding
saltshaker in automatic reflex. "The Southampton area has
more natural deep water, Ms. Hendriksson," she said.
"What did we run tonight?" Under minimal sail, for cau-
tion's sake.

"Ninety miles, ma'am."

There was more conversation, passing by her in a meaningless buzz as she lost herself in thought.

"Good morning, Captain." A cadet stood at her elbow.
"Officer of the deck reports the approach of eight o'clock.
Permission to strike eight bells on time."

"Make it so." She followed him up the companionway
ladder and faced aft to salute the steaming ensign on the
gaff.

"Captain on deck!"

"Captain Alston here," she said crisply to the quarterdeck watch, returning their salutes.

Alston strode around the radio shack to the wheel and
stood with her hands clasped behind her back. The morning
wind was fresh from the southeast, stiffening, and the sky
was blue but hazed around the horizon, a last few stars
fading as winds and shadows fell toward the west. No
weather satellites now; she cocked an experienced eye and
made an estimate. The smell was salt and intensely clean.
Perhaps it was imagination, but she thought there was a
keener scent to it than up in the twentieth . . . the currents
and winds seemed to follow pretty much the same pattern
as the one she knew, though.

"Looks to me like she'll quicken," she said to the sailing
master. "But not enough to give us another blow."

"I agree, ma'am," he said, stifling a yawn; he'd been up
since the relief watch was called at 0345. "Shall we let
her run?"

Alston nodded. It was time to resume full speed; they'd made good time across the eerily empty northern Atlantic, under full press ahead day and night. The last two days they'd been more cautious, working south around Ireland and up toward the southern English coast . . . or what would someday become the southern English coast, after Celt and Roman and Saxon and Dane and Norman had come and gone. . . .

"And you should get some sleep, Mr. Hiller," she said.

The sailing master had been on the ship years longer than she, and he regarded *Eagle* as he might a beautiful, willful, and rather retarded child that had to be watched and cherished every moment.

"Sail stations," she said, when he had taken his leave. "On the fore, on the main, set uppers and lowers."

"Uppers and lowers, aye!" Lieutenant Walker echoed her; he was OOD right now. They were a bit overofficered, even without all the cadets' instructors on board, and she'd suspended the practice of having upperclassmen stand watches for now. He turned and went on:

"Lay aloft and loose all sail!"

Orders ran across the deck. The crew swarmed up the ratlines and out along the yards, or prepared to haul.

"Let fall!"

The crew aloft released the gaskets that held the furled upper sails on the yards. She kept a critical eye on that; if anyone was slow the whole weight of the sail would hang on the unreleased gasket, and it might have to be cut. This time it went smoothly, leaving all the sails *in gear*, ready to be deployed.

We're gettin' a lot of practice, Alston thought.

"Sheet home the lower topsail. Belay!"

"Throw off the buntlines, ease the clewlines!"

"Haul around on the sheets."

The white canvas blossomed free, running up the masts from bottom to top. The ship gathered way, a living feeling that came up through the feet and legs as she bounded forward. Alston laid a hand on a backstay to sense the huge strain as the standing rigging passed the force of the sails to the hull.

"Walk away with the halyard! Ease the upper topsail braces!"

Almost done now, smooth curves stretching taut over her

head. No need to overhaul, plenty of wind to set the foot of the sails against the weight of the lines.

"A little to starboard, if you please, Mr. Walker," she said quietly, without taking her eyes off the sails. Her legs felt the heave of the deck and the way the long sharp bows cut the waves, and her skin gauged wind and spray.

"Ease starboard, haul port, handsomely port!" the junior officer shouted over the quarterdeck rail.

The *Eagle* gathered way, heading northeast on a course that might have been drawn on the water with a ruler. The sun still had its lower edge dipped in the water, turning the low cloud there fire-crimson. Alston looked at the polished brass clinometer on the deckhouse. The ship was heeled to eighteen degrees, and they were making a good twelve knots. Excellent, but the wind was favorable, twenty degrees off her stern to starboard. Four cadets were draped over the lee rail, their safety lines snapped on, returning their breakfast to the ocean whence it came, but the rest were settling down nicely. If anything, the enlisted crew were showing more in the way of problems, which was a little surprising. There seemed to be a hump for everyone, when suddenly they stopped just knowing what had happened to them and *believed* it, down in the gut and blood. That was the crisis point, and if they got through it, they were safe enough. Keeping them working, hands blistered and backs aching, helped them over the hump. It reduced the feeling of unreality, of being lost in a nightmare dream.

She shook off the thought. All that could be done about that problem had been; and there was a raft of new ones about to descend. The rigging lines were humming, like a huge stringed instrument all tuned to a single harmony. A voice cried from the mainmast:

"On deck there! Ease the t'gallant buntline."

Feet thundered across the deck. Alston's eyes followed the motions that let the line out a trifle and then secured it again with automatic ease. The blue-green swell raised the *Eagle* in its rhythmic grip, and the big ship heeled deep to port. The masts and the humans on them traced circles against the sky and began their cycle again. Alston went forward of the wheel and into the pilothouse.

"Ms. Rapczewicz," she said to the woman at the chart table. "Do you have the plot?"

"Here, Skipper," she said. One of the watch handed Alston a cup of coffee; that was something she was going to miss, when they ran out. "We should make landfall about here, this afternoon. Assuming there's an England here."

"There'll always be an England," she said, and looked at the XO's pointing thumb. Just east of the Isle of Wight, Southampton Water. "In a geographical sense, at least," she added.

"Mr. Arnstein," she said to the professor. He was there with the astronomer, come up from the cubbyhole where they'd been deep in the books from the Nantucket Athenaeum. "Is there anywhere we could expect to get coffee, here and now?"

"Hmmm?" Arnstein looked up, preoccupied. "Coffee? Oh . . . um, that is, it comes from Ethiopia, originally. Kaffa province, fairly far inland. It went from there to the Yemen, and from the Yemen to everywhere. The Arabs spread it."

"I don't suppose . . ."

"Well, Captain, there's no mention of it for more than two thousand years after this date. Tea, maybe—"

"Boat ho!" The lookout's voice came faint from the tops through the door of the deckhouse.

Alston turned and went out on the deck. "What do you make?"

"Captain, small boat off to port, a mile and a half!" the lookout cried. Sailors crowded to the port rail.

"Mr. Walker, get those people back to their posts!" she said crisply. "Helm, come about. Stand by aloft, ready to take in sail. Mr. Walker, we'll heave to once we're near."

"Lower a boat, ma'am?"

She shook her head. "Not immediately. I want to take a look at them first. Ms. Rapczewicz, you have the deck."

"Ms. Rapczewicz has the deck, aye!"

Alston walked down into the waist, securing binoculars to her belt. Then she crouched, leaped to the bulwark, caught the ratlines, and swarmed upward, tarred rope harsh under her hands. She climbed, past the tops—triangular railed platforms halfway and three-quarters of the way up the mainmast—higher still, until the ship was a tiny lozenge far below. She nodded to crewfolk as she passed; the rigging was no place to waste hands on saluting, and she was up here fairly often, for exercise's sake. At last she came to the uppermost yard, the royal, where the steel tube of the mast was barely as thick through as her waist. A leg over the yard and her foot hooked through a line gave her a secure brace.

The wind whipped at her, chilly and strong, and the sail bellied out below in a pure white curve. She turned the focusing screw of the binoculars with the thumb whose fingers held the instrument, according to the old nautical rule of one hand for yourself and another for the ship. The boat grew; it was an oval about a dozen feet long, low in the water, with neither mast nor sail and a curious double prow. There were five men—five human figures, at least—lying prone in it, some half covered by blankets or cloaks. The boat rose, hesitated on the height of a swell, then skidded downward. The sluggishness of the motion told her it was taking water and would sink in a few hours. The crew certainly weren't in any shape to bail. She watched until she could see limbs flopping loosely. It would be disappointing if they were all dead. . . . No, one stirred feebly.

"On deck, there!" There was a trick to calling down so you could be heard, a matter of pitch rather than raw volume. "Ms. Rapczewicz, bring us alongside!"

"Alongside, aye!"

Alston went down the ratlines to the middle top, then slid down a stayline, using the soles of her shoes to brake against the hard ridged surface of the cable. When she sprang to the deck the small boat was visible from this level, and a cluster of figures were by the port rail, peering themselves.

"I've never seen anything like it," she said. "Professor Arnstein, what do you make of her?"

She handed over the binoculars. Arnstein pushed his glasses up on his head and adjusted them more clumsily. At last he gave a surprised grunt.

"I've never seen one either," he said. "But I think it's a coracle, a boat made out of sewn hides on a sapling frame. The Irish were using them well into the modern era. Isn't it a bit far from land for a boat that size?"

"Two hundred miles from the nearest shore, and God knows where they put to sea," Alston said. The distance was closing rapidly; she took back the glasses and watched. "There are half a dozen people in that boat. They're not movin', but I thought I saw . . . Wait, one *is* moving."

She turned her head. "Get the medic ready," she said. "Severe dehydration, salt poisoning."

"How do you know that, Captain?" Arnstein asked curiously—he was always curious, which was annoying sometimes but a large part of what made him useful.

Not to mention interesting. Her own reading in history had been largely maritime and military. Talking with Arnstein, you always learned something. It might be completely useless, but it would be fascinating . . . and she suspected that many of the facts that *seemed* useless would turn out to be valuable later. Glad to return the favor for once, she continued:

"If you're lost at sea in a small boat, and it's not cold enough for hypothermia, the commonest way to die is thirst," she replied. "Or salt poisonin' from drinking seawater; that'll kill you faster, unless you're very careful to take small sips. And from the look of them, I'd say these people were blown out to sea and mighty thoroughly lost."

Ian Arnstein watched with queasy interest as the sailors went down ropes and climbed into the coracle. It bobbed and heaved as two of them climbed aboard, made fast, and began examining the bodies lying in the shallow water that sloshed in its bottom.

One of the sailors vomited over the side. Even at this distance the livid faces and swollen tongues weren't pretty, and seagulls or something had been at them. The other went on with her task, checking the inert shapes one by one.

"Only one alive, sir," she called up after a moment, her fingers on the neck of a figure hidden under several cloaks, as her companion returned to his work. "He's pretty far gone, though. I need a sling lift."

"Lot of weapons," Arnstein said thoughtfully. "Not fishermen."

Alston nodded. "The survivor probably had enough willpower not to drink from the sea." Louder: "Send up the gear, after you've recovered the live one."

Doreen pushed her glasses back with a finger and peered, fascinated beneath her nausea. The bodies were all men, all fairly young. Weapons lay beside them: spears, bows, quivers, axes with yard-long handles and long narrow heads of bronze, the drooping edges shaped like a hawk's beak. The rest of the boat's load was bundles wrapped in hide or basketwork lashed with thongs.

The ship's physician and his helpers swung into operation
as the body came inboard. The rest of the crew hung back,
but nobody objected when Ian pushed close, Doreen beside
him. The stranger was a little above average height, perhaps
five-eight or -nine. His body was sunburned and his face
and lips swollen, but you could see that he was young,
probably in his late teens. The sparse yellow beard bore
that out too, merely thick down. His hair was twisted back
in a braid that reached halfway down his back, bound with
bronze rings. For clothes he wore a thigh-length leather kilt
pyrographed with cryptic designs, cinched by a broad belt
of sheepskin worn with the fleece side in; his feet were bare
and heavily callused. The face was generic European of a
northern or eastern variety, narrow and long-nosed on a
long skull, although the nose had been broken at some time
and had healed a little crooked. Arnstein could see a blue
eye when the doctor peeled back an eyelid and shone a
light into it.

"Quite a bod," Doreen murmured, playing with a lock
of hair.

Ian nodded; the youth was broad-shouldered and narrow
in the hips, smooth muscle running over an athlete's long-
legged body. He also had an interesting collection of scars
for a young man. A deep pucker on one leg, still a little
red; thin white lines on his forearms; a deep gouge out of
an upper shoulder. There were scars on his back as well,
parallel ones dusty-white against the smooth pale skin.

"Those are whip marks," Alston said. "He could be a
prisoner, or a slave, I suppose?"

Doreen spoke thoughtfully. "Aren't there cultures where
boys are flogged as part of their initiation rites?"

"Yes," Ian said. "Sparta for one. The other scars look
like fights to me. Fairly recent ones."

The ship's doctor had hooked up an IV. "Dehydration
and sunburn," he said. "Looks like a pretty healthy young
man. He should be all right in a few days."

"When will he be conscious?" Ian asked.

"Any time."

Doreen looked at the materials coming over the side.
Besides the weapons, the bundles held mostly extra
clothes—kilts, and simple T-tunics of linen or wool, woven
in plaids or dyed in soft natural colors, blanketlike woolen
cloaks, and a few pairs of shoes made out of a single piece

of soft leather, rather like moccasins. There were baskets of dried meat, fish, hard crumbly cheese, and crackerlike hard bread. And there was an array of shields, difficult to see at first since they'd been laid down as seats. They were round or oval, frames of wicker and shaped wood covered in hide and painted in gaudy shapes, the swastika-like fylfot, or animals. Horses, wolves, bears, the head of a bull, or a figure half man and half elk, with horns growing from his head. A few had bronze rivets as well.

"What's this?" she said, prodding at a string of varicolored bits of leather with straggling fur attached. A thought struck her, and she backed away and wiped the hand frantically down the leg of her trousers.

"Human hair," the doctor said, glancing aside. "Scalps."

A murmur went through the crew. Doreen swallowed and forced her mind back to the task at hand.

"This man's people use representative art," she said. "Why don't we get some pictures? We can show them to him and ask the names. There's a set of *National Geographics* in the wardroom that would be perfect."

"Special court-martial is now in session. When did this happen, Ms. Hendriksson?" Captain Alston said.

"About half an hour ago, ma'am. Cadet Winters and several other members of the crew came to me, with Seaman Rodriguez in custody, and I had him put under arrest."

The lieutenant was young, looking as stern and efficient as someone with freckles and a snub nose could; her eyebrows and lashes were as white-blond as her hair, standing out against tanned skin. Cadet Winters had a black eye and an arm in a sling; Seaman Rodriguez was standing between two guards, sullen and hangdog, a scowl on his acne-scarred face. His lower lip was wrenched and swollen, with a deep bite mark sending a trickle of blood down his chin, and his nose was going up like a balloon. From the look of it someone had stuck fingers into it and pulled hard. Every so often his hand made an abortive movement, as if to rub his crotch, and he stood slightly bent over. Most of the off-duty crew hung back a little, close enough to hear what was going on on the quarterdeck.

Alston sat behind a table, the XO and a chief petty officer on either side of her. It was a little odd for a special court-martial, but the circumstances were more so.

"Seaman Rodriguez, what's your explanation?" Alston asked.

"Ah, ma'am, she said she'd go into the paint locker with me." Which was strictly against the rules, but it happened now and then. "Then she changed her mind and started yelling and hitting me. Ma'am."

Winters was spitting angry, Alston saw—which was all to the good, much better than depression. "Cadet Winters?"

"He grabbed me and tried to stick a sock in my mouth and drag me into the locker," she bit out. "I gave him a knee where it'd hurt, ma'am, and then he punched me and dislocated my arm, so I went for him and yelled."

"Ms. Hendriksson?"

"Several of the crew heard screaming, ma'am, and ran to the locker. They found Seaman Rodriguez struggling with Cadet Winters; her clothing was torn, and they were both injured. Seaman Rodriguez had been drinking."

Others stepped forward to confirm the testimony. Captain Alston fixed Rodriguez with a basilisk stare. There was sweat on his face, and he looked around unconsciously for support and found none. She thought for a moment, and the three judges bent their heads together to consult in whispers.

"Court will now pronounce its verdict and pass sentence," she said aloud, in a formal tone.

"Hey—I mean, ma'am, this isn't no real court-martial."

"No, it isn't, Seaman. However, since it's unlikely we're going to get back to a base in the near future"—*or the distant past, you noxious little shit*—"it'll have to do. We're not under the Uniform Code of Military Justice anymore; we're operating under the authority of the Nantucket Council. I think," she went on to the others behind the table, "that we're agreed this goes beyond sexual harassment."

"Attempted rape, aggravated assault," Rapczewicz agreed.

"Ten years minimum, dishonorable discharge," the CPO said.

And concealing liquor, she thought; Rodriguez seemed to be the sort who couldn't win for losing. Aloud: "Seaman Rodriguez, you are found guilty. As imprisonment is impractical, under the circumstances I think discharging you on the nearest shore would be equitable."

Everyone knew what the nearest shore was, and they'd all seen the contents of the coracle or heard about the scalps. Rodriguez lunged forward, face crumpling. The guards grabbed him by the arms as he tried to go down on his knees.

"Oh, *madre de dios,* please, Captain, no—" They shook him into silence.

"But heinous as your crime is, under the law it isn't punishable by death, which marooning you probably would cause. Get him a lifejacket."

Hands shoved the bright-orange float jacket onto the man and laced it tight. "Get a rope sling and secure it on him. Reeve the other end to the fantail railing. Chief Master-at-Arms, execute the sentence," Alston said, her face like something carved from obsidian.

Two of the ship's noncoms obeyed with gusto, with the sole of a boot in the small of Rodriguez's back. The push sent him out like a screaming meteor, to fall in the curling blue water and white foam of the ship's wake. The line paid out and then sprang taut where it had been secured around the rail's metal supports. He wouldn't quite drown, but being towed behind the ship would be considerably worse than the flogging Rapczewicz had suggested. That water was cold, too. Not North Atlantic frigid, but chilly. He probably wouldn't die of hypothermia either. Not quite.

"Court is adjourned," Alston said. "Hands to their stations, if you please."

She caught the tenor of their murmurs. *Not bad,* she thought. That would preserve discipline, without making the crew think she'd started doing a Captain Queeg. And Coast Guardsmen were as much policemen as anything; they didn't have much sympathy for criminals. Plus more than two-thirds of the crew were cadets and one-third were women. All in all, she'd done the right thing. For justice, and for the good of the ship.

It wasn't her fault if she'd enjoyed it. She didn't like criminals either, particularly that kind. *I hope there are sharks out there, you little piece of shit.*

Walker coughed discreetly. "The . . . man we picked up is awake, ma'am," he said. "You said to let you know."

*   *   *

The stranger thrashed and moaned as Marian Alston bent over him. His eyes were blue, and right now they were showing white all around the iris.

"I think you'd better back out of sight, Captain," Ian said. "I don't think he's ever seen a black person before, and this environment is strange enough as it is."

Alston nodded and stepped back with some difficulty; it was crowded in the little one-bunk sickbay. "I'll be on deck," she said. "Report when you've found out anything significant."

"And don't exhaust him," the doctor warned. "He's still weak as a kitten."

The stranger stopped his feeble struggling and let himself be pushed back into the bunk, although his eyes still flickered across bulkheads and porthole, electric lights and metal shapes—alien madness, terror building on strangeness. "He must think he's dead and among evil spirits or something," Doreen murmured.

Ian leaned forward. The sight of his bearded face seemed to reassure the stranger. Ian put a cup of water to his lips, and the man sucked greedily at it; the IV they'd just removed had pumped a good deal into his system, but it wouldn't have soothed the throat. He said something in a fast-moving language and sighed, wiping his mouth with the palm of one hand and then letting the arm flop back to the sheet.

Ian looked over at Doreen, who shook her head. *Well, that was a long shot,* he thought. "Give it a try anyway," he said.

"Ar . . . mane . . . spurantate?" Doreen said, leaning close and speaking slowly. *Do you understand me?* in Lithuanian, her mother's tongue.

That brought a puzzled frown and more of the gibberish, but in a different tone. "I think he *almost* understood that," Doreen said regretfully. I may have caught one or two words. I think."

Ian smiled at the stranger—*Well, first things first, that's obvious,* he thought—and pointed at himself.

"Ian. Ian Arnstein."

The narrow blue eyes frowned, then flew wide in understanding. "IanArnstein," he said, prodding a callused finger with a rim of dirt under the nail at the man who sat beside the bunk. "IanArnstein, *p'tos.*"

Ian mimicked the gesture, pointing at the young man's bare chest. He nodded and rattled off a string of incomprehensible syllables. Ian sighed and made a rapid gesture through the air, then a very slow one. After a couple of repetitions the other got the idea and sounded out his name very slowly:

"*Ohotolarix,*" Doreen said. "Ohotolarix son of somebody. I think," she added, making a note on her pad.

Ohotolarix nodded vigorously, smiling and revealing very white teeth—except for one missing at the front.

"Let's try him on the numerals," Ian said. "They're stable over time. You start."

Doreen leaned closer again and held up one finger. "*Vienas,*" she said. Two fingers. "*Du.*" Three. "*Trys.*" Four. "*Keturi.*" Five. "*Pieci.*"

"*Eka!*" Ohotolarix said. He held up one finger himself, then the rest in sequence. "*Aonwos, duo, treyi, k'wethir, penkke!*"

After a few tries the two Americans caught the pronunciation, and Doreen noted them down. He grinned at the woman, then glanced aside at Ian, looking a little abashed.

Which is a significant datum in itself, Ian thought. It was probably impolite to look at another man's woman, where this kid came from. Ian cleared his throat and went up the number scale; Ohotolarix seemed to have increasing difficulty, speaking slowly and counting on his fingers as they climbed.

Damn, he thought. This was going to take a while. In most of the fiction he'd read, there was some ingenious way around language difficulties—a Universal Translator or a wizard with a spell, or the side effects of a dimensional gate. Here he was, living it instead of reading it, and he'd have to trudge dismally through the basics instead. *I should complain to the author.* He smiled at the thought; back when he'd written those thud-and-blunder heroic fantasies, he'd had a nightmare about meeting his own characters in a dark alley and having them revenge themselves on him for what he'd put them through.

"Hundred," he said, slowly holding up ten fingers ten times.

"*Simtas,*" Doreen echoed.

"*Kweadas,*" came the reply.

"It's a *centum* language," Ian said to Doreen. "Western branch of the family."

"Show him the horse."

The picture was a photo of a drawing, rather than a photograph of the animal; they'd decided that would be more familiar. Awe stood out on Ohotolarix's face as he handled the glossy paper. Ian pointed to the animal.

"Horse?" he said.

"Hepkwos!" Ohotolarix said delightedly. "Hworze. *Hepkwos!"*

Next she held up a picture of a timber wolf. *"Vilkas,"* she said.

"Wolkwaz!"

Ian ran his thumb down his list of words. *Proto-Indo-European* wlkwos, *wolf,* he read. Almost unchanged. *God, we* are *a long way back.*

The exchange went on until Ohotolarix dropped suddenly and irrevocably asleep, and the doctor chased them out of sickbay. Alston looked at them sharply as they came up to the quarterdeck.

"Well?" she said.

Doreen waved her notebook. "It's definitely an Indo-European language, ma'am. A lot of the words were *very* close to Lithuanian, and some of the inflections and syntax, even. He caught a few phrases I spoke right off—'give bread,' things like that. I think I could learn it in a couple of months—for very very simple things, in a week."

"That could be extremely useful," Alston said. "Anything else, Professor?"

Ian shook his head. "Not much. It's a highly inflected language, and if I knew more Mycenaean Greek . . . I *think* it *might* be an extremely early form of Celtic. Some of the sound shifts between what he speaks and what the references list as Proto-Indo-European forms suggest that it might be a sort of Proto-Celtic. I'm not a linguist, though— my knowledge is very general, and I'm not sure we're transcribing accurately. Hell, the language might just as well be Proto-Tocharian, or some subfamily that never got—"

"Anything else we can *use,* I meant, Professor," Alston said with heavy patience.

Ian reined himself in. "Apart from that, this guy's a *wirtowonax,* which I think means warrior, or possibly something like freeman or tribesman or citizen; and he's got a chief, or king, or panjandrum, a *rahax,* named Daurthunnicar. I'm probably playing hob with the inflections there, by the way. From sign language as much as anything, this Daurthunnicar and his warriors, and women and children and horses, were crossing a body of water. To fight someone, presumably. Our boy—his name's Ohotolarix, by the way—and his friends were caught by a squall and couldn't find the land again. I'd guess they paddled in circles until they dropped. Ohotolarix hates boats, incidentally, and loves horses."

"Oh, joy," Alston muttered. "We're sailing right into the middle of someone's war. Hell of a situation to trade in."

"Oh, I don't know," Ian said. His face slowly creased into a smile. "It might just be the best possible situation to trade in, if you know what I mean, Captain."

"They come," the scout whispered. "Back along their track, as we thought they would."

They could hear how hooves pounded dirt away down the forest trail, louder and louder as the invader war band neared. Human feet slapped the earth, wheels creaked, an axle squealed, a horse blew out its lips in a wet flutter of sound. The war-car held a near-nude adolescent driver and a warrior in leather armor and bone-strapped leather helmet. The ponies stamped and snorted, their breath visible in the early-morning chill as the blur of the eight-spoked wheels slowed.

Swindapa of the Star Blood line of Kurlelo slowly drew the sling taut between her hands. The early-spring leaves made scanty cover, but the band hidden here were all hunters with the Spear Mark tattooed on their chests; most of them were from lands overrun by the invaders, the Sun People, too. Thirty of them, more than enough for this. She was the only woman, but the others had allowed her along for the sake of her birth, and the weapons she had brought . . . and after she'd shown them what she could do with the leather strap she carried. These were desperate men who cared little for law or custom or the will of the Star Blood who had not protected their homes.

For herself. . . . Her mother had forbade, her aunts and uncles—even the man who was probably her sire—had shaken his head and said it was a wild youngster's fancy. Yet here she was. Fear and excitement wrestled in her belly, like the Moon Woman pursuing the Sun. The Sun People had brought her pain; they'd broken the knee and the life of her man, they'd killed and burned. It was time to drive them out. She swallowed through a mouth gone dry and picked her target.

Two dozen footmen stopped and squatted around the chariot, light winking off bronze spearheads, glinting on polished leather. They talked among themselves in the harsh tongue they'd brought across the water, or swigged from skins. The chief waited for a moment, then called out to his followers. One threw back his head and laughed, and then they rose and spread out in formation behind the war-car, like a flock of geese spread back from the leader in wings on either side. The charioteer clucked to his ponies, and the warrior beside him hawked and spat over the side to clear his throat.

"Shoot!" the leader of the Earth Folk band bellowed, bounding to his feet. He drew his yew bow to his ear and obeyed his own order.

Bowstrings snapped and arrows whickered as men sprang erect. A pony went down, screaming like a woman in bad labor. The other reared, and the driver and warrior leaped down from the cart. Swindapa sprang forward, ululating rage, whipped the sling in two swift circles around her head, then cast. The polished egg-shaped stone within was heavy basalt, and flew almost too fast to see. When its arc ended in a snarling Iraiina face there was a half-seen splash of red and the man pitched backward to lie sprattling. She shrieked glee and tossed another stone into the soft leather pocket at the bottom of the sling. Men were running forward with spear and club and knife. Others shot over their heads; she darted about, looking for a clear path to a target. The fight boiled to close quarters; the Sun People stood shield to shield and cast back the first disorderly rush, but there were fewer of them left on their feet. The Earth Folk prowled around their line, rushed forward, retreated with blood on their weapons or on their own rent skins. Metal and stone and wood banged on each other, on the leather of shields. Men screamed in rage, or pain greater than they had thought flesh could feel.

The natives fell back, panting, and men glared at each other over a dozen paces of space empty save for the dead. The invaders had no missile weapons left; they'd thrown their spears, and few of them were bowmen. The Earth Folk archers had space to shoot again; they came near and stuck their arrows ready in the ground at their feet, grinning mockery. Swindapa ran to join them, yellow hair blowing behind her like a banner beneath her headband, light on her feet as a deer—in the old tongue her name meant Deer Dancer. She tried to see the fight as a whole, tried to ignore the men who wailed or groaned or lay silent on the grass. Perhaps because of that she was the first to see other figures moving through the woods.

"More of them! Run!" she shouted. *The hunters have become prey. The Barrow Woman will eat us unless we flee.*

The men nearby were too intent on their revenge to hear her. She ran up behind one and slammed a callused foot into his backside, dodging back as he whirled. His face went from rage-red to fear-white as he followed her pointing finger. In a few seconds the ambushers-turned-ambushed were ready to flee, but those seconds were too many. A bison war horn dunted in the woods, lowing and snarling. Two more chariots rumbled forth onto the green turf of the clearing. The drivers leaned forward, slapping the horses' backs with the reins to urge them into a gallop, and they circled to cut the Earth Folk off from the sheltering trees. Behind them their clansmen ran, almost as fast as the horses, in no fixed lines but in better order than any host the Earth Folk could muster, each man keeping his arm's-length distance from his neighbor. Now the numbers favored the Sun People.

"Forward!" they cried. She could follow their tongue; most children of the high families learned it, to deal with traders if nothing else. "Forward! *Mirutha* with us! Tauntutonnaurix with us! *Addadawiz Diawas Pithair!* Forward with Sky Father!"

Swindapa had listened to her uncles and their nephews talking of skirmishes with the longer-settled clans of the Sun People in the valley running to the sea northeast of here. In one such her lover had been crippled, his knee smashed with an ax. She grabbed at the shoulder of the band's leader and shook it.

"We must break through," she said. "If we get into the thickets, they can't follow us. Woods Woman will hide us."

The man nodded, the wild flickering of his eyes growing steadier. "We go," he growled.

Swindapa never remembered much of the fight that followed. She managed to sling most of the stones left in her pouch, breaking a horse's fetlock and striking men—one she thought had an arm broken beneath his shield. Then the loose mass of the Earth Folk's charge struck the running line of the Iraiina war band. The first line buckled before their packed weight, but more ax-bearing men leaped howling into the fray from either side, each aiding the other like a pack of wolves. Swindapa darted into the melee, jumped on the back of a Sun People warrior, and whipped the sling around his neck, twisting as hard as she could with crossed wrists. The axman choked and flung up his hands to scrabble at his throat, then collapsed. Swindapa flung herself backward to roll free and run, jinked past a spearthrust, dropped flat under the swing of a chieftain's bronze sword, and bounced back to her feet.

Something struck her across the shoulders. Her face plowed through the turf; her palms burned as they took the impact of the fall. For a single instant she lay dazed, long enough to see the last of her companions die under the tomahawks and spears. A sandaled foot tried to stamp down on her hand, and she flogged herself back to alertness. She snatched out her bronze dagger and slashed at the hands trying to seize her. A man tumbled backward with a yell as the razor-sharp edge drew a line across his thigh. Swindapa was on her feet now, twisting, dodging. Another slash scored along a hairy muscular forearm, and the man dropped his ax and swore.

His companions hooted mirth at him. More rushed at her behind shields. She leaped to try and vault one, stabbing at the man behind. The other slammed into her side, sent her staggering. A spearshaft cracked against her wrist and the knife went flying through the air. Arms grabbed her from behind, around the chest. She shrieked and bit down into a wrist, kicked, tried to gouge an eye and ripped skin across a cheek as the man twisted his fork-bearded head. A fist rocked into her jaw, another into her belly, another into her head above the ear.

The world went away in whirling colors. Everything was very faint. She could only mumble and push feebly as they threw her down and ripped off her thong skirt. Two men pulled her legs wide, and a third knelt between them, fumbling at his kilt.

* * *

"The *rahax* won't be pleased," Shaumsrix son of Telenthaur said.

He scowled around the clearing. "Four good warriors dead, and eight more wounded—" he counted only those too badly hurt to trek and fight, of course—"one of those so badly he'll be crippled if he lives. *And* three good horses lost."

Men were moving around, hooting and puffing and slapping each other on the shoulder. They gave rough aid to the wounded, retrieved arrows, scalped slain foemen, made repairs, skinned the dead horses. Unless they'd lost an oath-brother, the clansmen were content with their victory. A chief had to think more deeply.

"We fed two-hands-three-times of them to the Blood Hag," his brother Merenthraur said recklessly; she didn't like to be called that, better to use her praise-name of Crow Goddess. He counted on his fingers and then said: "Two-hands-less-two of them for every one of us, nearly."

Night Ones eat your eyes for a blockhead, the elder sibling thought. You couldn't say such things to a chief's son, not to his face, of course, even if you were the elder brother by the senior wife. Aloud he went on: "Thirty Earth Folk farmers are a poor bargain for four of our clan's warriors. We're not so many we can afford to lose men every day. We lost too many back in the homeland."

And lost the war, he did not add, not in words.

That still clawed at him, the memory of tumbled broken chariots and burning thatch, fear and flight. He forced his shoulders to unknot and pulled his lips back down on his teeth. It was different here. The Kcruthinii who'd driven them off the mainland were Sky Father's children too, even if they called Him only by His praise-name Long Spear. The Earth Folk here were not; they worshiped the devil-bitch Moon Woman. Only Sky Father's children had victory-right in war. The Iraiina would win here. *If* they were wise as well as strong. No Iraiina lacked courage—they tested their boys too well and saw that cowards did not live long enough to breed. But all the gods and warrior spirits would spit on a fool and send him bad luck, even a brave fool.

Merenthraur shrugged; the bone scales on his leather jerkin clattered. "We won. And we can't let bands of them skulk in the woods, either, or how are we ever to set up our own steadings?"

Shaumsrix nodded reluctantly. "Too many of these had good weapons," he said. Most of them had had metal knives, and there were a fair number of bronze spearheads, too. Even the girl had had a good bronze knife. Used it pretty well, too, as well as any of the rabbit-men she'd been with.

A thought came to him. "You, pick the Fiernan slut up," he said, walking over as a man finished with her.

"Plenty for all," he said resentfully.

The chief looked down at the woman—girl, rather; she'd never dropped a youngling, from the look of her hips and belly. Probably pretty when she wasn't bruised and battered; there were streaks of semen and blood down the insides of her thighs and bite marks on her high breasts, and one of her eyes was swelling shut. Long yellow hair trailed out on the grass, and there were red marks across her chest where a necklace of gold-rimmed amber disks she wore had been ground into her skin by the men mounting her. Nobody had bothered taking it from her yet; let loot carry loot. Shaumsrix leaned down and yanked the necklace free. Her head flopped loosely as he pulled the ornament away. There was no mind behind the eye left open.

"Ordinary Earther bitches don't wear things like this," he said, waving it in the clansman's face. "This one may be useful, or she may know something. The *rahax* will decide. Put her in my chariot. Not that way, fool."

The man who'd grabbed her by an ankle dropped it and sulked off. Two others, older men, picked her up and slung her onto the wicker floor of the war-car; Shaumsrix ordered his driver to bind her wrists and ankles. *She'll live,* he decided. If the blows to the head didn't kill her, sometimes there were convulsions and death days later. He tossed the necklace in his free hand, scowling; a nice piece of plunder, fine smoothed amber disks rimmed in worked gold—but he'd rather have his warriors back, for all the scalps and bronze they'd taken. Their axes were the strength of the tribe, and the strong could always get booty. He looked down at the girl again.

He had a feeling that there was something important about this one; perhaps a warrior *Mirutha* was whispering in his ear, perhaps an ancestor's ghost . . . or perhaps it was a land spirit, even a Night One. Shaumsrix shivered. He'd ask the Wise Man when he got back to camp, and make a sacrifice.

The chieftain slammed the flat of his ax against the side of his chariot. "Get ready, you slugs!" he bellowed. "We move in—"

His axhead caught the light as it pointed to where the sun would be in twenty minutes.

CHAPTER FIVE

April, Year 1 A.E.

"We're going to try and find this boy's people," Alston's voice said through the earphones. "We have a few words of his language, and presumably there'll be a goodwill factor for handing him back."

"Unless he dies of the common cold," Cofflin said gloomily.

"Our medic doesn't think so. He did get the runs, but a few pills cleared him up." A pause. "How are things back there?"

"Everything's more or less on schedule," Cofflin said. "Enough to eat, just, but everyone's getting tired of fish. There's been some tension, people are upset—I think it's really sinking in that we're stuck here."

"Here too, but this situation is a little more exhilarating," Alston said. "Perhaps because everything is strange. In any case, I'll keep you informed of developments, Chief Cofflin. Over."

"Likewise, Captain," he said. "Cofflin out," he added, and laid down the radiophone.

"Reception's good," the operator said. "Better than I can remember it ever being, before."

"Nobody else on the air, Karen," he said, looking out over the little airport from the control tower.

It already had a deserted look. The small planes were all in the hangers, or staked down under tarpaulins; Andy Toffler was doing the air scouting for the fishing and whaling, with what gasoline they could spare. Out beyond, thick columns of smoke marked fields where the brush was being fired.

He looked down at his notes. Quick passage, no trouble so far, and they'd made a beginning on talking to the locals, picked one up at least. *I wish everything was as smooth here.*

At least his stomach didn't hurt every time he thought about the food situation anymore. You could live on fish. He still dreamed about that burger he'd been about to buy when all this started; they'd eaten the fresh meat almost overnight, with no more coming in. Except whale meat, which was oily and always had a slight fishy overtone. Well, hell, whole peoples had lived off salt cod. The clearing was mostly done, planting going well . . . and everyone was going a little crazy.

Or most people were. "Well, I've got a dinner date," he said.

"Martha Stoddard?" the operator said, grinning.

"None of your business, Karen."

The phone rang. "It's for you, Chief. Pastor Deubel is at it again."

"Science has no explanation for this thing that has happened to us," the clergyman said.

There were over a hundred people listening to the open-air service outside the little church on Milk Street. Normally there wasn't a church on the island that got that many on a Sunday, not on Nantucket, where the biggest congregations were Unitarian and Congregationalist. The day was fine, mild, a breeze from the south that kept the smell of whale blubber boiling from creeping up from the docks. The people . . .

Cofflin leaned his bicycle against the wall of a house built for whaling skippers—it crossed his mind, an irrelevant fragment, that they'd be perfectly at home with the faint smell of oil and fish that hung over the crowd. Their faces were rapt as they watched the man on the steps. He paced back and forth, as worn as they—the able-bodied clergy had been pitching in, like everyone else—but his face glowing with conviction.

That's a good way to put it, Cofflin thought. It *was* a fire, and sparks were catching in the dull faces of the onlookers, lighting them from within.

"Science cannot explain it. We must ask ourselves, brothers and sisters in Christ, *why has this thing happened to us?* For this is a mighty and terrible thing that has happened, a thing to shake the earth. Not only earth: a thing to echo from the walls of Heaven, and make the gates of Hell rejoice."

"Fallacy," muttered a voice beside him.

Cofflin started. He had been caught up in the sermon, despite himself. Martha Stoddard was not; her gray eyes were cool and appraising.

"Fallacy," she said again. "Two, in fact. Science couldn't explain how the sun kept going, before Einstein. That didn't mean science was inadequate, simply that it hadn't gotten around to solving that problem yet. And just because something big falls on you doesn't mean there's an intention behind it. That's the pathetic fallacy, historical division. Mount St. Helens didn't blow up because God was mad at the bears."

Cofflin grinned. They were *all* off balance psychologically, with a few exceptions. Martha Stoddard seemed to be one of them.

Pastor Deubel was winding up: "All this I have said to you before, my brothers and sisters. Today we must ask a new question. If science cannot explain this thing that has happened to us, and if some great purpose is here, *what is that purpose?*"

He wheeled and pointed out into the crowd. "What is the purpose for which this miracle—for it can be nothing else—has been accomplished?"

Cries of *God!* and *Jesus loves us!* punctuated his gesture. He raised his hands.

"Why would God, a loving God, a God who watches as each sparrow falls, thrust the blameless into danger and hardship?"

"Oh, Lord have mercy, doesn't that man's church teach any theology at all?" Martha hissed through clenched teeth.

"We have been thrust into the past *before Christ*," Deubel shouted. "Christ's sacrifice is not yet made. Moses has yet to bring God's holy word down from Sinai to the Jews. We are lost in a world of pagans and devil-worshipers, cut off from the healing blood of the Lamb. To take the blood and wine now is *blasphemy*."

This time there were moans and cries of *no!* from the crowd. Many were weeping. Cofflin felt a touch of apprehension himself; he was a believing man, if not much of a churchgoer. *Come on, now,* he told himself, remembering something his own minister had said once. *God's not in time. God's outside time, He's eternal.*

"Some mighty power of the other world has done this thing. I tell you, there can be only one answer: *Satan!* And his purpose? Haven't we all thought how our presence here must change the history of humankind? Can there be a Herod, if history is changed? A Roman Empire? Can there be an Augustus who sends out a decree that all the world is to be taxed? A Pontius Pilate? Will there even be a House of David?

"What else can the Evil One intend than to frustrate God's plan by *preventing the birth of our Lord Jesus Christ?*"

This time the reaction from the crowd included screams of fear. Many fell to their knees and began to shout prayers.

"Well, that's original, at least," Cofflin said quietly. He moved forward half a step, so that the clergyman could see him. It cut through the exaltation on the man's face. The rest of the sermon was a call to pray for guidance.

"Man's dangerous, Jared," Martha said.

"Ayup. On t' other hand, I was a policeman, and now I'm head of state, God help me—but this isn't a police state. So long as the man does nothing but talk, I can't stop him."

"Later might be too late."

Cofflin took his bicycle by the handles, and they turned and walked toward Martha's house, not far from the Athenaeum with its white columns. The house she was using, rather; she'd moved into one of the fancy pensions on Broad Street, since the owners weren't there and neither were the guests booked for the summer. A number of teachers had followed her; one thing the Town Meeting had been firm about was that the schools had to continue, somehow, at least part of the week. She and they weren't the only ones that had switched dwellings. Some families were doubling up, and many single people were taking over the empty boardinghouses in groups. It saved on cooking and housework and made child care easier, and without television or radio or recorded music, or even electric light, most people found a whole house too cheerless for one person.

"No sense in allowing perfectly good broiled scrod to go

to waste," Martha said practically. "Held off on it when I heard you had trouble with Deubel."

"Ayup," Cofflin said, and nodded greetings to several of the people passing by.

She pulled back a cover on the basket she was carrying. "Dandelion greens, chicory, and pigweed, with sliced raw Jerusalem artichokes. Salad."

Cofflin's mouth watered, and he swallowed. "Thoughtful of you, Martha," he said.

"Ought to get some use out of being a Girl Scout leader."

They walked up the porch, through the dining room, and out into the backyard. Several of the teachers were sitting around, fiddling with a whale-oil lamp. They'd found hundreds of the lamps, maybe more, in antique shops, in the hotels as ornamentals . . . most of them functional, with a little work. The whale oil was abundant now, since they were harvesting the whales for their meat more than anything else. More of the oil had started off the wood in the barbecue, but the coals were low and glowing now. A pot burbled on one corner of it, sending out a savory, almost nutty odor.

"Dulse," Martha said, jerking her head toward it and picking up a platter with two large breaded fish on it. She slipped them onto the grill. They began to sizzle immediately. Meanwhile she rinsed the wild greens from a bucket of water standing in the kitchen—the running water was on one hour a day—and dumped them into a bowl, adding something else from a Styrofoam cooler. "Sea grass," she added. *"Ulva lactuca."* She tossed them with a little oil and vinegar.

Both her own suggestions. *Bless her,* Cofflin thought. He'd never considered seaweed as anything but stuff that washed up on beaches and smelled, and him a fisherman and a fisherman's son.

"Well, make yourself useful, Jared," she said.

He flipped the fish, which were just firming up, and then slid them back onto the serving platter. They went into the dining room and sat; it was just about sundown, and someone had lit the lamp bracketed to the wall. It cast a puddle of yellow light around their table.

"Fine eating on these scrod," Jared observed after a moment. "Haven't been doing this well myself."

"Bachelor," Martha observed, serving the dulse.

There were some mussels cooked with it, in a thickened broth. Jared savored the green nutty taste of the cooked seaweed and the contrasting flavors of the wild herb salad. His forehead was sweating slightly, and not from the eating or the mild spring weather. Martha ate with the same spare economy she did most things; he was a bit surprised when she brought out a half-bottle of white wine and poured them both a glass.

"Ill wind that blows no good," he observed after a moment. "Been meeting people I wouldn't have, before the Event."

Martha nodded. "Think I can guess what you're leading up to, Jared," she said.

He paused with a forkful of fish on the way to his mouth. The sweat rose more heavily on his forehead. *Christ, man, what sort of a fool are you?* he thought. *A high school graduate fool.* Just because the world had turned upside down didn't mean *everything* was changed. If Martha Stoddard wanted someone, it would be someone from her own level.

"And I'm not saying no," she added.

"You're not?" An effort of will prevented his voice from turning into a squeak.

"Wouldn't have asked you over if I were," she said. "Or seen this much of you since the Event. I'm not a cruel woman by nature, though I can't abide fools. Which is why I'm still single, despite a few offers. There was a man in university, archaeologist, did some excellent work on Mogollon pots, but then he started to talk about football. . . . Mind you, I'm not saying yes either."

An even greater effort of will prevented him from saying *You're not?* in idiotic counterpoint to his last contribution to the conversation.

"And the world was crowded enough as it was," Stoddard went on meditatively. "None of that applies now, of course . . . and I'd say you're not any kind of a fool, Jared. But we do have to find out how we'd suit, and that should take a while. Plus we're none of us ourselves, right now. Best not to be hasty."

"Bundling's a little out of style, even here," he said, feeling a laugh welling up. He let it out as a dry chuckle, and felt his shoulders relax. It seemed that some things went on despite glowing domes of light and journeys into the past. Even tentative middle-aged romance, apparently.

"It may come back, with a cold winter and no central heating," she replied. They touched their glasses.

The Cappuccino Cafe was still open, although the days when it served what Cofflin had always thought of as yuppie fast food—quiches and such—were long past. There were still customers, although the food was made mostly from the same basic rations as everyone was eating. A new exchange system was growing up using the work chits the Council issued. They could be exchanged for food and fuel, but a lot of people preferred to trade some of them in and eat at a place like this now and then, rather than cook at home. *Barter, too,* he thought, watching two teenagers come in with a brace of rabbits and a duck and begin haggling with the proprietor. Their bicycles were leaned up against the lampposts on Main Street outside, and they had slingshots stuck in the back pockets of their jeans. It was the end of a chilly, foggy spring day; outside a few windows showed lit against the gray gloom. The light had an unfamiliar yellow tinge, lanterns or candles rather than the white brilliance of electricity.

"At least we're not short of whale oil," Cofflin said to Dennis Brown, the manager-owner, when the youngsters had collected their chits and IOUs.

"I should hope not," Brown laughed.

He jerked his head toward the counter behind him. The pots and warming pans were suspended over improvised whale-oil heating lamps. Back in the kitchen an equally improvised stove with a chimney of sheet metal had replaced the electric ranges. It burned wood well doused with the oil, and twists of rendered blubber. The smell of the blubber was a little more ripe than the nutty odor of the oil itself, but they'd all gotten used to it . . . a little, at least. Here it was just an undertang to the scent of cooking.

"What'll it be, Chief?"

"A turkey club sandwich, and a fresh green salad, with a banana and a couple of peaches for dessert," Cofflin said. They both laughed. "What've you got?"

"Lentil soup with rabbit, mixed seafood chowder, and whaleburger. Or whaleloaf, if you want to call it that. And biscuits."

"Rabbit and biscuits! Hot damn! The lentil with rabbit, and biscuits," he said. "Three hour-chits do it, or do you want some sort of trade?"

Dennis shrugged. "I've got two kids, Chief; I figure we're pulling through because of the way you got things organized. It's on the house."

"The town pays me to do my job," Cofflin said gruffly. "I'm not taking freebies." He held up a hand. "Not even when it's all right. Bad example. Thanks anyway. Two orders, then."

Dennis nodded. One of his people dipped out ladlefuls of the soup into bowls and surrounded them with the biscuits. There were only two each, but he still felt saliva spurt into his mouth at the sight and smell of them. Flour was getting scarce; there just wasn't much on the island.

He took the tray and ambled over to a table, sitting with a bit of a groan of relief. He'd been on his feet all day, or pedaling the damned bicycle, and whatever Coleman said about it being good for them, he still missed cars. For a moment he sighed and remembered; you just got in, turned the key . . . and suddenly five miles wasn't all that far. Less than ten minutes' travel, warm and dry and comfortable. The power seemed almost godlike. At least Nantucket was relatively flat—although he'd become painfully conscious, mostly in his calves and thighs, that a rise that was barely perceptible behind the wheel was all too obvious when you were pushing pedals. Cofflin looked at his watch. Martha had said she'd be here at six, and it wasn't like her to be late.

The bell over the door rang, and a man pushed through. Cofflin looked up, and smiled to see Martha behind him. The smile ended when he focused on the man's face again. It was scraggly and unshaven, but no more than many in town these days—Cofflin had given up shaving more than twice a week himself, what with the razor blade situation, until he found an old cutthroat straight razor in the attic. The man stank of dried sweat, too, for which there was less justification, and his coat was crusted with food stains and dirt. Before the Event, Cofflin would have figured him for a bum—homeless, the jargon was—and seen that he got on the ferry back to the mainland first thing. These days, he looked like an islander who'd been letting himself go a bit.

Have to see about that proposal for bathhouses, he

thought. It was just too *hard* to heat water yourself and then haul it upstairs to a bathtub, particularly when you were exhausted already.

A few people gave the man room, wrinkling their noses at his smell. He marched over to a table, one where a quiet-looking woman in her thirties was sitting with a half-eaten bowl of chowder and a book. She was as worn as he, but considerably cleaner. When she looked up at him, she frowned and snapped:

"Donald, what part of *no* don't you understand? It's over. Learn to live with it."

"Do you understand this, bitch?" the man said.

Something in his voice froze Cofflin's smile. His head was turning even as the Glock came out. Time slowed; he could even see the rims of dirt under the man's fingernails, and the yellow color of his teeth as he snarled through a matted beard glued in clumps with old food.

"Do you?" the man—Donald, Cofflin supposed—said thickly. "Do you understand this?"

Donald Mansfield, he remembered. *Up on assault charges for attacking Angelica Brand a couple of weeks ago.* Sentenced to extra hard labor and reduced rations; his wife had left him shortly after that. Evidently he hadn't been adjusting to the Event as well as she had. There was a fair amount of that. Men seemed to be slightly less psychologically flexible, on average.

All that took just long enough for the expression on Martha's face to freeze and her eyes widen as they slid sideways toward the man with the gun. Cofflin's hand dropped toward his, and found only an empty belt holding up a pair of blue jeans. George Swain was head of the police these days. *Maybe I should have kept the gun.* He began to surge forward, cursing the decades that had slowed him down.

The woman's face had gone fluid with shock; her hands came up in a pushing gesture in front of her and she turned her head aside. That left it facing toward Cofflin. He could see the features twist, not so much with pain as incredulous shock as the bullets punched into her torso. Blood leaked from mouth and nose. She toppled backward and the man grabbed at her. He caught her with one arm around her body and staggered backward himself, to rest with his shoulders against the rear wall of the restaurant, sliding down to sit on the built-in couch. The dying woman slid across him, lying in his lap in a parody of affection. Somewhere in the room a scream tailed off into a choking, retching sound. *Ricochet*, Cofflin thought. No time to turn around and check who.

"You wouldn't listen to me, Michelle," the gunman crooned. "It'll be better now. We're together again. I'm sorry I had to hurt you. . . ."

The gun came up and trained on Cofflin. He stepped slightly sideways, putting himself between it and most of the people in the room; those to the side were moving away on their own.

Now, what do you say to someone who's utterly, completely, incontestably bugfuck? Cofflin thought.

"Mr. Mansfield, why don't you put the gun down before anyone else gets hurt?" he said, his voice calm and controlled. *High pucker factor here.* "You can't hold on to it forever."

"Michelle will be with me forever!" he said. "You'll never take her away from me!"

He was a little over twice arm's length away. Cofflin was quite close enough to see his hand begin to clench on the gun, much too far to cover the distance needed to stop the 9mm bullet punching into him.

Whack. Something struck the wall near Mansfield. *Whack.* This time it hit him in the body, bringing a grunt of surprise and pain. The gun roared, loud in the confined space of the restaurant, and the bullet went by with an ugly flat crack. Then they were swaying chest to chest, grappling. Even then Cofflin had time to notice the man's sour stink. The frenzied wiry strength was inescapable, wrenching and twisting at his hand where it held the automatic by the slide and strove to force it upward. Then blackened fingernails clawed for his eyes. He ducked under them and jammed his head into the filthy cloth of Mansfield's coat. *Can't let go.* Too many people behind him, *Martha* behind him. He hooked an ankle behind the madman's and pushed. They fell, toppling bruisingly through chairs and marble-topped tables and rolling about.

Whump. This time the gun's discharge was muffled by the press of their bodies. Cofflin felt hot gases burn his skin, and waited for the battering pain of ripped flesh. Nothing happened except a fresh set of stinks. The body locked against his began to thrash convulsively, and blood spurted into his face. He rolled free, spitting and wiping at his face, his hands coming away red as crimson gloves. One look told him that Mansfield was dying, his body jerking as he drowned in the blood pouring into his lungs. The messy, undignified process would be over in less than a minute. His wife—ex-wife—was already limp beside him, in the crimson pool that was spreading around them; Cofflin put fingers to her throat to check for a pulse, knowing it was futile. Blood was splashed everywhere, walls, the mirrored pillars, even droplets on the pressed steel flowers of the ceiling. More on Martha, where she stood with the teenager's Y-fork slingshot in her hand. He moved toward her.

"None of it mine," she said, in a voice like ash.

One of the teenagers lay at her feet, with his companion and another islander giving him first aid; from the way he clutched at his lower stomach, he'd need it to survive until the ambulance got here. *And there should be a helicopter to take him to a hospital on the mainland. This shouldn't have happened at all.*

He stooped to pick up the Glock, ejecting the magazine. Three cartridges left, out of twelve. "Damn," he said hoarsely. "We've got to do something about this."

The vehicle arrived, sirens wailing; someone must have heard the gunshots. The paramedics leaped into action, injecting a painkiller, cutting away cloth, and rigging a plasma drip. One swore softly as he exposed the wound in the youngster's stomach. They moved the torso quickly, slapping a pressure bandage on the larger exit wound and lifting the victim onto the stretcher. Another was already calling instructions into her radiophone from behind the wheel of the ambulance.

Martha dropped the slingshot, shuddering. Cofflin slipped an arm around her. "You saved my life," he said quietly.

"Had to," she said. "Wasn't anyone else. You saved us all. Take me out of here, please."

He did. *We've got to do something about this,* he thought grimly. People were just too near the edge. *Get the guns and explosives under control for a while.*

"Thought so," Cofflin said to himself, as the phone in his jacket buzzed.

They were sitting side by side in the chair swing on the front porch, holding hands. The grin he'd been suppressing—he'd never live this down, and several people had passed by close enough to see him in the light of the whale-oil lanterns—slid away unnoticed. The expression left behind was one generations of Cofflins had shown to the sea in its wilder moods, or to a boatload of Papuans trying to storm a whaler cast aground in the South Seas. Charles I's troops might have recognized it, coming at them behind a three-barred lobster-tail helmet at Marston Moor.

He pulled the phone out and listened. "Go ahead with it," he replied briefly, then rose and tucked it away. He checked the action of his pistol and reholstered it.

"What's wrong?" Martha said sharply.

"You weren't wrong the other day, about Deubel," Cofflin said shortly. "I couldn't arrest him before he did anything . . . but that didn't mean I couldn't have him watched. Now he's doing something. I'm a cop again, for a little while."

"Setting fires?" she asked.

He looked at her sharply. "Deduction," she replied. "The town was nearly wiped out by fires in the 1830s, and he knows it. And it'll serve his crazy purpose if we're just damaged enough to die off. The history he's interested in protecting ends after 30 A.D., and he doesn't care about what Europeans will find in the Americas."

That is one hell of a woman, he thought. The grin threatened to come back for a second.

"We do think alike, Martha," he said. "Have to go. See you at the Council meeting tomorrow. Thanks for the dinner."

The man fumbled with the oil-soaked rag. One match went out, then another. At last the cloth caught, flames running up it in sullen yellow and red. It dropped to the ground as the yard-long club made solid contact with the back of the arsonist's head.

"That's enough," Cofflin said sharply, stamping on the torch. The flame sputtered alive again and again, until he kicked dirt over it.

The militiaman—volunteer police reserve sworn in last week, technically—was winding up, wild-eyed, ready for a solid blow that would have cracked the arsonist's skull. The man on the ground was moaning and trying to crawl; abruptly he began to vomit. It wasn't as easy to knock a

man out as the movies could make you think, and when
you did he didn't wake up a little later as if he'd taken a
nap. A member of the TV generation with no training or
practical experience was all too likely to hammer a skull
into mush and expect the recipient to get up and fight again
like Jean Claude Van Whatsisname.

"Watch him," he said. "The rest of you, follow me."

The volunteers lined up with their shields and wood-
dowel clubs. No guns tonight, thank God. The island had
turned out to have an appalling amount of firepower, but
it was all safely under lock and key now. Cofflin led his
party of volunteers up Main Street. A few of Deubel's fanatics fled before them. None had had enough time to do
much mischief, although he could hear the wail of the fire
engine from the station off to his right rear. At the head
of the street he met George Swain. He could barely recognize him in the gloom. Speaking of which . . .

He took out the phone. "Ready?"

"Ready."

"Throw the switch."

He squeezed his eyes to slits as the streetlights came on
for the first time since the second night after the Event.
Amazing how bright it looked, after a few weeks without
electric light.

"Let's get the rest of them rounded up," he said. "Then
we can figure out what the hell to do with them."

The volunteers trotted down the street after him. He
could hear the other squads, but such of his attention as
could be spared was on the houses around him. Wood,
mostly. They couldn't keep the pumping system going all
the time. The last time a real fire had broken loose here
back in the nineteenth century, half the town had been
leveled. If it happened now, there would be no aid from
the mainland. His stomach clenched at what it would be
like, trying to survive with most of the town in ashes.

What the hell are we going to do with them?

The circle closed in on the little church. A few fights
broke out, and ended with more stunned or weeping men
and women sitting on the curbsides, handcuffed or hugging
bruises. More and more ordinary townsfolk were following
along behind, drawn by the noise and the appearance of
the streetlights. Deubel's congregation were hammering on
the door and calling on their leader, but the door was

locked against them, and the church's windows showed empty and dark. A last surge of pushing and shoving, and the would-be aronists let themselves be led down between the ranks of club-bearing volunteers and regular police.

"You're all under arrest, under the emergency powers invested in me by the Town Meeting," Cofflin said harshly, when they'd been gathered together. "You'll get a fair hearing. Now sit down and be quiet, will you?"

It was less formal than the pre-Event procedures, but it'd serve. "Hell of a thing, George," he said. "Better than twenty of them."

"Just glad you called it ahead of time, Chief," the younger man replied.

"So am I—but this's as far as I thought. Get the doorknocker, would you?" A piece of law enforcement equipment rarely used on the island before, but they did have one in stock.

It came up with four of his old officers staggering up the stairs under its weight, a steel forging with handles; shooting the lock out of a door was also something that looked a lot easier—and safer—in the movies. In real life the ricochets and flying metal made it a last resort.

"Pastor Deubel, please open this door. We don't want to damage your church." True in the literal sense; in the metaphorical, he wanted to get *rid* of Deubel's church and congregation, and get the people in it acting sane again. "Pastor Deubel, this is your last warning."

Cofflin sighed. It had been years since he had had to break down a door, and he'd never liked it. There ought to be a place where a man could go and lock the world away; on the other hand, people ought to be able to sleep secure in their beds without fear of a lunatic burning the roof over their heads.

Suddenly a sound cut through the murmur of voices and the distant wail of fire-truck sirens. A huge thudding *boom*, coming from the east, down toward the harbor. A cloud of smoke rose skyward, shot with sparks of firelight.

"Uh-oh," Cofflin said. "That was—"

George Swain took the phone from his ear. "—the warehouse with the guns and stuff, Chief."

Cofflin winced. *Maybe that wasn't such a bright idea after all,* he thought. Then: *No, goddammit. Think what Deubel might have done with some firepower.*

"Get some more volunteers down there," he said. "All right, Ted, Caitlin, Matt, Henry. Go for it."

He signed everyone else back from the steps and drew his pistol, holding it up in the two-handed grip that made it more difficult to grab. Only the second time he'd drawn iron as a policeman, other than to clean the piece. *Deubel's crazy enough for anything.* Sometimes he wondered what God thought of the number of people who claimed to act in His name. What had that old book said? *A fanatic is someone who does what he knows God would do if only the Almighty knew the facts of the case.*

Boom. The police officers staggered back as the steel rebounded from the stout doors, but there had been splintering as well. Stronger than a house door—those gave in at once. *Boom.* This time the splintering was louder. *Boom.* The doors swung open, and the team staggered a few steps into the aisle, drawn by the momentum of their ram. It was nearly pitch-dark in there, only a few gleams from the streetlamp up the road penetrating. Cofflin unhitched the L-shaped flashlight from his waist and shone it within.

"Christ," he whispered.

Deubel was there, all right—swinging from an iron light bracket, the cord that had once fed the light deep in his swollen neck. Matter dripped from his feet to the floor below, the usual release of bowels and bladder, and the stink was heavy inside the musty closeness of the church. He'd made a hash of hanging himself, too. Not enough drop, and his hands were still fastened to the cord where they'd scrabbled to stop his slow choking.

"The poor man," a voice said behind him. Cofflin looked back; it was Father Gomez, from St. Mary's.

Cofflin nodded to the priest. "Excuse me, Father." Louder. "Ladder in here, and a stretcher." Not much doubt about the cause of death; no need to rout someone out for an autopsy.

"The poor deluded man," Gomez said again, crossing himself, as the blanket-covered body was carried out. Deubel's followers looked at it as it went by, some weeping, some impassive, a few cursing or spitting at the dead cleric who'd left them to face the consequences of his preaching.

"Manichaeism is always a temptation," Gomez went on. "Chief Cofflin, I think if I talked to some of these people . . ."

"Do you think it would do any good, Father?" Cofflin asked. He wasn't Catholic himself, but he had a fair degree of respect for the little priest. Certainly he took his job more seriously than some of the other clergy on the island, and he'd been a voice of good sense since the Event. "They're not exactly of your denomination."

"We're all Christians, Chief Cofflin," Gomez said.

"What was that . . . Manni-something?"

"A perennial heresy—imagining that Satan is as strong as God. Poor Deubel thought that the Incarnation could be halted—which is to say that God's will could be defied. But even Satan is part of God's plan; He is omniscient and omnipotent, or He's not God at all. I don't pretend to understand what's happened to us here, but then there are many things we're not supposed to understand or can't understand. Mystery is at the heart of life. If God makes many worlds, He'll arrange them as He pleases—including when and where to send His son in this one."

Cofflin looked at him thoughtfully. "You know, I think it might be a good idea if you *did* have a talk with these people," he said.

"I will." Gomez hesitated. "Not to tell you how to do your own job . . ."

"Go ahead—everyone else does. It's a free . . . island."

"But it might be better if any formal trial, any Town Meeting, were held off for a week or so. People were frightened enough without this, and . . ."

" . . . frightened men are vicious, I know," Cofflin said. *And by then I can figure out something, I hope. I'll ask Martha.*

Cofflin rubbed a hand across the back of his aching neck. "I hate this job," he muttered.

"And that's a very reassuring thing, my son," Gomez said.

CHAPTER SIX

April, Year 1 A.E.

The coast of England was green and silent, save for birds in numbers that made the sky restless. It might have been a morning before man, except that—she focused the binoculars—there was a haze of smoke a little farther to the northeast.

Well, well, Marian Alston said to herself. Then, aloud: "Soundings."

"Forty feet and shoaling, ma'am. Twenty-three feet under the keel."

"Twenty-three feet, aye," Captain Alston replied. "Keep it comin'."

At least they had the depthfinder; she'd have to remember to have someone trained in throwing the lead line from the bowsprit nets against the day that it unrecoverably wore out. It made her teeth stand on edge to come this close to shore when her shoal charts were useless and the only repair facilities for a steel-hulled ship were a long, long couple of thousand years away. At least the weather looked fair and the glass was steady, just enough wind to scatter whitecaps across blue ocean. Water was lighter over shoals and mudbanks, of which the area looked to have more than its share. The low coast ahead stood green and wild, marsh and tossing forest and occasional clearings. Some of it looked like second growth, scrubby trees and underbrush. Now and then they saw a plowed field green with new crops, but some of the little clusters of round huts were burned and deserted.

What wind and wave there was would be broken a little by the Isle of Wight off to the southwest, and by the sides of the estuary on either hand, safe enough in anything but a really bad blow. She didn't dare go much farther up the

Southampton Water, though, not with the bottom shoaling like this.

"Eighteen feet under the keel, ma'am."

"Eighteen feet, aye."

And . . . *there.* They were coasting steadily closer to the smudge of smoke that marked a settlement of some type.

"Hampshire," she murmured.

She'd been here . . . before. It had looked nothing like this, of course. Perhaps if she was flying over it the resemblances would be more, but too many thousand years of human hands had shaped the lowlands of the coast, draining and ditching, clearing and planting. That land of tacky seaside resorts and naval bases, green fields inland with time-burnished villages and manors—it was all more distant than the moon, than the farthest star. She was adrift in the sea of time.

"On deck! Boats on the beach, there. Big ones!"

She trained her own binoculars. The beach came into view slowly, as the ship ghosted close at a bare three knots. Two boats, right enough; you could even call them ships, especially compared to the dozens of rafts and canoes and hide coracles also hauled up. About sixty footers, she estimated, pulled up on the shore above the high-tide mark. Prows curled up, carved in the likeness of a horse's head and gaudily painted; there were decked sections fore and aft, open amidships. Masts were stepped, rather short ones—probably they could be taken down at will—but the yards and sails were elsewhere, perhaps used for the big tents she saw a little behind the vessels. Two heavy steering oars, one on either side, canted up now and held by ropes. The hulls were fairly tubby, broader amidships, but with oar ports along the sides, and black with tar or pitch. Men crowded around them, sunlight flashing on their bronze spearheads. Alston scanned right and left. The camp sprawled for the better part of a mile, tents and huts, men in kilts and women in long skirts and shawls, oxcarts, fires and rubbish heaps and . . . yes, horse-drawn chariots driving down to the edge of the water. Pretty much like illustrations she'd seen, except that the panels around them were higher at the sides than the front. All too far away to see clearly, but it was plain enough that they were getting a reception party ready.

Sensible enough, she thought. If someone showed up off

her shore in a ship fifty times the size of anything she'd seen before, she'd have the troops out, and locked and loaded too.

"Sixteen feet under the keel, ma'am."

"Sixteen feet, aye. Prepare to strike all sail," she said quietly. "Stand by the starboard anchor. Three shots at the water's edge."

Most of the *Eagle*'s poles were bare already, except for a topsail, the gaff on the mizzen, and a few of the jibsails still up to keep steerage way on her. A minute of disciplined effort and the rest were struck.

"Let go the starboard anchor!"

There was a sharp *clung* as the blackened steel dropped into the water and the chain took up the slack. The *Eagle* checked as the flukes dug into the bottom, heaved forward a little, and swung to. The other splashed home as well and then they were still, rocking slightly to the longshore swell.

"She holds, ma'am!"

"Holding, aye."

The quartermaster's whistle rang out across the deck. "Shift colors!"

The steaming ensign came down from the gaff. The blue Coast Guard jack broke out at the bows, and the national ensign to the mainmast.

Noise grew on the shore, faint across the half mile of waters. Shouts, screams, a weird dunting *hu-hu-hu-hu-huuuu* that must be some sort of musical instrument. Tom Hiller came up beside her.

"That doesn't look like a permanent settlement to me, Captain," the sailing master said.

"No, I'd say they'd only been there weeks, maybe a couple of months," she said. "Let's get Arnstein's tame savage up here, Mr. Hiller."

Ohotolarix came bounding up the companionway with easy grace; the speed of his recovery had surprised the doctor. When he saw the shore he gave a great shout of joy, then threw up his arms in a gesture that looked religious somehow, palms up to the sky. They'd given him back his leather kilt; it looked a little incongruous with the blue T-shirt he was wearing.

Arnstein and the astronomer followed more slowly. They had all they could do to dam the flow of words from the young warrior, but at last they managed it. After a moment Ian turned to the captain.

"That's his king's camp—his *rahax*," the academic said. He rubbed a nose peeling a little from sunburn. "Daurthunnicar." He sounded out the name slowly. "And those are his people, the Iraiina."

"Eka, Daurthunnicar, rahax," the young man said happily, smiling and pointing. More gibberish followed. Then: "Iraiina *teuatha*."

"That means 'tribe,' or 'people.' I think."

"Can you make him understand 'we come in peace' and 'we want to talk to your leader'?" Alston asked.

"I think so," Arnstein said slowly. "We've been working on it."

"Ms. Hendriksson, get the boat ready. Boat crew of the watch, and six of your people fully armed." With the best Nantucket had had to offer, which wasn't much. "Remember, we don't want any conflict, but if they attack, shoot to kill." She was sending Hendriksson because she thought Walker might be inclined to jump the gun in a tricky situation.

"Ma'am."

"Mr. Arnstein, let's hand him the gifts."

First they returned the boy's ax, which made him seem inches taller as he thonged it to his wrist. The grin grew wider as they handed over a fire ax, one of the short swords, and necklaces of plastic beads. He touched his open palm to his forehead, bowed, seemed to glow with happiness as the sailors led him away to the boat.

Captain Alston waited tensely as it stroked in toward shore. They had the island's lone .50-caliber machine gun clamped to the rail, and a couple of sailors with scope-sighted hunting rifles, but it was still tricky sending people to within arrow range. The longboat stroked away, oars flashing in unison. It halted in shallow water, and she could see Ohotolarix jump overboard and wade ashore, holding his treasures aloft. A great screaming roar went up from the crowd on the beach; there must be at least a thousand, possibly two.

"I hope to hell this works," she muttered.

Daurthunnicar forced his hand to relax on the haft of his ax.

"He bleeds!" the *rahax* shouted. "He is no ghost!"

A sigh of relief went through the crowd as the young man held up his arm, a trickle of red running down it from where the high chief had scored it slightly. A Dead Walker back from his grave would be cold and bloodless and full of hunger for the living.

"This is a thing for the chiefs," he said. "All of you, back to your households. Chieftains, the Wise Man—and you, our ally," he added unwillingly, as Isketerol bowed. "Come, we will make council." Best to include the Tartessian, who had knowledge of strange lands and peoples.

They gathered around his chariot, casting glances out over the water. The *size* of the thing! It looked small with distance, but his vision was still good for things far away, had even grown better since the first gray appeared in his beard. He could see folk moving about on it, climbing up the mountain-high masts. Five times the length of the great ships of Tartessos, and those were the wonders of the world. Like a stallion beside a rabbit.

Young Ohotolarix was still grinning like a loon. Well, a man brought back from death had a right to feel joyful. He'd been a little less pleased to give up the strange things he brought, but he knew better than to gainsay his chief and knew he could await rich gifts in recompense. Besides, the Wise Man said the things must be purified, lest they carry a curse.

"This metal, what is it?" Daurthunnicar said, turning the strange ax in his hands.

"Iron," Isketerol said. "I think, for I've never seen more than a small piece shaped as a ring before. The Great King's artisans know the secret of it, in Hatti at the eastern end of the Middle Sea. But it's rare and very precious. Harder than bronze, I hear, and it takes a better edge, if you know how to work it."

The *rahax* took up the ax. The head shone like silver, and it shaved bare a patch of hair from his forearm when he tested the edge. He swung it tentatively; about the heft of his own war ax, or a little heavier—the strangers must be men of strong arms, since he swung more weight than most. Not badly balanced, either. He swung it down at a stump; the blade sank deep, and when he wrenched it out it was still sharp. The sword was an even greater wonder, finer by far than the goodly weapon the Tartessian captain carried. And no one had ever seen anything like the ornaments, smooth and shining and of colors brighter than the sun. Daurthunnicar felt his greed itch. If he had gifts like this to give out, warriors would flock to him from every tribe of Sky Father's people.

More than goods. What powers may these strangers have? His people were in need of strong allies.

"Say again how they treated you," he commanded.

"Lord," Ohotolarix said. "I woke a little as they hauled me to their great ship. The next I knew, their ruler bent over me. Their ruler is *black*, lord. With skin the color of charcoal."

A sigh that held fear rustled through the Iraiina chiefs. The robed Wise Man raised his staff to hold back evil magic, and talismans of bronze and bone clinked along its length. The Night Ones were black . . . although they did not walk in the light of day.

Isketerol leaned forward. "Was their chief flat of nose, with thick lips, and hair curled tightly, thus?" he asked.

Daurthunnicar frowned at the interruption, but felt new respect when Ohotolarix nodded.

"Strange," the Tartessian muttered. "A Medjay, here?"

"You know of them?" the *rahax* asked.

"At Pharaoh's court. He has warriors from far south up the Nile, in Nubia, the Medjay folk. Very fierce. And voyagers of my people who sailed far south of the Pillars say the folk there are black of skin, too, with features like that."

"*Eka,*" Daurthunnicar nodded.

From what he'd heard the sun shone brighter the farther south you went. The Tartessians were shorter and darker of skin and hair than most folk in these parts. Perhaps the sun baked the skin dark, as fire did clay, darker still as you went farther south. Pleased with his thought, the *rahax* signaled the young warrior to go on.

"Were all of them dark?" he asked.

"No, only a few, my chief. Others were like us, though their clothes and ways are strange. And some were brown, and some had skin the color of amber, and eyes aslant, so." He put his index fingers to the corners of his eyes and pushed them up. "But only a few. They treated me well, lord, like a son or oath-brother. They healed my hurts with strange medicines, and gave me a soft bed and food—

strange, and not enough meat for my liking, but plenty of it. And these gifts, as you see."

Daurthunnicar looked at Isketerol, and the Tartessian shook his head. Strange to him, then, too.

"The men among them mostly shave their chins," Ohotolarix continued. "And they dress strangely, both men and women, in garments sewn to fit their limbs, as a quiver fits arrows. Richly, richly, even the commoners are clothed from head to foot in fine woven things. Every one carries a knife and tools of metal."

The chief grunted. Women along . . . did that mean the strangers had come to settle? His gut hurt at the thought of another foe, but perhaps an accommodation could be reached. "Did you see cattle, wagons, children?" he asked.

"None, my chief." Ohotolarix hesitated. "It seemed as if all were one warband and its wives or concubines. Perhaps they hold them in common, for there were far fewer than the men . . . I think. When the black-faced high chief spoke, all others obeyed. The chiefs under him spoke, and his word was carried out, the others obeying like the fingers of a man's hand."

This time the chief's grunt carried envy. He'd always wished *his* underchiefs obeyed like that. They did better than the Earth Folk, who went each his own way, but . . .

"And what powers did they have?" the Wise Man asked, leaning forward. His seamed face was calm, but his eyes glittered with interest.

"Wise One," Ohotolarix said, looking more nervous than he had facing the *rahax,* "they had many. Light they could make appear in darkness, light as bright as the sun. They could make water appear in their bowls at will, and when they voided themselves into vessels of fine clay, the water came and took away their filth."

"Knossos," Isketerol muttered, then shook his head when the *rahax* looked his way.

"I don't think they showed me all their powers," the young man went on. "I learned a few of their words, they a few of mine—there was a man, an old man, very tall, and his woman, who tried to learn our tongue. And they had a curious magic they worked, one that I couldn't see the purpose of. They made marks on thin-scraped skins, so—" he picked up a short stick and mimed tracing on a square held in front of him—"and they would look at the marks, even hours later, and repeat my words."

The Tartessian started again, narrow dark eyes going wide. Daurthunnicar bared his teeth in the silence of his head. His ally knew something he did not, and wasn't telling.

"But I think," Ohotolarix said, "that I know why they come. They showed me pictures of grain, of bread, of cattle. They want these things, and they will give rich gifts for them."

"Ahhhh," Daurthunnicar sighed.

He looked at the ax, at the wonderful sword, at the shining jewelry. A chieftain who could open his hands and give such things to his followers would have power beyond power. A thought flickered through his mind: canoes, coracles, a night raid. Then he looked out again at the ship, its masts towering to pierce the sky, bulwarks like cliffs, the blood-red slash across its side and the cryptic symbols down the hull, the great golden eagle-god figure at its prow. No, no, he wouldn't raise blade against that power unless he must, for the lives of his folk. Better to deal in peace with such strength, if it could be done without offending the tribe's guardian gods. He would make parlay with these People of the Eagle.

"Wise Man?" he said.

The priest leaned on his staff. "I sense no great evil here," he said. "The Powers are at work, yes, but as likely to bless as to curse. Best I go to my tent, and ask of . . . others."

A few of the chiefs made signs as the old man stalked off. Daurthunnicar rapped the blunt end of his ax against the thin bronze panels that sheathed his chariot. "Hear the word of your *rahax*," he said. "We will send an envoy to these strangers, with a green branch and a white shield. You"—he pointed at Ohotolarix—"will go with him. We will bid them guest with us; they will share bread and meat and blood, and they will be peaceholy in all the camps of the Iraiina folk, unless I unsay the word of peace or they break it. Hear me! Any who raises hand against them, who insults them, will answer to me and to Sky Father and the Horned Man."

The chiefs bowed their heads. That was good, that meant they thought his word was wise. If they hadn't, he'd be hearing objections by now, loud and frequent. Most of the chiefs were his kin, and he was *rahax* as long as the most of them wished it, just as they were chiefs as long as the warriors respected and feared them.

"We will bid them to feast with us," Daurthunnicar went on. "We will speak of alliance and the giving of gifts. Sky Father is with us, and the Horned Man; they send us strong aid, much magic, much luck."

Swindapa lay motionless on her side, her knees drawn up to her chest, trying to ignore the aches and the itching and burning between her legs, and the cold feeling in her chest that never went away. The bonds that held her hands behind her back chafed, and so did the thick collar on her neck. That had a leash whose other end was braided around a wooden stake pounded into the ground. Even with her hands free she couldn't have removed collar or leash, not without a knife; they were twisted cowhide many strands thick. Everyone had gone away; she could hear the Sun People screaming and crying out down by the water. Her head lifted from the ground in a tangle of dirt-crusted hair. Nobody, not a dog, not the children who'd prodded her with sticks and thrown clods of earth, not the pack of older boys who sometimes hung around waiting for a chance to rush in and force her while her keepers' attention was elsewhere . . .

She shivered and ground her teeth, feeling herself starting to shake again. *No.* Instead she started working her bound hands down her back. If she could get her feet between them she could start gnawing on the hide that bound her wrists. With a grunt of pain she fell back on her side, panting. She was too stiff from lack of stretching and the binding was too broad. Tears of frustration ran down her cheeks. A tethered goat on the other side of a dead fire cropped at a bush and looked at her with unblinking eyes as it chewed.

Swindapa tried to whisper a Cursing Song, but it didn't feel right, as if the Moon Woman couldn't hear her in this place. She started again as footsteps moved toward her, from the other side of the two-wheeled oxcart. *Please.* It wasn't time for the woman who brought her food and water. Brought most days; sometimes they forgot. The big leather tent twenty paces away in that direction was Daurthunnicar's. Sometimes men came over from there and forced her or hurt her in other ways. That hadn't happened for twice seven of days; she'd tried to make herself too filthy, by voiding in the dirt instead of the trench they'd made her dig, and rolling in the mud. If they were drunk enough on mead or hemp they might not care—

It was the woman, and a few others with her, and behind them the whole crowd was returning to camp, chattering. There was a high note to their voices, excitement or fear.

The women paused around her. "She stinks," one said. "The guests will be insulted."

Swindapa stayed huddled on the ground, legs drawn up under her and ready to scrabble away. Sometimes the women were kind, but other times they kicked her, or dropped the food in the dirt.

"She did that to keep the men off," another voice said. This one was younger, and there was colored work in the shoes beneath the dyed woolen skirt. "They haven't been at her for two seven-days now. She'll look all right when she's cleaned up. The bruises are mostly gone."

Another voice chuckled. "It'd take more than a whiff to keep that boar-stallion away when he's had a few horns." The tone changed. "*Diasas.* Get up." The toe prodded her in the ribs.

"Yes, Iraiina," Swindapa said.

The tribe-name meant "free" or "noble" in the Sun People tongue. She came to her feet, gritting her teeth and stretching. The Iraiina women averted their eyes a little; it was shameful to go without clothes among the Sun People. That was why they'd kept her stripped, to shame her. Among her people, clothes were for warmth or comfort or show, but now she knew what their word *naked* meant. It meant helplessness.

A kinder voice spoke: "Come. The *rahax* says you are to be washed clean." That one made a *tsk* sound between her teeth. "He should have bestowed you long before this. He wouldn't treat a dog so, why a woman?"

"Wirronnaur's arm festered where she cut him," the younger woman explained. "And her kin wouldn't pay enough for her, they don't, you know—they say that if they pay for one, we'll take others, so it's against their law. The *rahax* was angry."

"Well, he still shouldn't have let them treat her like this, as if this were a raiders' camp. Come on, Earth girl, we have to clean you and see you're sound."

"Why?" Swindapa asked.

The woman sawing the leash tugged on it painfully. "The *rahax* says it."

"Careful," the older women said. To Swindapa: "Foreigners came today, in a great ship."

"Wizards," the younger woman said, spitting in the dirt and making the sign of the horns. "Night Ones, maybe."

"No, these Eagle People are men. Maybe wizards, and very strange, but men," the older woman said. She had a plump face, with four braids of graying black hair secured by bronze rings. Her voice was not unkind as she spoke to Swindapa. "Don't worry, you'll be treated better when you have one master to protect you. The *rahax* is to give you as a feasting-gift tomorrow. You'll be the stranger chief's. If you please him, you might be free soon, even become a second or third wife. You'll live well then—the strangers are rich and powerful. Come, we've got soaproot and sweet herbs, and then we're to feed you. That will feel better, won't it?"

"Why do we have to carry these pigstickers, sir?" one of the cadets asked, looking dubiously at the spear he'd been handed.

"Because the natives don't know what guns are, and we aren't going to let them know unless we need to surprise them, and we don't want them to think we're unarmed except for funny-looking clubs, either," Lieutenant Walker said. He looked around with a bright-eyed interest that was somehow also cool. "Now shut up."

Alston noted the byplay and forced herself to stop fiddling with her gloves. She was in dress uniform—well, mostly, damned if she was going to wear a skirt—and a lot was riding on the impression she made. The medal ribbons were ridiculous, but that was one of the Coast Guard's little foibles. You could get four or five of them just for getting out of boot camp or the Academy.

There were twenty in the shore party: herself, Arnstein, Rosenthal, Walker, and an escort of cadets, picked largely because they still remembered how to march smartly in step, not something the Coast Guard generally put much emphasis on. The cadets all had Army Kevlar helmets from

Nantucket, a little incongruous but better than anything available locally. They carried spears and shields made up in the island machine shop, for show, and likewise short swords. The pistols at their waists and the rifles and shotguns across their backs were for emergency use. If it came to that she supposed they could shoot their way out without much problem; people who'd never been exposed to firearms of any sort would scatter at the first blast and not stop running for a while.

And it had better not come to that. They *needed* the grain back on the island. Badly. Besides, she didn't relish the thought of gunning down men virtually unarmed.

She was wearing a sword herself, one she'd saved several years to buy, back in her early twenties in San Francisco, and a shorter companion on the other side of her belt. She wondered for a moment what Sensei Hishiba would think of where the set of *katana* and *wakizashi* had ended up. . . .

"Let's go," she said. "Ms. Rapczewicz, you have the deck."

The boatswain's pipes squealed. "*Eagle* departing!" rang out as she stepped into the boat and the davits swung out to lower it. The ship's bell rang three times, then again a single time.

Oars bit the water; the boats threw long shadows ahead of themselves as the sun sank behind. Bonfires blossomed ahead, up and down the shoreline, but the forest inland was a rustling sea of darkness. When full dark came, the sky overhead would be a frosted blaze of stars, as it never was ashore in her own time. A low chanting was running through the crowds ahead, backlit against their fires, deep men's voices and a keening female oversong weaving among trumpets that sounded like nothing so much as Tibetan *radongs*. Drumbeat thudded under it . . . no, she realized, that was the sound of feet, pounding the earth in unison. A crawling went up her spine, less fear than sheer lonesomeness. The oars caught slightly.

"Steady there," she said.

The boats' keels grounded on sand and shingle. Oars flipped up in unison, and the landing party disembarked. The sailor crews pushed the boats off again, to wait ready just in case.

Marian Alston stepped ashore onto dry land that crunched under her boots. The chanting and stamping cut off. A bristle of trumpets sounded again, upright shapes six feet long with gaping mouths shaped like the heads of wolves and boars. The cadets formed around her and the other officer, except for those who were lugging the bundles of gifts. She blinked aside strangeness and the failing light to see what awaited her.

More of the green boughs, for starters—evidently a peace signal, like the Biblical olive branch. A group of men waited, in the leather kilts she'd come to expect but with brightly dyed tunics and leggings as well, bracelets and neck rings of chased gold, pendant necklaces of amber and gold, silver pectorals set with colored stones. Behind them their chariots were drawn up. The horses wore headdresses of nodding plumes, and hangings of felt covered with writhing colored appliqué shapes of animals and monsters along their flanks.

"Captain," Arnstein murmured into her ear. "Look at the ones standing off to the left."

Her eyes moved that way. Several men. Shorter than the ones about them, black-haired and olive-skinned, clean-shaven, dressed in linen tunics, their ornaments more restrained and subtly . . . different. She gave an imperceptible nod and kept up her steady pace. A man was moving out to meet her, flanked by warriors of his own. Big, easily six feet, three inches taller than she and towering by the standards of this age, she guessed, and massively built. His chest strained at his sheet-bronze breastplate, decorated with raised hammered spirals over the nipples and gold studs along the neck and waist. The impression of height was increased by the bronze helmet he wore, rounded at the front and back, flat sides rising to a peak embellished by a fore-and-aft crest running from brow to nape of neck.

Talk about your dickheads, she thought irreverently; it helped break the hieratic mood.

A gold disk engraved with the sun hung on his chest; the haft of the war ax sloped over his shoulder was set with rings of bronze and gold, the falcon-bill head inlaid in silver, and he bore a long bronze sword at his waist. His beard was glossy brown streaked with gray, forked and held by more rings of gold where it trailed down on his barrel chest. The beginnings of a potbelly added to his impression of thick-armed strength. He raised the ax in a curious gesture and rested it on the ground, spoke in a rumbling bass.

"Daurthunnicar son of Ubrotarix," came through eventually, with Arnstein helping out. "*Rahax* of the Iraiina folk."

Alston saluted; it seemed to suit the occasion. "Marian Alston, captain of the *Eagle*," she replied firmly, meeting the impassive blue eyes. That got through too; Ohotolarix had known what to call the ship's gilded figurehead. "American," she added.

A slender boy came forward with a platter of basket-work. It held a golden cup, a piece of coarse dark bread, a slab of cheese, and a knife. Daurthunnicar picked up the knife and pricked his thumb, squeezing out a few drops of blood into the cup. Alston felt her own hands move in dreamlike precision, stripping off a glove and placing the razor-edged bronze against her skin. Her own blood fell into the liquid in the cup; that was yellow, the color of straw. The native chief picked up the cup in both hands; it seemed to vanish in their hamlike vastness. He raised it to the setting sun and pronounced something long and sonorous; she caught Diawas Pithair, the name of their chief god. Sky Father; cognate with Zeus and Jupiter and Tiwaz and the old Norse Tyr, according to Arnstein. Others, a list of them—Mirutha, which seemed to be some sort of angels; a Horned Man or god of beasts and forests; Hepkwonsa, who was the Lady of the Horses, and her sons the Twin Riding Brothers; the Crow Goddess, whose true name was Blood Hag of Battles . . .

He drank, slurping, then handed the cup to her. About half the contents were gone; on impulse she took it in both hands as he'd done, tilting it back until the last drops ran down her throat. It was alcoholic, no doubt about that, and sickly-sweet.

The crowd gave a long sigh. The *rahax* proceeded to cut the bread and cheese and sprinkle them with salt. She ate her portion and gave a polite smile as he grinned back at her out of a crumb-filled beard. This time the watchers cheered, waving weapons and torches over their heads.

"That makes us guests," Arnstein murmured again. "At a guess, we're now holy and inviolate."

"Hell of a thing to have to guess at," she said. It made sense, though.

Daurthunnicar waved a few others forward. *Introductions,* Alston thought. She tried to keep the names straight—or they might be titles, of course—but she was glad of Rosenthal busy writing on her pad.

Arnstein stiffened beside her when the one of the other men, the dark clean-shaven ones, was introduced. "Isketerol of Tharatushus."

"Tartessos?" he echoed.

The Latin-looking man nodded. "Isketerol. Tharatushus," he replied, pointing southeast.

"Tartessos!"

Arnstein burst into another language. Isketerol replied, and Arnstein turned to Alston, excitement ablaze on his face.

"Captain, he speaks Greek! It's very archaic, and he's got a thick accent, it's not his native language either, but I can catch about one word in every two—more, with a little practice. He's Isketerol, and those ships on the beach are his. They're from Tartessos—it's a city-state in southwestern Spain, not much known about it except that it was wealthy and important in the late Bronze Age and down into early classical times. I didn't know it existed this early, but nobody's ever found the site of it—very obscure."

Finally! Alston thought. "You can translate through him? Excellent. Tell the sachem here we've got gifts for him. And by the way, be careful with the Iberian." Anyone who could survive as a merchant adventurer here was likely to be on the ball, and her antennae were prickling anyway. "He's sharp."

Isketerol smiled and inclined his head, before turning and speaking in the harsh choppy Iraiina language. Daurthunnicar seemed to sigh with relief as well.

"He says that he's got gifts for us too, we're his guests—'guest-friends' is the term, it's fairly serious if it means the same thing in this dialect of Greek and if he's translating accurately—and we're to come to the feast, you and your warriors, and eat with him and his."

"Lead on," Alston said.

"Be careful," his cousin said to Isketerol. "Whether or not they're wizards, you can see these strangers aren't as brainless as the local oafs."

Isketerol nodded, legs folded gracefully before him as the feast began. "That grunting boar Daurthunnicar hasn't realized that the Nubian is a woman, did you notice? I

think he knows about the one with the man who speaks a
little Achaean—you can scarcely mistake those breasts—
but he hasn't spotted the leader, or the ones among her
spear-bearers."

The trader chief's cousin nodded. It wasn't surprising that
the Tartessians saw deeper, although stay-at-home kin in
their native city might have been fooled as well. When you
sailed all over the Middle Sea, though, and the shores of
the River Ocean, you met innumerable different styles of
dress, of custom. Your eyes saw more, after a while. Tartessians were *real* voyagers, not like the Achaeans, who composed an epic on their own bravery if they spent one night
out of sight of land.

"The plump woman is writing," he said to his elder.
"That looks like papyrus, don't you think?"

"A little, but that isn't Egyptian script . . . although
women learn to read there, sometimes, noblewomen. And
they had a woman as Pharaoh long ago, what was her
name . . . Hatshe . . . I can't remember. But they don't
have woman warriors. How does the ink get on that pen,
I wonder? Or is it like a grease stick?"

"How did they learn Achaean? You hardly ever see
those reaver bastards west of Sicily—for which thanks be
to Arucuttag of the Sea. Should we tell Daurthunnicar
about the Nubian?"

"Don't be more of a fool than the Womb Goddess made
you," Isketerol said. "Of course not. It might be useful
sometime. You know the saying: Give away your goods for
nothing, rather than a secret."

His eyes glittered. "Look, they're laying out their gifts.
Have you ever *seen* the like?" A rhetorical question. "The
king himself back home doesn't have anything like that.
The Crone take me, Ramses in Memphis doesn't have anything like that, and they're throwing it away on these savages as if it were a wad of grass they'd used to wipe their
arse!"

Both the Tartessians looked over at the strangers with
profound respect. Wealth like that deserved it.

"Well, that worked," Alston said to Arnstein.
"So far," he said.
The gifts had been received with rapture, particularly the
bolts of brightly colored synthetic cloth, the glass bowls and

tumblers, and most of all the leaf-spring longsword in a sheath of wood bound with brass wire and glued-on polyester; Daurthunnicar kept that by his side, stroking the hilt occasionally. Lieutenant Walker had demonstrated it by hacking through a bronze spearhead, and the warriors had roared and pounded their fists on the ground.

Now they sat in a small circle between two fires; other circles were dotted around the open meadow. The *rahax* had a heavy wooden chair; it was ancient, made of blackened oak and bone, with eight-foot wooden pillars at its back in the shape of men—or perhaps of gods—with erect phalli; the carvings moved like something alive in the uncertain light of the bonfires. A smaller chair was placed across the circle from him for his guest of honor; everyone else sat or squatted on blankets or furs over straw. Women in long skirts, shawls, and what looked like primitive sweaters came through and handed everyone a horn; many of them wore copper or gold stomachers and jewelry. Arnstein sipped at his, and found it was some sort of mead, honeybeer. The savory scent of roasting meat filled the air.

Damn, he thought. You couldn't put a hollow cowhorn down while there was anything in it; that probably meant everyone was supposed to get thoroughly blasted.

Isketerol sat a little forward of the throne, then leaned forward and began to speak in deliberately slow Greek:

"You understand, now the *wannax*—absurd to give this tribal chief the title of the High King of Mycenae—will give you gifts in return. Tonight everything must be an exchange of gifts, for honor's sake. Tomorrow they will dicker. Badly."

Arnstein heard the Tartessian through two or three times, wishing that the surviving Mycenaean texts weren't all inventories and taxation lists, in a script badly adapted to the sounds of Greek. With a wrenching mental effort he made himself *think* in Homeric Greek, and kept the Linear B word lists in the forefront of his mind. Doing that and talking at the same time made his forehead and scalp shine with sweat.

"They're going to give us gifts," he said to Alston. "It's a big symbolic thing. We'd better look pleased."

"That won't be hard, I imagine," she said.

Isketerol spoke again: "By the way, Ianarnstein, did you want our host to know that your leader is a woman?"

"You mean he *doesn't*?" Arnstein said, his voice half a squeak.

"By no means. He may listen well to his wives or even fear their tongues in private, but a man of the Iraiina does not sit at council or feast with a female. They make a great concession by allowing your woman to attend you."

Again, repetitions were needed to make meaning plain. Swallowing, Arnstein relayed the information to the commander.

She smiled thinly. "Don't deny it, but don't make an issue of it, either," she said. "I've run into the same thing abroad. If the people you're visiting have got really strong and rigid dress codes for the sexes, and you don't have the sort of figure that pushes itself on the eyes, it's not uncommon to be mistaken for a man. They don't see past the costume and the way you're acting."

Ian nodded and spoke in turn to the Tartessian, careful to shape his handling of the language to the merchant's.

"Very perceptive of your captain," the Tartessian said. "Ah, here are the gifts."

Weapons piled up at Alston's feet: spears, axes, a long leaf-shaped slashing sword with a broad bronze blade inlaid with swirling patterns and a beautifully worked hilt in gold wire. Jewelry, barbarically splendid and often skillfully made. Some of it didn't seem to be in the same sinuous, whirling style as the rest. *Plunder,* he thought. These people were obviously invaders here. Furs, glossy and well-tanned, wolf, otter, fox, martin, ermine, a couple of huge bearskins big enough for grizzly. A leather bag made of a whole sheepskin that Isketerol said contained wine from his homeland; Alston received another cheer when she had that opened and shared out. It was too sweet for Arnstein's taste, halfway between Manischewitz and a coarse sherry, but an improvement over the tooth-hurting mead or the thin sour beer flavored with spruce buds that were the alternatives.

Well, now we know why there wasn't any Mediterranean pottery of this era for archaeologists to discover, he thought sourly. It wasn't because there was no trade in wine and oil this early; it was just that the Iberians transferred everything to skin containers before they left home, and those rotted away untraceably. He reached into his knapsack, took out the reference book, and flipped to the illustrations, ignoring Isketerol's fascinated glances as he held it to the firelight, comparing the images with the heap of gifts and muttering to himself:

"Flame-shaped spearhead with short socket . . . yup . . . round shield . . . sword with solid-cast flanged hilt . . . Celt-socketed ax . . . collared thin-walled pottery . . . yup, Penard-group stuff—very early Urnfield. Okay, that settles the question of how the Deverel-Rimbury period ended. These guys chopped it into dogmeat. Mid and later thirteenth century B.C., spot on." He closed the book and looked at the spine. *The Age of Stonehenge*, by Colin Burgess. Martha had dug it up out of a private library in a summer vacationer's house. "God bless you, Colin Burgess, wherever you are."

The food came in, heaping mounds of fresh bread, cheese, onions, steamed roots, stews in clay bowls, pigeons and ducks on skewers, sausages, and endless roasts of pork, beef, mutton, and what he learned was horsemeat. The old man in the long robe stood and blessed the food with a staff topped with looped holly branches, and everyone fell to.

It wasn't quite the Henry VIII scene of two-fisted gorging and swilling he'd expected. The women laid slabs of tough dark bread down on the basketwork platters, then piled on the meat and other dishes, or brought clay bowls marked with waving patterns. There seemed to be an elaborate etiquette about who got what, and Daurthunnicar sent several pieces over to Captain Alston. Men cut portions with their belt knives and ate with their fingers, wiping their mouths and fingers occasionally with more pieces of bread ripped off loaves nearby; those might be eaten, or thrown to the big hairy dogs that also lay about. The serving women kept the horns refilled unless a man held his hand over the mouth—which few did. He noticed that while the chiefs and guests here had one horn or cup apiece, most farther from the throne of the *rahax* shared a beaker. The food was seasoned with sage, dill, sorrel, fennel, basil, and herbs he didn't recognize. Salt went around in wooden bowls, to be sprinkled between thumb and forefinger.

He sipped again at the heavy wine. The glaze it put over things seemed familiar, like the glassy sense of unreality that had been plaguing him and most of the others for the past few weeks. It was one thing to study history, or to imagine it. This was something else entirely.

The Iraiina cheered again. Ian looked up as he felt Alston stiffen with rage beside him. The last gift was brought forward.

"Captain," he hissed in her ear, as her hand fell to the Beretta at her waist. "Not here, not now. Please!"

"Ah, that thing at her waist is a weapon," Isketerol said in Tartessian as the last gift was presented.

His cousin Miskelefol nodded. "And she's angry to be offered the slave girl," he said. "I wonder why? Indifferent would be understandable, but why angry?"

Isketerol ran an experienced eye over the naked woman of the Earth Folk. The bruises had faded to very faint marks, so the Iraiina weren't offering spoiled goods; that couldn't be it. Except that she wouldn't be a virgin, and as the saying went you didn't find a slave virgin or a sweet olive, and anyway the Earth Folk didn't even have a *word* for virgin. A good enough figure, looking to be even better when she'd been fattened, young, very pretty. Although there was a good deal of unbroken spirit behind the downcast eyes. That was probably why her hands were bound behind her, as well as having a rawhide leash and collar around her neck. If the strange woman didn't want her for a servant or otherwise—he knew nothing of their taboos; these folk might be as odd a tangle as the Iraiina for all he knew—she'd be a valuable item for resale.

"I wouldn't mind taking her off the stranger's hands myself," Miskelefol said, echoing his thought. "I'd pay well in bronze or wine, and make it back again twice over on Tartessos dockside, four times over if I fed her up first."

Daurthunnicar's rumble interrupted them, demanding a translation

Isketerol sighed behind a bland exterior. Achaean wasn't his favorite language, but it was still a pleasure to speak next to the local hog-tongue. Someday he would be rich enough to sit at home in Tartessos and send younger relatives out as his skippers on these long dangerous voyages. He would lie on a soft couch in the courtyard of his house and eat grapes and count the ingots and bales in his storehouses, the fields and workshops he owned. But for now he must work; he set himself to translate into Achaean simple enough for Ianarnstein to understand. Odd. The stranger spoke sometimes like a poet with a mouth full of ornate kennings, and then like a child who hadn't mastered the endings of words . . . but he'd improved even in the few hours they'd spoken.

Where had he learned his Achaean?

"We can always turn her loose later," Arnstein was hissing into Alston's ear.

"I realize that, Professor," she gritted out through a broad, false smile. "What's that potbellied pervert with the beard saying?"

"Ah . . . this girl's a . . . high one? Something like that." He paused for back-and-forth with the Tartessian. Translating through three languages, two of them not native to the interpreters, was like trying to get the last garbanzo out of a slippery salad bowl without putting it over the edge. "She's a . . . princess or something of that nature, of the 'Fiernan Bohulugi,' the . . . I think it means People of the Soil, Earth Folk . . . the locals here. Daurthunnicar's men captured her and he was going to hold her for ransom, but he gives her to you as a sign of his friendship. I think that means the negotiations fell through."

He translated that back to Isketerol. The man from the south nodded with a cynical wink. "Knowing the Earth Folk, they were afraid she'd contracted bad luck," he said. "They think everything in a man's life is governed by the stars at his birth, and it's misfortune to interfere with it."

Alston tugged unwillingly at the leash, and the girl crouched at her feet. "Tell our host I'm delighted."

Daurthunnicar grinned back and made a joke that sent the other Iraiina laughing and hooting; the girl looked down at her feet, her mane of yellow hair hiding the disturbing glint in her eyes. That prompted Arnstein to ask another question.

"Yes," Isketerol said. "She speaks the Iraiina tongue, or one close to it, as well as her own. Daurthunnicar's people aren't the first to invade the White Isle; there are other tribes kin to them living north and east of here, who've been settled some generations."

Marian Alston had always considered herself a calm woman, even phlegmatic. Inch by inch she won back to full command of herself, controlling her breathing and forcing rage-knotted muscle to relax in the manner the Way had taught her through nearly twenty years of practice. At last she could pick up another morsel of food without choking on it, even smile and nod across the firelit circle.

I must be calm by nature after all, she thought ironically, looking at the girl crouched at her feet. *I can get that angry and not kill someone.* She'd come to get what she needed to help her people, and that was what she'd do.

But I'm damned if I'll sit here looking at those hands. The collar was four-ply twisted rawhide, it would take tools to remove, but the bonds on the girl's wrists were simply thongs. The horn was empty; she laid it beside the wicker plate and leaned forward with her knife in hand. It was a Swiss Army model, with a built-in fork and spoon, which had aroused a good deal of attention. The girl gasped, shivered, and stiffened in well-hidden terror as hands touched her wrists. She'd been casting sidelong glances at the *Eagle*'s captain, which was no wonder when she'd probably never seen a non-Caucasian before.

"Hold still," Alston said. The words didn't mean anything, but the tone did.

She cut carefully at the tough leather; there were raw chafemarks beneath it. More hoots from the Iraiina warriors made the girl clench her teeth. Alston could hear them grind, very faintly, and smell the faint woodsmoke-and-sweat odor of the blond hair under some soapy-herbal scent. The eyes that glared across the circle were cold blue. They turned and focused on Alston with the same wariness and hate, perhaps the more so because of her strange skin and features. Then they went wide, flickering up and down the other woman's clothes. She blinked in puzzlement, then carefully lowered her eyes again, rubbing at her wrists where the thongs had worn through the skin and left it angry.

Well, no flies on this one, Alston thought. Evidently the . . . Earth Folk could see past unfamiliar clothes. "Professor, tell her to eat, would you?"

The cold hate in the eyes dimmed a little, down to wariness. After a moment's hesitation she scooped food off the platter and ate with wolfish concentration. *Not too well fed lately,* Alston thought. The bruises told of a savage beating some time ago, and lesser ones since. She could guess the rest.

Looks English, she thought; evidently physical types endured longer than languages or cultures. Straight-nosed oval face, bowed lips, long-limbed shape. Under the recent gauntness she looked to have been well fed most of her life, which her five-six of height bore out, and she had a dancer's or a gymnast's muscles. The teeth that tore at bread and meat were white and even; the notoriously bad British record with cavities and crookedness must have entered later in the island's history, if she was at all typical.

"And what's her name?"

That took some doing, until Arnstein suggested that Isketerol ask her directly.

"Swindapa."

Think about this later. Perhaps they could drop the girl off with her own people . . . a good deed for the day, and if she really was of an important family, an opening for trade. *No way to tell if they're any less disgusting than this bunch. Later, later, keep your wits about you, woman.*

She glanced over at where her cadets sat in a clump. They were eating heartily, smiling meaninglessly at equally uncomprehending smiles from their neighbors, and drinking very lightly, with the upperclassmen keeping a watchful eye. *Good.*

One of the men near Daurthunnicar stood up; the old one with the robe and odd staff. He stretched the staff out, and near-silence fell. Then he threw back his head and began to sing, his voice occasionally cracking but still astonishingly full and sweet; a younger man beside him accompanied the song on something like a harp—not much like a harp; it was semicircular rather than triangular with the strings stretched over a parchment-covered soundbox, and the effect was closer to a guitar or mandolin. She had half expected the music to be wholly alien, but it was instead hauntingly familiar, the tone and scale easy to follow. The verses were rhythmic, not exactly rhyming. . . .

Arnstein leaned close to Isketerol to whisper, then back to the captain. "It's the ancestors and deeds of our host," he said. "Sort of like the begats in the Bible, with an occasional blood feud or war thrown in. Takes his bloodline back to their gods."

"Great, saga-singing biker gangs of the Bronze Age," Alston muttered, and settled down to listen. This wouldn't be the first long ceremony she'd sat through . . . and the food was good, at least. She'd been getting damned sick of fish.

The bosun's pipe whistled as the captain came back up the hanging stair and over the bulwarks. "*Eagle* arriving!" barked the watch. Three bells rang, and another as her foot touched the deck.

The welcome stuttered a little as he saw who was included among the party following her, but made a creditable finish.

"*Eagle* aboard. Captain on deck!"

"As you were," she said, returning the salutes of the watch. "Ms. Rapczewicz has the deck." Then, with the same toneless precision: "Get me a pair of bolt-cutters, and some clothes for Ms. Swindapa here. On the double."

They came quickly, the tool and a blue sweatsuit. Swindapa had been glancing around, her eyes enormous. She bit her lip at the sight of the long-handled cutters.

Probably thinks it's some instrument of torture, Alston thought grimly.

Carefully—the collar was tight—she maneuvered the blades under the tough rawhide. The leather parted with a dull snap; Alston pulled off the broken collar with her hands and threw the pieces overside. An ungovernable impulse made her spit after them.

"What's that phrase for 'You can go home' and 'You are free'?" Alston asked. Arnstein relayed it, and Swindapa's eyes went very wide. Alston mimed bound wrists, and then breaking them. It took a moment more to show her how to put on the clothes, and turn her over to the surgeon's assistant. Especially when she threw herself to her knees and clutched at Alston's legs, weeping.

"You'd better do the examination," she said to the assistant, who was also a woman. "Check for infection and so forth.

"Well, that's done," she said more normally to the officers. "Yes, things went fairly well. We were lucky; there are a couple of people there who speak a form of Greek that Professor Arnstein halfway understands. The natives are friendly, and we can probably do the business we came for, PDQ. Our trade goods seem to have enormous relative value here."

Sandy Rapczewicz rubbed her chin. "You don't seem to like the taste of it much, skipper," she said.

Alston shrugged. "No, I can't say that I do. I really don't approve of handin' out human beings as party favors."

The XO blanched. Alston went on: "But that buys no yams. It won't be the first time I've done something that stuck in my craw in the line of duty."

Several of the others nodded; they'd been on the Haitian refugee patrol too, turning starving people back into the hellhole of junta-ruled Port-au-Prince.

Rapczewicz shrugged. "At least it's in a better cause than rescuing some politican's credit with the voters," she said.

CHAPTER SEVEN

April, Year 1 A.E.

Someone was screaming. It was not until after she had opened her eyes that Swindapa realized it was her own voice. Her hands flailed about, until a painful knock on hard wood brought her shuddering to full consciousness. She sat bolt upright in the small soft bed, heart beating as if it were a bird trying to escape the basketwork cage of her chest. Sweat ran down her forehead, neck, flanks, turning clammy and chill. She put a hand to her neck. The collar was gone, was gone . . . nothing there but the ointment the Eagle People healer had put on it and her other scrapes.

The Burning Snake had me, she knew. The Dream Eater. It had taken her back, made her feel again the crushing weight and the tearing, splitting pain. As if she were being wedged apart like a log for planks.

She looked around, breath slowing. It was the Red Swallowstar time, just before Moon Woman led the Sun into the sky. Light came through the round window by her side, a window covered in crystal and rimmed with metal like an amber button, but huge. The bed was soft, made with very thin cloth like a fine tunic and thick warm cloaks, but a frightening distance from the floor. Walls surrounded her, straight on two sides, sloping on the other that bore the windows. Enigmatic objects filled the little chamber about her, things whose shapes shed her eyes, making them slip aside. She could hear footsteps and voices above, and the room itself was moving. The great thing she was on was floating, then; her memory did not twist but flew on a true curve. Out the round hole she could see the shore, and the Iraiina camp. She was away from it.

That gave her enough of herself back to swing her feet

out of the bed and stand, stretching gingerly. She was thirsty, a little hungry, and had an urgent need to empty her bladder. The door swung open under her hand, after she'd fumbled with the handle for a while.

Wait, she thought. The black chieftain had given her clothes, the same sort of clothes the Eagle ship-people wore. The chieftain who'd taken the collar from her neck, who'd led her back from living death to the Shining World. *I had better wear them, to show that I honor her.*

The worst things in the world had happened to her, and then something from beyond the world had lifted her out of it. There must be a meaning in this, a track among the stars making a path for her feet.

The . . . *head,* was the word . . . was just across the passage. Swindapa forced herself to walk erect and calm toward it; the narrow walls and the ceiling above her were terrifyingly like a barrow grave, the places where the Old Ones laid their dead. Inside was a *mirror,* something else both frightening and wonderful beyond words. In it she could see herself, really *see,* not just catch a blurred glimpse as in a pond or polished bronze.

The face that looked out was strange to her. Not the face of the reckless youngster who had gone into battle to avenge her man's ruined leg and life. Not the student who watched the stars with the Grandmothers. Not the beaten slave of the Sun People, either. *Three times have I died-to-myself and been reborn. Moon Woman has drawn me through the earth and Her light has changed me like a tree.*

Whose face was it, then? She would have to learn who it was, and how to be that one.

"Don't offer too much," Isketerol said.

Alston looked over at him. *Why does he give a damn if we're overcharged?* she thought.

Daurthunnicar and some of his chiefs were standing before big wicker baskets of grain—emmer wheat, club wheat, barley, rye—and several types of beans. The representatives from the *Eagle* had their own samples on display, the same sort of thing they'd given as gifts the night before. The eyes of the Iraiina chieftains kept straying back to the glass tumblers, cloth, plastic, steel tools, and weapons. Some of them licked their lips as they stood leaning a hip or buttock on the hafts of their axes, using them as their remote British descendants would a shooting stick. Today they were less flamboyantly dressed, though still sporting the odd gold arm ring; the *rahax* had a square silver plate on his belt. He also wore his new steel long sword on a baldric over one shoulder, rarely taking his hand from its hilt.

Arnstein spoke with the Iberian for several minutes. "He says he's a merchant here too, and if we pay too much we'll ruin the market," the Californian said.

"Ask him what he buys here," Alston said.

"Ah . . . copper and tin in the ingot, and gold dust and nuggets, mostly. Also raw wool, honey, beeswax, flax, tallow, hides and leather, and, ah, slaves. Among other things."

Alston nodded coolly. In a world this thinly populated, with these crude ships, she hadn't expected long-range trade in bulk commodities like grain to be of much importance. Isketerol had his own priorities, and keeping the price of wheat down wasn't one of them.

"Don't worry, Professor. I realize we're in another era with other mores." *Damned if I'll put up with this sort of thing forever,* she thought. *But for now, no alternative.* "And what does he sell?"

"All sorts of handicrafts, fine cloth, dyes, drugs, olive oil, wine." Another moment's consultation. "And Isketerol says he hopes to establish friendly relations with us, if we're coming here again. So he gives you his knowledge of local conditions as a gift of friendship. He also says that the locals—the word he uses probably means something like 'savages' or 'natives'—don't have much conception of bargaining. To them, this is sort of an exchange of gifts, and the *rahax* gets status by giving as well as getting. Our goods are very high-status. Daurthunnicar maintains his position partly by what he can give away. If he takes your gifts and doesn't gift you lavishly in return, he'll lose face." ·

"Does that sound plausible, Professor?"

"Very. In pre-urban economies with no money, gift exchange is nearly as efficient a way to conceptualize handing stuff around as trade. Wealth is a means to power through prestige, face. Warlike tribal cultures like the Iraiina often think that way."

"And I suspect that losing face among this bunch has very unpleasant consequences. That's probably a hint from Isketerol, by the way, as well. Assure him he'll get his share, tactfully. Now, those baskets seem to hold about a couple of bushels each. Let him know that we need . . ."

The slow, cumbersome business of dickering through two sets of interpreters went on. After a while Iraiina women brought stools for the leaders to sit on, and the tribal idea of breakfast: more of the coarse bread and cheese, leftover meat, and clay pots of the thin, flat sour beer. *At least it's weak, too, praise the Lord. A possum couldn't get high on this stuff.* Alston noticed one younger subchief staring at her, more and more intently. A baffled look grew on his face; after a half hour he leaned over and tried to speak quietly in his lord's ear. Daurthunnicar brushed him aside with one thick arm, then barked him into silence.

"Past noon," Alston said at last. "Tactfully suggest that we break for lunch."

Daurthunnicar rumbled agreement; there was more mutual confusion, as three different ideas of reckoning time met and clashed. At last they settled on what Arnstein thought was probably two in the afternoon.

Alston turned. There was a sound of scuffling behind her, footfalls, a quick warning shout of *Captain*—

A hand fell on her shoulder; she could feel the strength of the grip even through the cloth of her uniform jacket. Daurthunnicar bellowed in anger in the background, but there was no time for talk. She let herself fall backward in the direction of the pull that would otherwise have spun her around, swaying her hips aside and snapping the hammer end of her clenched fist back and down.

There was a choked-off screech of pain as she turned, a quick pivot in place. The young subchief was bending over convulsively, hands cupping his groin in uncontrollable reflex. Her own left hand flashed up to meet his descending and unguarded throat; the Iraiina warrior had neck muscles like braided iron cable, but that didn't matter a damn if you sank your thumb and fingers in precisely . . . so. There *wasn't* any muscle protecting the trachea or carotids, no matter how strong you were. The Iraiina choked again, this time as his windpipe closed and blood stopped flowing to his brain. Her right hand had gone into her pocket and closed on a short lead bar; she pulled that out, poised the fist, and struck with a snapping twist to the side of the head as she released his throat. The Iraiina dropped bonelessly to the ground, breathing with a rasping whistle. She restrained the automatic follow-through which would have brought her heel stamp-kicking down on the back of his neck.

Captain Alston looked up, meeting Daurthunnicar's eyes. "Ask him if this is the way his people treat guests," she said.

A bristle of leveled spears surrounded her as the cadets closed up. In back, a few more were unobtrusively bringing their shotguns and rifles around. Most of the Iraiina seemed shocked, bewildered; she saw naked horror on some of their faces. Daurthunnicar looked nearly as purple as his subchief had when her chokehold clamped on his throat. He drew his own dagger and brought it up to his face. Slowly, deliberately, he cut two lines there—shallow, but enough to bring a trickle of blood. Then he stepped forward, sheathed the dagger, and kicked the fallen form of his subordinate hard enough to do far more damage than she'd inflicted.

"Daurthunnicar, *rahax,* begs forgiveness for this shame," he rumbled; or at least that was how Isketerol relayed it through Arnstein. The *rahax* kicked the fallen warrior again. "How may he wipe out this shame, this attack on a guest, to avert the anger of his gods?"

Alston looked down at the figure of the Iraiina, recovering just enough to writhe. She remembered the screams that had echoed through her ship that morning, and what the ship's doctor had told her.

"Tell him that his oath is between him and his gods," she said curtly, making a chopping gesture. "Then tell him to treat this one as his people deal with oathbreakers."

Daurthunnicar grunted as if he'd been belly-punched; she turned and strode away, her people falling into position around her, back to the waiting longboat with none of the locals but the Iberian trader with them.

The chief's voice rose in bellowing protest behind her as the tribesfolk milled and shouted into each other's faces, waving their arms. A few women started to keen. The *rahax* stopped shouting and began to groan and sob; from the thudding sounds he was literally beating his breast as well.

"I didn't realize that the Coast Guard taught that sort of unarmed combat," Arnstein said, wiping his forehead.

"They don't," Alston said bleakly. "Only a little of the basics. The Way is a hobby of mine."

Isketerol spoke: "A very shrewd move, honored captain," he said. "That fool saw that you were a woman. Now none will dare think so—even if they suspect, they will keep silence. To admit that a woman beat one of their own hand to hand would be unbearable shame, so they cannot admit it even to themselves. Also Daurthunnicar will have to give you a better bargain, for his honor's sake."

"Tell Mr. Isketerol," Alston said, without looking around, "that I thank him for his assistance. Also that I have *nothing* to hide."

"Damn," Cofflin said softly, with a touch of awe. "I just don't by God *believe* it."

He looked out over Sesachacha Pond and suppressed an impulse to take off his cap as if he were in church, instead of out in the country at the eastern end of the island. His mind groped for a description of what he was seeing. "Flock of birds" was completely inadequate, the way "large building" would be for the World Trade Center. He was looking north to Quidnet across the ash-black remains of the arrowroot and scrub oak thickets Angelica Brand's people had cleared, over the water to the low barrier beach that separated the pond from the ocean. *And I can't see a damned thing but birds.* Birds so thick ashore that the ground *moved* with them, like a rippling carpet of feathers and beaks. Their sound was a gobbling, honking thunder, a continuous rustling background loud enough to make speech difficult at less than a shout. The explosions of wings were louder still.

"The smell's awesome, too," he added aloud, to hear himself talk and bring things back to a human scale. "Like the Mother of all Henhouses."

He raised his binoculars, peering through the vision slit of the plank-and-brush hide and suppressing the slight quiver in his hands. Big brownish birds with white-banded necks, Canada geese right enough. Ducks . . . mallards and canvasbacks and big black ducks, ducks beyond all reason, more varieties than he could name. On land . . . *Some sort of pigeon,* he thought; enough of them to outnumber the waterfowl, which he wouldn't have believed possible if he wasn't seeing it with his own eyes.

"Martha," he said, "what sort of pigeon is that? Foot long, sort of a pinkish body, blue . . . no, a blue-gray head, long pointed tail."

"What?" she shouted, and snatched the glasses out of his hands.

Cofflin stared at her; it was about the most un-Martha-ish behavior he'd ever seen from her. Martha Stoddard did not lose her composure.

"Passenger pigeons," she said, after a long moment's study. "Passenger pigeons, as I live and breathe, *passenger pigeons.*"

Hairs stood up along Cofflin's forearms, and he felt them struggling to rise down his spine. *I'm seeing something no human being has seen in over a century,* he thought with slow wonder. Then: *No. I'm seeing something common as dirt.*

"I almost hate to do this," Cofflin said softly.

Part of him did. The rest of him, particularly his stomach and mouth, was downright eager. Roast duck, crackling skin, dark flavorful meat with a touch of fat that fish just didn't have. . . . Jared Cofflin swallowed and gave the lanyard lying by his right hand a good hard yank.

Bunnnf. Bunnnf. Bunnnf. Bunnnf.

The modified harpoon guns had been dug into the fields at a slant. Now the finned darts shot into the air, dragging coils of line behind them . . . and then a rising arc of net soaring up into the sky, catching the birds as they flung themselves aloft in terror. All across the fields around the pond other nets were rising. From the edge of the water itself came a deeper sound as giant catapults made from whole sets of leaf springs flung weighted nets out over the waterfowl.

If the sound of the birds at rest had been loud, the tumult that followed was enough to stun. Cofflin dove out of the hide, waving his arms and yelling. The shouts were lost in the cannonade thunder of the rising flocks, but hundreds of islanders saw his signal. They ran forward, waving lengths of plank, golf clubs, baseball bats, leaping and striking at birds—the vast majority—that had escaped the nets. The air was thick with feathers and noise, thick with birds in numbers that literally hid the sun, casting a shadow like dense cloud. It drifted through the sky like smoke; bird dung fell from the air and spattered his hat and the shoulders of his coat, falling as thick as light snow. He ignored it, looking at the carpet of feathered wealth that lay around him . . . and there would be others waiting to take a similar harvest at Gibbs Pond and Folger's Marsh.

"I hope they don't take off elsewhere for good," he said. A broken-winged pigeon fluttered across his feet; he struck at it automatically, to put it out of its pain.

Martha came up beside him, brushing at her sleeve. "I don't think so," she said. "Bless their hard-wired little brains, they migrate pretty automatically. Unless we did this every day . . . and for that matter, it's not the same flocks every time—we're seeing a segment, like a moving rope touching down once a day. At that, this is just the edge of the main flight path down the coast."

Cofflin nodded, looking at the islanders standing and panting. "Now we've got to collect all this up," he said. "Hope we can store it all—didn't expect this much."

"Who could?" Martha said, shaking her head. "I still don't believe it, and I'm looking at it. . . . Well, we can make more ice, I suppose. There's plenty of salt, they can be packed down in oil, pickled in brine, smoked, the offal will go on the fields . . ."

He sighed and shook his head in turn, feeling a little of the wonder of it leaving him.

"Let's get to work," he said, pulling up his sleeves. "Big job today."

"It's stolen, isn't it?" Doreen said quietly. "All the things we're . . . buying."

Arnstein nodded, not taking his eyes away from the scene he was watching, a historian's secret dream made flesh. Every once in a while he would snap another picture.

An Iraiina chief was wheeling his chariot about in the open space before his gathered warriors, its wooden wheels cutting tracks dark green and soil-black through the silvery dew on the grass. The dyed heron plumes on the horses' heads bobbed and fluttered, the bronze and gold of the trappings glittered, and the chief's cloak blew back from his shoulders like the wings of a raven. The chief sprang up, his feet on the rim between the holders for bow, quiver, javelins, and long thrusting spear with its own collar of feathers.

Arnstein had read once—and now seen, these past few

days—that chariot riders could run out along the pole that linked the horses' yokes at a full gallop.

Studded shield and leaf-shaped bronze long sword shaped the air as he harangued them. At first they cheered and waved arms and spears and axes. After a few moments they screamed, hammering their weapons on their bright-painted shields, roaring into the hollows of the shields until the sound boomed across the camp. When the chief leaped back into the body of his chariot and the driver slapped the reins to spur the horses forward, they poured after him in a leaping, shrieking mass. Before they passed out of sight among fields and scattered copses of oak they had settled down into a loping trot behind the war-cars, silent and all the more frightening for that.

Doreen went on: "They're going out to kill people and take everything they have and sell it to us! Why don't you *do* something, or tell the captain—"

Arnstein rounded on her: "Because there isn't anything I *can* do, because we need the food or we'll starve, and because Captain Alston knows both those things perfectly well!

"Sorry," he added after a moment, as they turned and trudged through the tumbled, rutted confusion of the Iraiina camp. They were getting used to the smell, a thought that made his skin itch—although to do them justice, it probably wasn't so bad when they spread out in their normal fashion. In fact, some of the subchiefs had already moved out, up or down the coast, or inland.

A naked brown boychild ran up to them, a four-year-old with a roach of startling tow-white hair. Daring, he reached out and touched the stranger's leg and then ran away, shrieking his glee. An Iraiina woman scooped him up and paddled him across the bare bottom, then tucked him under her arm and walked away, casting an apologetic smile over her shoulder as she headed back to her tent.

"Sorry myself," Doreen sighed, and tucked her hand through his arm. "I . . ." She shrugged. "I don't want to quarrel. There are too few of us for that sort of thing."

"Agreed," Arnstein said, and patted the hand. *And so few of us who can hold an intelligent conversation.* Captain Alston, of course, but her interests were rather specialized, and in any case she was . . . *intimidating*, that was the word he was looking for.

Doreen gave his arm a squeeze and changed the subject. "I'm surprised they've gotten so . . . casual about us so soon," she went on.

"We're marvels," Arnstein said, relieved. "But they live in a world of marvels, magic, ghosts, demons, gods who talk to men in dreams or father children on mortals—they don't just tell folk tales, they *believe* them, more so than any Holy Roller back home. Like a dancing Hasid drunk on God. We're friendly marvels."

For now, he thought uneasily to himself.

From what he'd seen of them, the Iraiina had their virtues, all of them more comfortably observed from a distance. They were brave, of course. Unflinchingly stoic, loyal to their tribe and chiefs, usually kind to their children and positively affectionate to their horses. Surprisingly clean, for barbarians. They were also callous as cats to anyone outside their bonds of blood and oath, cruel when they were crossed, and they had tempers like well-aged dynamite sweating beads of nitroglycerine. Not just the warriors either; he'd seen two women lighting into each other with distaffs, and then rolling around trying to bite off ears and succeeding in pulling out hanks of hair. The laughing spectators had thought that great sport.

Let them feel insulted, or let some incident make their superstitious fears boil over, and . . .

"Sooner we leave the better," he said.

"Yes, it's sort of like being on safari . . . only, you have to make camp with the lions," Doreen agreed.

They wound their way through the early-morning bustle of the camp, between the huts and tents of households large and small. Women fetched water, cooked over fires or in crude clay ovens, kneaded bread dough in wooden troughs, tended the swarming children, gossiped as they spun thread on their distaffs or sat to weave on broad looms with stone-weighted warps set under leather awnings. Children had chores of their own, starting with minding younger siblings while their mothers worked. A slave could be told by her collar and the non-Iraiina way she braided her hair; she was silent as she knelt to grind grain on an arrangement of two stones much like a Mexican *metate*, but she didn't look spectacularly ill-treated. A woman went by with twin buckets of milk on the ends of a yoke over her shoulders. Three more in colorful checked skirts chanted a song as they swung a sloshing bag made from a whole sheepskin suspended under a tripod of staves; making butter, he supposed.

A brawny redbeard poured molten bronze from a crucible into a mold with exquisite care, while his apprentices blew through hollowed rods to keep the charcoal in his clay hearth hot. Other men cut leather shapes from hides stretched on the ground, braided thongs into ropes, worked with bronze chisel and adze and stone scraper on the growing frame of a chariot, knapped stone into everyday tools for tasks too mundane to rate the precious bronze. The ungreased wooden axles of oxcarts squealed like dying pigs.

Only a few of the men were slaves. He'd learned that free men were all warriors at need, but except for the chiefs' few household guards they mainly herded, farmed, and practiced crafts; the chiefs themselves were not above turning their hands to a man's work. *No real leisure class,* he decided. *This economy's not productive enough to support one.*

Many more of the menfolk here would be out with the cattle; herding large beasts was male work, while milking and making cheese and butter were for women. When they'd settled into their new land they'd build houses and start plowing and reaping as well, although he got the impression that farming was secondary to livestock with the Iraiina. Sights, smells, sounds reminded him of what he'd seen on vacations in the backlands of Mexico or in Africa or Asia, but always with differences. He finished one roll of film and snapped another into his camera; they were used to that, now, too.

They came down near the water, where a broad stretch was kept clear around the Tartessian ships. That section was cleaner and less cluttered, if only because the Iberians didn't have women, children, or domestic livestock along. They also looked more disciplined than the Iraiina. Not having much to do, the crews were lolling about in loincloths or less—they lacked the Iraiina nudity taboo—sunning themselves in the mild spring warmth. A few stood leaning on their spears in front of their leader's tent of striped canvas, standing to attention not having been invented yet. Some of the idlers made signs with their fingers and spat aside as the strangers walked past; others called invitations which Doreen needed no Tartessian to understand. They fell silent when Isketerol ducked out from under the canvas, walking over to the Americans with a broad smile.

That didn't reassure Arnstein. It reminded him too much of a man who'd sold him a car once, in San Diego. That car had cost more than its purchase price in repairs the first six months he drove it.

"Hello," the Tartessian said. "Ianarnstein. Msdoreenrosenthal."

Arnstein started to reply, then checked when he realized that the Tartessian had spoken in English . . . sort of. "Hello yourself," he replied.

White teeth showed broader in the lean olive-skinned face. "Rejoice, as well," he added in his archaic, gutturally accented Greek. If Arnstein ever met a real Mycenaean, he was probably going to sound extremely Tartessian himself, but comprehension came easily to both of them after a week of practice. He wasn't doing as well with Iraiina, but Doreen had made some progress there and was beginning to pick up a little of this Greek.

"I seek to honor you with your own people's greeting," Isketerol added.

"Rejoice," Arnstein said dryly. "My captain wished to speak with you this morning."

"Ah, she does me honor!" Isketerol said. He looked out toward the *Eagle.* "The loading must be nearly complete," he went on. "I and my cousin will come."

They came to the shore reserved for the Americans' use. There were disused rafts scattered up and down the beaches where the Iraiina camped, not yet disassembled for timber or firewood. The *Eagle*'s crew was using them to tow basket after basket of grain and beans out to the ship. Another cast off as they came to the water's edge, the crew of the longboat towing it bending their backs to the oars. Today the shore also held pens full of pigs—not the pink sluggish creatures Arnstein knew, but lean bristly vicious things like piney-wood razorbacks, three-quarters wild. All of them were young females in farrow except for a brace of boars penned separately; those watched with cunning beady eyes, their long curved tusks ready for anyone who came near. They'd already loaded calves, colts and ewes, for breeding with their stock back on the island.

"Those pigs're going to be a joy to get on board," Doreen remarked. Arnstein felt his mouth watering at the potential bacon, hams, and chops. There were advantages to being selective about the traditions of your ancestors. He was also acutely conscious of the woman by his side. Different generations, but they had a lot in common. There was nothing like being among aliens to make you realize that.

She ignored the days-old head that looked down on the beach from a pole, drastic reparation for an insult to a guest. The body was buried, with the head of a sacrificial horse in place of its own, an offering to appease the anger of the gods. Doreen blanched slightly at the memory; the young oath-breaking warrior had danced to the sword with a spring in his step and a face as composed as if he were strolling home to dinner. Probably he thought he was going to his gods. . . .

"Ah, Professor, Ms. Rosenthal," Alston said, handing a clipboard to a cadet. "And Isketerol of Tartessos."

The Iberian bowed, hand to breast. Alston nodded her head with its cap of close-cut wiry hair. "Translate, please, Professor. Tell Mr. Isketerol that I have a proposition for him."

There was a tray nearby, with one of the wardroom attendants standing behind it. Arnstein poured small glasses of wine, despite the early hour, diluting it half and half with soda water. You had to serve refreshments, at least symbolically, or you weren't trusted. He didn't think Isketerol trusted them much anyway, but there was no sense in open insult.

"First," the captain of the *Eagle* said, "thank him for the help he gave us."

Isketerol made a purely Mediterranean gesture with hands and shoulders; Arnstein had seen its like in Sicily and Greece in his own era. "Of course, you were still cheated, if not so badly as you might have been. In Tartessos, or any of the civilized lands around the Middle Sea, your great ship would have been stuffed to bursting three times over with grain and cloth for half—for one part in ten—of what you lavished on these barbarians."

Alston nodded, expressionless. "We may make other arrangements later. Right now, we're planning one more voyage here this season, after the harvest."

"Alas, by then I will have departed. My own ships are nearly ready."

Alston turned to Arnstein. "Phrase this very carefully, Professor. Tell him that we want to hire him for the summer, and we'll pay well. We want him to return with us to the island, teach some of our people the languages he knows, and then come back here in September when the local harvest is in. In return, we'll give him a fair sampling of our trade goods."

Arnstein sputtered. "Captain Alston! Would you buy a used car from—"

"You told me who he reminded you of, Professor, but we need him. Learning languages without one both sides can understand is just too *slow,* and he speaks how many?"

"Iraiina, several related dialects, the thing the Earth Folk speak, Greek, Tartessian, Egyptian, and some Semitic language I'm pretty sure is ancestral to Hebrew and probably to Phoenician as well. Plus a smattering of others." Part of the cost of doing business for a Tartessian merchant, evidently. "But Captain, impressions aside, I'm certain he's a slave trader and pretty sure he's a part-time pirate."

She shrugged slightly. "It's a calculated risk. I'm afraid I must insist."

The words were polite, and so was the tone. Behind it was a will ready to grind like millstones. He sighed and spread his hands.

The shouting crowd fell silent as the American approached. William Walker craned his head a little, looking over the tops of theirs; he was a tall man even by twentieth-century standards and he'd seen only one or two men bigger here. Two Iraiina warriors had been wrestling in a circle of yelling, cheering onlookers. They were stripped to their kilts, chests heaving and eyes glaring as they backed off warily, looking at him out of the corners of their eyes, panting amid a strong smell of sweat and dust.

Well, not exactly wrestling, Walker thought. One of them—it was the wog they'd picked up at sea, Ohotolarix—was bleeding slightly where a handful of his sparse young beard had been pulled out. The other man looked roughly handled, too. *More like catch-as-catch-can.*

Everyone was looking at *him,* one of the mysterious, magical strangers from across the sea. A little fear in the eyes of the men, in the women fear and . . . *Well, well,* he thought, smiling at one bold-eyed girl. She was probably not very respectable by local standards, the collar and short dress that showed her ankles indicated that, he thought. But he'd never let that bother him.

"Go ahead," he said, backing up with an urging gesture. "Don't let me stop the fun."

Tentative smiles met his. He nodded and looked at the two contestants. The other warrior was black-haired, more densely bearded than Ohotolarix, and more heavily built, a few years older and sporting a couple of missing teeth. He spat something at the young blond and lunged with hairy arms spread.

Ohotolarix met him chest to chest. *Catch-as-catch-can, all right,* Walker thought. *Butting, biting and . . . yup, attempted gouging allowed. Pathetic.*

They were fast and strong, but neither man seemed to have any idea what to do with his fists and feet—wild hay-makers like something out of a 1930s movie, and they didn't even attempt to kick. At last they closed again, and grappled at each other's heavy padded belts, straining and grunting. The older man lifted Ohotolarix bodily into the air and slammed him down again on the hard-packed ground. Blood was running from his mouth and nose now too, but he doggedly began to get up. The victor waited panting until he was on his hands and knees, then delivered a solid moccasined foot to the ribs—evidently kicking wasn't against the rules, they just didn't know how to do it effectively.

Ohotolarix collapsed, wheezing. His opponent dropped on him and grabbed him by the braid, pounding his head on the clay. When the younger man went limp he rose, dusted himself off, and walked toward the girl who'd smiled at Walker. He collected some trinkets from the bystanders, grabbed her wrist, and began to jerk her away; all around him men were laughing or scowling as they exchanged small items, knives or ornaments.

Bets, Walker realized. *Girlie there's the main stake.* Ohotolarix was hauling himself up, wheezing and snarling as he clutched at his ribs. *Tsk. Not fair; he must still be weak. On the other hand, life isn't fair.* On the other hand . . .

"Wait," Walker said easily, putting out a hand. "Hold it, Mr. Macho. Why don't we discuss this?"

The Iraiina flinched a little, then visibly gathered himself and began to brush past.

Maybe that was a mistake, Walker thought. *On the third hand, the guy just dissed me.*

He put a hand on the man's face and pushed, moving his foot in a simple heel hook. The Iraiina landed on his backside in a puff of dust. There was an amazed buzz from the crowd, then a rising note of excitement as Walker stripped off his jacket and shirt, holding them out with one hand. The girl took them, moving back to the edge of the reforming circle.

"No sense in prolonging this," Walker said easily, suddenly feeling alive. *Feeling like I'm really* here, *not watching it.*

He made a gesture that he'd seen among the locals, one that evidently hadn't changed its meaning in three thousand years.

"Mithair," he said. It was a pity he didn't know the word for "your" as well as "mother" yet, but the motion of arm and finger was unmistakable. The victorious warrior screamed at him and leaped.

"Well, maybe they take motherhood more seriously here," Walker said.

He swayed aside, grabbed arm and belt, set his feet in stance, and turned with a snapping flex of his waist and shoulders. Momentum turned into velocity, and the leap turned into a windmilling arc that ended in a crowd of laughing spectators. They broke his fall, and he came up shaking his head. Eyes fixed and pupils wide to swallow the color, lips curled back from teeth, a trail of mixed drool and blood coming from one corner of his mouth.

"Uh-oh," Walker said. *I don't think this is a sporting contest anymore.*

The Iraiina snatched a long bronze dagger from the belt of a man next to him and charged, shrieking something high-pitched. Walker's reaction was automatic: one hand slashed upward and cracked the edge of his palm into the knifeman's wrist. The blade flew free, twinkling in the evening sun as it spun end over end. A continuation of the same motion sent the American's hand around the Iraiina's arm, locking it under his armpit and torquing it up with the elbow locked against its natural bend. Walker's other arm slammed forward, fingers curled back to present the heel of his right hand as the striking hammer on the anvil of his opponent's breastbone.

"Disssaaa!" he shouted, deep and loud, the focusing *kia*. He had just enough control left to pull the blow as it rammed into the Iraiina's chest over the heart. Bone bounced it back at him, and the other man dropped, limp, rasping for breath, and clawing at his chest while his face turned purple.

Walker wheeled, crouching and dropping into stance before he realized that the crowd weren't attacking. Instead they were cheering; men pressed forward to slap him on the shoulders and back, pressing things on him—gold bracelets, worked bronze rings, even the knife the fallen man had used to attack him. The girl handed him back his clothes and made shooing motions at the others as he dressed. He straightened, wary, then grinned and held his hands over his head.

"I've got to control these chivalrous impulses," he muttered to himself.

Ohotolarix was on his feet, smiling wryly—either that or his mouth was too sore to do more. He limped over to the American and started to speak. Then he sighed, shook his head, and took the girl's hand, laying it in Walker's. She looked at him with another smile, this one broader and more appraising, before she cast her eyes down modestly.

"Oh, God *damn* the captain and her fucking floating Sunday school," Walker groaned.

He took the hand and put it back in Ohotolarix's. The Iraiina looked puzzled, then the beginnings of anger showed on his puffy, dust-and-blood smeared face.

"Uh-oh again," Walker muttered. *Think, dude.*

He mimed fighting, then stood by Ohotolarix and held a protecting arm above him. Then he stepped behind the Iraiina, taking his arm and raising it in fighting position as if to shield Walker; last of all he pulled the bronze knife he'd tucked through his belt and held it out to the warrior, hilt first.

"Listen, you dumb wog," he said, in slow solemn tones. "I don't have your spear-chucker's script handy, but this is some sort of heap big medicine. You're going to like it and not make trouble, because while I could talk my way out of this I'd rather not. You savvy, blondie?"

Something seemed to have gotten through to the young Iraiina. He took a step back, peering at Walker's face, then slowly went to one knee and took the knife. He grasped the American's hands and put his between them, touching them to his forehead and heart.

"*Pothis,*" the Iraiina said. A string of machine-gun-rapid syllables followed.

"Uh-oh again," Walker muttered. *What did I just get myself into?*

Ohotolarix seemed to want him to follow. He did, through the dusty tangle of the Iraiina camp, to a small hollow. Two fair-sized leather tents stood there, with a fire between them and bundles and baggage in leather sacks all around; a tripod of spears, a shield, and a long-hafted bronze tomahawk completed the picture. A swaddled infant was propped up against a heap of baskets, and a woman bent over the fire doing something with a big clay pot. She gave a small shriek at the sight of Ohotolarix, rushing forward and then halting in alarm at the sight of Walker beside him.

Wifey, Walker decided, nodding to her as she drew her shawl over her head. The young woman was about Ohotolarix's age, five months pregnant, and quite pretty, with dark-blond hair done up on her head with long bronze-headed bone pins and a round, cheerful face. *No collar, longer dress, more jewelry.*

The young warrior spoke, and the woman went back to the fire; the other one went into the smaller horsehide tent. Walker sat at his host's urging, and the pregnant girl brought them both bowls from the pot; it turned out to be mutton stew with barley, and hunks of rather dry bread to go with it, along with mead.

"This would be a lot more interesting if I could understand you, or knew what the hell was going on," Walker said. "You know," he went on, finishing his stew, "I sort of like it here. You guys have a lot to learn, and I could—"

The smaller tent's flap came half open and a voice called. Walker looked over; the girl with the collar had shed all her other clothing, and was kneeling on a heap of sheepskins, beckoning. He let a slow grin creep over his face, looking back at Ohotolarix. The young Iraiina gave him the same expression back, with a wink, and made the same gesture Walker had used on his opponent before waving at the tent.

"But oh, context is everything," Walker laughed, nodding and moving toward the tent, where a bare arm wiggled fingers at him. He picked up the cup of mead as he went.

"And the captain *did* say we should be careful not to offend. Quickest way to offend wogs is to turn down their hospitality."

He ducked inside and closed the flap behind him. The girl leaned back on her elbows, tossing a mane of rust-colored hair behind her; it wasn't very clean, and she smelled fairly strongly of sweat and woodsmoke.

But I don't give a damn, he thought. *I like this place. It's more . . . straightforward.*

And God, but there was an opening for someone with his talents here. Heading back to Nantucket with a cargo of pigs and the prospect of a year spent fishing suddenly looked rather dull.

Hold on, boy, he said, stripping and looking down at the girl. *You don't know the languages or the customs, and you* certainly *don't want to get marooned here by your lonesome.*

"I'll have to think," he said, taking a breast in each hand. The woman shivered and arched her back. "Later, that is."

"You can't be serious!" Miskelefol shouted. "Has the Jester stolen your wits?"

"Quiet!" Isketerol hissed. The tent's walls were thin, and too many ears listened outside. They were alone within save for a single native slave he'd bought from the Iraiina, crouched in the corner, but he suspected several members of the crews spied for rivals.

The senior Tartessian leaned forward on his stool and caught the neck of his cousin's tunic, hauling him close. Firelight stole through the slit of the tent's flap, underlighting the younger man's face. The smells of dinner cooking came through with the reflected flame, and the voices of men preparing for the night, doing chores about the camp, or playing at stones-and-squares. A woman giggled in the hull of the ship whose horse figurehead reared above them.

"Of course I'm serious," Isketerol went on. "All the gods and goddesses have given me this opportunity, I'd be mad *not* to take it!"

He sprang to his feet and paced in the slight room the tent allowed, his step lithe and springy as a youth's although he'd seen nearly thirty winters.

"They *need* me, cousin. They haven't *anyone* who can speak anything but Achaean, and that badly; and more than that, they know nothing about the lands on this side of the ocean. Forget what they've promised me for a summer's stay—even though it's ten times ten times the profit we expected on this voyage. Think of what could come of being their adviser and go-between when they come to negotiate with the king, or with Pharaoh, even! You know how our house has fallen from the wealth we once had. Why else are we here, risking our hides dickering with savages? This is our gods-given chance to do more than restore it."

He returned to the stool, forcing calm upon himself. He leaned close, hissing in his kinsman's ear. "Think of learning their secrets, and how to wield them!"

"Their magic?" Miskelefol whispered back, spitting aside and making the sign of the horns.

"Perhaps. A spell is a tool. But not all their secrets are magic. The Great King's men in Hatti get iron out of the rocks and know how to work it; that's a mystery, but not one you need to be a mage to understand. These Eagle People, these *Amurrukan*, they have arts that we don't, just as we have knowledge the barbarians don't. And they're not good at keeping secrets, most of them. With what I can learn . . ."

"You think you can build a ship of iron?" his cousin said. It had taken them both days to grasp that, but two visits to the *Eagle* had made them sure.

"No, fool!" Isketerol grabbed patience. "Your pardon, cousin. I misspoke. No, but it isn't magic that pushes her, it's sails—better sails than we know how to make, better arranged. It's smithcraft that forges those swords and spears. Weavers and dyers to make that cloth, artisans to make glass . . . glass shaped into pitchers, glass clear as spring water, common enough to give away when one beaker would buy riches at court! Listen, cousin . . ."

His voice sank, tempting, promising. At the last, Miskelefol nodded dubiously. "You're a bolder man than I, kinsman, to risk your life and soul so."

"I'm bold enough to risk the Crone's knife for a small profit among the Iraiina—why not with the Amurrukan for riches beyond dreams?"

"What do you wish?"

"You take the *Foam Treader* and the *Wave Hunter* home; my helmsman's well able to handle the *Hunter* on a safe run. Report to the king . . . but play down everything.

Say we saw a big ship from an unknown realm, whose crew said little but who had wonderful trade goods to offer. Give him some, but not of the best; the Corn Goddess knows the dregs are enough to satisfy even a king's greed. Our men will gossip, but everyone discounts sailors' lies, and by the time they reach home no two versions will be the same, and the truth is too strange to believe anyway. Summon my father, yours, our uncles, and meet in family conclave . . . hmmm, and my eldest wife, she's a shrewd one and has friends in the palace. You'll tell them everything you've seen and heard, and all I tell you this night. You'll make plans. They'll have to be tentative, since so much will depend on what I learn. And our elders will have their own ideas. Here's . . ."

The talk went far into the night, with just enough wine to sharpen wits. When his cousin left, Isketerol was still too taken with dreams to sleep, even though the strangers would be leaving on the morning tide. He snapped his fingers and signed, and the slave went over to the pallet, stripping and lying down. As he seeded her, it seemed that visions of glory burst before his eyes, a road of gold and fire stretching to the west.

"No, she definitely doesn't want to return home," Arnstein said, his voice sounding harassed.

They were all feeling harassed, not to mention sleep-deprived; loading seven hundred tons of cargo on a ship not designed for it, and without any equipment save block and tackle and sweat, had been a nightmare. Not to mention that most of them had come down with at least a mild case of Montezuma's Revenge—they were calling it British Belly—at one time or another. Now this.

Alston frowned. "You're sure?"

"Unless Isketerol is lying to me, and I doubt it," the academic said, running a hand over his balding scalp in a gesture of angry helplessness. "Doreen's got enough Iraiina now to confirm it, too."

Swindapa spoke unexpectedly in English. "No home. Go." She pointed west. "Stay, am me Eagle. Go."

The captain blinked in astonishment. "You've been teaching her English already?" she said.

"No," Arnstein said, shaking his head. "She's just got the most amazing goddam memory I've ever run across—

so does Isketerol, by the way, not as good as hers but still very impressive. Neither of them forgets a word once they've heard it twice. He's much faster at picking up syntax, but then, he's already learned six languages to her two. If you don't care about fine points of grammar, you can communicate pretty fast that way. Incidentally, Isketerol can also do some formidable arithmetic in his head, especially considering the clumsy numeral system he uses."

Alston looked at the Earth Folk girl. In sneakers and blue overalls, with blond locks escaping from a ponytail and blowing in the sea breeze on the deck of the *Eagle,* she looked like a corn-fed cheerleader type. Except that everything else was different, the way she moved and stood and the way the language she spoke had shaped her face. Now she folded her arms and looked stubborn in a way that crossed cultures and millennia, saying something in her own language and then repeating it in another.

"The . . . ah, the stars put her feet on the ship and she's not going to disobey them," Arnstein interpreted. "It's a religious thing, Captain."

Alston clenched her hands behind her back and rose slightly on her toes, thinking. *Stubborn,* she decided, and shuddered mentally at the thought of trying to force her into a boat. *She's got guts, too, to come through what happened to her with her will still strong.* She nodded approval.

"Very well," she said. "But make it plain she has to keep out of the way and follow instructions." Swindapa beamed; she seized Alston's hand and pressed it to her forehead, then kissed it. Alston disengaged it, firmly.

"And teach them both English."

The girl would probably be a much more reliable translator than the Tartessian . . . and besides, Alston could scarcely throw her over the side, all things considered.

As guests, the locals were allowed on the quarterdeck; Isketerol seemed to have enough sense to keep out of the way, and he'd taken a hint from a gift of soap and abandoned his habit of cleaning himself by rubbing down with olive oil and scraping it off, a massive sacrifice on his part. His eyes scanned about like video cameras, missing nothing. Swindapa tended to hover, until Alston gently motioned her back.

The captain looked about. Crew standing by, hands at the wheel, the smooth machinery of the *Eagle* ready to swing into motion. Wind from the northeast, which was just right, and not too strong, ten knots' worth—also good, in these narrow uncharted waters. If there had been any hope of refueling in the immediate future . . . but instead she'd do it the old-fashioned way, sail the anchors out of the main.

"Tide's on the ebb, ma'am," the sailing master said. "Four knots."

"Very well, Mr. Hiller. Prepare to weigh anchor," she said. "Make ready."

"Ready, aye." He turned to face his subordinates. "Sail stations, sail stations, on the fore, on the main, all hands to stations!"

The crew poured up the ratlines and out along the yards, their dark-blue clothing almost disappearing against the morning sky. Deck teams poised ready to haul.

"Put the royals in gear, fore and main. Jibs as well. The minute the anchors come free."

"Royals, fore and main, jibs, ma'am."

"Make it so, Mr. Hiller."

"Up and down!" The anchor chain was vertical.

"Anchors aweigh."

"Anchors aweigh, aye!"

White canvas—Dacron, really—blossomed a hundred and fifty feet above their heads. More sail spread down the stays to the bowsprit, the triangular swatches of the flying jib, the outer jib, the jib and the foremast staysail. Teams heaved them up the stay lines that reached to the foremast.

The quartermaster's whistle rang out again.

"Shift colors!" Jack and ensign came down, and the steaming ensign went up the gaff over their heads.

"House the anchor."

"Thus, thus," Alston said, giving the course to the helmsmen. They strained at the triple wheels as the great square-rigger came about and settled her prow to the south. "Mr. Hiller, the mizzen, if you please."

Alston kept one ear on the smooth sequence of orders, the rest of her mind sketching the ship's course. The fore-and-aft sails on the rearmost mast went up in a series of long surges as the deck crew heaved at the ropes and raised the gaff.

A boatswain's mate bellowed: "Now lower your butts, flangeheads, and haul away, haul away!"

"Heave!"

"Ho!"

"Haul away and sheet her home!"

"Heave!"

"Ho!"

The wind jerked the boom over their heads, swinging it out until it caught against the tackle that controlled its lunge. The green line of the shore wheeled and began to slide past, the cheering throng on the beach dwindling and falling astern. On the port, marshes slid by, ducks and geese and snipe rising thunderous. The air was heavy with the smell of silt and brackish water, a tang that blew away the odors of the Iraiina camp. Marian Alston smiled slightly and looked at the clinometer. Only a few degrees off vertical as yet.

"She trims well, Mr. Hiller."

"She does, Skipper."

A bit of a surprise; the *Eagle* had never been designed to carry cargo as a regular thing, and it had taken days of sweating-hard labor to arrange it so that it didn't throw the ship grossly off-balance. That could be crucial to her sailing performance, and as it was she rode four feet deeper. And the pigs were squealing and stinking in their improvised pens forward; she'd helped raise pigs as a girl, they were too smart by half, and could be downright dangerous. Her younger brother had toddled right into a pen once, and if her father hadn't been nearby . . .

Eating well is the best revenge, when it comes to pig.

"Ms. Rapczewicz, what's our status on fresh water?"

"Fifty-one thousand gallons," she replied.

Also good; they didn't want to waste fuel producing drinking water, either.

"Five knots, ma'am. Ten feet under the keel."

"Five knots, ten feet, aye," Alston said. "Mr. Hiller, we'll keep her so for now."

She'd decided to be conservative and take what the old-timers had called the String, down south to just north of the Azores and then across the Atlantic on the edge of the trades. Longer, but you got consistent easterlies that way most of the year. You *could* work across on the Viking route way north, up around Greenland, there were intermittent easterlies and the East Greenland and Irminger currents . . . she shuddered at the thought. There would be berg ice, this time of year—*any* time, actually, but worse just now.

She waited, expressionless, as the land fell away astern and on either side. The ship's motion changed as they came out of the estuary, a longer plunging roll as they came into waves that ran uninterrupted across three thousand miles of ocean; that always made her feel more alive, more free. The breeze stiffened out of the north, and a quiet order brought the yards braced around. She looked west. *Odd.* And in all that space, nothing but fish, birds, and whales. No other ship, until you got to within dugout-canoe range of the Americas . . . would they be called the Americas here? *Probably, if we live to do the naming.* Not a submarine beneath the waves, not an aircraft over it, no lights to pass in the night or float by overhead.

"Helm, south by southwest."

"South by southwest, aye."

"Mr. Hiller, make all plain sail."

"All plain sail, aye."

He turned and began to shout orders. White sail blossomed upward toward the tops of the *Eagle*'s masts, as if a huge sheet were being shaken out in the wind. As each sail came taut she could feel the ship lift and heel, moving more quickly as the vast horsepower of moving air was caught and channeled through the standing rigging into the hull. The yards were braced around at not quite right angles to the keel and the crew crept down off the yards and out of the rigging; others hauled and set lines across the deck. Slowly, slowly, the big ship leaned to port. The bow wave turned from a gentle swelling to white water, and that foamed higher and higher.

In twenty minutes it was spouting out the hawser holes and along the forecastle decking, to drain out the lee scuppers around the feet of the inevitable seasickness cases. Isketerol of Tartessos looked well enough, holding on to a line and staring incredulously overside as he mentally estimated the speed. Swindapa had turned green, and blundered helplessly until a couple of cadets snapped a safety line to her belt and draped her over the leeside bulwarks just in time.

The port rail was nearly under; Alston looked at the clinometer. Twenty degrees. "Speed," she said.

"Twelve knots and rising, ma'am."

"Twelve knots, aye. Ms. Rapczewicz, you have the deck; keep her thus, but reef if the wind freshens. I'll be in my cabin."

And she should give Cofflin a call, let him know things had gone well. They probably needed some morale-boosting back home. She checked in midstride for an instant. *Home? Well, our trip here was instructive, at least.* Compared to anywhere else in the world of 1250 B.C., Nantucket was very homelike indeed.

"Whazzit?"

Ian Arnstein came awake with a violent start. The little cabin was dark except for a trickle of light through the closed porthole, and for a moment he was lost, torn from a dream of freeways and shopping malls and teenagers on Rollerblades. Fear made his heart race.

Someone's here, he thought. There shouldn't be; he had the tiny room to himself. Captain Alston had left a fair number of her officers back on the island to oversee fishing and matters maritime, the ones who'd been there mainly as instructors for the cadets.

"Who's that?" he whispered.

There was a rustling at the edge of the bunk, and a vague shape in the darkness. "Me," Doreen's voice said.

"Oh." His heart still beat faster, but it wasn't quite the same sort of fear. "Why . . . oh."

A hand took his and guided it to close on a full breast. "You're an intelligent man, Ian. Don't be silly. Why do you *think* I'm here?"

I should be thinking, he knew through the hammering in his temples. *We've only known each other for a few weeks . . . I'm too old for her . . . all this stress has got us acting in ways we wouldn't . . .* His hands held the blankets up and slid down her back as she slid into the narrow bunk beside him, warm and smelling of clean woman and soap. Her first kiss landed on his nose in the dark, but the second was on target.

"Oh, yeah," she murmured. "The beard tickles nice."

"Yeah," he echoed in the same breathy whisper.

To hell with thinking. Before he'd expected it she had rolled underneath him and her legs were clamped along his flanks. He moved convulsively and bumped his head against the overhead.

"Damn these bunks!" he hissed.

Doreen chuckled and wrapped her legs around his waist instead, then gave a sigh that was half groan as he slipped into her. "Come on then," she whispered into his ear as they began to rock together. "God, come *on*, then."

Some immeasurable time afterward they lay in a tangle of arms and legs and stray bits of sheet caught between and under them, amid a pleasant smell of sweat and sex.

"It is cramped," he said, and sighed. "For the first time since this whole thing started, I feel as if I'm really *here*."

"Why, thank you, sir," Doreen purred into his ear. "The feeling's mutual."

A thought jarred him. "Wait a minute—you're protected, aren't you?"

"It's a bit late to ask, but yes."

Ian sighed relief. "It'd be a shame to waste this waist." He ran a hand down the damp smooth skin of her back. "Many happy returns of the night," he said, then checked himself.

"Mmmm-hmm," Doreen said affirmatively, nuzzling into the curve of his neck. "Hoped you'd say that."

Silence ticked away. "I'm a bit, well, *old,* middle-aged really, and—"

"I'm not a teenager either, I'm nearly thirty," she said. "Well into spinsterhood, by Bronze Age standards, I suppose." A chuckle fluttered across his skin, cool on the dampness. "Besides, you're certainly the most eligible Jewish man around. Even if you're not a *medical* doctor. Unless I sail east and put the make on Moses."

"We'll see how it goes, then," he said drowsily, feeling an enormous peace. A minute later he tugged his eyelids open. "God, we can't go to sleep, or she'll tow us at the end of a rope at dawn!" Captain Alston had impressed him as the type who enforced regulations with an old-fashioned absolutism.

"Mmmm, no. I asked. She said as civilians all we had to be was discreet."

They rearranged themselves with some effort, smoothing the sheets a little and drawing up the blanket, then settling down spoon fashion. It was a long while since he'd slept—in the go-to-sleep sense of the term—with a woman, and never in a bed so narrow. After a half hour his drowsiness faded.

"My, for a middle-aged man . . ."

CHAPTER EIGHT

April, Year 1 A.E.

"Well, people, we have a problem," Jared Cofflin said. He looked out over the crowd. Attendance at Town Meeting was certainly up from the days before the Event; of course, the stakes were a lot higher now. *But I don't like the look in their eyes,* he thought. *They're still scared.* Deubel's crazed arson plot had put the fear of death into them, like nothing since the Event. He could smell it in their sweat, and hear the shrill undertone in the murmurs as they adjusted their folding chairs. A few young children cried in their mothers' arms, ignoring the patting and shushing.

"The trial's over," he went on. "Judge Gardner can testify it was fair."

The judge nodded. "However, under the circumstances, sentencing is a problem. Arson generally carries a fairly long term of imprisonment."

"It's time we faced some facts. Look, we want a government of laws, don't we?" There were nods throughout the crowd. Cofflin felt sweat running down his collar, and was extremely glad that Martha Stoddard was sitting next to him at the table on the dais, spare and precise in a gray dress and single string of pearls.

"But let's face it, the laws of the United States don't run here any more. There isn't any United States, no Congress, no president, no Supreme Court. Sure, we want the same *sort* of laws—"

"Like hell," someone said from the ranks of townspeople. "The IRS can stay lost for all I care."

That brought a gust of laughter; Cofflin joined in for an instant. "Generally speaking, I mean. In the end, though, this—this Town Meeting here—is the source of law on this island. *You* are. You're the Congress, you're the Senate. You can make peace and declare war; you decide what the penalties for crimes are. You bind and loose.''

That brought silence for a long moment, except for the angry hiccuping of a fretful baby. "All right, then. Here we've got eighteen men and women who tried to burn down the town, which would probably have killed us all, one way or another.'' There had been twenty to start with, but two had managed to follow their ex-pastor into suicide.

"We've given them a fair trial, and they've mostly confessed anyway. The question is, what do we do with them?''

"Hang 'em!'' someone shouted, and there was a menacing snarl from the crowd. Together on a bench before the dais the prisoners shrank together.

Cofflin hammered his gavel. "That's one solution,'' he said calmly. "And you're the ultimate authority here. If you vote for it, it'll be carried out. Now, I just want you to think about that. Eighteen nooses. Eighteen people with broken necks hanging there—if we don't botch it and just strangle them slowly. I'll insist that it be done publicly; people should see the results of what they order. And then I'll resign.''

There was an uproar at that. Cofflin gaveled it into silence. He recognized the woman with the crying baby. She stood, anger crackling off her:

"I'm not going to let those . . . those *lunatics* loose to threaten my baby again.'' A growl rose from the crowd.

Cofflin nodded. "Ms. Saunders, I agree completely. I'm not against the death penalty as such in the ordinary course of events. This is a little different. We need to come up with a way to keep ourselves safe from these people here, without killing them. You're also right; they *were* acting like lunatics. Haven't most of us felt like running mad lately, now and then? Hell, a couple of us *have* run mad.''

With a Glock, in one case.

Saunders blinked. "What do you think we should do?''

"Well, we can't just keep them in jail. For one thing, it'd cost too much—we'd have to feed them. What I had in mind was a productive form of exile.''

Martha leaned forward and spoke into the microphone. "You'd better listen carefully,'' she said. "Jared Cofflin's the best man to head our Council, and you'd be well advised to keep him.''

"You're partial, Martha," someone said from the crowd. "You're engaged to him, after all."

Cofflin felt a small glow at the thought, even then. He'd enjoyed the engagement, too; all three days of it, so far.

"John Detterson, if you think I'd flatter a man just because I'm going to be married to him, you're more of a fool than I thought you," Martha said tartly.

The tension he could feel in the air crackled a little lower; there was not quite a laugh, but a relaxation.

"Everyone hates the salt-gathering detail," Cofflin went on. "We've been drawing lots for it. What I'm saying is that we should send these people down there, for a year at least and then further until they're safe to have back among us. We can send a boat down to pick up the salt and drop off supplies every month or so. It's a hard sentence, yes, but we don't have to kill any of our own, and we don't have to waste time and resources we can't spare on them."

More murmurs. Cofflin pointed the gavel. "Winnie McKenzie."

"That's an indefinite sentence, Chief," she said. "How are we going to tell if they're really safe? What's to prevent them lying about it and getting up to the same tricks when they get back?"

"I'll let Father Gomez answer that," Cofflin said.

"These poor people were deluded by a man who was deluded himself," the priest said, rising from his seat in the middle of the meeting. "I have volunteered to go with them to Inagua and help them. Father Connor can run the affairs of the Catholic parish here while I'm gone. With God's help, I think I can bring these unfortunate people back to reason, or at least tell if they haven't changed their thinking."

"And I have full confidence in Father Gomez's judgment," Cofflin said. *Since he suggested this whole scheme in the first place,* he added to himself. "What's more, I think a year spent shoveling salt and eating flamingo down on Inagua is at least equivalent to ten in a mainland jail. No way to escape, either." *No way to escape and live,* he amended. If they chose to drown themselves, that was their problem and a solution to his.

"Anyone second the motion?" he asked. A double dozen of hands went up. "Let's put it to the vote. All in favor, raise their hands. Now, all opposed." He swung his head from one end of the crowd to the other. "Joseph?"

"Carried," the town clerk said. Nobody objected; the ayes had outnumbered the nays by at least five to one.

Cofflin looked down at the prisoners; one or two defiant, a woman weeping softly, most of them simply stunned. "By vote of the Town Meeting of the island of Nantucket, you are hereby sentenced to exile on the island of Inagua for a period of not less than one year. Your exile will continue until Father Gomez, as authorized by the Meeting, determines that you are safe to live here again. You'll have one day to say your farewells, and the *Yare* will leave with the evening tide tomorrow. That's all."

The police officers shepherded the prisoners out. *Well, that's a hell of a lot simpler than it used to be,* Cofflin thought. Aloud: "All right, let's get on with it." He pointed the gavel. "Sam Macy."

Sam Macy was a house carpenter, and a very good one, island-born. "Chief, it's the way we're running things," he began, setting himself stubbornly. "This telling everyone where they have to work and such. It's too much like communism for my liking."

"Sam, you're one hundred percent right about that," Cofflin said. "The problem is, it had to be done—still will, for a while. Joseph"—he pointed at the town clerk—"and a couple of our potato-planting bankers—"

That *did* get a laugh, a rueful one.

"—are working on getting a money system going. After we've got the crops planted and the fishing steady, we can start swapping things around more as we please. People will still have to work or contribute stuff to the Town, though—otherwise we just can't pull through. Next year we can loosen up some more, and more still the year after that. Believe me, the last thing I want is to be a tin-pot Mao. If anyone can come up with a better way of doing it, they're welcome to ask the Meeting to give them this job . . . *more* than welcome," he added sincerely, running a hand over his hair.

Angelica Brand spoke: "We've been running most of the plantings as a single unit because there wasn't time to do otherwise," she said. "But I'd be just as pleased to split them up into smaller farms. Trouble is, not many of us know how to run a small farm with hand tools and animal traction. One thing I *can* tell you, it's damned hard work."

There was a general murmur of agreement on that. Cofflin went on: "We can reopen some of the stores pretty soon now, too, as soon as Joseph gets this chit system going. Satisfied, Sam?"

"Not altogether," Macy said. "There's that order collecting up all the guns."

The townsfolk groaned; Macy was a bit of a monomaniac on the subject of the Second Amendment.

"Sam, you know what happened at the Cappuccino Café. Everyone thought Don Mansfield was as sane as any of us and he goes and kills three people—one of 'em a kid. Then there was Johnstone—"

"Guns don't—"

"—kill people, people do. Ayup, I agree—but guns make it so much *easier.* By the way, Sam, if you want a crossbow, you're welcome to one. Once things settle down, all the firearms will be handed back to their owners, unless the Town needs them—we're going to have to handle our own defense, and from what Captain Alston says there are some mighty rough people out there over the water."

"We'd have more if you hadn't—"

Cofflin nodded. "Putting near all of them in one place was a bad mistake; I'll say that myself. But imagine what Deubel would have done with automatic weapons!"

Macy looked around, hesitated, and sat down; he was an opinionated man, but far from stupid.

"And hell, Sam," Cofflin went on, "if you want to make a motion, propose it and we'll vote."

Macy stayed down, unconvinced but aware that the Meeting was moving from boredom to irritation.

"All right, next item. Ron Leaton here needs more people who want to apprentice as metalworkers and machinists. The worst of the clearing is about over, so we can spare some hands. I'd like to suggest . . ."

When the Meeting was over, Cofflin ran a handkerchief over his face. "I'd rather face a half-dozen drunk coofs on the spree anyday," he grumbled.

"You did very well," Martha said. "Very Athenian, really." Cofflin raised his brows. "Aristotle thought about three thousand citizens was the largest number who could meet in assembly and decide issues," she went on. "Well, we're about the right size for his ideal city-state, aren't we?"

"Greek to me," Cofflin grinned. The librarian slapped his shoulder in mock reproof.

"Come along to supper, then," she said, sliding a hand into his. "And maybe we can do something about that bundling you mentioned."

"Er—" he said, flushing slightly.

Martha smiled. "This *is* the twentieth century," she said. "Or at least it was."

"You do, what is?" Swindapa asked.

Nearly mash my toes, that's what I do, Doreen thought, wiping her palms and picking up the length of wood she'd dropped.

"Practice," she said aloud, running through another slow form. Trying to get the rhythm back where breath and movement, body and feet and hands, united into a single flowing unity. Instead her thighs and shoulders ached and her eyes stung despite the terry-cloth headband she was wearing.

The deck was stable as the ship ghosted along at a crawl, creeping past the edge of a Sargasso that seemed to be larger in this era. Part of the crew were busy swabbing, painting, and chipping, but the rest were doing unarmed combat drill, under the tutelage of Lieutenant Walker and the captain —Doreen supposed that Alston had ordered it on the principle that the devil made work for idle hands. Ian was infuriatingly reading a book in a deck chair, smugly satisfied with his argument that he was a civilian and far too middle-aged for all this "chucking about." It was hot, too; they were down about the latitude of Bermuda. Doreen panted as she rested on the *bo*, the T-shirt sticking to her breasts and shoulders. The deck was full of yells and thuds as the fit, limber nineteen-year-old cadets ran through holds and throws or hammered at each other through padding.

"Practice who?" Swindapa said again, handing her water.

Doreen gulped it gratefully. "Practice *with what,*" she said.

Swindapa had a superb memory and a mimic's ear for sound, but too many of the grammatical conventions of the English language seemed to make no sense to her. Her own language was an agglutinative horror that made the complex inflections and declensions of Lithuanian or Iraiina seem straightforward. Three *separate* forms of the "r" sound, all of which were distinct to her and indistinguishable to the English-speaking ear. . . . Doreen shuddered at the memory.

"Practice with what?" the Fiernan girl repeated agreeably.

"Staff. *Bo*." They repeated the conversation in Iraiina for practice's sake. That was merely a complicated language, not impossible.

The *bo* was a piece of polished hardwood, five and a half feet long and about the thickness of her paired thumbs. She'd kept it on half a dozen moves after she stopped going to the dojo, never quite certain that she'd given up the art for good, but never having enough time to actually attend, either.

"For what?"

"To hit," Doreen said. "I'll show you."

She stood in front of the younger woman, the staff held slantwise across her body.

"Spear?" Swindapa said, and made jabbing motions.

"No. Like this."

Very gently, she ran the rounded tip of the staff into the weak point of the other's solar plexus, just below the breastbone. Even in the strongest, fittest set of abdominal muscles that was an empty spot, and it was right under the heart and lungs. The other woman folded over with a surprised mild *oooof*. Doreen followed through with a slow uppercut that would have smashed the jaw if it had been for real. That led naturally into a turn, the *bo* tossed up and allowed to slide between her hands as she pivoted so that the movement became a two-handed sweep. Step forward, sliding the left hand to the center of the staff, point down, use it to scoop behind the knee . . .

Swindapa went down realistically, grinning. Doreen smiled back; everyone liked the Fiernan girl, the more so since she'd relaxed—and stopped waking up *every* night screaming. She play-acted ramming the staff into the other's throat, then gave her a hand up.

"You show?"

Doreen hesitated, then nodded. "That's 'Will you show me?' "

"Will you show me?"

Training a novice might be just what she needed to keep her motivation up. "Stand like this," she began.

"Lesson over," she wheezed twenty minutes later.

Swindapa was just working up a sweat, but she reluctantly handed the *bo* back to Doreen, rubbing at a few bruises where the wood had gotten away from her.

"We'll get you one of these," the American said. The Fiernan was in good condition, a natural athlete, and she'd seemed to enjoy it. "We'll do more tomorrow." *And by the time you know enough, I'll have some endurance back.*

They turned to watch Isketerol trying a fall with Lieutenant Walker. Doreen didn't like the too-cheerful junior officer; for one thing, he gave off God's-gift-to-women vibrations. She disliked the Tartessian rather more, so it was a point up whoever got thumped. The Iberian trader moved in cautiously, crouched with hands held high and low, rather like pictures she'd seen on very old pottery in museums. Walker waited until the other man made a grab. She knew what came next.

Thump. The Tartessian landed on his face on the foam mat, winded and stunned. Nobody here seemed to know how to fall. Walker landed astride him—in a real fight the knees would have driven into the fallen man's back, probably crushing his ribs and snapping the spine.

"That's enough," Marian Alston said; she was barefoot, in calf-length cotton *gi* pants and an armless singlet, dripping wet from the work she'd been doing. Her skin shone like wet coal over long lean muscles, and she was smiling slightly. "Playtime's over, boys and girls. Classwork next."

The sparring circles and drill lines began to break up amid good-natured groans. Walker called out: "Try a few rounds, Skipper?"

Doreen frowned; the words were right, informal to suit the occasion, but there was an overtone. A few cadets paused to watch.

"Surely," Alston said quietly. "Light contact?"

"Sounds good, Skipper," Walker said. "Somebody call it."

They walked onto the mat, faced off, bowed slightly. Walker put his right fist to his left palm as he did; Alston bowed with her fists held before her thighs. An impromptu referee raised a hand between them.

"Asume . . ."

Get ready. They fell into stance. Then the hand flashed down.

"*Kumite!*"

Fight.

Doreen could make some sense of what followed. Korean-style kicking attack by the man, heels scything. Block and spinning kick in counterattack, straight-on, by the woman . . . *shotokan*, she thought. It was like the captain to have trained in a straightforward power style. Then there was a flurry of movement, fast and fluid. It ended with Walker skidding backward on his backside, clutching his gut, and Alston standing in a straddle-legged horse stance, shaking her head and wiping blood from her upper lip.

"Sorry . . . Skipper," Walker wheezed.

Wheeze he should, Doreen thought indignantly. That last backfist *hadn't* been pulled. *Lousy control, for all he's fast.* Serve him right if the captain hadn't pulled her thrust-kick, and given him a ruptured gut or broken pubic bone instead of just the wind knocked out of him.

"No problem, Mr. Walker," Alston replied. "And now I think we have work to do."

"Scumbag," Swindapa muttered beside Doreen, glaring, her hands clenching. She'd picked up bits and pieces of English from other members of the crew besides her official teachers. "T'row in water one him over side, fuckin' A."

"Ah, Swindapa, that's not a . . . nice thing to say," Doreen said.

The guileless blue eyes met hers. "Nice?"

"Not . . . ah, 'fuckin' A' is *low*." She held her hand down by her knees. " 'That's right,' or 'A-OK,' are better—are high." She held her hand up.

Swindapa shrugged. "Captain give life me," she said. "Cut one him neck—" she made a violent slitting gesture while she glared at Walker—"A-OK. That's right."

Isketerol picked himself up and rubbed his neck ruefully. *And here I thought I was a* good *wrestler and boxer,* he thought, squinting against the sun. He'd practiced at home, as any boy of good family did, learned tricks from Ugarit to Pi-Ramses, and by the time he was a man grown he'd been able to hold his own in a tavern brawl in Memphis with off-duty *nakhtu-aa* of Pharaoh's guard, the well-named strong-arm boys. Those tricks had saved his life more than once, and let him put much bigger men on their backs among savages like the Iraiina. Which had been useful in winning respect, and hence profit. But this . . .

The challenge to the *Eagle*'s captain caught him by surprise. *For the captaincy?* he thought wildly, moving back. Then: *Surely not.* Even the Iraiina weren't quite that primitive. *No. Why, then?*

Perhaps for face, in a campaign of prestige? He knew an ambitious man when he saw one, even if the nuances must wait. *I must learn Inglicks—no, that's Eng-il-ish—faster.* He already understood it far better than he spoke, or than anyone suspected, but the "sh" sound was maddening.

The brief fight ended. Isketerol's eyes widened. The Nubian had nothing worse than a nosebleed. Walker wasn't bleeding, but he'd been helpless for a few seconds, and seconds was all it would have taken to kill. He stepped back as the young officer went by. There would be a time later to talk to this Walker. A dissatisfied man could be a useful man, to the Tartessian.

Marian Alston toweled herself down quickly and thoroughly, enjoying the sensation of the rough cloth against clean skin and exercise-warmed muscle. The captain's quarters of the *Eagle* were spartan enough, but they did rate a private bathroom with a shower.

"That's one problem solved . . . for now," she said to her reflection in the mirror, feeling it at her nose.

Swollen a little, but that would pass—and her nose was wide-arched and set close between high cheekbones, harder to injure than a long thin *buckra* beak. Lieutenant Walker was *good,* as well as more than a decade younger. She didn't know why he'd taken up the Art seriously. Going beyond the rudimentary basics taught by the military ate a lot of an officer's sparse spare time. But he had, and not wasted his lessons, either.

Alston herself had decided in her teens that men were bigger and heavier and usually stronger. If she was going to make her way in the world she had to have something in reserve to compensate for it, as much for the confidence-breeding knowledge at the back of her mind as for the extremely rare actual violence. The more so when she decided to enlist as her ticket out of the Carolina low country;

she'd picked the Coast Guard at the time because she loved the sea and the Navy had still barred women from operational assignments. Well worth the effort and trouble in different dojos since, although it was easier to make the fourth dan above black belt for people like her with no social life to speak of. Even in the Guard, it still helped to know deep down that you could handle men *without* the protection of the uniform and the rules when push came to shove.

The only man who'd ever struck her and gotten away with it had been her husband, and that for the sake of the children in the brief while before the divorce. Everyone was entitled to at least one major misjudgment in her life, though.

So Walker got his little lesson, she thought. *And I will watch him.* Probably he'd just wanted her to lose face, but that indicated some sort of long-term plan. And she *was* on her own now. No high command to back her up, unless you counted Cofflin on the island—and how could he have enforced orders, if whoever ran the *Eagle* simply decided to sail away? Walker had had fun in England—you could see the possibilities churning behind his glass-green eyes. Walker wanted power badly, and would use it badly—because his only loyalty was to William Walker.

She dressed quickly in the little white-painted cabin, feeling loose and relaxed except for the slight throb of her nose, a spring in her step as she walked the dozen steps to the wardroom. One of the shoats had broken its fool neck yesterday, climbing out of its pen, and she thought that contributing ribs and crackling was the least it could do to make up for the clutter and stink its kind had made on *Eagle*'s decks. It had dressed out at about a quarter pound per head for the crew, counting chitterlings.

They sat; lunch started when the captain appeared. Walker was his smiling self, cheerful, polite . . . *and you'd better stay that way, buckra boy.* The professor and Rosenthal were at the table, along with the two locals, as guests of the ship, which made things a little crowded. A cadet came up to the table as she was shaking out her linen napkin, another of the ship's old-fashioned touches.

"Good morning, Captain. The officer of the deck sends his regards and announces the approach of noon. Chronometers have been wound. Request permission to strike eight bells."

"Make it so," Alston said, with a mild enjoyment of the small ritual.

It was homelike; about as homelike as they could get, now. The whole daily routine was invaluable, from reveille through falling in for quarters after lunch to the clean sweepdown fore and aft. Ordinarily they'd have tested the ship's alarms and whistles, too, but the electrical systems were powered down as far as was possible without actually endangering the ship.

"Excuse," Isketerol said. He was handling knife and fork with some skill and confidence now. "Why is high sun . . . noon . . . why is noon big?" She looked at him. "Excuse, why im-por-tant."

"Navigation," she said, taking a mouthful of the pork and swallowing. The crackling was exactly right, and the meat was good too, although stronger-tasting and stringier than the pork she was used to. When Isketerol looked blank she went on: "Finding where the ship is."

"Ahhh. How?"

Isketerol might be loathsome to modern sensibilities— she was never, ever going to find it in her heart to think well of a slave trader—but he was a seaman, in his way. She went on:

"First, the world is round—like a ball. You understand?"

Ian Arnstein looked as if he would like to make shushing noises. Both Isketerol and Swindapa looked at her with shocked surprise.

"Captain knows true?" Swindapa said.

Alston looked at her and smiled back, which was easy enough. *Can't say it's unpleasant to be hero-worshiped. Embarrassing, but not unpleasant. . . .*

"It is true," she assured her.

"No—I—" She looked frustrated, and then marshaled her thoughts. "People Swindapa . . . Swindapa's people know round earth. Swindapa . . . did . . . not . . . know . . . Captain know."

Alston felt her fork pause again. "You know the earth is round?" she said. Jaws had dropped up and down the wardroom table.

"Only . . ." She spoke a phrase in her own language.

"Star-Moon-Sun Priests," Isketerol translated automatically, through Arnstein. "The Grandmothers."

"Grandmothers know. Watched stars, sun, moon, many many winter-summer. Make—" She pushed salt and pepper shakers into a circle and mimed squinting through them.

"By God," Arnstein said. "I think she's talking about Stonehenge!"

A flurry of questions through the Tartessian settled that.

"Stonehenge," Swindapa repeated, and added the name in her own tongue. "The Great Wisdom. Watch, measure. Long time know. Secret, for Star Priest, families."

"Well I will be dipped in . . . ah, salt," Alston said, with a rare laugh of delight. "Live and learn." Swindapa beamed back at her. She turned to Isketerol:

"So you see, it *is* round," she said.

Isketerol nodded. "Tartessian captains know. It is secret of . . . circle of captains?" he raised a brow at Arnstein.

"Guild," the historian said.

"Guild of captains. Only we teach to sons." He made a curving motion through the air. "If watch you the mast top of a ship, sail aways, hull go, low mast go, top mast go. Same on ship sails away from shore. Tall tree, mountain, tower. Bottom go, middle go, top go, can't see them. How except—" He made the curving motion again, and shrugged. "Others may know, but don't say. Low people . . . common people don't know."

The officers looked at each other. Arnstein nearly rubbed his hands together. "It makes sense, in a way," he said to Alston. "Sailors and astronomers—"

"Astrologers," Doreen said sharply, giving him a covert nudge with her elbow.

"Astrologers might well figure it out. They just wouldn't *tell* anybody. The really new thing about the first Ionian Greek natural philosophers was that they *wanted* other people to know what they'd found out."

"Which made it possible to build on previous discoveries," Alston said thoughtfully.

"Sun?" Isketerol said hopefully.

"Oh. Well, if you measure the height of the sun at noon, you can tell exactly how far east or west you are," she said. *I'll leave the bit about chronometers for later.* "How do you tell on your voyages, Mr. Isketerol?"

The Tartessian's grip on his fork was bending it, and his

expression was like feeding time at the zoo, in the carnivore section. "Birds," he said. "Wind, taste water, throw rope with wax and look at sand, mud, rock, shell—shells—from the bottom. Look at clouds, landmarks. Know in here." He tapped his stomach.

In other words, by guess and by God, Alston thought. No wonder crossing open seas was daring for these people. It wasn't the size of their ships. The Tartessian merchantmen she'd seen drawn up on the beach back in Britain were big enough. Bigger than Columbus's *Nina,* or some European vessels of the Age of Discovery that had sailed the Atlantic dozens of times, even if not as seaworthy. But they had no way of knowing where they *were,* unless they'd been that way before. In a way she was sorry for him. He stood at the beginnings of a nautical tradition, and he was meeting the end of it, the culmination of four thousand years of sailing-ship knowledge.

"Stars," Swindapa said. "Dark sun-away . . . at night . . . Eagle People look stars. Why?"

"This would go faster if you could read," Ian Arnstein said in frustration.

Isketerol shrugged. "That would take years," he said. "How do I say that in English?"

" 'That would take years.' "

"That would take years." In Greek: "It was hard enough learning our script, and I was a boy then. How the scribe beat me, and how I yelled! Most gentry don't bother."

The phrase still came out *Dut wuld tika ye-arrrs,* but the Tartessian was making very rapid progress. Even faster than Swindapa, who was across the other side of the cadet mess deck, drilling with Doreen; Isketerol seemed to make her a little uncomfortable. An ewe gave a soft *baaaaa* from a pen in the corner beyond.

"Why would it take years?" Arnstein asked curiously, falling back into Mycenaean.

Isketerol looked at him, arching black brows over russet-colored eyes. "Why, to learn all the signs, noble Arnstein, and the determinatives, and the . . . the context that lets you know what the sign means in any written word. Some of them have fifty or sixty alternate meanings, after all."

"Ah!" Arnstein grinned. For someone who was so anxious to learn, Isketerol still gave off know-it-all vibrations;

it would be interesting to see his reaction to this. Unpredictable, too; when he'd first realized what a clock did, he'd been so frightened that he'd stayed in his bunk for half a day before he came out.

"There are only twenty-six symbols in our script," Arnstein said. "A man with your memory could learn them quickly."

Isketerol frowned. "Twenty-six? How is that possible? The Achaean one has over ninety, not counting denotative signs, and each can mean several things."

"Well—" A thought struck him. "Doreen, Swindapa, you should sit in on this."

The two women came and joined them. When the explanations were complete, he resumed.

"Each symbol stands for one sound, and that sound is the first one of the name of the symbol." He pulled a piece of paper toward himself and wrote down the letters of the alphabet. *Alpha, beta,* he remembered. *God, the snake's really swallowing its own tail with a vengeance.*

"So you take the symbols for, say, 'dog.' That's d . . . o . . . g . . . Put them together." He did. "Dog."

Swindapa frowned, moving her lips; she'd had to get the explanation mostly through Isketerol, and her language seemed to lack some of the words involved. The Tartessian stared. His lips moved as well, and beads of sweat broke out on his brow.

"So . . . but there are still thousands of *words*," he said. "This—" he pointed to the word DOG written in block capitals—"is as hard to remember as one of the Egyptian symbols. Harder, for they sometimes look like what they represent. And some of them are for sounds, too."

"No, no, you don't have to remember what the *word* looks like," Ian said. *I'll leave the horrors of English spelling for a little later.* "You just have to remember the *sounds* each of the twenty-six letters represents. They *all* represent single sounds—not things, and not groups of sounds, and it's always the same sound. Then you put the sounds together to make words, and you can read a word from the sounds—you don't have to have seen it before."

As long as you were taught with phonics, he added mentally.

He blocked out SWINDAPA and ISKETEROL, leaving spaces between the letters. "Here are your names. S . . . W . . .

I . . . N . . . D . . . A . . . P . . . A, and I . . . S . . . K . . .
E . . . T . . . E . . . R . . . O . . . L."

"My name?" the girl said, awed. Her eyes went wide.
"You take my name, on paper? Take my name away?"

"No." *Oh, God, she's probably afraid of magic.* He re-
frained from giving a reassuring pat; she didn't like to be
touched, he'd noticed. "No, just the *sound* of your name."

*And let's hope you can tell the difference between the
symbol and the referent. Whole schools of French so-called
philosophy couldn't in the twentieth century.* On the whole
the Event had been a disaster, but at least he'd escaped
the deconstructionists and semioticists.

Isketerol closed his eyes and bit a knuckle. "I . . . think
I see," he said, after concentrating for a minute. "So . . .
so you could write *any* language with this script? And anyone could learn it quickly?"

Arnstein nodded happily. Isketerol slapped the back of
his palm to his forehead twice, evidently his people's gesture of amazement.

"Teach me this!" he cried. In English; he'd learned *those*
words quite well.

Alston stopped. "Not quite right," she said.

"Captain?" Doreen said.

"That stance," she said.

Swindapa and her teacher came erect. The *Eagle* was sailing northeast now, slanting across a warm gentle breeze from
the south at eight knots, her deck canted slightly and moving
like a tired rocking horse across the long low swells. They
were off what would never be the Carolinas; the captain had
been standing and staring eastward, musing; crewfolk were at
make-and-mend, or lounging about on the forecastle deck;
the waist was scattered with cadets studying. A few were
scrubbing at the results of a visit by a huge flock of pigeonlike
birds with pink breasts. There had been enough of them to
blacken the rigging, and they'd been exhausted by the wind
that blew them out; it had taken half a day to drive the last
of them away. They made good eating.

"More like this," Alston said, demonstrating. "Feet at
right angles, back knee bent, and weight on the back leg.
Leading hand out in a fist, other hand ready over your
solar plexus. You should be able to lift the front foot with-

out shiftin' your point of balance. That's better." She shifted her attention to Swindapa. "You understand?"

"Speak pretty good, okay," Swindapa said. "Too, am I writing, now. Engelits crazy language." She paused. "Captain, Doreen, sound different speak why?"

She has a pretty good ear, Doreen thought. Aloud: "We come from different places. Far apart."

"Ah. I understand," Swindapa replied, evidently familiar with regional dialects. She'd shifted the sound of what she said, too, closer to the broad soft vowels that Alston used: *ah unnahstaan.*

The captain smiled. "Doreen speaks better English," she said. "And you're learning to write, as well?"

Swindapa pulled a scrap of paper out of her pocket and displayed it proudly. It held a shaky alphabet written in pencil. Her own name, Doreen's, Arnstein's, Alston's, the *Eagle*'s.

"Like birds," she said.

"Birds?"

"Words fly like birds. Write, catch, put in basket. There you there when want them."

Alston laughed, something unusual enough to make a few of the other Coast Guard personnel on deck glance over. "Keep it up—you'll find it very useful," she said, and nodded for them to continue.

"A-OK," Swindapa said, taking up a perfect backstance. "You start, Doreen."

Alston turned back. "I presume Mr. Isketerol is learning to read as well?"

Doreen paused and nodded. "Ian's teaching him. And Lieutenant Walker."

The *Eagle*'s brass bell struck three. Swindapa could tell the time to within half of one of the Eagle People hours, anytime she could see the stars or the sun, but she had to admit that it was convenient to have something tell you exactly. The nights were getting a little chillier as they coasted north, but were still spring-mild; the blue sweatsuit was more than warm enough—much warmer than she'd have been in the normal Earth Folk woman's dress of string skirt and poncho, this time of year at home. She crouched under the bulwark and hugged her knees. Tonight would have been a bad night to sleep, she could tell that, so she'd come on deck instead. The Burning Snake would have taken her back to the time of the Iraiina, and broken her with fear in her sleep when she could not fight it. Awake, she could hum the Warding Song and keep the Snake at bay. Especially under the friendly stars, with Moon Woman casting her silvery light. She talked silently with Moon Woman and played the Constellation Game for a while, tying every visible star into more and more intricate patterns, but the way the sails swayed across the sky distracted her. There weren't many of the crew on deck. The weather was mild, and they could be summoned quickly at need.

Instead she began by naming all the ropes and sails on the ship, stumbling a little over the more difficult ones like *main topgallant staysail downhaul*. Then she began counting over the list of stars; it would take a while, since there were over three thousand, and the names changed eight times a year according to the season. It had taken her to her twelfth summer to learn them; she'd never been more than an indifferent student.

Swallowflitting, dragonfly-in-amber, moonblood dewdrop, angry fly . . .

After a while that reminded her too much of home. She ran through a Building Wisdom instead; safely abstract, since nobody had actually *done* a Great Star-Moon-Sun Wisdom in so long. Her grandmother's voice sounded in her ear: *Take a circle of forty Building Rods where you will erect your stones. Align the circle and draw with your cord the southern half. How do you flatten the northern half to keep the curve smooth and avoid splitting the length of the outside of your Work into parts-of-a-whole-length?*

She shut her eyes and squeezed out distractions. The problem was to make the length of the outside of the circle come to *exactly* three of the cross-length, instead of the three-and-a-bit of a natural circle. Well, take your cord, knotted to the right length, then stretch it in a line. . . .

She smiled. *Yes, that's it.* The forms lay perfect in her mind. Swindapa began to put the numbers into the figures, holding her fingers out before her and tapping them together in the patterns of the Counting Chant. *Forty* laid out *circle means* twenty—

Voices sounded on the quarterdeck above her, startling her out of the calculations. She huddled deeper into the shadow where the bulwarks met the rise to the quarterdeck, not wanting to be seen. Only her hair would give her away, so she pulled up the hood of the sweatsuit jacket.

It was the captain. She looked almost invisible, dressed not in her usual garb but in a long black jacket of loose cloth tied with a broad black cloth belt, and baggy trousers that ended just below the knee. She carried something long and curved in her hands; she placed it on the deck, knelt, and bowed her head to the boards.

Should I go? Swindapa thought. These might be private devotions.

Then the captain took up the curved thing, and Swindapa saw that it was a sheathed sword. Her eyes widened, recognizing it from the night of the Iraiina feast, when her captivity ended. Swords were rare even among the Sun People, very rare among hers, and always two-edged. This had a curve like the crescent moon, and it was silvery as it was half-drawn—

A sword from Moon Woman! she thought suddenly, excitement choking her. Moon Woman had sent the captain to rescue her. A silver sword against dark skin, dark like the night sky. She focused to quivering attention. *The Eagle People guide themselves by the stars.* Not in exactly the way the Earth Folk did. Perhaps a better way?

The black woman tucked the sheathed sword edge-up through her belt and went to one knee, her left hand holding it horizontal, right resting on the hilt. A moment of absolute stillness. Then movement, the blade flashing out and up and down in a blurring arc of brightness . . . and frozen stillness again, the sword's curved cutting edge not quite touching the deck, arms and shoulders upright, legs crouched. No sound but the chuffing pulse of exhaled breath that had accompanied the motion. Another strike, equally swift, the sword reversing and thrusting backward, the wielder's body swinging to follow it and the sword slicing diagonally with a hiss of cloven air, another turn and a downward cut with the left palm sliding down the back of the sword to add force to the strike. Again the *hunh* of breath at the moment of impact. Swindapa could almost see the target falling away cloven—Daurthunnicar with his forked beard, down, dying.

She clasped her clenched fists to her heart, feeling its beating. This dancing with the sword was a thing of beauty, deadly and lovely like the Eagle chieftain.

I will study harder, she thought. *When I have learned all the others can teach me, I will ask the captain to show me this thing.* She raised her hands to the night sky in prayer. *Moon Woman, be my friend!*

CHAPTER NINE

April, Year 1 A.E.

God, it'll be good to get my ship clean again, Alston thought. The *Eagle* had a faint but unmistakable barnyard odor of pigshit, despite all they could do with pumps and swabbing. At least with the breeze on the beam most of it was carried off beyond the forecastle deck, little reaching her here on the bridge over the pilothouse forward of the wheels. The *Eagle*'s bowsprit was swinging around to the east; at noon they'd come up past Muskeget, the little islet off Nantucket's western point.

"I'd better look Cofflin up right away," she said to Sandy Rapczewicz. "See if we can't arrange a barbecue or something for our people."

The XO nodded, a little oddly, she thought. She'd also radioed ahead to have accommodation prepared for Swindapa and Isketerol. *I'll have to find a place myself,* she noted. Probably not a problem, with so many houses vacant. *And some office space.* She hoped Cofflin was as competent as he'd seemed in the brief time between the Event and the *Eagle*'s departure.

"We'll have to—" she began, about to order the engines fired up.

"Ma'am, it's the island. Chief Cofflin."

Alston blinked surprise and swung down the stairs. She walked back past the helm—only two sailors on the knee-high platforms beside the wheels, on a fair April day with an eight-knot wind—and into the radio shack.

"*Eagle* here."

"Chief Cofflin here," the familiar voice said. "We've got a little surprise for you—a tow, so you don't have to waste fuel getting into harbor."

"This ship's a little heavy for rowboats," Alston said. Not

that the *Eagle* couldn't be warped in that way, but it would be extremely labor-intensive.

"Too true, Captain. Take a look." Cofflin's voice held a smile.

"On deck! A . . . something off the port bow!"

"*Eagle* out," Alston said dryly. She really didn't much like surprises.

A plume of gray smoke was approaching. She leveled her binoculars.

Well, I will be dipped in shit, she thought. The hull looked to be a medium-sized powerboat, a forty-footer, cut down to a flush deck. Wooden paddle wheels framed within a steel circle churned on either side. Each was driven by a peculiar arrangement that looked a little like a Texas oil derrick, nodding up and down. *Rocking-beam engine,* she thought; they'd been common on steamships a hundred and fifty years ago. Each rocking beam was moved by a single steam cylinder, mounted with the piston rod upward. Between them was a boiler that looked like welded sheet steel, and a tall chimney of the same material. Crewfolk were throwing split logs into a furnace underneath it; someone pulled on a lanyard, and the unmistakable melancholy hooting of a steam whistle greeted them.

Cadets and crew lined the rail, cheering and waving their hats. Alston let them, for a few minutes; it was a special occasion. Isketerol came up beside her, peering as the tug came closer.

"More diesel magic, Captain?" he asked.

She shook her head absently. "Steam," she said. "Heated water. The fire heats the water, the water becomes steam, the steam is confined in metal pipes and pushes, doing work."

The Tartessian blinked and nodded, moving aside and staring hungrily. *Did I do the right thing?* she thought with slight unease. *Just because he's ignorant doesn't mean he's stupid.* Neither of the Bronze Agers was that. But the languages would be so useful. . . .

"Ms. Rapczewicz, strike all sail, if you please," she said aloud. "Rig for tow. We're home."

". . . and you've done a good job, one that's important in the survival of thousands of our people," Alston said, finishing the brief speech. It wasn't a part of her role that she enjoyed, but they deserved to hear it. The waist was packed solid, orderly ranks as if for Quarters. "I'm proud of you all."

The crew of the *Eagle* cheered. "Chief Cofflin tells me that he's declared today and tomorrow public holidays, and I've arranged for everyone to draw some of the Town chits we're using for money these days; they're good for beer, at least. Liberty for everyone but the posted skeleton crew. Behave yourselves—but have fun. You deserve it. Dismissed from quarters!" The cheers grew wilder, and hats flew into the air.

Alston looked grimly at what awaited them on the dock. The noise had alerted her first, as the *Eagle* came through the harbor entrance. Cofflin had said that the Town Meeting had voted a public holiday; she'd expected the harbor to be quiet. Instead there was a surf-roar of noise, and the quays were crowded with people.

"They did say some people would be on hand to say hello," Tom Hiller said.

"Some people . . . Cofflin didn't say anything about *this*, the lying hound," Alston snapped.

A huge banner stretched across the steamship dock, WEL-COME EAGLETS, with a big gold-painted wooden eagle above it. The quays and streets were densely packed with people; there was even a high school band, complete with drum majorettes and trombones tootling away.

She stood glowering at the three-ring circus. The crew were hiding smiles. Swindapa looked impressed; she suspected Isketerol had seen ceremonies more grand, traveling about the Mediterranean. Alston turned an accusing eye on her sailing master.

"You knew about this, didn't you?" she said.

"Well, the chief, the XO, and I discussed things a bit," Hiller said, grinning.

"Traitor. You *all* knew."

"We knew you don't like public occasions, at least in theory, Skipper. Consider it a surprise party."

She snorted and relaxed. *No use in fighting the inevitable,* she decided. Cofflin and most of the Council were waiting to greet her on the dock. And the crew certainly deserved a rousing public reception and cookout.

That reminded her. "Mr. Isketerol, Ms. Swindapa, we'll arrange quarters for you ashore," she said.

Isketerol bowed silently. Swindapa frowned, an edge of panic in her face. "Not stay captain's with . . . place?" she said. "Send away?"

The Tartessian had reverted to his native dress for the occasion, saffron tunic with a complex folded belt holding knife and short sword of bronze, and a long blue cloak. Swindapa kept to the *Eagle* working blues she'd been given, the spare pair of a cadet about her size. The hands that clenched the baseball cap were quivering slightly now, matching the desperate look on her face.

"I'm sure there will be room," Alston said hastily. *Damn. I'm a sailor, not a trauma therapist! This is as bad as having a chick imprint on you when it hatches.* Swindapa relaxed and put on the cap.

Not much choice in the matter. *Have to get her some things,* Alston noted. She'd have to organize a good deal, get a regular shore establishment going, if she was going to run Nantucket's maritime endeavors as well as captain the *Eagle* herself. A number of ideas had occurred to her, along those lines. *I need a good* long *talk with Chief Cofflin.*

"Ms. Swindapa." The blue eyes turned to her, pools the color of hyacinth flowers. "I'd like you to see the doctor here," she said.

"Already seen Eagle doctor, ma'am. Feel goods—I mean, better."

"All the same, I'd like you to see the one here, please." The Fiernan girl ducked her head in a shy nod. She had an appealing face, really . . . *Careful,* Alston reminded herself.

The gangplank swung out and crunched into place ashore. Alston set her own hat in place and walked down the gangway to the waist, past the rows of sailors and cadets now braced to attention. The boatswain's pipe sang out:

"*Eagle* departing!" The bells rang. Cofflin shook her hand at the bottom of the gangway and handed her a microphone.

"A few words, Captain," he said.

"Ah—" Alston cleared her throat, and Swindapa and Isketerol jumped and started at the amplified sound. "It's all right," she said, flicking the thing off for a second.

Then: "We're all happy to be back, and back with the food the island needed. The trip was . . . interesting . . . and there'll be a report, film, and photographs handed out. We accomplished our mission, and we'll probably be able to trade in Britain again later this year. The crew of the *Eagle* have worked very hard for the community, and in their name I'm honored to accept your thanks." She paused. "That's all. Thank you again."

"Short but to the point," Cofflin murmured, and took the microphone from her. "Three cheers for Captain Alston and the *Eagle*!"

At least nobody can see me blush, Alston thought as she endured it.

Cofflin led the way. Trestle tables had been set up on Main Street, and from the looks of it Nantucket's abundant cooks had been at work. Mostly seafood, of couse, but well prepared, and a surprising abundance of poultry, roast goose and duck, and big plump birds that looked a little like chickens but weren't. They'd raided the accumulated stores, too; there was even a butter sculpture of the *Eagle*. Sitting in crisp brown glory with an apple in its mouth was proof of why Cofflin had been so considerate in getting the first load of pigs off the *Eagle* via the tug; glazed with the honey that had also been a part of the cargo, it waited on a bed of rice. Alston shrugged with a rueful chuckle, sat next to the chief, and poured herself a glass of wine—the island's own vintage, she noticed. Cadets and crew were already pouring ashore and filling the tables below her, interspersed with the townsfolk.

"Thanks—my boys and girls deserve a blowout," she said to Cofflin.

"They and the town," Cofflin said, sharpening a carving knife and falling to.

"What's this?" she added, looking at a bowl surrounded with crackers, full of a jellylike substance. Daubed on a cracker, it had a creamy, salty taste. "Tastes interestin' . . . some sort of seafood?"

"Caviar," Cofflin said. "It's sturgeon-spawning time over on the mainland. We sent some boats to the mouth of the Connecticut River." He nodded down the table.

Alston looked and gave a silent whistle. "Now, that's a *big* fish." The section sitting in the middle of one of the trestle tables was three feet thick and ten long, resting on a base of steamed seaweed.

"Half a ton," Cofflin said, smiling a little. "We had to harpoon it, and nearly lost the first boat that tried. Things've been a bit . . . hairy here at times. It's a good idea to give everyone some time off, throw a party, celebrate—and you've given us a fair bit *to* celebrate."

"Starting with this most excellent pig," she said, loading her plate; the mashed potatoes were the instant type, but edible. "Pass those drumsticks too, please. . . . Ms. Swindapa, Mr. Isketerol, Mr. Jared Cofflin, our chief executive officer."

Hell, I deserve a holiday, she thought, as the two Bronze Agers leaned across her to shake hands with him. *And here's everything necessary. Of attainable things,* she thought, looking wistfully at a young man and woman freed of the *Eagle*'s rule on Public Displays of Affection and holding hands as they ate. *It would be nice to have someone myself. Or even just to get laid.*

Isketerol of Tartessos sipped at the odd-tasting, bubbly beer and watched silently as the feast wound down into the night. He'd left the public square when most of the others did, finding his way to this half-underground tavern in the basement of another of the strange, magnificent houses; he could tell what it was, from the sounds and scents making their way out the door. He sounded out the words written on the wooden sign above.

Brotherhood of Thieves. The sign pictured a man with short bullhorns on his head, holding a small chained woman on one hand and a sack on the other. A god of trade, perhaps? But it was a Brotherhood of *Thieves*. . . .

His eyebrows rose at the thought. The Amurrukan seemed like far too orderly a folk to have an open thieves' den flaunting itself here in this impossibly clean city . . . but he was confident enough of what he'd read. His English was as good as his Egyptian now, and he'd spent many months, in visits over the years, to learn *that*.

"Brotherhood of Thieves," he sounded out aloud, and looked around. This street was one of the ones with the strange smooth dark substance coating it, not the honest cobblestones of Main Street. The buildings were mostly wood, covered in shingles and white or gray paint; some had little courtyard gardens. He could see the spire of a temple . . . no, they called it a *church* . . . not far away. Large trees grew on either side of the street, which was broad—enough for two loaded wagons to pass abreast, at least. The temple tower had another one of the *clocks* in it. He shuddered. Cutting away your life, second by second, the way the Crone's knife did at the last when she put you in the Cauldron. *Seconds,* he thought. Only the Amurrukan would divide time up into pieces like that, like a cook dicing onions for soup.

"A name for every street, and a number on every house," he muttered to himself.

Oh, he could see how useful that would be, but it was a bit daunting. What was really useful was the counting system. It had taken him two days of questioning—driving Arnstein and his woman almost insane—before it sank in that there was some use in a symbol for *nothing.* Humiliating, that the Earth Folk slave girl had grasped it earlier. He scowled slightly. It would be more convenient if the bitch weren't along, or if she'd been too stupid to learn a new language. Scant hope of that; the Star Priest families bred for wit.

He mustered his courage and walked through the door; there was a short corridor, two more doors with the symbols for the wonderful better-than-Cretan interior latrines the Amurrukan had (but why separate ones for men and women?), and a half-door to the left where the taproom was.

Even before William Walker waved him over to a table it was reassuring. After so much that was alien, things so strange that he had to force his eyes to *see* them, this was only middling unsettling. The lights on the walls came from lamps of wonderful design, glass and bronze, but they burned with honest flame—he recognized the smell of whale oil. So did the candles in more glass holders on the tables. There was a fire of wood in a tiny alcove set into the wall, with an opening above to take away the smoke through a brick tunnel—now, *that* he could use at once, back home. Wooden tables with benches and chairs, floor of smooth lime mortar, brick walls—different in detail but not in essence from things he'd seen before. The smells were familiar too, fire, cooking fish and meat, wine, beer, a little sweat . . . and the strange cleaning fat they called soap.

He slid onto the bench across from Walker. The Amurrukan had his arm around the shoulders of a girl, wonderfully and scandalously dressed in nothing but a halter for her breasts and short breeks tight enough to show the shape of her mound. Her jewelry was strange, but would have bought a good-sized farm in Tartessos, although her hands were work-roughened. She had long black hair, skin the color of old ivory, a tiny nose, and eyes that seemed to tilt up at the corners, lovely in an exotic way. The one on his bench was even prettier, nicely plump, dark-haired and colored like an Egyptian herself. Need stirred. It had been a long time since they left the White Isle, and the Amurrukan had not allowed him to bring a servant.

Careful, careful, he told himself. The easiest way to get yourself into killing trouble in a strange land was over women, if you didn't know the customs. It wasn't enough to know formal laws, you had to understand the ways those were bent or changed by unspoken taboo. These probably weren't harlots and certainly weren't slaves; the Amurrukan had none, none at all. He decided to think of them as young priestesses of the Grain Goddess, to be courted.

"Greetings, friend," Walker said in mangled Tartessian. Then in English: "Alice, Rosita, here's my friend Isketerol who I told you about—a prince of Tartessos, which is a kingdom in Iberia. Isketerol, Rosita Menendez, and Alice Hong. *Dr.* Alice Hong."

Isketerol bowed slightly, hand to chest, and flashed his best smile. The women smiled back. He wasn't exactly a prince, if he understood the word rightly, although his family were relatives of the king. There certainly wasn't any need to tell the women the details, though.

"All Tartessos has nothing more beautiful," he said carefully in his best English.

Jared Cofflin smiled as the last of the deck cargo trotted down to Steamboat Wharf. Those waiting with handcarts and a few improvised horse-drawn vehicles managed to raise a cheer as well, although this load was not grain but several dozen loudly argumentative pigs, the last left on the ship.

"I'm surprised they can stand to make any noise, after the homecoming celebration," Captain Alston said. "A few of my cadets and crew still can't, and the aspirin are rationed."

She looked around the dockside. Cofflin tried to see it as she would. Not much had changed in the time away . . . *only six weeks, Christ.* The main difference was the absence of motor vehicles. The sailing boats which had ridden at mooring poles in the enclosed basin to her left were mostly out fishing; so were the trawlers and the converted scallop boats. Work went on to turn the cabin cruisers and other motor craft to something useful. Two steam tugs waited over in the Easy Street marina basin, next to an improvised barge they'd towed over from the mainland. Perhaps the smell was the biggest difference, and that had crept up on him so gradually that he hardly noticed anymore. They did their best to scrape up every fragment from the fish landed here, if only because it was needed for the fields everyone else had been laboring to clear. Still, there were scales, and a definite smell.

"The town needed a rest," he said. "And what you brought back, that's going to make a big difference."

"A third of a pound of bread per person per day for a year," she said, and looked around. "Y'all have been busy."

The pigs were being herded into the carts, with barriers of wire netting set up to give them only one route. Enraged squeals sounded, the whack of poles on bristly hides, and the shout of someone whose hand was saved only by the thick glove he left in a pig's mouth.

"If y'all only knew how glad I am to see the last of those things," she muttered; he presumed the remark was directed at the world in general. "I hope we can feed them. Seventy-five sows made it, say three batches of eight piglets per year each, and they start breedin' within a year themselves—"

"We'll manage. Feed 'em alewives, if nothing else," he said. They weren't particularly good eating fish, but they were certainly abundant—no wonder the Pilgrims had used them as fertilizer. "Good thing Steamboat Wharf is deep enough for you to dock," he said.

"It's a menace," she replied absently. "The land around the harbor here isn't really enough to break a first-class storm. We could lose the ship, if she was caught here in a bad norther, and we don't have much warning without a weather service. I'm inclined to park her over on the mainland in the winter. Providence harbor ought to do—it's deep and sheltered up there at the end of Narrangansett Bay. Inconvenient as hell, though."

"Well, we've got a sort of base there," Cofflin said. "The ferry's there now, for one last trip before we lay her up.

We're bringing back timber—you wouldn't *believe* the quality of the lumber we've been getting. Seems a pity to use so much of it for firewood. We figured it was worth the fuel, and now we've got the tugs on the same run, and some sailboats. They're bringing salt-marsh hay, too, for the livestock."

"You won't regret it come winter," Alston said. Her voice took on a more serious tone: "Look, Chief, that grain will help, but we'll need more."

He nodded. "Farming here never was more than a scramble, and a chancy one at that."

"Damn right," Alston said. "My family were farmers down South; it's a nice hobby and a hell of a way to make a living. I've got some ideas about how we should trade this fall."

"Not with the same crowd?" Cofflin said, one brow arching.

"Not if we can avoid it. I'm not what you'd call squeamish, but . . ." She shrugged. "Besides, they don't control a big territory as yet, and they're making war. Not the situation to produce good crops."

"Are there any others likely to do better?" he said.

She frowned and clasped her hands behind her back. "I think there may. We could just pick another spot, somewhere else in Europe or even the Mediterranean, but . . . I told you about Ms. Swindapa?"

"Seems to be a nice girl," Cofflin said cautiously. "Doc Coleman is taking a look at her, as you asked."

"Speak of the devil."

The doctor appeared, wobbling in on a bicycle. He coasted to a halt beside them and dismounted. "Whooo," he panted. "I've known for years that I should get more exercise." Then he looked up at Alston. "Well, I confirmed what your ship's surgeon said. She's in remarkably good condition, for someone who was beaten to within an inch of her life and gang-raped to the point of internal lesions. Anal and vaginal."

Cofflin sucked in his breath. The radiophone report had said "badly abused"; he'd assumed something like this, but . . .

"I think they make them tough in the here-and-now," Alston said thoughtfully. Only someone who knew her rather well could have interpreted the slight tightening of the skin around her mouth. "The ones that live, anyway."

"And the pelvic inflammation's cleared right up," Coleman went on. "Nice to see a bug that doesn't sneer at sulfonamides. There's probably fallopian scarring, I'm afraid. I've given her and that Isketerol fellow every vaccine and shot in the armory, just in case, too. Apart from that she's in fine condition. Full set of teeth, not one cavity, twenty-twenty vision . . ."

"Right," Alston nodded. *God, she's a cool one,* Cofflin thought. He was angry, himself; policeman's reflex, if you were a good one.

"Ms. Swindapa is connected with a prominent family in the . . . I don't think it's a kingdom or a country, exactly, but it occupies most of southwestern England in this era," Alston said. "I hope to learn more when she speaks better English, and she's learning remarkably fast."

"Can't Dr. Arnstein translate?"

"Only through Isketerol, and I'd rather not."

Cofflin's eyes narrowed. "You're thinking alliance," he said.

"I'm thinking we should consider it," she said, and held up a pink-palmed hand. "No, I'm not dreaming *conquistador* dreams. We've only got a couple of dozen real firearms left, with pitiful stores of ammunition. But we could make a difference helping one side or the other . . . and Ms. Swindapa's people are being attacked without provocation. They also have plenty of what we need: foodstuffs, livestock, linen, wool, and eventually metals. Copper and tin already, and we could show them how to mine and smelt iron. A few simple innovations . . ."

Cofflin whistled silently. "That's something the whole Council will have to talk about, and the Town Meeting too," he said. "You certainly don't think small or dawdle, Captain."

Alston shrugged again. "The iron's hot. But yes, this is all tentative now. We've got photographs and video footage you should see, too."

He nodded. "Let's take this further. We have your baggage moved into the quarters we found for you—we can go there and talk in privacy."

They turned and walked south along Easy Street, then west along the ankle-turning cobblestones of Main. The shops were mostly shuttered and locked, but there were ladders against many of the cast-iron lampposts, and the glass frames had been taken off their tops.

"Putting in whale-oil lanterns," Cofflin said, to Alston's look of inquiry. "The field clearing and planting's done, most of it; Angelica can get the grainfields sown in a day or two with her machinery—they're ready and waiting. We've got a little leisure for other things."

"Too much," Coleman said grimly. "How many suicides did you have, Captain?"

"One . . . wait a minute."

Coleman smiled bleakly as he saw the woman blink at the implications. "We've had over a hundred and fifty," he said. "In a population of less than eight thousand, that's . . . quite a few. Plus a rash of depression. The work was good for that. The suicides have tailed off, thank God, but there's still a few every week. I'm afraid of what might happen if everyone has much time to think."

Cofflin sighed. "It just seems to *hit* people, particularly when they have a chance to sit down and think," he said. "Did me, for a while."

A whole day when he could not summon the energy to get out of bed or answer the insistent voices, and nothing seemed real. The memory still haunted him, worse than things he'd seen in his naval service, and not just because it was more recent. This had been a failure within himself, a failure of his *will*. A failure of the thing that kept him going, and if your will could fail you, what could stand?

"I noticed something similar on the *Eagle,* but we were extremely busy . . . and a ship's company is a self-contained group anyway," she said. "Hmm. I'd give odds that most of the suicides were adults, and not many of them were Council members."

Coleman looked at her in surprise. "Average age thirty-eight, and no, only one of the selectmen killed himself," he said.

"It makes sense," Alston said. "Upward mobility's great for your self-confidence."

"None of us *wanted* this catastrophe!" Cofflin said.

"Didn't say that; I'd rather it hadn't happened too. But you, me, the others who've . . . taken charge, for us the catastrophe has meant scope for our talents."

"*Everyone's* been stretched to the limit."

"Planting potatoes, fishing; hard labor, for people who aren't used to it, mostly. The whole world lost, even the little things—morning TV, hot water from a tap, hamburgers. We, though, we've been suddenly promoted from lower middle management to president-Cabinet–Joint Chiefs level. Everyone's life depends on us, and that's a burden to crack your back, but you *can't* put it down."

Cofflin's anger faded. "You may be right," he admitted. "That's what pulled me out of it, I think—knowing that too many people were depending on me."

"I definitely think you're right," Coleman said. "But how should we apply the knowledge?"

"Keep people busy. The Lord knows there's enough to do," Alston said. "Beyond that, I'd try to get them involved in the planning more."

Coleman laughed aloud. "Funny you should say that. People seem to be planning for the future already, in their way. With all those suicides it took a while to notice, but the number of pregnancies is up too, about three times what it should be."

"More mouths," Cofflin grumbled.

"More hands, eventually," the doctor replied. To Alston: "And along the lines you suggested, the Chief's been pushing this Project Night thing . . ."

"Project Night?"

"Sort of like a suggestion box," Cofflin explained. "I figured there must be a lot of good ideas out there about things we should be doing. Had Martha Stoddard over at the Athenaeum screen out the crazies, and God but there are enough of those. Then, I figure, once a month the serious ones get to do a presentation, and the month after that the Town Meeting votes which projects to tackle. Martha had a good one herself—have Angelica Brand turn part of her greenhouses over to growing orange trees, lemons, that sort of thing. We had the seeds, after all. Even got some coffee plants—ornamentals, but they'll grow coffee beans, right enough."

"Not enough yield to be worth the trouble, surely?"

"Ayup, not here—but we keep sending the *Yare* down to the Caribbean for salt, anyway. They can plant seedlings, leave 'em, and let them grow wild. Martha tells me explorers used to do that, whenever they touched at a newfound island. In a few years we'll have the fruit."

"Now that *is* clever," Alston said respectfully.

"Martha's a clever lady," he said. They had come to where Main Street veered to the left, forming a Y-fork with Liberty. "It's along here. Right here, as a matter of fact."

He enjoyed the look of well-hidden surprise on Alston's face. The house was one of the Three Bricks, a big Federal-style mansion with two white pillars on either side of the entrance. There was a flagpole above it, now bearing the Coast Guard's banner, and a square cupola on the roof flanked by two chimneys at either end. Someone had even put up a brass plaque over the entrance, *Coast Guard House.* It stood four-square and peaceful, two more like it to their left.

"Ah . . ." she said. "Chief Cofflin, Ah did have thoughts 'bout a big house with white columns as a girl, but isn't this a bit . . . grand?"

Cofflin laughed. "It's also Town property, since the owner didn't make the voyage with us. Don't worry; we're turning it over to you as your headquarters, as well as someplace to store your toothbrush ashore. Room for some of your officers, as well."

"Thank you kindly," she muttered, craning her head up at the facade and accepting the key ring.

"I'll be off," Coleman said as they opened the door. "While I can still do some good." The humor left his seamed, elderly face as he pushed his bicycle to a start.

"Definitely a little grand," Alston said, looking around the lobby.

There was a curving staircase to the upper floors, rising from an entrance papered in Empire style with gold medallions against cream. Two large sitting rooms flanked it on either side, each with a black marble fireplace and eight-foot windows; the colors were gray and green and beige, picked out with coral and yellow. The furniture was quietly sumptuous, Persian rugs on the wide-plank floors, pictures . . .

"I'd hate to have to dust all this. . . . Does the doctor have a problem?"

Cofflin nodded somberly. "Things running out. Insulin, specifically."

"I . . . see."

"He's trying to save some of the diabetics with special diets and exercise," Cofflin said. "Martha dug out an old treatment, a tea made from parsnip leaves, believe it or not—lowers the blood sugar."

"That won't work for most of the Type Ones," Alston said clinically.

Cofflin felt anger flare again, and throttled it down. *Make sure he said what you think he said,* his father had always told him. *Almost as many fools ruined by their ears by as their lips.*

"You're a cool one, aren't you?" he said.

Alston caught the tone and faced him. "Chief Cofflin," she said quietly, "practical is what I am. I try to do what I can, and that takes all I've got, so I don't wail and beat my breast over things I can't do an earthly thing about. It's what's kept me sane through this . . . thing. I hope that's all right with you, because I have no intention of changing. Gave up tryin' to make myself over to other people's patterns when I filed for divorce."

Cofflin spread his hands. "I can't argue with that." A wry smile. "Or with someone who does their job. Too few of 'em."

Alston returned the smile. "Too right," she agreed. "Look, we do have a lot to talk about. Let's get to it. Does this place have a kitchen?"

Blue collar reflexes, he thought—like him. They walked through a dining room under a brass-and-crystal chandelier. The kitchen beyond had been thoroughly modernized, in a meticulous-restoration style. Much of the equipment was of the latest and completely useless with only a thin trickle of rationed electricity available, and that earmarked for the clinic and machine shops, but there was a big black cast-iron wood stove as well. Alston's eyes lit up at the sight of it.

"Now *that's* going to be fun," she said.

"You cook?" he asked, a little surprised.

"I was a complete failure as a mother and not cut out for a wife," she said, "but yes, my momma did whack one feminine accomplishment into me. It's relaxin'. Splice the mainbrace? Think I saw a liquor cabinet back there."

"One won't hurt."

She came back with two glasses and a bottle. "I see someone told you my tastes, or whoever owned this place knew whiskey."

"It's your local brand?"

"It's Maker's Mark," she said, pouring a finger into both glasses and adding water to hers. She raised an eyebrow; at his nod she splashed a dollop of water into his as well. "Also known as Kentucky Champagne. Where *I* came from, the local brand went right from the still into pint jars."

They sat across the carefully scrubbed pine boards of the table. "To a long and successful association, Chief," she said.

He sipped; the whiskey went down smoothly. Nothing but the best for the man who'd owned *this* place. For a moment he smiled at the thought of an enraged stockbroker wandering through the primeval woods of the 1250 B.C. Nantucket that—presumably—was dumped into 1998, looking for his three-point-seven-million-dollar investment. The smile was without much sympathy. In his book financiers were right up there with publicans and sinners among the people only a mother or Jesus could love.

"I'm not sure that I can drink to that," he said. "A long association means I have to keep this miserable job they've pushed off on me." A sudden thought struck him, and he glanced at her speculatively.

"Oh, no. No way this woman-chile goin' fall fo' that, Yankee." Flatly: "Wouldn't work. I'm an outsider here, a woman, and black."

"I'd noticed," he said dryly. "I don't think you'd have much trouble that way here. It's a pretty open-minded place, Nantucket."

"Let me be the judge of that," she said, in the same flat tone.

He shrugged ruefully. "Well, I suppose you *would* be in a better position to judge."

"Not necessarily, Chief—"

"Jared."

"—Jared. If you're black, there are people out there who are going to do their best to mess you up, and if you're a woman it's twice compounded . . . and one of the subtle ways they get you is to tempt you into using their prejudice as an excuse every time you screw up, and if you make excuses for failin', you'll do nothing but fail. Huggin' resentments isn't very productive, even if they're justified; gets to be one of those self-fulfillin' prophecies."

She smiled wryly. "Besides, you don't know the half of

it . . . and I'm doing *exactly* what I'm suited for." Meditatively: "They were going to lay the *Eagle* up, did you know? I think that's why I got her after Quillman broke his neck in that damn-fool accident, they thought I'd make a good PR choice as last captain. A good thing it was brought back with the island."

"Some useful things came along," Cofflin agreed. "The problem is when they run out. All the makeshifts and replacements we come up with take so much more *time*. Paper towels," he went on. "Did you ever think how many man-hours of washing up paper towels save?"

"My own thoughts along those lines were a little more personal," she said. "I still remember vividly my first thought when you told me about Rosenthal's notion that we were back in the Bronze Age." Her eyes went wide in mock horror: "What, no more Tampax, *ever*?"

They shared the chuckle and lifted their glasses to meet with a chink. "Well, let's get down to business."

Isketerol of Tartessos sat in the garden outside the tall white columns of the Athenaeum, with his face in his hands.

"Three thousand years," he whispered to himself.

It was a number—meaningless, not real like three thousand ingots of copper or three thousand sheep or three thousand paces. "Three thousand *years*. Three *thousand* years. *Three—*"

He stopped himself with a wrenching effort of will, shuddering, and the few folk passing by under the cruel brightness of the sunshine gave him only a glance or two.

Why didn't they tell me? he asked, anger bubbling up under eeriness. "Because you didn't have enough command of their tongue, fool!" he snarled to himself.

He probably wouldn't have believed, then. Now it made too much sense, with what he'd seen and heard. This island was only the fragment of a greater realm; *that* was why there were so many people and so little farmland.

"Hardly even a memory of us survives," he whispered.

He looked down the corridors of the ages, and saw his city and his people and his very gods forgotten, dust and ashes and a few corroded remnants pored over by strangers indulging an idle curiosity. His father's house, that he had hoped to build strong for the years; his wives, his children.

S. M. Stirling

The little crooked lanes where he had run as a boy, the bay where he had learned to handle a boat, the dock where he left on his first real voyage.

Tartessos, and the whole *world*. He remembered the pictures the Amurrukan woman inside the white building had shown him, the shattered wreck of the Lion Gate of Mycenae, the Egyptian temples stripped of their colors and crumbling away amid the sands. He remembered standing in the crowd and watching Ramses return from his campaign in Canaan, like the graven image of a god in the chariot behind high-stepping horses. The blaze of faience and gold from the temples and palaces, great colored streamers hanging between the pylons. He remembered the sheer awe that had gripped him when he saw the pyramids, those mountains made by men like gods . . . and the pictures of them stripped of their smooth shining coats of limestone, lying jagged and worn beside the Nile. . . .

Dizziness swept over him, and he moaned. Gradually, fighting as he'd done to bring the *Wave Hunter* through a storm on the River Ocean, he won back to himself.

Think, he told himself. The Womb Goddess and the Lady of Tartessos had given him wits; he was no brainless savage to cower before the unknown.

Yes, a mighty magic had taken this island, this Nantucket, and set it adrift in the sea of time. The anger of some god, for no sorcerer could do this, could bestride the universe and compel the Powers. The Amurrukan themselves, with all their arts, had no inkling of how or why. *Yes, yes . . .* And their arts were deserting them, they said so themselves. Only the simpler ones remained.

He took heart from what the wisewoman in the temple of writings had said. Now the course of the world was turned on a new tack. A new heading, on which anything might happen. Nothing need be as it was shown in those deadly, lying pictures. He was free.

Slowly his breathing slowed. He wiped his face on a linen handkerchief, a gift of Walker, and looked around. He had known he was faring into strangeness, beyond the world he knew—and he had seized the opportunity with both hands. Well, it was still there. He was learning much; already he had learned enough to make his house the greatest in the city. How to make a ship sail against the wind, the secrets of the *rudder* and the north-pointing needle. Something of the currents and winds of the River Ocean far beyond the coasts, and if they were as reliable as the Eagle captain said, that was much.

You are in no danger here. Not unless the wrath of the gods struck again, and against that he could do nothing. If a curse rode these shores, so be it.

No danger. He had the promise of rich rewards, beyond what he'd sent back home with his cousin. They had quartered him in a house that was not large, but furnished like a king's. He had a friend, of sorts, in Walker. He even had a woman. Isketerol made himself dwell on that, and grinned; a very inventive woman, better than any he'd ever bedded, and a mine of unintentional information. He was a merchant adventurer of Tartessos, who'd dared storm and beasts and wild men in unknown waters. Abide the summer, teach the languages he'd promised, and see what opportunities offered. Snatch them when they came.

Swindapa sat on the soft bed and bounced experimentally. It creaked and the four posts at the corners swayed a little, fluttering the fringe of the canopy all around. She looked around the room, awed. The floor was planks of wood, smoothly fitted together like the wood on *Eagle*'s deck. The walls were smooth too, showing no sign of the potlike baked clay lumps—*bi-ri-ks*, she told herself—on the outer walls. Patterns of blue and green flowers covered them, so lovely she wanted to kick off her shoes and run dancing barefoot through the spring meadows they showed. There were fitted wooden windows, with panes of the clear icelike glass, and folding shutters. One wall held a hearth, with faint traces of ash and a metal rack for holding wood.

Strange. Where is the smoke-mark? Smoke was useful—it kept vermin out of your thatch as it soaked through, and dried the straw. A hearth like this should leave a broad band of smoke up the wall and on the roof, but that was smooth and white, looking like the gypsum plaster used to coat some Star-Moon-Sun workings. She went over and knelt, looking up. There was a tunnel of bricks leading away upward for the smoke. The room didn't smell of smoke, and the hearth only very faintly.

It smelled like flowers. Swindapa followed her nose. Yes, a bowl of dried petals on the wooden shelf over the hearth. That was homelike; bunches of dried herbs and flowers hung around any Earth Folk dwelling. There were flowers on the rug that warmed the floor, too, somehow drawn in cloth.

A big wooden box on short legs stood by the bed. It had real metal fastenings on it, polished bronze. *I wonder if this might be like the thing in the wall on the ship?* She tugged on one brass handle, and a sliding box within the larger box came out, filled with things of fine cloth. She pulled one out. It was an Eagle Folk loincloth, the type made from two triangles of cloth and an odd stretchy belt that clung and stayed up by itself. You could put one of the little pads inside it to catch your Mourning blood, too, when your womb wept with Moon Woman. Another wonderful thing of the Eagle People.

"Surely even Tartessos has nothing this fine," she murmured to herself, looking around the room. "Not even Egypt."

It was getting dark, and she remembered something the captain had showed her. This place didn't have the ship-magic that made a little star glow when you touched the wall. The lamp screwed to the wall was almost as delightful. You took off the tall glass bulb—carefully, carefully, the clear stuff was as fragile as a snowflake—and lit a *match*. That was a pleasure in itself, when you thought of how long and uncertain using a fire drill was; no wonder the Eagle People didn't have to keep a fire going all the time for folk to take splinters from. Then you touched the flame to the flat strip of thick cloth that ran down into the cup of oil below. She put the chimney back on the lamp and turned the brass knob. Warm yellow light filled the room. A fire in the hearth would have been good too, even though the night was warm, but the lantern was pleasant.

She yawned, full and sleepy, remembering to cover her mouth in the way the Eagle People considered polite. *A whole bed that size to myself.* She'd gotten used to lying so far off the ground, and no longer worried about rolling off the edge in her sleep, but she'd never expected to have so much space to herself. *That's good, though.* Outside your kin, it was extremely bad manners not to share pleasure with someone sleeping in the same bed if he wanted to, and she didn't think she could stand to have anyone touch her that way right now. Even the gentle old healer's impersonal hands had made her struggle not to weep and scream.

Her teeth ground together in rage. Another thing the Iraiina had stolen from her. She forced herself to relax again. Vengeance was coming. Moon Woman had taken her out of the world to find it; or brought this place *into* the world, perhaps. She couldn't quite understand what the Eagle People had tried to explain about that yet, but she would.

She padded down the corridor to the washing place, and did the Eagle People ritual of tooth-scrubbing. Many of them seemed to have trouble with their teeth, so chewing a cedar twig wasn't enough for them. *Although the captain's are beautiful, shining like pure salt.*

Perhaps the Powers which gave the Eagle People so much sent them that trouble to balance things.

"It *is* fun to have more room," Doreen said.

Ian laughed as he came back to the big four-poster bed with two glasses of sherry. He'd had to turn over all the provisions he'd accumulated on that panic-stricken morning right after the Event, but the Council's regulations had let everyone keep his booze. The island was out of bottled beer, although the local microbrewery was ready to start malting the barley they'd brought back. God knew what it would taste like with the supply of hops so limited, but it ought to be drinkable. That was all you could say about Nantucket's own wine, though. The real surprise was that grapes would grow here at all, probably because the island sat in the middle of the Gulf Stream.

He checked half a step, then climbed back into the bed.

"Penny for them," Doreen said, snuggling close and taking her glass.

Ian propped pillows up against the headboard and leaned back into them. "I was just thinking that when things settle down, it might be an idea to look into a wine-importing business," he said. "That Tartessian wine wasn't half bad—it reminded me of sherry, which is why I thought of it just now—and with a few hints, they could probably do even better."

Doreen tweaked his chest hairs. "It reminded *me* of Manischewitz," she said.

"Oh, not *that* bad—well, actually, that was my first thought too."

"You're just looking for an excuse to go do historical research in the first person personal," she said.

"I wouldn't mind seeing a few things," he admitted. Isketerol had let fall a few hints about Egypt that made his scholar's mind drool; and the thought of seeing Agamemnon's Greece . . . *God! To get there with a camera!* "But there's still the matter of making a living."

He glanced down. "Making a living for us?" he said tentatively.

Did I really say that? he thought. *Yup.*

Doreen grinned up at him through the fringe of her abundant, rather coarse black hair. "Trying to make an honest woman of me?" she said. He nodded.

"Thank you, Ian," she said. After a long moment. "Yes."

They clinked the glasses gently together. "Strange," Ian said. "I've only done that once before, and the results weren't all that great."

Doreen knocked her knuckles against one of the posts of the bed. "Avert the omen. I've never said yes before . . . haven't been asked all that often, either."

"I can't think why," he said sincerely. "Smart, agreeable, good-looking."

She laughed ruefully. *"Zaftig,"* she corrected. "A lot better looking on this enforced diet and exercise program God's sent us on."

She *had* lost a good twenty pounds, in the right places, although she'd never be the ballerina she'd once wanted to be. He ran a hand down her back to her hip. "I've got no objections at all," he said. "When?"

"Well, Chief Cofflin's getting married . . . after that?"

He nodded. That would be a town-wide blowout; they could have a quiet ceremony with only a few friends. *Odd. I actually have more friends here than in California.* A thought struck him. "Should we apply for a house of our own?"

"Why bother?" Doreen said. "There's nobody else in this building. We could convert the other rooms to office and library space, and there's a nice living room and solarium downstairs."

"No kitchen, though," Ian pointed out. The place was part of the John Cofflin, with three suites on each of its upper two floors. Each held a bedroom, bathroom—largely inoperable now—and sitting room, of variable sizes.

"I'm not the hausfrau type, particularly not with wood stoves or whatever we're going to be using. The main building's just across the way for meals. Later on we could put an attached kitchen out back—there's plenty of room."

Ian sighed. *Nice to be thinking about something normal . . . relatively normal.* "And it's right downtown," he said. "The location will be convenient while we're working for the government." The term came naturally now.

"You're the head of the State Department," Doreen giggled. Her eyes took on a thoughtful look. "That could be a pretty dangerous job, here. It isn't a nice era, from what Swindapa said. Interesting, in the Chinese sense. We'll be back across the Atlantic in August, maybe September."

Ian nodded uncomfortably. Doreen had spent more time with the Fiernan girl than he. "She's, ah, recovered fairly well, hasn't she?"

"I'm not sure," Doreen said. "She's a nice kid, but weird—well, with that background, you'd expect it. We talked astronomy, did I tell you?"

"You mentioned it. Do they know much?"

"It's all tied up with their religion, but once you strip out the stuff about Moon Woman and her children the stars—and boy, do they believe the stars control your destiny!—they've actually got a pretty good grasp of things. Pre-Copernicus, but very sound. They even know the sun's a star and the planets aren't, although the sun's the bad figure in their mythology."

"The devil?"

"More like a wayward child who needs a lot of discipline," Doreen said. "I'm not sure; the theology's as complicated as the Kabbalah, and I get the feeling this astronomical stuff was overlaid, a *long* time ago, on an older religion. The thing is, they've got an amazing grasp of stellar motions for people with no instruments to speak of and no way of writing any of it down like the Babylonians did. And their math, geometry in particular. Even something like algebra. No wonder Swindapa's got a good memory—the amount of stuff the poor kid had to memorize! She says some of the mnemonic songs they use are so old the language has changed beyond recognition."

We are *made for each other. Make love, lie here with a glass of wine, and talk about anthropology,* Ian mused ruefully.

Doreen thought for a second. "It's really odd how much they know, and how little hint of it there is in the history of the field," she said. "Really. They've got a good idea of the size of the earth, for instance, and of the distance to the moon. As good as the Greeks, better in some respects. Yet there's no trace of it in the records at all."

"I don't think that's surprising," Ian said grimly. "Let's put it this way. Imagine everything the same as we saw in Britain, only we didn't arrive. What would have happened to Swindapa?"

"She'd have died, the way they were treating her," Doreen said at once. "Or gone mad. Oh."

Ian nodded. "The Iraiina, or their relatives, are—were—would have—hell, you know what I mean—were scheduled to blot her people out. At least Swindapa's class, the ones who hold their accumulated knowledge. There's no trace of their language in our history, either. All that'll be left is their monuments and burials, which nobody will really understand."

"Poor kid," Doreen said again. "At least that's one thing we improved on." She sighed, then brightened and returned to a more personal subject:

"There's plenty of room here for a nursery, too." Ian stiffened in momentary panic. "No, I'm not pregnant—back a while I got Norplant." She rolled her arm to show the five little tubes under the skin.

"Were you, ah, involved with anyone?" he asked. *Odd that I waited until now to ask that.* A convention was growing up that you didn't lightly inquire about what links a person had had off-island before the Event. Irrelevant, and often painful.

"Not recently. I was overoptimistic," she sighed. "It'll wear off in another year and a half, and we can decide what we want to do then." Her grin turned wicked. "No reason we can't *practice*, though, is there?"

"None at all." He finished the sherry and put his glass beside hers on the side table.

CHAPTER TEN

May, Year 1 A.E.

"Ahhh," Swindapa sighed under her breath.

Everyone in the huge building was sitting on padded chairs of stone, like steps ringing the wooden platform ahead of her. Hundreds of people; she did a quick count. Nine hundred eighty-six, with a dozen children carried in their mothers' arms, almost as many as a Midwinter Moon ceremony at the Great Wisdom. The chairs had been enough for wonder, that and the building itself—like a Star-Moon-Sun work, only more vast and stately. Now the banner of white cloth up at the head of it was showing flickering images, colored, with sounds. The sounds of an Iraiina chant, of their magic.

Shivering, she huddled a little closer to the captain sitting beside her, reached down and seized her hand. She and the others were watching the moving shapes of light as if they were . . .

Something went *click* inside her head. She remembered the shadows of dancers thrown against the walls of a hut as they leaped and whirled around the fire. *Ahhhhhh!* The images were shadows of things past, like a memory taken out and put on the banner of white cloth! She relaxed a little. This was a seeming, and the captain wouldn't let the magic hurt her.

Figures walked through a meadow at dawn. Iraiina figures, stalking between two high-leaping bonfires and a double line of warriors. One was huge, heavy-bodied, scarred and hairy, swag belly above pillar legs, barrel chest and bear-thick arms above. *Daurthunnicar.* Naked save for the kilt and the mask over his face and shoulders, the head and neck of a horse, skillfully tanned and mounted on wicker. Equally naked in his hand was the long sword of silvery metal that he'd been given by the Eagle People. The younger man had designs painted over his body in blue and ocher-red.

The Iraiina priest came forward, with two acolytes leading a chariot; they unyoked the right-hand pony of the team and brought it to the magus, who raised his staff and began to chant. The words were strange, like Iraiina but longer and twisted. *Old speech,* she decided. The Grandmothers used an old speech for some of the most ancient Star Working Songs; Moon Woman might not like it if any of those were changed. Maybe the Iraiina sky god felt the same way.

Behind the priest and the horse a hole gaped in the earth, with dirt piled up on either side of it. The Iraiina warriors began to dance in a great circle around it, stopping now and then to drink deeply from skins of mead, tossing their heads and neighing; it was the *hepkwos-midho,* the horse-drunk.

Daurthunnicar danced too; the Dance of the King Stallion, knees flashing high as he pranced. The chant filled the hall, and she could hear the Eagle People murmuring beneath it. Then the Iraiina chieftain stopped, standing straddle-legged. The horse was led forward, and the holders urged it to its knees. The young man in the kilt came forward, and took up a stone-headed maul. With a shout he swept it up and then down into the forehead of the horse, stunning it.

Daurthunnicar struck as well, two-handed. The sword severed the horse's spine; five more strokes cut through its neck, until the head rolled free. Blood splashed the *rahax* from head to foot, until scarlet dripped from his beard and from the mane of the horse mask. The younger man stooped, then stood with the horse's head held stiffly over his own, corded arms straining at the weight. Both men danced again, younger following older, the muzzles of the horses jerking and swooping in unison.

At last they halted. The young man laid his burden down beneath his feet and faced the rising sun, singing in a strong clear voice with both palms raised. Gradually the arms lowered, but the song went on. It was still ringing out when Daurthunnicar's sword blurred in a horizontal circle.

Very sharp sword, Swindapa thought. Cutting through a neck like that was *hard,* even for a man of Daurthunnicar's huge strength. She gritted her teeth and wished it were the chieftain's head falling.

The images showed men laying the body of the horse in the grave. Dirt went over it, then the body of the man-sacrifice, with the horse's head in place of its own. Lights came up, and Swindapa breathed out a long sigh of wonder.

The captain gently disengaged her hand, putting Swindapa's firmly back on her own side of the gap between the chairs. She rose and went to the front of the room, with the Spear Chosen of the Eagle People beside her; he was very tall, with thinning blond hair cut short like a mourner's. They began to speak; Swindapa strained to hear the language. She could follow it pretty well now, and make herself understood on all ordinary matters.

Strange people, the Americans, the Eagle People. Strange but wonderful.

Pamela Lisketter spat to clear her mouth, then rinsed it with water from the bucket by the sink. The image of the horse, falling, falling, blood spurting over the man with the sword, and then the sword flashing again and interrupting the song . . . her stomach nearly rose again, but she pushed the scene away until it was distant—words, images on TV, not so *real*.

She walked back out into her living room. The house was mostly that single long space, furnished with futons and her own creations, smelling faintly of incense . . . and now of whale oil. The loom stood by one wall, the windows next to it flooding it with light. Her friends were scattered about. She'd been planning to have a few over for dinner, and ready to sacrifice the last of the tofu, until the revelations tonight. They'd hit some of the others even harder; Cindy Ganger was still sitting silent, with her face crumpled in behind her thick glasses, but then, she was a Wiccan and really believed that her religion went back to ancient times. The only ones who looked at all collected were the Coast Guardsman, Walker, and his friend from Europe, Isketerol. They were sitting with Alice and Rosita. Lisketter frowned a little. The two young women were dilettantes, in her opinion; Hong dabbled in pagan circles for the sexual aspects. Also feckless, as witness who they'd taken up with—but that could be useful now.

"Shocking," she said at last. "Obviously sexist, patriarchal in the worst way, abusive of animals. And we did business with them."

"The Iraiina are savages," Isketerol agreed.

Lisketter felt her lips thin, then forced herself to remember that the . . . *indigenous person,* she decided . . . had learned his English in the wrong place, among people no better than police. "Savages" was a Eurocentric term. *Or Nantucket-centric, I suppose,* she thought with an attempt at gallows humor.

"They are the ancestors of the technolators," her brother David said. "Remember, oh, what was the book, *The Chalice and the Blade*?"

"Yeah, they're pretty hard-assed, the Iraiina," Walker nodded, sipping at his bottle of homemade beer. He looked down at it and grimaced slightly, then continued: "We shouldn't be selling them weapons."

"I should hope *not,*" Lisketter said. "Or anyone else, for that matter." Thoughtfully: "Perhaps we should talk to Ms. Swindapa about *her* people. They seem more . . . more harmonic. If we could get her away from Captain Alston."

"You couldn't separate those two with a crowbar," Walker said. At her raised eyebrows: "You do know the captain's a dyke, don't you?"

"That is a homophobic term in this context," Lisketter said stiffly, flushing with anger.

Walker smiled charmingly. "Sorry. Force of habit. I haven't been around the right sort of people much, I'm afraid."

"That's all right," Lisketter said, brushing a lock of her long straight hair back. "She does seem male-identified, obsessed with patriarchal rules, and logocentric."

"Damned right," Walker said. "Saluting, heel-clicking . . . did you know she had a crewm . . . crewperson dragged behind the ship on a rope? He nearly died."

There was a shocked murmur in the big brick-floored room. Lisketter tried to remember what she'd heard of the incident, but it *did* seem the sort of thing a power-oriented person would do.

"I'm certainly not going to spend the rest of my life working for her," Walker said. "It was bad enough, a temporary assignment—but here and now, she's set to run the *Eagle* and everything else that floats for life. An empire-builder."

"The imperialism has already begun," David said. "All those Native Americans dead of our diseases, and Chief Cofflin has a settlement over on the mainland already, stripping the forests of trees and butchering the animals."

Pamela nodded somberly. It had begun, and if they didn't do something it would be *worse* than the Conquest of Paradise that her ancestors had wrought.

"We have to do something," she said.

"Well, yeah," Walker said smoothly. He and the Iberian exchanged glances. "We're ready to help, of course. Alice and Rosita have opened our eyes."

"It is . . . what is your word, reassuring," Isketerol said to William Walker.

They had halted their bicycles under a stand of pines, with a few last daffodils still nodding yellow beneath. No one was near; the road was empty, and only heath and fields stretched away on either side, potato vines already bushy and rows of grain just showing like a faint green fuzz on the gray-brown soil. The loudest noise was the sough of the wind in the trees, the buzz of insects. Hot resin scented the air, baked out of the trunks behind them. The noon sun was warm, full of the sound of bees and sleepiness.

"Reassuring?" Walker said.

"That you Amurrukan can also produce your share of fools," Isketerol said. "That is what they are, isn't it, Lisketter and the others? I didn't understand much of what they said, but I haven't been a trader for this long without recognizing an . . . easy mark, you say."

Walker laughed, a loud rich sound. "Oh, they're fools, all right," he said. "But for you and me, they're *useful* fools. Useful idiots."

"We should cultivate them, then," Isketerol said.

"Like a garden ripe for the harvest," Walker replied, slapping him on the shoulder. They both laughed as they pedaled on, back toward the town.

"The woman become one the man's thing only? Like among the Sun People?" Swindapa whispered.

Marian Alston moved aside a little as the breath tickled at her ear.

"No," she whispered back. There was still a hum of conversation in the big church, as they waited for the bride to appear at the foot of the aisle. "They can leave each other if they please. I did."

"You had a man of your own?" Swindapa asked eagerly. She knew that questions were impolite, but she'd been trying to learn Alston's background.

"Such as he was. A mistake."

"So this is like the . . . the, you say, party, as have we, when a woman's man goes to live with her kin?"

"Yes . . . more or less. The ceremony calls the blessings of God, and settles things like who inherits property and children."

"Oh," the Fiernan girl said, frowning a little in puzzlement.

Evidently her people didn't have anything closely resembling marriage. A man went to the woman's family grouping, and the relationship could be broken by mutual consent at any time. What Alston thought of as the father's role in a child's life fell more to the mother's brothers or other male kin, since they'd always be there. Property passed through the female line. Not exactly a matriarchy, though; nothing she could easily understand. She pushed the thought aside, concentrating on the ceremony.

The church on the hill was crowded, every seat full; the chief's marriage to the head of the Athenaeum was an event. *Royal wedding,* Alston thought wryly. She'd gotten a pew for herself and the *Eagle*'s wardroom, plus Swindapa . . . *who is a very nice girl, but clings like a burr.* Not intrusively, just refusing to go away for long; it was like trying to push the wind. Isketerol was there too, observing with his usual cool detachment.

All were in their best; she sat stiffly in her dress uniform, thinking wryly of the last time she'd worn it at Daurthunnicar's feast. Although this time it was *with* the regulation skirt. Swindapa couldn't have looked more different, in a white dress with lace panels, a broad-brimmed hat beside her on the pew, her hair fastened up with pearl-headed pins. *Certainly an improvement on a collar and leash.* Fancy clothes were going cheap on-island these days; overalls were harder to get. Still, it looked wonderful.

The organ started, thundering in the high vaulted white spaces of the church. She'd attended Baptist churches in her childhood, of course—mostly built out of weathered pine, down sandy tracks and surrounded by rattletrap cars.

Not much like this Congregational one, three-storied snowy spire and stately white walls on what passed for a hill on this sandspit island. *We had better singing, though.* Everyone stood. The sound was like a subdued slither under the trembling of the instrument, a rustle of cloth as people looked back toward the entrance.

Martha Stoddard stood there. She held a bouquet of flowers; otherwise she wore only another of her subdued but elegant gray suits.

"Silly to pretend I'm a girl," she'd said. Alston's lips quirked slightly. *No side on that woman. Good-looking, too.* In a spare sort of way; excellent bones, and those eyes would be full of mind and will when she was ninety. *Now why don't I ever meet anyone like that?* That wasn't quite the problem, of course, but . . .

Cofflin was waiting at the head of the aisle, sweating under the collar of his formal suit, looking pale. Looking rather like a bull waiting for the second blow from the slaughterhouse sledgehammer, in fact, or a man wondering desperately if he'd done the right thing.

The minister stood at the altar as the bride and her party walked down the isle. "Dearly beloved," she began.

"Well, there's one superstition disposed of," Alston said.

"Hmmm?" Cofflin asked.

He'd recovered most of his color by the time the outdoor reception began to wind down, and he was wandering about with his wife, talking to people and nibbling at the cake on his plate. Irreplaceable nuts and sugar and candied fruit had gone into the wedding cake, as well as flour made from grain the *Eagle* had brought back from Britain.

Alston looked over at him, and when she glanced back the remains of the piece on her own plate were gone. Swindapa was licking her fingers, grinning unrepentantly. *Sometimes you can remember that she's still a teenager.* Just turned eighteen, to be precise.

"What superstition?" Cofflin asked.

"About catching the bouquet," the captain said. It had been pure accident; the thing came flying at her face and she grabbed by instinct.

"It might come true," Martha observed.

"When pigs fly," Alston said.

"Congratulations again," a voice said; Ian Arnstein, with Doreen. They were holding hands.

Damned mating frenzy, Alston thought, smiling slightly. *Maybe there's something in the air here in 1250 B.C.* Or maybe it was just that people felt the loneliness pressing in on them and sought comfort where they could find it.

The ex-professor went on: "Have you mentioned what we discussed to the chief yet?"

"I didn't want to impose," Alston said dryly. "It *is* his wedding day, you know."

"Oh . . . sorry . . . bit of an obsessive-compulsive . . ." Arnstein floundered in embarrassment. "Always was socially challenged . . ."

"What *did* you discuss?" Martha Cofflin asked sharply.

"Well, the captain and I had this appalling thought."

Best get it over with, Alston decided. "We were talking about Isketerol's ships, and I mentioned that they could sail the same course to the Americas that we did, if Isketerol was keepin' his eyes open. Which he was."

Cofflin seemed to choke on a piece of the cake. "They *could*?" he wheezed, looking around.

"Easy. It's followin' winds most of the year, on the southern course. Ships no bigger did it routinely back in the early days after Columbus. Damnation, people have taken *rowboats* across the Atlantic. It's all a matter of knowing what's where, and how far, and the wind and current patterns. I may have made a mistake persuading him to come here, but he's so damned *useful.*"

"Tartessians are sneaky," Swindapa said. "And greedy. They don't liked we trade our own bronzework to anyone. At sea they sink boats coming from, ah, you call it Ireland? Yes, the Summer Isle, we say. And amber traders from the mainland they sink, toos." Her features thinned to rage for a moment: "Theys help the Sun People invade our land."

Doreen nodded. "They want a monopoly," she said. "Tin's scarce here. Britain and northwestern Spain are the only sources these people know west of Bohemia and the Caucasus."

"The Tartessians are sort of upstarts, who've been getting quasi-civilized over the past century or so," Arnstein added. "They've copied the eastern civilizations somewhat, adapting them to their own patterns—rather like the Japa-

nese with us. They're not as set in their ways as most people here-and-now."

Cofflin brushed a few crumbs off his jacket. "Well, so
the locals could sail here. That's a bit startling, but why's
it appalling?"

"Because piracy's hōt, here," Alston said. "Down in the
Mediterranean, from what Isketerol's let drop, anyone will
attack anyone, if they think they can get away with it—
ships, and 'longshore raids, that's where pirates make most
of their loot anyway. And this island is the richest prize on
earth. We underestimated the value of our goods. Badly.
One small shipload would make a successful pirate the richest man in the world."

"Oh." Cofflin thought. "They couldn't do much against
guns, could they?"

"Not the first time. After that we'd be out of ammunition. What's more, we're so short now that we can't even
train people to use the few guns we do have. I saw the
locals in operation in Britain. These people—peoples—are
warriors; they don't scare easy."

"You're right," Cofflin said, wincing. "Those Indians we
met the first day, a couple of them kept right on coming.
Guess they realized all a gun can do is kill you, and they
just weren't that scared of dying."

"We'd better start training a militia to use weapons we
can manufacture," Alston said.

"We'll have gunpowder eventually," Martha observed.

"That's then, this is now. Even when we do, the locals
are going to pick up tricks fast. Possibly not democracy or
women's rights, but weapons? You bet. And we *can't* stay
out of contact with the locals, not if we want to do more
than decay into a bunch of illiterate potato farmers in a
couple of generations. This island's too barren." She
paused, frowning. "It might be better if Mr. Isketerol
stayed here, rather than returning to Tartessos. . . ."

"Thank you for that delightful end to the day," Cofflin
said, turning on Arnstein. "Sorry, Professor, but I was just
beginning to think we could relax a little."

"No, no, no, man, it ain't a sick cat, you can't tell its
temperature by running a thermometer up its ass. You've
got to, like, look at the color. Really look."

Marian Alston stopped a moment at the anguished cry,

watching the group around the forge. *Always a pleasure to watch someone who really knows what he's doing,* she thought.

The blacksmith was a tall man, lean but with ropy muscle all along his bare sweat-slick arms and running under the thick canvas apron he was wearing. He was mostly bald on top, but a long ponytail of brown-streaked gray hair fell down his back, and a walrus mustache of the same color hung under sad sherry-colored eyes, like those of a basset hound hoping for a pat and expecting a kick. He held a rod of metal in a pair of pincers, turning it to show how it went from black to cherry-red to a fierce white at the tip.

"That's welding color, the white. Okay, get me the other piece."

More clumsily, the apprentice—an ex–office worker in a veterinary clinic—took up his own pincers in his gloved hands and wrestled another piece of steel out of the charcoal.

"Now down on the anvil," the smith said. "Okay, this stuff is mild steel. It won't weld as easy as wrought iron, so you have to dust it with a little flux—" he added a sprinkling of powder to where the two strips of metal overlapped each other—"and shed some righteous sweat. Here goes."

The big shed was noisy with a dozen metalworking benches, but the steady *clang . . . clang . . . clang* of the smith's hammer was the loudest. The metal flowed under it, merging. "Here's where we reheat and hammer some more," the smith said happily, putting the joined pieces of strapping back in the coals. "Meantime, drink some water. Important to drink water, man, keep your natural fluids in balance."

He dipped a cup into a bucket hanging on the wall, drank, then poured another over his head, holding his wire-rimmed glasses with their tiny round lenses out as he did so.

"Hey, Captain! What's happening?" he said cheerfully, peering at her.

Well, at least it isn't "How're they hanging," Alston thought resignedly. John Martins had been up in the hills of northern California since 1970, and stayed when the commune dissolved around him. A quarter century of lonely effort lay behind the skills he was trying to impart to a dozen apprentices.

"I warned you," the smith said. "I can't make anything like that Nip beauty y'showed me. No way, man. That's some excellent smith's work in that sword, truly righteous."

"Those take too long to make," she said, inhaling the scent of hot charcoal and scorched metal. It wasn't unpleasant, in its way, although the heat in here was fierce. "If it'll work, I'm satisfied."

He went over to the wall and took down a sword. She drew it from the plain leather-bound wooden sheath, raised it in both hands and tried a simple downward cut in slowtime, the pear-splitter. It followed the shape of her *katana* exactly, and the weight and balance were much the same. Not quite the living feel hers had, but much better than the cheap copies you got in most martial arts stores. The hilt was bound with cord, and the guard was a plain brass disk.

"I welded a sandwich of mild steel around a strip of 5160 for the cutting edge—y'know, the *moroha* way. Lotta fun, rilly."

This *moroha* blade wasn't quite the marvel that you got from the *ori awasi san mai* or *shihozume* methods, but it didn't take a year to produce, either. Alston turned the blade cutting-edge-up, admiring the wavy *yakiba* line in the steel that marked the hardened edge; she smiled, imagining Swindapa's face lighting up when she saw the sword. The Fiernan girl was a natural, too; teaching her was a real pleasure. So you couldn't really say it was favoritism to let her have this. . . .

Ron Leaton came up wiping his hands on an oily rag. "Our anachronism doing right by you, Captain Alston?"

"Peace. I love you too, man." the smith said, and turned back to his work.

"I have a horrible feeling he's the wave of the future and the machinery is an anachronism," Alston said, snapping the sword back into the sheath.

"Well, we're fitting out a whole building just for him and his apprentices," Leaton said; she suspected it would be a relief to both of them to part company. "Meanwhile, things are going pretty well. I found another three Bridgeport milling machines, eight engine lathes larger than twelve-inch, three larger than fourteen-inch, and one eighteen-inch—that was a pile of rusting parts down at the Electric Company, but it's restorable. What we're really short of is tool steel for drills and working edges, and stuff like Teflon lagging tape, hacksaw blades, files, sandpaper . . . we've swept every basement on the island and it still isn't enough."

She looked around. The boat-storage-cum-engineering-shop had changed, beyond the appearance of the big charcoal hearth and its surroundings in one corner. Dozens of people were laboring with hand tools at workbenches scattered through the cavernous interior; many of them were assembling crossbows from parts turned out on the lathes and cutters. The five machine tools they'd moved here from Seahaven Engineering's original basement setting and the ones Leaton had scavenged out of attics and forgotten storerooms were all set up, and they'd . . . *spawned* was the best word, she decided. There were another four lathes, and heavy six-foot-by-three platforms were being built to house more. Metal shapes and curves lay scattered about, with men and women working on them, assembling a gearcutter. The new lathes had been converted to work from leather belts taking off a power shaft rigged near the ceiling, and she could hear the chuffing of one of Leaton's prize steam engines. A big flywheel was going up against one wall, and beside it a bulky clumsy thing like a miniature stripped-down locomotive, the old choo-choo kind.

"Where did you find *that?*" she asked.

"Oh, Martha and Jared dug it up. Steam traction engine. Someone imported it years ago for the tourists, then stuck it in a storage shed and forgot it. Nearly got it working again; it eats wood, and by God we've *got* wood. We're going to hook it up to a generator, for times when the wind's down, and then we're going to duplicate it, maybe modify it a little. I'm doing some plans for a steam road hauler, too."

She nodded. *That* will *be useful,* she thought, and continued aloud: "How's that project I started you on going?"

"Better than we expected," Leaton said. "No shortage of sheet metal and bar."

He sighed, halfway between pleased and sad, and she knew why. The Steamship Authority's big motor ferry had been laid up for good. Useless, with no fuel oil available, and the thousands of tons of steel in the hull would last the islanders for many years. For that matter, the *Eagle* had nearly four hundred tons of pig-iron ballast in her, now being laboriously brought out and replaced with granite from the mainland. Then there was the fuel barge, another fifteen hundred tons of metal, and the old lightship, as much again, and structures like the oil storage tanks.

"The first set's ready, the first we're really satisfied with. Over here. Made to your measurements, by the way, Captain."

It rested on a workbench. The first part was a jacket of tough quilted canvas. The elbow-length sleeves were chain mail, rustling and clinking as she touched them; so was the collar, and a patch below the waistline at front and rear. Two workers nearby were winding sanded coathanger wire around wooden rods and cutting off links for more.

"Might as well try it on," she said. It pulled over her head. *Not too bad.* Not comfortable, of course, but you couldn't expect that.

"Not bad," she went on, "but you ought to make the mail inserts removable—lacing, or somethin' like that, so the padding can be cleaned without getting the metal wet."

The breastplate was a smooth shallow curve, basically Japanese in design like the rest of the armor but somewhat simplifed; the backplate hinged to it at the shoulder, and clasps fastened at the flanks. She'd drawn the plans from what she was familiar with, and what Martha could find in her references, modified to make it possible for one person to put on by herself. She lifted the set, ducked her head through and pressed it closed, then fastened the brass clips under her left arm and pulled the loose mail collar out to rest on the surface of the armor. The metal extended to waist level, and hinged to it were jointed skirts of sliding curved plates to protect the thighs. Fitted armguards for the forearms went on next, and greaves for the shins.

She *hadn't* told the metalworkers to enamel everything green with yellow trim, and put a golden eagle copied from her ship's figurehead across the chest. "Bit bold, isn't it?" she said, jerking her chin toward a mirror that leaned against the wall.

I feel like an actor in a pageant. Against people armed with flint-tipped arrows and bronze spearheads, though, this was high-tech weaponry.

"We had the paint on hand, and it wasn't any great effort to bake on the enamel," Leaton said virtuously. "And it'll keep it from rusting, too."

Alston grunted noncommittally. She bent, twisted, squatted, rose, did a few long low stances to test the equipment. Heavy, of course, but she'd carried far more weight less well distributed on camping trips, and it was no more awkward than practice armor for a *kenjutsu* bout—very similar to that, in fact. This was flexible enough not to impede movement much, too. She did a slow forward roll and came to her feet with a grunt, clattering a little. *Have to wear this a lot to get used to it.* Then she settled on the helmet and snapped the chin strap.

"Cool!" someone said. "Just like the ones in *Star Wars*!"

Alston gritted her teeth, and bit back *Lucas and I both copied from the same source.*

"It'll do," she said. "But plain green for the rest, if you don't mind. How many, how quickly?"

"Thirty a week, given the priorities the Council's set," the engineer said. "Scaling up to a hundred."

"You, sir, snore," Martha said, sipping at a cup of hot herb tea.

"Well, a man can't tell his fiancée *everything*," Jared said reasonably. "Or his bride. Not before the end of the honeymoon, at least. Where's the romance and mystery in that?" They'd anticipated the parson, of course, but not by all that much—and never actually *slept* together before moving in after the wedding.

She gave a dry chuckle. "Unsuspected depths; even a sense of irony. What will it be next?"

They looked at each other and smiled. *Well, we're neither of us nineteen,* he thought with satisfaction. Forty and fifty-plus-six-months, in fact. She set her cup down on the kitchen table and sat on his lap; not what you'd call well upholstered, but damned pleasant nonetheless. *We suit, that's the best way to put it,* he decided, and grinned.

"A penny for them. Or a pound of dulse, in our barter economy."

"Thinking of how different I felt about a woman on my lap in the morning thirty years ago. Not," he added hastily, "that it doesn't—"

She put an arm around his neck. "Jared, from puberty to their thirties men aren't human beings. They're hormones with feet. I prefer one with enough functioning mind to be interesting . . . which you are."

A few minutes later: "But the hormones still seem to be functioning, too. Not on the kitchen table, dear, and not before breakfast. The griddle cakes, I think," she went on, slightly breathless, sliding away to her own seat. "You didn't tell me you could cook, either."

Functioning indeed, Jared thought, with a slight trace of smugness. "I was a widower for five years, and a hunter for twenty-three. Breakfasts I can do," he said, getting up and going to the counter.

"Have to look into making baking powder—we'll be out soon," he added, as he got out the jar of oil and the frying pan and wound a cloth around his hand to open the wire-handled oven door to check the coals.

"Mmm," she said, watching him.

He poured a little oil into the iron frying pan and set it to heat, mixed the dry ingredients and beat the whole-wheat flour into the water and eggs, and added some of the syrup to make up for the lack of richening milk. The oil was ready when a drop of water flicked off the end of a finger hopped and sputtered. One big spoonful three times, and you could do three at a time.

"Baking soda . . ." she said thoughtfully, straightening her bathrobe and hair. "Sodium bicarbonate and an acid. Cynthia at the high school might know. I'll look into it."

"These'll be better when the blueberries ripen in July," he said mildly. "Here we go."

He edged the spatula under the crackly, lacy brown rim of the griddle cake; the top surface was just browning a little, and spotted with bubbles. He slid the first three onto a plate, covered it with a dishtowel, and put it on the warming tray at the rear of the cast-iron stove. When there were enough for two he took the lot back to the table with the crock of maple syrup. *Now, all we lack is—no, by God, we don't.* There was a little bit left of the wedding present from Angelica.

"Here you are," he said cheerfully, putting a tray with a lump of butter the size of a peach pit down beside the pancakes and removing the cover with a flourish. "Luxuries of the island elite; welcome to the ruling class."

Martha looked cheerful herself, in her subdued way, as she loaded her plate. Right up to the moment she raised the first forkful to her mouth.

"Oh, dear," she said then, swallowing and staring at the syrup-laden pancake. "Oh, my. Oh *shit*."

Her fork clattered to the plate and she bolted from the kitchen. He sat frozen for an instant, fear tasting of acid at the back of his mouth. Then he levered himself to his feet and followed her; she'd made it as far as the small downstairs bathroom, and he could see her kneeling in front of the toilet. A hand waved him away.

All right, then, he thought, a little of the fist that was squeezing under his breastbone relaxing. *Bad fish?* They'd had problems with that. He padded back into the kitchen, his slippers scuffing on the floorboards, and got a dry towel, a damp one, and a glass of water—there were a couple of large buckets sitting on the counter, filled during the hour the town mains were running. He carried the glass and cloth back into the small washroom after a discreet pause, and found Martha sitting on the closed seat lid of the toilet, breathing deeply.

"Here," he said. She rinsed, spat into the sink, and wiped her face gratefully. "Shall I go get Doc Coleman?"

His wife shook her head. There was a little color back in her face again. "Later. It's not urgent."

"It isn't?" he said, puzzled. "Food poisoning can—"

"It isn't that . . . I think. We'll check with Coleman, but I think the bunny just died."

"The . . . oh, sh—, ah, oh dear."

Her smile flickered wan; she stood, bracing herself with one arm against the wall. He gathered her to him, lips shaping a silent whistle over her shoulder.

"What was that saying on the tombstone?" she asked. "*I expected this, but not so soon?* At our ages . . . and on this diet, I've been irregular anyway, thought it might be early menopause coming on. . . ."

He nodded into her graying brown hair. They'd discussed the possibility, but only in an abstract sort of way. This . . .

"Sort of risky," he said after a moment.

"At my age, you mean?" she replied. "Jared, we're in the year *1250 B.C.* Risk . . ." She sighed and shrugged. "Risk has assumed a whole new meaning. Let's go talk about this. There's still some RU-486 if that's what we decide, but let's go talk." A moment. "I'm even hungry again."

*   *   *

"Turnabout's fair play," Alice Hong said, pouting.

"Nope," William Walker said, pulling on his trousers.

"Well, untie me then. I've got roomies, remember."

"I believe in spreading the joy of life."

He looked around the room. A little untidy for his tastes—he was a man of fastidious neatness—but not bad. A series of Escher prints, and others he didn't recognize, heavy-metal varieties with a lot of skulls, candle flames behind their eyes, and people tied up with barbed wire, pentagrams, bat wings, real symbolism. A good modern bed, not the four-posters so common in this antique-happy town. Alice Hong was lying on her stomach in the middle of that bed, ankles lashed to wrists behind her back with padded ties. A number of her other toys were scattered about. She squirmed over, which left her arched like a bow and spread-eagled. He admired the view; she was deeply into this stuff, and it had its points. Probably tedious as a full-time diet, but not bad as a change. There was a full-length mirror opposite the bed; he admired the view in that, too. *In even better shape than I was,* he decided smugly. Washboard stomach carrying a full six-pack, broad shoulders, narrow waist, every muscle moving just so under tanned skin. A heavy investment there, but worth it. William Walker had to live in that temple, after all. He smiled at himself.

"Yeah, you're gorgeous," Alice said, collapsing onto her side. "*Sure* you don't want to try it from this side? It can be fun."

He stepped over to the bed and jerked her head back by her hair. She gave a gasp, smiling at him. The sweat running into the marks the cane had made across her back had to sting too, but she didn't look any the worse for it.

"I'm strictly a pitcher S&M-wise, darling," he said. "Not a catcher, and you shouldn't have been quite so honest on why you got blacklisted in every pain club on the East Coast. Besides, I'm on duty in a while. The captain has an uncivilized attitude toward unpunctuality."

"Mmm," Alice said, the tip of her tongue touching her lips. "You're a workaholic too. . . ."

"It's how you get places, babe." He pulled her head back a little farther; she shivered and clenched her teeth. "How'd you get that medical degree?"

"Took a five-year holiday from life," she said. "Everyone

needs holidays. What's the captain like, anyway? Everyone talks about her. Real mysterious. Cute, too."

"I don't think you're her type, Alice," he said. "She's surprisingly straitlaced, if you know what I mean." They both laughed.

"And you get to go back to those fascinating places with her," Alice said enviously. "That sacrifice, that was *wild*. Sure looks like more fun than dancing around in night-gowns with a bunch of middle-aged hausfrau geeks who think they're witches. All the stupid bitches ever want to do is bless the crops, anyway. Dull."

"Why, I don't think Pamela Lisketter would like to hear you talking that way," Walker chuckled.

"Fuck Lisketter—on second thought, no thanks."

"You know, Alice, I really like you. You're my kind of lady. How'd you like to travel to beautiful Bronze Age Europe yourself?"

"Oh, *yeah*," she said, skeptical.

"I mean it. Can't you see yourself as the Great White Queen—Great Asian-American Queen—of a tribe of adoring barbarians? Stone palaces, silk blowing in the wind, some *really* kinky stuff. Sacrifices. Flames in the dark. Screams. No more make-believe, no taking turns . . ."

She gave a complex shudder. "Tease. Now let me loose, c'mon. Rosita's coming back any minute, and Isketerol will be with her."

He buttoned his shirt and tucked it in, tying his tie and picking up the uniform cap from a dresser. "I'm sure all three of you will enjoy that thoroughly," he said. "*Hasta la vista,* and call me when you're not all tied up."

"Asshole!" she cried after him.

He stopped, turned, and stuck his head back around the doorjamb.

"Yes," he said, with a brilliant grin. "I am. But I am no *ordinary* asshole."

Walker went down the stairs two at a time, chuckling, with the woman's curses ringing in his ears. *She* is *my kind of girl,* he thought. *And maybe* . . . A doctor could be very useful, in a number of different ways.

"Hunff!"

The *katana* flashed in the evening sunlight, halting just above the ragged surface of the grass. Marian Alston looked critically out of the kitchen window; Swindapa was still hard at it, doing the *kata* long after Alston had gone in to oversee dinner. Saturday afternoons were supposed to be free time; she'd been doing paperwork until noon herself. Doreen was running through staff forms doggedly. She'd never be really good, no natural talent, but she'd improved considerably. Ian was watching from a deck chair, his thumb keeping place in his book.

The Fiernan flicked the sword aside to shed imaginary blood, sheathed it, and went to one knee. A long quiet moment and then she drew and thrust straight back without turning, flicked the blade up for a straight cut, blocked, blocked, backing . . . Alston looked at her feet and the set of her shoulders.

"You're forcing it," she called through the open kitchen window. "Relax. No tension until the end of the stroke. Let the sword do it."

"Do," Swindapa panted. "I that."

She stood, relaxing and shaking out one wrist and then the other, then began the *kata* again.

Still hasn't got English syntax quite *down,* Alston thought, smiling. She caught her own expression in the slanted glass of the window. *Uh-oh,* she thought. *Watch it, woman.* There was enough grief in life without courting it.

Instead she looked down at the loaves, tapping them out of the sheet-metal pans with a cloth to protect her hands. The bottom of the bread was light honey-brown; she tapped it with a fingernail. Just the right sound, slightly hollow.

The kitchen door opened. "Damn, but that smells great, Skipper," Sandy Rapczewicz said. "What is it?"

Rapczewicz and Lieutenant Victor Ortiz went over to one of the sinks and washed their hands, using economical dippers of water from the buckets beside it. Both the Coast Guard officers looked worn—everyone did—and their working blues were stained with engine oil.

"Duck," Alston said. "Bread-and-sage stuffing." That didn't get the groans that seafood would have. "Sea lettuce and pickerelweed salad, courtesy of the Guides. Cattail stalks and dock. And fresh bread, of course."

"Good," Rapczewicz said, sitting down at the kitchen table and slumping wearily. "Max is up and running, Skipper," she went on. "But God alone knows for how long. Those bearings . . ."

"We're almost out of diesel oil anyway," Ortiz said.

"Worth it, to keep the trawlers running as long as we could," Alston said, wrapping a corner of her apron around her hand and opening the oven door, blinking through a cloud of fragrant steam. She prodded a serving fork into the birds and looked at the color of the juice. "Ah, just about—"

Swindapa bounced up the steps into the kitchen, ducking into the sunroom for a second to rack her sheathed sword.

"I help can I?" she said. The two scholars followed her, Doreen still panting.

"That's *can I help,* 'dapa. Toss me those potholders, and get those cattail stalks ready, would you?"

They worked in companionable silence for a few moments as Alston finished the gravy and began to dismember the ducks.

"Shouldn't—" Alston began. Then: "Speak of the devil."

Dr. Coleman came through the door; Sandy had invited him again. *Hmmm. Seeing a lot of each other,* Alston thought.

"Not exactly the devil," he said. "Been mistaken for Daniel Webster, though." His long nose quivered. "Smells wonderful."

"All the more dishes to wash," she said. "And it's served."

Everyone carried plates to the pinewood table, and for a few minutes there was no sound but concentrated eating. Long days of hard physical labor had taught them all exactly what *hungry* was, and it wasn't much like just being ready for dinner. The duck was good if she said so herself, and the boiled dock tasted hauntingly like spinach, or like spinach with a squeeze of lemon; cattail turned out to have a flavor a little like sweet corn. Alston sat next to the Fiernan girl, conscious of a slight summery odor of clean sweat; more agreeable than a lot of islanders, with soap and hot water both difficult to get.

Coleman plied his fork with a will. "Wouldn't have thought you were a chef, on top of everything else," he said to the Coast Guard officer.

"I'm not fancy enough to be a chef," she said. "I'm a cook . . . it's, mmm, relaxin'. Everyone should have a hobby."

"Better this butter—" Swindapa stopped and frowned.

"This would be better with butter," she went on carefully, dipping a piece of the bread into the fat.

"So it would," Alston said. "We don't have enough cows yet."

Swindapa frowned. "Why not?" she said. "Understand that the island Nantucket is-and-was only part of United States, here, but every part of the White Isle has always cows—how could not? Everyone needs butter, and cheese and milk and hides and meat."

"We had ways of keeping those from spoiling, and of sending them a long way very quickly," Alston said.

"Ah," Swindapa nodded. "Steam engines." She tapped a book at the end of the table: *The Great Inventions*. "Reading is *fun*," she added. "Especially at night."

When she's given to nightmares, Alston thought, nodding. Not surprising. Aloud:

"We might think about a steam auxiliary for *Eagle*, when the last diesel's gone," she said thoughtfully.

"Bulky, though," Rapczewicz said.

Swindapa sneezed and raised a hand. Alston made an admonitory clucking noise. "Sorry," the girl said, pulling out a handkerchief and using that instead of her fingers.

"Useful for short distances," Alston said. "She couldn't carry any great amount of wood, but wood's not scarce, either. Victor, why don't you look into it? Have a talk with Leaton, see what you can come up with. It's a long-term project, though."

The Cuban-American officer made an inarticulate sound of agreement around a mouthful of drumstick. "I'll get Will . . . Lieutenant Walker in on it, Skipper," he said. "He's got an eye for machinery, and he's a good draftsman, too."

"By all means, Victor," Alston said.

She thought she heard Swindapa mutter *scumbag* under her breath. *I can't completely disagree,* she thought. *On the other hand, I can't completely agree, either.* You had to be fair; a gut feeling wasn't enough to justify coming down on a capable, hardworking officer. *On the other hand, there's that administrative reprimand over the junk that went missing from the evidence locker.* Nothing proved, not even enough evidence for a decent suspicion. Still . . .

"I understand he's found permanent quarters ashore," she said.

"Moved in with Dr. Hong—Alice Hong," Ortiz said.

Coleman cleared his throat. "She's a very capable physician," he said, with a neutral tone that spoke volumes. Alston raised an eyebrow. *These Yankees can say more with the words they* don't *speak. . . .*

"Well, we can hardly insist that everyone live in barracks," Alston said, after swallowing a mouthful of duck. "One thing we can do . . . " She turned her eyes to the Arnsteins, at the foot of the table. "And I'd like your help on this. We've got to get a classroom schedule going again for the cadets. Academics may not be as important here as back up in the twentieth, but I want those young people to have something *approachin'* a liberal education, as well as specialized things."

Ian nodded. "Well, I'll be glad to teach a history course . . . God, maybe 'current affairs' would be a better description? Will we have time?"

Alston nodded firmly. "We'll *make* time."

Doreen pursed her lips thoughtfully. "I should talk to Martha about this too. She's been worrying that we don't have anything past high school on the island."

Alston's eyebrows went up. "Hadn't thought of that," she admitted. *There's a certain comfort to having a limited sphere of responsibilities,* she thought. All she really had to do was oversee matters military and maritime, including the Guard . . . which was a hell of a job, but not nearly as nerve-racking as Jared's. He had to be responsible for *everything,* and she didn't envy him in the slightest.

The site of Providence that would never be was beautiful in the summer sun. Water glimmered broad across Narragansett Bay, like a field of hammered metal under the sunlight. Water purled back from the steamboat's prow, churned foam-white from its thrashing paddles; the steady whunk-*chuff* of its engine echoed back from the great trees that lined the shore as they headed northwest up the bay. On the hills above the bay, green waves receded into blue distance, the edge of a climax forest that stretched from Florida nearly to Hudson Bay and inland to the Mississippi, rustling mystery ten stories high.

It was thicker, ranker, the trees growing straighter and taller than those which had greeted the first of Cofflin's English ancestors. Birds flocked thickly, gulls, pelicans, duck, geese, and the hawks and eagles and falcons that preyed on them. He saw a bald eagle swoop by within a hundred yards of the noisy steamboat and snatch a two-foot fish from the surface of the bright water. Its wingtips dimpled the wave once, twice as it flogged the air, and then it was a dark soaring shape heading back toward the shore with its quarry in its talons.

He winced a little at the thought of the Indians. The islanders had come, very cautiously, and found abandoned huts. The ones near Boston had been full of the dead— whole families lying rotting. Perhaps the worst had been the children who hadn't died of the virus out of time, who'd starved or died of thirst as they lay beside dying parents. . . .

We didn't know! he cried out inside himself. At least all the local tribes seemed to have fled inland, plenty of coastal campsites but no people. Nobody since had reported any contacts, and overflights hadn't seen any fires that weren't natural. He pushed the matter out of his mind; no help for it, and too much else to consider.

Cofflin stood and watched as the shore drew nearer. A piledriver mounted between two rafts went *thunk . . . thunk . . . thunk* over and over as rope and pulley and hand-powered crank drew the stone-weighted oak pole up and released it with a downward rush. It was driving seventy-foot logs into the mud of the bay, in a row four trunks broad and already twenty long. As he watched another log came slithering down a steep trail, pulled by a brace of hairy-footed horses, with cursing humans steadying the great baulk of timber with ropes snubbed around stumps and trunks to keep it at least mostly under control. The bottom of it had already been shaped into a rough point. Other logs were being pegged and mortised into the vertical piles, webbing them together. Near it a barge-shaped raft of rough-cut timbers held a cargo of charcoal in wooden tubs, piled firewood, and slatted wooden cages full of captured wild turkeys gobbling in indignation.

He stepped out onto a floating pier of smaller logs as the teams pushed the big timber into the water. Rowboats hitched on and began hauling it toward the end of the growing wharf; he walked carefully shoreward, feeling the surface bob a little beneath his feet.

"Making progress, Sam," he said to the man who waited for him. They shook hands.

"More to be done," the burly carpenter turned lumber boss said. "Wharf'll be ready come July." He shook his head. "Feels odd, having timber cheap and nails scarce like this. But she'll be ready."

Cofflin felt a glow of satisfaction. That would give the *Eagle* a secure, protected deepwater anchorage for the winter. In the meantime, it meant cargo from here could be loaded directly onto her decks, at an enormous saving in time and effort. They were all becoming fanatics for the labor-saving device; there was simply so much to *do*.

Sam Macy waved him toward the shelters, and they fell into step. Half a hundred yards away stood a row of log buildings. The timbers had been roughly squared on top and bottom, then notched at the ends and pushed up sloping poles into position; Martha had done up an instruction pamphlet on the technique, culled from history books and more recent hobbyist magazines. Stable and barn with hayloft, smokehouse for the venison, bear, and duck the crews hunted in their spare time. Hides were tacked to its outer wall, stretching and drying. Bunkhouses, another divided into apartments for the married couples; storehouse, cookhouse, mess hall. Last but not least was the one beside the stream, a framework of upright timbers instead of horizontal logs. A flume guided water to the top of an overshot wheel on its side, and from within came the *ruhhhh . . . ruhhhh . . . ruhhhh* of a vertical saw ripping its way through the tough wood.

"We're getting beam and plank in some quantity now, as well as the firewood and charcoal," Sam Macy said. "But Jared, it burns my butt to use trees like this for fuel, it really does. Planks four feet across and twenty yards long, and not a single knot!"

"No choice, Sam."

The logging boss nodded gloomily. "At least we've managed to get some wood alcohol out of the sawdust and chips," he said.

"Doc Coleman'll be glad. Needs it for disinfectant." Someday they might get enough to use as motor fuel.

"We could do more if Leaton could send us someone who could do real repairs on the metalwork," Macy said. "That's one of the big things holding us up, sending broken parts back to the island. That and the fact that only a few of us have even a faint idea of what we're doing. God, some of these people, they can't lift a sandwich without putting their backs out—and making charcoal is *dangerous*. Get airing the pile just a little wrong, and it can *explode*, not just spoil the load."

Cofflin chuckled. "You think you've got problems that way," he said. "You should hear Leaton." His face grew serious. "Now let's settle this little matter."

They stepped into one of the big cabins. The floor and the fireplace at one end were local rock, hastily shaped and then cemented together. Light came from windows cut through the logs, but it was a little gloomy inside nonetheless. The pothooks and andirons that held a black iron cauldron over the low flames were a hundred and eighty years old, and had spent the last couple of generations in a museum, but they were still functional. Two figures sat at a table made of a single great plank, holding hands. They stood defiantly as Chief Cofflin walked in. He peered.

"Why, I thought . . . Sam, you can build a house, you can run a lumber camp, but you can't send a message to save your life. I thought you said it was Ed Smith who'd gotten her pregnant."

"That's *Fred* Smith. I swear, Jared, I said *Fred*."

Edward Smith was this boy's father, in his fifties, married with three children. Jared Cofflin had come over from Nantucket ready to kick some molesting butt, full of righteous anger.

Cofflin sighed. Another thing that was hard to get used to, not being able to call up and settle details over the phone. Radios were precious, used for emergencies, batteries even more so—though Sam was talking about hooking a car alternator up to the waterwheel here once they had time to get the necessary gearing done back at Seahaven.

"Let's sit down and talk this over, why don't we?" Cofflin said.

Nice girl, he thought. Black hair in a ponytail, blue eyes, scrubbed outdoors look. The kid had a scraggly beginning brown fuzz of beard; a lot of the male islanders were sprouting chin fungus these days. Muscle swelled at the sleeves of the young man's T-shirt and stretched it across his shoulders, probably a lot of it added since the Event, like the hard callus on the palm of the hand he offered.

"Fred Smith, Tiffany Penderton?" Cofflin asked.

The camp cook brought them four mugs of hot liquid from a smaller pot over the fire. It was sassafras tea, deep red and a little astringent despite the honey added to sweeten it. *Sure as hell isn't coffee.* Still, having a cup of something in your hand helped to break the ice.

"Son, there's been a misunderstanding here," Cofflin said. The boy's hand tightened on the girl's. "The report reached me secondhand, and I heard it as *Ed* Smith being the man responsible."

Tiffany giggled, looking much younger. Her companion went blank for a second, and then said: *"Dad?"* After a moment he went on: "Sir, when I heard you were coming, and we were supposed to drop everything and meet you, I thought that Tiffany's parents had, um . . ."

"Got to me, yes, I know, son."

The tension around the table dissolved into laughter. "All right. Now, I understand you two are willing to do the right thing?"

They nodded. "Yeah. We've been planning on it for, oh, months now."

"That long?" Cofflin said dryly. "Well, it's breaking out all over, isn't it?" They looked at him as if he were an alien being, or a different order of creature at least. "Mrs. Cofflin is expecting as well."

Polite bafflement this time, and perhaps slight horror. *Well, it must seem unnatural, people our age,* he thought charitably.

"Remember, taking care of a baby is a lot of work—on top of everything else you have to do."

"I'm not afraid of work," the boy said.

"Isn't, at that," Macy amplified. "Good hand, learned as fast as any of us. Tiffany's a dab eye for edible greenery, too."

As if on cue, the cook came back with four bowls and a platter of thick-cut bread. There wasn't any butter, but the bread was still hot from the oven, and there were mushrooms and some sort of chunky root in the venison stew. "Pity you don't have much time to hunt," he said. "Some people back on the island would kill for this." *Wild mustard leaves and chives, too,* he decided.

He went on: "Well, do you want a church wedding back in town, or what?"

"No, sir," Smith said earnestly. "We really like it here, and our parents, well, ah, actually Tiffany's parents, well . . ."

"I understand," he said. The Pendertons were coofs, and pretty well-to-do at that. Ed Smith had been a garage mechanic, before the Event. "When do you want the ceremony?"

He certainly rated as better than a justice of the peace, all things considered. As long as it was performed in public and duly witnessed, they weren't being technical about weddings.

"Tonight, Chief?" Tiffany Penderton said quietly.

"Why not?"

He ate another spoonful of the venison stew. You could probably get sick of this—he'd gotten tired of lobster lately—but it was a very pleasant change. The deer on Nantucket would be killed out soon. When they had time, maybe they could send some more hunting parties ashore. . . .

Time, he thought, smiling at the youngsters. Time was he'd have thought the pregnancy a sign of trouble to come, and the kids far too young; plus they'd probably never have been thrown together enough to meet. Not everything about the Event had been a disaster.

"I wish Ms. Stoddard—I mean, Ms. Cofflin—could be here," Tiffany said wistfully. "It was a lot of fun, being in the Scouts with her teaching us things."

Not everything, by any manner of means.

A man pelted in. "Boss!" he called. "Chief!"

Cofflin looked around at the tone in his voice, and waited while he controlled his breathing.

"Chief, there's an Indian up the track—just where we were cutting those black walnut. He's just standing there, keeps putting his hand up empty and talking Indian at us."

Cofflin and Sam Macy looked at each other. "Solve one problem . . ." Macy began.

". . . get another," Cofflin replied. "I'd better go take a look."

"There!" Swindapa whispered close to her ear. "There, see?"

Marian Alston bent slowly and peered through the thorny scrub, squinting. It was a gray day, low cloud scudding by overhead like cavalry of the sky, with an occasional spatter of rain; the air was so moist it would have been fog, if the wind hadn't been at twenty knots from the south. A flicker of brown ears . . . a deer, its lips and tongue cropping delicately at the new growth.

No harm there . . . but beyond this thicket was the rolling

surface of one of Angelica Brand's new grainfields. Shoots
of wheat ran bluish-green over what had been thicket and
moorland a few short months ago, rippling nearly calf-high
in the wind. Except for some near the edge of the cleared
zone, eaten down to the roots. There were a thousand deer
on Nantucket, or had been when the island was covered in
scrub and moorland. They had to go, now that it was to be
farmland once more. Fencing was out of the question this
year at least, and couldn't be deer-proof anyway.

Besides, I crave *red meat,* Alston thought. Hunting was
useful recreation, in the intervals between taking the *Eagle*
out, training, overseeing the militia, getting the fishing fleet
built and maintained. She enjoyed it; Swindapa gloried in it.

The deer bent its head again. The crossbow came up to
her shoulder with studied slowness. Snuggle your cheek
into the stock. Curl finger on the trigger, stroking it. *Altogether too much like making out,* she gibed in some recess
of her mind. Now. Bring the foresight down until it settled
in the notch at the back. Distance . . . about thirty yards.
Raise the angle a little, then. The crossbow bolt didn't go
anything like as fast a bullet. Exhale. Squeeze.

Whunnnng. The butt kicked back against her shoulder.
The short heavy arrow whipped out through the thin-
branched scrub. And . . .

The deer leaped convulsively. Alston cursed and leaped
up herself; the worst possible result, a wounded deer ca-
reering off. Swindapa drew her knife and bounced forward,
eeling through the spiny growth. Alston followed more
slowly, sharp thorns snagging at her jeans and denim jacket,
wondering at the young woman's skill. She'd said that she
was an indifferent hunter, that being mainly men's business
among her people. Blood spattered the trail, drops and
then thick gobbets of it, smelling of copper, salt, and iron.
The deer was lying on its side a hundred steps farther in
under a dwarf pine, with the crossbow bolt sunk past the
fletching behind its shoulder. Its hind legs kicked a final
time as she came up; the graceful shape laid itself limp.
Swindapa trimmed a branch and dipped it in the blood.
She stood and flicked it north, south, east, west, murmuring
in her own language as she did so. Then she crouched by
the deer and began breaking it, butchering with easy skill.

"Bad that we can't hang it up," she said, red to the elbows.

Her English still held a strange lilt and roll, but it was fully fluent.

"Easier that way . . . *unHUojx*, look, the liver." The girl sliced off a bit and popped it in her mouth, chewing with relish. "Best part. Want to start a fire and grill it?"

"Nnno, I don't think so," Alston said. *For a number of reasons.* She squatted as well to help with the messy task; not unfamiliar, she'd helped butcher animals as a child. "I prefer it with onions, and we've got some back home. Besides, we don't have much water here. Dried blood is sticky."

Vegetables were more precious than gold—those Brand had planted back in the spring were watched like ailing first-born children, or perhaps the ailing firstborn children of hungry cannibals—but red meat had scarcity value too. For an occasional haunch of venison, you could do wonders trading on the quiet. She didn't feel that was cheating, not like using her official position; after all, she *did* kill the deer herself.

They occupied themselves in companionable silence for a moment. "I've been meaning to ask you," she said. "What's that mark?"

Swindapa was wearing a shirt, unbuttoned partway down in the warm weather with the tails tied off under her bosom. Just between the upper curve of her breasts was a small tattoo, shaped like an arrowhead.

"That?" she said, peering down. "That's the . . ." She considered for a moment, her lips shaping words. "The Spear Mark. When I was fifteen . . . years, I think, we count by thirteens of the moon . . . I took the Spear Mark, nearly three years ago when I was young. I stalked a deer close enough to kill it with my spear, and came back with the antlers on my head and the hide wrapped around me, and jumped the fire trench, and they put the Spear Mark on my chest."

"Everyone does that?" Alston said.

"Oh, no. Some-many boys every year, and some-few girls sometimes. My—the one I did the Moon Spring Rites with, you'd say, my boyfriend?"

" 'Lover' might be more appropriate, I think."

"My lover was a big—no, a great—hunter, didn't study the stars even though he was part of the Egurnecio family. A warrior, too, a . . . Spear Chosen, someone who leads warriors. I wanted to be with him." She looked bleak for a moment, then sighed and shook it off. "The Sun People hurt him, smashed his leg, he couldn't run or hunt or fight anymore. He got angry all the time, got sick with too much mead, then he died."

And I know the rest, Alston thought.

They'd finished gralloching the deer; they left the entrails for the ants and birds, packed heart, liver, tongue, and kidneys back in the stomach hollow, and removed the head. Then they ran a pole between the bound legs, brushed the blood off their hands and arms with sand as best they could, and lifted it with an end of the carrying pole on each shoulder.

"Do some more sword work tonight?" Swindapa wheedled.

"If you don't mind the others," Alston replied. She'd started classes for some of her cadets and a few islanders who showed promise. *In our copious spare time.*

They came out onto the road and dumped the deer carcass into the wire baggage holder at the rear of the two-seater tricycle; it was a fairly robust thing, one of many worked up since the Event by Leaton. Alston looked at the sky; not long to dinner. Deer liver and onions sounded more wonderful all the time.

"No problem, more fun with lots of people," Swindapa said. She went on, "Good hunt today," giving Alston a quick hug before jumping onto her seat.

I wish she wouldn't do that, the captain thought. Evidently Swindapa's people embraced and touched at the slightest provocation, and she was gradually starting to do that again as her memories healed over a little. *She has no idea how . . . difficult that makes things.*

Well, life was difficult. They began pedaling in unison, enjoying the cooling effect of the breeze.

"We'll stop at Smith's," Swindapa said happily.

Smith was an enterprising soul who'd put the hot-water shortage to work and opened an Oriental-style scrub-and-soak bathhouse; much more economical of fuel than trying to heat water and pour it into a tub in a single house, now that the electrical and gas heaters were useless. The Council had approved, since it was just the sort of thing that was needed to jump-start the island away from the emergency-collective setup that necessity had forced on them. Unfortunately, Smith didn't run to individual tubs yet, just one big one for men and another for women.

Oh, well. Life is *difficult.*

"No, I'll sponge down at home," she replied. *And avoid all temptation. My own virtue sickens me at times.*

CHAPTER ELEVEN

July–August, Year 1 A.E.

"I say the last thing we need is foreign entanglements!" Sam Macy said.

There was a rumble of agreement from here and there in the Town Meeting. Cofflin sighed inwardly. He could understand Sam's position only too well; the problem was that while that sentiment *felt* right, the balance of facts was against it. Macy was a nice guy to sit down and have a beer with, he did his job well—hell, he'd turned out to be a genius at logging, sawmilling, anything to do with wood—and he kept his people over at Providence Base happy with their boss. The problem was that when Macy got onto politics, he had certain fixed opinions that couldn't be shifted with plastique and bulldozers.

"We're just getting things going right," Macy went on, flushing as eyes turned to him all across the big room. The microphones were long gone, and his voice came out in an untrained foghorn roar. "We've got plenty to eat, it looks like the harvest will be good—" he knocked on wood—"and we've got plenty to keep us warm this winter—"

"Good job, Sam!" someone said. Macy stuttered and then went on:

"—and we're learning how to do lots of stuff. We all saw the pictures and video Captain Alston brought back. I'm not saying we shouldn't have sent the *Eagle* over to Britain, but those aren't the sort of people we want to get involved with. Why should we risk the lives of good American boys and girls for those dirty savages? It's worse than Bosnia."

Another mutter of agreement, louder this time. Swindapa's hand went up. She stood as Cofflin pointed the gavel.

"My people are not savages like the Iraiina," she said simply. "They come to take our land for no better reason than they want it, and to make us slaves because they would rather take our crops than work to grow their own." Her face was flushed, but she spoke firmly under the lilting singsong accent her birth tongue gave to her English. "We don't ask them to walk the stars with Moon Woman. All we want is that the Sun People leave us *alone*."

Silence fell after she sat, crossing her arms on the dark-blue sweater with *Nantucket* woven on it in yellow cord.

Poor kid, Cofflin thought. *Still comes up and bites her when she thinks about it.* Post-traumatic stress disorder, a fancy name for very bad memories that wouldn't leave you alone.

"Pamela Lisketter," Cofflin said.

"That's all very well," the thin woman said. On most people the results of hard work and a fish diet were an improvement, but she'd started out gaunt; that made her yellow-green eyes seem enormous by contrast. "But isn't it true that the real reason you want to interfere in the affairs of these people is to *exploit* them?"

"Nope," Cofflin said. "Fair exchange is what we've got in mind. Professor?"

Arnstein stood and stroked his bushy reddish-brown beard. "This island can't produce enough to do more than keep us alive," he said. "It doesn't even have much timber, much less metals or fuel. Seven thousand-odd people—call it five thousand working adults and teenagers—that just isn't enough to keep civilization going, if most of us have to spend all our time producing food. We can't have teachers and engineers and clerks and, oh, silversmiths and everything else, all the specialists, because there won't be enough food or enough raw materials or enough markets. But if we can trade widely, we *can* have those specialists, and exchange what they make for what we need. The question is, do you want your grandchildren to have something like a decent life, or do you want them to be illiterate peasants?"

A thoughtful silence fell. "Ms. Lisketter."

"There's nothing wrong with a simple life! We should all learn to lower our expectations and walk lightly on the earth, not kill its whales and cut down its trees and . . . We've got an opportunity to *escape* from a culture dominated by machines, and cultivate our skills and the spiritual—"

A chorus of whistles, catcalls, and boos shouted her down. "I've had all the fucking simple-life blisters I want or need!" someone shouted, and there was a roar of approval.

Cofflin kept his face impassive as he hammered for order. Inwardly he was grinning; Lisketter had a hard core of supporters, but the numbers had dropped off drastically. Imagining a world without internal combustion engines and electricity and actually living in one were two entirely different things.

"Let's keep it polite here. This is a Town Meeting, not a football game. Ms. Lisketter has a right to say what she believes whether anyone else likes it or not."

Lisketter was quivering, but the tears in her eyes were rage, not chagrin. "You're making exactly the same mistakes that people back home did, wrecking the earth and any chance of living in peace with each other!" she said. "Please, *please* don't be so blind! There aren't very many of us now, but if you start the same cycle all over again that won't matter. The real frontier isn't out there." She waved at the world beyond the darkened windows. "It's in ourselves. If we're not at peace with ourselves and the earth, what does it matter if we have material wealth?"

"Dane Sweet?"

The manager of the bicycle shop—nowadays he was more like assistant secretary for transportation—stood. "Pamela, you and I go back a long way. We agree on a lot of things. But can't you understand that we're not back home any more?"

"This isn't Kansas anymore, Toto," someone said.

Sweet waved them to silence and went on: "If you want to preserve the environment and the Native Americans, and I do too, you're not going to do it by making the people here want to lynch you. It's one thing to tell people who've got too much to cut back, but you may not have noticed we're not exactly living in the lap of postindustrial luxury here."

"Anything more to say, Ms. Lisketter? Then I suggest you sit down." She sat. "Joseph?"

Starbuck stood. The town clerk was as near to a minister of finance as they had. "And we're not doing as well as Mr. Macy thinks, either. We're living off our capital—off what we had before the Event. Yes, we're growing and catching our own food, but we're not building our own

houses, making our own clothing, or shoes, or even tools
for the most part—and what we are making, we're largely
making out of accumulated raw materials that were here
before the Event. Consider the effort needed to find and
smelt metals, for example. Or to find fiber and leather to
replace what we've used, or glass. What Dr. Arnstein said
is quite correct."

That brought a thoughtful silence. *He's got a point,* Cofflin mused. He pointed his gavel into the midst of the
crowd. "Professor?"

"We do have an opportunity to do things better,"
Arnstein said. "That doesn't mean sitting on our behinds
and finding infinite Mandelbrot sets in our navels. Let me
tell you, people have *never* lived in harmony with nature.
Goats and axes and wooden plows can ruin countries every
bit as surely as bulldozers and chemical plants; it just takes
a little longer. We've got three thousand years of knowledge to apply to a fresh world. Let's do it right this time."

There was a smattering of applause, growing louder and
then dying away. Cofflin saw another hand raised. Surprise
held him for a moment, and then he pointed the gavel.
Can't let Swindapa speak and can him, he thought.

"My hosts," Isketerol said, bowing in several directions.
His guttural English flowed, as fluent as a native speaker's
apart from the accent and an occasional choice of words.
"I, a poor foreigner, cannot advise you . . . except that if
you wish to trade, why deal with the poor and warlike
savages of the White Isle, the island you call Britain? Instead, send your wonderful ships to the Middle Sea, where
men dwell in cities obedient to law, not like bears in the
forests. In Tartessos, my home, or Mycenae rich in gold,
or splendid Egypt. Grateful for your many favors, I will be
ready to advise and guide in whatever small way I can. You
will find rich return, I promise you."

That is one smart son of a bitch, Cofflin thought. Yes, he
was a slave trader and probably a pirate when occasion
offered, but this was the thirteenth century before Christ—
you couldn't expect him to act any other way. He'd lived
up to every bargain he made with the islanders, that was
for sure. Nobody had any complaints about the way he'd
behaved since he arrived, either. *But that proposition has
its own risks.*

"I think Captain Alston has something to say to that," he said aloud.

Alston stood, her face the usual impassive mask she wore in public. "Once we're in regular contact with the more . . . advanced peoples of this era," she said, "they're going to be able to sail here; that's why we've been drilling our new militia. We have a military edge, but not a very large one, frankly. Consider the numbers, as well. And this island is a glittering prize, by local standards. If we wave that relative wealth in front of the locals who can come and make a try for it, I won't answer for the consequences. It's my opinion that we should limit our contact with the higher civilizations for the next few years at least. The British peoples of this era are no such threat."

That caused an uproar; Macy was on his feet demanding to know why they couldn't seal off the island from all outside contact.

"Because the ocean is a very big place," Alston replied. "And we have only one large ship to date. Buildin' others means we have fewer people growing food." She indicated Arnstein with a jerk of her chin. "It's the professor's point again. Everyone we have do *anything* but produce essentials means fewer essentials, unless we can get resources from elsewhere."

Cofflin tapped the gavel again. "We need trade," he said. "We need to trade somewhere where the locals won't be a menace to us. We could use allies, and extra hands, as well. Ms. Swindapa tells us, and our own experience in Britain bears out, that her people are basically peaceful—not saints, mind you—and they can produce most of what we need. Especially if we give them some help. That'll include some military help, but not much; more a matter of showing them how to do things."

Advisers and military aid, he thought with a wince. *Well, by God, we can do better than LBJ and McNamara. At least I hope so.* Aloud: "Ms. Swindapa."

The Fiernan girl rose again. "My people don't have a, a government," she said. "There is nobody who can order everyone to do things. But there are families and Spear Chosen who many will listen to. My family, the line of Kurlelo, is a family like that. We welcome peaceful traders, and we need strong friends. Please, be the friends we need."

Another hand shot up. Cofflin sighed and pointed the gavel. This was bad enough, and they were only discussing a hypothetical situation. Wait until they got the report about the Indians approaching Providence Base and offering to trade. *That* was going to send Lisketter and her crowd completely ballistic.

The core of the Nantucket Council stood and watched the new militia at practice.

"Big turnout," Jared Cofflin said, surprised. *Wouldn't have thought so many people would volunteer for more sweat,* he thought. Of course, with harvest still some time off and the fishing going so well, people weren't nearly as hard pressed as they had been in the spring. And this was a novelty.

Alston nodded, her armor rustling and clanking slightly as she moved. "It'll thin out when it sinks in how much work it is, I expect," she replied cynically.

"I'm surprised we have the time," Martha Cofflin said thoughtfully. "I assumed that without machinery, we'd be working every hour of the day and night."

Cofflin the fisherman-turned-policeman chuckled; so did Angelica Brand the farmer, and Marian Alston the farmer's daughter.

"I said something funny?" Martha inquired tartly.

"My daddy used to say that farming is two kinds of butt work," Alston said. "Bust your butt working fit to kill yourself, then sit on your butt 'cause there's nothing to do."

"Fishing's a lot like that, too," Cofflin added.

"Seasonal," Martha said. "So there's time for this."

The big sandy field held several hundred men and women. All the *Eagle*'s cadets and off-duty crew, of course, for whom it was compulsory, and nearly as many volunteers. The islanders present were a mixed bag, mostly younger; a good many were friends the cadets and crew had made in the months since the Event. There were enough crossbows for practice, and shields with foam rubber bound around their rims, spears with blunt cloth-bound tips, extra-weight wooden short swords. A few worked with *bokken*, wooden replicas of the *katana*. Nearly half the *Eagle*'s complement were in the new armor Leaton was turning out, getting accustomed to the weight and heat. Trainees attacked wooden posts and practiced simple formations.

Grunts, Rebel yells, and the thump and clatter of wood on wood and metal sounded across the dust raised by so many feet. The *Eagle*'s instructors were busy hammering home the basics of close-order drill. Cofflin watched with interest as a column of about thirty countermarched, each pair's spears crossing in an X as they turned. A little farther off two rows with crossbows faced a hastily-erected wooden wall backed by earth.

"Front rank!" the officer drilling them shouted. "Ready!" crossbows came to port-arms position, held across the chest. "Aim!" The weapons came up to their shoulders with a unified jerk. *"Fire!"*

WHUNNGGGG! The strings released in near-unison. "Reload! Second rank, *fire!"*

The first rank braced the butts of their weapons on their hips and pumped the levers built into the forestocks. The second rank took half a step forward and fired in their turn. By the time they stepped back, the first rank were clipping bolts into the firing grooves of their weapons.

"Think that'll do much good?" Cofflin asked.

"I think so," Alston said; she'd been looking at her watch, and gave a grunt of satisfaction. "It's what Maurice of Wassau originally developed drill for. Few of us can match"—she pointed eastward—"for individual ferocity and skill at arms just yet, but the Iraiina aren't much at coordination, which can be more important. From what I saw and can get out of our guests, battles are a series of individual brawls here."

Cofflin nodded. "They're having a lot of fun, too," he said. "Working off some energy."

Martha chuckled. "Human energy we seem to have enough of. Amateur theatricals, people giving lessons in the guitar and piano, quilting bees, glee clubs, learn-how-to-make-it groups, debating societies, mushroom-collecting circles . . ." She shook her head. "We're going to have to move the notice board out of the Athenaeum and put a few more in down by the Hub convenience store. Getting in the way, it's so crowded." She looked thoughtful. "Blackboards and chalk, perhaps?"

"No more mass media, it isn't surprising people've turned back to making their own pastimes. We've got a lot of Internet junkies going through withdrawal pains, as well," Dr. Coleman said. He smiled, a not altogether pleasant expression. "Not to mention real junkies. Suicides are down, though. I guess most of those inclined that way are gone." His smile turned rueful. "The rest of us are getting disgustingly healthy. Lots of exercise, low-fat diet, no cigarettes, and not much alcohol. Did you know that the average islander has lost ten pounds?"

"If you could sell it back up in the twentieth, you'd be set for life, Doctor," Cofflin said.

That brought a chuckle from the rest of them. The group began to split apart, only Cofflin and Martha accompanying Alston toward the circles where individuals sparred. *Alston looks quite natural in that stuff,* Cofflin thought. There was a sort of archaic handsomeness to her face above the enameled metal, and she swung along as if oblivious of the weight and the hot summer sun, which must make the inside under the padding like a solar oven. Her long sword was slung across her back in a special baldric tight-cinched to the armor, and it rattled slightly as she walked, clinking occasionally against the neck guard of her flared helmet.

He grinned mentally. In fact, he knew she still felt hideously self-conscious in the armor, even though she'd issued an order, backed by the Council, making it the equivalent of working and walking-out dress for Guard and militia members.

As they reached the chalk circles for individual sparring, Swindapa fell backward out of one, winded, armor clattering. She lay stunned by the impact for a moment, blond hair leaking out from under her helmet brim. The islander she'd been fighting advanced his practice spear and tapped her on the chest; then he looked up and saw Alston. He came to rigid attention, blanching a little under the flush of exercise.

"Sorry, ma'am, I, ah, got carried away, and—"

Alston frowned. "Middleton, you were doing what you're supposed to be doing. If you ever have to use that pigsticker, it'll be for real. And Ms. Swindapa wouldn't thank you fo' playin' patty-cake." She turned and hauled the blond Fiernan girl up with a forearm-to-forearm grip. "Here, let me show you."

She took the *bokken*, the oakwood practice *katana* that some of the advanced students were using rather than shield and short sword. In shape and weight it was exactly the same as the real weapon, although the aerodynamics were different, since the wood was thicker.

"Slow-time, Middleton. Here's what you did, 'dapa." She stood with the hilt at waist level and the point slanted up toward her opponent's eyes. "*Chudan no kame*, for starters."

The young man advanced, thrusting the spear with both hands. Alston brought the wooden sword up under the cloth-bound point, hands braced widely on the long hilt.

"So far, so good." The wooden shaft rose as it slid across the sword until the breastplates met with a *cling* sound. "Here's where you went wrong. Come on, Middleton, *push.*"

"You were tryin' to *stop* his impetus like a wall. Bad idea. If you fight, you'll be fighting men, and they'll likely be bigger and stronger, and weigh more. Don't try to oppose strength with strength."

"I was trying to get into a place . . . a *position* to cut strong," Swindapa said, a frown of concentration on her face.

"It isn't cutting strongly or weakly that's the point, 'dapa. '*One is totally involved with getting the opponent to die,*'" she quoted. "Watch. Middleton, we'll go through this again. Slow-time, please."

They set themselves. The spear came forward, and the sword rose to meet it. This time it circled from left to right, pushing the spear slightly aside and down. "Don't stop the thrust, redirect it." Her right foot skimmed forward. "Now turn yo' hips at a forty-five-degree angle. Turn the edge of the sword to face your opponent—it's just a motion of the wrists. You're inside his guard and he can't stop moving toward you, or not quickly enough. From here you can strike at the upper arms, at the throat, or at the face, snapping your hips into the movement for added force, then follow through."

Her *bokken* tapped the areas indicated. "Again."

"If you can't step aside, redirect the spear, not the man." She faced the thrust directly, snapping the *bokken* up from right to left.

"That puts you in position for a diagonal cut. His spear is over your left shoulder, and so is your blade. Let it fall back until the point is almost touching your back. Now *quickly,* elbows out, hands light on the hilt, you bring it down. At the same time, your legs go down, your arms come around as your hips pivot, elbows moving together, wrists clench, breathe out, and the blade strikes *so*." It tapped at the young man's right shoulder and slid down across his torso. "Drawing the cut."

And opening him like a can of sardines, Cofflin thought with a shudder. He'd seen men blown open by flying shards of steel, and a lot of accidents with heavy machinery. It didn't take much imagination to fit those memories to what he'd just watched.

Swindapa nodded. "But what if he has armor?" she asked. "Or a shield?"

"Good point. Then you redirect *here*—" she turned the blade back to its starting position and swung it higher, across throat level—"or down at the thighs, or you use his thrust to turn yourself three-quarters 'round." The circling motion of the sword pushed the spear aside, and Alston's feet landed in a cramped-looking position that moved her eighty degrees with a fluid speed he could see even in the slow-motion mime. "And that puts you in position to strike here, here, here." The sword tapped at the armpit, the back of the knee, stabbed toward the inner thigh and groin. "Again, use speed and precision against his weight."

Swindapa frowned. "What if he's just as fast and skilled, and still stronger and heavier?" she said.

Alston met her eyes. "Then you probably die," she said quietly. To the young man: "Full-speed, please."

The spear came punching forward. *Crack.* The *bokken* snapped up and met it with a sound like a gunshot. There was a whirling and a clang as Alston pivoted on her bent front leg, the knee half-collapsing as she went, her left leg coming around like a scythe. It struck the man behind his knees, and he flipped backward to land on his back. That left him looking up at Alston as she came down in a wide-footed straddle stance. The point of the *bokken* came down and stopped precisely over the hollow of his throat.

"Well, that's your lesson, Middleton," Alston said, smiling slightly. "Don't focus on the weapon. There are no dangerous weapons, only dangerous people. Fight the whole enemy." She gave him a hand up. "See you later, 'dapa." She tossed the wooden sword back to her.

"Does that work as well as it looks?" Cofflin asked as they walked away. "It *looks* as impressive as hell, but then so does Olympic fencing, and that's got damn-all to do with real fighting, I understand.''

"Well, that's the sixty-four-thousand-dollar question," Alston said. "I think so. The unarmed parts do work; I've used them in real-life situations a few times, back before the Event and here too.''

She reached over her shoulder and touched the hilt of the *katana*. "The Japanese were in their equivalent of the Middle Ages until one long lifetime ago, and men fought to the death with these almost within livin' memory. My *sensei* learned in a school that's been—would have been— in operation continuously in the same place since the year 1447, at a shrine to the Shinto sword god. It teaches *bu-jutsu*, the war arts, not the sport or spiritual-learning versions. So, chances are it'll work in practice.''

She held up crossed fingers. "Best we can do. I'd rather win by intimidation than fighting any day, but you have to calculate on the worst possible case.''

She turned her head slightly. "I wonder why Middleton looked like I was going to cut out his liver for a moment there, though?'' she added.

Cofflin coughed and looked away. Martha touched Alston's elbow and said gently: "Ah, Captain, there have been, well, certain rumors about you and Ms. Swindapa.''

"Oh.'' She paused for a moment. "He thought I was going to annihilate him for beating up on my girlfriend? Oh. Hell, and here I thought I'd kept everyone in the dark by avoiding the softball team and not leavin' old copies of *Deneuve* around.''

Her mouth quirked at his expression. "Sorry, in-joke.'' She shook her head. "What really annoys me is the idea that anyone would suppose I'd be unfair like that.''

"Umm—'' Cofflin began. He could see Alston's face take on a set calmness, like a mask carved from obsidian. By now he knew her well enough to realize what that meant: total determination. When she went on, it might have been a machine speaking.

"If you're asking, the rumors are wrong in particular— she's, ah, not suitable—but true in general. Yes, I'm gay. You might even use the dreaded l-word.'' The eyes met his, dark within dark, seemingly all pupil in the smoky whites. "Do you have a *problem* with that, Chief Cofflin?''

"Myself? Absolutely not,'' Cofflin said.

I think, he added to himself. You met the occasional queer in the Navy, of course, and while he had no objection in principle he didn't like the reality. On the other hand, those were men. Women just didn't bother him like that, which was illogical and probably unenlightened, but what the hell. . . . And Alston was simply too valuable to alienate, besides being damn likable in her chilly way. The thought of trying to handle this mess without her was enough to give him the cold willies.

"But some other people might, eh?" she said, relentless.

"If they do, that's *their* problem," Cofflin said. "I'm behind you. You're doing your goddam job, lady, and as long as you do I don't give a flying . . . curse whether you sleep with men, women, or sheep."

"Mostly by myself, actually, worse luck," Alston said, with a slow grin. She offered her hand. "Here's to the league of people who do their jobs, then." He took it in his, and Martha laid hers on top.

"Amen," she said.

"More?" Alston said politely, indicating the venison ragout and the single remaining new potato; they'd fallen on those pretty ravenously.

The cadets shook their heads. "Great, Captain," one of them said. "But I'm stuffed."

"Clear up, then, please," she said, turning and pulling a roll of mapping paper from a sideboard.

The three young men and two women made short work of cleaning the table. She'd made a regular thing of these off-duty meetings, to keep in touch with the cadets. Dining in on *Eagle* was a little too formal, considering the gap in rank, not to mention the cramped quarters. For that matter, cruises on the *Eagle* had been a small part of a cadet's education, just enough to familiarize them. The Academy at New London was a very long way away, now.

A whale-oil lamp in the center of the table gave a glow good enough for reading, quite passable if you made yourself forget what electric light was like.

"Take a look at this," Alston said, leaning over the table and unrolling the plans.

She weighted the corners down with saltshakers and candlesticks. The upperclassman cadets picked up their cups of sassafras tea and leaned over it.

"It's the *Bluenose*, isn't it, Captain?" one of them said, interested.

The plans showed a two-masted schooner with a long sleek hull curving up to a prow like the point of a laurel-leaf spearhead. The design breathed speed, but not the fragile swiftness of a racing yacht—there was hard work in every line of her.

"Not quite, though it's based on it," Alston said. She nodded to the ship model. "That's the *Bluenose*. This here—" she tapped the plans—"is a little smaller, two hundred tons displacement; she's shallower-draft, with a longer straight run below, and doesn't carry as much mast. Probably not quite so fast, but even better suited for inshore work. Look at it well, ladies and gentlemen, because you'll be officers on something like this in the not-too-distant future."

The cadets sat down slowly. Alston smiled at them. "I'm not deaf. Now that we've a little leisure to think, you're all afraid that you'll spend the rest of your lives hauling ropes and reefing sails on the *Eagle* . . . and you signed up at the Academy to be officer-trainees, not deckhands."

"Yes, some of us have been thinking about that, ma'am," one of the cadets said slowly. McAndrews, a big soft-spoken black kid from Memphis. "We didn't like to complain, though. Not your fault, after all."

"That's appreciated."

Another half-raised her hand. "Won't we be building more steamboats?"

"Certainly, for tugs, whale-catchers, 'longshore work generally. But it'll be a long time before we can make deep-sea steamers. For long-distance work we need ships that don't need fuel or machine shops and that can be repaired with local resources where they make landfall, at a pinch. The *Eagle*'s a fine open-ocean ship, but she wasn't built to haul cargo, and she's too deep in the keel for inshore work in this era, without made harbors.

"This"—she nodded her head at the drawings—"is just right. Wood-built, and we're not short of good timber and masts. Big enough to go anywhere on earth and haul a useful amount of cargo, fore-and-aft-rigged, nimble, and not requirin' a heavy crew. Eventually we'll have a dozen or more, in the carrying trade, exploring, swapping our manufactures for food and raw materials. Guarding the is-

land, too, and whatever settlements we make elsewhere.
I've talked it over with the chief, and we'll be putting a
proposal to start building to the Town Meeting, fairly soon.
There's enough seasoned timber on hand now."

Alston saw enthusiasm kindle. "Since we're stuck here,
it's better to think of it as an opportunity, not exile."

"Sort of like Francis Drake and those guys, ma'am?" one
of the cadets asked.

"Mmmm, not quite, I hope. But lots of exploration, yes."

The conversation broke up some time later. "Stay for a
moment, McAndrews," she said. "You had something you
wanted to say?" She leaned back, watching the young man
twist a little. "I won't bite y'head off for speaking your
mind."

"It's . . . we're going back to England, right, ma'am?"
She nodded.

"What I was wondering was, why England, ma'am?"

"Trade," she said. "We need to develop a secure base
for it."

"Yes, ma'am, but why *England?*"

"Oh," Alston said. "Ah, I see what you're driving at.
You'd rather we try, say, Africa?"

"Yes, ma'am!" McAndrews beamed.

"You're thinking that instead of giving the buckra a leg
up, we should sail to Africa and get in contact with the
great kingdoms and empires there? Ghana, Mali, Dahomey,
the Ashante? And with our technology, they'll grow to
dominate the world?"

"Yes *ma'am!*"

Alston sighed. She reached up and removed an invisible
hat. "All right, Cadet, for just this once I'm going to take
off my captain's cap and speak to you as sister to brother."
She leaned forward. "You ever heard the saying 'Free your
head and your ass will follow'?" He nodded.

She went on: "Well, I'm afraid your head's gotten stuffed
with something that'd fit in better down below, boy. None
of those empires and kingdoms exist now, and they won't
for a long long time. Thousands of years. South of the
deserts it's mostly still hunters, with a few farming villages
in the grasslands. Sail to West Africa and all you'll find is
jungle and pygmies. And maybe malaria and yellow fever."

McAndrews's face fell. Alston sighed internally. *I won't
ask him who he thinks* sold *our ancestors to the white slav-*

ers, she thought. That had been one of her more disillusioning personal discoveries. At least, the West African kings and merchant princes were the ones who'd sold *her* personal ancestors, seeing as she was black as tar. McAndrews was a sort of rye-bread-toast color; more than a few buckra in his own personal woodpile. *Let him down easy. He's probably stuffed with shit about ancient Tanzanian jets and the black Cleopatra and suchlike.*

"North Africa is mostly filled with people who look like Isketerol, only they're savages," Alston went on. "The only place in Africa that isn't full of savages is Egypt." At his look, she continued: "Have you ever *been* to Egypt, Cadet?"

"No, ma'am."

"I have. Up in the twentieth, the Egyptian slang for a black person is *abdeed,* which means slave, in case you hadn't guessed. Look, when Isketerol first saw me, he thought I was a Medjay. Ever hear of them?" He shook his head. "Neither had I. They're mercenary soldiers from Nubia at Pharaoh's court. The only other black folk there are black slaves."

At his look of shock, she pushed on ruthlessly: "Who do you think *started* the slave trade, Cadet? You go to Egypt as of 1250 B.C., you're just another nigger barbarian, as far as they're concerned, and so am I. Of course, they'd consider Isketerol a nigger too, or Lieutenant Hendriksson. *Anyone* who isn't an Egyptian is a nigger to them."

"I . . . suppose I see," he said after a long minute's thought.

"Don't take it so hard, Cadet," she said kindly. "If things work out well here, there'll never be a Middle Passage. And we've got plenty of *real* heroes. Frederick Douglass or Sojourner Truth is worth a dozen imaginary African princes any day."

He frowned. "Then what's going to happen to us, here, ma'am? I mean, as a people."

The island had less than two hundred black residents, and fewer still of other minorities; she'd checked the figures, discreetly. The population was 96 percent white. She'd always regarded white people as sort of like the weather; they were *there,* sometimes pleasant, often not, and you had to deal with them as best you could. Here-and-now they were pretty well the whole damn climate, and that was just that, whether she liked it or not.

Alston shrugged. "What happens when you squeeze a drop of ink into a glass of milk and shake, Cadet? It mixes in and pretty soon it's gone." Alston spread her hands. "From now on, you'd do best to think of this island as home and everyone who lives here as your people. We really don't have much choice."

Seahaven Engineering was getting more crowded by the day, even though Martins and his forge had been moved out to their own quarters, and the sound of metal on metal was deafening.

Ronald Leaton and Cofflin stood in one corner, looking at the latest development, and occasionally moving aside as someone went through with a handcart of materials or parts. Sweat ran down their faces; the sun was bad enough, beating down on the sheet-metal roof, and the steam engines turning shafts and pumping compressors added to the heat and noise. The machine shop stank of hot metal, hot whale oil, sweat, and smoke. The big doors to the water were open, giving an occasional draft of welcome cool air, and you could see smudges of black woodsmoke drifting out over the smaragdine brightness of the harbor. Sails speckled it, and the ocean beyond; closer too a Guard officer was overseeing the loading of a large handcart, yelling out his checklist to the Seahaven clerk:

"Breastplates, twenty-five, size A1!"

"Check!"

"Helmets, twenty-five, size A1!"

"Check!"

Cofflin shook his head. *Busy as bees,* he thought. There was just so much to *do*, before winter set in—and never enough time or hands.

"It's a blow-drier for fish," Leaton explained, kicking the frame and handing over a sample. "Desiccator, if you want to get technical. I figure it'll cut down the spoilage rate to nearly nothing."

Cofflin nodded, turning the slab of dusty-white, rock-hard cod in his hands and looking at the wood-and-iron . . . *thingumabob,* he decided. The rack for the fish wasn't much different from the improvised ones they'd been using, looking a little like a giant bedstead, except that it had a mesh cover over the top to keep the flies off . . . and they'd lost far more cod than he liked to think about to maggots.

Off to one side of it was a contraption of sheet metal and wood, with a flat covered steel pan, a round metal chimney, and a shaft running down from that into a wooden box that underlay one edge of the drying rack. Leaton took pieces off the sides of each.

"See, you light the fire in the pan here—ordinary wood fire, and there's this grating underneath for the ashes."

Cofflin nodded solemnly. Wood ash was prime fertilizer, and it had half a dozen other major uses—you needed it to make soap, for instance, which wasn't something he'd suspected before. There was a Town ordinance now that everyone had to keep ashes for collection.

"Then some of the hot air goes up the chimney and turns this fan. That turns this metal shaft running down here, which turns this wooden fan, and that blows more of the hot dry air . . ."

A ton of fish sounded like a lot, until you remembered how much seventy-two hundred people ate in a day. Every pound counted, and this would save a lot of spoilage.

"Good work," he said sincerely. "How many, how fast, and what do you need?"

"Well, we can make up the metal parts here. Thornton's can do the carpentry"—another new industry, working with the hand and simple power tools Seahaven turned out, and Macy's shipments of timber from the mainland—"and I thought we'd take over another boathouse or something for the assembly work. It gets in the way here."

"Say another forty, maybe sixty people all up," Cofflin said. "Damn, we're running short—particularly of people who know which end of a hammer to pick up."

"It'll save in the long run," Leaton said earnestly. "You don't need nearly so many watching the drying racks."

"A lot of those are kids," Cofflin mused. "But yeah, I think so. Okay, go for it."

"And you can use it to make jerky, any kind, and dried sausage as well, or dry vegetables for keeping—"

"Ayup. You've struck oil, Ron, you can stop drilling," Cofflin said dryly.

The problem with being the one who can bind or loose is that everyone keeps trying to convince *you of things,* he thought wryly.

"Ah . . . thanks, Chief."

"Thank *you*, Ron. What's next?"

"Well, the barrel-stave machine is working now, and the one for the hoops." Cofflin grunted satisfaction; barrels for storage were a big bottleneck. "And we've got something here that'll make us all a lot more comfortable," the engineer went on.

He led Cofflin over to where two more samples rested against the wall. One was a simple steel box with a hinged front door and a section of sheet-metal piping coming out the back.

"Heating stove," Leaton said, taking a rag out of the back pocket of his overalls and wiping his hands—futile, since grease and dirt were ground into the knuckles. "An outer box, an inner box, the intervals filled with sand—retains heat, the way thick cast iron would if we could cast iron, which we can't yet—ashpan, grate, door for feeding wood, and an adjustable flue. It's about airtight, and the thermal efficiency is seven, eight times the best fireplace. You just stick it *in* a fireplace, and the pipe here goes up the chimney a bit."

"Excellent," Cofflin said. They'd all been chilly in the tag end of early spring. "We can start on these later in the year, though—after harvest."

Leaton nodded. "And there's this." The other stove was much larger, standing on legs. The top held what looked like solid-metal equivalents of heating elements on a normal stove, and there was a big oval tank welded to one side.

"Wood-fired cooking stove," he went on proudly. "We modeled it on the old style, with some improvements. That thing on the side is a hot-water tank—the exhaust flue goes right through it."

"Oh, *that's* going to be popular!" Cofflin said.

Not least with those who had to do dishes. People who couldn't do anything else had taken to filling in with housework, for those who were otherwise occupied. It let them earn Town chits of their own, and freed up the able-bodied for essential tasks.

"Wait a minute—you should put in a heating tray at the back. That done, you can put those into production right away, say twenty a week to start with?" he said.

"Can do, but I'll need more assembly space. They bolt together, and the parts are standardized."

"I'll get you the people, at least until the harvest," Cofflin said. "The Council will go along with it. Speaking of which, is the reaper working yet?"

"Ah—" Leaton's eyes shifted. "Well, we're still getting some of the bugs out, Chief."

"Goddammit, Ron, we were counting on that. . . ."

"God," Ian Arnstein wheezed, straightening up and rubbing at his back. "Now I know what 'stoop labor' really means."

Everyone had toughened up considerably since the spring, but reaping grain with a sickle and bagging hook evidently took muscles and degrees of flexibility they'd never called on before. Swindapa was proof positive, two people down from him in the row. She moved with an economical rhythm: stoop with leg advanced, sweep the wooden hook with the left hand to gather in a swatch of grain, bring the sickle up sharply head-high and slice downward and back, tip the hook to spill the cut rye in a neat row, step forward, stoop . . . despite the T-shirt and cutoff jeans, moving like that she didn't look at *all* American. She was well ahead of Alston and Doreen, and stopped occasionally to let them catch up, putting a better edge on her sickle now and then with a pull-through sharpener. Others were doing the same, punctuated with the odd yelp or curse as someone cut a hand. Ian had already, twice, and sweat stung like fire as it ran into the superficial gashes.

The rye stretched before him, waving in the sun with an evil brown-gold beauty, starred here and there with wildflowers; he'd have admired those more if he hadn't learned by painful, personal experience how much harder weeds made the work. It was a hot August day, sunny except for some high haze and a few puffy white clouds. The field was fairly large, about twenty acres, part of Brand Farms' winter cover crop let ripen. A hundred islanders were advancing across it in a staggered row, sickles flashing. As many more followed behind, gathering the ragged rows of grain into sheaves and tying them with a twist of straw. There was a buzz of crickets in the air, and a dusty smell of earth, cut stems, and sweat, mingled with the wilder scent of the weeds cut along with the stalks. According to the books they ought to be able to reap a third of an acre or so per day per worker. It was an hour past noon, and fairly obviously they'd be lucky to do a quarter of that.

If we had a hundred Swindapas *cutting this stuff, maybe,* Ian thought, bending again with a groan. A bell rang behind him, and he felt like weeping with relief. *The second shift.*

They were rotating people through the harvesting gangs, so as many as possible would have experience before the much larger fields of spring-planted grain came ripe. *A thousand acres of barley alone, Christ on a* crutch, *I'll never make it.* He looked at the sky again. When the time came, they'd have to go all-out. You couldn't count on the weather here, and rain at the wrong time could be a disaster—literally a disaster; it would mean the difference between eating well and going hungry. With the planting so late it would be touch and go, first to harvest, and then to get all the grain under cover.

Then we get to pull the flax and dig up the potatoes. And harvest and shuck the corn. And cut the buckwheat. And cut the last hay and turn it and dig the Jerusalem artichokes and harvest the sunflowers and . . . Oh, joy, oh, my aching back.

"And I thought 'bust your ass' was a metaphor," he said.

"Come and get it!" the cook at the wagon over by the pines shouted.

"About time," Doreen said.

She was wearing a T-shirt around her head like a headdress, with strands of her long black hair escaping, and a bikini top and shorts. Her skin was tanned to a deep olive brown, flesh firmed up and trimmed down and turned to something more like the opulent shape of a Levantine fertility goddess; even the sweat on neck and breasts and the bits of straw stuck in it merely completed the picture. At the moment he was too tired to really appreciate the sight, except in an abstract way. He trudged over to the wagon and the blessed shade of the trees, dropping his sickle and hook into the racks. Plastic trash barrels full of water stood there. He drank four mugfuls one after the other, almost shuddering with ecstasy as the cool water cut through the gummy saliva and dust in his mouth and throat. Then he poured more over his head; it felt icy as it cut runnels through the sweat. The towel he used to wipe his face and hands was limp and damp, but afterward he felt halfway human—as if he'd been dead for days, rather than months. Human enough that the smell of the stew penetrated and set his stomach rumbling like a wolf trying to claw its way out.

"Surf 'n' Swine, folks! Come and get it!" the cook said again. "Surf 'n' Swine! Come and get it!"

He got in line and took a big red plastic bowl of thick brown pork and lobster stew. The helper added half a loaf of rough dark bread, and Ian filled his mug again. The shade beneath the stubby pines where he and Doreen spread their blanket was infinitely welcome, but he could feel his muscles stiffen further as they cooled. He sank down with a groan.

"The chief is carrying this egalitarianism to extremes," he grumbled. "I notice *he's* not here."

"He's out harpooning bluefin tuna," Alston said from a few feet farther along the line of shade. "Those things go up to a ton weight; it's hard, dangerous work." She raised herself on one elbow; *she* wasn't looking particularly tired, although the singlet was plastered to her torso with sweat.

But then, she's an athlete and younger than I am, he thought.

"I know, I know, I'm being unfair," Ian said ruefully. "I'm also being a middle-aged man with blisters and a crick in my back."

"Easy work," Swindapa said, laying down her food and stretching on tiptoe with her fingers pointed at the sky.

Woof, woof, Ian thought. Even gaunt and terrified, the Fiernan had been pretty. Filled out, glowing with health and youth, tanned a light toast-brown that made even more vivid her blue eyes and the sun-bleached hair falling down her bare back . . . He looked back at his wife. *Damn, the view is good here all 'round.* Then: *I must be recovering.* He looked down at himself; he'd never been anything but lanky, but the middle-aged pot he'd added had about vanished. He was fitter than he'd been. He just wished it didn't hurt so much.

"Not what I'd call easy," he said.

"Try doing it with a wooden sickle with flint blades, Ian, or even a bronze one," Swindapa said. She frowned when he moved and then winced. "Lie down on your front."

Curious, he obeyed. The blond woman walked over and knelt beside him. "You Eagle People do some wonderful

things, but you aren't much as farmers," she said, beginning
to knead along his spine with strong skilled fingers. She
sang under her breath in her own language as she worked,
timing the motions of her hands to the slow chant.

He gave a small whimper of mixed pain and pleasure.
"We had machines to do this sort of thing," he said. "With
any luck, we will again—next year."

Leaton's attempt at a horse-drawn reaping machine had
been a spectacular failure, jamming itself every second step.
He swore that he could perfect it now that he had fields to
test adjustments on, but the crop wouldn't wait. Cradle
scythes would have been more efficient than the sickles
and easier to make than the McCormick-style reaper, but
it turned out that they required both unusual strength and
a lot of practice to use. They'd have to solve the grain
problem this first year by simple brute force and massive
ignorance, throwing every pair of hands not catching fish
into the fields for a brace of weeks. At least the *threshing*
machine looked like it would work, so they wouldn't have
to spend the winter beating this stuff with flails in the intervals between digging potatoes.

Swindapa finished the massage on the muscles of his
neck, then drummed the heels of her hands down from the
nape of his neck to the base of his spine. The knots loosened, and he gave a groaning sigh of relief. She moved
over to Doreen and began to repeat the process; Ian sat
up and spooned down the stew. He was beginning to understand why farmers usually ate their main meal at midday;
it seemed like a *long* time since breakfast. A few dozen
feet away another bunch of resting harvesters was singing
to a flute and guitar:

> Corn ricks and barley sheaves—
> And garlands of holly;
> No, I'll ne're forget the nights I spent
> Among the sheaves, with Mollie. . . .

He wasn't surprised at the plaintive-cheerful Old English
tune. Nantucket was just the sort of place for acoustic-
guitar folkie enthusiasts who drank home-brewed beer and
did Morris dancing.

Come gather golden honey
Come reap the tender corn;
And with me lay in new-mown hay
Before the winter's bourne. . . .

It was the fact that they had the energy to *sing* that astonished him.

He mopped the bowl with a heel of the bread, and belched with something approaching contentment.

Swindapa shook out her hands and moved back to Alston's blanket. "You next, Captain," she said cheerfully.

There was a moment's silence; Ian looked over at the sudden tension in the air. After a long instant Alston nodded and laid her head face-down in her folded arms. Swindapa moved beside her and crooned the same minor-key chant under her breath; she was smiling as she began to work, a slow dreamy expression.

"No rest for the wicked," he said to the air, rising and helping Doreen fold the blanket. As they walked toward their bicycles he inclined his head slightly back and raised an eyebrow.

"No, I don't think so," Doreen said. "The captain has a . . . highly developed sense of scruples. Almost as hyperthyroid as her sense of duty."

They picked up their cycles and began walking them down the dirt road out toward the pavement. Nantucket had had a system of bicycle trails before the Event, but the whole road system belonged to it now. The thickets along the path were mostly uncleared, and they had a wild sweet smell of feral roses. The blossoms starred the green undergrowth with red, with a few clusters of blushing-pink phlox for contrast. The main road had a narrow strip of brush and trees along it, and on the far side of that was a broad field of flax already eight feet tall, its blue flowers only a memory. Ian looked at it and winced in prospect. You harvested flax by pulling it up by the roots.

"Positively superhuman self-control," Ian said dryly. "And Swindapa has a powerful crush."

Doreen frowned. "I wouldn't exactly put it that way. She's not a kid, you know, not by the standards of her own culture."

Ian shrugged. "I don't want to let this sweat dry," he said, changing the subject. He liked them both as well, they were good people, but there were certain things that individuals just had to work out for themselves.

"Smith's?" she said.

"How about Quigley's?" he asked.

"You're not as tired as you looked," Doreen laughed. Quigley's was a new place, giving Smith fierce competition; it had individual cubicles for soaking after you scrubbed down.

"Let's see when we get there," he grinned.

They reached the pavement and swung into the seats of their cycles. *I may not have the captain's nobility of character,* he thought, looking at Doreen's hair flying in the wind. *On the other hand, my life's a good deal less complicated, and there's something to be said for that.*

CHAPTER TWELVE

August–October, Year 1 A.E.

"**S**he's a fine ship," Isketerol said. "What does this name mean, *Yare*?"

William Walker thought. He'd heard the word in a movie once . . . yeah, HBO Classics. The one with Katharine Hepburn? *What a fox*, he thought irrelevantly, then concentrated. "Yare means . . . fit, ready, eager," he said.

"Ah, a good name for a ship!"

The yacht had about a hundred feet at the waterline, two-masted and flush-decked except for a low cabin directly ahead of the wheel and binnacle, with a burden of a hundred and ten tons. Not as fast as the *Eagle*, of course, Walker acknowledged to himself. Twelve knots at most, given optimum winds; she was a topsail schooner, fore-and-aft-rigged except for two square sails at the top of the foremast. On the other hand she could go three or four points closer to the eye when tacking upwind, and she drew only six feet to the big windjammer's seventeen. That was why she was scheduled to go along on the next voyage to Europe, for scouting and inshore work. Plus she was wooden-built, thirty years old but still as sound as the day when the boatyard in Nova Scotia had sent her down the ways. Injury to her hull need not be an irreparable disaster, with tools and carpenters along.

The deck was broken by a low coaming, its cover aside for the present. Hammering and sawing noises came from within, where carpenters were installing a proper hold. The cargo for it waited on the dockside where the ship was moored, under an improvised loading crane also under construction. There were ingots of pig iron from the *Eagle*'s ballast, barrels of salt fish and meat, barrels of hardtack, and others to hold extra water. A complete set of blacksmith's tools and forge-furnishings, including Martin's best homemade anvils, and bar stock for it. Drills, planes, augers, axes, sledges, kegs of nails, two-man saws. A small lathe, and a set of measuring gauges run up on Leaton's Swiss instrument-making machine; knocked-down metal-work for a sawmill and gristmill. Books, most of them bound photocopies, carefully wrapped in multiple layers of green plastic garbage bag to make them thoroughly water-proof; books on shipbuilding, metalsmithing, agriculture and mining. Trade goods, useful and ornamental, rounding out the heavier load the *Eagle* would be carrying.

Couldn't have done it better myself, Walker thought. Of course, he *had* done much of it himself. With a crew of fifty and the cadets, *Eagle* was grossly overmanned for routine work; Alston had them all working half a dozen projects ashore as well, herself more than any. Getting the schooner ready was his job. He'd impressed the captain with his zeal and perfect discipline, but it was Hendriksson who was slated to command the *Yare.* Alston still wanted him close under her eye.

"Bitch," he muttered to himself.

But a *smart* bitch—she didn't miss much. He was still kicking himself for blurting out his half-formed dreams that first night after the Event. Granted he'd been dazed and disoriented, everyone had, but it had still been a stupid thing to do. *Hmm. Victor would like the* Yare *too . . . could I recruit him over that?* No, probably not. The Cuban-American lieutenant was too much of a straight arrow.

"Come on," he said to Isketerol.

Careful, careful, be *very* careful. He hated Captain Alston, but he respected her brains and courage thoroughly. He'd have been more than ready to follow her on an expedition such as the one he planned . . . but she'd never do that. *She'll stick with shepherding these sheep on this damned island.*

They walked up the gangplank onto the ship, dodging men and women with tools and materials for the refit, and walked back to the little fantail behind the wheel. There was an awning stretched over it like a tent with the miz-zensail boom as a ridgepole, and a couple of chairs. The day was hot and clear, with little trace of yesterday's fog; the breeze off the harbor smelled of fish and salt and tar. Gulls went noisily overhead, their harsh cries thick in the

air. A big load of barrel staves and planks sat on the wharf
not far from him, just in from Providence Base, adding the
vanilla tang of fresh-cut oak to the mixture; beside it were
oozing casks of pitch and turpentine from Cape Cod. A
chattering party of junior high students were sitting around
mending twine nets. Hammering and the hiss of the last
cutting torches sounded from the ferry's upperworks as
teams labored to disassemble it from the top down; carts
were going back and forth with loads of steel plate, beam,
and girder as the work went on. Other working parties
were ripping the air-conditioning and partitions out of
Eagle, undoing her last refit in '79.

Isketerol sat and accepted a bottle of beer from the
cooler; he went on in the Mycenaean Greek that Walker
now spoke well, since Iraiina lacked the concepts and vocabulary for much of what they had to discuss.

"I have confirmed what you told me," Isketerol said.
"They plot to keep me here, always among strangers, never
to return to my home, fearing what I might do with the
knowledge I've gained." He bared his teeth. "By Arucuttag
of the Sea, they'll regret that."

"So they will," Walker agreed.

Actually they haven't decided *to screw you over, good
buddy, they're just* thinking *about it,* he mused. In Alston's
position he would have put Isketerol over the side with a
stone tied to his ankles as soon as he'd told all he knew,
but Alston was squeamish, to a point. *Only to a point.
Don't forget that.* Underestimating your opposition was stupid, and stupidity was the only real sin he recognized.

"We can help each other, then," Walker said. "You need
a friend who will guard your back, and so do I." Solemnly,
they clasped hands. "Now, tell me more of the lands of
Mycenae. How would they welcome a stranger with powerful gifts?"

"No, I don't think you should seek out the Achaean lords
right away," the Tartessian said thoughtfully. "They're too
hard and greedy, and not very forethoughtful, most of
them. . . . But they hire many mercenaries from the barbarian lands."

Walker sipped at the beer. It was too sweet without the
hops, but otherwise not bad; only middling cold, though.
There were plans for ice pits to store frozen lake ice over

the summer; that could probably be done in the Aegean, too.

Greece looks like the best bet. The Hittite Empire was too big and too tightly centralized, a god-king autocracy. He'd learned Troy was a prosperous city-state that controlled the approaches to the Black Sea; but he'd have to learn yet another language to operate there. Greece, now—Greece sounded a lot like Renaissance Italy, or the more turbulent medieval European countries, say the Holy Roman Empire. He grinned like a wolf. According to the reference books, in about fifty years or so the whole Aegean basin was due to go under in a mad-dog scramble of internal warfare and barbarian invasions, with refugees and savages squatting in the ruins, a Dark Age. In other words, a perfect situation for an able, realistic man like himself—provided he had an edge, so that he could establish himself among the locals and work up to a position of strength gradually.

William Walker, King of Men, he thought. *Has a nice ring to it.* It was even altruistic, in a way. These goons were going to wreck their own civilization. He'd be doing them a favor—and they'd return the favor to him, and his children after him.

Provided he had an edge. . . . Leaton was already working on a musket, and anyone who could cast a bronze statue could make cannon. Sulfur was probably available, and there were black-powder enthusiasts on the island who knew the whole technique of making gunpowder; he'd drop in on them and pump them for tips. But for all that he'd need a secure base for a while, and preferably more men, as well, before he showed up in the Mediterranean. Isketerol needed a sweetener too.

"The question is, where to get a strong band of men?" Walker said. "I can't recruit more than a few here. Someone would talk, no matter how careful I was."

"There is the White Isle," Isketerol pointed out. "And the lands around it. Of course, for that you would require a ship, and then passage from the White Isle to the Middle Sea."

Passage for a couple of hundred, the American thought. *The* Yare's *useful, but with good carpenters and some time I could reproduce her. . . .*

"How would you like this ship for your own?" Walker said.

The Tartessian raised the beer bottle to his lips and looked out over the blue horizon. "Tell me more, my friend," he said.

Nantucket was never hot for long. Fog had rolled in and filled the streets as the sun fell; the air was cool, cool enough that the small blaze she'd kindled in the bedroom fireplace was pleasant, even on a summer's night.

Alston sipped at her bourbon-and-water and opened the first page of *Master and Commander,* ready for another run-through of the whole set. Luckily she'd had most of her O'Brian collection on board *Eagle* during the Event, and she'd been able to replace the others here. There'd never be any more, of course, but she'd reluctantly come to the conclusion that *The Commodore* was the natural end of the series anyway. The big house was very quiet, although an occasional voice came through the open window, and once the slow ringing clop of shod hooves on stone. A grandfather clock ticked the evening away downstairs. She smiled and glanced around the big room. You could get used to this sort of thing, although she liked her cabin on the *Eagle* well enough, and the lack of running water ashore was a surprisingly hard adjustment. The books and ship plans on the walls, those were hers, and the armor on its stand in a corner with the swords beneath, and the squared-away neatness. It smelled of wax, the nutty-scented lamp oil, metal polish, and flowers.

"Not in the mood," she murmured after a while, setting down the novel.

In fact, I'm feeling restless, bitchy, and itchy-skinned. She'd been having a hard time suppressing the impulse to bark at people, which would be fatal. A commander was the last person on earth who could afford to lose her temper. If she hadn't known for a fact her period was two weeks off, she'd have put it down to PMS.

"Well . . ."

She picked up another volume; her favorite poet, something she'd stumbled across in a little out-of-the way used-book store in Boston once, many years ago. She'd opened it in idle curiosity, and fallen in love at once; now she whispered aloud, hardly needing to read:

High on the bridge of Heaven whose Eastern bars
Exclude the interchange of Night and Day,
Robed with faint seas and crowned with quiet stars
All great Gods dwell to whom men prayed or pray.
No winter chills, no fear or fever mars
Their grand and timeless hours of pomp and play;
Some drive about the Rim wind-golden cars
Or, shouting, laugh Eternity away.
   The daughers of their pride,
   Moon-pale, blue-water-eyed,
Their flame-white bodies pearled with falling spray,
   Send all their bright hair streaming
   Down where the worlds lie gleaming,
And draw their mighty lovers close and say:
   "Come over by the stream: one hears
The speech of Nations broken in the chant of Spheres."

"Damn, can't escape the blue-water-eyed daughters," she
said. "Ah well." An immense and not unpleasant sadness
filled her, like the soft silvery fog creeping through the
streets outside. She went on:

Between the pedestals of Night and Morning,
Between red death and radiant Desire
With not one sound of triumph or of warning
Stands the great sentry on the Bridge of Fire.
O transient soul, thy thought with dreams adorning,
Cast down the laurel, and unstring the lyre:
The wheels of Time are turning, turning, turning,
The slow stream channels deep, and doth not tire
   Gods on their Bridge above
   Whispering lies and love
Shall mock your passage down the sunless river
   Which, rolling all its streams,
   Shall take you, king of dreams,
—Unthroned and unapproachable for ever—
   To where the kings who dreamed of old
Whiten in habitations monumental cold.

"Seize the day, in other words," she told herself. Nobody
else was here tonight; Rapczewicz was on board *Eagle*, the
other officers who'd roomed here temporarily had moved

into the two buildings next door, and Swindapa was over at Smith's Baths—

"I'm back," she called, from the entrance hall below. Alston heard the door click shut, and feet bound up the staircase and down the hall. "Foggy out tonight."

"Hello, 'dapa. So you are, so it is."

The Fiernan was wearing a knee-length T-shirt and plastic sandals, with her hair loose and damp around her shoulders, the yellow of it darkened by the water. She came in and sat cross-legged by the fire, holding her hands out to either side with the hair draped over them to dry. The cerulean-blue eyes looked up at her, vivid by contrast with the summer tan, warm and full of affection. *And here I thought Whitney Houston was the very definition of hot stuff,* she thought. *May have to revise that.* Marian Alston closed her eyes for a second and sighed, then tried to concentrate on the book again, thumbing through the pages at random:

> We that were friends tonight have found
> A fear, a secret and a shame:
> I am on fire with that soft sound
> You make, in uttering my name . . .

It seemed even the poet had turned against her tonight, she decided ruefully. *Well, it isn't the first case of unrequited love you've blundered into, woman,* she thought, scolding herself. Uusually she had better sense, but there was no way to get *away* on the island; in retrospect it'd probably been a mistake to have Swindapa living here, but she'd been much more fragile back then and needed a familiar, trusted face around. Alston recognized the symptoms in herself with mournful accuracy, although not until they'd been stealing up on her for a while. That combination of overwhelming tenderness and lust . . .

"I talked to Cindy Ganger at the baths," Swindapa said after a while, smiling. "She asked me if I was your girlfriend."

Alston choked, spraying bourbon across the page. Swindapa jumped up in alarm and pounded her helpfully on the back, then sat down beside her on the couch.

"Are you all right?" she asked, a little frown of worry between her brows.

"Yes. Just, mmm, surprised," Alston said. *And my si-nuses have diluted bourbon in them, goddammit.* She used a handkerchief to mop the page and blow her nose, which gave her a moment to collect her thoughts. *God damn all rumormongers.*

When she looked up, Swindapa had an arm draped over the back of the blue Directoire sofa and one leg hooked up under the other. She was still smiling. "I don't really understand you Eagle People," she said after a moment. "I don't know how to . . . hear what you're saying when you're not speaking, not really well. So I make mistakes like that."

"Body language?" Alston said, her mouth a little dry. She took another sip of the whiskey. Swindapa picked the glass out of her hand and sipped herself before returning it.

"Yes, that's a good way to say it—body language." The smile lessened. "I'd like to be your girlfriend, you know. But you move away when I touch you, even though I think you like me. Back home it's bad manners to come right out and ask someone older than you—you have to wait for them to ask you when you show you want them to. I keep showing you, and you never ask!"

"Ah . . ." *Oh, hell, what can you say to that?* " 'Dapa, that's very flattering, but it's impossible."

"Don't you like me?" Swindapa asked, her eyes going wide and beginning to fill. "I thought you were getting to like me, not just feel sorry for me."

Oh, hell *and damnation.* "Of course I like you. I like you a great deal. But you're too young, and you're my . . . guest."

"I know you want me. I can tell that."

Alston's tongue locked on a denial. She hated lying, par-ticularly to friends. The necessity of doing so in the service had rasped her soul.

Swindapa frowned. "I'm not a child," she said angrily. "I wish you wouldn't act as if I was. I've got the Spear Mark; lots of girls my age back in the White Isle have babies and their own hearths. Do you Eagle People have some rule against sleeping with people who are your guests?"

"No, we don't, not exactly," Alston said. *Christ, I must have been a* monster *in a past life to deserve this.*

"Is it because I'm ugly, too pale, not beautiful like you?"

"*Christ* no."

Swindapa's voice took on a note of exasperation. "Then *why?*"

Alston opened her mouth to reply, then closed it. It was true; Swindapa was young, but not a child, not in the way an American her age would be. She wasn't someone under Alston's command, either, nor a dependent. What reasons did that leave? *Sheer cowardice,* she thought, and leaned forward. *Fear of rejection. Fear of public opinion. Rationalizations.* Their lips met. *This may be just the worst thing I could do, but the hell with it.*

Minutes later she sighed breathlessly into the fine-spun blond hair. Deer Dancer certainly didn't need any instruction on kissing. "I've wanted to do that for some time now."

"Me too." Softly. "I was afraid I never could, after the Iraiina. But I can." They kissed again.

Alston felt a cold knot untie itself in her chest, then travel down from neck to spine as the warm closeness dissolved doubt and tension. After a moment the hug turned into a moving embrace. The T-shirt floated to the floor. She gave a sigh of wonder as her hands glided over the Fiernan's back and stomach and moved up to cup her breasts. Swindapa wiggled and gave a little chuckle of delight, arching into the caress. Her hands began undoing the buttons of Alston's uniform tunic. After a moment:

"How do you take this off?"

No bras in the Bronze Age. "The catch is at the back." Fingers touched her. "Does that feel nice?"

"Oh, yes." *Any nicer and I may faint.*

"Stand up for a second, I can't get at this buckle."

Well . . . Alston stood, grinning. *No bashfulness problem.*

"Oh, good! I *wondered* if your hair was lovely and . . . what's your word . . . nappy down here too."

I never did like bashful types, anyway, Alston thought, dizzy. "Come *here,* girl."

They lay on the bed, wrapping arms and legs around each other, kissing and nuzzling. A thought struck Alston:

"Ah . . . 'dapa, you *have* done this before, haven't you?"

"Of course. I told you about my boyfriend, didn't I?"

"Ah . . . I meant with another woman."

"Oh." Alston shivered as the other's fingers traced up her spine and lips nibbled down her neck. *That feels* incredibly *good.* Involuntarily her thighs squeezed together with one of Swindapa's between them.

"Not really," Swindapa whispered.

Tickling fingers found the base of her spine. Alston shivered again and arched her back. *The Bronze Age isn't all backward.*

"Not—*ah!*—not *really*?" she said. She hadn't thought it was the sort of thing you could be uncertain of.

"It was dark . . . some friends, after a feast, lots of mead . . . you know how it is. Does it matter?"

"Not really," Alston laughed. The Fiernan Bohuguli seemed a lot like Trobriand Islanders in some ways.

"I like it better with these wonderful lamps," Swindapa said. She looked down to where their breasts pressed together. "See how we go together, like the moon and the night sky. Isn't it pretty?"

"Yes," Alston said throatily. *It is also better to give than to receive. Or at least pleasantly excruciating to start with.*

She pressed the girl back and stroked her lightly with her fingertips, just touching the fine down-hairs. Lips touched breasts and tongue curled around a nipple. The other's soft explosive sigh made her own skin tingle from head to toe, like being caressed with heated mink gloves. After a while she worked her way downward, caressing the other's inner thighs and urging them apart. The hands that stroked her head trembled, and she smelled the delicious musky scent of desire. She slid down, stroked a hand onto either hip, and began. Swindapa gave a shocked cry of surprise and delight at the delicate caress; then a whimpering moan.

Well, well, something new has *been invented since the Bronze Age,* Alston thought happily.

"Yeah, it was a lot too much like hard work for my taste," the man said.

William Walker nodded, straddling the chair and resting his elbows on the back. "Over there in Europe, they've got peasants to do this sort of thing," he said.

They were watching the parade from a roadside café on Easy Street, before it turned west on Main and stopped in the upper section near the Pacific Bank. The floats were a little amateurish, made up with what was to hand. The commonest theme was sheaves of grain, appropriate considering this was a harvest festival; some of them were made up into big human figures, and everyone wore a wreath of it. Most of the floats were horse-drawn, apart from one pulled by a chuffing steam traction engine, a miniature model about the size of a Volkswagen. People milled along in the parade as well, carrying torches; the school band tootled away. At the front rode the Bronze Ager, Swindapa—wearing a wreath of wheat around her hair and carrying a sheaf, and a sash with "Best Reaper" on it over a white dress. She was laughing and waving, and the hair falling past her shoulders had the same wheat-blond color as the ripe grain she carried in the crook of one arm.

What a fox, he thought. Wasted on the captain, although he couldn't fault her taste, and it *was* the traditional reward for rescuing the beautiful princess, although the application was a little . . . unorthodox in this case.

Chief Cofflin was waiting up on Main; there would be a speech and a barbecue, patting everyone on the head for working hard. *Suckers,* Walker thought. The priests and pastors would be there too, to bless the fruits of the fields and invoke Big Juju. *The oldest sucker racket in the world.* He made a mental note to himself to become *very* pious, once the Plan was in place. Nothing like having the supernatural on your side. People who thought Big Juju was looking over their shoulders, why, that was better than all the secret police ever foaled.

The man—Cuddy, he was called, Bill Cuddy—flexed his hands. "I can still feel my blisters," he said.

"Yeah, like I said, it's ridiculous we should be doing this stuff, as if we were Stone Age wogs," Walker went on. "I mean, think of what our technology and what we know could do over across the ocean. Those spear-chuckers would be *glad* to do the donkeywork."

Cuddy looked at Walker, his eyes narrowing thoughtfully. He was a nondescript-looking man a little older than the Coast Guard officer, brown of hair and beard, wary gray eyes in a tanned face.

"Look, Will," he said. "You've been fan-dancing around this for days now, you and your friends there." He nodded; Seaman Rodriguez and Cadet McAndrews sat behind Walker, lounging at their ease. "Gold and dancing girls, yeah, it sounds good. A lot better than shoveling shit for a living. How, though? Cut to the chase, man."

"Okay, Bill," Walker said. "You want to stay here all your life?"

"Not particularly," Cuddy said. "Leaton's a pretty good boss, but I don't want to be a machinist, it's just the best thing available. And I certainly don't want to bust my ass cutting fucking wheat or chopping down trees. On the other hand, I don't want to go live in a mud hut, either, even if it's the biggest fucking hut in the village."

Walker nodded with a charming grin. "There's a lot more than mud huts over there, in some places," he said. "There's my friend Isketerol's hometown, for example, or Greece. Shit, they've even got running water in the Mycenean palaces—flush toilets. Which we don't, anymore. Plus we can get the natives to build what we want. Plenty of places a bunch of us could pretty well write our own tickets."

"If the locals didn't *punch* our tickets," Cuddy said.

"Timid?" Walker asked, a slight edge of mockery in his tone.

"No, just cautious. We don't have any fucking tanks, man."

"Yeah, that's a point. That's why it'd have to be done in a group, with some organization."

"And you to head up the organization?"

He shrugged. "Somebody has to," he said. "Why not me? I've got the training, I know some history, and I've learned the languages. There'll be plenty for everyone when it comes time to share out."

Cuddy sipped at his drink. "Why me?" he said.

"You don't have any local ties, you've learned a lot of useful stuff from Leaton, and I think you're the ambitious type . . . but reasonable about it," Walker said. "And hell, it's not even illegal. The law's back up in the twentieth. Nobody declared Cofflin's goddam Town Meeting a sovereign state. The captain's authority came from the Department of Transportation and the UCMJ; it ended when we got shoved here. They've got no right to tell us we have to stay here and make like farmers."

The other man put down his glass. "They've got the power, though. Most people are behind them. What if I go to the chief, or your captain, and tell them what you've told me?"

"Then I'd be in deep shit, and you'd be back to blisters,"

Walker said. The grin slipped off his face, leaving an expression more like something out of the deep woods. "For the rest of your life."

Cuddy looked slightly nervous for the first time. *However long the rest of your life was* ran unspoken between them. He nodded slowly.

"Okay, I'll think about it." He looked around. "Even with things the way they are, this place still has some of the comforts of home. Doctors, for instance."

Walker flipped one palm up. "Give me credit for some brains, Cuddy."

"Ah, right, you'll have gone looking for other people who know things you need. Like, I did a hitch in the Crotch, too."

Walker clapped. "Give the Marine a great big cigar!" he said dryly. "Semper Fi, mac. Now's the time, Cuddy. Are you in, or are you out? Last chance to be out and just keep your mouth shut. Once you're in, you do it my way."

Cuddy finished his drink and looked after the procession. The music and lights were fading into the darkness of the summer night, a little cool here near the waterfront even in this season. The road was littered, straw and flowers and fresh horse dung. Walker saw his face harden in decision.

"Okay," he said. "You've got the brains for it, if you've come this far without getting caught, and you've got the balls for it, looks like." He nodded and offered his hand. "I'm in . . . boss."

"Kemosabe, me think it *too* quiet," Cofflin said.

"That's right up there with 'What you mean *we*, white man?' " Marian Alston quoted. "What's too quiet, Jared?"

September was a good time for a civic holiday; the grain harvest was in, and everything else was well in hand, well enough for the school year to be starting up again soon.

Not that there isn't enough to do, Cofflin thought. He was beginning to see why socialism was impractical, something he'd simply taken on faith before; there just wasn't a mind alive that could soak up all the information needed to make all the economic decisions, even for this miniature city-state. It was a profound relief to get the government—which had somehow turned out to be himself and his friends—out of more and more, after the desperate scramble of the first weeks after the Event.

Private schemes were bubbling up on all sides: to make iceboxes to replace refrigerators; to cut and store ice in underground pits; to start a manufactury to weave sailcloth, once the flax was cut; another to put up a ropeworks—*Eagle* alone had five *miles* of running rigging.

Now at least he could deal with priority projects, like the schooners Marian wanted built, and public policy . . . and one policy was that everyone not superessential had to take a few days off after the harvest party.

The beach wasn't crowded, there was too much of it and too few people for that, but there were parties clumped along it as far as he could see. Flying kites or playing volleyball, throwing Frisbees, playing the guitar and singing, or just sitting around talking. More out in the water swimming; Nantucket's offshore water got fairly warm in the late summer, up in the seventies, in vivid contrast to most of the New England coast. From what he'd heard, there were even a few hardy souls *surfing* today, over on the south shore. Rod-fishermen were casting in the waves for bluefish, and families with rakes were gathering scallops. It might have been an evening some year back before the Event . . . except that everything was different. Even the way people looked; they'd acquired the roughened, weathered patina of outdoor workers.

Bonfires cast sparks into the sunset, down the long curve to the point. The evening was warm enough for his T-shirt and jeans to be comfortable, or Martha's single-piece bathing suit and sunrobe, or Marian Alston's cycle shorts and muscle shirt. A rummage of children went by shrieking down at the water's edge, chasing a soccer ball and kicking up spray. Their noise was soon lost in the vastness of sea and sky.

"Ah, the hell with it," he said. "The only thing that really worries me is that Pamela Lisketter has shut up."

He got up and went over to the pit. There was an art to a successful clambake. First you had to have lots of rockweed, and after all the soul-butter he had to hand out in this damned politician's job they'd saddled him with, wading out to collect it—Polpis Harbor was the best spot—was a relief. You couldn't soft-talk a wave; go at it wrong and it dunked you, and that was that. The pit he'd dug in the sand behind a dune was properly shallow. He'd lined it with wood—driftwood was best—and then carefully packed the stones and surrounded them with a mound of more wood.

"That's the tricky part," he said to Alston as she came up, beer in hand. "You've got to build the rocks up so there's room for air to filter around every rock, but not too much."

"Looks hot enough," Alston said. The rocks were beginning to flake, glowing and cracking with dangerous popping sounds.

"Ayup." Cofflin cast a critical eye on them, then picked up a long-handled rake.

"I thought you'd be glad that Lisketter stopped talking about walking lightly and petitioning to stop all the trips to the mainland," Martha said, bringing up the baskets of food. She was just beginning to show, a rounding out of the stomach.

A father. Christ. He and Betty had never been able to have kids—something with the fallopian tubes—and had never got around to adopting. Doc Coleman said there shouldn't be any problems, but a first child at forty was always risky.

"That's my worry," he said, pushing at the stones. "She's stopped talking." The rocks slid into a thick red-white glowing mass, evenly spread across the pit. "All right, let's get the rockweed on."

The bags of damp weed were ready. They tossed it in a thick layer over the rocks, and clouds of fragrant steam rose, like the distilled essence of the sea. "Quick, now," he said.

The food went on top of the seaweed: clams in net bags, potatoes, young corn in the husk, a quartered turkey, lobsters still feebly waving their antennae in protest, and cheesecloth bags stuffed with homemade pork and venison sausage. Alston borrowed the rake and used it to add a thick closed clay pan with her contribution in it; more of her famous beaten biscuits. They threw another layer of weed on top, a tarpaulin over that, then spadefuls of sand.

Cofflin took up the thread again: "Lisketter's about as stubborn as . . . as you, by God, Martha. If she's given up speechifying at the Town Meeting, it's because she's got another angle."

They returned to the campfire and its thermos of sassafras tea and cooler of beer. "The other environmentalists are treating her like a leper," Martha said. "Dane and Terri and the rest."

"Yeah, but they're the sensible ones. Hell, they're some of our most useful people. They *know* things—marine biology, handicrafts, stuff like that. And they know I'll listen to them. But Lisketter . . . she's a True Believer."

Alston settled back on an elbow, the blanket dimpling into the sand and her full African features thoughtful. "You're the expert," she said; he couldn't tell if she meant on clambakes or political dissidents. Her eyes lifted.

Cofflin followed them. A group of youngsters in bathing suits—islanders and cadets—were throwing a football in an impromptu touch game. Swindapa leaped and caught it, ululated some ferocious-sounding warcry in her own language, and went pelting down the beach, fair hair flying in the wind. Doreen Rosenthal went after her, puffing. *Marriage suits her,* he thought. *Or our Bronze Age health spa setup.* From chunky the ex-astronomer had gone to a figure that turned heads in a bikini, particularly among men who liked the look of a woman with the promise of something to grab on to.

By contrast Swindapa had filled out a little, and gotten even more deer-graceful, if that was possible.

"Lisketter's been talking to me a good deal," Martha said. "Doing some research."

"Research on what?" Cofflin asked.

"Early Mesoamerican cultures," she said.

"Aztecs?"

"Oh, no, much earlier than that—Olmec and proto-Mayan, this century we're in. Really trying to learn something, too. Her brother's with her a fair amount of the time."

Cofflin frowned. Pamela Lisketter was odd, but functional. Her brother David, on the other hand . . .

Ian Arnstein stirred beside his copy of *The Oxford Illustrated Prehistory of Europe.* He yawned and woke fully when Doreen plopped down beside him, panting. "Dinner ready yet?" he said.

"Works up an appetite, snoozing does?" she said.

"You had me swimming for an implausibly long time earlier," Arnstein said. "Have mercy on an antique. Besides, I just finished harvesting an area equivalent to the state of Kansas."

Swindapa trotted up, throwing the football and a word over her shoulder. She settled down by Alston, giving her a quick brush of the lips and linking hands. *Glad we haven't had any more trouble about that,* he thought. The black woman hadn't flaunted it, but she hadn't made any secret of it either; they'd just quietly gone down to the Town Building and registered as domestic partners under the ordinance Nantucket had passed a year before the Event. And she'd been smiling a lot more. So had Swindapa. *Very, very glad we haven't had any trouble.*

The island depended too much on what *Eagle* and the Guard brought in; it had made the difference between bare survival at very best, and a sufficiency you could almost call comfortable. Of course, that was one reason why there *hadn't* been more than a fringe murmur among the more conservative; plus many Nantucketers had a Yankee respect for privacy. That and the fact that it would take a very bold man to stand up to the basilisk stare of Captain Alston in a cold rage; he'd seen it once or twice, and had no desire at all ever to experience it personally from the receiving end.

Oh, well, I'm in love myself. It made you feel sort of mellow and ready to think well of people, he found.

"Furthermore, I wasn't sleeping, I was thinking," Ian said virtuously. He turned his head toward Cofflin and Alston. "We've finally figured out something about the Earth Folk language—it's very distantly related to Basque."

"Ah, that's interesting," Cofflin said. "Should we try to find someone who speaks Basque?"

"*Very* distantly," Doreen said, sitting near her husband and combing out her hair. "The way we see it, the languages are about as close as English is to Sanskrit."

"Oh." *One more factoid for the Useless Trivia File.* He supposed there were people up in the twentieth who'd pay a fortune for information like that, to settle those perpetual feuds academics enjoyed.

"Tartessian is related to Basque too, we think, possibly ancestral to it," Ian said. "Or closely related to the ancestor of Basque, whatever that is and wherever it's spoken in this century. And therefore Tartessian is related to Fiernan. We think. And Iraiina, it's probably a bridge dialect between proto-Germanic and proto-Celtic. How's the clambake coming?"

"Dinner won't be ready for a while," Cofflin said. "Someone could hand around that bucket of oysters, though."

The boats brought them back by the hundred bushel; they were common as dirt over on the mainland coast, but you had to be careful about the size if you planned to eat them on the half shell—many were so big the only way to approach them was with a knife and fork. He began opening these with a knife and handing them around; there was no butter for the bread, of course, but somebody had managed to scavenge a half-bottle of Tabasco sauce.

Swindapa looked down at her oyster and blinked dubiously. Then she primed it with a drop of the Tabasco, slid it into her mouth, and swallowed, imitating the others. "These things are . . . interesting, you'd say?"

"You don't have them in Britain?" Ian asked, surprised.

"Not where I was live then-when-there—lived then, I mean, by the Great Wisdom. And I never visited the coast while they were in season."

She looked at the next he handed her. Her eyes went wide, and she began to giggle helplessly. Alston bent her head, and the Fiernan whispered in her ear.

". . . better warm." He caught the last words; with the full message, Alston was fighting not to laugh.

Cofflin cut another slice from the loaf. *Every couple's entitled to their own private jokes,* he thought—slightly irked, because the Arnsteins had also caught the byplay, and *they* were laughing too. So was Martha. . . .

"Later, dear," she said. "I'll tell you later."

The driftwood fire crackled, flames running blue and green, and the wind was full of the clean scent of the sea. Cofflin sank back on one elbow and watched the sun going down over the waves and headland to the west; Martha handed out blankets from the picnic hampers, and those in swimsuits wrapped them around their shoulders.

Pretty good day, Cofflin thought contentedly. It was amazing how much better all that wheat and rye and barley and beans and flax and dried fish in the warehouses made everyone feel. *Maybe quiet isn't so bad, after all.*

The knock was loud and insistent. "Ignore it and it'll go away," Cofflin advised.

The three couples tried, but it came louder and louder.

"I'll get it," sighed Martha. "The doctor says walking is good for me." She pushed herself to her feet, kissed Jared on the top of his head, and walked over to the curving staircase that led to the ground floor of the Athenaeum.

Marion Alston relaxed, tired after the long day at the beach, full from the clambake. She smiled with drowsy contentment, looking across the table at Swindapa. Her love life hadn't been much; the disastrous marriage with John, the even more disastrous affair with Jolene that had ended it . . . and since then the extreme discretion that someone in uniform had to practice, in her position. Discretion so complete it made any real relationship difficult to impossible.

Of course, Martha and Jared and Doreen and Ian were in the same boat. Had to leave the twentieth to find the right one. Truly *odd. Even odder that now* I *am the one who sets personnel policy for the Guard. Now it's the bigots who have to keep their mouths shut for fear of consequences.* That was intensely satisfying.

They were sitting at one of the tables in the lecture hall of the Athenaeum, a big room covering the second floor of the white neoclassical main building; a desk was to their rear, shelves of old books to either side, and at the head a stage where Frederick Douglass had once spoken.

Ian and Doreen were sitting side by side and holding hands, discussing anthropology or something of that nature. There were times when she was very glad she wasn't an academic.

"We're closed." Martha's voice came up, muffled by the distance to the front door. "Tomorrow."

"I know, Ms. Cofflin," a voice said from below. "Please let us in, though."

"I'll go down and help her run them off," Jared said, pushing himself upright and walking away with a sigh. "Damn, doesn't anyone realize we have to sleep too?"

Alston's mind divided between the final cargo loads that would have to be swung onto *Eagle* tomorrow and the way Swindapa was tickling her behind the knee with one bare foot under the concealing table. *If humans could purr, I would,* she decided. Love was wonderful; so was humping your brains out as an end to the perfect day, and when you put the two together . . .

Something in the voices from downstairs brought her

back to full wakefulness with a cold jolt. She sat up and signaled Swindapa's suddenly alert face to silence with a finger across the lips.

"What—" Ian began.

"*Quiet.*" He shut up as if she'd slapped him.

She didn't have a gun with her—nobody in the Guard wore one on the island except on duty, and that rarely—but their swords were bundled in a pair of blankets with the other things from the picnic, taken along to do a few *kata*. She slid the long steel free of its sheath.

"Wait here," she whispered in the blond girl's ear. "Be careful. Get help if things go wrong. Look after Ian and Doreen, and do *not* come charging in. Go that way."

She jerked her head at the sash window and drew the blade. "Understand?"

Unwillingly, Swindapa nodded. Just then a gun barked, a small flat crack; there was a cry of pain, and angry voices raised. Her mind clicked it off; pistol, very light caliber.

"Ian, Doreen, stay out of this," she said. Doreen had some training, Ian none. *Damn, this would have to happen with civilians around.*

She walked to the head of the stairs and looked down. Nothing. *Down the stairs and the circulation desk's to the left. Main entrance to the right, only a few feet away.*

She kicked off her sandals and padded barefoot down and out into the entranceway, the sword held in her left hand with the blade not exactly concealed, but not forcing itself on anyone's attention, either.

Pamela Lisketter was there, with her brother and a few more of her followers. Her brother had the gun. It was a .22 Hammerli auto target pistol, of all absurd things, looking oversized in his hand. His eyes glared behind the thick glasses, jumping from one point to the next, and the muzzle jerked around at her as she walked into view. A round cracked off, ricocheted somewhere to her right, and ended in a tinkle of glass.

Cofflin was down on the ground, swearing softly, and his big fisherman's hands squeezed a bleeding wound just above his knee. Either Dave Lisketter was a very good shot—unlikely—or he'd been dead lucky. Incapacitating a determined man with one light bullet was not easy, and from the way Cofflin was glaring at them he had all the determination you could want.

One of those little bullets between the eyes and you're as dead as if it was a rifled shotgun slug, she reminded herself. Everything was very bright and clear.

Martha was backed up against a desk, quivering with the anger she was keeping off her face, except for the two red spots on her cheeks. Pamela Lisketter looked out of her depth, but grimly determined to carry through. Her brother's twitching eyes and bared buck teeth gave him the look of a gopher on pure crystal meth, capable of anything, one way or another. Other figures moved behind Lisketter, taking boxes of books out of the Athenaeum.

"You'd better put that-there down, white boy," she said, conscious in some remote corner of her mind that the Gullah accent she'd fought so long and hard to control was back in full force. "Y'might hurt yoselfs wit it."

"Drop that sword!" he barked, shrill. She continued to walk forward, slow and soundless, then halted just beyond arm's reach. "Drop it."

"No, doan' think I'll do that thing," she said carefully.

"Drop it!" He looked bewildered and waved the gun. "You *have* to drop it!"

"That there's a gun, white boy. It ain't no magic wand," she said, and turned her head to Martha. "What's goin' on here?"

"Ms. Lisketter," Martha said, her voice frigid with contempt, "is going to save the Indians—"

"Native Americans!"

"Native Americans. By taking them our guns and a copy of the *Encyclopaedia Britannica.*"

Alston laughed deliberately, a deep rich sound. "Even crazier than Ah thought," she said. "Lisketter, tell your brother that if he puts that there gun down now, I won' hurt him." *Much,* she added to herself. These people didn't have any experience with violence, or much confidence in their use of it. If she could shake them enough . . .

Her senses expanded, taking in the room and the positions of everyone in it. One long controlled breath. Another.

Lisketter spoke: "Your own Lieutenant Walker is helping us," she said.

Alston laughed again. "Walker doan' help nobody but Walker," she said. "So . . ."

Lisketter wasn't going to back down. Her brother had so

much adrenaline in his system he was on the verge of going berserk, which would make him an utterly unpredictable factor. Time to act.

A number of things about swords were surprising to those who'd never trained with them. The first was how *far* a yard-long blade at the end of an arm could reach. A drawing cut sliced through David Lisketter's flesh, through the radius and ulna of his arm, hardly slowing at all. He shrieked and whirled, the stump of his forearm sending up twin jets of deep-crimson blood halfway to the low ceiling as the hand clutching the gun spun away.

In the instant that followed, Marian Alston knew two things with angry certainty. The first was that her training had betrayed her; she stepped forward into stance and whipped the blade back and around for the finishing stroke in drilled reflex, leaving Pamela Lisketter a crucial moment to react. The second was that Pamela Lisketter also had a gun, and that she'd fired it through the pocket of her coat.

Blackness.

Isketerol smiled as he pushed through the door and over to the desk. The partition—the *plastic* partition—had been taken down; the Amurrukan who lived here year-round didn't fear each other much. There was only one *police officer* sitting there yawning. Probably feeling resentful that he wasn't off-duty and celebrating the harvest like most of the island. It was dark on the street outside, save for the noise and lamplight spilling down from the Ocean Café half a block away.

"What can I do for you?" the policeman asked.

"You can die, foreigner," Isketerol said in Tartessian.

His left hand flashed out and clamped in the Amurrukan's hair, jerking the man forward, while his right flashed out from behind his back with the steel dagger the smith had made for him. It was double-edged and needle-pointed, about seven inches long, and sharper than anything he'd ever held before. The point punched into the side of the Amurrukan's neck just behind the windpipe; he could feel the stiff tissues crunching and popping as the broader shoulders of the weapon sliced in. He jammed the man's head down on the desk as he wrenched the blade forward. Blood spurted, covering the short tunic—the T-shirt—he was wearing. His victim's movements went spastic for an instant, then slumped away. Bowels and bladder released their smells to the iron-copper tang of blood.

"To You, Arucuttag of the Sea, I dedicate this offering. Take what I give, Hungry One, and grant my desire," Isketerol said. A wet finger outlined a red wave on his forehead.

He turned to the door and signaled the others in. One of them took a single look and bent over, vomiting. Isketerol hid his contempt. *Despite their powers the Amurrukan are womanish,* he thought.

"Get moving," he said, raising the barrier between the entranceway and the night officer's desk.

He pushed the body backward, so that it slumped off the chair and onto the floor. No sense in taking unnecessary chances. A moment served to strip off the gunbelt and buckle it around his own waist; he cleaned and sheathed the dagger, then took the crossbow one of Lisketter's followers handed him, instead of drawing the pistol as he longed to do. Best to use a weapon he'd practiced with, and one that made no loud noise.

"Harry? What's going on out there?" someone called from within the building.

Isketerol's lips skinned back from his teeth. *So. There is a second one.* He waited until the doorknob began to move; the panels were thin wood. Then he shot.

Whunng. The crossbow spoke its single musical note. There was a sharp crack as the bolt punched through the door, hardly slowing, then a heavy grunt from the other side. The door swung open toward him and the policeman toppled out, the stubby arrow sunk to its fletchings through his breastbone. The body sprattled and leaked, then went still.

"Quickly!" Isketerol snapped, reloading.

Lisketter's followers and Walker's men had come prepared, on the assumption that a sixteen-pound sledgehammer and a pry bar were the most versatile keys ever invented. They pushed through into the police station, where the shotguns were in racks, padlocked closed. Three ringing blows disposed of the locks, and the long arms went into crates and were manhandled out to the handcart. Ammunition was in locked boxes beneath; they simply carried those out, since they could be opened later. The door of the storeroom where the private firearms were being kept yielded to two strong men with sledges in less than a min-

ute of battering. Isketerol nodded approval. *The best pass-
word is an ax,* he thought. That was an old saying of the
Sidonians, and he'd found much value in it.

Inside was the smaller type of gun, *pistols.* Each was
neatly labeled with its owner's name; they were due to be
returned to the private citizens soon, perhaps within the
week—that had been one reason they decided on this night
to make their strike and flee. Hands dragged in two large
boxes, padded with blankets. Walker's man, the gunsmith,
began to toss weapons into each, carefully segregating out
the *magnums* from the *Saturday-night specials,* and seeing
that Walker's box for the *Yare* got the former. Isketerol
did the same for the long arms, where the differences were
less subtle and the pictures he'd memorized made the work
easy. Most of the best ones had already been sent aboard
Eagle—that was Will's task—but there were two that were
especially formidable; *Garands,* Will called them, weapons
with which the Amurrukan had fought a great war in Walker's grandsire's day. Improved somehow, something about
twenty-round magazines. Lisketter's people accepted the
others, the *.22 popguns* and the *kiddie can-plinkers,* without
dispute. Few of them were familiar with firearms, less than
he was, even; and those who knew anything were away
with Lisketter herself.

Metal clattered on metal. Seconds crawled by like minutes, minutes like hours. *Like a battle,* Isketerol thought,
working a dry mouth. Or rather like the waiting before
one; he could remember feeling like this as a stripling, out
with the city levy to fight off a raid by mountain tribesmen
on the valley farms tributary to Tartessos.

At last they were finished. Isketerol chivvied them out,
turning to check that all the other doors to the building
were locked from the inside. Then he shut the last one and
stuck a strip of soft brass into the slot for the key, hammering the end home with the butt of his dagger and then
breaking it off with a sideways blow. That would delay
whoever came to check on the station, and moments might
be crucial. He took a coat from the handcart and draped
it over his shoulders, hiding the weapons at his belt. The
crossbow went within, his hand on it as he stood beside the
cart in the position he would walk.

A quick glance up and down the street. Nobody was

looking this way. "To the docks," he said. "Walk as if you own the world."

If this plan succeeded, Isketerol son of Elantinin would own a good deal of it. *His* part had begun well. He could only ask the Powers that the others might do as well, and keep alert.

"*Go!*"

"Told you the blacksmith would be working," Walker said, looking down at his watch. "Right where we need him."

Time to go for it. Three coordinated strikes. *Yeah, Isketerol will bring his off. Lisketter . . . fuck it, I'm committed. Go for it.*

He could smell the fear-sweat on the men behind him, Rodriguez and McAndrews. *Casual, you dumb bastards, act casual,* he thought. *We're just some friends out for a stroll.* There were a fair number of people out tonight, dropping in on neighbors or heading for parties or whatever. Theirs wasn't the only lantern drawing a yellow light through the dark streets away from the streetlamps of Main. He could smell the clean hot scent of burning charcoal from the big shed up ahead of them, hot metal, sneeze-making cinders, the heavy frying smell of the oil bath used for quenching and tempering.

Dumb bastards. This is the safe part. You're not committed till we go through that door.

You took what material was to hand, but he wasn't impressed with either. The Puerto Rican sailor thought with his balls, and McAndrews had more nonsense stuffed into his thick head than one of Lisketter's flakes, just a different flavor. On the other hand, neither was a coward. McAndrews was even fairly bright, when his brain wasn't focused on the Glories of Africa; squeamish, though.

They could hear the clang of the hammer from the shed; it was a converted truck garage near Seahaven Engineering, chosen for its concrete floor. Smoke floated up from the new forge chimney, ghostly in the star-sheening night sky. Sheet metal had been laid around the brick of the stack, to lessen the risk of fire. Red light leaked out around the edges of the doors and through the big propped-open windows.

Good. Only Martins and his bimbo there. There were six

separate hearths inside, and a selection of special-purpose
anvils. Walker pushed open the door just enough for a
man's body and slipped through. Even with good ventilation it was hot inside, and Martins's bare skin shone with
sweat. He was standing by the oil bath, and it hissed and
bubbled smoke as he plunged the bright metal into it. Over
by the forge his girlfriend, Barbara, rested at the pedal-
worked bellows, her inevitable cat in her lap. She was a
comfortable-looking woman in her late thirties, given to
wearing long scarves; she'd run an herb store, before the
Event.

"Hey, man." Martins looked up and smiled, his round-
lensed glasses looking absurd on his long-nosed face. "Like,
what's happenin'? It ain't the time for your regular
lessons."

Walker jerked his head at the other two men. They
spread out behind him, covering the entrances. *I really need
this turkey,* he told himself. Martins knew his work; he was
even a good teacher, and Walker had put himself out to
learn the basics over the summer. Knowledge was always
valuable, and among other things he now knew how the
smith thought.

"Your friends want some lessons too?" Martins said, his
voice full of its usual dreamy mildness.

"Actually, John," Walker said, "what I'd like is for you
to come along with me. Right now."

The mild brown eyes blinked at him. "Okay, but like,
I'm sorry, man, I got some work I have to do. Another
time, Okay?"

"I'm afraid it'll have to be now, John," Walker smiled,
coming closer. "Really."

"Man, I *can't* go anywhere now. You know how it is,
you're tempering something, it like rilly has to be done in
its own time. It's the flow, man."

Barbara was looking up, blinking, an edge of suspicion
in her eyes. Something snapped in William's head. He drew
the Beretta from its waist holster under his jacket and
brought it around.

"*Now,* you dumb fossil hippie bastard!"

His voice had taken on a crack of command that usually
brought results. Martins only blinked again, his mouth setting stubbornly under the walrus mustache.

"Guns," he said. "Oh, I don't like guns. I'm sorry for

you, man. Heavy. You're carrying some heavy power trip there, like, authoritarian stuff? No way am I going to, like, reinforce that sort of negative trip." He turned away, lifted the blade out of the oil, and began to wipe it down.

Barbara had given a little scream at the sight of the pistol. Now her eyes flickered to the other two men, the hands resting under their sweatsuit jackets.

"Johnnie," she said breathlessly, "I don't think these guys are kidding. Maybe you'd better go with them."

"Hey, Barbs—you can't let stuff like this divert your energy, you know? It's Will's karma. He has to work it through."

William Walker smiled bleakly and holstered his pistol. This had not been altogether unanticipated. The *tanto* he drew from under his left armpit was one of Martins's own, a heavy-backed thing with a blade six inches long, very slightly curved, with a slanting chisel point. The edge was whetted to just short of razor sharpness. He took four lithe steps and grabbed Barbara by the ear, dragging her to her feet with a squeal of pain.

Martins rounded on him, his hammer going up. "Drop her, man! Drop her now!" His sheeplike face was transformed, forgelight gleaming in his eyes and turning them red. The twenty-pound forging hammer went up as if it weighed no more than a thistle.

Walker smiled and reached around Barbara from behind, letting the tip of his knife rest just under her eye. "Let's put it this way, John. You start cooperating, and I won't cut this stupid cunt here a new set of orifices. You do *anything* but what I say, and I'll start taking bits off her; she's a big girl, and there are lots of bits. You understand this concept, John? Do you grok it?"

The hammer dropped slowly. "Yeah," he said hollowly. "Careful, man, that's sharp."

Barbara was crying with short, sharp inhalations, tears gleaming in the red-and-white light of the bed of coals in the forge.

"Glad we're communicating at last, John. Here's what you're going to do."

William Walker swung onto the *Eagle*'s deck and turned smartly to salute the flag. "Permission to come aboard, Ms.

Hendriksson," he said, turning to the OOD and saluting her in turn.

"Very well, Mr. Walker," she said, returning the courtesy. Less formally: "What's up, Will?"

"Working party, Greta," he said. "A few last things the skipper wanted shifted to the *Yare* before you take her over tomorrow. Thought I'd get them done tonight so you'd have a clear deck in the morning and no distractions."

"Thanks," Hendriksson said, impressed with his zeal—it was a holiday, after all. "You've been doing a great job working her up."

"De nada," Walker said with an easy smile. He'd cultivated Hendriksson. In a very comradely way; she had a boyfriend ashore now.

He looked around the deck. Not much activity, as you'd expect with the ship at anchor and most of the crew on liberty ashore. The swell was slight, and the ship rode easily under a sky ablaze with stars, a frosted band against the night. Not quite deserted, though. There were still enough people to screw things up completely, if the alarm was given. Speed was the ticket, that and acting as if he had a perfect right to be where he was and doing what he was.

"Sooner done, sooner I can get to sleep," he said. Hendriksson nodded and returned to her post near the wheel, trotting up the gangway from the waist to the poop deck.

Walker fought not to wheeze relief. Sweat trickled down his flanks; it could have been very awkward if she'd stayed closer. A dozen men followed him up the companionway, moving with professional briskness; he'd drilled them in the movements often enough, although in fact only about half of them were Coast Guard.

"This way," he barked, waving them forward with his clipboard.

Lights were dimmed below; he led them down to the second deck, and the locked door that held the *Eagle*'s armory. Full now, since the ship was nearly ready to sail; full with the pick of the island's firearms, what was left after the warehouse fire back in spring. Gray steel door, and a plain gray lock.

"Jimmie," he whispered. Even in a small town like Nantucket you could find appropriate talents, if you looked. A small man eeled his way forward, knelt by the door, and went to work.

Four endless minutes later it clicked open; all he'd had to do was savagely hiss the restless into silence. The door swung back, and Walker shone his flashlight within.

"All right, get the light." A larger battery-powered item went on. "That's the machine gun. Get that and the ammunition first. Rifles next, then the shotguns, then the handguns, then the cleaning oil and parts. Keep it looking normal, no running, but *move*."

Seconds stretched agonizingly. When two men dropped a box of ammunition they were carrying by the rope-sling handles he had all he could do not to light into them with fists and feet as the deck boomed. Minutes crawled by, and exultation with them. *I'm going to do it, by God!*

The last boxes went up the stairwells and out on the deck. He never knew exactly what it was that woke Commander Rapczewicz, only that he heard her voice from above, raised in a sharp tone of command:

"You there! Yes, you. Who are you? What are you doing on the *Eagle*?"

She was the XO. She knew everyone authorized to be on the ship, at least by sight . . . and the approximations of uniform he'd slowly, painfully accumulated for his recruits were only that, makeshifts. He went up the companionway in four bounding steps and burst onto the deck. Willpower slugged him to a halt, made him walk over calmly with a smile on his face, extending the clipboard.

"Sorry, ma'am," he said. She was hastily dressed—buttons misaligned—and blinking sleep out of her eyes, but narrowly suspicious. "It's right here—"

That brought him within arm's reach. The heel of his right hand rocketed up, punching into the angle of her jaw. Sandy Rapczewicz was a solidly built woman, but his hundred and ninety pounds outweighed her mass by forty. She snapped backward with her heels barely touching the ground and lay in a crumpled heap with blood running from her nose and mouth. Luckily that brought her into the shadows by the bulwark. He looked around. Nobody.

"Get that crate down to the boat," he said, forcing himself out of his crouch. "Now, you fools. Move it." The flat calm of his voice was a better lash than a shriek. They fumbled it up and started down the companionway, feet clattering.

"Mr. Walker. Is everything all right?"

Walker turned at the hail from the quarterdeck. *Well, there goes any chance of quietly scuttling the* Eagle, he thought savagely. *Fuck, fuck,* fuck*!* Aloud: "Everything's okay, just dropped a box," he said.

Hendriksson turned to go. It was at that moment that Sandy Rapczewicz crawled into a pool of light and collapsed again, her blood-slick face ghastly in the yellow light of the lamps. Walker responded instantly, pulling out his Beretta and firing. Bullets thunked into teak decking and spanged off steel with vicious red sparks. The lieutenant threw herself flat. Walker whirled and raced down the gangway, half-throwing the two men and their burden ahead of him into the boat and leaping after. The rowboat swayed wildly and shipped water over one side; it was perilously heavy-laden, even for a calm night.

"Out oars and stroke!" he roared.

They responded, clumsily at first, then bending their backs to it. He turned and knelt, holding the pistol in a two-handed range grip, squeezing off the rest of the magazine at the side of *Eagle*'s quarterdeck, shooting at movement and lights. The boat gathered way, heading for the riding lights of the *Yare* where she stood out from Nantucket Town's breakwaters. Voices and shouts were rising on the *Eagle* . . . but he'd put the XO in the hospital for a while, at least, and Hendriksson was a by-the-book type. She'd send for orders; besides, there probably wasn't anything but a handgun or two left aboard the ship. If that. *Damn, I've got all the guns in the world!*

The boat came alongside the *Yare*. Lines came overside, and men made them fast to guns and crates. More hands hauled them up; Walker went up a line himself, hand over hand. Isketerol stood by the wheel, hands on hips, cloak flapping a little in the night breeze. He was grinning, and Walker felt himself answering the expression.

"We did it!" he said. A bit premature, but they *had* done it.

"Arucuttag of the Sea was with us," the Tartessian whooped.

Two women huddled behind him; Alice Hong, and what's-her-name, Rosita. Martins and his girlfriend were securely handcuffed below, and . . .

The last boxes came aboard and went below, secured with padlock and chain.

"A taste of things to come," he said to the Iberian. "The

guns weren't half as hard to steal as that bastard of a quarterhorse." As if to punctuate his words an indignant neigh came from the hold, and the drumbeat sound of hooves on wood.

Turning to his crew: "Start engines!"

The diesel coughed to life under his feet. That took longer and made more noise than he liked, but there was no point in trying to sail her off in the face of an onshore breeze, not with this scratch crew. They'd be clumsy at it despite the economical nature of the schooner's rig, much easier to set than a square-rigger of the same size. *You'll all be sailors by the time we reach our destination,* he promised himself. A vast wild exhilaration was building in him, and he struggled to keep it under control. Another boat was rocking not far away; smaller than the *Yare,* but more heavily crewed. Walker walked to the port rail and called across, cupping his hands:

"Thanks for the help, and good luck!" he called. *Thanks for all the fish,* he was tempted to say, but he doubted she'd catch the reference. "Also goodbye!"

Panic-stricken cries rose; the other boat's engines were turning over as well. That had been the plan, to run the engines dry building up a lead. The plan had been to do it together, though. He laughed, a barking sound.

"Where are you going?" Pamela Lisketter cried, springing up to the rail and cluching at a line. "We need you!"

"But I don't need you," he chuckled again, and shouted: "And wherever I'm going, it isn't fucking Mexico, you dumb bitch. Give my regards to the proto-taco-benders and Formative Period bean-eaters!"

He roared laughter again; it had been the hardest work of his life, putting on a convincing imitation of a would-be tofu muncher and humanitarian weepy for this collection of . . . *bathetic geeks and tree-hugging wimps*, he decided. That had a fair, objective sound to it.

Give her credit, though, he thought, still chuckling. Lisketter didn't waste any more time—didn't even stop for several of her crew, who went overside and began swimming back to Nantucket. She simply put the helm about and headed west . . . Isketerol already had the *Yare* moving east; he'd had a thorough grounding in how to use the wheel.

Walker went to stand beside the Tartessian. "I see you

brought Rosita," he said to the adventurer . . . *other adventurer,* he thought. Freedom was like wings, like striding over the earth, omnipotent.

"But of course," Isketerol said, looking down at where she huddled against the rail. "I promised her that I would take her as a wife. And so I will. Third wife, to be sure—but when we are finished, my third wife will be more than Pharaoh's great queen." He jerked his chin without looking around. "Your Alice, as well."

Hong got to her feet. "What the hell do you think you're doing, Will? This tame goon of yours comes along and strong-arms us—"

He swung around, still grinning, and pointed a finger. It didn't quite touch the young doctor's nose, but she jarred to a halt. "Shut up," he said. "You're along because I don't intend to entrust my precious personal body to the local witch doctors if I get sick. But I'm a healthy guy, so your value isn't infinite." She froze, clasping her arms around her nightgown.

Restoring order and setting watches took a few minutes. It left him still full of energy, bouncing on his toes, sleep out of the question, like a hit of cocaine—something he'd tried once or twice, on confiscated material that went missing. No more than that—William Walker wasn't going to wreck himself to make a bunch of Colombian greaseballs rich—but the sensation was pretty much the same. Except that this high was free, and high as the gleaming moon above him. The thudding diesel drove the schooner's sharp prow eastward at a steady ten knots, water curling back from it in opalescent wings. He grabbed Alice Hong by one arm and pushed her ahead of him down the stairs before the wheel, then sternward and into the captain's cabin. There were two big bunks on either side of a table, with a semicircle of padded seats under the fantail windows. Out of them he could see the *Yare*'s wake disappearing behind him.

The woman rounded on him. "What the fuck do you think you're doing, you son of a bitch?" she began.

Crack. His hand took her across the face, just hard enough to leave a red imprint. She staggered back a step and caught herself against the edge of the table.

"Hey, Will—" Her voice was tremulous. "No need to get rough."

"But you *like* it rough, don't you, Alice?" he said, sliding off his belt.

A combination of fear and queasy excitement brightened her eyes and made her moisten her lips. She did; he'd discovered Alice Hong had more kinks than a corkscrew, which made her more interesting . . . and more useful, in some respects. Leather whistled in his hand.

"Please, Will . . . what are you doing?"

"Whatever I want, from now on," he said. "I told you about it, remember?"

"I thought you were just bullshitting me, fantasies to get me hot!"

"No, Alice. I'm going to be a king . . . and those who follow me are going to have wealth and power beyond their dreams. As long as they obey me. Turn around."

She obeyed. He gripped the back of her nightgown and ripped it off with a single yank that brought a gasp from her. A hand between the shoulder blades bent her over the table.

Smack. The leather raised a welt across her buttocks. "Isn't that right, Alice? Anything I want." *Smack.*

"Yes, God, yes!"

He laughed and unzipped. "There are a lot of things you'd like, aren't there, Alice?" he said, and thrust into her. She yelped and gripped the edges of the table. *Wet,* he thought. *This is one sick bitch puppy.* Wet tightness around him. He began to move, eyes on the moonlit road across the waters behind the ship.

"You'd like to have a place where you could dish it out, too, when you felt like it," he said. "Gold and silk, wealth, girls, boys, do some *real* rough stuff of your own, with no laws and no place you had to stop. Real whips, real knives."

"Yes," she hissed, pushing back to meet him. "Yes, you bastard—you weren't just—*Jesus!*—you weren't just daydreaming."

He laughed, one hand gripping the back of her neck with painful force, thrusting into her with a savagery that battered her thighs against the edge of the table.

"I'm the man who makes dreams come true."

CHAPTER THIRTEEN

October, Year 1 A.E.

"She's coming 'round," Coleman said.

Cofflin rolled his wheelchair closer. The left leg was straight out before him, the wound a dull ache under the anesthetic. The other pain couldn't be dulled—he could feel it nibbling at the edges of his mind, roiling with a killing rage. But there was no time for it, not if he was to do what had to be done.

Alston's eyes fluttered open. They were bloodshot, wandering. Coleman leaned over her and shone a light into one and the other. A long-fingered black hand came up; Swindapa gripped it in hers and bent close. Alston's eyes closed again for a moment, and she sighed. Cofflin fought down a moment of sickening envy; it wasn't Alston's fault that he was the one left alone.

"Water."

A nurse cranked the hospital bed up. "Hospital" was a bit too grand for the little forty-bed clinic that was all the island had—all it had needed, when the mainland's hospitals and specialists were close. Morning sunlight shone through the open windows, and a breath of sea and flowers. The garden outside was heedlessly, cruelly beautiful with roses.

Swindapa held a cup to Alston's lips. The officer felt at the bandages above her left ear. When she spoke, it was quiet but coherent. "Hurts like hell."

"You're a very lucky woman," Coleman said, in the semi-scolding tone doctors always used in these situations.

"Ah'm lucky . . . the bitch was usin' a popgun," she said. "Concussion?"

"It skipped around the bone," Coleman said. "Light bullet, as you guessed. Some blood loss, minor concussion"—

which was better than a serious one, but that was all you could say for it—"and you'll have a small scar. White streak through your hair, maybe. It didn't even need a stitch."

Alston sighed again. Her eyes swiveled around to Cofflin. "Fill me in."

"It was Lisketter and her gang," he said. "They took a boat—the schooner, *Bentley*—and kidnapped Martha. And I couldn't do a God *damned* thing." His fist pounded the arm of the chair, once, twice.

"Not . . . with a bullet through your knee," Alston responded. "That the whole of it?"

Cofflin shook his head. "Your . . . formerly your Lieutenant Walker was in on it. We got a couple of prisoners, Lisketter's people who jumped ship. Evidently he and Isketerol, the Tartessian, scammed Lisketter—got her to help them hijack the town's weapons and create a diversion. Meanwhile Walker got a gang of his own together, some Coast Guard, most townies, and took the weapons from the *Eagle*'s armory, together with the *Yare*, its cargo, and John Martins and his lady Barbara. They were kidnapped too, evidently. Lisketter thought Walker was going down to San Lorenzo, Mexico, up the Coatzacoalcos River, to help her, some crazy scheme to arm the Indians there to protect them from big bad us. Then when the *Yare* and the *Bentley* were both out beyond the breakwaters, Walker gave her the finger and sailed east."

"I'm . . . extremely sorry, Chief Cofflin." Alston said softly. "Extremely."

"You did better than any of the rest of us," Cofflin said roughly. *Which isn't very fucking good.* "We got overconfident. We got lazy."

Alston nodded and winced. "How long?" she said to Coleman.

"I will not let you out of that bed for another two days," he said. "I'd *like* to have you under observation for another week after that."

"Not possible. Is *Eagle* still here?"

Cofflin cleared his throat and jerked his chin toward the next bed. Alston rolled her head slowly and carefully. Sandy Rapczewicz was there, her lower face immobilized in a brace. She held up a slate, marked in chalk:

Bastard broke my jaw, Skipper. Sorry.

Coffin saw something in her eyes that answered his. He nodded. "Can you catch them?"

"Which ones?" Alston said. "*Eagle*'s got more hull speed than either, but they can both cut closer to the wind. If *Yare*'s gone east, and she has, I can probably catch him. Those are following winds—best for a square-rigger. *Bentley* will be beating to windward most of the way down. *Eagle*'d be traveling three sea miles to her two. Plus it's a big ocean and we don't have spotter planes. *Eagle*'s radar is short-range."

"And besides, if you did run *Yare* down, he's got the machine gun, and most of the rifles. Unless you could ram him"—as a former fisherman he knew how nearly impossible that would be, especially for two ships under sail—"it would be a . . . hairy proposition."

Coffin waited; he saw with some amazement that Alston was suppressing a laugh. At last she spoke:

"Not all that bad . . . I've got a nasty paranoid mind. The firin' pin, bolt, and return spring for that Browning are in a box under my bed at Guard House. Plus the pins fo' the rifles, although he might be able to make more of those. Various other crucial parts, too."

This time she did laugh, a snarling chuckle which ended with a wince. Coffin grinned, a baring of teeth. He had a score to settle with Lieutenant Walker, someday. But first . . .

He looked at Alston. There were two hostages on *Yare,* as opposed to one on *Bentley* . . . four on *Yare,* if Menendez and Hong hadn't gone of their own wills; their rooms were suspiciously unpacked.

"*Bentley,*" Alston said. "We go after *Bentley.* More difficult . . . do that first. Then run down *Yare.*"

Coffin closed his eyes for an instant, shuddering, then opened them and met hers. His nod held a promise: *I owe you one.* Whatever the reason, she'd go after Martha first.

"Did I get . . . what's-his-name?"

"David Lisketter. We're not sure; they didn't leave a body, at least. They *did* leave the hand and the gun it was holding. They panicked, dropped any other plans and ran."

Alston nodded, closing her eyes and laying her head back on the pillows. Coleman stood and made shooing motions. "Let her rest; she'll recover faster that way. Out, all of you!

Well, you can stay, young lady, if you're very quiet. Out, the rest of you. Out!"

"You're not just a prick, Rodriguez, you're a *stupid* prick, you know that?"

The *Yare* was heeled over sharply, making twelve knots with a following wind. She was heading north by northeast, into the higher latitudes, and the raw wind was colder already over seas huge and ice gray. The schooner crested a rise, hesitated, then plunged downward with spray flying twice man-height from her bows. The others of her crew—twenty in all, not counting the women or Martins—were watching silently, except for the two at the wheel and a few more leaning over the rail, retching as the waves lashed their faces.

"I was just, like, trying to get some," the sailor whined. He was visibly forcing himself not to cringe, but there was a cornered viciousness in his eyes. "You got your squeeze, so does the wog—why shouldn't the rest of us get some?"

Crack. Rodriguez staggered back and grabbed at a rope, the imprint of Walker's hand across his face. Behind him Bill Cuddy picked a spare belaying pin out of the rack around the foremast and stepped forward, with McAndrews just behind him. Walker waved them back. This had to be settled right. He went on:

"Because, you dumb fuck, I told you to keep your hands off the blacksmith's woman. And you *do* what I *tell* you. What part of that is too complicated for you to understand?"

"You said we'd all get women!"

"You will . . . when you've earned it. Work to do first, fighting to do—and all of it when I say so. I say jump, you say 'How high, *sir*!' Got that? *Sabe?*" He grinned, slow and savage. "Or maybe you'd like to give the orders? Come on, Rodriguez, this isn't the Coast Guard. You want a piece of me, come and get it."

The Puerto Rican hesitated, wiping blood from his mouth, then whipped out his knife and lunged. Walker caught the wrist with a slap of flesh on flesh. *Let's do this the simple, brute-strength, old-fashioned way.*

He squeezed. Muscle stood out in cords along his forearm, and Rodriguez dropped the knife. It struck the deck point-down and the sharp point sank in enough to support it quivering by their feet. Walker kept up the pressure, until the bones in the smaller man's wrist began to grate together. He screamed and lashed out with the other hand. Walker caught that as well, twisting both arms until the seaman rose up on his toes, face livid and writhing with the unbearable pressure on his joints.

"And incidentally, Rodriguez, Isketerol is XO of this ship. So you don't call him 'wog.' You call him 'sir.' *Capiche?*"

"Sir, yessir!" came out in a gasp.

"And the reason I'm not pulling your arms out by the roots is that you're useful. But not that useful. So you're not going to try disobeying my orders again, are you?"

"Sir, nossir!"

This time it was more like a scream. Walker released him and he dropped to his knees, arms quivering with the released strain. The former Coast Guard officer raised his voice:

"Let's all get one thing straight. I'm in charge. Because I'm stronger and faster and meaner than any of you, but most of all because I'm smarter. I know the languages, I know the countries, I've got the plan. Without me you'd all be dead in a month—if you were lucky. Any arguments?"

There was a murmured chorus of agreement, a few grins and salutes. He went on: "And I don't remember saying *stop working*." The crew split like magnetized billiard balls, back to the duties he'd assigned. "Thanks, by the way," he continued to McAndrews and Cuddy, nodding. "I'll remember that."

Good timing, he thought. Good that it had come so soon, and in such a formless way. He turned and walked back toward the wheel, passing John Martins crouched with his arm around Barbara.

"You know, John," Walker said cheerfully, "you'd better pray real hard that I stay alive. Because without me, I don't think you or your little second-wave flower child there would live long enough to dance on my grave."

He turned aside from their glares, laughing. He was still chuckling when he settled by the wheel. Isketerol was standing there, his cloak flying in the wind and feet braced against the plunging roll of the ship, one hand caressing the butt of his pistol.

"You like not mutiny, do you, blood-brother," he said with a grin. The language was Tartessian.

"Not unless I'm leading it," Walker agreed, in the same tongue; slow and halting, but understandable. He switched to Iraiina. "Better this way. I don't have laws and custom behind me, only my own strength. Now they know my strength."

"Better still if you'd flogged him," Isketerol suggested.

Walker clapped the Tartessian on the shoulder. "Maybe with your people, but not with mine, brother. That would have convinced them I'd gone mad, and they'd have killed me to save themselves."

"You know them best," Isketerol shrugged. "Will they stay obedient when they learn about the guns?"

Walker shrugged in turn. "They don't have much choice. They can't go back, and alone they're just so much meat. We still have the shotguns and pistols, anyway." He shook his head admiringly. "That is one smart bitch," he said. "Of course, look on the bright side." The Iraiina word was *sun-turned*, but it meant about the same thing.

"Is there a bright side to the most powerful weapons being useless?"

"Of course. We can't use them without the pins . . . but Alston can't either, without the *guns*. And we have the two Garands—they're functional."

Isketerol nodded respectfully. "You are a hard man to discourage; that is good. No plan works perfectly against an enemy."

"Interesting; we have exactly the same saying."

Walker looked up at the sky, and took a glance at the compass and his wristwatch. "We're making two hundred miles today," he said. "But we may have to reef; I don't want to risk the sails."

Isketerol flipped a hand in agreement, looking around. "What a *ship*!" he breathed. "The *Eagle,* that was like sailing a mountain—it never seemed real to me. But this *Yare,* I understand her. Let me sail her into Tartessos harbor, and in a year I will have four more like her with trained crews."

"And she'll be yours," Walker agreed. "Just as soon as I'm in Tiryns, with my men."

"We will do much good business together," Isketerol said, pleased.

* * *

Up. Guard, guard, crosscut, crosscut, pivot, guard . . .

The swords moved in perfect unison, flashing in smooth controlled arcs. Their feet rutched across the sand of the beach as one, like a mirror image set side by side as they went through the *kata*. Alston held the last movement, crouched with the sword out and down, until her leg muscles began to quiver slightly. Then she sank back to one knee, sword snapping sideways in the move that was meant to represent flicking excess blood off the blade. Pull the cloth out of your belt, run the sword through it, slide it back into the sheath, sink back on your heels with hands on thighs . . .

That night was the first time I've ever actually cut anyone with this thing, she thought as she completed the movement.

Oh, she'd shot once or twice in the line of duty; hurt men with her hands and feet a few more times in self-defense. Never used the steel to kill before, though, or really thought she would—except in the trancelike way you were supposed to imagine it as you practiced. *Odd. I'd have thought it would affect me more.* Instead she simply felt irritated she hadn't been able to finish David Lisketter off. Perhaps it was the circumstances; she'd been *angry.* Controlled enough to use it rather than be used by it, but it was nothing like action against a boatful of drug smugglers. Much more personal; her friends had been in danger of death, one hurt . . . she'd never felt so lifted out of herself before.

"How are you?" Swindapa asked beside her.

Alston laid the sheathed sword down before her, bowed to it with hands and forehead to the ground, and sat back. "No pain at all. Just a bit of an itch," she said, touching the wound under a small bandage. *Of course, an inch this way and I'd have left brains spattered on the Athenaeum notice board.*

"I was so frightened for you," Swindapa said. "I asked Moon Woman to find the good star for you, one that would stand for your birthstar and namestar."

"You did the right thing though, sugar," Alston said. "Gettin' help." Rushing in like a berserker would have been the worst possible choice at that moment.

"But you're still hurt," Swindapa went on, the hint of a

smile at the corners of her mouth. "You shouldn't be all alone in that big cabin on the *Eagle*—"

Alston laughed. "I said no yesterday, no this morning, and the answer's no again at sunset. If I make a rule for my people, I have to keep it, just as they do."

The no-fraternization-on-shipboard rule was essential to discipline, in her opinion, and without discipline a ship was a snack for the sea to gobble down. There were a good many other things in the Uniform Code of Military Justice that she'd been glad to leave behind in the twentieth century, but that wasn't one of them.

Swindapa sighed and rolled her eyes. "There's always the paint locker. . . ."

"I have to keep the rule *better* than they do," she said. "Let's get going. We're not sailing until tomorrow morning, remember. And I am feeling better."

They picked up their swords and headed back toward town along the beach, running at a steady jog-trot with their arms pumping and bare feet light on the sand. To their right was a sand cliff, covered in low green scrub and topped with houses, trees, and a fringe of seagrass. Waves broke to their left, green-blue and white, hissing up almost to their feet. Out on the water were the sails of the fishing boats; whatever happened, the town had to be fed, something that had sunk home to just about everybody over the summer. The wind blew in from the sea, cool and welcome. Alston concentrated on her breathing, feeling for any trace of dizziness or pain in her head.

None. Good. The island didn't run to a CAT scan or MRI imager, and there was no way to tell if the trauma had produced an aneurysm or clot, short of waiting for her brain to burst. She grinned without mirth. They'd been thrown back more than three thousand years, but every one of the temporal deportees still moved forward an inexorable minute per minute in her own losing fight with Father Time. You could win battles, but entropy won all the wars.

"Let's go!"

They turned inland and raced for a long wooden staircase built up the near-vertical slope of the bluff.

From here she could see the masts of the *Eagle,* where it waited in the harbor. There were clouds on the northern horizon; she'd have to check the barometer. Bad to be caught on a lee shore in this shoal water, with the wind blowing toward the shallows. Hard to beat off, unless she fired up Max the engine and won free that way, got some sea room for tacking. Maybe they'd have the steam tug take them well out, a couple of miles.

Pedaling back along the smooth paved road was almost a relaxation. Chief Cofflin was waiting for her, standing with boulder patience before the police station and leaning on his crutch. The street there still had bloodstains, where the life of the two police officers had flowed out under the doorjamb. She strongly suspected that if Cofflin's leg hadn't been injured he'd be on board *Eagle,* all arguments to the contrary. The look in the blue Yankee eyes was worse than fury; a cold, grim deadliness, intelligent and calculating.

"I'm fit for duty," she said quietly, swinging down from her seat. "We leave at dawn tomorrow." Stepping closer and taking his hand: "I'll get her back, Jared."

She didn't add: *or die trying.* That was for losers.

"You've got the best chance," Cofflin said, returning a controlled pressure before releasing her. "That's why I waited two days." Hiller could have taken the *Eagle* west and south. She knew that Cofflin had vetoed that because he trusted her judgment better in a fight.

"They need her alive," she said.

Cofflin nodded, his face unchanging. "That bunch, they'll be lucky to keep alive themselves."

"Right. That's another reason I voted to go after *Bentley* first. Walker is almost as smart and tough as he thinks he is, and he needs Martins for his skills and Barbara to control Martins with. Lisketter will probably need to be rescued herself."

Cofflin's smile was icy. "Kidnapping's a capital crime, the Town Meeting decided," he said with a tone even colder. "I don't give a shit if she dies down there or hangs back here."

Not much to say to that, Alston thought. Swindapa reached out and touched Cofflin's shoulder.

"I will talk to Moon Woman and ask for a favorable constellation," she said. "The captain already carries great luck for the rescue of those in need, I know."

The edge of Cofflin's narrow Yankee mouth turned up slightly. "Thank you," he said, sounding sincere.

They turned to watch the last cargo going down to the docks, ready to be loaded on *Eagle.* Bundles of spears, of swords, of crossbow bolts. Suits of armor carried on poles run through the armpits; the sight prickled at Alston, a shadow familiarity . . . *yes, the Bayeaux tapestry.*

She hoped that was a good omen; William *cognomine bastardus* had sailed to victory. She looked eastward, unconscious that her expression was twin to Cofflin's. There was a debt to be paid there too, and she'd always believed in the full, precise, and punctual payment of obligations.

Not least, that this world didn't deserve to have Walker unleashed on it.

CHAPTER FOURTEEN

October–November, Year 1 A.E.

The beach in Bronze Age England had changed since
the *Eagle*'s visit in early spring. The great encampment
of the Iraiina was gone, most of it, emptied as they had
dispersed to take up their steadings. The land it had covered drowsed in the late-summer sunlight. Grass mantled
it, or red-brown fields ready to be sown with winter grain;
Walker supposed the accumulated filth of the temporary
city had manured the soil. Half a mile inland on a slight
rise was a cluster of buildings. He leveled his binoculars.
There was one largish oval hall, eighty feet by thirty across,
with smoke trickling up into the morning air from three or
four places on the thatched roof. The inward-sloping walls
looked like turf, with a framework of heavy timbers.
Smaller buildings were scattered around it, and piles of
trimmed logs he thought were probably for a stockade.
There were large stock pens up already, holding a herd of
scrubby cattle, hairy sheep that looked to be more goat,
and a dozen stocky hammerheaded little horses like Icelan-
dic ponies. Daurthunnicar's *ruathaurikaz*, the Iraiina term
for a high chief's steading. Evidently the *rahax* kept a good
lookout; men were boiling out of the buildings and hitching
up chariots.

Like home, he thought sardonically. *Minus a couple of
millennia or so.* He'd been raised on a ranch up in the
Bitterroot country of western Montana, a miserable little
cow-calf spread that had swallowed his father and his older
brothers and broken his mother in a lifelong losing battle
with the bank and the weather. *Back to the cowshit, but
not for long.* He'd gotten out at eighteen, working harder
to make the Academy than he'd ever done roping or
branding.

There was an additional factor drawn up on the beach. Tartessian ships, two of them. They *were* the ships that'd been there last year, he recognized the horse heads at the bows. Isketerol must have been extremely persuasive back last spring to get his cousin to bring ships north this late in the sailing season; Walker didn't like the thought of taking one of those glorified rowboats through a winter blow in the Channel, or the Bay of Biscay. The Tartessians didn't seem inclined to go anywhere either, since they'd run up substantial-looking huts on the shore above the high-tide mark.

"They'll be here for the winter?" he asked Isketerol.

The Tartessian nodded. "Sail home this near the storm season?" he said. "In the *Yare,* yes. In those, never. The Hungry One eats enough of us as it is, without tempting Him."

Now, just how far can I trust my good buddy Isketerol? Walker thought. *Oddly enough, rather far, I think.* For one thing, the Tartessian seemed to take certain types of promise very seriously; for another, their ambitions ran in concert. *Or so I think. But he's from a completely different background. His logic may be my madness.* For that matter, look at how differently he and Alston thought, and they *did* come from the same background, more or less. *Well, nothing ventured . . .*

"You go set up the meeting with Daurthunnicar," he said. They clasped wrists. "This is the beginning of something good."

He watched the Tartessian depart, then called McAndrews and Cuddy; they stood quietly, waiting for him to talk. The voyage across the Atlantic had established discipline, at least. He stood, pressing his palms together and tapping the bunched fingers on his chin. Then, spearing a forefinger at each:

"All right, this is going to be tricky. We have to get in good with the locals; and incidentally, we have to watch our Tartessian friends, just in case they decide to get a jump on their part of the bargain. McAndrews, you're going to be in charge of the ship while I'm ashore." The black upperclassman was the most reliable of them all. *He* was in this to save his beloved black Egyptians; Walker had promised to send him to Pharaoh's court with a ship and a selection of goodies, when he was well set up. "I'll leave you Smith, Gianelli . . ."

He rapped out the orders, most of his mind on the dickering ahead, and a fraction wandering westward. If his luck was very good, Lisketter would manage not only to get killed—that was more or less inevitable—but to take the captain and the *Eagle* with her. Alston would certainly go after Lisketter first, with Chief Cofflin's wife along on that particular Ship of Fools; that was why he'd persuaded Lisketter that Ms. Martha Cofflin would be indispensable. With only moderate luck, it would be spring before the captain arrived in England—and by then he planned to be ready to depart for points south, or to have an unassailable position here. He'd read up a little on Lisketter's destination, and without her blinkers. They were going to be *very* unhappy when they got there.

Good luck with the People of the Jaguar God, Skipper, he thought ironically.

"Duck!"

Everyone on the decks of the *Bentley* did. The booms swung across the deck and sails slapped taut as the schooner's bow swung through the eye of the wind onto the other leg of her tack southwestward. Martha Cofflin felt her stomach heave again and forced it down by an effort of will. She closed her eyes on the painful brightness of the day and sipped again at the cup of broth.

When she opened them again, Lisketter was standing near her, clutching at a stay.

"It won't work," she said to the kidnapper.

"I know it probably won't," Lisketter said with a sad smile. That was enough to surprise a raised eyebrow out of Martha. "But I have to try."

"Try *what*?" Exasperation drove out anger and even nausea. "Do you really think seven thousand people on Nantucket are going to overrun a continent and . . . and shoot all the buffalo?"

Lisketter shook her head. "It's not that simple, although who knows what might happen in a few generations? But you've already begun trading with the Europeans, and they'll learn things from you. Alston said it herself—in a few years, *they'll* be able to sail here. What do you think they'll do, if we don't give the Native Americans some defense? They'll conquer the Americas, three thousand years earlier than in the world we left. I know the people on Nantucket aren't genocides, not really. But the . . . the Iraiina, or the Tartessians, what about them?"

Martha finished the broth and crossed her arms. "I don't suppose it occurred to you that you might persuade the Town Council to open peaceful contact with the more advanced Amerindian cultures? There would be profit in it for the island, as well. No, you have to hare off on this crazy stunt—"

"They never *listened* to me! I was silenced!"

"You and Andrea Dworkin," Martha said scornfully. "They listened to you, all right; they just didn't *agree* with you. Which isn't surprising, considering the way you treated them like idiots or bad-mannered children. Did you think you could *scold* them into agreeing with you?"

"I told them the truth," she said quietly. "Now, Martha—"

"That's Ms. Cofflin to you, Pamela Lisketter."

"Ms. Cofflin. We're here, you're here, and I hope you'll be reasonable and help us. You have knowledge that will be crucial."

Martha regarded her bleakly. "I'll do my best to keep you alive," she said, laying a hand on her stomach in unconcious protective reflex. "I daresay you won't listen to me about that, either."

"I—we—intend to consider carefully anything you can tell us. Making contact with the Native Americans—"

"Olmecs, isn't it?" At the surprised look: "I do note what research people do."

"Yes, they seem to be the most likely to benefit from what we have to offer. In any case, making contact will be a very delicate matter. We don't want to frighten them, or disrupt their culture more than absolutely necessary."

Oh, Lord have mercy, Martha thought. *Does she really think that the Indians are so fragile that twenty people in a boat can bring them crashing down?* Their bacteria might, of course, but Lisketter seemed to have been very careful about that.

Instead Martha switched back to practical matters. "Do you really think you can get away with it? Think, will you? The *Eagle* is probably on our track right now."

"Unless they're following that . . . that . . . Walker to

Europe," she said. "In any case, what can they do? We took the guns."

"Those that Walker didn't hijack to Europe," Martha said with malice aforethought. There was a certain satisfaction in seeing Lisketter flush. "You shot Jared and Captain Alston, Lisketter, but you didn't kill either of them. Never do an enemy a small injury." *Particularly if the enemy is smarter and tougher than you'll ever be. You and your brother* both *seem to think firearms are Evil Magical Talismans that you can wave and everyone has to obey you.* No use telling her it didn't *work* like that.

It was amazing what a combination of strong emotion, faulty assumptions, and inexperience could do. Make a high-IQ type act like an utter natural-born damned fool, for instance.

The one good thing about this, Marian Alston thought, *is that tacking broad means we cover more ocean and are more likely to blunder into 'em.*

The *Eagle* lay hard over with her port rail nearly under and white water foaming from the bow and hawse holes; the wind was out of the south—a little to the east of south—and they were making sixteen knots with all sail set. She locked her hands behind her back and gritted her teeth, taking little of her usual pleasure in the dolphin grace of the big windjammer's passage or the blood-flogging breeze and spindrift in her face. Sixteen knots by the log, but they were tacking, zigzagging up into the teeth of the wind and making more mileage left and right than forward. *Eagle* was square-rigged on her two forward masts, which meant she couldn't point anything like as near to the wind as a schooner. That gave the *Bentley* a two-knot advantage in actual sea miles covered southward, overall, sailing straight into wind like this. She looked up into a cloudless sky. If the wind were to back and come out of the north, she could cannonball down at twice the *Bentley*'s best rate; schooners were at a disadvantage running before the wind, and the one she was chasing was no greyhound, nor was it well manned, probably.

On the other hand, if I could run her straight before the wind, I might well simply sail past Bentley. The ship's radar had a limited coverage, and it was a big, empty ocean. If Lisketter changed her plan and ran the *Bentley* into the

Chesapeake or one of the big Gulf rivers, there wouldn't be the chance of a Klansman at a Black Muslim convention of finding them. Everyone was keeping an eye out, too, not just the posted lookouts; that was an old Coast Guard tradition.

Tom Hiller cleared his throat. "Very well, Mr. Hiller," she said.

"Aye aye, Captain." Louder: "Ready about!"

The orders echoed louder than they had before the Event, without the continual burr of generators and fans; those were secured for emergency use only, now.

Feet thundered across the deck. At least they had a full crew—overfull. Walker had taken only six of the *Eagle*'s complement with him, thank God. None of them were men she would miss, except McAndrews, and she could guess how Walker had scammed the black cadet; no women among the deserters, she noted without surprise. As it was, there were a hundred and fifty sets of hands available for this maneuver where thirty would do at a pinch.

Commands cracked out, to the helm, to the hands on the lines across the decks. Everything had to be adjusted throughout the maneuver, and precisely, with split-second timing.

"Fore manned and ready," shouted the foremast captain.

"Main manned and ready."

"Mizzen manned and ready."

"Helm's alee!" she ordered. "Right full rudder."

The four hands standing on the platforms beside the wheels heaved at the spokes. Down in the waist and on the forecastle deck came a chorus of heave . . . *ho* as the lines controlling the yards that held the square sails braced to starboard were paid out and their mirror images drawn taut.

"Ease the headsail sheets!"

The ship's bowsprit began to move from port to starboard, left to right. Dacron thuttered and flapped in thunder-cracks up aloft. She could feel the ship's deck swaying back toward the level as the wind lost leverage on the sails. This was the critical part of the maneuver; unless they were hauled around sharp and the vessel's momentum was sufficient to carry her through the dead spot, she could be taken aback and held in irons—sliding humiliatingly sternward.

"Haul spanker boom amidships!"

"Rise tacks and sheets!" Clewlines hauled the square sails up, spilling wind.

"Mainsail . . . *haul!*"

The *Eagle* was through the eye of the wind, and the orders continued:

"Shift headsail sheets!"

"Ease spanker!"

"Ease the helm!"

The wheels spun, pointing her rudder amidships.

"Let go, and haul! Set the main!"

Eagle tilted to starboard. The sails swung, set, braced, filled out into lovely white curves. Feet moved across the deck in a dance more neatly choreographed than any ballet, making lines fast to belaying pins, cleats, and bits.

"On the port tack, ma'am," Hiller said, satisfaction in his voice.

Alston looked at her watch and the clinometer, and overside. They were almost back up to speed, slicing southeast instead of southwest. "Six minutes forty-five seconds. Very good, Mr. Hiller."

He nodded. That *had* been very good. There was an easier way to come about onto the other tack, but it meant going the wrong way for a few minutes, and took a bite-sized chunk out of your forward passage.

And there was no time to spare. One small consolation was that they knew, pretty well, where the *Bentley* was headed. The other was that Cofflin knew better than to nag her over the radio; she'd had superiors in uniform who hadn't grasped the futility of jogging a subordinate's elbow nearly so well. Even as it was, she felt an impatience that seemed strong enough to urge the *Eagle* faster through the water by a sheer effort of will.

Swindapa came bounding up the gangway stairs from the waist, where she'd been helping out on the line teams. *You never have to tell her twice, or find her work to do,* Alston thought, fighting back a grin she knew would be both unprofessional and silly. The impulse faded quickly, driven out by worry. There would probably be fighting at the end of this trip, one way or the other.

Loving means giving hostages to fortune, she told herself grimly. *Do your best; it's all anyone can.*

*   *   *

"That's the Coatzacoalcos River," the yachtsman among Lisketter's followers said.

Silence fell as the *Bentley* ghosted forward under an unmerciful noon. The air here where the Isthmus of Tehuantepec narrowed was hot, hazy and hot and damp, still and full of the smell of vegetable rot. The waters of the Gulf of Mexico—Martha supposed it should be called that, for want of another name—beat on the shores as the schooner coasted down along them; sometimes on beaches of white sand, as often on marsh and forest growing tangled to the water's edge. They had stopped at islands for wood and water, never seeing a dweller. There were Indians in the Caribbean, she knew, but they were few and scattered. Farming hadn't penetrated there yet, and wouldn't for some centuries. Mile after mile, white beaches that turned jungle-green at the high-tide mark, islands like lush emeralds in the unbelievably blue sea.

Martha listened to the conversation behind her at the wheel with half an ear, already convinced that the sailor was right. The maps were unreliable for the smaller things, lesser streams, shoals, reefs, the precise outlines of coasts; such had changed too much in the three millennia between now and the day the charts were drawn. That said, mountains and the great rivers were much the same as they'd be in the twentieth. This river was broad and deep, fringed by mangrove and marsh along the coast, rising up to dense jungle behind. Ebony, mahogany, dyewood, great buttressed trunks coming into view as the schooner slowed still more and breasted into the current. Vines laced them together, thicker than her thigh and running up to the tops of the canopy nearly two hundred feet above.

The engine of the *Bentley* burbled into life for the first time in weeks. Sails came down with a rattle, to be roughly lashed to the booms. As the diesel blatting echoed back from the near bank of the river, birds exploded out of it. There were thousands of them, showers of feathered shapes in canary yellow, red, blue, sulfur gold, and sunset crimson. Parrots, macaws, others she couldn't name, their cries loud and raucous in the heavy air. Alligators slipped off mudbanks into the water with little rippling splashes like lowslung dragons. Insects rose from the river and the swamps along it in clouds, and without the sea breeze to scatter them soon had everyone on the schooner's deck slapping and scratching.

"Do you have a depth sounder on this ship?" Martha asked.

"No," the yachtsman said. "But this looks pretty deep."

Oh, God, Martha thought, wiping at her face with a handkerchief. Sweat lay oily, refusing to dry. At least she'd stopped getting so sick.

Most of the crew—she supposed that was the way to describe Lisketter's followers, after a couple of weeks at sea—were resting along the rails of the schooner, pointing and chattering. Everyone was tanned dark, and they looked shaggy and ragged, but they'd managed to get here without sinking or running onto something, rather to Martha's surprise.

She turned to Lisketter. "You should have someone checking the depth," she said. "And shouldn't you break out the guns, after all the trouble you went to to steal them?"

Lisketter had been staring out at the passing wilderness of wood and jungle, transfixed. She came to herself with a start. "Whatever for?" she said. "There's nobody here but the Native Americans we've come to help."

Martha reined in her sarcasm with a massive effort of will. "They might . . . they might *misunderstand* you," she said. "After all, we can't *talk* to them until someone's learned their language. How do you expect them to know you're friendly?"

"Well, they'd certainly misunderstand any show of force," Lisketter said, shrugging. "We'll demonstrate them when we get to their leadership. From what I've read, the Olmecs had a deep spiritual relationship with nature, so it'll probably be priests or priestesses of some sort."

Martha closed her eyes and sighed, sinking back on the blanket, only to come alert again when voices rose in excitement. The river had narrowed, though it was still hundreds of yards across. On the north side was a village in a clearing, set on the natural levees that always flanked a lowland river like this, given to seasonal floods. Fields surrounded it; plots of maize stood green, overgrown with bean vines, and interspersed with cotton and other plants she couldn't begin to identify. The houses were rectangular, thatched, with sides of mud and wattle to waist height and rolled-up screens of matting below. Canoes were drawn up on the dirt beach that fronted the slow-moving river, some of them quite large; others were out on the water, fishing. The buildings straggled, except for some larger ones grouped in a square of beaten dirt around a rectangular earth platform in the center. That held something much larger atop it, still timber and thatch but with corner posts intricately carved. Smoke drifted up from hearths outside the doors of huts and from a larger fire on the platform.

Must be a few hundred people at least, Martha thought. They were dressed simply, a twisted loincloth for the men and a short skirt for the women; otherwise their brown skins were bare to the late-day sun. As the *Bentley* came into sight they stood for a moment stock-still and amazed. They were almost close enough to see expressions, more than close enough to hear the terror that sent men and women pelting screaming back toward their homes, that drove canoes ashore with flashing blades. A warbling, bellowing sound came from the low earth platform in the center. *Conch-shell trumpet,* she knew with a tremor that chilled even in this steam-oven heat. From there, order spread through the panic and chaos of the village. A small knot of men descended from the mound, the sun bright on their cloaks and masks and vestments, on nodding plumes and banners. They moved among the villagers, pushing and shoving them into silence, shouting, haranguing, slapping faces. Men dashed off to their huts, returned with spears and other weapons she couldn't make out. They moved down to the shore.

Despite herself, Martha leaned forward in fascination. Among the crowd on the riverbank, circles opened up, and men were swinging lines around their heads. From them came a whirring, thuttering roar that shivered down into the bass notes and back up again, each a little out of time with the others. *Bullroarers.* The conch trumpet wailed, and beneath it came the beating of a drum—a massive, booming, thudding sound that echoed down from the mound and against the trees on the other side of the river. Her head came up. Faint and far, another echoed it, the same irregular staccato rhythm.

"Signal drum," she said, touching Lisketter on the arm. "They're sending the news upstream."

They waited, sweating, as the sun crept lower in the sky.

She tried not to think about Jared, without much success. *Poor bear.* He'd be fretting so. . . . Lisketter paced, watching the shore.

"Why don't they send anyone out?" she asked fretfully, slapping at her face. A red splotch appeared where the mosquito had been. "What are they waiting for?"

"Waiting for us, I think," Martha said. Lisketter glanced at her, and she sat back against the rail. "No. This foolishness is your idea. You can force me into the boat, but you can't make me think or talk."

David Lisketter was thin and pale, but the wrist hadn't festered. He pushed forward. "I'll do it, Pam," he said. "I've been studying that Mayan dictionary."

Much good may it do you, Martha thought, but did not say. The archaeologists didn't have a clue what language the Olmecs spoke, since they hadn't left any written records. The theory that they'd been Mayan-speakers depended on a single very late inscription resembling the Mayan calendar. For that matter, the language ancestral to modern Mayan would be unrecognizably different in the thirteenth century B.C. Only a professional linguist would be able to tell that some barbarian dialect in Germany-to-be this night was going to turn into English in the course of the next three thousand-odd years.

There was a good deal of arguing, but eventually David Lisketter and three others lowered the boat that hung at the *Bentley*'s stern and tumbled down the rope ladder into it. She saw that he had a pistol strapped to his left hip; Lisketter saw in the same instant, opened her mouth, and then closed it. Silence fell as the boat approached the shore. The thudding drum on the platform rose to a crescendo and then stopped along with the conch and bullroarer; it was only then she knew how the great drum had come to dominate the scene, like the heartbeat of a giant who'd swallowed them all. Then she realized that it *hadn't* stopped, not completely. The upstream echo of the rhythm went on for three seconds after the drum in the village had halted. Then true silence fell, quiet enough that the cries of the birds were the loudest things they heard. Flocks swirled in toward the treetops backlit by the setting sun. The way the river bent southward here put a tongue of jungle between them and the west.

The schooner's lifeboat grounded among the beached canoes of the villagers. David Lisketter and his companions advanced toward the clump of brightly clad watchers, their open hands—only one, in his case—held out in sign of peace. Headdresses of plumes and fur nodded as the locals stood to meet them.

"I can't *see* what's going on," Pamela Lisketter fretted.

"It wouldn't do you any good if you could," Martha muttered. You couldn't *predict* what a people this alien were going to do on first contact. It all depended on how the strangers fit into the local belief structure. Did gods come from the east? Cortez had used that myth, which might or might not be present here-and-now. Or perhaps they had a belief like the Balinese, that evil came from the sea and goodness from inland. Or they might be perfectly ready to deal with strangers as humans, odd but otherwise like themselves.

A tossing confusion went through the meeting ahead. Shouts arose. Then a sound this river had never heard before: the flat snapping *crack* of a light automatic pistol. "What is he *doing?*" Lisketter cried, shrill fear in his voice.

Trying to save his life, Martha knew. It was the only reason someone like Lisketter's brother would shoot at his precious Olmecs.

Everyone on board had eyes glued to the shore now, difficult though the fading light made it. There was a swirling eddy in the crowd around the Americans, shouts and screams. Weapons moved, flourished overhead or driving forward; she couldn't see precisely what they were, except in a general way. Despite the danger, Martha felt a small chilly satisfaction. She'd been waiting for something like this since Lisketter's brother came into her library behind a gun. That gun cracked again and again, and men toppled—some of them men in elaborate cloaks, as well as the near-naked peasant spearmen. A bubble of space grew around the Americans for a second, and they took advantage of it, toppling backward into their boat and shoving off. Two dragged a third, and David Lisketter walked backward toward them, holding the gun threateningly.

Some of the Olmecs had fled—all villagers in loincloths, Martha noted, not the men in bright costumes. Others stood their ground, waving weapons and fists; several lay still, or writhed groaning on the ground. The ones still hale took fresh heart when the boat slid out into the water.

The . . . *priests? nobles? officers?* Martha wondered; men in authority, at any rate—pushed and yelled them forward. The boat went slowly. Pamela Lisketter's hands gripped the rail with a force that turned the fingers white as flung spears and darts beat the water around it or stuck quivering in the wood. Her brother fumbled with the pistol, reloading, then began to shoot back as the others rowed. Another Olmec toppled, but most of the bullets went astray or inflicted only wounds; it was too far, the boat too unstable, and the light too uncertain for the gun to be very deadly.

Then one of the rowers stood, screaming. A black-hafted dart sprouted between his ribs. He fell, thrashing and moaning, and the boat capsized with him. The others were thrown into the water. Lisketter screamed again and again. Others rushed aimlessly around the deck of the *Bentley;* a few with more presence of mind dashed below and returned with weapons. Martha intercepted one of them and snatched the gun away; it was a .22 target rifle, a bolt-action toy with a tubular magazine. She'd never done any shooting to speak of herself, but Jared had shown her some things on general principle. Men from the village danced and screamed triumph on the beach; others were manning and pushing off in canoes, emboldened by their victory over the pale wizards.

If we can beat them back, we can get out of here, Martha thought. Not even Lisketter would be crazy enough to linger after *this.*

Because she was looking northward, Martha was the first to see what came around the bend in the river. A moment later everyone did, as the flotilla of canoes whipped their torches into flaring life and the drums began to beat again. For a long instant she stared slack-jawed at the spectacle approaching them.

Most of the canoes were simple dugouts, holding four to twelve men. But leading them were a pair of giants, double-hulled craft with the floats eighty feet long and linked by a broad platform. Burning torches on tall poles gave detail a ghastly clarity. Each held forty paddlers to a side, standing and digging their leaf-bladed oars into the water with a chant of *hi-hi-ye-YI, hi-hi-ye-YI,* repeated endlessly. Flamelight glistened on the sweat-slick skin of their muscular bodies. Water coiled back from the prows, which curled up in a ten-foot figurehead carved in the form of a snarling jaguar pug face. Great drums stood on the platforms, man-high, with two drummers each beating out BOOM-ba-da, BOOM-ba-da with yard-long wooden mallets. Behind the drummers the platforms were crowded with warriors in garish cloaks and trappings, carved helmet-masks fantastically colored and sweeping up to impossibly tall plumes of flamingo and quetzal feathers. They waved spears and weirdly carved wooden club-swords and rakes edged with the teeth of sharks or with obsidian chips. At the rear of the giant catamarans hulked platforms on which the commander squatted, and above that more jaguars—this time in frozen wooden leaps. Every inch of the big canoes that she could see was carved, painted, inlaid, in a riot of grotesque imagery.

Both catamarans held at least forty armed men. Scores of canoes followed after.

Martha grabbed the yachtsman who had served as Lisketter's captain. "Get us *out* of here!" she screamed in his ear, shaking him, tasting sour vomitus at the back of her throat. Features slack with bewilderment and fear firmed a little, and he turned and dashed for the wheel. "Shoot, you fools! Shoot!" she called to the others.

"No—we came to *help*—" Lisketter began.

For once her followers ignored her. The diesel coughed and roared into life. When it did the men sitting cross-legged on the platforms at the rear of the catamarans sprang erect. They held up masks overhead in both arms, making pushing motions toward the schooner. *Magic of their own,* Martha thought wildly. She aimed at one of the men, remembering what her husband had told her—breathe out, squeeze the trigger—and felt the light kick of the .22 against her shoulder. The man looked up as the ceremonial mask tugged in his hands, then returned to his gestures. Martha worked the bolt and shot, again and again until the magazine was empty. She wasn't sure if she had hit anything. The schooner lurched under her feet as the helmsman tried to take her downstream and ran up against the anchor. The *Bentley* swayed and dipped, throwing people off their feet. Someone with more presence of mind than most ran to the bows and leaned far overside, chopping at the mooring line with a machete.

Martha saw a warrior in the lead catamaran set an atlatl dart in his spear-thrower. The arm whipped forward and

the American hung upside down, pinned to the side of the
schooner like an insect in a collector's cabinet. More of the
darts whistled by in flat fast arcs, and slingstones cracked.
The schooner's engine gave a cough and died. Martha went
down behind the meager protection of the low deckhouse;
some impulse made her pull Lisketter down beside her.
The catamarans swept in on either side, throwing grapnels
pronged with wood and stone. They bound fast to the bows
of the *Bentley,* and the rowers threw themselves flat. Over
them, vaulting off their backs, came the warriors in their
garb of feathers and skins and painted wood. What followed could hardly be called a fight. She saw one Olmec
slam a three-pronged pick shaped like claws into an American's shoulder, haul him close like a gaffed fish, and stab
into his belly with a knife of volcanic glass. Another crewman reeled back with his chest gashed open by a shark-
toothed rake.

The noise died, except for a screaming that went on and
on until a warrior stabbed downward to end the annoyance.
A few of Lisketter's followers fled belowdecks. Olmecs followed them, poking ahead gingerly with their spears and
holding torches high. Others scoured the deck. Martha
came to her feet cautiously, holding up empty hands, trying
not to shake. The onslaught had been so quick and brutal
that it was hard to grasp; it seemed impossible that people
who'd been whole just a few seconds before were now
bleeding lumps of meat. Eyes turned toward her, and
toward Lisketter where she crouched in shock-driven silence. Pride stiffened her spine; she crossed her arms on
her chest, resisting the impulse to lay protective hands over
her swelling belly. *They can kill me, but I'm the only one
who can make myself act like a disgrace,* she told herself.
And she didn't think that groveling would do much good
with this bunch.

The warriors seized her, and hauled Lisketter to her feet.
They were hustled forward to the clearer space near the
bow; there was only one other living prisoner, dazed,
bruised, and battered. The Indians were laying a gangway
from one catamaran to the deck of the schooner. The man
from the platform at the rear stepped up onto it, and it
shuddered under his tread. He was big, tall and massively
built, heavy muscle moving under a generous coat of fat.
Cross-straps over his shoulders held an ornate pectoral of

colored woods inlaid with rosettes of stone. Over it hung
a concave mirror that she recognized as polished hematite,
iron ore, polished until it reflected torchlight as brightly as
glass might have done. On his head was a mask-helmet in
the shape of a jaguar's head cunningly fashioned from
wood, bone, and real fur, with his own thick-lipped, heavy-
featured face staring out through the fanged muzzle. A
cloak of jaguar skin half-hid his massive upper arms, and
one hand bore a curious ceremonial weapon, four basalt
claws fixed at the end of a yard-long shaft.

He walked with an odd swaying gait, each foot turned a
little sideways as it went forward. *Of course,* Martha
thought, dazed. *He's trying to imitate a panther . . . no, a
jaguar.* Her glance darted aside. The warriors were much
like the folk she'd seen on visits to the Yucatan over the
years; darkish brown, of medium height, their faces al-
mond-eyed and big-nosed; these men were tremendously
lithe and muscular as well, many of them hideously scarred
under their finery. She remembered how they'd advanced
howling into gunfire, undaunted by death utterly mysterious
and supernatural. Their commander looked different
enough to be of a separate race, even discounting the obe-
sity. *Or maybe an inbred royal family? Priest-king,* she decided. It was a label no more likely to mislead than any
other.

There was no mistaking the look in his eyes, though.
Power, raw and absolute. It showed too in how the warriors
bowed low as he passed. Others held the prisoners forward
for his inspection. A word, and they were stripped as well,
and torches brought close to examine them. The big man
seemed fascinated by the strangeness of their skin and hair,
pinching and tugging. When he came to Martha his eyes lit
and he touched her rounded belly, smacking his lips as he
did so. His teeth were filed to points; they glittered in the
torchlight. The pupils of his eyes were wide, wider than the
dimness would have made them. Next he turned to
Lisketter.

"We came to help—" she began.

There were shocked cries from the warriors, and raised
weapons. Evidently you didn't speak until spoken to, with
Big Chief Baby-Face. The back of his meaty hand smacked
across her mouth, leaving blood trickling in its wake.
Lisketter's eyes went even wider with shock; she looked

around, as if the blow had brought her out of a stupor and
made her realize that this was *real*. The priest-king's hand
rose to strike again, and then froze. He gave back a step,
pointing at Lisketter's face. He shouted something in his
own language, a tongue that seemed to consist mostly of
"u," "x," and "z" sounds.

No, not at her face! Martha thought, with a trickle of
desperate hope. *At her* eyes, *that's what he's frightened by.*

What . . . *of course!* Lisketter had greenish-yellow eyes,
about as close as a human could get to the way the eyes
of one of the big cats looked. *Were-jaguar cult.* Nobody
knew for sure, but the Olmec myths—or at least some of
them—seemed to center on a mating between a woman
and a divine jaguar that produced a race of part-felines.
Evidently the archaeologists and anthropologists had
guessed right this time. *I get off because I'm pregnant, and
Lisketter because she's cat-eyed.*

Spared. Who knew for how long, and for what purpose?
But every moment you were alive was one you weren't
dead. . . . The fat chieftain recovered his composure,
enough to signal again with his claw-pick. The warriors
holding the two American women dragged them back a
few paces. More forced the next captive to his knees and
pulled back his head. A flat-bottomed ceramic bowl was
brought forward, one big enough to hold gallons. She
closed her eyes and swallowed hard, heard the brief desperate gasping and a long scream cut off in a gurgle. Slowly—
it was the hardest thing she had ever done—she forced the
lids open again. The warriors were dragging the corpse
away by its ankles—away to the catamaran, with the other
bodies, those killed in the fighting. She thought she knew
why. The priest-king held the flat-bottomed bowl up to his
lips and drank deeply, trickles of red running down from
the corners of his mouth, then passed it to his followers.
Then what she had expected happened; fire on a big
wooden ship was a menace they'd be unlikely to understand, not having anything with enclosed decks. Flame
belched out of a porthole, and the remaining Indians
poured up the companionways, yelling in panic.

The gangway thundered under the chief's steps as he
retreated to his own vessel. His followers hustled the
Americans in his wake and the rest poured after. The oarsmen rose from the crouch where they had waited like stat-

ues and pushed their craft away. By then fire was licking upward from every door and porthole, red tongues of flame casting a flickering light on the river, and the roar became loud. Martha watched motionless, ignoring the grip on her arms. Beside her Pamela Lisketter stood as silent, weeping slow tears that fell from her face. The canoes rowed for the land, with a last fierce heave by the oarsmen that sent the keels of the twin hulls riding up on the slick mud.

Out on the river the masts of the schooner fell into the blaze; there was chanting and singing ashore, dancing, fires built high in the hot insect-swarming night. Martha and Lisketter were dragged up to the earthen mound, past larger buildings of wood and thatch, past hearths being prepared for cooking. Behind a massive wood table was a cage; hands thrust them inside, and spearmen stood as guards. The giant priest-king seated himself on the table—*throne, perhaps?*—and sat like a statue with legs crossed. His warriors stood before him, then went to a resting posture on one knee, weight back on that heel. Their feather crests bobbed in the slight breeze, casting grotesque shadows as the feast was prepared; they and the platform-throne cut off sight of what was being done.

A little later a woman came with bowls of food: cakes of maize and cassava, fish, beans, and a small bowl of meat. The two Americans began to eat mechanically, after a while.

"I wouldn't touch that," Martha said quietly when Lisketter reached for the bowl of meat.

The kidnapper looked up dully. "Why not?" she said.

"You can't smell what's cooking out there, stuffed up like that." The other woman had been weeping until her nose ran. "I can."

Lisketter's eyes and lips framed a question. There was no need for speech. After a moment she pushed the bowl violently away and curled around herself on the earth platform stacked with cut grass that served the cage as a bed. Martha doggedly forced down as much as she could. There was a gourd of fermented maize as well, like a thin gruel-beer. She drank that too. Tomorrow and in the days that followed she would need strength, and the baby had to be fed.

When the time came . . . she looked around. *They'll need to know we're alive.*

*   *   *

Alston lowered her binoculars. "No sign of them," she said, keeping her face carefully blank. It was illogical to feel disappointed. Not sensible to expect the *Bentley* to be trapped neatly here, but there was a feeling of letdown all the same.

"They'll have gone upriver, Captain," Ian said. "That's definitely the Coatzacoalcos."

"Or they foundered on the way here, or passed on farther south, or stopped farther north," Alston noted. Still, this was the maximum probability. . . .

"Ma'am!"

The forward lookout called. "Something floating!"

The winds were faint, and the echo sounder showed these waters to be shallow. It took some time to maneuver the *Eagle* close to the debris, and a few minutes more to lower a boat to hook onto it. Alston stood like stone, feeling the sweat trickling down her flanks even under the light tropical uniform with its short-sleeved shirt. The heat didn't particularly bother her; it was even a little homelike—summers in the Carolina low country were much like this. Her gathering suspicions of what they would find, however . . .

The sailor in the ship's boat next to the flotsam prodded at something. "There's a body here, ma'am, legs tangled in something. Looks like one of ours, from the clothing. Been in the water a while, couple of days."

"Well, you were right," she said quietly to Arnstein. To the sailing master: "We'll anchor here, Mr. Hiller."

Tom Hiller looked around at the estuary of the Coatzacoalcos. The land was low and flat, and the sea stretched behind them like hammered metal. "We could get a nasty blow out of the Gulf any time, ma'am," he said. "It's hurricane season."

"That's not the only nasty thing 'round here," she said, nodding downward.

The body was—had been—an American; the clothing was unmistakable. She heard Doreen swallow a retch behind her, but the Coast Guard officers were all familiar with the bloating that went with a submerged body and the way the sea life ate its way in. What drew her eye was the broken-off shaft that protruded from the dead man's ribs.

"Think of a few thousand of the locals coming out under cover of darkness," she said. "Especially if we were farther in, where the banks are close and there's no room to maneuver."

He nodded. "How are we going to get up the river at all, then, Captain?" he asked.

"Cautiously, in small boats, and with difficulty, I suspect, Mr. Hiller," she said thoughtfully. "But first we'll have to find out what went on, and where everyone is. Call Mr. Toffler, and get his transport ready."

Assembling the ultralight was difficult in the cramped quarters of the *Eagle*'s waist deck; the wings were long enough to overlap the rails on both sides. It was essentially a big hang glider with an aluminum trapeze below, a tiny pusher prop and engine behind the seat, and rudimentary controls.

Sort of like a beginner's sketch of an airplane, the Kentuckian pilot thought. A far cry from going "downtown" in an F–4 Phantom; more like being a forward air controller, not a trade he'd ever wanted to take up before. The sodden heat was familiar enough, though, and the look of the shore. They were all sweating hard, and in this oily humidity it didn't evaporate, just got into your shorts and chafed.

Sailors and cadets finally mounted the frame on the cutdown metal canoes that served for floats and bolted the wing to it. The boom came around; two dozen hands held steadying ropes, while others hauled at the line that hoisted it free of the deck.

"Careful, there," he muttered; no point in saying it aloud.

They slid it out sideways, threading the wings between the rigging and then swaying them around bit by bit until they were parallel to the ship. After that it was fairly simple to pay out the ropes until the *God Help Us* lay bobbing slightly beside the big windjammer. He'd named it himself, after the first flight back on the island.

"*Eagle,* the Coast Guard's first aircraft carrier," he said as Captain Alston came up beside him.

She nodded, as expressionless as usual. Toffler wasn't quite sure about her. He didn't really approve of women in situations like this, and he certainly didn't approve of her private life; he was a good Baptist. On the other hand, he *was* pretty certain she wouldn't lose her nerve. If she went wrong, it would be the other way.

"Keep in close contact and follow the program," she said. He nodded. "Remember that they may have rifles. And good luck."

"Thanks, Captain," he said.

I am certainly *not going to forget that they may have rifles,* he thought, climbing over the side. You didn't necessarily get less brave as you got older, but you did start realizing that you could really, really, *really* die, and how easy it would be. Sometimes he wondered if war would be possible at all without that nineteen-year-old conviction of immortality. *Well,* you're *here, aren't you?* he asked himself sardonically. *And you're getting into this miserable goddam excuse for an aircraft, aren't you?*

Crewfolk were holding the ultralight steady for him. He stepped onto one of the floats, ignored the alarming bob and dip, scrambled up into the seat, and strapped himself in. The earphones went on next.

"This is *GHU,*" he said into the microphone before his lips. "Testing, testing."

"*Eagle* here. Loud and clear. Keep in touch."

"Roger wilco that."

The engine caught with a lawn-mower buzz. Toffler looked up to check the wind direction, came into it, and pushed the throttles forward. The little Rogallo-wing aircraft came up off the surface as if angels were pulling on rubber bands. He banked; the *GHU* was maneuverable enough, but only about as fast as a car. The height and stiff wind cut the muggy heat to something more nearly bearable, and he felt the exhilaration he always did aloft. Certainly more interesting than flying a puddle-jumper between Hyannis and Nantucket, ferrying tourists. Looking for whales and schools of fish had been getting pretty routine, too.

The river wound through the forest beneath. He looked at the map taped to the frame to his right, and then at the compass strapped to his left forearm. "Heading west," he said.

"Roger."

The lesser canoes peeled off to villages along the riverbanks as they headed west. Martha and Lisketter had a good view; they were kept near the throne-seat of the chief at the rear of the catamaran. The settlements were much like the first they'd seen, but they grew larger and more numerous, the jungle between them less, as they traveled. None were very far from the river's banks, though, or the banks of the tributaries that gave into it. Despite weariness, Martha found herself a fascinated spectator. *We knew so little. . . .*

Crops grew more densely on the rich silt of the riverbanks. Canoes and rafts passed ever more thickly, but the water still teemed with life and the sky was always full of wings. And the people . . . *Oh, damn, what I wouldn't give for a camera, or even pen and paper to take notes!* Part of her knew that the thought bordered on madness, but she pushed that away. Better than brooding on her helplessness.

The river narrowed and the current became stronger; the sun blazed down through a sky half-hazy, and she was glad of the shade at the rear of the craft. At intervals servants— she assumed that those near-naked figures were such— brought food and water or the weak maize-beer-gruel to the commander and his warriors, and to the two American women; this time it included small avocados juicy enough to be eaten by themselves, and once a hot liquid brewed at a clay hearth amidships. After a moment she identified it as unsweetened chocolate, harsh and bitter, and set it aside. Others fanned the obese figure that sat cross-legged and silent on his platform beneath the gaudy colors of the carved beasts, brushing away insects and bringing a little, little coolness to the constant clinging heat.

At last they came to a sudden fork, where the waters divided around an oblong island some miles across and more long. Most of it was covered with oxbow lakes, or drained for farming and speckled with thatched hamlets of clay huts. But the plateau at the southern tip had been sheered off and built up; suggestions of color and massiveness showed even at several miles' distance. The catamarans turned for the shore; the paddlers were too exhausted now to chant, grunting in unison instead. Ten yards from the edge of the water they stopped with a final panting shout, and the big vessel coasted forward, sliding to a halt with hardly a jar. Crowds of attendants waited for them on the beach; warriors, more villagers or servants in plain loincloths and skirts, other types she couldn't hope to identify. Drums beat, smaller than the great booming instrument in the bows of the catamaran; other instruments played, pipes, gourd rattles, shell whistles, and the people sang accompaniment. A dozen bore a huge litter, and those waded out into the water until the priest-king could step onto it dry-shod. They bore his massive weight without a bob or waver, walking back up onto the land and then swinging away in a disciplined lockstep trot.

"We're next," Martha said.

Another litter came down to the side of the catamaran. It was as ornately carved as its predecessor, but lacked the canopy above. Warriors shoved and pointed, indicating the two women should climb aboard it; around them were piled spoils from the *Bentley.*

"Why are they doing this?" Lisketter whispered, as the bearers swung up the beach and onto a packed-dirt road. She hadn't spoken since the previous evening.

"Who knows?" Martha said. "At a guess, we've stumbled into some sort of myth that's important to them—something to do with their primary god or goddess or whatever, the jaguar. We're starring actors in a play and we don't have any idea what the script is."

The bearers broke into a trot along the dirt road. It was embanked and neatly ditched, raising it a little above the soft black earth of the cornfields tasseling out around them and the cassava patches, vegetable gardens, groves.

"Why? It doesn't make *sense,* none of it makes *sense.*"

"For someone who's supposed to be a multiculturalist," Martha said, "you had a really naive faith that everyone else's sense would be the same as yours. That's a little logocentric, isn't it?" Lisketter winced as from a blow. Martha put a hand on her arm. "Sorry, but . . . no, sorry. Just keep your eyes open. I have a very bad feeling about all this, and if we're to come out of it alive we need to keep our wits about us."

Shouts broke out among the Indians crowding around them, and the workers in the fields. They were pointing southward, into the sky. Martha turned.

CHAPTER FIFTEEN

October, Year 1 A.E.

"The natives are restless," Alston said, listening to the drums as they echoed under the sound of the engines. Beside her Swindapa nodded gravely. Lieutenant Hendriksson cast a quick uncertain glance her way, then smiled wryly. Somebody farther back in the boat snickered.

Good for morale, Alston thought. Let her people see that the skipper wasn't oppressed by the alien weirdness of the surroundings. *Much,* she added to herself in blunt honesty. Besides, it *had* come to her spontaneously.

The boats from the *Eagle* were advanced up the twisting river in a broad wedge, with the motor launches to the fore acting as scouts. Behind them came the twoscore big inflatable lifeboats; their powerful outboard engines let some of them tow long whaleboats brought along for this voyage. On either side the jungle reared, a medley of greens and great gaudy slashes of flowers, flights of birds like living jewels with their long tails dangling behind them in streaming banners of blue and turquoise, showers of rainbow-hued butterflies. Birdcalls echoed, raucous or sweet. Now and then an alligator, now and then a cluster of tapirs on the bank snorting away in crashing, noisy panic. Once the unmistakable scream of a jaguar. Always the muggy, clinging heat; always the faraway stutter of the drums.

Sweat trickled down into the padding under her armor; a certain percentage were wearing theirs, the others keeping it near to hand, and the sets switching over at two-hour intervals. Practice and sound design meant that they could scramble into it in short order, even in the cramped quarters of the boats. Wearing it courted heat exhaustion, though; and anyone who went overside in forty pounds of steel . . . well, it was a long wet walk along the bottom to the edge. She blinked at the huge red disk of the sun, sinking ahead of them. Not always directly ahead; the river wound considerably.

What really worries me is how vulnerable these rubber boats are to flung weapons, she thought. And they were laden enough that the outboard engines gave them only a little edge of speed against a well-crewed canoe.

A buzzing came from the radio. "*GHU,* this is *Eagle,* over."

"*Eagle,* the village is just around the next bend in the river," Toffler said. His ultralight was circling at the edge of vision, perhaps a mile and a half ahead. "The sunken hulk is definitely the *Bentley.* Burned at her moorings, looks like."

"Sure they've cleared out, *GHU*?"

"Ma'am, they ran like hell. Over."

"Rendezvous there, then. Over and out."

For a moment the craziness of it struck her. An aerial scout, a flotilla of inflated boats of complex synthetics driven by engines, the whole coordinated by radio, and each boat filled with Nintendo-generation warriors in steel armor armed with swords, spears, and crossbows. *And the real irony is that this medieval metalwork is almost as far-future compared to the locals as the solid-state electronics in this radio.* That reminded her to make yet another mental note to be careful with that equipment. Nantucket wouldn't be making microchips in her lifetime.

She had a Colt Python .357 Magnum at her side, but less than thirty rounds for it—twenty-seven, to be precise, counting the six in the chamber. The machine shop back on Nantucket could make more, in limited quantities, but there was nothing to charge them with, nor fulminate for the primers. There were three other handguns with the expeditionary force, and another back on *Eagle,* and that was *it.* The *Bentley* had, or had had, more in the way of firearms, and it hadn't seemed to have done them much good. What Alston did have was two hundred trained, disciplined people. She hoped that would make the difference.

They sailed into gathering murk; it was quieter as the day's wildlife sought its lairs and roosts, and the noctural versions weren't out. A long looping curve and suddenly there were cleared fields, then buildings and canoes drawn up on the bank.

And the schooner's grave. The tip of one mast still stuck forlornly out of the water, not far from where Toffler's ultralight bobbed on its floats. She could see how fast it must have sunk by the relative lack of damage; it just looked like something had taken big black-fringed bites out of the sides. They'd brought an Aqua-Lung, but she didn't think the diver would find much useful. On the north bank the village waited, smoke still trailing up into the darkening sky but eerily quiet, not even a dog barking.

"We'd better get set up," she said, and switched the radio to the general frequency. "Smith, Bulosan, take first picket." Those were the motor launches; they also had the diver. "Group A, all personnel in battle order, and follow me. Mr. Ortiz, you'll maintain station with Group B until I give the signal."

She put on her helmet and clipped a small walkie-talkie to the belt about her waist; it still felt rather odd to have no specific sensation of pressure or weight there, but the armor took all that. The lifeboat rocked under her as crew scrambled into their armor. A dozen boats turned inward for the shore, cut their engines, and grounded. The Americans leaped over the sides, hauled their craft up, and fanned out to make a perimeter. Alston was with them, eyes peering into the gathering mirk. Nothing moved, except the rustling of scrubby-looking cornstalks and the buzz of insects. She raised the radio to her lips. "Lieutenant Ortiz, bring Group B in and take over here."

The others followed her as she walked down the single street of the village. The huts were laid out with some precision, and were bigger than she might have expected. Her followers inspected each, prodding at the recesses with blades to make sure nobody was hiding. She entered one herself, clicking on her flashlight. Bedding and tools lay tumbled, as if the locals had simply snatched up whatever was at hand when they fled the apparition in the sky. They must have been three-quarters terrified already, after the brush with the *Bentley*. The solid wattle-and-daub walls came only to waist height, leaving the hut relatively cool and airy with the woven mats rolled up under the eaves. Possessions were few: flat-bottomed pottery that looked hand-formed, not thrown on a wheel, and bigger globular jugs, both decorated with incised designs. One end of the hut held a terra-cotta figurine of a babylike figure with flat features and fangs; probably a shrine. Hooks, lines, barbed fishing spears, and stone hoes and adzes were in corners. A *metate* and grindstone lay abandoned, surrounded by corn and maize meal; beside it was a clay platter with a mound of oozing grated cassava.

"Captain!"

She dropped a hand to the pistol; that voice was urgent. A cadet dashed up. "Ma'am, Section Leader Trudeau says there's something you ought to see right away."

He led her and the others up the village street to the earth platform. It was about five feet high, a rectangle thirty feet by fifty, made of the same clay loam as the earth around. The sides sloped inward, smoothed and coated with colored stucco in patterns that looked abstract until she saw past the alien iconography to the shapes of men, animals, and birds. They went up turf steps to a platform that held buildings larger and more ornate than the village, but of the same basic style. The exposed wood was carved and painted in a floridly baroque style. *Damn, but those animals look like something out of Dr. Seuss,* she thought. Cooking hearths stood beneath gazebo-like roofs. Stone gutters led water away, keeping the surface dry; there were ornamental plantings.

Ruling-class housing, she thought. Or possibly the equivalent of a church. A place where power resided, at least.

"Ma'am."

That was Trudeau, his face looking pale and ill in the fading light. That reminded her that the enemy would probably be much better at sneaking around in the dark than most of her command. "Let's get some floods set up here," she called over her shoulder. "Mr. Trudeau?"

He was an upperclassman, near graduation; a slender dark blue-eyed young man, Maine-born of French Canadian stock.

"Ma'am, I've, uh, found where some of the *Bentley*'s crew went."

She began to suspect as he led her over to one of the hearths. The bones were unmistakably human, and the dental work in the skulls equally certainly of the twentieth century. The meat on the spits and in the pots . . . The smell was thick, like pork stewing or roasting, horribly appetizing. She swallowed heavily once; behind her came the sound of retching.

"Arrange a burial detail, Mr. Trudeau," she said. "But not until I give the word. There was something else?"

Lights blinked on as the equipment was carried up from the village. Trudeau turned away, obviously relieved. "This way, ma'am."

Like the village, the settlement on the platform was laid out on either side of a street. At one end was an open space, trampled hard and set down into the soil. Wooden scaffolds set with stone and painted figures held hoops at either end; in a weird way, it reminded her of a basketball court. At the other end was a wooden platform, smoothly pegged together. Its front was carved in the likeness of a cross-legged man wearing a jaguar mask and holding a rope in either hand. That led around the sides of the slab, to carved images of bound prisoners on either side. Behind the slab in turn stood a roofed cage, with a single door that could be securely fastened. The senior cadet led her toward it.

"It took a bit of looking, ma'am," he said. "And we were sort of, you know, shook up. But here it is."

They entered the cage, flashlights probing. Insects fluttered in and out of the beams. "Over here by the back."

The bars of the cage were hard wood, notched into a single huge undecorated foundation beam on each side. Part of their surface had grown soft and punky with rot, and doubtless they would have been replaced soon. In the meantime they had a surface soft enough to scratch. The shaky letters on one of them spelled one word: *Upstream.*

Behind her, Ian Arnstein spoke softly: "At least it's not 'Croatan.' Some of them were alive, then. One at least."

"And I know just which one, Professor," Alston said.

Deep in a fissure of the wood, metal gleamed. She went to one knee and dug carefully with the point of her *tanto* knife. The wood was hard below the weathered layer, but in a few seconds the metal popped free and she scooped it up. A plain golden ring, sized for a woman's hand. A wedding ring. She held it up and shone the flashlight on the inner surface.

"Martha Cofflin's," she said, and knelt silent for a moment, long black fingers curling about it. Then she rose and spoke briskly: "Trudeau, maintain your perimeter." With the handset in her grasp, she gave further orders: "Mr. Ortiz, please relieve all perimeter guards and workin' parties in succession. I want them all to come and see something up here."

It was a good thing to know your enemy.

"So, does this count as our first fight?" Doreen said, tight-lipped.

"We're not fighting, we're just *discussing*," Ian hissed back.

The expeditionary force had built up the hearths from stored firewood—except the ones where *that* had been cooking—and put a line of watchfires along their perimeter. Doubtless the eyes of the village's inhabitants saw that, where they huddled in the jungle and swamp that bordered the inland edge of their fields, and also the harsher brilliance of portable electric lights. Insects buzzed about; the stores of mosquito repellent were already running low, and huge bright tropical moths plunged into the fires. Despite the shock of what they'd seen, the camp was no longer funeral-quiet. Food was cooking, stored rations, fish and duck caught on the trip up the river, cornmeal and vegetables from the huts. For a while he'd thought he would never want to eat again, but the smell set his stomach rumbling. It had turned very slightly cooler, with a breeze from the river, as the sections assembled below the earth platform. The Arnsteins fell silent with the rest as Captain Alston stood to address them.

"You've all seen what was going on here," she said.

A snarling mutter went through the ranks below. *More angry than afraid,* Ian decided. Evidently Captain Alston knew them better than he did . . . which was, after all, her specialty.

"We have definite proof that Ms. Cofflin, at least, was still alive yesterday and was taken upriver toward these . . . people's main town. I intend to follow and rescue her. Because I really don't approve of Americans being tortured, killed, and eaten. These people need to be taught a good, hard lasting lesson along those lines."

The mutter grew into an angry cheer, guttural and full of menace. Alston nodded. "Good. Keep eager. Just remember that the difference between a real military force and a bunch of savages is discipline. We've got it, they don't, and that's why we're going to go up that river tomorrow and kick cannibal butt."

The next cheer was more like a roar. Alston cut it off with a chopping gesture of her hand. "So eat hearty and get a good night's sleep; you'll need your strength tomorrow. Dismissed."

"Where were we?" Doreen said, as the ranks broke, their noise louder and more cheerful.

"Ah . . . I think we were about to have a totally useless argument," Ian said.

"Yup, that sounds right," Doreen said. They met each other's eyes and laughed.

"It's not as if the captain would lay on a boat to take you back to the *Eagle,* anyway," he sighed. "Still, I wish you hadn't insisted."

"We're a team," Doreen said. They began walking toward their quarters. "How'd you put it . . . Speakers-to-Savages?"

A burst of laughter came from the next hearthfire down. "A little touch of Harry in the night," Ian quoted. Doreen chuckled. Most of the sections assigned to huts had kept the fires going at a low level even after their cooking was done, despite the heat and the insects it attracted. The flames were heartening, he supposed; ancestral memories.

"Odd to think we're actually going to be fighting a battle like Agincourt," she said. "Swords and spears and all. . . . Hi, Marian."

Alston sank down a little way from the fire that burned in its clay bowl before their hut, nodding reply to their greetings. "Fo' Christ's sake don't offer me another cup of that goddam sassafras tea, Doreen," she said. "I'm going to be up often enough tonight as it is." Her teeth showed white against the darkness, and her eyes; otherwise she almost vanished.

"Wait until you're my age," Ian grumbled. "Every bloody night."

"You should try being pregnant," Alston said, topping him neatly.

He blinked. *Yes, she was once, wasn't she?* Twice. Odd to think of it. Odd to think of her as a mother, too.

"Aren't you going to reassure us?" he asked.

"I might, if you were going to be anywhere near the

action," she said. "Assumin' there is action. I'd prefer to bargain Martha out and go." She paused, arms around her knees and chin on them. "Well, no, that's not quite right. I'd *prefer* to drop napalm an' cluster bombs on them. As it is, I'd rather not fight. Too much chance of our hostages bein' hurt, for starters."

"What do you think our chances are?" Doreen asked.

"Mmmm, pretty good," she replied. Little flames licked in the dark irises as she stared into the flames. "Cortez conquered Mexico at longer odds. I—we—could probably do the same."

"You think so?" Ian said, surprised.

She nodded slowly, with the faraway look of deep thought. Alston wasn't what he'd consider well read in history, but she had a good working knowledge of those parts of it that interested her.

"Cortez conquered Indians with Indians," she said. "He could do it because he came from a more . . . advanced military an' political tradition. Weapons didn't—won't—wouldn't have—mattered much. They outthought the locals as much as they outfought them."

"I see what you mean," Ian said thoughtfully. "That was Machiavelli's home century, near enough. Montezuma spent his time worrying about whether Cortez was the Feathered Serpent come back again, while good old Hernán was analyzing how the Mexica hegemony worked and taking it apart. We could probably learn the languages, find out who's enemy to who, and—"

"Exactly," Alston said. "We've got more of a technical edge than the Spaniards did, too. The only thing Cortez had that I envy was experienced troops to start with. Ours are green, 'specially at this hand-to-hand style of fightin'. That's the only thing that worries me, and that not much."

Doreen looked alarmed, and sounded it. "Surely you're not thinking of conquering this country!"

Alston showed her teeth. "What, *live* here in this rotting sauna, and get stuck *rulin'* these lunatics? I'd rather juggle live squid in a laundromat. Thought you knew me better than to think that's what I want, Doreen."

The fire had died down; many of the others were out, and the huts filled with sleep. *Not to mention snores,* Ian thought. He'd noticed that the young needed sleep less and got it more easily.

"What do you want, if you don't mind me asking?" he said, curious. As soon as the words were out he half wished them back. On the other hand, curiosity was one itch he'd never been able to resist scratching, and he doubted he ever would.

"Want?" She shrugged. "What does anyone want? A job doing something important, and doing it well, and enjoying doing it. To have good friends, and deserve them. Love too, of course." Her smile grew gentle. "Can't complain on any of those counts, now."

Doreen's hand sought Ian's. "Things must have been, um, difficult for you, before the Event."

"Oh, I wouldn't say that," Alston said judiciously. "Unless you'd call havin' any chance of a decent personal life destroyed by lying politicians who pander to the bigotry of a bunch of dimwit redneck peckerwood jackasses 'difficult.' Difficult." She snorted. "Thus do we protect our sacred family values."

"Sorry."

"Oh, no problem." She rose, and grinned again. "Got nothin' to complain about now that *I'm* making the rules . . . although they give you privileges I don't get, you lucky civilians, you."

After their goodbyes the two looked at each other. "She's right, you know," Ian said, straight-faced. "It would be unfriendly and ungrateful not to."

Still holding hands, they went into the hut. *And besides,* Ian thought, *tomorrow we may die.* Quite literally.

"What would you have done if they were all dead?" Swindapa asked.

The alien night pressed down around her; despite the heat she shivered slightly. They were sitting at the edge of the earthen platform, looking down at the village. Out on the water two more lights went like stars and glittered in the river, where boats guarded against surprise. Trees cut off the horizon on every hand, black against the frosted multitude of stars. Those glimmered in the water, bright and many. Even the smells of water and earth were different, strange in a way that the Island was not, scents like spoiled bread and yeast and brewing beer. She looked up. Moon Woman's home floated huge and yellow near the horizon, casting a soul-path across the ripples.

All this world is Your daughter, Swindapa thought. *So You are always with me.* Her hand reached out and touched the captain's. Fingers clenched, infinitely soothing; so much could be allowed, here where none could see. How good it would be to lay arms around each other in comfort! This place was like the things the Sun People believed about Night Ones; like a dream of Barrow Woman, clutching at the souls of the dead.

"I would have turned around and gone back, if they'd all been killed," the captain said, her voice equally soft.

"Not taken revenge?" Swindapa asked.

Almost invisible, the dark head shook. "Not worth the risk of lives," she said. "As long as Martha's alive, yes, we keep goin'."

"Many more may die than one, though, if there's a fight."

A soft chuckle. "That's not the same thing. We don't . . . abandon our own, not while I'm in charge."

Swindapa nodded. "That's a good law," she said, and sighed.

The fingers tightened on hers. "I know you want to see your home again," the other woman said. "This . . . we may not be able to, this fall. The storm season is coming."

"I know," Swindapa said, keeping the shiver of longing out of her voice. Her mother, brothers, sisters, uncles. *And the Iraiina. They must be put back.* "I know. I know you had to do this, too."

The fingers squeezed hers gratefully. She touched them to her cheek. *The journey will come when it comes,* she thought. There was a rightness to going and returning in the same season. But oh, the time seemed long!

Morning broke hot and fierce, the dawn coming up like thunder out of the jungle to the east and clouds that piled on the edge of the world, turning their black heights to crimson and burning gold. Alston finished stretching and watched. Mist lay on the river, drawn by the increasing heat. Tendrils of it drifted between the great trees, as twisted as the vines and lianas that laced them together. *I really do prefer the temperate zone,* she thought.

"We'd better get under way as soon as Toffler reports," she said to Lieutenant Hendriksson; she and Lieutenant Ortiz followed their commander's gaze and nodded. "I don't like the look of those clouds."

The village swarmed with cadets and sailors making ready. The ultralight was drawn up, Toffler overseeing as fuel was pumped into the tanks from cans brought along.

"Full gear today," she went on. "And be ready for—"

Voices broke in, shouting—a group of the perimeter guards were hustling someone along. Not a local; he was dressed in the tattered remains of shorts and T-shirt. He stumbled and jerked as one of the cadets behind him prodded at him with a spearpoint. Alston frowned; then her face relaxed for a moment into carnivore anticipation as she saw the man had only one hand. Hers twitched to take the long hilt of the *katana*.

Finish the job, she thought. Then, scolding herself: *Of course not. We'll take him home, give him a fair trial, and hang him right next to his sister, if we can. Still . . .*

David Lisketter stumbled to a halt before her. He was plastered in mud, his thin face blotched with insect bites that also covered much of his body. The green-yellow eyes were staring behind smeared spectacles. At last they blinked and focused somewhat.

"Captain . . . Alston," he said.

"David Lisketter," she said. "You are under arrest for robbery, assault with intent to kill, complicity in first-degree murder, and kidnapping. Oh, yes, and high treason, too."

He straightened. "All right," he mumbled. "But Pamela, they've got Pamela, and Ms. Cofflin too. I saw."

"Saw what?"

"Canoes, big double canoes, two of them."

Alston made a motion with her hand. "Get the Arnsteins."

The cadets pushed him into the shade, and someone brought food and water. He wolfed the dry cassava bread and drank in gulping heaves. Ian and Doreen came up and hovered. Lisketter's account of the attack on the *Bentley* was disjointed; he'd seen only glimpses as he swam downstream and hauled himself out among the trees.

"They wouldn't *listen,*" he said, again and again. "I tried the Mayan words from the dictionary, and I thought they recognized a few—'east,' 'sea,' a few—but they kept talking so fast. And then they grabbed me, grabbed all of us, and they kept pointing to my eyes and shining lights in them and they wouldn't let *go.* I had to shoot, I had to!"

Ian Arnstein leaned forward, face gone keen. "Your eyes are the same color as your sister's, aren't they?"

Lisketter peered at him. "Yes, yes," he said.

Ian hurried off to the hut where he'd slept, and came back with something in his hands. It was a wooden mask, of a face halfway between human and jaguar, the eyes inlaid with some polished stone. He held it up beside the one-handed man. The eyes of the living man were a shade of amber-green almost identical to the jade insets.

"I think we have something here," Alston said. She clapped Ian on the back. "Congratulations, Professor."

"What . . . what happened to the others?" Lisketter asked.

"The locals ate them," Alston said. Lisketter bent over abruptly and lost the food he'd just swallowed.

"Get him cleaned up, and handcuff him."

"Ma'am? What about the village?"

"Load everythin' we can use," she said. Her eyes swept over the buildings. "Then torch it."

"Why haven't they tried to stop us, Captain?" Lieutenant Ortiz asked, bringing his boat alongside. "They've got a *lot* of those canoes, and they did attack the schooner."

Alston nodded; she liked junior officers who tried to puzzle things out. "The *Bentley* was sitting still. We're moving without oars, making a funny sound, and we've got Toffler's ultralight flying overhead. At a guess, they're spooked. They'll fight eventually, though, when we get to their capital."

Another village was passing by on the north bank, much like all the others—including the crowd of armed Indians waiting at the landing. The chanting and war dances were pretty standard too. She did a quick calculation, counting huts and heads, focusing her binoculars to count the relative proportions of commoners and brightly bedecked men with elaborate weapons; also the number of adult males, women, children.

"Either I'm grossly overestimatin' the number of people per hut, or a lot of their menfolk are beating our time upriver," she said.

Toffler's ultralight came slanting in from the northwest, sun bright on the colorful striped fabric of its wings. The radio reports were brief and sketchy, just confirmation that

Martha Cofflin and Lisketter were alive and captive. Now she could debrief him and get the videotapes; they might not have enough electricity for washing machines, but there was ample to charge a few batteries, thank God.

The ultralight sheened across the sky; it was as if suddenly reality had broken through the veil of myth. Men bore Martha toward a city where they worshiped a jaguar become human; but a man she knew flew overhead. She stood and waved, saw the wings waggle again in acknowledgment.

The chattering throng on the dirt roadway scattered like drops of mercury on dry ice. Porters threw away their burdens, men their spears, their screams shrill and loud enough to drown the buzzing little engine. Only a few of the caparisoned warriors followed them. Most grouped tightly around their leader's litter. Both halted to his command, and the heavy figure stepped forth, down a living staircase of bearers. He stood, arms akimbo, looking upward at the thing that flew five hundred feet above them.

Doesn't know what it is, of course, Martha thought. Aloud, in a murmur: "He can't really *see* it yet. Too alien. No scale, probably doesn't realize what size it is, maybe doesn't see that it's artificial, and yes, these priest-kings probably do hallucinogens of some sort. He's used to visions."

Toffler circled lower. He steered with one hand; the other held a video camera. Lower still, and suddenly the Olmec warriors realized—not what the flying thing was, but that a man was within it, and steering it. A few more of them fled, but their comrades brought those down with flung darts. The others raised a bristle of points around their lord. Lower still, and a rain of darts sprang up from their atlatls. Even with the spear-throwers they arched well below the aircraft, which circled away and banked. This time it came barely above the reach of the flung spears, straight down the roadway from the plateau citadel. The commander of the guards, a man with a jade plug in his lower lip and a headdress even more fantastically feathered than the rest, snapped an order. Bellowing surprise, the fat priest-king was bowled back into the covered litter. Half a dozen of the warriors threw themselves across him to put their bodies between him and harm. The rest crowded around the litter and its burden, casting darts, waving their rakes and spears and clubs, screaming defiance. Toffler soared above them, then brought the ultralight's nose up in a sharp climb. He circled once more, waggled his wings again, and circled higher.

The priest-king surged out of the litter, scattering the men who'd protected him with a shield of flesh. He roared something and slammed a fist into the face of the commander of his guards. The man reeled backward, fell, rose with his face a mask of blood. His overlord struck him again; the commander stood passively under the blows until the other man halted, panting. Then he went down on all fours and prostrated himself. So did the others; the big man kicked a few of them, then climbed back into his litter. The bearers heaved it upright, Martha's along with it, and trotted forward.

She watched the ultralight bank away to the southeast. "They're not far behind," she said quietly.

But what can they do?

"Run that by me again," Ian Arnstein said sharply.

The cassette whirred into reverse. The display unit was small, compact enough to be carried along in the boat. That rocked as several officers jostled slightly to see.

"Freeze that," he said. A book lay beside him; he picked it up and skimmed rapidly through the pages, each a little limp with the humidity. "Look."

He pointed; the picture was of one of the monumental Olmec stone heads. He brought it close to the flickering screen. "Pretty close resemblance, isn't it?"

Alston sighed and shook her head. "Well, there goes another theory." He looked a question at her. "There was speculation that those heads were signs of early contacts with the Old World—West Africa, specifically."

He looked at the picture. The features *did* look a little negroid, if you assumed that the depiction was realistic. But even so, the likeness to the heavy-featured man in the litter was unmistakable.

"Go on," she said.

"The archaeologists thought these heads were portrait-statues of Olmec rulers," Ian said. "From the looks of it, they were right for once. And now look at this."

He hit the fast-forward button, to the minute where the

guards threw themselves over their ruler. "Does this suggest something?" he said.

"The Secret Service do the same with the president, up in the twentieth," an officer objected.

"Yes, but he doesn't beat them up afterward," Ian pointed out. "I think that's a significant datum."

"Proving that pudgy-face here is a son of a bitch?" Hendriksson asked.

"Proving he's an absolute ruler. I'd guess he was a god-king; it was a common pattern later in these Mesoamerican cultures. Common in a lot of very early civilizations, for that matter. Old Kingdom Egypt, or the Shang. We know they practice human sacrifice, too. So it's probably very tightly centralized . . . one royal or divine family that marries within its own boundaries, or maybe with the other Olmec principalities, if there are more than one. That would account for the unusual appearance, too."

"It's a thought," Alston said meditatively. "Possibly irrelevant even if accurate, but it *is* a thought." A slender black arm moved past him to touch the controls. "Let's take a look at the layout of that city."

Martha blinked as they came up the slope and over the crest. The single-minded determination that had leveled this plateau and covered it with the structures she saw was impressive. They climbed up a spur on the southern side, debouching onto a broad ceremonial avenue that stretched thousands of yards ahead. The surface was made of hard-pounded clay stained different colors, reds and greens and oranges, making patterns she could only guess at as they went by. Two of the giant stone heads like those she'd seen in museums flanked the entrance, twelve feet high and hulking in their brutal menace, but they were not the monochrome remnants of her day. Here they were painted: yellow spotted with brown for the faces, brilliant yellow-green for the eyes, crimson for the tight-fitting helmets. On either side of the avenue were rows of hexagonal basalt pillars on timber bases; beyond them stretched rectangular pools joined by covered stone drains; more drains led to fountains done in wood and clay.

Around the pools were statues by the score, each in its cleared space; the brooding thick-lipped heads, birds of prey, jaguars and men in every possible degree of merging.

Nor was that the only type of merging depicted: one huge statue showed a gigantic jaguar copulating with a supine human female. The same theme was repeated over and over again on the vividly painted carved stelae of flat stone and stucco that covered the sides of the low earth mounds marking the axis of the avenue and its side streets. The woman gave birth, and the race of jaguar-faced infants was swept up by men in elaborate headdresses like those of the warriors around her.

She thought of the labor needed to haul stone hundreds of miles through these swampy alluvial lowlands, to carve it into these intricate shapes with nothing better than rock and wood for tools, to heap up these thousands of tons of earth, to gnaw hard tropical woods into shape . . .

Atop the mounds were buildings, their exteriors lavish with colored stucco and carving. In the doorways and open sides stood more people, including women of the same flat-featured massiveness as the priest-king. Banners of colored cloth and woven feathers streamed from the buildings; the women were bright with jewelry of colored stone and cloth. The smell was surprisingly clean for a preindustrial city, none of the sewer reek she'd experienced traveling in some Third World areas . . . *but then, they have those drains.*

The knowledge wasn't particularly comforting. The Romans had had excellent sewers as well, and look at *their* taste in entertainment.

"Well, here's the sticking point," Hendriksson said.

Alston nodded, looking ahead. A line of canoes stood from bank to bank of the river; beyond them, faint in the hazy distance, she could see the flat outline of the plateau where the Olmec city stood. She estimated their crews at six to seven hundred men, mostly naked brown peasants with spears and clubs; some two hundred of the feather-clad warriors she'd decided to call jaguar knights made up the center of the array. Most of those were on the two big catamarans that made up the center of the opposing host. Their chanting and the boom of their drums was loud in her ears, louder somehow than the droning putter of engines. Light glittered off the glass and painted wood of their weapons, a different sight from the metallic gleam from the American forces.

Silence fell, save for the jungle noises. Sweat trickled

down out of the foam-rubber padding of her helmet, stinging in her eyes; she licked it off her lips. The inflated fabric of the boat dimpled under her hand. *Well, I certainly can't fight a naval engagement.* The inflatable boats were simply too vulnerable and the odds too steep. *The problem with technological surprise is that it's only a surprise once.* After that, a determined opponent could usually figure out some countertactic. *On the other hand, we need to survive the next couple of hours.* Drums beat louder, and the native canoes began to surge forward. There was a time when you had to expend an asset.

"Mr. Toffler," she said into the microphone. "Now, if you please. The two big craft."

The ultralight skimmed over their heads, rising beyond to just above spear range. Black pins arched into the air as the Olmecs tried to bring him down; they'd lost a good deal of their initial awe of the aircraft—inevitable, if it was to stay over their heads and report back.

A dot arched down from the rod-and-fabric aircraft, trailing smoke. It landed on the river before the lead catamaran and burst into a puddle of flame several feet across. The Olmecs hardly noticed. Closer, only a few hundred yards now. Toffler came around again, recklessly low. Another dot. This one crashed into the foredeck near the drummer.

"What are those?" Doreen asked.

"Gasoline, benzene, detergent flakes, in three-gallon glass jars with a burnin' cloth fuse," Alston said without looking around. "Poor man's napalm."

She trained her binoculars. The Olmecs weren't ignoring *this*. The flame had spattered wide, soaking into the reed matting that covered the catamaran's deck, into the dry wood beneath. Gobbets spattered warriors and rowers; they leaped into the river, howling. The elaborate panoplies of the warriors burned like tinder, tall plumes of flame replacing the feathers of their headdresses. The advance of the canoe fleet suddenly turned ragged. Smoke and yellow-white fire billowed up from the catamaran, and the frantic water splashed by the crew did little good.

A few seconds later the warriors abandoned the drifting, helpless hulk and let it ride down on the current toward the Americans. Toffler banked and dove toward the second; it turned and drove back the way it had come, angling for the docks nearer the city. The ultralight pursued. Another bomb missed; a third hit, and by the time the frantic paddles drove the catamaran onto the riverbank mud, half of it was burning. The smaller canoes fled also, some in the wake of the bigger vessel, some upstream with no apparent intention of stopping, and some to the far shore, where the crews took to their heels.

"Molotov cocktails, by God!" Ian whooped. Cheers spread across the little riverboat fleet.

"Just so, Professor," Alston said grimly. "Next time they'll realize that those things can't hit small moving targets. If the other canoes had pressed in, we'd have been in trouble."

She raised the microphone. "All boats, to the shore."

They turned, bows lifting as the engines revved. The buzzing of the ultralight faded as it chivvied the fleeing canoes toward the city; the Olmecs were thoroughly panicked for now, and unlikely to make a stand. The motor launches and inflatables grounded where the natural levee of the riverbank was comparatively low, covered in cornfield and laced with footpaths.

Marian Alston stepped off the side and quickly forward, out of the zone where her boots were driven deep into the mud. More armored figures dashed by on either side of her. Other hands were deflating the lifeboats, heaping up the flattened shapes and pulling a tarpaulin over them. She wet a finger and held it up. Despite the clouds westward, the wind was from the sea—southeast, blowing from here toward the hilltop citadel.

"Get it started," she said.

Islanders kindled torches and spread out. Even in this damp climate the cornstalks were fairly dry by this season. Soon a wall of fire and black smoke was walking westward, faster than a man could. The smell was heavy and rank; behind it the fire left embers, black glowing stalks toppling into ash, a foot-catching chaos of half-burned vines bearing squash and beans. They tramped through it, to the highest point of the levee's ridge. To their right stretched more fields, and patches of undrained marsh. Behind Alston the standard-bearers raised their poles. One streamed with the Stars and Stripes, the other with the Coast Guard flag. Both bore gilded eagles above, and each standard-bearer was flanked by six guards with short swords and big oval shields. The expeditionary force fanned out to either side, a broad shallow V facing toward what would have been San Lorenzo. Crates went forward; working parties donned heavy gloves and began scattering their contents.

Swindapa spoke softly: "I hate this," she said. "The children haven't harmed anyone, and they will go hungry."

Alston nodded. "Can't be helped, 'dapa. Lieutenant Ortiz! Get that line set up!"

The radio beeped at her waist. She brought it up in one gauntleted hand.

"They're coming, Captain," Toffler's voice said. " 'bout a thousand of them, or a little more. I dropped a Molotov, but they just opened out around the spot and kept right on."

"About as I expected. Keep me posted and watch for any activity on the river." She went on to the officers: "Aggressive to a fault. Let's make some use of that."

Behind her the corpsmen were setting up an aid station for casualties. The Arnsteins were nearby; a clear path led from there to the bank, not that many could retreat if things went wrong.

Ian Arnstein nodded; he was a little pale, but otherwise taking it well. "We've probably stepped into a myth," he said. "They're reacting to what they think we are."

"Haven't even tried to parley," she agreed. And they'd thrown things at every boat she'd sent forward to try and talk. "I've got to keep them off-balance, keep hitting them."

"What do you plan on doing?" Ian asked.

"Giving them a good thrashin'," she replied. "Then maybe they'll listen to reason."

Swindapa shivered a little as she watched the Eagle People spread out in response to the captain's orders. It was a strange and terrible thing, this *discipline*. There was none of the shouting and shoving and milling about you'd expect with a big crowd of people, or even the arguing at a Town Meeting on the island. Just quiet directions, and hundreds moved as if they were the fingers of a single hand. *Even stranger and more terrible on land than on the great ship.* The captain's face was closed and shuttered, gone away from her while she made this Working, as if a different Power were there behind the dark eyes. Still, they would fight side by side.

She kept her left hand on the hilt of her sword and raised a shading hand to her brow, looking westward. Nothing to be seen there but smoke. Her braided hair was hot on her head; the helmet would give some shade, but also more heat. Never had she been so hot, the weight of the armor and padding squeezing at her ribs. Her heart thudded; the last fight she'd been in had not gone well. *I am with the Eagle People now,* she told herself. *And the captain.* The evil luck had been taken away when Moon Woman bore her beyond the circles of the world.

The islander force was spread out on either side, seventy-five armed with crossbows on each wing, standing in two ranks. In the center were a block of spear-bearers with oval shields, three deep. Green-enameled steel armor gleamed and clanked as they settled themselves; the round shields slung over the crossbowmen's backs clattered. The captain walked through the ranks, up and down once in front of them, speaking a word here and there. Then she returned, at the same steady, even pace.

"They should be—right, there they are," she said softly, looking west. "Wish I had more of a reserve. . . . For what we are about to receive, may the Lord make us truly thankful."

The enemy host were coming out of the smoke, trotting along, a great humming wailing chant preceding them. Their spearpoints bobbed and rippled as they came, a huge clot nearly a thousand strong. Some limped or hobbled, from feet seared as they walked through the embers. Others leaped or stamped, jerking in circles, dancing their way to the ground of war. Hands hammered on drums, mouths blew shell trumpets, bullroarers whirled. The feather banners were eye-hurtingly bright and beautiful.

"Not in any order," the captain murmured beside her, raising the binoculars. "But those are their shock troops in the center, the ones in the fancy clothes. The others are farmers. How far would you say, 'dapa?"

"Seven hundred yards?" she estimated.

It was called the Socratic Method, after a great teacher of ancient times, teaching with questions. There was a trick to judging distances; look at the men and see whether you could tell the movements of their legs, their arms, the shape of their weapons. Each gave you a measuring point to judge the distance. It was as cunning as a Star Working, in its way . . . but more practical.

" 'Bout that," Alston nodded. "What do you think they'll do?"

"Come around our edges . . . our flanks?"

"That would be the sensible thing to do, but—ah."

The conch trumpets wailed again, and the Olmec host stopped, eddying and swirling. Silence fell over the burned fields, broken only by the small clatters of warriors shifting in place and the flapping silk of the banners overhead. A tall figure strode forth from the enemy ranks, his body gorgeous with a tunic of plaited feathers; more fringed his painted shield and waved from his carved helmet-mask; he brandished a long wooden rake set with flint as he walked slowly forward. His voice came high and shrill, an endless wailing chant.

"A champion, making a challenge," Swindapa said, setting her helmet on her head and buckling the chin strap in place. Shade fell over her eyes, and on the back of her neck.

Alston nodded. "Doubtless you're right," she said, and waited until he was within range. Then she lifted the radio to her lips. "Mr. Ortiz, have that man seen to."

An order was barked. A cadet stepped out of the ranks of the crossbows, leveled her weapon, aimed carefully, and pulled the trigger.

Whung.

The sound was small and tiny, lost in the wind and the chaotic mutter of the enemy warriors. The Olmec champion stopped dead, jerking backward a little. He tottered three steps on his heels and fell with arms outstretched, raising a puff of black ash as his back hit the dirt. The enemy host stopped moving, talking, chanting, everything. For a long second Swindapa could feel their unbelief, and afterward sense their swelling outrage coming in a wave that made the little hairs along the back of her neck struggle to rise. Then a united scream of rage came up from them, and their selves followed behind it. First one, then another, then clumps of them, even the musicians casting aside their instruments. The host moved in a dense clot, many deep and still overlapping the line of the Eagle People. The captain reached back and drew her *katana;* her other hand held the radio. Her lips curled to show her teeth, and the Fiernan girl knew that this was exactly as she'd hoped.

She shivered a little. Marian was wonderful, a true gift from Moon Woman . . . but there were times when she was a little frightened of her.

"Points down," she said. The order was repeated, and the long spears came down in a single rippling motion. "Ready."

Voices echoed back from either side. The front rank of crossbows knelt, and both brought their weapons to their shoulders.

"About—" the captain murmured.

The Olmecs' massed pounding run was building into a headlong charge that nothing could stop. Then suddenly it *did* stop, leaping and screaming with a different note—pain, instead of rage. Those behind piled into those in front, sending many of them rolling and screaming even louder. Their own momentum packed them together; not until the sharp iron was in their feet could they understand why those in the lead had stopped at all. *Caltrops,* Swindapa knew. Two pieces of sharp iron, twisted together so that one of the four points stood uppermost no matter how they landed. And the enemy went barefoot. . . .

"Just goes to show," the captain said, "that you shouldn't get so mad you don't look where you're putting your feet." Louder: "Commence firing!"

WHUNNNG. The kneeling front rank of the crossbows loosed. There was another sound, like a wind through reeds, and then a slapping like fists on flesh. She could hear the section leaders shouting: "Reload! Second rank . . . *fire!*"

WHUNNNG. The short heavy bolts sleeted out like horizontal rain. They punched through hide and shield and bone, and in that massed target scarcely a single point could miss.

"First rank . . . *fire!*"

WHUNNNG.

Again and again; she set her teeth and made herself watch. Toffler swooped down and dropped another fire-bomb; this time the enemy were bunched, immobile. Men burned, clawing at the fire that stuck to their skins.

"Ignore the ones running! Go for the fancy-dress brigade!" the captain barked.

Those warriors were at the front of the Olmec array, facing the islander spears. And they were *advancing,* twisting the iron out of their feet and coming forward, stopping to do it again, leaving red tracks through the ash behind them. *WHUNNNG. WHUNNNG.* A tenth or more of them went down with every volley.

"Why don't they *run*?" Swindapa cried.

"They're warriors," the Captain said. "Their whole lives are bound up in their courage and sense of their own honor. They *can't* let danger or pain turn them aside."

A trickle of warriors won past the caltrops and ran forward, screaming defiance. Crossbow bolts slammed into them, but now they were a more scattered target, and some did not fall.

Closer, and Swindapa could see the contorted painted faces within the mask-helmets. One reached the line of spears, hacked down at a point, pushed forward. The second line stabbed at him.

"Harder! Kill him, goddammit!" the captain barked.

The Olmec swung his stone-edged club-sword with desperate force. His shield went up to stop a spearpoint, but the long steel head punched through the light wicker and the arm beneath. Another caught him in the side, pulling back with a jerk. More probed at him, until the feathers of his costume were dyed fresh scarlet. The warrior went to his knees with blood leaking from his mouth, but a comrade vaulted on his back and leaped, howling. The third-rank islander stumbled backward under the impact, and more Olmecs were coming up, loping for the gap in the line.

"Shit," the captain said. "Stay on my left, 'dapa."

She ran forward at her lover's side. The warrior saw them coming and turned, roaring. The rake came down, and the captain's *katana* came up to meet it. Stone swept along steel with a tooth-grating sound and the warrior half-turned with the impetus of the blow redirected. Flexing wrists snapped the blade up again, up and back, foot stamped forward, and the blade came down in a blurring curve, just as they'd practiced . . . only this time there was a man reeling away with an arm hanging by a thread, reeling and falling. The captain moved forward into the next, sword rising to *chudan no kame.*

Another beside him, spear arm back for the thrust. Swindapa pivoted to deal with that one. *Keep your mind out of the way,* ran through her. It was true. Her hands had learned; the sword came up and turned as she thrust, cutting edge up, right hand just behind the guard to guide and left on the pommel to give force, body moving behind it. Down, hands loose, now clench, elbows out . . . the impact, and she continued through the curve of the circular motion, whipping the sword through the diagonal and drawing the cut. Ruin flopped down to lie at her feet.

Swindapa staggered slightly as an obsidian spearpoint broke on her breastplate, knocking her back two steps. Her sword snapped up, cutting into the underside of the Indian's arms above the elbows, and he fell backward. That put him in the rear rank of spear-bearers, and a shield edge slammed down, twice.

Then there was no one else to fight here. More Olmecs were out beyond the line of spears, caught and slashing as the wielders slammed the points forward. The crossbows were down, and the islanders were unslinging the shields across their backs and drawing the short stabbing swords slung at their right hips. An Olmec rake came down on a metal-faced shield and the cadet staggered beneath it, going to one knee. The warrior stepped closer for another stroke, froze for a second's incredulity as he saw how the obsidian edge of his weapon exploded into fragments against the metal, and ran onto the long point of the upflung *gladius.* The cadet's comrades heaved her back as she knelt staring; others closed in, four against one, stabbing. One reeled back yelling and clutching at an arm bone-bruised through the armor that protected it. The others thrust and thrust again. The Olmec staggered, swung his blunted rake in a final circle, and collapsed. Blood ran out on the ashy ground from the broad wounds the leaf-shaped short swords had made.

And then the remaining foemen were running, running back the way they had come. *Woods Woman has their souls,* she thought—panic had taken them, the wild fear that breathes out of the deep forest.

"Fire! Don't let them get away!" the captain shouted in an astonishing husky roar, enough to cut through the confusion. Crossbows twanged again, enough to bring down a man here, another there, a steady trickle until the last survivors were out of range.

Swindapa tried to swallow, felt her tongue dry as leather.

The hand she released from the hilt of the *katana* was sticky, coming free with a *tack* sound as she reached for the water bottle at her waist. The bodies were steaming under the hot sun, the smells of shit and iron-copper blood already underlain by a slight sickly scent as tissue began to go off. Insects swarmed, feeding.

"We won," she said huskily, staring.

It wasn't a pleasant sight. The captain was right about that, though she hadn't truly believed until now. It was certainly a lot better than losing, though.

A hand patted her armored shoulder briefly. She stood straighter, feeling the constriction around her chest easing.

"We surely did," the captain said.

"Thank God for morphine," the corpsman said.

Alston nodded. The aid station was busy; there were a dozen seriously wounded Americans, one with a raked-open face who might not live. *We should modify these helmets—hinged cheek guards.* There were a couple of other face wounds, or blades driven in under armpits, or in the back of the leg. The doctor sewed and bandaged, debrided and cleansed. Orderlies moved the treated back under the awnings and stood by to keep the insects off.

And all from a few seconds of hand-to-hand, she thought soberly. If it had come to a melee, or if the numbers hadn't been so grossly unequal by the time the last Olmecs came into arm's reach, she doubted the Islanders' armor and weapons would have been enough. *We need a lot more practice, most of us.* Or Uzis and M-16s, whichever they could manage to get first.

"Good work," she said to the last of the conscious wounded, touching him gently on the shoulder.

He managed a smile, eyes wandering as the combination of drug and shock blurred the edge of thought. "Kicked cannibal butt, didn't we, Skipper?"

"We surely did, son. Now you rest—you've done your bit."

She stood and moved forward. You could see where the Olmecs had hit the caltrops; there was a row of bodies there, some piled two or three deep. *Must have gotten a third of them that way, held up while we shot them,* she thought. Swindapa came up with a bucket of water and they cleaned themselves. Blood swirled into the silt-brown liquid. They drank again from their water bottles; everyone seemed to be thirsty. She could feel the sweat oozing through the padding under her armor, as saturated as if she'd gone for a swim. Looking down she saw a line of bright scratches and a dint across the lower part of her breastplate, and she didn't even recall the blow landing. Without the metal, that would have cut halfway through to her spine; those obsidian bladelets were *sharp*. And it had all taken barely half an hour. . . .

"Ma'am." She returned the young man's salute; her hand went *tick* against the edge of her flared helmet. She seemed to be noticing details like that. And sensations stayed with her, the ugly slicing, jarring feeling of the sword going through muscle and bone . . . *Enough. Think about that later.*

"Ma'am, what shall we do with the enemy wounded? There are a lot of them."

"Bring them back to the aid station, but carefully. Mr. Ortiz! Stretcher bearers and guards for the enemy wounded. We'll do what we can for them."

"Mr. Toffler," she went on. "Report."

The noise of the ultralight's engine came through the handset. "Captain, they're still running, most of them, the ones that haven't fallen down along the way," he said. "The fancy ones are making for the city; they stopped about half a mile on, and they're in a clump retreatin' at a walk. No sign of Martha or Lisketter there, since they took them into the big place on the main earth mound."

"Thank you, Mr. Toffler. Well done, by the way."

There was a slight hesitation on the other end. "Hell, ma'am, I just flew around up here."

"Nevertheless, well done. Refuel when you have to, and stand by."

Martha watched through the narrow slit. The room was featureless adobe, and the roof overhang was wide, but the ventilation slit gave a bar of light when the sun was at the right angle, a breath of air, and a few minutes' vision if she braced her toe against a projecting spot in the wall and hung on.

The warriors who straggled back up the broad avenue were a far cry from the host that had set out that morning. Plumes were bedraggled, or hacked away; most of them limped or hobbled, many bore bleeding wounds. Women and children and near-naked servants gathered along the edges of the broad roadway of colored clay, between the basalt pillars and atop the rectangular mounds. They didn't chant and sing as they had when their men marched out to fight, either. Their silence was like a dirge, compounded by the sound of keening grief that wailed from the interior of the houses. Her arm muscles were beginning to quiver. Gasping, Martha dropped down.

"What did you see?" Pamela Lisketter said. She was beginning to look a little more alert. *Which may be good if we can do something, but on the other hand, everything she's done so far has been harmful.*

Still, it was a little comforting. Having a zombie as your only companion in confinement was hard on the nerves.

"The . . . army has come back. Badly beaten, from the look of it. Less than half the numbers that went out this morning, and most of those wounded."

"Should I hope for rescue?" Lisketter said, mouth twisting. "What can they do to me that Cofflin and the Town Council won't?"

Martha looked around the room. It was absolutely bare, except for a tall-necked jug of water and an open pot for wastes. The room stank, of sweat and the chamber pot and their unwashed bodies.

"The town jail's an improvement on this," she said dryly. "And as to what they can do, I suggest a prayer that we don't find out."

She sank down in the far corner, concentrating on hope. *The* Eagle's *crew obviously beat them. They may be myth-besotted, but surely they'll respond to a whack across the face.* The problem was, she didn't know *how* they'd respond.

She heard the buzz of the ultralight's engines again, faint through the thick walls of the prison. She didn't try to climb to the ventilation slit again; the angle was wrong, and in any case it was unwise to strain herself, in her condition. Hours passed, in a silence broken only by the skitter and buzz of insects.

The door banged open. Warriors stood there, warriors with bandaged wounds and rough cloth wrapped around their feet. Behind the fanged, carved masks their eyes were as dark and hard as the obsidian of their weapons. Both

Americans had learned the local word for "come"; there was no point in being dragged. Outside was a corridor, and then a wooden colonnade enclosing a court. A ball game was in progress there. The object seemed to be to drive a rubber ball through a vertical wooden hoop on either side of the court. Knowing what she knew, Martha wasn't surprised when the three members of the winning team passed through a ritual and then knelt with their throats over a basin. She did turn her head aside, likewise when the priest came by flicking droplets of their blood on the two women.

That made her stare at their escort. She frowned slightly after an instant; he seemed to be ill in a way unrelated to the cuts and punctures on his arms and chest and thighs. He was swallowing convulsively, and now and then putting his hand to his throat, or rubbing at his loincloth.

A suspicion formed in her mind. Sharp terror drove it forth as they were prodded into another court. This encircled one of the oval pools, and more brightly clad members of the priest-king caste stood around it, men and women. The open side giving onto the avenue held one of the giant jaguar-and-woman statues, and all around it were panels of carved stone or stucco portraying the myth of the jaguar-men. A woman alone in the jungle, and the cat sprang upon her. The same woman hugely pregnant; her tribesfolk menaced her with weapons, and she fled into the jungle to squat and give birth, but the babe was born with fangs and talons. The jaguar returned, to devour mother and child, but the child turned within its stomach and the jaguar rose to walk on its hind legs like a man. . . .

"Shamanistic practices aimed at bringing about a complex of feline transformation," she quoted to herself. The archaeologists didn't know the half of it.

"Are . . . are they going to sacrifice us too?" Lisketter asked.

"I don't—"

A painful rap on the back of her head silenced her. A ripple went through the waiting crowd as the ultralight passed overhead, the setting sun red on its wings. Then they turned their attention back to their task. Imploring the help of their god, or gods, or ancestral spirits, she assumed.

Aromatic gums burned in clay holders. Brightly clad figures, men and women, acted out scenes whose importance—usually whose nature—she had no conception of.

The ritual went on and on. Objects were raised before the huge masked figure who sat immobile and cross-legged on yet another of the table-altars. The ropes he grasped in either hand led to prisoners on either side; ordinary peasants, by the look of them, naked and with one hand tied behind their backs. The other hand dangled limp, pierced by a stingray spine.

The drums began to beat again, a thudding in the same rhythm as a human heartbeat; flute and shell and bone xylophone. She was numb enough that the death of the two captives went by almost unnoticed, like a flicker in a movie someone else was watching. Lisketter's whimper as they dragged her away toward the pond cut through the glaze a little. Priestesses grasped her and stripped away the rags of her clothes, pushing her down and scrubbing her as they chanted. Then they pulled her onto the bank and began dressing her in an outfit that was mostly woven feathers and not many of those. The last touch was to dip wads of cloth in some murky, musky-smelling substance and wipe them across Lisketter's belly and inner thighs and genitals. Then they bore her between them to the altar, binding her over it spread-eagled.

Martha obeyed numbly as she was pushed into a position near the carved block of stone; in one hand she was to hold a stalk of maize, in the other a rod carved to represent a burning snake. It wasn't until warriors led in the muzzled jaguar on two thick leashes that she could bring herself to believe what was going to happen. Lisketter began to scream and heave against the ropes that held her, and the big cat's tail lashed as it licked its nose and took the scent.

The connection was through a relay on the *Eagle,* but good enough. Alston went on: "The good part is that we gave them a first-class lickin'," she said.

"Casualties?" Cofflin's voice.

Strange to think of him in the air traffic control tower back on the island. It seemed so far, here in the night where the drums boomed and the light of fires silhouetted the great buildings of the plateau-city ahead.

"Ours? One dead, one critical, twelve or so serious, and the rest walkin' wounded. Theirs . . . couple of hundred dead, maybe more. Plenty of wounded, too." She hesitated. "The bad part is I still can't get them to talk."

Silence came across the miles. "Can you get her back?"

"Not by direct assault. That city isn't walled, but it's over a hundred feet uphill, and they still outnumber us. Storming that . . . even if it worked, the butcher's bill would be ugly. Nothin' to stop them killing her right off, either. If I try to besiege them? Well, right now we've got them dazed, but they'll get their wits back, maybe call up overwhelmin' numbers to finish us off, or block the river back to *Eagle.*"

"You're giving up?"

"Didn't say that. There's something I'm goin' to try, but it's damn dangerous, bit of a long shot."

Another long silence. "I'm leaving things in your hands. You're the expert."

"Thanks, Chief. We'll be in touch tomorrow, one way or another."

She turned to her command group, where they gathered around the folding table with the photographs of the city made with the carefully hoarded Polaroid.

Town, really, she thought. For all the massiveness of the monuments and works, the housing didn't look to have room for more than a few thousand permanent inhabitants. She turned the screw of the oil lantern, and the yellow flame grew brighter. A big tropical moth beat its wings against the glass. She shooed it away and traced a line with her finger.

"This looks like the best approach," she said, drawing a line up from the south, where the tumbled outlying hills of the plateau came right down to the water. From the picture they were covered with thick scrub.

"This building here is where they were, and this courtyard is where the . . . ceremony took place?" she asked.

"Yes, ma'am," Toffler said. Beads of sweat glistened on his balding scalp. "By the big pond."

"That's it, then. Any questions?"

"Ma'am," Ortiz said, "I still think it's inappropriate that you lead this operation in person."

Alston nodded. "Acknowledged, Mr. Ortiz. However, I have certain skills that'll increase the probability of success. So does everyone else I've picked." From a very large pool of volunteers, surprisingly large. *Amazing how many people will clamor for a chance at probable death. Though I should talk.*

She looked at her watch. "Twenty hundred hours. Let's

get going. If they move the hostages, things could get very sticky indeed."

There were five in the party. Herself and Swindapa, of course. Lieutenant Hendriksson, who came from rural Minnesota and went bow-hunting for deer as a hobby; she had her weapon in her hand, a Bear compound, and a carefully padded quiver over her back. Pulakis and Alonski, cousins from a small mining town in west-central Pennsylvania. They were hunters as well, good shots with the crossbow, and both built alike—square young men the same width from pelvis to broad shoulders, long-armed, moon-faced under cropped black hair, their little blue eyes calm. Both of them could probably bend horseshoes with their hands. It was just as well to have a couple of heavy lifters along.

A final check. Everyone was in loose dark clothing; she and the Fiernan were carrying their twin swords, with the .357, a blowgun, and the sling for distance weapons. Swindapa and Hendriksson had stocking caps to pull over their light hair. Burnt cork for rubbing on face and hands also went around; Alonski finished and began to hand it to her, then halted, wincing in embarrassment.

"I'm covered," she said dryly. She took up a final piece of equipment from the table, a slender section of hollow tubing, broke it down at the joint in the middle, and tucked it into her harness. "Let's go."

She turned to Ortiz. "Lieutenant, in the event of failure, don't throw good money after bad. Withdraw. Is that understood?"

"Yes, ma'am." He didn't look happy about it, but on the other hand, she didn't intend to fail.

"Mr. Toffler, you have the signals?"

"Flashlight for Phase One, flare for Phase Two, yes."

"Then let's be about it."

Martha sat in a corner of the cell, head in her hands. It was very quiet. Lisketter lay staring; she hadn't made a sound or a voluntary movement since she stopped screaming, during the rite. When they'd pulled the jaguar off her and the priest-king in his costume of furs had come to take its place.

Catatonic shock, she thought. Probably better. The stucco friezes made it plain what Martha's part in tomorrow's ceremony would be, the cutting and then the feasting.

Now there was a sound—the intolerable taunting buzz of the ultralight going by overhead, freedom just beyond arm's reach. Her head sank wearily down on her knees again.

Then the sound altered; shouting came beneath it, a growing roar. After a moment, the faint light of watchfires that shone through the slit above her head grew brighter.

"Here," Alston whispered into the hot wet darkness of the river.

Slow and muffled, the paddles slid the rubber boat toward the shore. Trees grew almost to the edge, roots grew into the stream, amid thigh-deep water. *Do they have leeches here?* she wondered, as they gripped at branches and made the boat fast. The water felt tepid and stagnant, and smelled of swamp. She went over the side, holding her swords high in one hand, and waded up to dry—drier— land. The cotton of her trousers clung wetly; she slipped the long *katana* back into the carrier across her shoulders and the short *wakizashi* into her belt. Then she took out the pipe, fitted the sections back together, and pushed a round through the plastic mouthpiece and into the tube. It was a steel needle five inches long, with the base set into a plastic bead; a dozen more waited in a case at her waist.

Through a gap in the foliage she could see the riding light of Toffler's craft, circling over the city ahead. Binoculars brought it closer, although not close enough to see the figure beneath or the night-sight goggles on his face. Not particularly modern ones, Israeli-army surplus bought from a catalog by someone on Nantucket before the Event, but they worked. She brought up the flashlight, braced it against a convenient stem, and blinked it on. Three long, one short . . . and hope that nobody on the plateau was looking in precisely the wrong direction. The undergrowth buzzed with insects, and with slight crinkling and rustling noises. Nightbirds sang or croaked or screeched. Some-where close a bull 'gator bellowed, announcing his territory to the saurian world.

She waited, controlling her breathing and feeling the sweat slide gelid down her flanks and spine. *Might have to do it twice. . . .*

No. The riding light on the aircraft returned the signal. She turned her head; the others had the boat tethered and tucked away out of sight. There was just enough light to see their faces as they approached. She knelt in the damp earth and laid down the photograph, then shone a red-dimmed light on it for a second. Swindapa put a hand out to help her steady the curling square of paper, grinning in the dark. *Young,* Alston thought, with a wrench of the heart that she thrust aside with an effort of will. Calm, calm, she could only be centered and calm at this moment. *Don't try to hurry.*

In Heiho *speed is not the true Way. Speed is the fastness or slowness which occurs when the rhythm is out of synchronization.*

"This heading," she whispered, tucking the aerial shot away again. "Follow me."

Her head swung, sighting through the trees on pieces of easily recognized higher ground. It was appallingly easy to get lost in the dark, in unfamiliar brush. They moved forward, placing each step carefully. She pushed vines aside, unhooked from thorns, ignored unseen slapping branches that gouged for her eyes. Every thirty seconds she clicked her tongue softly and they all halted, listening. *Good. Quiet.* Swindapa quietest of all, and the others not much worse. Steeper ground, crawling on all fours. The lip of the plateau above them now, cutting off half the sky, and the rooftrees of thatched buildings beyond it. She looked at the compass and the landmarks, wiped the dirt and moisture off her palms on the sleeves of her jacket. *Excellent.* And it was about time for Toffler to—

A crash came from above, muffled by distance. Shouts. They waited; she could hear Swindapa trying to match her long slow breaths. A glow began to silhouette the rooflines ahead of her. She grinned, a silent snarl. *World's first fire-bombing.* The homemade napalm would send those roofs of dried grass up like tinder, and they were an easy target, even in the dark.

"Go!" she hissed.

They surged up the final steep section and then sank down again, flattened to an earth roadway of pounded, colored clay. A log retaining wall loomed ahead of them, probably set to prevent erosion along the edge of the plateau. Two guards were walking along it, looking northward toward the fire, talking and pointing.

Most excellent, Alston thought. These Olmecs seemed to make war to a rigid set of rules and conventions—duels by

champions, taking prisoners for sacrifice; she had an intu-
ition that they'd refused to talk because trying to get captives back was an outrageous defiance of custom. Their
fighting garb was a clue as well, designed for formalized,
almost ritual combat out in the open by day. She intended
to wring every possible ounce of advantage out of that.

She touched Swindapa's shoulder and pointed to the
right-hand of the pair; the men were only sixty feet away,
and at that range the Fiernan was eye-punching accurate
with the sling. An egg-shaped lead shot went into the
pouch. Alston raised the mouthpiece of the blowgun to her
lips, took a deep breath, aimed . . . *huffft.*

The man on the left stopped talking and went stiff. He
turned, shaking; she could see his jaws gaping wide in a
spastic yawn. Then he toppled forward like a cut-through
tree. *God. Must have caught him in the spine.*

Swindapa leaped upright as Alston fired. Her body flexed
as she swept the sling twice around her head and loosed.
A fraction of a second later there was a hard *thock* sound,
just as the second guard was drawing breath to shout. He
fell across the body of his comrade, leaking gray and pink
from a skull shattered above the ear. The Americans
dashed forward and flattened to the earth by the bodies.

"Uh-oh," Hendriksson muttered.

Another man was standing between two bestial statues,
looking over toward where the guards should have been.
Hendriksson rose to one knee and drew an arrow through
her compound bow; the four edges of the hunting broad-
head glittered slightly in the distant firelight. The wheels
on the tips of the stave flipped over as she drew to the ear
and loosed. Another arrow was on the way before the first
struck, but the man had time for one strangled shout. They
sprinted past him, into a lane between two buildings atop
mounds. Alston looked again at her compass and matched
it against the memorized image viewed from the air.

"This way. Go, go!"

They ran; speed was more important than stealth now.
A quick glance to her right showed the rooftops there
aflame, and people swarming about them, forming bucket
chains from the ponds and tearing at thatch with hooks on
poles. Toffler circled above, the firelight red on the wings
of his craft, now and then dropping another Molotov when
it looked as if the workers might contain the blaze. The

commando headed left, toward the larger building that crowned a mound at the avenue's southern end. There was a wide doorway, flanked by monumental stone heads, and a spear leaning against one—probably the men here had gone to help fight the flames. Inside was a courtyard surrounded by wooden pillars, with rooms leading off from it, and corridors at the corners. Men stood at the entrance to one. When they saw the raiding party they began to shout; two turned and dashed off down the passageway they guarded.

"There!" Alston shouted.

Crossbows snapped, the bowstring slapped against its guard, Swindapa's sling whistled. Two men fell, and another three retreated behind the angle of the wall. Their shouts rang loud.

"No help for it," Alston said grimly, drawing her *katana*. "Go for them."

They sprinted around the colonnade. The Olmecs were waiting, in the straight confines of the corridor, a splash of color moving in the darkness. *Sekka no atari:* the words flowed through her mind, but it was as if she were watching her own actions and commenting. *Spark of the flint;* to strike without windup, without raising the sword. *It is not possible to deal this blow without diligent practice,* Musashi had said.

She'd had sixteen years of it. Her edge flashed in under the Olmec's rising elbow, landing on the drum-tight skin just below his floating rib. Thumping jar of impact, elbows down, hands clenching as she ripped the curved blade across his gut. Ignore the falling body, turn as the blade swept around. Swindapa was backing up, parrying the blurring strokes of the stone-edged rake, clang and clatter and bang and rattle in the murk.

Fast, she thought, as her body reversed stance to point her the other way. The Olmec was very fast. The blade came up, and her body went forward with the downstroke. Another grinding thump as the vertebrae of the neck parted. Hendriksson and the others were swarming silently over the last Indian, shields pinning him back and short swords stabbing. Alston ignored them and sprinted down in pursuit of the two who'd run first. They were bent over a door set into the painted adobe wall, a door made of strong hardwood and secured with a thick hide knot. One of them turned at the last minute to meet the point of her shoulder.

"*Ufff!*" Their lungs gasped out air almost together, hers a controlled half-shout to add force to the blow, his an involuntary gasp; *mi no atare*, the body-strike. Even braced for it, she felt as if she'd rammed herself into a wall. The Indian was shorter than she, but half again as heavy and built like a solid block of mahogany. He staggered, though, falling backward. Her legs moved sideways again, sidethrust kick, the most powerful in the Empty Hand repertoire. Usually a bit slow, but here she was in perfect position for it. The heel caught him in the throat just as he started to straighten. She used the leverage of that to kick off and spin around, ignoring him—larynx crushed at least.

The last Olmec had managed to get the knot slashed open. She saw his back disappearing into the cell, dropped her *katana* and drew the shorter *wakizashi* as she plunged after him. The light in the corridor was faint, but this was like diving into an ocean of blackness.

She nearly died as her eyes adjusted. The spear whistled past, the shaft giving her a painful thump on the neck. She scarcely noticed; the Olmec was following his flung weapon, a dagger of volcanic glass in his hand. The ugly wind of it passed before her eyes as she jerked her torso back. Then it shattered against the curved steel of the *wakizashi*. The Indian shrieked a war-cry and drove in, reckless of the edge and point in her right hand.

Can't let him grapple. Not with his advantages of weight and strength. That was easier to think than do, in this dark confined space. Cut. Cut, and a hiss of pain. A second's blind flurry, and she drove the point home in meat—into the biceps of his right arm. His shriek was as much agony as rage, but his left hand came up and grasped at her wrist, momentum driving her back against the adobe wall with bruising, winding force. The back of her skull rang off the sun-dried brick, and she barely managed to twist as they fell down on their sides. The eighteen-inch blade of the *wakizashi* wavered between them as he strove to force her wrist back. The Indian suddenly rolled, gaining the uppermost position.

Can't hold him. Luckily she had one more functioning arm than he did. It groped downward, between thighs spraddled as he tried to pin her and gain possession of the knife. All she could see was his teeth snarling, but her hand found what it sought. She grabbed, wrenched, and twisted.

Some pains will reach even a berserker, and the Olmec wasn't quite that far gone. He reared up in a soundless gape of agony. Behind him something moved, a bright horizontal slash and a wet heavy impact. The body pitched sideways. Swindapa stood there panting, sword out in the follow-through, her eyes anxious in the cork-darkened face; Hendriksson had a flashlight out behind her.

" 'm all right," Alston gasped. And there was Martha Cofflin, thank *God*. Coming this far and not finding her . . .

"Good to see you," the Yankee said, showing teeth and pushing herself upright along the wall.

"Jared sends regards," Alston said, with the flash of a smile. *We're going to pull it off, hot damn!*

"Lisketter's in the corner."

"Oh, shit," Alston said, as the light speared empty, mindless eyes. There was drool running down her chin. "Pulakis, you carry her. Swindapa, take point; Martha, you go with Pulakis; Hendriksson, Alonski, we'll take rearguard. *Move.*"

The squat Pennsylvania Slav bent and took Lisketter's limp form across his shoulders in a fireman's lift, rising again with effortless ease. Alston recovered her *katana*, wiping it down and resheathing it; catching her breath as well.

"Right," she said after a moment. "Let's go home."

They moved out into the corridor, past the still bodies. The floor was wet with blood, enough to make the dirt tacky and slippery under their feet in the dark. None of the Americans had taken more than superficial bruises and cuts, but she had no illusions about that. They'd had surprise on their side. Now was time to get out, just as fast as they could.

Swindapa darted out into the courtyard, and called them on. The raiding party followed, retracing its steps. The fires were bigger now, spreading to more of the north end of the city as tufts of burning thatch drifted with the wind. They were beside the ornamental pool when Lisketter started screaming.

"That's torn it," Alston said, sparing the carved stone altar a single disgusted glance. "Run."

They did, at as fast a jog as was possible. When the

Olmecs came across the bodies of their fellows and saw the prisoners—vessels of sacredness to them—gone, their shrieks of rage sounded trumpet-loud. They pelted after the Americans, closing the distance fast. Alston reached the retaining wall, leaped down, and calculated the times.

"Damn," she said mildly. Aloud: "Swindapa, Pulakis, get Martha and the prisoner back to the boat. We'll take rear guard." When the Fiernan hesitated, she put a whipcrack into her voice: *"Now!"*

The three of them turned back to watch the pursuers. "All right," Alston said as the others behind them crashed down through the scrub on the hillside. "Let's discourage this lot."

Some of the Olmecs running toward them were carrying torches. All of them were backlit as the wood-and-thatch buildings burned out of control. She drew the Colt and leaned forward, her chest against the logs of the retaining wall and both elbows on the clay of the roadway. She wasn't an expert with the pistol, but this was as straightforward as any shooting range—silhouetted men running straight toward you. Beside her Alonski aimed his crossbow and Hendriksson reached over her shoulder for an arrow.

Crack. She slitted her eyes against the muzzle flash of the magnum. One of the men with torches down. *Crack . . . crack . . . crack . . .* Let the pistol drop back naturally after each shot. *Crack . . . crack.* Open the cylinder, work the ejector to spill the spent brass, slip in two speedloaders each holding three rounds. Snap it shut and get back into firing position. Spears whistled overhead in the dark, but the Indians were shooting blind. One of them landed uncomfortably close; well, they had the muzzle flashes to aim at. She shifted a few feet along the wall, firing steadily. The crossbowman and the archer shot, shot again, steady as metronomes. *Damn fine work, both of them.* Closer . . . then the enemy were tumbling backward.

"Go, both of you, go!"

They went, sliding down the trampled path on their backsides. Alston followed. Behind her she could hear voices, shouting, whatever the Olmecs used as officers rallying their troops. They certainly didn't lack guts; the past few days had shown *that* for certain. More war whoops through the darkness behind her. Branches and thorns clawed at her face, at her limbs, at her feet. Torches broke the darkness, cast wavering red gleams of light through leaves and vines. *Mistake,* she thought, turning to shoot. An atlatl dart thudded into a trunk near her. She crashed downward another dozen feet, shot again, retreated. They were down on the flat below the hillslope, mud catching at her boots; she turned and emptied the revolver, never knowing if she struck anyone. Back toward the edge of the water a little moonlight came in, reflected off the river. The pistol clicked empty.

Her hands swept the sword out. Starlight glimmered on its clean arc. She filled her lungs, gave a *kia,* and rushed forward. The Olmecs hadn't been expecting that; *tateki no kurai,* the way of fighting multiple opponents. The first took her point right in the face. She jerked it free and slashed another across the chest and upper arms. *Damn, but I'm glad Master Hishiba made us practice outdoors and in the dark.*

"*Diiiiissaaa!*" Alston shrieked.

She retreated a step, another, dodged a rake, beat a spearhead aside, and slashed the hand that held it on the backstroke. The Indians had never met anything like the continuous whirling menace of the *katana;* however brave they were, it threw them off their balance for a few crucial seconds. There was no way she could tell what her comrades were doing. Behind her something went *pop* and brilliant light washed across her shoulders, throwing her shadow stark before her. *Flare pistol.* The leading Olmec stopped, staring goggle-eyed at her face. *Never seen a black before,* she thought. Her hands took advantage of the moment and slashed the sword in a horizontal cut. The falling body tripped the man behind as he stumbled squint-eyed in the sudden light. The *katana* came down in the pearsplitter. She lost a crucial second as she tugged it free from his skull.

Something stung in her leg. The damp ground hit her as she fell and she was looking wide-eyed at a spear driven into her leg six inches above the knee. An Indian loomed over her, raising another spear in both hands. Then something silvery slashed across him and he staggered back. Swindapa came leaping after her sword-strike, darkness save for starlight on her *katana* and wisps of hair leaking out from under the wool cap, screaming something saw-edged in her native language. The Indian came back at her, snarling and drawing back his spear to thrust.

Above and behind him a great winged shape slid down out of the night like the god of all owls, its wings black against the bellowing inferno that topped the plateau. Red dots fell from it, to blossom into fire amid the scrub of the slope, and then it was by only a few feet over their heads and banking out over the river. Swindapa caught the spearman as his head whipped around in shock, a gash across neck and chest that sent him back gurgling and thrashing; the sword in her hands swung in red arcs that drove the Olmecs beyond arm's reach for an instant. Other hands grabbed at Alston, and she bit her tongue in the effort needed not to scream; the shock was wearing off, and the pain of the wound flooded into her.

Water, then inflated rubber flexing under her back, firelight red all around them. The flat twanging snap of crossbows; the whaleboats were out on the water where they'd been waiting all night, just beyond spear range. Swindapa tumbled over her, bringing an involuntary grunt of agony as the haft of the spear was jarred, and paddles dug frantically at the water. Indians waded into the river after them, fell as the Americans in the longboats pumped crossbow bolts into them. Darts fell around the rubber boat, struck into the body of it, and it hissed as air began to escape.

The last flicker of consciousness left her as she was dragged again, into the whaleboat. Her mind clamped down on her right hand, bringing the sword with her, and then there was darkness.

"She won't live long," someone was saying in a hushed voice.

Marian Alston knew where she was without opening her eyes—in the flag cabin aboard *Eagle*. Her thoughts seemed clear enough, but distant and slow. She forced her eyelids up.

"Surely not that bad," she said quietly.

The ship's doctor was there, and most of her officers; also the Arnsteins, and Swindapa sitting beside her bunk. Hendriksson had her arm in a sling and a bandage around her head.

The voices fell silent, then all broke out at once for a moment. The doctor overrode them: "Not you, ma'am. Pamela Lisketter. Javelin under the short ribs as you were leaving. Alonski was wounded badly too, but he ought to pull through. You lost a lot of blood, though—one of the big veins got nicked. Be thankful you've got a fairly common type."

Swindapa smiled at her and held out her left arm; there was a patch of gauze taped over the inside fold of her elbow.

Alston nodded slowly; that seemed to take an inordinate amount of effort. "Ms. . . . Cofflin?"

The doctor smiled. "Fine, ma'am, and the baby."

"Mr. . . . Hiller?"

"We're under way, ma'am. Heading north-northeast. I don't like the look of the barometer. We're in for a blow, and I wanted sea room."

"Very well," she sighed, closing her eyes again.

Martha Cofflin clung to the line as the quarterdeck canted under her feet. No nausea, thank God, but the sky looked dirty, clouds brassy and black at the same time. The wind was increasing as well, a shrill piping sound in the rigging. David Lisketter went by between two sailors, his hands—hand and stump, rather—bound before him.

"Hello, Mr. Lisketter," she said flatly, and just loud enough to be heard above the gathering scream of the wind. "There was something I wanted to ask you."

His eyes stared at her like those of an ox in the slaughter chute, and she almost left it at that. *No. It's necessary. This musn't happen again, and Jared might be too forgiving.* Her hand rested on her stomach; it would have been so easy to lose it. . . .

"Have you ever had mumps?" she asked.

Slow thought stirred. "Mumps?" he said. "I'm . . . I think so. Most people do, don't they?"

"Most people aren't asymptomatic carriers," she said. "A few are. I noticed several of the Indians showing the symptoms, though. So one of your party must have been; but you were here long enough for the eight-day minimum incubation period to run . . . and of course, eating undercooked meat is a wonderful way to catch something. Congratulations, Mr. Lisketter."

"Con . . . gratulations?" he whispered.

"On your revenge."

"People don't die of . . ." He stopped, appalled.

"Oh, the fatalities will be heavy," she said. "But it's the long-term effects I was thinking of. You do know that adult-onset mumps often causes male sterility, don't you? I expect that in a population that hasn't been previously exposed, that will be nearly universal. Congratulations, Mr. Lisketter. You've avenged your sister and your friends quite thoroughly. You've single-handedly wiped out the first Mesoamerican civilization, and all the ones which followed from it. Genocide."

Martha turned and headed for the companionway down to the cabins. She had the captain's, with Alston recuperating in the flag suite. There was a shout behind her, and a scream. The splash did not carry over the noise of the birthing storm. Some people were simply too dangerous to have around her friends and family.

CHAPTER SIXTEEN

October, Year 1 – February, Year 2 A.E.

"Jared," Martha said, stooping to kiss his forehead where he sat in the wheelchair.

"Martha," he replied.

Thank You, he added in silence to God; he wasn't much of a praying man, ordinarily, but this was a special occasion. Jared cleared his throat and looked up the gangplank at the *Eagle* and her crew. It was a cool, bright day, and the flags were flying at her masts in a wind that smelled of salt and fish.

"Best we get out of the way, I suppose," he said.

She nodded, and they stood to one side as the others came down—crew and cadets by squads, and the wounded, limping or on stretchers. He tried to look each one in the face and print the features on his memory forever, returning their greetings with solemn nods. The crowd spilling up the dock behind him, filling it and Broad and Easy streets behind him, was almost equally respectful, parting for the ambulances . . . and nobody begrudged the precious remnant of gasoline they burned.

"*Eagle* departing!" the boatswain's voice barked.

A pipe shrilled, and the ship's bell rang three times and once again. Marian Alston stood at the top of the gangplank, crutches under her arms. She blinked as a voice called from among the cadets and crew crowding the dock:

"Three cheers for the skipper!"

Cofflin joined in the three crashing shouts, self-conscious but loud as he felt his wife's fingers squeeze his. Alston nodded, then drew herself up slightly and saluted the dock; those who'd sailed south with her answered in snapping unison. Swindapa came up to steady her as she maneuvered slowly down the gangplank, then sank into a wheelchair beside the Chief's.

"Christ, we're a matched pair," she muttered, as they endured the necessary formalities.

"Not all that long, I hope," he said.

"The medic says it was a nice clean puncture—blade went in with the grain of the muscle, not across it. Should heal without any loss of function."

When the street emptied somewhat, their partners wheeled them about and began pushing them up it.

"You up to that, Martha?" Cofflin asked anxiously.

"Jared, I'm pregnant, not ill," she replied tartly, then stroked his head for an instant. A smile went between her and Swindapa.

Cofflin's head turned to Alston. He swallowed. "There . . ." He cleared his throat and began again. "There aren't any words except *thank you*, and that isn't enough," he said. "And, ah—"

Alston's broad-lipped mouth quirked. "You're welcome, Jared."

He turned in his chair and reached out a hand. "Look, I mean it. I owe you Martha's life, and our child's. That's one hell of a big debt. When you need me, I'll be there, whatever it is. All right?"

She took his hand in reply; it was narrower than his, the fingers long and slender, with a grip like steel wire in his big fisherman's paw.

"I was doin' my job . . . but I may take you up on that, someday." She sighed. "It's going to be a while before we can go after Walker and finish the job," she went on. "We aren't ready. Weren't ready for what we just did, but we were lucky."

Martha snorted. "I don't believe in unearned luck," she said.

"Earned or unearned, we were still lucky." She looked down at her leg. "Well, *I'm* not going anywhere for a while. Spring, then." Alston looked over her shoulder and smiled. "By the way, you should probably thank 'dapa here, too. She saved *me*, at least."

The Fiernan beamed. "Yes, I did—Marian was hurt, and all at once Moon Woman filled my bones with fire and my liver with strength. . . . We're here."

The two women watched the Cofflins negotiate the stairs;

someone had put in a ramp for the chair. Swindapa
frowned slightly as she pushed Alston's back down Orange
toward the junction of Liberty and Main.

"They didn't say much when they saw each other," she
said.

"Well, they're Yankees," Alston replied, smiling. "They
like to squeeze all the use they can out of a word, or an
expression." Then she yawned. "Tired."

"Of course you are. Home soon, and you'll get better
fast." She shook her head. "You need lots of sleep, and—"
She continued in her own language. Alston looked over
her shoulder and raised her brows. The Fiernan continued:
"Someone to . . . keep your spirit warm. Cuddle, you'd say.
Everyone knows that speeds healing."

Alston laughed. "I believe it may," she said. "It very
well may, 'dapa."

Her head turned eastward, and her voice went harsh and
flat for an instant. "And I'm going to need all my strength.
Yes indeed."

With the Tartessians acting as go-betweens, the formal
meeting with Daurthunnicar was delayed several days for
ceremony's sake. When all was arranged the sun was near-
ing the edge of the world, on an evening that fell clear and
warm for autumn.

"Glad of the delay," Walker said, looking critically at
the quarterhorse stallion. "Bastard here needed to get his
land legs back."

The horse still wasn't fit for hard work; standing idle in
a cramped stall in *Yare*'s hold all the way across the Atlantic had lost it some condition. Still, it had enough energy
to try to rear a little. Walker slugged it down with a hand
on the bridle, pulling up and back as it rolled an eye and
stamped.

"None of that, Bastard," he said. "You're not some yuppie's pet now."

He'd been raised a cowboy on an old-fashioned working
spread, and didn't have sentimental illusions about horses.
They were near-as-no-matter brainless, often malicious, and
dangerous, a primitive, less valuable form of organic pickup
truck. Rich hobbyists could afford to spend years coaxing
a horse into doing tricks; when you worked the range, you
needed it to do what you wanted, right then and there.

Walker swung into the Western saddle and looked behind. His followers were drawn up, except for the few on the ship; he'd left them the firearms, save a Colt and shotgun for himself, but everyone wore island-made armor and carried spear, sword, crossbow. They marched across the fields in good order, following a beaten track that ran down to the beach. Isketerol walked at his stirrup, with his cousin and a clump of men from the ships.

The *rahax* came a third of the way to meet him, standing tall in his chariot; a considerable concession, implying that Walker was a guest of rank, rather than merely a suppliant. The American swung down from the saddle, put his hand to his heart and bowed.

"Greetings. The favor of your gods—" he listed them, which took a while—"and great good luck be with you always, Daurthunnicar son of Ubrotarix, *rahax* of the Iraiina."

The shrewd little eyes in the heavy, bearded face blinked at him. After a long moment, he nodded. "Come, you are peace-holy in my steading, welcome beneath my rooftree. Be my guest, drink and eat of my bounty, and we will talk."

"Okay, boys, we're guests," he said, turning to his followers. "Keep your hands off the women, unless you hear me say different, and watch your manners. This is tricky and I don't want any of you queering the deal."

Jared Cofflin reached out and cut the ribbon. Above him the vanes of the new windmill began to turn with a rumbling of gears. Water gushed from a thick pipe onto the sloping inner face of the holding tank. Cheers rang out behind him, first from the crews who'd built the pumping engine, then from hundreds of islanders behind them, most of whom had spent pick-and-shovel time on the basin that would hold the water. The big wind machine was much like the eighteenth-century Old Mill in outline, a round cone of beams and planks on a circular base of mortared stone, ending in a timber circle twenty feet above.

Steel ground on steel from within. The wind was brisk out of the north, carrying scudding tatters of iron-gray cloud with it, from a dark horizon. A few spatters of cold rain came flicking into their faces. *Hard to believe it's November already*. It seemed longer than eight months since the Event; and it seemed sometimes as if it were still a dream, that he might wake any morning to the sounds of cars and television.

Cofflin turned to face the crowd, leaning on his stick to spare the healing knee. Coleman allowed that, as long as he didn't overdo it. He smiled inwardly; Alston was still on strict bed rest, and snarling abominably. Swindapa must be a saint.

"When the rest are finished," he said, pointing to the foundations of five more spaced along the earth berm of the reservoir, "we'll have twenty-four-hour running water again throughout the town. Three cheers for Ron Leaton and Sam Macy and their teams!"

The cheers were long and heartfelt. *Twenty-four-hour flush toilets again, by damn,* Cofflin thought, grinning. That was one thing few people could get used to doing without. *And the composting sewage works is so useful.* The engineer and the carpenter waved and smiled themselves.

"Civilization, brick by brick," he said to the two men and their workers, as the gathering broke up.

"Plank by plank," Macy said, looking pridefully at the structure.

"Gear by gear," Leaton said with equal conviction. "And those cogwheels are six feet across, the main ones. The bevel gears weigh a hundred and fifty pounds each."

"Good piece of work," Cofflin said, clapping them each on the shoulder. "Now, when can we get the whole project wrapped?"

Whump.

Walker fired the last shot and held the shotgun to his face, blowing into the open breech. The first rifled slug had killed the aurochs, but he'd put the whole six-round magazine into the beast, all at the head. What was left looked as if something very large had chewed on it, and then spat it out again. The locals were suitably impressed.

He walked around the animal. It had stood a good seven feet at the shoulder, and the hump was still level with his eyes now that it had collapsed upright. "Wild cattle" didn't give any idea of its size and ferocity; it made a bull bison look like a Jersey milker. *Sort of like a cross between a cow and a rhinoceros,* he thought. Blood pooled out on the sere yellow leaves and dead grass that carpeted the little clearing. The oak trees roundabout still bore a few leaves, but mostly their huge gnarled limbs reached for the sky like a giant's arthritic fingers from the massive moss-covered trunks. It was chilly enough that the Iraiina were all wearing thick leggings and double tunics as well as their usual kilts and cloaks. The American wore mackinaw and ski pants, and a cap with earflaps. He didn't want to blend in too much. A touch of mystery helped with his purposes.

All hail the wizard-chief, he thought.

Thumbing more shells into the breech of the shotgun, he looked around. Some of the Iraiina chiefs looked as though they'd prefer to be running just as far and as fast as they could; they made covert signs with their fingers, spat aside, stared out of pale faces. The half-dozen young warriors who'd sworn service with him looked terrified but even more proud as they drew knives and advanced to begin skinning and butchering the ton-weight of animal. After a moment one of them came over to him with a slice of the heart; the man's arms were red to the elbow.

"Yours is the hunter's right, lord," he said to Walker.

"My thanks, Ohotolarix," Walker said and took a piece between his teeth, cutting it off with his belt knife and chewing the hot rank meat.

Tough as boot leather, he thought. The chiefs' followers were building a fire. He chewed with relish. *Well begun, half done.*

"There's nothing men have ever made more beautiful," Cofflin murmured.

"*Men* in the generic sense, yes," Martha said, nodding agreement with the sentiment.

It was raining outside, freezing rain that turned to glistening treacherous black ice underfoot; the big sheet-metal building drummed to the beat of it. Even with the steampowered compressor thumping and shedding heat in one corner, the interior was chilly. The huge shed had been built for storing boats overwinter; now it was used for building them. Saws whined and drills whirled, filling the air with the fresh sappy scent of cut wood. The ribs of the schooner curled up from the keelson like the skeleton of some sleek sea beast cast ashore, embraced by the cradle that held them in place while the frame was spiked and treenailed together. The interior braces were mostly in place, and the shell of planks was starting to go on. A crew heaved at a line as they watched, and a big curved shape of oak went up on a pulley rigged from the roof and swung down to where the deck would be. Other hands reached up and guided it down. Already the half-built ship looked as if it yearned for the water, to turn its sharp prow southward and race for the unknown seas.

"How does she shape?" Cofflin called up. "Everything looks good from here."

Marian Alston came out from behind a rib and climbed down the board staircase stiffly, limping over to them with a roll of plans in one hand.

"Shapes like the beauty she is," she said. "We'll have her ready to come down the slipway by the beginning of February, and then we can fit her out and mount her sticks and start on the next."

"Fast work," Cofflin said.

"The next one will go a lot faster, with what we've learned. And Leaton's made up some more compressed-air power tools. It'd take a year, if we were usin' hand methods only."

"Decided what to call her yet?" he said.

"Well, that's not entirely my say-so . . ." Alston began.

Cofflin snorted. "The hell it isn't, after what you did."

"*Frederick Douglass,* I thought. He worked as a caulker in a shipyard for a while, you know, before he got free. And *Harriet Tubman* for number two."

Martha nodded. "Excellent choices, Marian," she said, sighing and sinking back on an upturned bucket. Her stomach curved out the loose dress she wore. "More sore ankles."

"You work too much, Martha," Alston said.

"Hell, those are my lines," Cofflin grinned. He tilted his head up and looked at the bulk of the schooner. "I envy you something . . . straightforward like this."

"Speaking of straightforward," Alston said, tapping the rolled plans into her other hand, "I'll need to make some promotions when we commission the schooners. Bump Ortiz and Hendriksson to lieutenant commander and give them each a couple of ensigns and lieutenants. I have my eye on some of the upperclassmen for that."

"Sounds good," Cofflin said. Alston was always conscientious about recognizing the supremacy of the civil authorities, and he didn't interfere in her bailiwick. "I assume your second-in-command agrees?"

"Certainly. I'd like to move Sandy up to commander as well, for symmetry's sake. For that matter I'm going to be leaving her in command of *Eagle* a good deal of the time, when we get to Britain."

Cofflin nodded. "Again, no problem. We can put together some sort of ceremony, I suppose. I wish everything went as easily."

"Don't tell me—y'all've just come from another Constitutional Committee meeting?"

"Almost as bad," Cofflin said, shuddering slightly for effect. "Finance." He dug in one pocket of his parka. "Here. Three bucks."

He flipped the coin to Alston. She caught it; it was gold, about the size of a dime, with LIBERTY on one side beneath an eagle's wings, and *Republic of Nantucket: 1 A.E.* on the other. The picture inside that was a lighthouse—specifically, Brant Point lighthouse at the northwestern entrance to the harbor.

"I thought you were going to use the Unitarian Church tower?" she said. "Don't tell me . . ."

"All the other denominations objected. One-tenth of an ounce fine gold, though, eighteen-karat—smelted down from jewelry. Starbuck *swears* gold-based money'll work. God knows we need a currency. Swapping is so damned awkward."

"Useful for trade, once the locals get the idea." She looked down at the coin. "Can't say 'queer as a three-dollar bill' anymore, can we?"

"Ah . . . hadn't thought of that." He gave a dry chuckle; it *was* funny, when you thought about it. "Starbuck's bad enough on Finance, but everyone on the Constitutional Committee has a bee in their bonnet."

"We need a constitution, and that's more important than this." She jerked her head at the schooner. "Much as I hate to admit it."

They both sat on stacks of boards, and began to massage their injured legs with an identical gesture. "The Twin Gimps," Alston said.

Cofflin snorted. "You could spend more time on the Constitutional Committee, then," he said. "Since it's so damn important."

"A cobbler should stick to her last and a sailor to her ship. I just don't have your capacity to endure fools," she said, with a slight momentary smile he'd learned was her equivalent of a grin. "Didn't I get the Arnsteins to enroll? Aren't they a help?"

"Too *much*. Every time I turn around they're telling us how the Republic of Venice or the Hanseatic League or ancient Athens did it—Ian's always trying to pin some unpronounceable Greek name on everything we do, at that. It's as intimidating as hell. Then Sam Macy loses his temper with them, and I have to smooth it over."

"Thus getting your own way," Martha pointed out. "Politics may not be your trade, dear, but you're learning it."

Damn, but it's . . . energizing . . . being married to someone smarter than you are, he thought.

"How's it look, basically?" Alston asked, leaning forward to get out of the way of someone carrying two buckets of hot tar on the ends of a shoulder yoke. The strong scent made Martha hold her breath for a moment.

"Oh, a republic with a chief executive—everyone seems to like the name—and a Council, reporting to the Town Meeting and with appointments subject to confirmation, and the Meeting to pass laws and review and vote on all the major decisions," Cofflin said. "That's the bare bones. Right now we're thrashing out whether the militia should be separate from the Coast Guard, and whether the commander of that should be called an admiral or not. Want to be an admiral?"

"Only if I can wear one of those fancy fore-and-aft hats and gold braid," Alston said dryly.

"Talk of calling you people the Republic of Nantucket Navy, too."

That brought her upright and indignant, as he expected. "Look, Cofflin—" She saw his grin, and relaxed. "Sorry, but tell them Guard people would rather barbecue their mothers. No offense—I know you were a squid."

"None taken," he said. "*And* they're debating whether the Town Meeting can amend the constitution with a simple majority or not; Arnstein's strong for a two-thirds vote two years running. Goes on about something the Athenian Assembly did." He lifted a brow. "Hung some admirals for losing a battle, it was."

"Sounds reasonable," Alston said. "Christ, you know

how a crowd can get, 'specially when someone tells them what they all want to hear."

"You could come and tell the committee . . ." he said.

"You've got a fund of low cunning, Jared, you know that?" she said. "Maybe. If I've got time. After Christmas."

"So at this point, you just pack up and go home," William Walker said.

Shaumsrix scowled; he was an experienced war chief by Iraiina standards. "Of course. We can't take the fort, we don't have enough men, and if we wait here too long many will get sick in this cold and wet. Or nearby chiefs will come and overfall us with numbers we can't match, even though this chief is at feud with all his neighbors. We've taken many cattle and sheep, and horses, yes—I admit that your riders let us surprise them that way. Now we should go home and guard against their revenge."

Walker leaned his hands on the pommel of his saddle and looked around at his own followers. Most of them were mounted; chariot ponies broke to the saddle easily enough, and at thirteen hands were big enough to carry a man if he changed off every so often. They stamped and fretted a little, their newly shod hooves squelching in the damp earth, breath blowing white from their flaring nostrils into the chilly air of late fall.

"Time for our next surprise, boys," he said. "Break out the axes."

An ox-wagon creaked up behind them. Not the local kind, two solid wheels and two beasts; this was as close as he could get to a Boer trek wagon or a Conestoga, with eight yoke pulling it via a stout iron chain. It wasn't fast, but it could carry a couple of tons of weight pretty well anywhere.

"More magic?" the Iraiina said fearfully.

"Just a little applied mechanics," Walker said. Shaumsrix made a sign with his fingers.

It took all that day and most of the next to set the engine up. At last Walker stepped forward and took the lanyard. A swift tug . . .

Thack-WHUMP. The long arm of the trebuchet whipped upward.

It was nothing but an application of the lever: the short arm carried a timber box full of rocks, the long a sling at its end to throw rocks or other projectiles. The bigger medieval examples had been able to throw a ton of weight half a mile. This was a bit smaller, but ample for his needs.

"Devil's in the details," Walker snorted to himself, watching the barrel of lard wrapped in burning rags arching up into the blue November sky. *At least we've got some decent weather for a change.* Most of the time he'd been wading in mud while he worked on the damn thing back at base.

He leveled the binoculars and watched. The target was a round earthwork *dunthaurikaz,* a little fortlet with perhaps a dozen big huts inside, and a stockade surrounding it made of upright logs rammed into the top of the earthwork. Pathetic even compared to the Western forts he'd seen on TV when he was a kid, but nearly invulnerable by here-and-now standards. The defenders had been standing on the platform behind the ramparts, shooting an occasional arrow and yelling insults. He could understand them, more or less; their language and the Iraiina tongue weren't far apart—about like the difference between BBC English and what a small-town Texan spoke. The screams of fear as the barrel flew toward them were understandable anywhere. It struck near the sharpened points of the logs and snapped two off as it shattered. Burning tallow flung in all directions, spattering. Wood began to catch.

"Haul away, boys!" he called.

Four horses were waiting. They were local chariot ponies, but he'd had proper horse-collar harnesses made up, not the choking throat-strap yoke these people used. A strong rope ran back from them to the pulleys, and the longer throwing arm began to swing downward with a creaking of its raw timbers, hauling up the great box of rocks on the other end. *John did a good job on the ironwork,* he thought. But then, the blacksmith always did a good job, it was a habit with him . . . and Walker had done enough work with him back on the island to know exactly what he was capable of, and how fast.

The crew snapped the iron hook into the loop bolted into the arm. Ohotolarix came up beside him.

"Lord, that thing is a marvel—but we don't want to burn all the loot, do we?"

The young Iraiina swaggered, hand on his new steel

sword, but there was plenty of deference in the way he spoke to his new chief.

"Good point," Walker said. To the crew at the trebuchet: "Give 'em a stone this time, men."

Four of them lifted a three-hundred-pounder into the heavy leather sling. McAndrews adjusted the stop ropes, frowning in concentration.

"That ought to do it, sir."

. "Go for it."

The tall black jerked at the cord that tripped the release. *Thack*-WHUMP. The rounded boulder spun through the air. For a wonder—aiming this thing was by guess and by God—it struck not far away from where the barrel had. Four logs snapped across, raw white splinters showing in their heartwood, and a man arched out to land crumpled in the wet pastureland between the fort and the invaders. The chiefs and warriors who'd agreed to come along on this raid shrieked and beat their axes on their shields in glee.

"Reload."

"We'll batter them to sausage meat, lord!" Ohotolarix said with wild enthusiasm.

These people are like kids, Walker thought, not for the first time. One minute they were all agog over a novelty, then next sulking in the corner or stamping and waving their fists in quick anger . . . not what you'd call dependable. *On the other hand, they can learn. At least the younger ones.*

"No we won't," Walker said. "Because they can figure that out themselves, and any minute now . . ."

The narrow gate of the fort was hauled open. Hands thrust a gangway through, over the muddy ditch that surrounded the settlement, and two chariots thundered across. Behind them ran forty or so men, all the adult free males in this chief's following, bellowing their war cries. The Iraiina whooped themselves, and ran to meet their foes.

"Remember what I told you!" Walker barked. "Shoulder to shoulder! *March!*"

His own little band tramped forward, spears lowered and crossbows ready, swinging around the clot of combat where chieftains hurled javelins and taunts from their war-cars and footmen met in milling, deadly chaos. Grossly outnumbered to begin with, none of the enemy fought long. Walker met one of the last, an axman bleeding but still wolf-swift. The tomahawk chopped at him, trailing red drops. He brought his *katana* up in a looping curve to meet it, and the ash-wood slid off steel. The American planted his feet and swung, drawing the cut across the native's neck. The con-torted fork-bearded face went slack and dribbled blood, then collapsed. A few others, perhaps seven or eight, threw down their weapons.

"Don't kill them!" Walker yelled, pointing his blade to the warriors who'd surrendered. "I want prisoners."

"Well struck, lord!" Ohotolarix said. His own short sword was red. "Now we plunder!"

The flanking move had done more than end the fight quickly; it had also put Walker's band nearest the gate. "Double-time!" he shouted. *First plunder,* then *burn.*

The inside of the fortress was stink and chaos; the locals had driven much of their stock inside, and brought them-selves from steadings all around, packing it far beyond its usual capacity. Hairy little cattle bawled and surged in panic; sheep milled in clots; women and children ran like-wise. One or two of the mothers had already cut their chil-dren's throats and plunged daggers into their own chests, or hung themselves from the carved rafter ends of their houses.

"You, you, you, get those fires out!" Walker barked. "The rest of you, round these people up! They're no use to us dead. Get their stuff over there."

He pointed to the . . . porch, he decided . . . of the biggest building in the fort. Almost certainly the fallen chief's dwelling; the roof ran out a dozen feet or so beyond the wall, supported on wooden pillars, and there was a raised floor a bit out of the mud, covered with the same cut reeds used inside.

The other Iraiina were surging into the fort in his wake, but even their chiefs were a little overawed by the foreigner who'd won the favor of the *rahax* and shown such com-mand of war-magic. Instead of flinging themselves on the plunder and women they shouted commands to their own followers, enforcing them with an occasional cuff or shove. The burning sections of the palisade were put out or dragged away, the livestock herded out to await division, the survivors kicked and pushed and spear-prodded into a mass.

"Chief Hwalkarz," one of the charioteer lords said. "As you wished, we have done."

Men were shouting in glee as they dragged out their booty. Bolts of woolen cloth, clothing, furs, bronze tools; some gold and silver ornaments, more of bronze and stone and shell. Pottery jugs and skins of mead and beer were added; they called out reports of stored food, grain, cheeses, smoked and pickled meat.

Happy as kids at Christmas, Walker thought, smiling and wiping his sword.

"Here's what we'll do," he said to the two Iraiina chiefs. "You can have all the bronze and cloth, and half the gold and silver."

They whooped and pounded him on the back; Ohotolarix looked a little startled, then relaxed. The bronze tools and weapons weren't much use to them, and they could trade for cloth.

"We divide the food and livestock equally—half for me, half for you two to split. Half the prisoners are mine, and I get first pick. Is that just?"

"Just and more than just," the senior of the two Iraiina leaders said; he was about Walker's years, although he looked a little older with his weathered face and several teeth knocked out in fights. The dark-brown braid of his hair was bound with leather thongs and wolf fangs; it twitched as he looked around. "Never shall you or your men lack for meat and drink at the steading of Shaumsrix son of Telenthaur."

"That is good," Walker said politely. *Sucker.* He had an eye on several of Shaumsrix Telenthaur's son's followers, and he suspected the Iraiina would be less than pleased when they switched allegiance.

"We should make a thank-offering to the gods," he went on.

"Else no few of our fear-despising heroes will lie sleepless in dread of Dead Walkers," the Iraiina chief agreed. "Hmm. One horse and, *eka,* four cattle? That will make enough fresh meat for the victory feast." He grinned, a carnivore expression. "We've given enough man-meat to please the Mirutha and the Crow Goddess. He of the Long Spear was with us, and the Blood Hag drank deep."

"Your word is strong," Walker said, clasping wrists with the other man. "Let it be as you say."

He walked over to where the prisoners waited, weeping or stoic or watching with silent dread. The men and older boys had been bound at wrist and ankle and shoved into a hut with a barred door. The locals were surprised he hadn't just cut their throats . . . but then, the Iraiina had little idea of how to make men work. Three among the remainder caught his eyes, two girls about twelve and an older one of eighteen or so, holding the younger ones against herself. They looked enough alike to be sisters and probably were, with seal-brown hair and gray eyes. Their clothing was good by local standards, the bright plaid wool of their long dresses woven in a sort of herringbone twill, and the older wore a gold bracelet; they all had shoes, which was swank among the natives. The way their hair tumbled loose to their shoulders meant they were unmarried.

Alice said she could use some more household help, he thought. Fair enough; it was wasteful to have a qualified medico doing scutwork, and he wanted to keep her happy. *Not to mention . . .*

"You," he said, smiling and beckoning.

The younger ones whimpered, and the older girl clutched them tighter. "You, come here," Walker went on. They stumbled to him. *I must look strange,* he thought. Rumors about the new wizard who'd taken up residence among the Iraiina would have spread far, too.

He gripped the older girl by the hair, just hard enough to immobilize her, and checked her over. Some of these women carried razor-sharp little triangular bronze knives tucked away in the most unexpected places. There was nothing beneath her clothing but girl though, shaped very pleasantly . . . and these people didn't wear underwear. Walker looked around while his hand moved beneath her skirt. The girl trembled and closed her eyes, biting at her lip. She didn't seem very surprised, though; this was what happened after a lost battle, here.

"All right, boys," he said in English. "Party time. Pick one each. Remember, the supply's limited, and you'll be taking these back home, so don't get too rough." Then he repeated it in the more formal phrasing of Iraiina.

There was going to be a lot of work, getting all this stuff and the people back to the base he'd named Walkerburg. No reason not to relax tonight, of course. A raw whoop rose from his followers, and the war bands of the other chiefs jostled, waiting their turn to pick. He noticed McAndrews hanging back. *Can't have that,* he thought.

He released the brown-haired girl for a moment and grabbed another, a full-figured blonde in her twenties who was wiping away her tears and trying to smile at the conquerors. *Obviously one with an eye for the main chance.* The ones glaring defiance or standing slumped in despair wouldn't do for a shrinking violet like the cadet from Tennessee. The eyes went wide in alarm as he ripped the dress off her shoulders and shoved her over to McAndrews; nobody around here had ever seen blacks before.

"You're entitled to your share, Ensign," he said. The younger man stuttered, obviously torn between horror and temptation. "You wouldn't want anyone to think you were looking down on us, would you?" Walker said. His smile was cold. "Not hurt anyone's feelings? I'd just purely *hate* to have you hurt m' feelings, McAndrews."

"Ah . . . no, of course not, sir."

"Good man. Have fun."

Laughing, he turned and pushed the brown-haired girl he'd chosen into the hall, scooping up one of the jugs of mead as he passed; her younger sisters tailed along uncertainly. It was dark and smoky within, but the turf walls and the fires smoldering in pits down the length of the floor kept it reasonably warm; there were a few low wicker partitions, but otherwise it was just one big room, with tools and bundles of herbs and hams hanging from the low rafters. He led the others behind one of the woven barriers; the younger girls huddled in the corner, clinging to each other. Furs and wool blankets covered straw.

"What's your name?" he asked, shedding his sword belt and hanging the weapons carefully behind him. *No sense in taking chances,* he thought, undoing the latches of his armor and swinging out of the suit.

"Keruwthena, lord," she said, clenching her hands and looking down. Then she forced her eyes back up. She seemed a little reassured that he looked like other men beneath the steel.

"Lord, my sisters . . . they're very young," she went on, as she unfastened the pins that held her gown at the shoulders.

Meaning, please don't throw them to your men, he supposed. "Don't worry," Walker said. *Not often your fantasies come true so precisely,* he thought, laughing at the hammering of his own heart. "They're safe enough, if you're going to be sensible."

Some time later he rose and began dressing. Keruwthena did too. "I . . ." she said. "I am glad you are not a cruel man, lord," she said after a moment. "The stories . . ."

Walker finished off the jug of mead. "Not cruel unless I'm crossed," he said genially.

A woman in her position's best hope was to end up a prominent warrior's possession, and work her way up to minor wife and personal freedom, or as much freedom as a woman ever had among the eastern tribes. She doubtless thought she'd lucked out, with him. Then he laughed; Keruwthena tried a shaky smile, and the two young girls stared at him in terrified awe.

You're lucky so far, he thought. *But then you haven't met Alice yet.*

It was still near-dark along Main Street, and cold fog swirled about the iron lampposts and the trunks of the great elms, blown in the damp chill air from the sea. Jared Cofflin ambled slowly up the street, past the small crowd already gathered near the bulletin boards at the Hub, the store halfway up Main; there wasn't enough paper to print a newspaper yet, but the *Inquirer and Mirror* continued its hundred-and-seventy-year tradition by posting a newsletter in strategic places. He inhaled deeply, taking in the cold salt air, as familiar as breathing itself. *Snow tonight, most likely. Or mebbe not.* Everything else had changed, but walking up the brick sidewalk in a December fog still felt the same.

As if to give him the lie, a shrill steam whistle split the air. That must be one of the tugs, heading out to haul back another raft of mainland firewood and charcoal and planks while the sea allowed. Moisture dripped down his collar, and he hurried his pace a little. Another new smell reached him, one he didn't mind at all—the scent of new-baked bread in wood-fired ovens.

His stomach rumbled. *Smells great, tastes delicious, doesn't keep worth a damn,* he thought; so it had to be baked fresh every day, which meant a couple of dozen new bakeries to use the fruits of the harvest. A couple of slices with an egg or two and some cranberry preserve made a decent breakfast. *Possibly we'll have coffee again about the time I die,* he thought. Angelica Brand was growing several hundred seedlings in her greenhouses, and the plan was to drop a boat down to Puerto Rico in the spring and plant them out along with the oranges and lemons and whatnot. God knew if it would work; the birds might eat them all, or something.

In the meantime it was pleasure enough to walk without pain in his leg, even on a damp cold morning. Lucky the bullet hadn't done much damage to bone and tendon as it drilled its way through; lucky it hadn't been a hollowpoint, too. He nodded greeting to friends and acquaintances, and once to a mainlander, an Indian struggling not to gape around him, a blanket wrapped about his shoulders. The sight set his teeth on edge. It was impossible to avoid all contact, he knew—if nothing else they were within canoe-paddling distance of Martha's Vineyard and the continent—and Doc Coleman was taking every possible precaution, but still . . . *What will happen will happen.*

At least the locals had proved reasonable enough, once you learned how to approach them. Eager to trade for cloth and tools, too; pelts, deerskins, birch-bark containers of maple syrup, gathered nuts and dried berries, roots and herbs.

He heard feet on the sidewalk behind him and turned. Alston and Swindapa were running side by side, sheathed swords in their left hands pumping back and forth with the movement of their legs. *She's not limping either anymore,* he thought with satisfaction. Alston must be back in fighting trim. He was glad of that, for her sake, and . . . *And frankly, she was like a penned she-wolf for a while there.* They slowed to a walk as they came up to him, wiping the sweat from their faces with the towels slung around their necks. You could work up some heat even in this weather, and they were wearing thick track suits and gloves.

"Mornin', Jared," she said, breathing deep and slow.

"Morning, Marian, Swindapa," he said.

"You're out early, I see."

He shrugged. "Martha didn't feel well last night, so I thought I'd let her sleep when she finally could." One drawback of marrying late was that she'd never gotten used to having someone else in the same bed; and when you piled morning sickness on top of it, a lot of rest got lost. "The doctor says it's natural enough. Why do they call it *morning* sickness?"

"Don't worry," Marian said. "There's a lot of variation. I was sick at unpredictable intervals right into the seventh month. And everythin' went smoothly enough come the time."

" 'Bye, Jared. I got to get breakfast ready, it's my turn," Swindapa said, giving Alston a kiss. "French toast today. Maple syrup!" She dashed off, vaulting smoothly over one of the sidewalk benches and pelting up past the shuttered Pacific Bank.

"Glad to see you're back in shape. Must be a bit of a trial, keeping up with all that youthful energy," he said, grinning.

She rolled her eyes. "Oh, *tell* me 'bout it, Jared. 'Sides, I've got sisters—and both of them hit two hundred and thirty pounds by their second baby. Powerful incentive to sweat."

He turned his head sharply. ". . . that the sort of role model we want in front of our young people—" came from behind him. Sound was tricky in a fog like this.

Alston's head was turning too, the friendly expression congealing into that flat glare she had. She'd gotten a lot less likely to let that sort of thing pass recently. Coffin turned on his heel and stalked back down the street, halting when he came to Lisa Gerrard. He'd recognized her voice; she was on the School Committee, and spoke often. Very often. He thrust his face into hers, conscious of the cold anger in him and holding it back. The words came out slow, deliberate, and bitten off:

"Well, actually, Ms. Gerrard, I *do* consider Captain Alston an acceptable role model. Considering that she saved Martha's life and nearly got killed doing it, and that she led the expedition that got us the food we're eating this winter, and everything else she's doing for this ungrateful island, I consider her an *excellent* role model. And when you, Lisa Gerrard, have done one *tenth* as much for the common good, maybe—just maybe—you can criticize her. Until then I suggest you shut . . . the . . . hell . . . up!"

He'd started loud, and the last part rose to a bellow. Whistles, cheers, and clapping came from the crowd around the bulletin board, and Gerrard retreated in confusion. Cofflin gave a curt nod to them and stalked back to Alston, who stood waiting with her brows raised.

"Why, Jared, I didn't know you cared," she said. "Thanks, by the way."

He snorted, but the tension relaxed out of his shoulders. "How's the ROATS program coming along?" he said, slightly embarrassed.

"Not bad, considerin', although we surely miss Martins. Leaton says the turntables and hull bracing shouldn't be any problem. Come on, I'll fill you in. 'Dapa's learned to make a *smokin'* piece of French toast with turkey eggs and barley bread."

John Martins turned away from the open end of the smithy. From here he could see the workers—slaves, in iron collars—putting up a new building, with a couple of the Americans supervising. There were already half a dozen frontier-style log buildings around a square, William's house, accommodation for his retainers, storehouses and workhouses and stables, and the smithy. The square itself had been roughly cobbled with round stones from the river, and the whole settlement kept reasonably dry with drainage ditches—refinements not current in these parts. Another working party labored to hollow out split logs, the chain-link hobbles between their ankles clinking as they moved. The logs would be strapped back together with iron bands and used to pipe in water from a spring not far distant.

One slave stopped a little too long to stretch his back, and the overseer's cane whistled. There was a *pop,* a yelp, and the man began working again with furious speed. Walker had mentioned that he was using Roman methods, including the *ergastula,* the windowless half-underground jail where most of the male slaves were kept shackled at night.

"Oh man, that guy is, like, an *orc,*" he muttered to himself.

"What say?" one of the apprentices said.

There were four other men in the smithy with him, two of Isketerol's Tartessians and two Iraiina who'd sworn service with Walker. Not counting the poor bastard in the collar working the bellows, of course. He and the men learning from him were communicating fairly well now, in bits and pieces of each other's languages, despite the way

Walker kept sending him new ones. Eventually you got across what you needed to, and teaching helped take his mind off the general shittiness of the situation. The smithy was warm and close inside, well lit by the glow of the big charcoal hearth as well, despite the rainy dimness outside. He turned back to the forge, explaining:

"Like, this is *cast* iron, man," he said, taking a piece that had originally been in the *Eagle*'s ballast out of the forge and laying it on an anvil. "It won't forge like the wrought stuff we've been working—it's too brittle."

He demonstrated with a blow of his hammer. The iron split, showing gray at its heart.

"You gotta get the carbon out. So y' heat, sorta stir the puddle of melted stuff around, y' hammer to get the slag out, and heat again."

"Eventually," he went on, "it gets to be, you know, *wrought* iron. Then you can work it like we've been doing, or harden it up again to steel. Like, you need a rilly *big* hearth for a finery, not just a forge like this—this is just to give you an idea."

He picked out a piece farther along and bent it into a curl shape with a few skilled blows. Each of the others duplicated the process under his critical eye.

"This *cast iron*," one of the Tartessians said, "it is the same as will come from the *blast furnace* when it is finished?"

"Yeah, man, right on. You got it."

The twelve-foot-high fieldstone furnace was nearly complete, and there was ore and limestone and charcoal in abundance; mineral deposits didn't change, and they had the Ordnance Survey maps. They did need cylinder bellows and water-powered draft, though, which was taking a while. Judging from the way things had gone with other stuff, they'd have to fiddle around a good long while to get it to work really right—there were lots of little things the books never mentioned. Meanwhile they stockpiled materials.

"That little sucker will put out a thousand pounds a day, and then—"

"Good work, John," a voice said from the entryway.

Martins turned, gritting his teeth. Walker was standing there, holding the reins of his quarterhorse stallion. "Bastard here needs a shoe on his left fore. Kicking again."

Martins grunted wordlessly and took a blank from a rack

on the wall and flipped it into the forge to heat. Then he took up pincers and rasp and walked around to the left side of the horse. Walker gripped the bridle more tightly—Bastard was well named and found the bent-over rump of a blacksmith an irresistible temptation, teeth-wise—and Martins pulled up the left forefoot, gripping it between his knees. He took the pincers and began drawing the nails on the loose shoe.

Behind him Walker spoke to one of the Tartessians: "You learn?"

"I learn a great deal, lord! Already we can do many of the simpler tasks. In some ways this iron is easier to work than bronze. A great pity it's so difficult to cast, but it works well beneath the hammer. The *blast furnace*"—he used the English phrase—"goes well too, soon it will be ready, and we learn how to find the ores of iron. There is much of it back home, I think."

The hoof hissed as the hot iron touched it, and the glowing shoe gave a *shuffffff* as it was quenched in a bucket of water after he'd tapped the final adjustment; he drove the nails home that held it in place, and crimped them. Both the Iraiina apprentices could already do that much, but it didn't hurt to show them again. He hated the thought of anyone messing this up and hurting a horse's feet.

"Be seeing you, John," Walker said, swinging into the saddle. "Promised Daurthunnicar I'd bring Bastard over to cover some of his mares." He slapped his mount's neck. "Now that the locals've seen what he can do, he's in stallion heaven."

"Aren't we all, boss?" laughed one of the three riding escort; it was Rodriguez, the ex–Coast Guardsman.

The four horses clattered across the cobbles and then their passage turned to the softer thudding of hooves on dirt.

Martins stared sullenly after them. It was bad enough when Walker was around, but much as he hated to admit it, it was worse when the renegade was gone. Some of the things that Hong woman did . . . his eyes slid away from the big two-story log house across the courtyard. Of course, he'd thought about running.

Shit, I think about it all the time, man. This is, like, totally Mordor here. That dude's head is in a truly fucked-up place.

But he'd seen others who ran brought back with hounds,

flogged . . . and once, crucified. *He* might make it, especially if he could steal a horse, but Barbs certainly couldn't. She wasn't the outdoor type, and their natural-method contraceptives had failed, badly. At least Walker didn't have him in an iron collar or chained up at night. Not yet. Plus there wasn't anywhere to run when you thought about it. From what he'd seen most of the locals were every bit as ferocious as Walker, just less systematic. He'd heard the Earth Folk were more mellow, sort of laid-back, but they lived a long way away to the west.

Barbara came out of his own smaller cabin and banged a spoon against the bottom of a frying pan. "Time to break for lunch," Martins said gratefully. "C'mon, you guys."

"Well, I'll admit that you're a pretty good pool player, but nobody could make *that* shot," Cofflin grumbled. "Besides, don't you have to go baste that turkey again or something?"

The basement recreation room of Guard House was dominated by the billiard table; the other end of the room held only a set of well-used weights and some Nautilus machines, both brought in since the Event. The oil lantern over their heads provided more than enough light, and it was no more than medium chilly, something everyone had gotten used to since the beginning of their first winter without central heating.

Marian Alston grinned like a shark as she chalked her cue and pulled back the sleeves of her sweater. *Got him,* she thought. Not a bad player, but you needed killer instinct for pool. Good to have someone to shoot with, though. You could really relax over this game, and it bored Swindapa like an auger.

Although there are some *drawbacks to hanging out with straights. Wouldn't understand the turkey-baster jokes, for instance.*

"Know, Oh Cofflin, that my state of karmic spiritual enlightenment puts me beyond all need for your praise. Yet not beyond need for your beer. Extra bottle on this shot? Thirty-seven up and with anothah three I win."

"Well . . . all right."

Smack. The white caromed off a cushion, kissed one ball, then tickled the twelve. It spun on the edge of the pocket, wavered, and settled again.

"Damn! If you hadn't reminded me about the turkey, I'd have done it," she swore.

The smell from upstairs was getting better and better, mingling with the lingering aroma of the baking she'd done earlier in the day.

"All right, then, I'll *split* that beer with you." He ambled over to the cooler and took out a bottle, part of the Cofflins' contribution to the Christmas quasi-potluck dinner. "One good thing about this weather is you can get the beer really *cold*."

"Amen." She looked at her watch. "I will have to go look at that turkey—"

"Marian." Martha's voice. "You'd better come up, I think."

"Oh, hell."

She laid the cue down and took the stairs at a bounding run. The other early arrivals—Martha and the Arnsteins, Sandy Rapczewicz and Doc Coleman—had been sitting in the kitchen, for the warmth and to nibble. Swindapa was standing by the black-iron stove, long spoon still clutched in one hand, tears streaking down her face in slow trickles.

"Hey, honeypie, it's all right, I'm here," Alston said softly, reaching for her. " 'Sall right, sweetheart. There, there, Marian's here, sugar."

Swindapa dropped the spoon and gripped her convulsively. Alston made a waving gesture toward the stove with her free arm and led the Fiernan out into the vacant sunroom. They sat on one of the sofas, and the tears became racking sobs. Outside snow fell in huge soft flakes, batting at the windows like slithery cold kitten-paws.

"I miss my mother! I want my family!" The words trailed off into unpronounceable Fiernan consonants, gasped out into the hollow of her shoulder between sputtering heaves of grief.

And this time of year is a big family feast over there, too, Alston thought, making a low humming in her throat and rocking the other, stroking her back through the check shirt. *Fiernan don't leave home, at least not the women.* From what Swindapa had said, a girl usually just moved elsewhere in the greathouse and built a hearth of her own when she started having babies, staying in the same huge extended family all her life. The other's misery wrung at her; she buried her face in the silky hair and crooned.

After a while the tight grip around her chest relaxed and the sobs faded into sniffles. She pulled a handkerchief from her pocket, wiping her companion's face and smiling wryly as she remembered the screaming Valkyrie figure who'd stood over her on the shore of the Coatzacoalcos. After another while of silence, Swindapa sighed and blew her nose.

"I feel better now," she said, smiling, cuddling with a mercurial change of mood.

Didn't apologize for crying, either, or say thanks, Alston noted. An American would have. At least she'd learned to use a handkerchief instead of her fingers. *Well, the fact that you love someone doesn't make them more like you.*

Her mouth quirked. She'd always—well, ever since Jolene left—had dreams about the ideal Significant Other. Someone black, of course. About her own age, and with similar interests, just enough difference to be interesting. . . . *And here I'm settled down with a blond bukra teenager from 1250 B.C. who prays to the Woman in the Moon,* she thought. Well, you had to work at any relationship worth having.

"Glad you do feel better, 'dapa," she said tenderly.

They went back into the kitchen. Sandy Rapczewicz had the oven door open and was standing over the turkey with baster in one hand and spoon in the other, looking irresolute. "I have the deck there, Ms. Rapczewicz," Alston said. "It's nearly ready, anyway."

"Thanks, Skipper," the XO muttered. She was still a little tender about the face, but the bones were knitting well, the rather lumpy Slavic countenance unaltered.

"The secret to a really *good* turkey," Alston went on easily, "is keeping the flesh moist—'specially with these lean wild ones."

The bird weighed about twenty pounds, the upper limit with the woods-caught types from the mainland the island was rearing now. She prodded a fork into the joint between drumstick and body. The juice ran clear. "Right, let's take it out and let it stand for a little while. Now everyone but volunteers out of the kitchen—this is the tricky part."

Getting everything to the table at the same time and neither overcooked nor cold was *difficult.*

"I feel as if I were mutilating my eldest son," Miskelefol said dolefully. "And this climate! It's bad enough in summertime. In winter the damp would rot the testicles off a Sardinian."

"You've seen what the *Yare*—the *Eager*—can do," Isketerol said cheerfully. A Tartessian crew was training on her, under the supervision of Walker's men. "Think what this will be capable of. And it keeps the men busy over winter."

Both men peered out the door of the hut. They had broken up the hulls of the *Wave Treader* and the *Foam Hunter* for their wood, and put up improvised stocks to hold the frame of another ship. One about two-thirds the *Yare*'s size, considerably shorter but broader in the beam. Back home on the Middle Sea, a ship's hull went up first, with the boards fitted to each other tongue-and-groove, and the frame put in later as strengthening. The Eagle People method was to build the frame first, cut the planks straight, and then nail them on, twisting them as necessary. It was just as strong, and much easier . . . once you were used to it. The sailors practically had to be driven to it, full of mutterings about bad luck. Not to mention doubts that caulking would hold out the water, even when they'd seen with their own eyes.

The other cause of delay had been the need for iron smithwork. Isketerol looked out from the edge of his hut and smiled as the distinctive *clang . . . clang* came from another hut closer to the beach. Now he had two men of his own skilled in the ironsmith's art, at least the beginnings of it, and they were teaching others. And they'd helped with every stage of setting up the *blast furnace,* learning that mystery as well.

"When the *Sea Wolf* is finished, we'll load her with a cargo of sixty tons of *iron,* cousin," he said. He slapped the younger man on the back. "Then we'll sail her and *Yare* into Tartessos town and be richer than the king. You saw what tools and armor made of iron can do."

Turn a bronze spearpoint as if it were made of lead, for starters. *Everyone will pay high at first,* he thought. *But the price will come down.* No matter. He'd charge high prices to have his smiths teach the skills to begin with, and meanwhile sell widely.

And then . . . who knew what he'd do then?

The turkey was a skeleton, and the mashed potatoes, peas, squash, and carrots mostly memories—cherished memories, because vegetables were a strictly rationed luxury this winter, doled out in grudging lots to hold off scurvy. The pumpkin pie tasted a little odd with honey as the sweetener, but lacked nothing but whipped cream otherwise—milk was still worth its weight in gold, almost literally. Sandy Rapczewicz looked down at her plate for a second. Then she looked out of the corners of her eyes at Coleman, who nodded; Alston could see her gathering herself for an announcement.

"Think I didn't know?" she said, forestalling it.

"Yeah, well," she said. "We were . . . well, sort of waiting, you know, Skipper?"

Waiting to be sure we were here for good, Alston thought. Rapczewicz had been married, back up in the twentieth. But the Event was as final a method of divorce as death, and considerably more so than a *decree nisi.*

"Congratulations," Alston said aloud, glancing from her to Dr. Coleman. *A bit May-September, but I'm not in a position to talk.* "Just one thing, Sandy. Get married by all means, but if you get pregnant before this spring's operations, *I'll* perform an operation on *you.* A hysterectomy, with a blunt butterknife. I'm goin' to need my XO."

"Sure, Skipper," Rapczewicz said, grinning in relief. "Wouldn't miss it for the world."

The guests joined in carrying the dishes back into the kitchen, then trooped back into the front parlor with drinks, and plates of dried-cranberrry muffins and cookies. Alston looked at them a little wryly. *Lost in time, and we still play bridge and have Christmas dinner parties.* It was such a workaday crowd, among the period-piece splendors of the mansion. One of the better things about the Event was that it had amputated the social pyramid at both ends, though. No masses of poor, and by definition nobody on the island could be rich these days.

They exchanged the gifts piled under a miniature tree, then Coleman sat down at the piano and began tinkling something vaguely Straussian from the book of sheet music someone had given him. Swindapa pulled her up by the hand and did a creditable waltz. *Where the hell did she learn that?* Alston wondered. They'd never danced together before; she felt rusty by comparison. *Damn, this is nice. She really is graceful as a deer.* Sweet-smelling, supple, strong, looking at her with that guileless smile she knew full well covered an unself-conscious, inventive randiness. *Damn, and here I thought I was the cold, self-contained type. . . .*

Several of the other couples rose to dance as well. "Can I cut in?" Cofflin asked after a moment.

"Sure, but with who?" Alston said, smiling secretly to see him blush. "And who leads?"

"You were really warning Sandy, weren't you?" he said quietly as they danced off. His style was basic-competent. "I don't think fighting's an 'unlikely contingency we should be prepared for' with this British expedition, is it?"

"Hell, no." They swayed aside to avoid a table. "Should have cleared the room for this. . . . Unlikely? No, not with Walker over there. If he's cleared out of Britain, that's one thing. If he hasn't . . ."

"You get to kick some Iraiina butt?" Cofflin said gently.

"I confess, wouldn't be the least pleasin' thing in the world." Her eyes touched Swindapa, where she led Ian Arnstein through the steps. "Think, though, Jared. King William Walker, wherever he is, is a deadly threat to us. We're not talkin' about a Lisketter here. He knows too much. The knowledge will make the locals dangerous to us, and if Walker gets enough power, *he'll* be dangerous to us—as the only potential limit to his power, he *has* to strike at us. It's the way he'll think, believe me."

"I do believe you," Cofflin sighed. "Worse luck. Ayup, I'll back anything within reason at the Meeting." His face hardened. "God *damn* Walker."

"May God damn him indeed. But I'll do my best to help."

"Friends come!" Walker shouted at the top of his lungs. "Friends come! Friends come!"

That was Iraiina law; if you didn't call out three times when you approached a steading, you were assumed to be hostile. In this case it was purely formal; Daurthunnicar's scouts had seen him some time ago. Several of them were mounted, with simple pad saddles and stirrups. Bastard trumpeted a challenge at their mounts, and he reined him in sharply; the quarterhorse swiveled its ears back, but he'd taught it to know better than to buck. Walker would still be very glad when there were a couple of his get old enough to break to the saddle—mares would do, a gelding by preference, of course. Riding an uncut stallion was taking machismo to absurd lengths.

He threw back the hood of his cloak. It was a typical English winter day of the better variety: fleeting patches of sun, interspersed with gray overcast and occasional chill drizzle. He'd almost prefer a hard freeze and some snow, but that didn't happen often in southern Hampshire. It was amazing how cold the Nantucket-made armor and underpadding were, when you thought of how uncomfortably hot they could be in warm weather. He'd be glad to change over to the set of fancy duds in the leather trunk the packhorse was carrying. The fields were a sodden sort of green, patched with brown and occasional puddles. Mud sucked at the horses' hooves, coating their lower legs and spattering the trousers of their riders. The smell was rich and earthy, mixed with damp wool from their cloaks. Those were woven from raw fiber, unfulled, with the grease still in it; he was surprised at how well they shed water, almost as good as a rubber slicker.

There were other changes around Daurthunnicar's *ruathaurikaz*, besides stirrups and horseshoes. It had gotten bigger, and one of the new buildings was made of horizontal logs. A couple of wheelbarrows were leaned up against the walls of buildings; it was amazing how much difference those made. Beside the bronze-casting workshop was a small ironworking smithy, and instead of all the women grinding grain by hand, two male slaves walked around a rotary quern pushing at a beam, linked to it by chains from their iron collars.

The heads nailed above the hall doorway were very much in the local tradition, though. None of them had had time to weather down to skulls.

Cuddy nodded to the gristmill. "Great what you can find in books, isn't it, boss?"

Walker grinned. "Actually, I got that one out of a movie, Bill," he said.

He'd suggested they use horses here on the mill when he built it for them; that would be quite practical with the new harness he'd introduced. Everyone had looked at him as if he'd recommended eating their own children. Odd people, the Iraiina.

"You know, if we *did* stay here, we could be running the

place in about five years," he said to Bill Cuddy. "Running the whole of England."

The former machinist grunted and looked around at the trampled mud, pigs rooting for slops, a blue-fingered girl in a tattered shift milking a scrubby little cow into a bucket carved out of a section of log.

"This?" he said. "Run *this*, boss?"

"Well, Walkerburg's already a lot better. Not as much already built as in Greece, yeah, but less opposition, too."

"You thinking of changing the plan, boss?"

"Just a notion. The climate here sucks dead dog farts, I give you that. I'll think about it."

They swung down out of the saddle, armor clanking. He'd kept the conversation with Cuddy quiet; Ohotolarix was picking up English fast, and there were things he preferred to keep private. Retainers came up to take their beasts, and two unsaddled Bastard and led him gingerly off to the round corral where the hobbled mare waited. By the time they got there they were being dragged by the horse, rather than vice versa. His enraged squeal cut through the air.

There were a lot of horses in the other pens, and four extra chariots stood in a wicker-walled shed. *Well, well,* he thought, drinking off the ceremonial horn of beer that marked you as a guest. Another tribe, ready to talk alliance with the Iraiina. *Our efforts are bearing fruit.* And some Tartessians were there, lounging about the entrance, trading warmth for fresh air.

"Good to see you again, blood-brother," Isketerol said, shaking wet from his own cloak; by the look of him, he hadn't been here long. "We should talk, later."

"That we should, later."

The *rahax*'s hall was thronged with warriors and guests tonight, heavy with the smells of woodsmoke and cooking and beer and damp dog from the hounds that lay growling amid the feasters' feet. Daurthunnicar came down from the carved seat along the southern wall to greet him and lead him to the stool of honor at his right hand. Over to the left were half a dozen visitors; they wore their long fur-trimmed woolen jackets and went without the leggings Iraiina wore this time of year, and their hair was in twin braids rather than the single ponytail of Daurthunnicar's folk.

Easterners, an embassy from one of the Kentish tribes. Looking rather sullen, but polite enough. *Or scared.*

A huge platter of smoking roast pork was borne in before the *rahax*. He directed the server to carry a portion of the loin to Walker. The American smiled at her; she was Daurthunnicar's daughter, a statuesque blond young woman with gold on her wrists and in her braids. The *rahax* was really doing him honor. That was the champion's portion of the carcass, too.

As he reached for the meat, someone shouted. Walker looked up sharply.

"No! No!"

It was an Iraiina, one of Daurthunnicar's own followers, with a holding not far from the high chief's. A big man, but not one ounce of it fat; his shoulders were a solid knot of muscle. Face and arms were seamed with scars, although the man couldn't be more than thirty, and he had a formidable collection of gold arm rings, a torc, and a checked plaid tunic that clashed horribly with both. He stamped and roared:

"No! Why should this outlander get the hero's meat? Let him eat husks with swineherds!"

The whole hall was thrown into confusion. Men stood, yelled into each other's faces, shook fists as pro- and anti-Walker factions coalesced. Some of the women were screaming too with excitement, and the easterner guests weren't bothering to hide their smiles. Daurthunnicar surged erect, frowning like a thundercloud, and waved his sword—everyone else had to hang his weapons on the wall—until the uproar died off to a low babble. He yelled at the big Iraiina:

"You shame your *rahax* by insulting his guest! The man he has made *wehaxpothis*, a chief among our tribe. You shame the brave warriors who have sworn to follow him."

Ohotolarix certainly seemed to feel so; he was half off the bench, fingering his eating knife and glaring blue-eyed murder. Walker reached out and put a hand on his arm, gently urging him back to his seat.

"No, this is good," he murmured. "Wait—remember what I told you. Anger is like fire, a fine servant but a poor master. The fool will fall on his own words."

Daurthunnicar was shouting: "He has brought victory and much booty to the camps of the Iraiina, new things to make us strong. Your forefathers are ashamed, Tautanorrix son of Llaunnicarz!"

"No!" the strongman declared. "He is nothing but a wizard. He offends against old custom and law, his slant-eyed wife is a witch, and the gods and Mirutha will shun us for harboring them, stealing our luck. Send him away, lord, or better still, cut his throat in the grove and make a bonfire of his goods and followers, to appease the Mighty Ones."

More uproar, with Daurthunnicar shouting louder than anyone. Walker stayed relaxed, leaning back with his horn of beer. *Totally clueless,* he thought. These people didn't have the least conception of government, or even of war, really. They fought like tigers individually or in small groups, but their sole idea of a war was a series of big raids, until one side or the other got sick of it and moved out or paid tribute. And this near-riot was their concept of how to settle policy questions.

He waited until the shouting had passed its peak, then rose to his feet. "Hear me, lord," he called, not raising his voice much but pitching it to carry through the swell as if it were storm-roar at sea.

"Hear me. This fool and son of slaves—"

Tautanorrix roared again, wordless, his face turning purple.

"—has offered you offense by breaking the peace of your hall, like a mannerless swineherd. As your handfast man, let me punish him."

Near-silence fell through the firelit dimness of the big turf-walled hall.

"And since he might fear my sword is enchanted, let us fight here and now with only the weapons the gods give to every man," he went on, holding up his clenched fists. That provoked a surprised rumble. "To the death, of course."

Laughter at that, fists and the pommels of knives pounding trestle boards until the pottery tableware rattled. *That bitch Alston wasn't completely wrong,* he thought. *This* is *a lot like a biker gang.* Guts and toughness were everything. He'd put his stock up considerably by challenging Man Mountain here, and he'd have lost everything if he'd backed down.

Daurthunnicar's fork-bearded face swung back and forth between them, little blue eyes narrowed. On the one hand, Tautanorrix was a valued supporter. On the other, Walker had made the chief rich—and unlike virtually every other subchief of the tribe, he'd consistently deferred to his patron, thrown his weight behind him in council, and given him shrewd advice on how to increase his own power, make himself a real king. The idea was strange to the Iraiina chieftain, but he'd taken to it like a Russian to vodka. And Walker had a strong following of his own among the younger Iraiina warriors.

The rumbling voice of the high chief went on:

"You are both warriors of note, forward in shedding blood and manslaying, generous in feeding the Crow Goddess. Indeed, it might be said that you're among the best of us. If you fought, the tribe would lose whoever died." A long pause. "But words have been passed which cannot be brought back. Hear the word of the *rahax*! Let these men fight. Let the Wise Man see that no enchantments are used, only strength and skill and luck."

More rousing cheers from the warriors and warrior guests and their women, and cat-yowls of excitement as the betting began. Daurthunnicar was a shrewd leader in his way; he knew when to rule by taking this pack of wolves in the direction it wanted to go. Tautanorrix bellowed with glee.

The *rahax* held up his sword again. "The tribe must be one, here in our new lands. So I, your *rahax,* will pay the blood and honor price to the kindred of the man who falls. Let both of you swear, in the name of your kindred, that they will take the price and not seek blood for blood; that is honorable, because this is no killing by stealth, but an honest challenge."

Walker nodded. "Hear the wisdom of our *rahax!*" he said. *Sotto voce* in English, to Cuddy: "If I lose, kill the bastard."

Tautanorrix sneered: "I will break him between my hands and give his body to the Blood Hag. Yet the word of our *rahax* is wise."

Daurthunnicar went on: "And the victor shall be acknowledged by all men as the champion of the *rahax,* first among the warriors of the Iraiina folk, with an honor price of a hundred horses and two hundred cattle. In acknowledgment of this, he who is victor here shall take as his wife my daughter Ekhnonpa."

That brought full silence. The *rahax* had no living sons,

although he was well provided with nephews. That made
the marriage all the more significant, since whoever wed
the chief's daughter would be a member of the chieftain's
kin by tribal law, and eligible himself to become *rahax*.

Oho! Walker thought. *Well, maybe I will stay.*

He vaulted over the trestle table into the open space
between the firepits. Isketerol was leaning back with a
raised eyebrow; Walker slipped him a wink as he stripped
off coat and shirt and T-shirt. Tautanorrix blinked surprise
but did the same, save for the gold bands on his arms and
neck. His chest was shaggy with the same yellow hair that
swung in a braid down his back and cascaded from his chin;
the skin was almost blue-white where it hadn't been exposed to the sun. Blue-and-crimson rings of tattoo circled
his biceps under the gold armlets.

The American looked at him critically; about two-forty
on the scales, he judged, and built like a Swedish weight
lifter. *So, he's fifty pounds heavier, stronger, and probably
fast too,* Walker estimated, taking slow deep breaths. He
put right fist to left palm and bowed slightly, then brought
both fists up.

Normally he thought of fair fights as something for suckers, but this time there had to be a real battle, something
the audience could understand.

Tautanorrix bellowed and leaped, arms wide to grip
and crush.

The attackers came at her steadily, unintimidated, moving the shields just enough to block. Alston took a deep
breath and launched herself forward in a shoulder strike,
pinning the other short sword back as she did. Her armored
shoulder punched into the shield before her with a metallic
crack. The man behind the shield staggered backward,
away from his companion. She followed up, slamming at
him until the shield boomed and he was wavering back on
his heels. Then she had to wheel herself as his companion
came up, boring in and stabbing.

"Stop," she called.

The trainees did, leaning on the shields and panting, the
double-weight wooden training swords dangling from their
hands. Elsewhere in the high school gymnasium the noise
continued unabated, the whack of wood on the pells, or on
the metal of armor. Most of the trainees were wearing wire

face protectors as well; they'd had quite a few accidents involving broken noses or lost teeth, and Alston had been utterly intolerant of any toning-down of the regimen. Others were doing unarmed combat, or climbing up ropes and over barricades in armor. There was a heavy smell of whale-oil lanterns and sweat, and a cold damp tang to the air; snow lay a foot deep outside, and the huge empty spaces had been designed for central heating, not wood stoves.

She controlled her own breathing, keeping it slow and deep as she felt the sweat soaking her padding turn chill, and watched the purple faces of the two youngsters. Siblings, Kenneth and Kathryn Hollard, about two years between them; they had the Yankee look, light brown hair and blue eyes, long bony faces.

"You two have been really practicin'," she said.

"Yes ma'am," they chorused, with grins of enthusiasm.

"Why do you want to volunteer for the expedition?" she said.

They looked at each other. "Ah . . ." the young man said. "It needs to be done."

Good answer, she decided. More thoughtful than most his age. They weren't talking about the other reasons, of course: boredom, longing to travel, even the desire for adventure. Her mouth quirked slightly at the corner.

"Mr. Hollard, Ms. Hollard, remember that adventure is someone else in deep trouble a long way away. I can tell you that having a spear through your leg is no . . . fun . . . at . . . all. Sterowsky!"

The sailor barking at a group ramming spears into a wall-mounted target came loping over. He'd recovered reasonably well from the blow of the obsidian rake across his face, but the scar was still purple along its edges and his beard was growing in white along the line. It pulled up his mouth into a continual half-sneer.

"Want to show me off again, ma'am?" he said.

"If you don't mind."

"*De nada,* ma'am."

The two young islanders had turned a little pale.

"Not everybody can come, and there's militia work to be done here, too. We'll need qualified instructors. Listen, you two—people are going to get killed, people are going to get cut up, crippled for life."

"Ma'am . . . I'd rather go with the expedition." They spoke in almost-unison, like a bad mixing job on a record.

Alston nodded. "You understand that you'll be under military discipline?" she said.

"Yes ma'am. Our dad was in the Marines."

"All right then; you can both sign up and move into barracks." She wanted the teams that would be fighting together to live tight for as long as possible first. You did better with people who knew each other than with strangers. Her eyes went to the girl. "After you report to the clinic and get the IUD fitted."

Kathryn Hollard blushed; her brother grinned at her with an elder sibling's lack of compassion. "Ah, ma'am, I'm, uh—" she began.

"No exceptions. Virginity isn't a reliable contraceptive." *As opposed to mister-ectomy, but that was a minority taste.*

She could see them deciding whether or not to smile. Good kids, most of the islanders were, not many attitude problems—but not very deferential either. They settled on shy grins; she nodded in reply.

"Meanwhile, back to work. Mark 'em down, 'dapa."

Swindapa made a note on her clipboard; she'd more or less fallen into the role of aide-de-camp and general factotum. Alston sighed and went over to the side of the big room for a dipper of water.

"Oh, 'lo, Jared," she said, looking up.

"Still trying to discourage volunteers?" he said, nodding greetings to Swindapa.

"Just making sure they know what they're getting into," she replied, drinking deep. *Ahhhh. One of the best things about exercise is the way it makes water taste.* She shook her head. "Seems to be a lot of enthusiasm."

He chuckled. "Farmers and fishermen used to be the best recruiting grounds," he said. "Now we know why. Even soldiering is easier."

"How's Leaton coming with the reapers?" she said. That would remove a crucial time constraint on the expedition, if they didn't absolutely have to get those hands back by harvest.

"Looks like they'll really work this time. *Nobody* is going to miss those sickles. Once was enough."

She nodded. "We should take a couple of reapers along,"

she said thoughtfully. "They'd be a big productivity boost over there."

Cofflin snorted. "*Everyone's* getting their oar in this thing. It's the clergy, next—they've scheduled a meeting with me for next week."

Alston sighed: "Almost as many as want something brought back from Britain. Still, there's—"

Her face took on the flat, blank calm of intense concentration. Suddenly she smiled and snapped her fingers. "That's it!"

"That's what?" he said.

"Old military saying. *Amateurs talk tactics, dilettantes talk strategy, professionals talk logistics.*"

He frowned. "I've heard that, but just how does it apply—"

"'Scuse me, Jared." She hefted her *bokken* and headed back toward one of the practice groups, quickening her stride. Someone had just tried something that Jackie Chan would have had trouble pulling off on his best day.

There was a clattering thump, and a trainee landed half off a mat. She lay gasping while her opponent leaned on his spear and panted.

"Don't tell me," Alston said. "You watched a lot of martial-arts movies, right?"

"No ma'am," the young woman said. "It was TV—*Xena, Warrior Princess.*"

Alston closed her eyes for an instant. *Lord, give me strength,* she thought. "Well, let me show you why lifting your leg above your head is a *bad* idea. Especially when you don't have a scriptwriter on your side."

Tautanorrix swung a fist the size of a ham. Walker slashed the edge of his palm into the Iraiina's wrist. His heel flashed into the back of the bigger man's knee, and the warrior landed face forward in the dirty rushes. His face was thoughtful as he rose, shaking a numb arm.

That's the last thing we need, Walker knew.

"Looking for your mother down there?" he asked. "Or for your mare's heart?"

That brought another bellowing charge. He met it with a front stamping kick that flashed between Tautanorrix's outstretched arms and thudded into the big man's chest; the flat of it, not the deadly heel. The Iraiina stopped as if he'd run into a brick wall. Walker felt as if he'd kicked one, as the impact jarred into the small of his back.

Christ, but this fucker's built. Tautanorrix's hands came up to protect his torso; his face was a splotched pattern of purple and white. This time Walker's foot went out like a frog's tongue darting for a fly, aimed low. The heel slammed into the top of the Iraiina's kneecap with a sound like a maul striking wood.

Tautanorrix tried to grab for the foot and nearly fell. The warrior's quick downward glance showed the kneecap twisted offside, like a lumpy growth under the skin on the side of his leg. He bent down and twisted it back into place with a *pop. Talk about your high pain tolerance*, Walker thought. He circled, and Tautanorrix pivoted on his good leg to follow.

"I thought you were supposed to *hit* me, swineherd," the American said through a grin.

This time Tautanorrix ignored him, utterly intent. Well, overconfidence could last only so long. . . . The granite fist flashed out toward his taunting grin. This time both his hands met it, slapping it aside and then locking around the bigger man's wrist. He pivoted on his rear foot, leaning far over and pulling Tautanorrix with him. His left foot slashed upward into the Iraiina's armpit. Tautanorrix came up on his toes, mouth gaping in a hoarse grunt. Walker released him and flipped away with a fancy handstand and twirl that ended with him back in fighting stance. Tautanorrix stood swaying, his right arm dangling useless and dislocated.

"Time, big fellah," Walker panted and came back in, fluid and fast. "Time to die."

The left hand struck at him. He blocked, grabbed the thick wrist, and locked the other man's arm tight with a twist, pivoting. His own right forearm slammed into the locked elbow, and it broke with a sound like green branches snapping. Walker screamed out the *kia,* launching a flurry of fist-strikes, face, belly, throat, slashing with the tips of bladed fingers at the other man's forehead and eyes. Tautanorrix lurched and stumbled, swaying like a cut-through tree, his ruined features sheening with blood. Walker grabbed him by the belt of his kilt and the base of his braid, bending him over and smashing his own knee into the Iraiina's face over and over again. Bone splintered. He looked down, panting, naked torso slick with sweat and the dead man's blood. *First time,* he realized. First time he'd been able to keep on with the hand-to-hand until the other fucker was *dead.* He turned, feet dancing, fists flung over his head in an instinctive gesture of triumph. The Iraiina were roaring out his name, Durthunnicar among them.

His daughter Ekhnonpa stood watching the victor with shining eyes, her hands clenched at her breasts, chest heaving. Walker met her eyes and grinned.

Man, this is great, he thought, as his followers pushed forward with blankets to wipe him down and a horn of beer for his thirst. *It doesn't get any* better *than this.*

"Thank you," the Catholic priest said, accepting a cup of sassafras tea. "You understand, Chief Cofflin, that the division of the Visible Church of Christ has long been a scandal."

Father Gomez looked tanned and fit; he'd been shoveling salt along with the prisoners he was supposed to rehabilitate . . . *had* rehabilitated, Cofflin reminded himself. He trusted the little priest's judgment.

So did his colleagues, evidently. The Town Building office held the pastors of the Episcopal and Baptist churches as well, the Congregationalists, the Methodists . . . even the Unitarians. Only the Quakers and Jews were missing, and neither were very common on Nantucket, particularly the former—ironic, since the island had once been a stronghold of the Friends. Cofflin looked out the square-paned window for a second, as wet snow clung to it and more fell down onto the quiet dockside. The hulking shape of the big motor ferry sat there, dim and dark in the winter's afternoon, looking chewed on where half the superstructure had been disassembled. *Symbolic,* Cofflin thought. Old things broken up for material to make the new. He stirred uneasily. This sort of thing made him embarrassed.

"I know you gentlemen and ladies"—the Congregational minister was a woman—"have been holding a conference."

"We have indeed," Gomez said. "We've been trying to come to some understanding of what God meant by the Event, in a specifically religious sense. Some things are obvious. Questions of episcopacy and papal supremacy are . . . well, completely moot. We think that this means that God is telling us to fall back on the simple wisdom of the early church; wherever two or more of us are gathered in His name, there He is . . . and all believers are one."

Cofflin nodded. That made sense. For that matter, there'd been something of a religious revival on the island since the Event. Not showy, and there'd never been many fundamentalists here—Unitarians and mainstream Protestants were in the majority, with the Catholics a not very close second. More people had been showing up of a Sunday, though.

The Congregational minister went on: "At the same time, God is also telling us something by the very fact that it was *Nantucket* that was thrown into the sea of time. And not, say, Sicily or an island in Indonesia."

She looked at her colleagues. "There's a certain balance of denominational forces here that's pretty well unique. And we're in a world where, say, Islam or Buddhism is completely absent, even Zoroastrianism. No other what you might call competing higher religions."

"So you're going to unite and form a single church?" he said.

Gomez spread his hands. "More of a federation."

"Congratulations . . . but there's no question of a *state* church, I hope you realize that."

"Of course."

"Well, then, what exactly is the point of all this?" Cofflin said.

The clerics looked at each other. Gomez cleared his throat and took up the thread: "Well, Chief Cofflin, you must realize that God is also telling us something by putting us in a world still wholly pagan. Some of it reasonably clean paganisms like . . . oh, like Ms. Swindapa's. Others abominations like the Olmec jaguar cult. Obscene by worldly standards, and possibly of demonic inspiration."

Cofflin nodded grimly. Cultural autonomy be damned, that *deserved* to be scrubbed off the face of the planet. The problem with eliminating undeserving customs, though, was that it was hard to do it without wiping out the people who held them. He was a lot less enthusiastic about that.

"Well, the obvious inference is that God wants His word brought to these people. . . . There are some technical issues to do with the effect of the Incarnation on man's fallen nature, but I won't bother you with that. Basically, we're called to spread the Word, and to do that, we need some help from the government of our new republic here."

"Oh. Missionaries?"

"Certainly. On a more secular note, conversion will also make trade and other peaceful relations easier."

"Hmm." Cofflin pondered. "What exactly did you have in mind?"

Funny, William Walker thought. The Iraiina verb for "to marry" was *wedh.* It also meant "to carry away," which was precisely what you did with the bride. Ekhnonpa was a big young woman, but he lifted her easily onto his saddle-bow; a pleasant armful, and her face was nice enough—not exactly pretty, but it wasn't paper-bag-ugly, either. It would have been a chariot in an *entirely* traditional upper-class wedding. She shivered a little through the fur cloak and leaned against him; he waved and called back greetings to the guests who thronged Daurthunnicar's steading. They roared out good wishes, mostly of an obscene nature, with plenty of puns on "riding home," the bawdy mirth of a stockbreeding people. The women crowded close, pelting them with handfuls of wheat and barley for fertility. Ekhnonpa had been in high good spirits all through the cere-mony—the viewing of the dowry, the handing over by the father, the bride and groom eating from a loaf cut by the man's sword—but now she became a little subdued.

The grass in the fields was silvery with frost where tips lifted out of last night's snow. The branches of the oaks were a tracery of silver where the path ran beneath, and a mist of ice crystals drifted down, reddened by the morning sunlight. Breath puffed white from men and animals. Walker fell back beside the light horse-drawn cart that drew up the rear of the procession.

"Here, wife," he said. "This will be more comfortable for you."

She made a small sound of surprise at the heaped wool and bearskins under the padded leather canopy, more so at the smooth ride the springs gave, glowing with satisfac-tion at this demonstration of her man's status. Her two attendants were already sitting there; he could hear them chattering to each other as he rode back to the head of the line. His men called congratulations, waving spears or slapping him on the back as he passed.

"No, I don't have any objection," Isketerol said, taking up the thread of the conversation as their horses paced side by side. He'd adopted trousers and jacket and cap with earflaps for winter wear. "Even better, if you stay here. More for Tartessos in the Middle Sea; and richer trade— you'll want to buy wine, oil, dried fruits, things like that."

"It'll depend on what happens this winter and spring," Walker said. "I think I can build a position the Nantucketers won't care to mess with, particularly not if I'm prepared to be reasonable about trading. Which I will be." *For a while,* he added to himself. "And then again, if I can open peaceful relations with the island, I can attract more specialists here. I can certainly offer them a better deal than they have back home, and good luck to Cofflin and the captain if they try to stop it. Pretty soon you'll have ships on that run." *And so will I, of course. You're a good buddy, Isketerol, but I'm not giving you a monopoly.*

The folk of his own steading came out to greet them as they arrived around noon; the winter sun was fairly low in the southern sky. He stopped to put Ekhnonpa back on his saddlebow. She looked around, awe plain on her face as they rode into the courtyard.

"Walkerburg," he said.

"It's larger than father's *ruathaurikaz* already!" she said, startled. "And no palisade?"

"It's our enemies who need walls," he said, and tried to see it with her eyes.

All the buildings of horizontal logs, with split strakes for roofing, and fieldstone chimneys carrying away the smoke. The stone pavement of the courtyard showed, the snow brushed off it; the barn and stables were built to the pattern he remembered from his boyhood. Martin's hammer went *clang . . . clang* from the smithy, but otherwise everyone was here. He'd throw a party for the common laboring slaves as well; letting them get blasted and laid on high occasions was good management practice. There were a row of smaller log cabins for his free followers, and the big house he'd put up out of logs from the palisades of plundered settlements.

All in all, it didn't look like his family's ranch in the Bitterroot country of southwestern Montana any more. It looked like the little crossroads hamlet where his grandfather had gone four times a year to lay in supplies.

"Nut a izzy plessta mekka livvin'," he quoted softly, remembering Gramps. *"But kip y'feet uffa m' prop'ty. Ent much but it's mine."*

"My husband?" she said.

"Nothing," he replied. "Old memories."

He swung down, swept up the Iraiina woman in his arms, and carried her through the big house door. He'd built the place on the shotgun principle, four rooms up and down separated by a hall, with a lean-to kitchen out back. It was fairly comfortable, too. Squared-log walls made good insulation, and Martins had run up some Franklin stoves.

"It's warm!" she said in amazement as he put her on her feet again. An arm stayed around his waist. "Warm as summer!"

Warm as a sixty-degree English summer, maybe.

Ekhnonpa gasped again; she'd never seen a floor of split logs, sanded smooth and covered with rag rugs, or plumb-line-straight walls hung with native tapestries, or a staircase, or proper hinged doors. Nor the brightness that glass-chimney oil lamps and molded wax candles allowed.

"This is like the palaces of the *gods,*" she blurted.

Actually more like summer camp, Walker thought with some pride. *But it's a start.*

Alice Hong came up. Ekhnonpa made a bobbing gesture, halfway between a curtsy and a bow, as was due to the senior wife.

"Greetings, my elder sister," she said quietly.

Hong nodded to her, smiling, and went on to Walker in English: "All right, if you like big blond horses. Being a cowboy, I suppose . . ."

"Tsk, tsk, meow," he replied in the same language. "Everything ready?"

"Yes, oh Master," she said, leading the way into the dining room. "The runner got here an hour ago. And I delivered a baby and set a broken leg in my *abundant* spare time today."

"Cut the sarcasm—I'm hungry."

The table was set for a dozen, his principal followers. Ekhnonpa looked around at the room, the table with its place settings and candelabra, the chairs—those were only for chieftains, among the Iraiina—and laughed nervously. "I can see that there is much I must learn about helping to run a household of the Eagle People. Much my elder sister Alauza must teach me."

Alice had enough Iraiina by now to understand that. She began to laugh into her wineglass. The other Americans joined her, and the Iraiina looked at the ceiling or the table, anywhere but at the chieftain's bride. Servants scurried in with platters of food and baskets of bread, the candlelight flashing on their silver collars.

"I teach well," Alice said, looking aside at Walker. "Don't I, Will?"

"Not this time," he said in English. "Political considerations, my sweet."

She pouted slightly. "You get all the fun, with this bloody log-cabin harem of yours."

"You've been having a good enough time."

"Pickles and ice cream are nice, but they're no substitute for beef," she said. "There isn't enough of you to go 'round, Will, and now there'll be less, and you've developed a really medieval jealous streak."

"This *is* the Land of the Double Standard, Alice my medicinal *querida*." For an instant his face went utterly cold, until she looked aside. "I don't give a shit personally, but I can't afford to lose face, which I would if you strayed. If I lose face, you lose your face. Clear?"

"Clear," she said sullenly. "Pass the peas."

Walker did, then helped Ekhnonpa fill her plate. A fork could be surprisingly difficult if you'd never used one before, and he helped her with that too. He kept her wineglass filled. Before long she was blushing and giggling at him, and leaning closer unconsciously. He grinned inwardly. Iraiina men had no technique. In bed they just put a woman on her back and leaped aboard, and outside it they socialized mainly with each other. A little American smoothness went a long way here. And for the present, Ekhnonpa was going to be *very* useful to him.

"That's *fun*," Swindapa said, swinging down out of the saddle.

Ian Arnstein stifled a groan. *Well, young women are* supposed *to like horses,* he thought. He didn't, and besides that he looked ridiculous on any but a fairly large one. On the Bronze Age ponies . . . he'd be lucky if they didn't walk out from underneath him and leave him standing like a straddle-legged statue. There'd been a Viking chief with that problem; they'd called him Hrolf Ganger, Hrolf the Walker.

The big barn had two sawdust riding rings inside it, and the board walls cut the chill a little . . . a very little. It smelled of the sweat and other by-products of horses, despite the snow that lay three inches deep outside. Cynthia Kelton had rented stable space before the Event, to support her habit—the habit being horses, of course. She was about thirty herself, and she'd been plump before the Event; that showed in the looseness of her jodhpurs. There was a visible glow to her as she tutored *Eagle*'s officers and selected members of the militia who'd be going east with the expeditionary force. She would be along herself, to break in local horses they planned to buy on the other side of the ocean, which was considerably easier than carrying any with them.

"Of course it's fun," Kelton said to Swindapa. "And a very promising student you are, too. Nice seat and good hands."

"Better her than me," Arnstein muttered under his breath.

He'd always been convinced that the only purpose a horse served was to take up space that might otherwise be occupied by another large quadruped, say a cow or a camel.

"It's not that bad, Ian," Doreen said, turning out a leg with a riding boot on it to admire the curve.

"I'd rather hoof it myself on shank's mare than saddle myself with one of these things," he said, heading toward the mounting block. "What is it with women and horses?"

"They don't make puns, for starters," she said. "Or leave cracker crumbs in bed."

Marian Alston doubted anything like the Dance of the Departing Moon had been done in Nantucket before. Certainly not by someone in pink bikini briefs spangled with blue flowers. Swindapa was humming to herself as she danced, turning, whirling, leaping, crouching, then slowing to a stately gliding walk in the intricate measure; it was like a ballet laid out by a mathematician with a taste for geometry. Long blond hair spun out in a final spiral as she collapsed gracefully into a pattern of limbs, the fixed look of religious ecstasy fading from her face.

Well, that explains how she picked up the Art so quickly. With that sort of training . . .

"That will bring our journey luck," the Fiernan said, rising and kneeling up on the sofa at the foot of the bed, elbows on the back and palms supporting her chin. "Oh, it will be good to see my family again! And I'm looking forward to showing you off to everybody, my friends and my uncles and aunts, and having you meet my mother and sisters."

Alston blinked a little. The Fiernan Bohulugi had plenty of taboos. Swindapa wouldn't eat swan, for instance, or eat at all on certain days, or wash clothes or plant in the dark of the moon. But they evidently had *different* taboos. The thought of acquiring a whole new set of—*well, might as well call them in-laws*—was a bit daunting. Plus that meant more culture clash. The memory of the day they'd spent going over the concept of monogamy wasn't pleasant; the Fiernan language didn't even have a word for it. *And what if she wants to stay home?* With an effort, Alston put that thought out of her mind.

She looked out the window; dawn was just breaking, gray through early-spring clouds. "Not worth trying to go back to sleep," she said. The Arnsteins were coming over for a working breakfast, planning diplomatic strategy.

"No, it isn't worthwhile going back to *sleep,*" Swindapa said.

Alston looked down to the foot of the bed. The Fiernan was skinning out of her briefs and crawling up toward her, grinning through a fall of tousled wheat-colored hair. She'd never considered herself a very passionate woman, until now. *Live and learn,* she thought.

A hand knocked at the door a little later. "Go away!" Swindapa shouted, laughing.

Alston found herself laughing too; then stiffened as it turned into a long shivering moan. They lay clasped together, and then the knock came again—louder this time, and Ian Arnstein's distinctive mumble. She rolled off the bed and snatched up her bathrobe, belting it on as she strode over to the door.

"This had better be good, Arnstein," she said as she flung it open, trying to make the words a bark and knowing she still had an ear-to-ear smile on. "In case you hadn't noticed, breakfast time isn't for another hour and a half."

It was the scholar, looking extremely nervous, and then blushing slightly as he looked over her shoulder.

"Sorry, Captain." He didn't call her that onshore unless it was a formal occasion or he was *very* nervous. "It's Martha."

Her irritation vanished into a cold clench of worry. "She's all right?"

"So Coleman says, and the baby's doing fine for someone only fifteen minutes old—but they want you there."

Alston blinked; she hadn't realized the labor had started yet. "Oh. Give me a minute, Ian, I'll be right with you."

Swindapa was dancing again with excitement as they scrambled into their clothes and downstairs to where their bicycles waited. They kept to the sidewalks to avoid Main Street's bone-shaking cobbles, then swung onto pavement. Rainwater misted up from the asphalt, soaking her lower legs. For a moment she remembered her own children, something she'd carefully schooled herself not to do. *Forget it, woman,* she scolded herself. *They're a long way away. Three thousand years is an even better wall than a divorce decree.*

The streets were quiet, and so was the maternity ward—section, rather—of the hospital. Martha was lying in a freshly made bed with the baby in the crook of her arm; she was tired but triumphant, the baby was as crumpled and formless as babies usually were, and Jared Cofflin had the same sledgehammer-between-the-eyes look that he'd had on his wedding day, only more so.

"Congratulations," Marian said inanely. "Everything went well?"

Coleman was still in his green surgical gown. "For a primigravida in her forties, very smoothly. Nice healthy bouncing eight-pound baby girl," he said, with a workman's pride.

"You wouldn't say *smooth* if you'd been doing it yourself," Martha said tartly.

"No indeed," Marian said emphatically.

"Does it get better the second time?" Martha asked.

"No, can't say that it does," the black woman said. "But you sort of expect it more." *And afterward you feel very, very—*

"Is there a *kitchen* in this torture chamber?" Martha asked sharply.

—hungry.

"You *are* recovering well," the doctor said. "Someone will be along with a tray shortly. And if you'll pardon me . . ."

Cofflin cleared his throat. "We've got a name for her," he said. "Marian Deer Dancer Cofflin. Hell of a moniker, but it seemed appropriate."

Alston felt the blood mount to her face, glad that it couldn't be seen. "Ah . . ." she said. "Er, ah . . . why, thank you, Jared, Martha." She stopped her feet from shuffling with an effort of will.

"We'd like you and Swindapa to be the godparents, if that's all right," Martha went on. "As neither I nor the baby would be here if it weren't for you. We can have the baptism before you leave."

Marian looked down at the wrinkle-faced form and stroked one arm with a finger. A tiny hand closed around it, rose-pink against black, the nails perfectly formed miniatures.

"That's fine," she said. "Mighty fine. We'll just have to see that there's a good world for her to live in, won't we?

"Ayup," Cofflin said. "Amen."

CHAPTER SEVENTEEN

February – May, Year 2 A.E.

Daurthunnicar scowled and gripped the arms of the huge carved oak chair. The *ruathaurikaz* of the Tuattauna folk's chieftains had stood here for many generations, time enough to accumulate many treasures. The timbers of the hall were carved and painted in the shape of gods and heroes, and they seemed to move slightly in the red-shot firelit dimness like the smoke-darkened wool hangings on the walls. By the wall across from him was a Sun Chariot and horse, cast in bronze and bearing a great golden disk as high as a man, incised with endless looping spirals. The Iraiina had nothing like that. They had never been a wealthy tribe, and they had been plundered of much of what they did have in the lost war on the mainland. The eyes stared at him through the murk, full of holiness and dread.

But we have victory here. The Sun Lord, the Long-Speared Father of the Sky, gives us victory now, he told himself firmly.

The Iraiina *rahax* scowled at the Tuattauna high chief as he stood before him, and at the other enemy leaders. They bore themselves proudly, for beaten men looking at a foreign chief in their own high seat . . . except when their eyes strayed to his son-in-law, where he leaned on his spear beside the throne. *Men fear me because Hwalkarz is beside me,* he knew. *They fear our tribe because Hwalkarz lends it his wizardry and his might.* He was not altogether happy with that, not now. What was given could be withdrawn, and if the outlander's hand was taken back, the Iraiina would have many foes and face much hatred.

When you have the wolf by the ears, you cannot let go, he reminded himself. And had he not bound Hwalkarz to him by the closest of ties? His daughter's belly swelled with this man's get, which was more than his witch-wife had ever given him.

True, he's a wizard. But he was also a warrior beyond compare, a never-failing fountain of wealth, and a giver of deep and crafty redes. Some said he was a god. . . . And the old stories *did* tell of times beyond number when gods or half-gods or warrior Mirutha walked among men and took part in their quarrels in man's shape. It would be a thing of high glory if his grandson was the son of a god. Such a one could make the Iraiina mighty. Such a breed of men could bestride the worlds. If he could not turn the wolf loose, he would wrestle it to the ground, set it to hunting for him.

"You come to hear my word," Daurthunnicar said to the envoys of the defeated. "That is good. Sky Father has given victory to the Iraiina folk and the tribes who have sworn on the oath-ring with them. It is unlucky to strive against the gods."

One of the ambassadors answered, speaking boldly. "Sky Father gives no man victory forever," he said, in the whistling nasal accent his people had. "His favor is fickle."

The defiance would have been more impressive if melting sleet hadn't been dripping off the envoy's beard and hair. Among the tribes of the White Isle it was not the least of grudges against Hwalkarz and the Iraiina that they had broken the old good custom of making war only between spring planting and first frost.

"Sky Father is not so fickle that there will be a steading of the Tuattauna standing whole by next harvest season, if you try to meet us on the raven-feeding field of war," Daurthunnicar said. "Your warriors' flesh feeds the Crow Goddess, your gold is on our arms, your cattle roast over our fires, our women wear your cloth, your wives and daughters spread their thighs for the stallion-cocks of our warriors. This is truth."

The envoys' fists clenched and they growled in their beards. But their eyes flickered to the iron-mailed line of spearmen who stood unmoving along the wall on either side of the Iraiina chieftain. Hwalkarz had taught them that unnatural stillness, and the arts of riding with footrests, arts of moving their warbands in ways that somehow always left their enemies at a disadvantage. Outside the captured hall

rested one of the stone-throwing engines that battered
down palisades like the fist of the Horned Man. And in
two of the greater battles the sorcerer had struck men and
horses dead at five times the reach of a bow, throwing bolts
of thunder-death. The sorcerer, or the god?

"We . . ." The chief of the envoys stopped and ground
his teeth. "We will pay tribute for peace. A tenth of our
herds, a tenth of our bronze and gold, a tenth of our cloth
and of this year's harvest."

There was a time when Daurthunnicar would have accounted that triumph and to spare, and taken it gladly. *And
spent the next year in fear of their revenge,* he thought. Instead, he inclined his head slightly toward his son-in-law,
holding out a gold-chased drinking horn. A woman scuttled
over to fill it with captured mead.

Hwalkarz stepped forward; Daurthunnicar made a gesture, granting him formal leave to speak. When he did he
used the Iraiina words with only the slightest trace of an
accent. Was that the mark of how they spoke in the halls
of the sky?

"You strove against us bravely," he said, turning his
spear and grounding the point in sign of peaceful intent.
"It's no fault of yours if the gods fought against you. And
you're wise to offer us peace. It's a chief's duty to safeguard
the life of the tribe."

The envoys relaxed a trifle, knowing that the Iraiina did
not intend to grind their faces in the dirt further.

"Of the tribute you would give, we'll ask only half of a
half," he went on. Their eyes went round in amazement.
"That is, if you give your yes to our other offer."

"Offer?" one said suspiciously. "You've beaten us—we
acknowledge it, may the Dead Walkers suck your blood
and the Night Ones ride your dreams forever. Why do you
speak of offers?"

Hwalkarz smiled. Daurthunnicar shivered slightly behind
his face. That smile did not mean what an ordinary man's
did.

"The Tuattauna still have most of their warriors," he
said. "If we take your tribute, their axes remain—and may
strike at us some other time. So if you remain our foes,
better that we grind you into nothingness. What we offer
instead is that you become our friends."

"Friends! You take our cattle and horses, burn our steadings, kill our men, force our women, and we should become *friends*?"

Hwalkarz's voice was soothing. "After war, peace may be made. No feud should last forever; else the kin die out and there are no living to make sacrifice for the spirits of the dead. The Iraiina have already made peace with the Zarthani, the Maltarka, many of the eastern tribes. Their chariots fight side by side with ours, and they share in our plunder—and in our new arts of war and making."

"They are your dogs, you mean, to run at your heel!"

Daurthunnicar could see that the envoys were thoughtful, despite their bold words. He nodded smugly. This was a talking he had heard before, with the other neighbor tribes.

"Who speaks of dogs?" Hwalkarz shrugged. "Speak of *wolves*, instead." He touched the fanged wolf's head that shone on the green-enameled steel of his breastplate. They had seen his wolf banner on red fields, and the same emblem was more and more common on Iraiina shields. "The wolves run in a pack, and for each pack there is a leader—but all the pack share in the kill. Run with us, be our pack-brothers, and you will feast richly. More than enough to make up for your losses."

"Run against who?" the envoy said dubiously.

"Against all who oppose us," Hwalkarz answered. "In another year, perhaps two, all the tribes of Sky Father's people in these lands will go to war behind Daurthunnicar, high *rahax* of the White Isle. Already warriors come by the score from the mainland to join our banners and take meat and mead from our *rahax*, famous for victory-luck and his open hand to those who pledge loyalty."

Daurthunnicar felt himself swelling with pride. It was true. He'd received envoys hinting that whole clans might follow, taking land to hold of him and joining the Iraiina folk. A tribe shrank with defeat but grew in victory.

"Then who will we go to war against?" the Tuattauna chief asked.

Hwalkarz's grin spread. "Against the Earth Folk of the west and north, of course," he said. "That will be a fat carcass big enough for us all to feast on. And in return for our friendship, we ask only a light tribute—every year—and that you make no war without the consent of our *rahax*. In return, you will share with us as comrades, and your chieftains will take council with ours."

Daurthunnicar signaled the waiting women to bring in the food and drink. "Come, feast with us, be guests and peace-holy," he said. "We will speak more of this."

This session of the Constitutional Committee's core group was fairly informal, a dozen people sitting around a table with notepads and plates of cookies, and Swindapa at the foot taking shorthand notes—she'd proved to have a natural talent for that.

Informal, hell, it's in my living room, Cofflin thought. The Meeting had given him and Martha a former boardinghouse-cum-inn just past the upper end of Broad, where it turned into Gay Street—Marian had given one of her rare full-bore laughs when she heard, he on Gay and she on Main. They'd pulled out the extra bedrooms, except one for guests and another for a nursery, and turned most of the space into offices of a sort. *So now I can't ever get away from the goddam job.* He had to admit it was a nice place, and more practical for his work than the old house farther out, which was just too damn far to commute on a bike, especially in winter. There were more fireplaces, too; it was an older house, 1840s, like most in this section of town, and honestly built. Rain beat against the streaked antique glass, and the lilac bushes tapped on them like skeletal fingers. The streets were dark, drizzle falling through chill fog; a good thing nobody had to walk or bike far to get home.

On the other hand, it was just too convenient at times. This meeting around the long dining-room table was going to go on long past the dinnertime it was supposed to end at. *On the third hand, with the committee meeting here Martha can go nurse the baby when she has to.* Extremely fortunate; the supply of infant formula was strictly limited.

"Look, let's stop squabbling about details for a minute, shall we?" Cofflin said, washing down a bite of oatmeal cookie with lukewarm sassafras.

Because otherwise I may strangle somebody. The dull roar of argument subsided along the long table.

"Most of you were here for the first meetings we had right after the Event. We worked together well enough when we were figuring out how to avoid starving to death, nearly a year ago. Let's apply a little of that spirit."

"Good point, Jared," Martha said. "Everything we do

will have repercussions down the road; look at what happened with the original Convention, back in the 1780s. Let's stand on their shoulders and perhaps see farther. Concentrate on principles, and on making them clear as crystal."

"I still say the Meeting should be the final authority," Macy said stubbornly. "Remember the way Congress got, back up in the twentieth? Say one thing, do another, and their hands always out to whoever would give 'em the biggest contribution. Let the voters decide themselves."

"*For now,* that's fine," Ian Arnstein said. "What happens when it gets too big? It's awkward enough now, when we get a big turnout for a Meeting."

Oh, please, *not more about ancient Greek city-states, please.*

"How's this?" Doreen said. "We set a maximum size for Towns—say when their Meetings have five thousand members. Bigger than that, they have to split into two. Towns elect delegates to a, oh, let's call it a House of Delegates. With an automatic setup for admitting new Townships. We can put in a formula for how many delegates per voter, say a percentage of the total so the ratio automatically goes up as the number of voters increases. That way the House would always be a manageable size."

"Okay," Macy said cautiously. "I can see that. But changes in the constitution should still be referred back to the Meetings. And the Meetings ought to be able to recall their delegates, too."

"How about a two-thirds majority in two-thirds of the Meetings to approve a change the delegates propose?" Ian said.

"Okay. I can go with that. We need a way for ordinary people to propose changes too . . . say, the same two-thirds and two-thirds voting on a petition, what do they call it—"

"Voter initiative, we called . . . will call . . . would have called it out in California," Ian said. "Damn, those tenses trip you up. We could use the same formula for a recall."

Macy nodded. There was a group that generally followed his lead; they gestured agreement as well.

"All *right*," Cofflin said, trying hard to keep the sarcasm out of his voice. "All in favor?"

Hands went up along the table. He ruled a line through that item on the list before him. His stomach rumbled complainingly; dinner was being long delayed. The smells coming from the kitchen didn't help.

"Next, the military," he said. "I move we use the Swiss system, suitably modified."

Martha frowned. "Does that really need to go into the *constitution*, dear?" she said. "Couldn't we just say where the warmaking power lies and then leave the details to the laws?"

"Ayup, the basics do need to go in, I think. How's this? Everyone registers at eighteen, serves the equivalent of Basic, and does periodic training after that. Meeting—or this House of Delegates, later—has to approve any prolonged call-up, or sending the . . . hell, let's call it the Militia abroad. Details beyond that by legislation."

"I'm for it, Jared," Macy said.

Cofflin looked down the table to Marian Alston.

She nodded. "Sound, as our basic defense. We'll need the Guard for operations abroad, ships and landing parties and so forth. I think that should be at the chief's discretion, with the Meeting as an overall check. We can't be too centralized, particularly with communications so slow."

"All in favor?" He glanced around. "Passed by acclamation. All right, next item, the Declaration of Rights. Let's see, we got the first seven down last session—religion, speech, assembly, franchise, property, privacy, fair and speedy trial by jury."

"What about bearing arms?" Macy said.

"Sam, that comes under 'military service' up the list, in case you hadn't noticed. Everyone's in the militia and they keep the personal weapons issued 'em at home, unless convicted of a felony. Satisfied?"

"I suppose," he grumbled. After a moment: "Ayup, Jared, that about covers it."

"Good. All right, there's a short codicil after all of 'em, to make what we mean clear. Like this bit about the freedom of religion not meaning the town can't put up a creche at Christmas, the speech not including fornicating in the streets, assembly not including rioting, property subject to legal usage, and trial not meaning damnfool stuff like throwing anyone who knows anything off a jury, things like that."

Joseph Starbuck held up a page, his glasses at the end

of his nose. "Phrasing here's a bit more elegant than that, Jared," he said dryly.

"Blame Martha." That brought chuckles. "And Father Gomez, he did most of the religion codicil."

"Good," someone farther down the table said. "For a moment there, I was afraid we had a lawyer on the committee."

There was another chuckle at that. "We're ahead of the Philadelphia Convention there, at least," a man said. He'd been a candy-maker before the Event, and still did amazing things with honey and maple sugar now that his chocolate truffles were merely a sadly happy memory. "They were lousy with lawyers."

"All in favor?" Jared asked. "Passed by acclamation. Next item, the everybody-means-everybody-no-exceptions part of the Declaration of Rights. No abridging citizens' rights on the grounds of race, religion, origin, gender, or sexual orientation. The codicil covers things for damn fools again, in case we get many down the road. We didn't put in anything for green-eyed dwarves with two heads, on the assumption you can't cover all the angles."

"Excuse me, Chief." He looked down the table; it was Lisa Gerrard. *Might have known.*

"Yes, Lisa?" He tried to keep the coldness out of his voice. Gerrard wasn't a *bad* person, exactly. She did good work on the School Committee, though the closest she came to children of her own was seven cats. *Just can't keep her mouth from flapping when she hears certain words. What was that Russian doctor . . . Pavlov?*

"Why do we need to include, um, sexual orientation? Isn't that special rights for some and not others? Those people are covered by the general rights, aren't they?"

Alston touched him on the arm, and he nodded to her. She leaned forward, looking coolly down the stretch of mahogany. "As one of *those people,* Ms. Gerrard—three times over, black, gay, and female—it's my experience that we're not covered by general provisions unless it's made quite plain. Which is why, fo' example, I lost custody of my children, in fact couldn't even *ask* for it. Accordingly I'm for that provision. Strongly. Very strongly."

"All in favor?" Hands went up; close enough this time that he had to count. "Abstentions? Opposed? Passed."

He made a mental note to start talking people around.

About sixty-forty. If it was that close, it might not pass the Meeting without some work—mainly on getting people to attend; the constitution was being passed in chunks, and not everyone bothered to attend every session, so a small band of enthusiasts could be disproportionately influential if he didn't watch out. *Maybe we should make voting compulsory, like the Aussies did?* Ian Arnstein had brought that up a couple of sessions ago. *On the other hand, no.* People too damned lazy to vote didn't deserve a say. He'd pass the word to Sandy Rapczewicz, and she'd see that the Guard people showed up en masse; most of them would vote for legally protecting cream-cheese three-way llama bondage if they knew Captain Alston favored it, but Marian'd never dream of using her position to influence the turnout. Cofflin had no such inhibitions, and neither did the XO. *Hmm.* Father Gomez, he'd noticed, abstained—which might mean either . . .

Christ, I hate politics. Even when you were doing the right thing it could make you feel like you had rancid oil on your soul.

"And that's the last item on tonight's agenda. The minutes'll be posted at the Hub and the Athenaeum as usual, copies of the proposed articles in the Warrant, and we'll all vote on this chunk next Meeting. Thanks, people."

"What my husband means is that he's ready for dinner and would all those who aren't eating here please leave," Martha said.

Cofflin's stomach rumbled again in counterpoint, which brought a general laugh. He stood at the door, shaking hands as people opened their umbrellas and Martha helped them find their coats. The chill night air crept in, raw with the fog and rain.

The door closed finally, leaving only himself, Martha, Alston, and the Fiernan; the Arnsteins were going to settle for sandwiches at a meeting of their chess club. Cofflin winced slightly; he'd taken on Ian in a friendly game once, and it had lasted a whole six moves. Doreen beat him in three. Doc Coleman could give either of them a run for their money, though, and the game had become quite popular over the winter. The four remaining looked at each other and sighed, then a thin wail came from upstairs.

"Our overlord's voice," Martha said resignedly. "Now if only I could learn to tell the 'I'm hungry' cry from the 'I need to be changed' cry. Or the 'Pay attention to me' subvariety."

"I come too," Swindapa said eagerly, joining the older woman on the stairs.

Cofflin smiled to himself; according to Martha, the Fiernan thought cloth diapers were the greatest invention since matches.

"Better you than me, Martha," Alston said. "*I'm* going to check the roast. Lordy, how some of those people love to hear themselves talk."

He busied himself clearing and setting the table, taking out the middle leaves that had extended it for the committee meeting and rummaging in the sideboy for the plates and cutlery. The carving knife and sharpening steel rasped together; the pigs the *Eagle* had brought back from Britain last spring had thrived—there were nearly a thousand of them now—but you couldn't say they were tender eating. Flavorful, yes. Tender, no. Then he uncorked a bottle of the island's red wine, which Martha told him needed to be done to let the stuff breathe. *I can't tell the difference, myself.*

"Drink?" Cofflin said, when Alston came back.

"Wouldn't say no," Alston replied. "The roast's standing. Ready to carve in about five minutes."

"Thanks for making the time to attend these meetings. It's pretty dull stuff," Cofflin said, handing her a bourbon-and-water. This was her sixth committee meeting, but the first time she'd spoken more than a few words.

"No, I wouldn't say dull," she said, her voice remote as she sipped at the drink and bared her teeth at the bite. "Interestin', more like. Seeing history up close." She paused for a moment and then went on: "You know, before . . . all this, I'd never met many Yankees. The real thing, I mean, not just people who live no'th of Mason and Dixon's line."

The silence stretched. They leaned back in their chairs, looking into the low blue-red flicker of the heartwood coals. At last he looked over at her. "Penny for 'em," he said.

She turned and looked into his eyes. "Jared, I love this place."

Cofflin blinked surprise; that was a bit effusive, for her. "Well . . . thanks."

"No, I mean it." Her voice was still remote and calm,

but there was a flat intensity of purpose in it. "I was in the Guard a long time, since I turned eighteen, a lot of it down in the Gulf. DEA liaison shit, Columbians, refugees . . . when we weren't pulling drunken speedboaters out from under after a three-day lovefest with the eels and crabs. Staring up the ass end of the world."

"I was a cop too . . . well, ayup, you've got a point. I was a small-town cop, here."

"Still and all, I started out thinking I was doin' something worthwhile for the country, you know? And that meant a lot to me, because the country did—does, for that matter, or I wouldn't have kept wearin' the uniform. . . . After a while, I got convinced I was standing at the bottom of the sewer drain, tryin' to push the flow back up with a plumber's helper. A while more, and I got to thinkin' the whole country had flushed itself right down that drain and we were just waiting to hit the septic tank. Got posted to *Eagle,* training duty, and sometimes at night I'd think . . . am I just giving these kids a shuck-and-jive?"

They sat listening to the crackle and soft popping sounds from the hearth, and the rippling tap of rain on the windows.

"Here . . ." she said.

"Here . . ." Cofflin went on. "No gangbangers, no Wall Street downsizers, no nutcases on a mission from God, no 'national media,' no redneck black-helicopter paranoids, no multi-cultis, no animal rights lunatics—not anymore, thanks to the Jaguar God—no trial lawyers, no Beltway crowd with their collective head so far up their butts they're looking at their tonsils from the rear. Our own share of natural-born damn fools as Martha likes to call 'em, but they're nothing by comparison."

She raised her glass. "Exactly, my friend. Exactly." The full lips quirked in a wry smile. "No *damnosa hereditas* like the foundin' fathers had on their backs, either. Tom Jefferson talked about havin' the wolf by the ears, but hell, the wolf's ears get mighty sore too. Here we don't have all that."

Slowly, he said: "That's why you finally gave in and started coming to these committee meetings?"

Alston nodded. "But Jared, I'm . . . not qualified. Oh, I can give advice on stuff in my area, but basically what I do is kick ass and take names. I'm a hammer. To me, all the problems look like nails, and they *aren't*."

"We're none of us qualified. I was a fisherman and a cop; Martha was a librarian; Macy's a carpenter turned contractor; Starbuck was a small-town businessman turned town clerk; the Arnsteins barely knew or cared that the real world existed."

"Christ, that's better than a bunch of sociologists and politico lawyers. Ian and Doreen are as bright as anyone I've ever met, and between 'em it seems like they've read every book in the world, sometimes; Martha's about as smart, and less naive. Macy drives me nuts, drives *ever'body* crazy, but he's got a conscience like a bedstead carved out of granite rock—uncomfortable, but it's solid to the core. And Jared, you know people, and you'll do what you think is right if you have to head-butt your way through a brick wall to do it. Plus you've gotten really good at persuading, in your own way."

"Ah—" He flushed, looking down into his glass uncomfortably. "I'll do my best."

"Know you will. Just . . . be careful, okay? Because it's for the whole *world*."

That thought had occurred to him, now and then. It was a sobering one. "Bargain on that, lady." They touched their glasses.

Alston sighed. "I wish my kids were here, you know? I really do. For their sakes."

As if on cue, Martha and Swindapa came down from the second-floor nursery. "She's asleep, at last," Martha said, wiping her hands on a towel. "For a while. As much as half an hour, if we're lucky."

"She's a beautiful baby—very good, as sweet as new butter," Swindapa said, smiling. "If I had a baby as good-natured, I'd . . ."

Then the expression ran away from her face, and she stood with her eyes closed, tears squeezing out from under the lids. *Poor kid,* Cofflin thought. Evidently having children was *real* important to her people. A fully equipped fertility lab back up in the twentieth might have been able to do something, but weeks of a raging untreated pelvic inflammation had probably put her beyond any benefit from the island's clinic.

Martha put an awkward arm around her shoulders. Alston came over and led her to the seat by the fire, pressing the glass of bourbon-and-water into her hand and perching on the arm of the easy chair beside her.

"Your older sister has some children, doesn't she, honeybunch?" the black woman said gently, stroking her hair. "What're they like? Tell me."

Martha drew him out into the kitchen, snagging the long knife and fork along the way. "She'll be all right by the time you're finished carving," she murmured.

"It's called *division of labor*," Walker said to Ohotolarix.

The phrase was in English; Iraiina didn't have the words for it, not without a paragraph of cicumlocutions. You couldn't say *mass* or *table of organization* in it either, not really.

The long shed was filled with men and women and children at work; most of them wore iron collars with a loop at the back for attaching shackles. At one end of the building thin rods of metal went into a machine of wooden drums and crank handles. Four strong men heaved on levers, and the iron rod was drawn through cast-iron dies until it became wire wound on a length of smooth round oak. There was a smell of hot iron and stale sweat, and the raw timbers the shed was fashioned of.

The wire went from bench to bench; some of the slaves cut the links into circles, others flattened the ends, still others fitted the rings together into preset shapes. At last the rivets were closed by lever-operated presses, and the end product was tumbled in boxes of sand to polish it, then washed and wiped down with flaxseed oil and rolled up for packing and transport. Chain-mail hauberks, in six standard sizes that he'd found would fit nearly everybody; kneelength, with short sleeves and a slit up before and behind so that the wearer could ride a horse. Not quite as good as the plate suits Leaton made back on the island, but almost infinitely better than the local equivalents.

"I see, lord," Ohotolarix said thoughtfully when he'd explained further. "Because each task is *division* among many." The Iraiina frowned in puzzlement for a moment.

"But why is this better than having each of these slaves and workmen make a whole set of this fine armor?" He wore his own now, did so virtually every waking moment, in fact.

"If a man does only one thing, he works faster," Walker said. "And if you only have to teach him one thing, he can learn it quickly—little skill is involved in doing only one step over and over again. And if he does only that one thing, it's easier to check that he does it well and quickly, and to drive him on."

A sort of primitive assembly-line system, although he'd gotten the idea from Adam Smith's description of how pins were made in the eighteenth century.

The young Iraiina frowned, thinking the matter through. "I see it must be as you say, lord," he said at last. "*Eka,* truth, I've never seen so many work so swiftly for so long. It's like . . ." He searched for words. "It's like the spokes of a wheel, going 'round and 'round."

Walker nodded, unsurprised; these people were burst workers. At crisis times like the harvest they labored at a pace that would kill most residents of the twentieth, but much of the rest of their working days they spent loafing along, stopping when they pleased. None of them had any precise time sense, either, and they absolutely *hated* working regular hours at high intensity as a steady thing.

Not as much as they hate flogging or the hotbox or the cross, though, he thought with some satisfaction. Or Hong's patented special gelding without anesthesia, although that was reserved for extreme cases. He grimaced a little; he wasn't what you'd call a squeamish man, but there were times when Hong's kid-in-a-candy-store approach to torture made him a little uneasy, not to mention this cult she'd started, with herself as the avatar of the Lady of Pain. . . .

Outside a bell rang to mark the noon hour, echoing across the buildings and fields. At a shout from an overseer the workers in the shed downed their tools. Wheeled carts came in with tubs of food: porridge for the slaves, meat and bread and beer for the skilled freemen and overseers, a covered plate of ham and eggs for the American supervising the whole operation—Rodriguez, today. That would probably get a little cold; the sailor had taken one of the women back into the little wicker cubicle where the accounts were kept the minute the bell went, and the grunts and moans and rhythmic rattling were already loud. Walker grinned; Rodriguez was becoming something of a legend for the amount of action he got.

Still thinks with his balls, he thought, slightly contemptuous. *But he's learned to keep it out of working hours.* And he'd become downright devoted to the boss.

Walker and his chief Iraiina follower walked out into the courtyard. Walkerburg had grown considerably over the winter; he had sixty full-time warriors and retainers now—some from the new allied tribes, as well as Iraiina—plus their wives and children and dependents and the Americans and *their* women; most of them had a steady squeeze now, or more than one. And the slaves, who outnumbered all the rest put together. Plus the horses, milch cows, and draft oxen they needed, with corrals on the pastures downwind toward the river, and the watermill, the workshops, the warehouses. They'd logged off most of the heavy timber in the area over the cold months, and muddy ground interspersed with stumps spread around. New leaf was showing on the trees he'd left for shade and appearance, and a haze of grass and grain across the fields; the sun shone on wind-ruffled puddles and cuffed at the hair he'd let grow long in accordance with local custom.

Warriors drilled, marching, thrusting in unison with their spears or firing crossbows under McAndrews's direction, or rode their horses around an obstacle course. An Iraiina he'd taught was breaking horses to the saddle in a corral, cowboy-fashion. Laborers unloaded a broad-wheeled Conestoga wagon full of iron bars and barrel staves and charcoal and tanned hides. Another was being loaded with small barrels full of the output from his latest project, a still for homemade white lightning. That was wildly popular among the natives despite being rawly undrinkable; he supposed that was because they'd never been exposed to distilled liquor before, but it was another hold on the chiefs.

"Can we plow and herd enough to support so many?" Ohotolarix said, worry fighting with pride in his tone. None of the native settlements was as big as this; they didn't have the organization to feed large numbers, and disease was a constant threat to any substantial group.

"No," Walker replied. "We don't need to."

They walked across toward the main house; he nodded to followers of his about their errands, and took a deep breath of the fresh early-spring air. Apart from woodsmoke and the odors of baking and cooking, there was little taint in it. Alice had seen to the sanitation, with his full power behind her. He'd even set up a bathhouse, and made the

slaves wash regularly with soap, another of his innovations.
The natives were already talking in awe of how few died
here, particularly children. The placc was certainly swarming with rug rats.

"No, we won't plow that much," he went on aloud. "But
we'll get ample grain and beans and beef from our share
of the *rahax*'s levies on our tributary folk, and from our
Earther tenants. Here we'll raise just enough for garden
truck, and fresh grazing for our beasts. Thus we'll be freed
to fight, and work on other things."

And he'd had Martins run up a few plows and nineteenth-
century-style seed drills, miles better than the simple
wooden crook with a stone share the locals used. Nobody
here had much grasp on stuff like liming the soil or rotating
crops, either. Not that he intended to spend his time on
agriculture, but he'd spread that sort of thing around, first
of all on the lands the *rahax* had given him directly to work
with slaves and tenants. It ought to be easy enough to double or triple productivity, which would be essential when
he got around to the sort of building he had in mind. You
could round up all the slaves you pleased, but they weren't
much good if you couldn't feed them; that went double for
armies. He was a young man; plenty of time.

Ohotolarix nodded and strode off to his own house; he
had a growing family, and his youngest son was named
Hwalkarz. The American walked into the hall of the two-
story log dwelling, waiting while a servant knelt to take off
his muddy boots and fit felt slippers. Alice Hong looked
up from her papers on the table in the dining room and
rang a bell for more food, then rubbed out some notes on
a flat slate and chalked in others. Keruwthena's young sisters sat on either side of her; Hong was training them up,
easier than with someone older. That was the main drawback of ruling primitives. You could make them do things,
but you had to show them how first.

"Welcome, Oh Lord of the Manor," she said.

Walker grinned; Alice might take her perversions with
excessive seriousness, but it was refreshing to have someone who wasn't *totally* in awe of him. Of course, he could
relax around Alice. The locals would never follow a
woman, witch or no, and she knew it. She was crazy, he
supposed, but not in the least stupid.

"How are things going?" he said.

The serving girl brought in a tray of sandwiches, thin grilled beef with onions on crusty almost-French bread, plus cheese and pickled vegetables. Hong had taught the kitchen staff well—she liked to eat properly herself—and *none* of them disobeyed her twice.

"Well, I told that cow Ekhnonpa to stay off her feet more—she's still puking in the mornings and probably will be until she drops her calf. I don't like the spotting she had, and I've cut her salt intake," the physician said. "Speaking of that, do you know *half* the females in this place are pregnant? It's not decent—as soon as I've got one trained to do something, somebody pups her. I'm going to start spaying some of them, or doing some D&Cs, or we'll never get any work done. Anyway, four births and one death this week—brainless bitch fell into the boiling tallow in the soap shed and got scalded, nothing I could do. A beam fell on a slave's foot and crushed it; he'll live and I saved the foot, but he's laid up for months. No more dysentery, thank goodness, just the usual rash of minor injuries, and my assistants could see to most of those. The food stores are holding up with the latest delivery. We're finally seeing some real production from the spinning and weaving shed."

He nodded approval as he swallowed the last of his sandwich and took a bite of strong cheese. A lot of the tribute was in raw wool and flax. Building the kick-pedal flying-shuttle looms and the spinning jenny hadn't been any problem, but getting the machines into actual production was another matter. Hong had taken the project under her wing for something to do, now that her regular clinic was well organized. It also made work for all those pregnant women, work they actually liked, and if you wanted decent sheeting or pillowcases here you had to make them yourself. The local linen was more like canvas.

"Good job," he said. The kitchen girl came in to clear away the wood and pottery plates. "As a reward, come along upstairs."

He rose. Hong dropped her chalk beside her quill pen and followed suit, grinning at him and slowly licking her lips. "You too," he added to the servant.

"You girls work on your times tables," Hong said to her helpers.

"Yes, Ms. Hong," they chorused, eyes firmly down on their slates.

The two Americans went out the door into the hallway, pushing the kitchen girl between them and up the stairs. Their hands met on her shivering back. Hong was smiling, and twirling a little silver-handled crop of bone and leather she always wore thonged around her right wrist.

Life is good, Walker thought, moving his hand down to the girl's rump. They turned left down the hall to Hong's room, which had the frontal mask of a human skull nailed to it with golden spikes.

"Wake up! Wake up!"

Ian Arnstein yawned and stretched, shaking off a dream in which he was trapped in a seminar without end, populated exclusively by illiterate surfer dudes who kept quoting Foucault at him; or even worse, Paul de Man. It was still dark outside, just the slightest hint of gray in the windows. It was his turn to make up the morning fire, and he snuggled down under the blankets and coverlet in reluctance. It might be March—now that he came a little more out of sleep he realized that it was the anniversary of Event Day, the morning of the expeditionary force's sailing date—but it was still cold and damp after a week of storms.

"Wake up!" Doreen said again, shaking his shoulder. "Ian! We're back in the twentieth! The Event reversed! There's a jet going by right over us and a Navy helicopter landing down by Steamboat Wharf!"

Ian hit the floor with a bellow and tripped, tangled in the sheets. His elbows thumped on the floor; he ignored it and scrambled to the windows, throwing up the sash.

Cold wind and the drizzle it blew in raised goosebumps on his naked body. Below in the street a cart pulled by two cows went by, piled high with bundles of salted fish under a tarpaulin. A steam whistle sounded mournful and remote; he could smell burning whale oil from the lanterns. . . .

A giggle from the bed brought him around. Doreen squeaked and hopped off the mattress, keeping the four-poster between them. "Now, darling, it was just a joke—"

He kept coming. She dodged and somersaulted over the bed. "Joke my hairy arse!" he roared. "That rain was *cold,* goddammit."

He chased her around the room. By the second circuit

he was laughing as well; he took time to throw a few dry sticks on the fire before she let him catch her. They were both still smiling when they dressed and went across to breakfast, and so down to the wharves.

The two schooners *Frederick Douglass* and *Harriet Tubman* were already being hauled out from the dock by the tugs. *Eagle* still waited. She didn't look quite so pristine as she had a year ago; they were still short of paint, and would be for years. Extra davits for more boats had been added to her stern and sides, and other shapes crouched at the rails, covered in tarpaulins. Umbrellas and rain slickers crowded the dock; there were hugs and tears as friends and family members said farewell. Father Gomez—who'd been chosen as head of the new church, rather to his own surprise—led a blessing service.

Then Jared Cofflin climbed onto a board between two barrels.

"Bad weather for a send-off, so I won't keep you long," he said. "We did all the speechifying necessary at the Town Meeting. This is something that has to be done. Lisketter's bunch got themselves killed, but we don't know what Walker and his gang have been doing, and we have to go, for our safety and that of our families and our homes. It isn't that far to Britain."

Not too far for Walker to come back with a horde of pirates, if we give him enough time, Ian thought soberly. *Or for the Tartessians to do the same.* That fact had sunk home well and truly over the winter; three-quarters of the Meeting's votes had gone to sending an expeditionary force and giving Alston plenipotentiary authority. Even Sam Macy had gone along with it, with a convert's zeal. Now that the spring plowing was mostly done, the islanders were anxious to see the expedition on its way. Not enthusiastic, certainly, except for some youngsters, but very willing.

He wondered whether it was the situation that made Town Meeting government work relatively well here, or the fact that this was a community whose core was people with real roots. *I doubt a random collection of seven thousand Angelenos would have done nearly as well.*

"I have complete confidence in Captain Alston's judgment and leadership," Cofflin finished. "With that, I'll turn this slippery plank over to her for a minute."

There was a friend's malice in the smile he gave the

commander of the Republic of Nantucket's fleet. Ian knew
they both detested public speaking. It was a bit of an irony
that they'd both landed jobs where it was an essential part
of the work.

Alston went up on the plank, yellow slicker over her
working blues, and stood with hands behind her and feet
braced wide. "I'm glad Chief Cofflin and the Meeting have
confidence in us," she said. "This is an essential mission,
and I intend to see that it's done right and at the least
possible cost."

Well, that's the captain, he thought. Mission first, people
second. She included herself among the expendable, of
course.

"Cheer up," Doreen whispered in his ear. "Think of the
adventure, Oh Speaker to Savages."

*Adventure is somebody else in deep shit far away, as Mar-
ian so eloquently puts it.* "Think of the cold, the wet, the
cramped bunks, the salt meat and hardtack"—without re-
frigeration the *Eagle* and her consorts were back to traditional seafaring provender, "the natives throwing things at
us," he whispered back.

"If all goes well, we'll make sure that there's no long-
term menace to Nantucket's safety, and gain friends, allies,
and trading partners," Alston went on. "Every one of us
will do her or his best to see that things *do* go well."

*"Or they'll answer to me and wish they'd never been
born,"* Doreen whispered, in a sotto voce impersonation of
the icy soprano Alston used when angry.

"We appreciate your support, and please keep us in your
thoughts and prayers," Alston concluded. "Thank you."

She stepped down, and the last of the expeditionary force
trooped up the gangplank.

"Almost wish I were going with you," Jared said.

"I don't," Martha added bluntly. "I just hope you all
come back safe." She looked down at the baby sleeping in
its carriage.

"You're right," Alston said. "That's important work
too."

"You will come someday," Swindapa said. "There will
be many voyages. I'll show you my birth-country." She bent
and touched the baby's cheek. "You too, little Marian, *iho-
jax.* You will see the midwinter Moon rising over the
Great Wisdom."

Ian looked aside at Doreen, and smiled. "Remember our honeymoon cruise?"

"Time to break the mold," Walker said. "Hoist it out."

Men in thick leather aprons and boots and gloves went cautiously close and fastened a three-bar iron grapnel to the top of the mold. A ten-ox team bent their necks to the yoke and pulled in the muddy yard outside, and the long clay tube rose slowly out of the casting pit to the creak of harness and rattle of the block-and-tackle. The workers stood watching and blowing on their hands until it was free, then moved forward to guide it onto a timber cradle as the oxen walked backward and let the great weight down again.

A whistle blew, and slaves attacked the clay of the mold with wooden mallets and chisels. Large sections of it peeled away, revealing the dull brown-gold color of the bronze, still painfully hot to the touch. Walker and Cuddy stepped close, examining it with painstaking care from the thick breech down through the trunions and the extra foot of spongy, pitted metal at the muzzle. The center was still full; they'd hollow-cast it with a water-cooled core for greater strength, the outer layers shrinking in as they solidified.

"We'll saw this last foot off, and then we're ready to bore it out," Walker said, slapping the metal. *There's a thrill to it,* he thought. Sort of like having a giant hard-on, in a rarefied intellectual sort of way.

"Yeah, but that boring, that's going to be a bitch, boss. The tool pieces and the gearing for the boring machine— that'll be mostly a hand-filing job."

"You've got the gauges for measuring results, don't you?" Walker asked, crouching and looking along the top of the barrel.

"Boss . . . ah, hell, yeah, I can do it. I can build a tool-and-gear cutter, too, it's just a shitload of work."

"Nothing worthwhile without sweat," Walker said cheerfully. "You've got those locals understudying you, don't you?"

"Right. Boss, have you tried to get the notion of doing something *exactly* into these wogs' heads? It's like *on time,* they just don't have that file on their hard drive."

"Actually I have, Bill. It just takes persistence and a boot up the ass now and then."

Perfect, he thought, touching the cannon again.

The sights were elementary, a blade at the front and a notch at the rear, just like the model, the Civil War twelve-pounder Napoleon. Saltpeter was still the bottleneck in gunpowder production, and Isketerol was working on that—his people used it as a medicine, and it was just a matter of scaling up the leaching process. When it was solved, he'd have the same power at his command that stopped Lee's men at Malvern Hill and Gettysburg.

"Ultima regio regnum," Walker said, patting the barrel again. "The last argument of kings." If the Nantucketers wanted to fuck with him, he was going to give them a right royal welcome.

Bill Cuddy blinked at the sound of Walker's laughter, and several of the slaves made covert signs with their fingers as they cringed.

"Oh, God," Doreen said, looking up the companionway stairs that led to the fantail of the *Eagle* and at the tumbled slope of foaming water beyond.

"Quickly, please, Ms. Arnstein!" the yellow-muffled figure at the head of them said. "Can't keep this hatchway open!"

Ice-cold sea spray was blasting through, already hitting her face and trickling down into the layers of quilted parka and wool sweater beneath her waterproofs. She took a breath and ran up the slippery treads; the fact that the ship was riding up the slope of one of the huge waves made it a little easier.

At least the air and cold cut the nausea. Seasickness had never bothered her before, but the four unbroken days of a high-latitude North Atlantic gale had triggered it well and truly. The crewman grabbed her as she came out and snapped her belt onto one of the safety lines that ran down either side of the quarterdeck. The wind snatched the breath out of her, leaving her gasping as she pulled herself slipping and crouching along past the radio shack and toward the great triple wheels.

She looked at the waves and felt her stomach heave one last time, but mastered it. *It isn't really storming anymore,* she told herself. *Not really.* Not the way it had been for the previous four days. Then she looked back over a sea like a long range of mountains in labor, white water from horizon to horizon except in the troughs between the great waves. Appalled, she turned her back on it—had to, because otherwise she couldn't breathe. Somewhere up there it was near noon, but the light was a somber gray wash.

The *Eagle*'s bow climbed until it was pointing at the growling iron sky. Wind moaned and whistled through the rigging, loud enough to drown out a voice five paces away. No sleet today, but spray still came in sheets. The ship seemed to pause and then pitch forward under a mountain of gray and steel blue streaked with white, plumes of white throwing back from the twisting lunge of the bows. The rigging changed its note as the height of the wave itself sheltered them a little from the force of the monster wind raging down out of Greenland. Dim in the sheets of water coming over the side, figures in yellow slickers fought with the ropes in the waist or aloft.

The wave broke behind them and poured across the port rail, cataracted across the waist deck, hip-deep to the crew. Doreen felt her feet slip out from beneath her and clung for sheer life to the safety line; it bent like a bowstring under the terrible leverage, and her head went under—or she thought it did. With wind and water so intermingled there was no real surface to the billow streaming about her, only a zone of increasing density. Then like some great dog *Eagle* shook herself and roared upright again, with a Niagara pouring overside and through the scuppers.

Oh, God, thank You, she thought, coughing and wheezing to get the water out of her lungs as she fought her way to the wheels. Eight crewfolk wrestled the savage leverage of the following seas as it played through the rudder and the gearing.

"Sharp weather," the captain called, bending to shriek into her ear. "This is real sailin'!"

"You're out of your mind!" Doreen yelled back.

White teeth split the black face dimly seen under the slicker's hood. "Yeah, I am. Ain't it cool?" Alston shouted in turn.

Swindapa laughed beside her. She was bareheaded, long wet hair streaming like a yellow banner in the gale.

One advantage of weather like this was that you could mutter and not be heard. "Oh, great, I stop puking my guts out for the first time in sixty hours, and what do I get? The Loony Lesbian Sailors' Comedy Hour."

She pulled herself closer, holding on to the safety line. "How are we doing, Captain?"

Alston seemed in a playful mood. "Do you take Band-Aids off slowly or rip 'em quick?" she yelled.

"Slow—why?"

"I'm of the rip-'em-quick school," Alston replied. "This blow was just what we needed, to see how the crews settled in, test the schooners' seakeeping . . . and get us across fast."

"The schooners aren't sunk?" Doreen said, looking around.

Nothing. The *Eagle* came to the crest of a wave, and she couldn't even tell where sea and sky parted company. *The Queen Mary couldn't live in this.*

"Not as of the last radio check, half an hour ago. Good weatherly little ships—they float like corks. And we've been making three hundred sea miles from noon to noon, or better. This blow's dying, though; we'll rendevous off Ireland in two, three days. Fast passage."

"I'm glad we're not in danger."

"Oh, there's danger. Let a couple of sails go in this and we'll broach to—be turned broadside on to the waves in a flash."

"Would that be bad?"

"We'd capsize and go down like a rock," Alston yelled cheerfully. "But don't worry—it's a sound ship and the crew's shaken down somethin' wonderful."

"I'll take a 747, thanks, given my choice," Doreen shouted back. "Anyway, Ian says he's finished."

"Lead along then," Alston said. "Ms. Rapczewicz, you have the deck. Keep her so."

They went down the companionway behind the radio shack and forward of the emergency wheel. The narrow passageway on the port side was dimmer than it had been when the electric lights were on; even the smell was different, a very slight fishy-nutty tang from the whale oil, and the officers' galley to their right gave off an occasional whiff of woodsmoke. They turned left, past the usual captain's quarters and back to the flag cabin at the rear.

Ian was sitting at the table, gnawing on a crackerlike piece of ship's biscuit. "Is it still blowing hard up there?" he asked innocently. The two rooms of the flag cabin were warm and dry and fairly well lit, but the swooping lurch was still the same—possibly even worse without the distraction of the heaving sea to watch.

"Excuse me while I strangle my husband, Captain," Doreen said, dripping.

Alston went into the head and returned with towels. Doreen and Swindapa wrapped them around their hair; the captain rubbed her inch-long wiry cap a few times and sat. *I wish I could just ignore discomfort like that,* Doreen thought.

"Well, Mr. Arnstein?" Alston said.

"I think I've come up with a diplomatic strategy that might work," he said cautiously. "What we discussed, but refined a bit. It turns on a nice little piece of linguistic reconstruction Doreen and Martha and I did back on the island."

Alston's eyes narrowed. "Oh?"

"It turns out the Iraiina and their relatives, what Swindapa calls the Sun People, weren't the first Indo-Europeans to settle in Britain," he said. "They were probably just the first ones to make it stick—would have without us, that is."

He pulled several sheets of paper out of a folder. "Damn, but this almost makes me wish I'd been a comparative philologist; as it is, I'm a rank amateur out of my depth. But look at these words in Fiernan."

He drew a list: *bronze, wheel, axle, plow, yoke.* Each had a phonetic rendering of the Earth Folk equivalent beside it. "Now look at these Proto-Indo-European equivalents, and the Iraiina ones."

"They don't look very similar to me," Alston said dubiously. "I mean, the Iraiina words do, very similar, but not the Fiernan."

Doreen took up the explanation: "You've got to strip away the grammatical features—and that's damned hard in this language, with this crazy—no offense, Swindapa—prefix-suffix system they've got. Sometime a long time ago, hundreds of years, Swindapa's ancestors borrowed the words for these concepts. From something even closer to the ur-language than Iraiina."

"Oh," Swindapa said, looking at the list. "Yes. I see what you mean; that makes sense. Why didn't you ask me, though?"

Doreen felt her stomach lurch again. *Oh, shit. We got too tied up in our research and assumed that preliterates couldn't have a historical sense.* Preliterates like the Iraiina couldn't, perhaps; they lived in mythic time, not historical. The Earth Folk were obsessed with memory and measuring natural cycles, though, as much as the Mayans had—would have—been.

Aloud, feebly, she said: "What do you mean?"

"Well, in your years . . ." The blue eyes took on a remote look; her lips and fingers moved in a mnemonic chant. "A thousand years ago, or a little more."

"The . . ." She paused for a moment, and her accent grew stronger, as it did when she shifted back to thinking in her native tongue. "The Daggermen, we called them; the Brawlers, the Mannerless. They came from the east—the Sea-Land Country. A few at first, trading, and sometimes stealing things, then more of them. They built their houses in places that weren't good for farming, at first, and raised animals. They had no manners, but they had wonderful things—mead, and copper, and plows, and the very first horses to be seen in the White Isle. They made pots marked with cords for the mead-drinking, and new types of bows, ways of herding cattle, and oh, all sorts of things. There were a lot of fights."

Doreen put her face in her palms. Ian pummeled his temples lightly with the heels of his hands. "Bell-Beaker burials," he said.

"So the Grandmothers sent their daughters to them, to teach them about Moon Woman, and when they learned, they helped us to make the greatest of the Building Wisdoms." Swindapa smiled. "That was eight hundred and fifty-two of your years ago. And they took the Spear Mark, that our hunters had always had, and became part of the Earth Folk."

"Assimilated," Doreen said to Alston. "But not completely. I think that's partly why the two institutions in Earth Folk society don't cooperate very well."

Swindapa shrugged. "The Grandmothers and the Spear Chosen don't *have* much to do with each other," she pointed out. "Moon Woman and . . . oh, I see what you mean."

Alston was nodding slowly. "You're right," she said. "Now, let's figure out how to use it."

Ian made an eager gesture and pulled out another sheet, this one with a flow chart on it. "It's a wild coincidence, but there are some similarities in the Earth Folk setup to recorded cultures—particularly the Iroquois. They're matrilineal and matrilocal, for starters, and there's a Sacred Truce celebrated by a gathering at . . ."

It was a fair spring day when the men of Walkerburg made ready to ride out to war; tender leaves fluttered, and wildflowers starred cornfields and meadows. William Walker pushed the modified Garand into the saddle scabbard and tied the thong that held it in place as he looked around in pride. Not bad, considering that he'd only been here since last September. The seed kernel of an empire. *Archaeologists may dig it up someday. The place where the dynasty that ruled the world for a thousand years was born.* If things went well, he'd move somewhere more convenient in a couple of years—the site of London, probably—but this was the first ground that had been *his*.

Alice Hong rode back up the line and handed Walker a piece of birch bark covered with notes. He looked at it and made yet another mental note that he'd have to get going on making paper someday; there was plenty of linen to make the pulp. Hong rode with reasonable confidence, able to stay on at least and keep her horse going in pretty much the direction she intended, which was all you could say for most of the people here. A Browning automatic was belted to her waist.

"Good," he said, returning the list, a last-minute check of the stores.

Unlike most of the others in the war host gathering through the Iraiina lands and Kent and the Thames Valley, *his* people weren't going to spend half their time foraging. And they weren't going to lose ten men to disease for every one killed in battle, either.

He looked down the column. Sixty riders, all in chain hauberks and conical helmets with bar nasals except for four Americans wearing Nantacket-made plate suits like his. They'd all ride to battle but fight on foot; it took longer than seven months to train a real cavalryman, or to train the horse for that matter. It still gave them unprecedented mobility and striking power by local standards; every man had a steel sword, a spear, and a crossbow slung over his back, although most of them kept their native axes or copies Martins had made at their saddlebows as well. More followed on foot, also all in iron, half of them with spears and half with crossbows. None of his original crew from the *Yare* among them, except for four as officers; the Americans were more useful at base, mostly . . . and not really up to local standards in hand-to-hand fighting, the majority of them. They and the ten native warriors he was leaving would be more than enough to keep the slaves in order.

For the rest there were a dozen servants; Hong and her native assistants; the train of big wagons and a smaller two-wheeled one he'd modeled on the farrier carts Civil War cavalry units had taken along, with a portable sheet-iron forge and small anvil for Martins's best pupil. Plus spare horses, and some cattle driven along for fresh meat.

And the *pièce de résistance*, two long bronze tubes on wheeled mounts with limbers behind four-horse teams. A nasty surprise, if he needed to pull a rabbit out of his hat.

Good little army, he thought. They actually had some notion of discipline and coordinated action by now. Combined with the natives' built-in ferocity and hardihood, it was a formidable combination.

He turned and led Bastard back toward the steps of the Big House. Ekhnonpa stood there, with the smile that brought luck. She was showing now, five months along; Keruwthena was even bigger, standing back with the lower-status staff. *Odd.* He'd never had any particular or urgent desire for fatherhood—it was far too much trouble and expense and time taken from his own ambitions up in the twentieth. And here he was going to be a daddy twice over . . . probably more than that, actually, but those were the two he was sure of. It did change your perspective a little; there was a certain satisfaction to thinking of your genes heading down the ages, enjoying the wealth and power you were piling up after you were gone.

He turned and looked out over the gathered folk of his settlement, raising his voice to carry. "While I am gone, my handfast man Bill Cuddy stands as steward in my place," he said.

He looked down at the machinist. "Don't fuck up, Bill," he continued in English.

"*De nada,* boss," Cuddy said. "No problem."

"And my second wife, Ekhnonpa has charge of household matters," he went on in Iraiina.

She looked at him with worried adoration. "Return to us victorious and hale, husband," she said.

"You are to take care of yourself," he said, patting her stomach. "Remember what Alice told you about straining, and diet."

"Yes, lord," she said, looking past his shoulder at Hong.

A mixture of awe, terror, and fascinated loathing was in the glance. He hadn't let the doctor play any of her little games with the *rahax*'s daughter, but they were no secret.

Alice is very *useful.* Good wizard/bad witch was as workable as good cop/bad cop.

He swung into the saddle and stood in the stirrups. "Once more we ride out to victory!" he called.

Local tradition guided most of the speech that followed— uncomfortably florid to American ears.

Wood and metal boomed on the sheet-steel facing of the shields as they hammered their weapons on them and screamed out Walker's name. Success accounted for a lot of that; he'd led many raids, all of them profitable and most of them easy work.

"Yo!" he said at last, waving his hand forward. His standard-bearer raised the banner, topped by a wolf skull and aurochs horns. Cloth went streaming out in the chilly breeze—a black wolf's head on a red ground.

Women made their last farewells; McAndrews tore himself away from his heavily pregnant blonde. *Can these mixed marriages work?* Walker thought with a flicker of sardonic humor. At least it seemed to have settled the man down; he doted on the wench. A romantic temperament.

Hooves thudded on turf, axles squealed, oxen bellowed as they leaned into the traces.

"I suppose I'm a romantic too, in a way, in a way," Walker whispered to himself. After a while, he began to sing—you didn't get music here unless you made it yourself. The locals just couldn't deal with rock tunes, but the Americans took it up with him.

And it's so right, he thought. *I* am—

"—Bad to the bone!

"Bbbbbbaad! . . ."

CHAPTER EIGHTEEN

April – June, Year 2 A.E.

"Hard to remember," Swindapa said, looking over the rail, her hair lifting around her face under the baseball cap.

Eagle and her consorts were beating southeast, down the Irish Sea after rounding Anglesey and the bulge of Wales. No land was visible now, save perhaps a distant smudge to port.

"Remember what, 'dapa?" Alston said, brought out of her own thoughts.

If they spoke quietly by the fantail nobody was likely to overhear. The ship lay over at eight degrees, making ten knots with all sail set, its motion a slow smooth rocking-horse plunge. The waist was crowded, ex-cadets and militia volunteers straining for their first sight of the wild lands.

"The sea. Hard to remember that I've only sailed on it this last year. There is so *much* of it—and always something waiting beyond the edge of it. Always something new to see."

Alston smiled herself. *That does sound good.* And there was a whole world out there, once Walker and his bloodthirsty ambitions were seen to. *Moas,* she thought, *if we get as far as New Zealand. Great flocks of them, fourteen feet high.* Or the elephant bird of Madagascar, extinct a thousand years in the twentieth, the creature that had given rise to Sinbad's legend of the roc. *Dodos, too. I'd like to see what San Francisco Bay looks like when it's not all mucked up. Babylon. I'd really like to see Babylon.* Or Africa, despite what she'd told McAndrews. Egypt—with an escort big enough to impress the locals—and maybe the Serengeti. . . .

"Someday, 'dapa," she said. Then she turned and took

a few paces forward, looking into the radio shack. "Ms. Rapczewicz, signal to the *Tubman;* it's about time, I think."

The signal lantern clacked, and the schooner dipped her ensign in acknowledgment. Faint and far, the orders echoed across the water and the *Tubman's* prow turned west of south, heading to round Penzance on the point of Cornwall. Alston clasped her hands behind her back and looked east.

"It's begun," she said. *Chess with lives for pieces, and not knowing how your opponent moves until too late.* And she could not afford to lose. *So I'll win.*

"Arucuttag of the Sea!" Miskelefol of Tartessos blurted.

Isketerol ducked out and leveled his binoculars. The shape that loomed out of the morning mist was not quite like anything he'd seen before. A little like the *Yare,* except that there were no square topsails on the forward of the two masts. A gilded eagle flung back its wings below the long bowsprit, seeming to take to the air with every bound across the whitecaps that patterned the estuary. The hull cut the water like a knife slicing flesh, its prow throwing a sunlit burst of spray twenty feet in the air as she rounded and tacked in toward shore. The Tartessian's eyes went wide behind the lenses as he saw how close she cut to the wind that blew from the north, and did a quick estimate of her speed.

"Quiet!" he roared into the chaos of the camp. His thumb turned the focusing screw and his lips moved as he read the name on the bow, just forward of the diagonal red slash. "*Harriet Tubman.* Odd. Sounds like an Amurrukan name." It was unlucky to give a ship a person's name, splitting a soul in two.

He cased the binoculars and looked around. "Quiet, I said. Get to your posts!"

With his cousin's help he put down the disorder. *Yare* was anchored close offshore, and *Sea Wolf* drawn up on the beach; he'd built her to be capable of that, since it was so useful. *How deep does that . . . schooner, that's what they're called . . . draw?* he thought. Eagle People ships tended to have deep keels, but that was a lot smaller than the *Eagle* herself, if bigger than the *Yare. Hmm. Eight feet or so, I'd say, perhaps a little less.* That meant they could get to within three hundred yards of the shore without touching mud, with the tide full like this.

"I *told* you we should have sailed for home last week!" his cousin was saying.

"Quiet, and get your thrower ready," Isketerol said. His cousin departed at a run.

How many aboard her? He studied the Nantucket schooner carefully. Hard to say, but somewhere between twenty and forty, unless they had the belowdecks packed with men. "You!" he pointed to a crewman. "Run over to Daurthunnicar's huts and tell him we've enemy in sight. Diketeran!" One of his trustier men, steersman on the *Foam Hunter* in the old days. "Get your horse, ride to Walkerburg, and report. You, fetch my war harness. Now!"

Men scattered to their tasks as they recovered their wits. The Tartessian camp was a half-circle backing onto the sea behind an earth rampart and palisade. At each end where the rampart met the water was a platform of timber and earth; on it crouched a shape of beams and cords. The trebuchets creaked as the Tartessians heaved around the crank handles of the geared windlasses. Isketerol finished snapping the clasps on his Nantucket-made suit of armor, checked his pistol, and walked over to the left-hand stone thrower. The crew had had plenty of time to practice over the winter, especially after *Sea Wolf* was finished. More hands were dragging obstacles of logs studded with iron blades down to the water's edge, in case of a landing.

"Ready, Skipper," one of the trebuchet crew said to him, teeth flashing in his olive face.

Isketerol made his own estimate of time and distance. *Moving target* . . . "Up one on the stayrope," he said. "And . . . *now*."

The two-hundred-pound boulder whipped into the air as the machine crashed and creaked and thumped. It turned into a tumbling dot, seemed to pause at the height of its curve and then arching down. He used his binoculars again; a hundred yards behind the enemy ship the rock dropped nearly into its wake. Isketerol hid his surprise at how close they'd come. Just then his cousin's emplacement fired; they were loaded with a large barrel of tallow and pine pitch and turpentine. The barrel—even then Isketerol found himself thinking how sheerly *useful* barrels were, and wondering why nobody in this age had thought of them—landed farther from the schooner than his rock had. The deliberately weakened hoops burst as it hit the waves, scattering the contents. The patch of burning oil floating on the water was probably more intimidating than the splash of the boulder, though, and so was the trail of smoke through the air. Nobody on a wooden ship took fire lightly unless the Jester had eaten their wits.

Evidently the Eagle People commander wasn't mad. The schooner whipped around, heeling far over, and let the booms of her fore-and-aft sails swing far out, wheeling and running south along the shore away from the Tartessian camp. The spearmen, archers, and crossbowmen grouped behind the spiked log barricade cheered and waved derisively.

"Good shooting," Isketerol said to his cousin.

"*Now* shall we head home?" Miskelefol said. "We can sail with the evening tide—"

"And meet the *Eagle* out on the open sea?" Isketerol said, grinning.

"Maybe she's not here."

"But probably she *is*. I don't think I'm ready to go to the Hungry One just yet, son of my uncle."

"Shall we wait for *Eagle* here, then?"

"Why not? She can't come close to shore. This camp is strong and we can call warriors from inland if they try to send men ashore. If we run here the Amurrukan may well come for us in Tartessos. Walker is right; we have to teach them that it's too costly to interfere with us, or we'll never be safe anywhere near salt water. Besides, I gave him my oath."

The other Tartessian sighed. "As you will."

"Indeed," Isketerol said.

His glance went inland. What was it Walker was fond of saying? *Nothing ventured, nothing gained.*

Swindapa leaped over the side of the longboat as its keel grated on the shingle and ran up the beach with the quiet water cold on her shins. Then she went to her knees and took a double handful of the dirt there, grass and weeds and soil tight between her fingers. Her chest felt tight too, and tears prickled at her eyes as the nettles did at her skin. They didn't drop free to land on her native earth, though. If she'd felt this way a year ago, they would have. But the Eagle People wept seldom; they kept their thoughts and their joys and their sorrows more within themselves. Part of them had entered into her, she knew, in the time she had spent among them, and in Marian's arms. She would not weep, nor dance her joy along the seashore. Instead she let the bittersweet happiness fill her, like something growing behind her breastbone. A rose, with beauty and with thorns.

I am not what I was, she thought, standing and looking around. That was both bad and good; more good, perhaps. The Earth Folk would have to become other than they had been, or they would cease to be at all. *Moon Woman has turned time itself to give us this.*

The land lay green and bright about her, beneath a hazed-blue sky empty of all but a few high clouds and swirls of wings as birds took flight from the reeds to the southwest. There was a hamlet not far away, several compounds, one quite large. She'd been here before; it was an important place, boats from the Summer Isle—Ireland—came here, and people from inland to trade. Long ago the bluestones for the Great Wisdom had been brought this way, from far in the Dark Mountain Land—what the Eagle People called Wales. The soil was firm right down to the water's edge here, not like the tidal flats and marsh to either side; and not far north two rivers met, the long Hillwater and the shorter Glimmerfish. There were beaten tracks through this pasture, and between the square fields of the settlement. Young wheat and barley cast bluish-green waves over those; farther away were cattle with red-and-white hides and long horns, and youngsters watching over them. Between the grainfields came others hurrying toward the strangers—light blinked off metal, spearheads, and the bronze rivets of shields.

Marian came up beside her. "Hostile?" she said.

Swindapa shook her head, touching the other's arm briefly for reassurance. "No, making sure of us," she said.

They were talking the Fiernan Bohulugi tongue; Marian worked doggedly at it even though the sounds were hard for one of the Eagle People.

"There must be war in the land, or they wouldn't turn out in arms without sending a scout first." She looked around at the *Eagle,* lying at her anchors well out on the broad waters. The *Douglass* spread her white wings beyond it, cruising inland cautiously. "Or, well, the ship may have frightened them."

Crewfolk were forming up around them as they spoke; the Earth Folk party slowed and then halted as they saw so many spears. A cadet trotted up with a green branch, and the *Eagle*'s emissaries moved forward, waving it in sign of peace. Light twinkled as the Fiernan spoke among themselves, waving arms and spears; then some of them trotted back to the huts. The sun beat down, warm enough to make you sweat under armor. More of her people came from the settlement, hesitated, then came closer once more, and halted in speaking distance. One of them bore a branch as well, and several young men carried a wicker chair padded with blankets, holding an aged woman in a long patterned cloak. The rest were men in their prime, some with the Spear Mark on bare chests, others in tunics and leggings; one with gray in his beard wore a sword and a belt with gold studs, and a necklace of bear teeth and gold and amber. They flinched back at the strangeness when Marian took off her helmet and showed her black face and alien features, then visibly nerved themselves to come on again. Sweat shone on their faces. Their eyes flickered over the foreigners, and then out over the water to the great ship and its smaller consort.

"Greetings, if you come in peace," the sword-bearing man said in the charioteers' tongue.

"A fortunate star rule our meeting," Swindapa replied in Fiernan. "Moon Woman send it so."

A gasp went up from the little group, and an excited babbling.

"You speak like one of ours!"

"Like one of those turn-up-the-nose snobs from the downland country," someone muttered toward the back of the group.

"I am Swindapa of the Star Blood line of Kurlelo," she said.

The old woman exclaimed, then hobbled close. Swindapa bent her ear to the other's whisper, and whispered in her turn, exchanging certain words.

"She is as she says," the Grandmother said to the men, probably her son and grandsons. "The Kurlelo line who dwell by the Great Wisdom."

"Don't you know my face, Pelanatorn?" Swindapa said. Not really fair, she'd been four years younger the last time they'd met, and that had been brief. Who paid attention to one youngster among many?

As far as the Grandmother was concerned the Words settled matters, since Swindapa was obviously not a captive. No line was wiser or older than the Kurlelo. Her son looked dubiously at the twoscore or so foreigners already ashore.

"Who are these?" he said to her. "Yes, I am Pelanatorn son of Kaddapal," he added, remembering his manners, and naming his mother to her in the same sentence.

"These are the Eagle People, from across the waters beyond the Summer Isle," she said. "They come friends. Last little planting season they rescued me from the Sun People—the Iraiina, the new tribe, caught me, they held me captive—and I have been a Moon Year in their land, guesting. This is their . . . Spear Chosen," she said, touching Marian on the shoulder. "Marian Alston. My lover," she added proudly.

More gasps and murmurs; she might as well have claimed to have spent the year among the stars and brought back Moon Woman's heart.

"They come friends?" the man said, looking at her with respect shaded with awe, taking half a step back. "That is well. We have need of friends."

"There is war?" she asked anxiously.

"When hasn't there been, since the Sun People came?" the man said bitterly. "But since last year, it's worse in all ways. They have a sorcerer to lead them now, a child of Barrow Woman's own suckling. Instead of fighting each other mostly, they beat us like threshers flailing out the grain. And their Tartessian friends raid along the coast in their ships."

Swindapa's eyes went wide in fear as she turned to translate.

The captain of the *Eagle* looked down at the picture again. It had been taken with a telephoto lens, from the deck of a moving ship, but it was clear enough.

"Will you look at that," she said, throwing it down on the folding table with a tightly controlled gesture of disgust.

It was growing dark, the sun a fading crimson in the west, but the sides of the tent were still rolled up and the lantern hanging from its peak made the inside bright enough. The officers gathered round and leaned over the glossy photograph, exclaiming. Alston scowled out through the open side of the tent as they pointed out the details.

With three hundred and fifty pair of hands working, the American camp was going up rapidly. She'd had it laid out in the shape of a pentagon; there had been a few smiles at that, but it wasn't really a joke. The five-sided figure gave you enfilading fire on the flanks from all the points where the lines met. A few locals—*Do* not *think of them as "natives,"* she reminded herself firmly—stood by and watched, gaping. They'd picked a stretch of firm meadow not far from the high-tide mark, and the ditch went in quickly, dirt flying up. It was six feet deep and twelve across, with the earth piled on the inner side to make the rampart; inside went laneways flanked by ditches, with tents in neat rows and a clear central space for a parade ground. Working parties carefully cut squares of turf and laid the grass on the soil of the embankment; without cover the whole thing might well erode into a mudpie at the first hint of rain.

Time for refinements later, Alston thought, hands clasped behind her back. A palisade, of course, when they had time to cut the necessary timber; huts for stores . . . and a central platform for Leaton's pride, the centerpiece of the ROATS program.

"That's the *Yare,* isn't it?" Ian Arnstein said, peering at the photograph. "And that other one doesn't look at all like the Tartessian ships we saw this time last year."

The Coast Guard officers looked at him, silent. "Well, I'm not an expert," he said defensively.

"It's a bloody brigantine," Alston said. "*Look* at the thing, the way it's rigged. Oh, she'll have a lot of leeway sailing close and she's too beamy to be really fast, but that bastard Isketerol didn't waste his time on Nantucket, if he could build that from scratch."

She saw his incomprehension. "Remember what I said, about sailing across the Atlantic in the ships they had?"

He nodded. She stabbed a finger into the picture and went on: "With this, he could sail across the *Pacific.* He probably broke up a couple of those ships we saw last spring to make it. You could circumnavigate the world in this—Magellan did it, in somethin' less seaworthy—or carry a hundred men to Nantucket."

"This brig isn't just a copy, either," she continued. "It's

a clever *adaptation* of our ideas for local use. That shallow draft . . ."

"You can beach it without damage," Sandy Rapczewicz—she'd kept her maiden name in her second marriage too—said mournfully. "That'd be handy, for inshore work."

"Or an invasion," Alston said, nodding. "Well, taking Isketerol with us—I made a bad mistake, there. We've got to put a stop to this now, if we can."

She looked up at Lieutenant Commander Hendriksson. The young Minnesotan drew herself a little more erect. "What did you make the water there, Ms. Hendriksson?"

"I had twelve feet, but that was quarter of a mile offshore," she said. "From the color and the look of the bottom on the lead line, it shelves quickly."

Alston picked up the photograph again and measured with her eye. A man was standing upright beside the beached hull of the Tartessian brig to give her some idea of the size. Somewhere between seventy-five and a hundred tons displacement, she decided. Slightly less than half the size of her two schooners, but much stubbier and tubbier than the *Tubman* or *Douglass*. Which meant . . .

"This thing may draw less than four feet," she said.

"*And* the brig's got oar ports," Hendriksson pointed out. "That could be useful, inshore, given a calm or a wind right in her teeth."

"Well, at least we know the range of those rock-throwers," Alston said. "What did you make of their camp?"

"Ma'am, that wall and ditch they've got . . . I wouldn't like to try and storm it."

"No, you're right on that," Alston said. "If I know Walker, he's had the Tartessians put underwater obstacles in, too."

She spread her fingers on the table and looked around at the others. "I hope I don't have to say keep a careful lookout," she said dryly.

There were somber nods. Together the *Yare* and this brig could carry almost as many fighters as the expeditionary force numbered, at least for a short coasting voyage.

"From what Ms. Swindapa's people were able to tell us, Walker has a strong position in the east—either he's in charge, or nearly so, with a real army under his control. Plus we're not nearly as completely in command of the sea as we'd hoped. We obviously need better intelligence, and we need help. This is the back crick of the beyond, by local standards. We'll have to send a party inland."

She smiled, a shark's expression. "And perhaps we'll give *him* a surprise or two, busy little bee that he's been."

"Ma'am? Lieutenant Commander Ortiz is back."

She ducked her head out of the tent for a second; the commander of the *Frederick Douglass* was coming up from the improvised dock. She returned his salute.

"I've got 'em," Ortiz said. "And ma'am, you're welcome to them."

Alston nodded, hands clasped behind her back, watching the livestock coming ashore from the schooner. All of it safely dead, at least; there was slaughter stock for sale a few hours' run up the channel. They'd put in a small wharf, enough for the ships' boats, and wheelbarrows and handcarts and strong young backs began trundling the carcasses up into the camp. Several dozen locals were among them, led by Pelanatorn's sons and nephews, daughters and nieces.

"No problems, Mr. Ortiz?"

"Well, the locals are damned light-fingered, ma'am," he said. "Anything metal particularly. And, ah, some of them are so friendly that it creates problems. Otherwise no; once we convinced them we weren't pirates, they were eager to trade."

"Good. Have a look at this, Mr. Ortiz—Ms. Hendriksson hasn't been idle."

He exclaimed over the picture of the *Yare* and the Tartessian brig. Alston stood deep in thought, rising and sinking slowly on the balls of her feet with her hands clasped behind her.

"Which brings me to a matter of standing orders," she said. "Now, you've all read the briefing sheet. These people here don't have anything like what we'd call a government. If we want to get them on our side—and we need them—we have to win them over small group by small group. Ms. Swindapa and the Arnsteins and I are working on the, ah, the Grandmothers—fairly soon we'll be taking a party off to consult with more of them inland. However, they've also got a series of local councils and another great council covering most of the southwestern part of England that meets near Stonehenge. It's a more of a *religious* institution, in charge of what they call the Sacred Truce, but it has a lot of influence. It's composed of men, but they're *selected* by the Grandmothers. On top of all this, there are the Spear Chosen, who are the closest thing the Fiernan have to military leaders. They're not elected or appointed at all; anyone who gets a good reputation as a leader and who throws a lot of parties gradually becomes accepted as one—sort of a potlatch thing. Land here is owned by lineages; trading or owning a lot of cows is the only way you can become really rich. Evidently among themselves the Fiernan Bohulugi don't really fight, they skirmish in a sort of ritual way with livestock as the prize."

"Jesus, what a marvel of organization," someone muttered. "Real Prussian stuff."

Alston frowned; Swindapa was scowling at the slight on her people. "So if we want to get the Spear Chosen on our side, the way is to lavish hospitality and plenty of gifts. Hence this series of barbecues. Clear?"

"Yes, ma'am," Ortiz said. "Ah, the locals, they evidently have a rather, ah, wild idea of a party."

Alston smiled thinly. "Well, that brings me to the next order of business. As you know, I've always insisted on enforcing the nonfraternization and public-displays-of-affection orders strictly on board ship. I intend to continue to do so."

Nods went around the table. Shipboard was enough of a pressure cooker as it was.

"However, onshore, that's a different matter. We have nearly four hundred healthy young people here, and they aren't going to live like Cistercians indefinitely. Never give an order you know will be ignored." Emphatic nods; doing that made the next one more likely to be ignored as well.

"I'd like to emphasize, however, ladies, gentlemen, and have you pass on to your commands, that any misuse of rank, in fact any fraternization up or down the chain of command, is going to be goddam painful for all involved. In short, I'll come down on it like a ton of wet cement, and so will each and every one of y'all. Ditto anythin' else that interferes with discipline or combat readiness. Every officer will take a personal interest in seein' that any such individual will *suffer*. Clear? Off-duty, however, we'll apply the consentin'-adults rule."

She relaxed slightly. "However, that brings up another

problem. Our expeditionary force is about two-thirds male, as you know. This can cause . . . awkwardness."

More nods; in fact, it had created fairly serious problems back on Nantucket. The cadets were numerous enough in the island's small young-adult population to throw the balance between the genders off, and there had been fights and tension over it.

"I anticipate that our position vis-à-vis the locals will, ah, lessen the problem."

"God, yes, ma'am," Ortiz said. "Like I said—very, very friendly around here."

And we'll probably end up with a fair number of war brides, Alston reflected. *Nothing wrong with that; I could scarcely complain even if there was, all things considered.*

She smiled secretly to herself behind an impassive face. Swindapa had also said, privately and emphatically, that if they were going to do this monogamy thing they could at least do it frequently. *Not much danger of Lesbian Bed Death there.*

"Now, as soon as a fair number of locals come in," she went on, "we'll have to start outfittin' and trainin' them."

A crewman saluted. "Ma'am. The locals are at the gate."

"Very well," she said, returning the courtesy. "Ladies, gentlemen, we have guests." Alston drew on her gloves; dress uniform again, even if it meant nothing to the locals. *Strange. Last time here it was for Daurthunnicar.* And hadn't that been a total fuckup . . . she looked at the Fiernan girl. *Well, not quite. Not at all, personally speakin'.*

She ducked out of the tent, returning the sentries' salutes, and toward the gate; it was local courtesy to greet guests at the door.

"So Walker is a king already, as he wished," Swindapa said, while they walked toward the inland apex of the pentagonal fort.

"I'm sorry, 'dapa," Alston said quietly. "If we could have come again last year . . ."

"That wasn't the way the stars moved," Swindapa replied in a murmur. "It's Walker's fault, not yours."

"Besides"—Swindapa shrugged—"if things weren't bad, they might not listen to you. They might not anyway."

They'd certainly *talked* a good fight here, full of anger against the Sun People, but Alston didn't know how much of that was telling her what she wanted to hear. From what the Arnsteins and Martha had told her, most primitive people took hospitality very seriously—if you traveled at all, it had to be as a guest. *No HoJo's here.*

The locals were back—not the old woman in the intricately checked and embroidered cloak, but the middle-aged man and his sons, and this time some girls as well, dressed in string skirts and short-sleeved knitted shirts and colorful shawls. They looked around in awe, and there was well-hidden fear in the older man's eyes. *Pelanatorn*, she remembered. The younger Fiernans called greetings to the sentries on the walls, and seemed surprised and a little hurt at being ignored; even more surprised at the way the gate guard braced to attention and saluted as Alston came up.

"Better explain, 'dapa," she said.

"I have—I told them that it's prayer, to please the Eagle People spirits of war."

Alston's mouth quirked. *That's actually not far from the truth.* Most of the Fiernans were holding baskets, two had a gutted and dressed pig on a carrying pole thrust between its legs, and several children drove a pair of cattle and four sheep.

"And thank them for the gifts," she said, after calling for a detail to come and take them.

"Oh, no—that would be impolite, thanking them for being hospitable, as if they might not be," Swindapa said. "Just smile and nod."

Well, thank God for interpreters, Alston thought. They slowed things down so you could avoid putting your foot into it too badly. *I feel like Captain goddam Cook.*

"Stop there, outlander. Who are you?"

Two warriors stepped out from behind the smooth, mottled bark of a huge beech. Isketerol reined in his horse. *I'm a man with a sore arse,* he said to himself; he'd learned how to ride over the winter, but doing twenty miles in a day still told. His horse seemed to agree, lowering its head and blowing out its lips.

"Isketerol of Tartessos, oath-brother of Wehaxpothis Hwalkarz of the Iraiina," he said. "These are my handfast men," he added, jerking a thumb over his shoulder at the others and the train of packhorses.

"Oath-brother to the sorcerer?" The bearded faces behind the spearheads—steel spearheads, he noticed—went pale. "Pass."

The weapons dipped in salute. The Tartessians booted their horses up out of the vale and onto the hillsides. The war camp of the Iraiina and their allies lay sprawled about them, a vast shapeless mass in clumps and clusters across the downs. There was no problem in finding his blood-brother. The Walkerburg men had pitched their tents in neat rows, northward and upstream of the others; some of them were still digging the latrines their lord insisted on, grumbling as shovelfuls of chalky subsoil flew. Sentries paced the outlines of the camp, full-armed; most of the rest lay around their cooking fires, throwing dice or talking, working on their gear or already rolled in their blankets and asleep. Servants carried grain and cut grass to the pick-eted horses, or tended the trek oxen near the wagons that made a wall around half the camp. Wind blew the scents of wildwood from the great forest to the north, overcoming the stench of massed humanity and animals. Meat roasted over the flames, and flat griddle cakes of wheat flour cooked.

Sentries cried him hail as he reined in, and men dashed over to care for his horse and his followers'. All the Walk-erburg folk knew the friend of their chief, who guested with him so often. The Tartessian took the hot mead one offered and drank it gratefully, walking over to the *wehaxpothis*'s pavilion. It wasn't a cold day, by the standards of spring in the White Isle, but the wind could still flog your blood to racing.

"Good to see you!" Walker said, in English. "Did you get the saltpeter? And the barrels from base?"

The Amurrukan were like that, abrupt; he meant no in-sult by it. "That I did," he said. "And I left the saltpeter at Walkerburg. What do you need it for? All it's good for is cooling the blood, as far as I know." Isketerol sat in one of the folding canvas chairs before Walker's tent.

Walker laughed and rubbed his hands. "My friend," he said, "I'll let you in on a little secret that may brighten your day." He shouted for food and drink.

"I could use that," Isketerol said frankly, as they ate; the usual Iraiina fare, roast and boiled meat and bread and a few vegetables, but better done than usual. *I would pay gold for a handful of olives, or good tunny cooked with goat cheese, and a decent salad.* "From what my scouts say I don't dare put to sea," he went on. "Not with *Eagle* and those two new ships about. So far, we know nothing of what Alston and the *Eagle* are doing, except stirring mischief."

A man screamed, not far away. "Odd that you should mention that," Walker said. "We took an enemy messenger, and he's been telling us some interesting things. Come take a look."

They rose and walked around the back of the pavilion. A series of leather panels between poles with a canvas awning overhead made an enclosure there, with two full-armed guards standing stock-still outside the entrance; Isketerol smelled fear on them, and saw it in the sweat that rolled down their faces under the helmet brims despite the cool evening air. Over the entrance hung a mask, the frontal bones of a skull mounted on a hemisphere of polished gold with a light burning within. The flames flickered through, red through the eye sockets and teeth, translucent through the thin-worked bone. Inside a hearth and living area were set up to one side, and a place of work to the other. Ingenious cabinets of folding wood and drawers stood open on the close-cropped sward; between them was a jointed table, now adjusted to a sloping surface. The man fastened to it screamed again as the figure in the green gown bent over him and made an adjustment to some metal tool that burrowed in under his rib cage.

Hong straightened up and pulled down her cloth facemask. "Hi, Will. Hello, Isketerol, glad you could make it," she said. Then to one of the early-adolescent girls standing behind her, also in green surgical garb, "The number-four extensor, Missora."

The girl giggled and stood on tiptoe to whisper something in Hong's ear. The Amurrukan woman laughed and swatted her assistant lightly on the bottom. "Not yet. Later, when he needs to be cheered up." Her sister giggled too, crouching over the little brazier where still other instruments were at white heat.

An Iraiina stood by the man's head; *his* fear was undisguised. "Ask him again, Velrarix," Hong said.

The tribesman bent over the prisoner and shouted in his ear; the language was the purling glug-glug-glug sound of the Earth Folk tongue. Isketerol caught most of it, although the translator had a vile accent.

The figure strapped to the table tried to shake his head against the clamps that held it. Drops of blood went spattering on the waxed leather covering of the wood, and slow fat tears ran down his cheeks. The glass jar dripping saline solution down a tube into one arm rattled in its holder.

"No?" Hong said. "Well, maybe we'll advance the schedule again. Scalpel and clamps, little one."

She selected an instrument from the offered tray and flashed a smile over at the two men. "This is fascinating, you know. Sort of like an operation in reverse. The human body is absolutely amazing, the way it clings to life. And the way you can shape it like wood or marble. I'm developing a true art form here."

To her assistants: "Kylefra, leave those cauteries and crank his head up a little. Velrarix, explain to him what happens next. After this he'll be a lot calmer. No bothersome hormones."

The other girl in the green surgical gown came and turned a screw that pushed up the victim's head. When the sharp metal tickled the base of his scrotum he began to scream again, and then shout words—numbers, places.

"Got all that?" Hong asked the interpreter, when the Fiernan began to repeat himself for the second time. He nodded, pasty-faced. "Kylefra. We don't need to hear him speak anymore."

The men walked back to Walker's tent. *Demons spare us*, Isketerol thought. *Will is a braver man than I, to bed with that. I'd rather put the Crone Herself on my staff.* He picked up a glass bottle and poured a little of the *lightning spirit* into a cup, knocking it back with a jerk of his wrist. He'd seen men put to the question before, beaten or burned or flogged, but this . . . The meal sat heavy on his stomach; he drank again. "You learned what you needed?" he said.

Walker poured himself more mead. "Better watch that hard liquor," he warned. "It creeps up on you if you're not used to it. . . . Yeah, I think I've got what we need. And I've got a plan for a coordinated action. Here's what we'll do."

Hong's laughter rang over the sounds from behind the

tent. Isketerol shuddered. "I hope you can rule her," he said.

Walker chuckled. "She has sort of blossomed into her opportunities, hasn't she? Don't worry, I can keep her in line . . . and if she goes completely 'round the bend, there's always—" He made a cutting gesture across his throat. "Now, let's get down to business. Here's what sulfur and saltpeter and charcoal are good for. . . ."

In the screened-off area, Hong was singing as she worked:

> "I've bought myself a new knife
> You'd be surprised at what my knife can do;
> Guns can jam; bombs are complex;
> Sometimes grenades fail to explode.
> My knife is simple—this is true;
> Part of it I hold . . . the other part of it's for *you*.
> A girl needs a knife . . . oh, a girl needs a knife . . .
> And I've got mine!"

"How do you like my country?" Swindapa said proudly.

"Beautiful," Alston said sincerely, touching a heel to her horse.

The long column of Americans stretched back along the trackway. They'd finally made their way out of the ancient oakwoods and up into rolling downs under a mild spring sun. It shone bright on polished steel, and on the gilt eagles that tipped their flagstaffs and the spread-winged version on every breastplate and shield. A drum beat, *triiip-trip-trip*, and a hundred and fifty feet hit the earth as one; spearheads swayed rhythmically.

Not much like it was in the twentieth, she thought.

Not even the shape of the land. In the England she'd visited, these uplands were mostly bare moorland. In the White Isle they were still covered with a coating of loess, light fertile soil that had yet to erode away. Small square fields were laid out, green with wheat, barley, rye, oats, a few turning yellow with mustard, others shaggy with nettles or yarrow. Most of the fields were already calf-high, and they rippled and fluttered in the brisk south wind that streamed out the flags. Copses of wood covered hilltops or wound across the dales along the sides of streams, birch and beech and oak, leaves fresh and clear-cut, almost glistening in their newness. Flowers starred the grainfields and meadows, thick along the sides of the rutted dirt trace. Hawthorn hedges bloomed, filling the air with a faint elusive scent of wild rose when the wind dropped.

"Absolutely beautiful," she said, reining aside.

The horse snorted and obeyed, and Swindapa's followed it. Their Nantucketer expert had broken in enough for a few officers, mounted messengers, and scouts in the weeks since their landfall. They turned and cantered down the line; she exchanged salutes with the officers, fingers going *tick* against the brim of her helmet.

The ordered alignment of the Americans made a stark contrast to the great shambling clot of Fiernans who walked along with them, their own numbers again or more; adventurous youths and maidens, a few Spear Chosen with their followers, traders with a shrewd eye to the main chance and trains of donkeys loaded with packs, or livestock driven along to sell to the wealthy strangers. More ran to gawk from the settlements all around. Most of those were farmers, men in sleeveless tunics of coarse wool, women in string skirts, sometimes bare above the waist, sometimes with a shirt and poncho; children were often naked or nearly so, accompanied by lean whip-tailed dogs. The dwellings they abandoned were mostly huts, round or rectangular, often grouped together and sometimes surrounded by ditch or bank or thorn hedge; the livestock enclosures always were. The thatch was cut and sculpted in attractive abstract patterns, and the wattle walls whitewashed and painted over in geometric shapes; the effect was as much African as anything else, reminding her a little of pictures she'd seen of Ndebele villages. Somehow it looked right for the landscape.

"But . . ." Swindapa said, an edge of trouble in her voice.

"But?"

"It looks . . . it looks *smaller* than I remembered it, somehow," she said, swiveling her head. "And sort of . . . messy."

You can't go home again, Marian didn't say. That was one lesson everybody had to learn . . . *or maybe not, here.* Here things *stayed* the same, usually. They didn't build time-share condos and golf courses over the place you were born and the churchyard where your great-grandfather was buried.

A changed note ran through the burble of Fiernan Bohu-

lugi conversation. Someone was coming running down the
trail from the east, stumbling as he ran. A minute, and she
could see there was blood on his face, and running down
the arm he held cradled in the other. He stopped in shock
at seeing the obvious foreigners, but some of the locals who
were tagging along with the American column caught him
as he started to buckle.

*On the other hand, raiding arsonists can also rearrange
the landscape.*

"Lieutenant Trudeau," she said. "Deploy from column
of march into line, if you please. Nyugen, scouts out
forward."

She and Swindapa spurred forward to the group around
the wounded man. He stared from one to the other, wide-
eyed. A torrent of Fiernan consonants followed, and Swindapa answered; both were too fast and complex for Alston
to follow.

Swindapa's eyes went wide as well. "A big Sun People
raiding party—many of them, a great host, more than a
hundred men. Not far up the track—he ran for perhaps an
hour. But there shouldn't be, not this far west and north!"

"Walker has changed things. Get some details, numbers, weapons."

That took some time. Alston used it to remove her helmet, get out her binoculars, and stand in the stirrups, scanning slowly from left to right ahead. *There.* A faint trace
of smoke. Burning things seemed to be a Sun People fixa-
tion. *Time to stop ambling along being a tourist.* And very
faintly came the *huuuu-huuuu* sound of an aurochs-horn
war trumpet.

She looked back. The wagons were drawing up in a circle, frontier-style . . . or Boer style, which was irony, if you
thought about it. The three-hundred-odd Americans were
fanning out, running to take up position in a line perpendic-
ular to the rutted, muddy track on which they had been
marching, with their left wing resting on the wagons and
their right . . . *well, hanging in air.* And the locals . . .

Alston spurred her horse out in front of them. Most of
the farmers were running for their huts—probably to get
their spears and bows. The noncombatants were streaking
for the tall timber or local equivalent, or herding their stock
and children toward the big palisaded roundhouses. And

the Spear Mark men who'd come along were starting to run *toward* the smoke-smudge, all seventy or eighty of them.

"Well, you can't fault their guts," she said; the Fiernan might not be long on organization, but they had a terrier courage which made it more understandable how they'd held out against the invader tribes so long. She trotted out ahead of them.

"Stop!" she shouted. "Stop now!" That much Fiernan she could manage.

The leading Spear Chosen was a rangy young man with freckles and a fiery head of copper-colored locks trained in dozens of braids. "Why?" he said. "We come to fight the Sun People; they burn our houses, attack our kindred."

"Swindapa, tell him we'll show him how the Eagle People fight. Remind him that they usually lose fighting the charioteers, but tactfully."

Swindapa broke into voluble, arm-waving speech, a little odd to see from horseback; eventually they started listening to her. Alston put her helmet back on, swinging down the new hinged cheekpieces and clipping them together under her chin. The padding was rough against her skin, and the world took on a hard outlined shape from beneath the low brim. About half of the Fiernans stopped, sullen and restless, shifting their feet; the steel-headed spears the Americans had handed out danced in their hands. The others pelted by, heading for the invaders. Light-armed riders fanned out ahead of her, crossbows bouncing at their backs. They came back minutes later, galloping.

"Ma'am, they've taken a village about two and a half miles up thataway. Seven chariots, say a couple of hundred men. They've stopped to loot."

"Any sign of out-time equipment, weapons, armor?"

"Hard to say for sure, ma'am. Most of it was straight Bronze Age stuff, right out of the briefings."

"Carry on." *Well, they won't stay stopped to loot when that gang of wild men that went haring off down the lane hits them,* she thought. They'd beat the Fiernans like a drum; for starters, they outnumbered them eight to one. *And then they'll chase them, all the way back here.*

Other fires were puffing smoke into the sky, from hilltops around about or from the big round enclosures. "Alarms?" she said to Swindapa.

"Yes, to show that the Sacred Truce is invoked. Many

Spear Chosen and their bands will come soon now. Well, in a while."

Alston nodded; about what she'd expected. From what she'd been able to gather, none of them had ever been able to take land *back* from the invaders, though. And there was only one end to a game where the rules went *what's mine is mine, what's yours is negotiable.*

Swindapa rode back to the injured man, now being treated by an American medic. She swung down out of the saddle, going to one knee beside him, then led her horse over to Alston again.

"Marian, it's odd. From what that man tells, those were Zarthani, from one of the eastern tribes of the Sun People, east of the Great Forest. Not Iraiina at all."

"Walker has made some friends," Alston nodded. She studied her position, then rode over to the Spear Chosen.

"Maltonr, put all your men with bows and slings in there, on the beds of the wagons." The canvas tilts had been rolled up until they offered only overhead protection. The Americans were linking the vehicles together with chains and spiked steel bars. "The spears, to the right of my line."

Maltonr scratched his red head. "Why?" he said. "First the shooting, then the fight hand-to-hand."

"They'll be more effective shooting all together. Trust me. And when the Sun People hit us, your archers can fight from behind the wagons, like a fort."

The Fiernan shrugged; the Eagle People were strange, but he'd go along. *Lord have mercy if I don't win this fight,* Alston thought, licking dry lips and fighting down an urge to drink from her water bottle. Stopping to pee in this armor was just too damned difficult, particularly for a woman.

Instead she rode down the American line. "No different from the cannibals, boys and girls," she said. More than half had been with her among the Olmecs, and the rest had been drilling with them for months, five days a week. "Hold steady, listen for the word, then shoot straight and hit hard. Remember, we fight as a unit. Anyone who gets carried away will have his or her ice cream ration reduced." Laughter, a little nervous, and some grins.

She called the unit commanders together, sketched plans, shifted a squad over to provide backup in the wagon circle, checked that the handset radios were all working, then dismissed them to their troops. Very faint, the sound of combat came from over the rise ahead. Lieutenants and petty officers checked equipment, and quietly blistered ears over loose straps or clasps unbuckled for marching and not done up again. Then the Americans stood at parade rest, spears vertical with the butts resting on the ground and both hands clasped on them at chest height, or loaded crossbows carried at the port. No time for fancy tricks with caltrops this time, and no heavy equipment along. A straight stand-up fight. Good ground, at least. It looked like the enemy thought they were just going to stomp straight over everything in their way.

Christ, I run away to sea and here I am, in the goddam Army.

A thousand yards, mostly level, straight ahead; steeper ground to the left and right. Open, except for a few hurdle fences, not even much planted ground. Then a dip down to the creek, and the enemy would have to forge uphill from the water to reach this plateau.

A spatter of Fiernans came past first, the fastest ones, many wounded, many weaponless. The others murmured, milled about, then slowly settled down again. One of her scouts came trotting up over the rise, galloped across the open ground, then drew rein and saluted.

"Here they come, ma'am, just like you said they would," he said, grinning from a painfully young face. "Three hundred and fifteen by my count, seven chariots, nothing fancy, just heading straight for us as fast as they can."

"Very good."

She glanced aside. Swindapa was watching the rise to the east, her face gone milk-pale under the light tan, hands quivering-tight on the reins. *Christ, I forgot. These are the same sort of people who captured her.* She brought her horse a little closer and rested a hand on the girl's armored shoulder.

"'Dapa, you're not alone now. We're going to kick their butts and send them off howling for their dead." She paused. "Don't let me down."

A start, and a flush, then a tight smile. "I won't, Marian."

"By the *Dagadevos*, who are you?" Dekarchar son of Wirronax, high chief of the Keyaltwar, asked. "You look like a Tartessian to me."

Lieutenant Commander Victor Ortiz, born in Havana, raised in Florida, commissioned by the United States, and currently serving in the Coast Guard of the Republic of Nantucket, smiled and spread his hands. They'd assigned him to slip around to the east coast of the island and raise some trouble in the enemy rear because he'd picked up the language faster than the other ship commanders.

"Some of my ancestors came from there," he said. "I'm of the . . . Eagle People."

The chieftain scowled and looked through the door at the end of his hall at the schooner rocking at its moorings in a channel that wound through the marshes. "You mean you're a friend of that turd of a wizard Hwalkarz and his Iraiina shit-eaters and Tartessian arse-lickers?" he rumbled menacingly.

The Keyaltwar chief had reddish-gold hair and the pale complexion that went with it, liberally starred with light brown freckles, and rather protuberant blue eyes in a narrow, beaky face. The way he clenched his hand on the handle of his ax was probably unconscious, rather than a direct threat to his guest. So was the red flush of rage that crept up his cheeks under beard and scars.

"Are all the children of Sky Father friends of the Iraiina?" Ortiz asked rhetorically, following the script the captain and the Arnsteins had mapped out for him.

"Well, no," the chief grumbled, sinking back in the chair.

"So not all the Eagle People are friends of Hwalkarz. He is an outcast among us; oathbreaker, murderer by stealth, thief. A wolf's head, we call such a man—that's why he uses it as his banner."

The Americans' visit had coincided with spring cleaning; women and slaves were raking out the old reeds from the dirt floor, and a winter's accumulated bones and garbage with them, and replacing them with fresh. The fires were out—rekindling them would be one of the year's most important ceremonies and the hall was rather fusty and disarranged.

Ortiz sank down on the stool before the chief's seat and smiled, moving one hand in a spreading gesture. "You haven't bent the knee to Daurthunnicar yet, I take it."

"Never! Never!"

The chief *did* rise this time, waving his ax in the air. The other warriors hanging about his hall did likewise, stamping and screaming. Some of them dyed their hair with lime, which made it stand out in spikes. They looked like enraged daisies as they waved their weapons and shrieked; the noise grew so loud that other folk from the hamlet put their heads in to see what was going on, and they shouted too. Eventually even the animals got into it, loud enough to startle clouds of ducks and geese and storks out of the tidal marshes that stretched for mile after mile along the north bank of the Thames.

Ortiz waited out the spontaneous demonstration. *So this is what they fake at political conventions,* he thought.

"Our folk came here as conquerors!" the chief brayed.

Probably chased here by stronger tribes on the mainland, Ortiz thought, remembering his briefings. *Like the Iraiina.* Possibly *by* the Iraiina, generations ago. There seemed to be a billiard-ball effect to these migrations, with the end ball getting bumped out over the Channel. The original impetus might have started as far away as the Ukraine or even Central Asia.

"We live as free men! We sent Daurthunnicar's dogs back with a boot under their tails, and he and his wizard haven't done a thing but puff and stamp!"

Actually you're just too difficult to get to; too much swamp and bog forest in the way, Ortiz thought.

"Why don't you raid them, for such an insult?" he said. "Why don't the Keyaltwar show the wizard and his dog what they think of him?"

"Well, now," Dekachar said, sitting back. He signaled for more beer to be brought. "Well, now, we Keyaltwar are men of honor, but we aren't fools. Daurthunnicar has too many allies now, curse him, and the wizard has given his men fine weapons—armor of this *iron* stuff. And they're far away, many days' journey."

"Farther than that," Ortiz said. "The Iraiina and their allies are moving west, against the Earth Folk. Their steadings lie stripped of fighting men. Stuffed with cattle, bronze, gold, women, cloth, the new iron tools and weapons."

"What?" Dekarchar leaned forward eagerly. "You know this?"

"I know it. My . . . high chief fights them even now, in the west."

Dekarchar counted on his fingers, called for counsel from his advisers. "No, no," he said regretfully. "It would take too long for a raiding party to strike at the Iraiina lands and return—they'd catch us in the open with numbers we couldn't withstand. They move too fast these days, curse them, all this riding." He shivered slightly. "And the wizard . . . no, no."

"That's if you go by land," Ortiz said helpfully. "My ship could carry three, four hundred warriors for a short journey . . . say over to the south bank of the river, west of here. From there it's less than a day's march to the northernmost Iraiina steadings, or to tribes allied to them. Or we could carry you and your warriors to a point on the south coast near Daurthunnicar's own *ruathaurikaz*. Stuffed with the plunder of a dozen tribes . . ."

Dekarchar began to breathe heavily. "Tell me more of this," he said.

Here they come, black as hell and thick as grass, Marian Alston thought, with a slight ironic twist of her lips. That had been the cry of the British sentry at the battle of Rorke's Drift, during the Zulu War. The Sun People war band coming over the rise wasn't as numerous or as disciplined, but they had a good deal of the same ferocious impetus and will to combat. *These buckra mean business.* They fought to kill, and defined winning as being the only one left standing.

"So do I," she muttered to herself. She also remembered something else from the Zulu War, and urged her horse over to the Fiernans.

"Maltonr," she said, "have your men turn around, walk forty paces, and sit down with their backs to the enemy."

"What?" he said.

"Swindapa, interpret for me. Explain it's a magic. When I tell them to turn around and fight, they'll each have the strength of two." *Because they won't charge in when their feelings overflow.* "And lay their spears flat, to gain strength from the earth."

The Fiernan girl broke into enthusiastic speech. Interest dawned on the faces looking up at them, replacing sullen bewilderment. They turned and squatted on their heels, holding spear and shield before them, a buzz of excited conversation rising over their heads.

"Oh, and tell them if anyone looks behind him before they're told, it'll spoil the magic."

Maltonr gave her a doubtful look, then smiled ruefully and sat with his followers and the spear-armed peasants. "How are you going to do that?" Swindapa asked, as they cantered back to their position. "Make each of them strong as two, that is."

Alston shrugged. " 'Dapa, a properly timed flank attack *does* double the effect," she said. "Now let's get down to business."

They halted by the standard-bearers. She looked down her own line as the chariot people milled on the lip of the rise a thousand yards to the east. The circle of wagons, with the Fiernan archers and slingers inside. More were trickling in every minute, to be shoved into the ring of the wagon-fort or called there by their friends. Others straggled over to join Maltonr and his crouching spearmen. Call it forty or so in the wagons, as many again or a little more with Maltonr, double that soon. Then her own force, a central block of fifty spears three deep and a double line of seventy-five crossbows on either side. She kicked her horse out again, a hundred yards in front, and looked over the line from the enemy's perspective. *Good.* The Fiernans weren't at all conspicuous; Maltonr's bunch were nearly invisible, what with a slight dip in the ground.

This is going to be ugly, she thought, returning to her station.

The Zarthani had paused for a moment to work out what was waiting for them; then they spread out in a line, blowing their ox-horn trumpets and shouting. Even at this distance she could see bronze and gold and bright felt trappings gleaming on the horses, the heron-feather plumes nodding as they snorted and tossed their heads.

"Nyugen, Trudeau," she said. The two senior lieutenants stood at her stirrup. "Remember, infantry usually breaks before a chariot charge here. When ours doesn't, the chariots may wheel off and try and shoot us up while their infantry close with us, or they may just ram in close as they can. In either case, concentrate fire on the chariots—go for the teams—and then switch to those following. Any questions?"

Both shook their heads. "Good luck."

The tribesmen had shaken themselves out, seven clumps behind the chariots of their chieftains. They started toward her at a walk, yelps and hoots and the odd high shriek coming as they worked themselves up. Wooden axles squealed like tortured pigs, wheels rumbled, hoovcs pounded the short dense turf, bare human feet slapped dirt. The chariots loomed larger and larger. Now she could see the men in them, the near-naked youths driving, and the leather-armored aristocrats standing behind, although one . . . she focused the binoculars. *Chain mail, by God.* Walker had been a busy little bee; and wouldn't one of these suits be a potent bribe here. The riders stood easily in the jouncing unsprung carts with their feet braced wide and knees bent, javelins and bows in their hands. *Must train them from toddlers to do that,* she thought. The horses trotted as the drivers slapped their backs with the reins, and behind them the hairy kilted warriors began to lope, keeping up effortlessly.

Four hundred yards. "Now," she said.

"Spears . . . *down!*" the officers barked. The Nantucket troops gave a single deep shout and raised their polearms high. Drums beat, and the cool English sunlight sparkled on the edges and points as the nine-foot shafts swung down into line.

"Prepare to receive cavalry!"

The first rank knelt, propping their oval shields on their shoulders and the ground ahead of them, slanting their spears out. The next two lines stood in staggered formation, points reaching out to make a bristling three-layered forest of knife-sharp heads poised to stab.

"Prepare to fire." The front rank of crossbows knelt. *Three hundred and fifty yards.* A bugle call. "Fire!"

Alston swung down off her horse, and Swindapa followed. The standard-bearers and their guards and the twelve sword-and-buckler troops formed up behind them. The easterners were at a full run now, horses galloping, pulling the chariots ahead of the footmen. The long shadows of the spears seemed to reach out toward them.

WHUNNNG. Seventy-five crossbow bolts flickered across the space between the two forces, moving in long shallow arcs blurred by their speed. Men fell; the short heavy arrows would punch right through the light hide-and-wicker shields, through the arm holding the shield and then the breastbone, and crunch into the spine. A chariot went over in a tumbling, splintering whirl as both its horses were struck by several bolts apiece and collapsed in mid-stride.

WHUNNNG. The second volley brought another two chariots down, and a dozen men; the range was closing fast. A slight ripple through the spearpoints as the troops braced themselves. *WHUNNNG. WHUNNNG.* The ratcheting click of the mechanisms as the crossbows' cocking levers were pumped. A chariot veering and going off on a wild tangent, a bolt standing in the rump of the off-lead horse and the animal plunging and bucking with its eyes bulged out, squealing piteously. *WHUNNNG.* More men down, but not as many as with the Olmecs—the easterners had a better formation than that, irregular but strung out so that men could support each other without crowding. So had their ancestors conquered, spreading out from the steppes of inner Asia, west to the Atlantic and east to the borderlands of China.

WHUNNNG. More chariots out of action, the man in chain mail dismounting and running forward, screaming hatred at those who'd wounded his precious horses. The remaining war-cars edged away from the sleeting death of the crossbows, heading toward the massed spearpoints at the bottom of the American formation. Then still farther to the right, as the Fiernan archers and slingers in the circled wagons opened up, ragged but enthusiastic. Arrows whistled, and slingstones cracked on shields, whunked into flesh. *WHUNNNG.* Very close now, a hundred yards, and the bowmen among the Zarthani were shooting as they ran. Shafts arched up into the sky, slammed down. Bronze and flint sparked and bent and shattered on steel armor and pattered on metal-faced shields. Here and there one slipped through to find vulnerable flesh, and a few Americans were dragged backward by the stretcher-bearers; their comrades closed the ranks.

Half the Zarthani were left on their feet, many of them wounded. One chariot came on, its horses streaming blood and foam, bolting, but bolting in the direction their driver wanted them to go. Alston could see snarling grins, shouting faces, axes whirling overhead in blurring circles.

"Bows down!" barked the officers. Trumpets reinforced the orders. A last spatter of bolts, and the crossbows went over their users' shoulders. The round bucklers slung across their backs went forward, and hands slapped down to the hilts at their right hips. *"Draw!"*

Long months of practice made the motion a single flicker

of light as the leaf-shaped stabbing swords came free of their wood-and-leather sheaths.

"Give 'em the Ginsu!" someone shouted. Alston's teeth showed in a not-quite-smile. Ian Arnstein had wanted the short sword called a *gladius*, after the Roman blades it was modeled on. Public opinion had proved stronger. Ginsu it was.

Alston reached over her shoulder and drew her own sword, head moving back and forth as she kept the whole action in sight through the intervening ranks. A long rattle of thrown spears came from the Zarthani, in the moment before impact. An American not far ahead dropped on his back kicking; a spear had bounced off the rim of his shield and up into the unprotected underside of his jaw. The driver of the last chariot was leaning back, hauling on the reins to try to skim along the line while his warrior shot arrows. He almost made the quick turn, but the horses were too far gone in hysteria to respond as they'd been trained. Their too-tight curve put their legs into the thicket of spearpoints, and they collapsed. The chariot cartwheeled sideways; its crew were thrown out straight onto the waiting points, but the wood-and-wickerwork vehicle followed right behind.

"Oh, *shit,*" Alston said.

It was the worst possible thing that could have happened; the line of spears disintegrated just where it formed a junction with the right-wing crossbows as the chariot's flying body bowled into them. You couldn't have gotten any horses ever foaled to do that voluntarily, or most men, but the accident had sent a kamikaze into her formation.

" 'Dapa, tell Maltonr to face about and bring his spearmen, *now.* The rest of you, follow me!"

She ran for the spot where the war-car had crashed into the American line just as the howling clansmen leaped to follow the chariot into the gap it had made.

CHAPTER NINETEEN

June, Year 2 A.E.

Bill Cuddy listened to the panting messenger. His Iraiina was pretty good now, more than enough for this.

"Keyaltwar for certain," the messenger gasped. "Hundreds of them, maybe others of the northeast tribes—burning, killing, looting. They came from the coast."

Somebody had to have given them a lift. Not hard to do—there was plenty of deserted beach along the south shore. "The Guard got smart," he muttered to himself, looking around.

Everyone was looking at *him*. He thought of what the boss would say if he came back and found Walkerburg burned . . . and without Walker, there was no place at all for him in this world now.

Okay, he thought. *Let's see what we can do.* "How's the *rahax*'s place holding out?"

"The stockade holds, but they ravage among the holdings outside. A strong band is coming this way—they must know where you are."

"We'll deal with them first, then," he said. "All right, get the *ergastula* filled. The rest of you, get your weapons and fall in."

There were twenty free men left here, half and half Iraiina and Americans. The slaves had learned their lesson, though, the ones left alive after the past year; they turned and shuffled toward the low-set building at the sound of the settlement bell rung three times and then three times again. Nervous hands shoved and prodded them down into the odorous darkness.

The women were running out of their houses, or from the workshops. "Fuck this," Cuddy muttered, then shouted: "All of you, back to your houses!"

Ekhnonpa appeared beside him. "I will deal with them, and see that a meal is prepared for the warriors, and the *first aid equipment*"—that was in English—"is made ready."

"Thank you, lady," he said in Iraiina. In his mother tongue: "Charlie, John, Sam, c'mon. We've got to get the Mule ready."

They slung their shotguns and dragged open the doors of the carpenter's shed where the catapult rested. The men he'd named ran to hitch the four-horse team. That reminded him.

"Shaurshix, Llankwir, you get your horses and scout down the track to Daurthunnicar's place." He pulled out a key and unlocked the door of a new storehouse, a small stoutly timbered one standing some distance off by itself. Inside were shelves with rows of small ten-pound kegs. He grabbed one under each arm and ran toward the Mule with them. "Get over to the smithy and get me some scrap iron. And I want some bigger barrels, about twice this size— doesn't matter what's in them as long as it's dry—dump it and bring them. Fast!"

Swindapa ran to deliver the message to her waiting countrymen, her feet jolting on the hard sheep-cropped grass. The forty pounds of jointed steel she was wearing did not hinder her much, not after nearly a year of practice almost every day. It was the sight of the Zarthani that squeezed at her chest, the leather kilts and long tomahawks and the yelling snarling faces so close on her left. Sweat poured down her face and flanks, and memories opened and bled. When she reached the waiting band of her people she could scarcely gasp out the command.

The wheeze was enough. Only conviction that strong magic was involved had kept them still. They trembled too, and sweat dripped from them, but it was eagerness. With a single long, savage scream they leaped up and swarmed past her, the bright metal of their weapons gleaming in the light of noon.

She followed, feeling her feet weighed down as if with heavy stones. The enemy had lapped around the right end of the Eagle People's line; the ones there were fighting back to back. Convinced that they each carried the *mana* of two, the Fiernans struck into the backs of the Zarthani and pushed them back, and now the Sun People were squeezed in turn. It all seemed curiously remote, something happening far away. All she could remember was the flexing, pounding feeling of fists hitting her, the world whirling away, herself strengthless as they threw her down.

Trotting past bodies writhing or still; Fiernan, Sun People, a few of the Eagle People as well. No lines now. A figure turning on her, a young Zarthani warrior snarling past a sparse brown beard clotted with blood from a light slash along his jaw. He had a shield painted with a bull's head, the sun between its horns, and a long one-handed ax with a bronze head that drooped like a falcon's beak. He nearly ran onto the point of her *katana,* bounced back, and came at her again. Her sword came up but the movement seemed dreamlike. Invisible hands twisted inside her stomach, shooting pain, and she tasted sour vomitus at the back of her throat. Parry, parry, wrists crossed on the long cord-bound hilt; the steel rang under the fast savage blows of the ax. Her heel caught on a clump of grass, and she staggered. The tomahawk rang off the curved surface of her breastplate, leaving a line of bright steel where it scored through the enamel. Again, again, three times in five seconds the armor saved her life. The shield slammed into her and she was over backward, down, hitting with a thump that knocked the wind out of her and drove the edges of the armor into her skin. The sword flew spinning.

Everything was still very slow, except the Zarthani warrior. He alone moved quickly, leaping forward to stamp a bare foot down and hold her in place while the ax went up for a looping chop at her neck. The muscles of his chest and arm knotted as the weapon went up; she could smell him, sweat and greased leather and smoke.

Don't let me down.

No. Her left arm came off the ground and slammed into the back of the Zarthani's knee. *I won't leave you alone.*

The man heaved backward with a yell. She surged half upright and hammered a gloved right fist up under his kilt. The yell turned to a high yelp of agony. Swindapa kicked her legs free and shoulder-rolled, sweeping the *katana* up from where it lay. The Zarthani was up too, gray-faced and sweating but still fast. She lunged forward, and the point jammed through wicker and into the warrior's arm. He croaked rage and swung the ax. Her hands pushed up and her wrists crossed, presenting the blade at a precise forty-five-degree angle, the point near her own shoulder blade. Tough ashwood, the shaft of the ax slid down the metal and the force of the blow turned the Zarthani half around. She planted her feet and lashed the sword back at him; a frantic leap and twist still left him with a gash leaking red along the outside of his right arm, a flap of skin and flesh dangling. She moved in, *jodan no kame,* sword up over her head.

Cut, and a section of the wicker shield spun away. Strike up from the follow-through, and her blade met the descending arm, already weakened by the first cut. This time the edge jarred solidly into meat, and she pivoted from the hips, a snapping twist that grated the blade into bone and past it. The follow-through sent a fan of red drops across the grass, and the sword seemed to fly of itself back into the high-stroke position for the killing blow.

"Quarter!" the Zarthani yelled, falling back and putting up a hand against it in a futile warding gesture. "I yield!"

For a long moment Swindapa stood, feeling fire torrenting through her blood.

"I won't let you down," she whispered, in her lover's tongue.

The Zarthani swarmed into the breach howling, striking at Americans still dazed on the ground, or still cumbered by their long spears. The bang and clatter and crash of hand-to-hand combat sounded all around them, like a load of scrap metal dropping on a concrete floor.

"Follow me," Alston said firmly, as Swindapa dashed off to bring the Fiernan reserve into action.

The standard-bearers fell back a little as the command party moved forward, and the dozen sword-and-shield guards closed up in a blunt wedge behind her.

"Rally!" she shouted. "Rally, there!"

The American line was starting to reform, yielding flexibly without breaking ranks, rallying about the flag. But too many of the barbarians were through; a knot of them hacked and trampled their way to the rear of the formation. Alston led her band directly at them, forcing them to turn and meet her. At their head was the chieftain with the chain-mail hauberk; he carried a small shield painted with paired thunderbolts and a long steel-shod spear whose head was surrounded by a collar of white heron feathers. Armored, he still moved lightly, a lithe fast knot of bone and gristle and tough muscle.

The spear punched at her. Worry fell away; you couldn't think, not in a fight. You *reacted*. He leaped backward frantically as her katana slammed down in a blurring arc, but the tip still burst links; without the armor it would have gashed his shoulder to the bone. Pale eyes went wide . . . and he'd gotten his first real look at her face.

"Night One!" he said in his own tongue.

Beside her one of his followers struck, and the ax boomed off an American shield. That trooper stepped in, stabbing and punching the shield forward. The whole wedge of guards was pushing forward, stepping into place and sealing the breach in the line.

Alston thrust two-handed at the chief's face, shrieking the *kia*. He yelled back and caught the blade on the face of his shield, short-gripping the spear and stabbing underarm. The point skittered off the lower part of her breastplate and the thigh guards. He backed again, but she followed closely, keeping herself too close for his longer weapon to be fully useful. The brass cap at the base of the *katana*'s hilt punched up at his face, taking him at the angle of his jaw. Bone broke, but the Zarthani's shield edge whipped around and struck her across the head and shoulder. She tasted the iron and salt of blood in her mouth and went with the stroke, letting her right knee loose. Weight and momentum pushed her down on one knee, and the long curved blade took the warrior on the back of the leg, just above the knee. He fell backward with a scream, one that ended in a gurgle as the *katana* came down across his neck.

Alston spat blood and came to her feet. The fight was ending, knots and clumps of the Zarthani turning and running lest they be caught between the Fiernans swinging in from the right and the Nantucket line. *Training pays off*, she thought, dragging her mind back to the chessplayer's state a commander needed. *True for the Romans, true for us.*

"Shall we pursue?" Lieutenant Nyugen said.

"No," she replied.

No point; they couldn't possibly chase down unarmored men, not without cavalry, and those took years to train.

She shook her head. "Let the locals do it."

The Fiernans were hallooing off across the stretch of pas-

ture, spearing running Zarthani in the back or wounded
ones on the ground with the ruthless enthusiasm bred by
old, old scores that they'd never had a chance to pay off
before. That reminded her . . .

"See to the prisoners." Where the Fiernans had passed,
there simply weren't any—which was a pity but also a load
off her mind; there weren't any facilities for them. "We'll
need a few for interrogation."

Stretcher-bearers were taking the wounded off to the circle of wagons where the doctors waited. There were already
birds circling above, ravens and crows, waiting for the living
humans to get out of the way. And . . .

Swindapa. For an instant she could be an single human
being, not the head of a hundredfold body. Fear and love
roiled under the shell of control. The Fiernan girl wasn't
far away, cleaning her sword and standing over an enemy
prisoner. As Alston came up she pushed back the cheekpieces and removed her helmet, turning a wondering look
on the American.

"I beat him. He gave up," she said. "I beat him, and he
gave up."

Alston put an arm around her shoulders. The armor
made it like embracing a statue, but she squeezed anyway.
"Damn right," she said, grinning in relief and fierce pride.
"I didn't waste all that teachin' time."

"I didn't let you down."

"Never."

The Zarthani warrior lay not far away, rough field dress-
ings on a couple of bad wounds on his right arm. His look
of sullen fear turned to amazement, doubled as Alston
bared her head to the cooling breeze and his suspicious
eyes studied her throat.

"Women?" he blurted, horror in his voice. "I surrendered to *women*?"

Alston and Swindapa looked at each other for a long
moment. Then they began to laugh.

"Here they come," Ian said.

"Get *down* from there," Doreen said nervously, pulling
at the back of his bush jacket as he stood above her on the
floor of the wagon.

"I *really* don't like battles," she said.

Ian nodded, climbing down, his eyes still glued on the

onrushing . . . *barbarian horde. A real, live, very ugly barbarian horde.*

He didn't like battles either. He remembered the one with the Olmecs all too vividly—in dreams, at times. Not that he'd seen much of it, from his post well to the rear, but he'd seen the aftermath close up . . . and smelled it. Right now all he could smell was his own sweat, the fairly powerful odor of the threescore Fiernans massed in the forward part of the ring of wagons, and the strong disinfectant the medics were getting ready.

The doctors and orderlies were pulling their steel-tube folding tables out of the supply wagons and setting up, lighting a fire to heat the pressure cookers that would sterilize their implements. The Arnsteins helped them; it felt rather odd, since the orderlies were in armor.

"Periods all jumbled up," Doreen said, holding the platform of a table while an orderly spun the wing nuts that secured it to the frame.

"Bronze Age, medieval, twentieth," Ian agreed.

"Excuse me, sir," a petty officer said. "Is that loaded?"

"What loaded?" Ian said.

"The *gun,* sir," the noncom said, her voice heavily patient. "The one you're wearing slung across your back."

"Oh, *that* gun," Ian said.

It was a 12-gauge double-barrel model, cut down. He clicked open the breech; empty.

"You should load it, sir. We're not supposed to need 'em here, but you never know."

The shells were double-ought buckshot, and had an unpleasant weight and solidity as he slid them into the breech; the *snick* and *click* as he closed the weapon had an evil finality to it. He could hear the crossbows firing now, and the shrieks and screams of the enemy were much closer. Stretcher-bearers came trotting in with the first of the wounded, an American with an arrow through the biceps and into the bone. He was cursing, a steady flat-toned stream of obscenity and scatology, until the painkiller took effect. As he went limp an orderly cut the shaft of the arrow off an inch above his skin with a pair of pruning shears. The surgeon pulled an instrument from a tray, one Ian recognized—an arrow-extractor spoon, an ancient model that probably hadn't been used in centuries . . . or wouldn't be invented for millennia, depending on how you looked at it.

He looked away, himself, as the doctor's intent face bent over the wounded man. As he did there was a long whirring *shoooosshh* sound from the east-facing side of the wagon fort, underscored by a flat twanging. *Bows,* he realized; he was hearing massed archery. Here and there a slinger stood in a circle of open space, flicking his leather thong around his head with a one . . . two . . . *throw* motion; he'd seen Swindapa do it, in practice. The lead eggs the Americans had provided their allies as ammunition blurred out almost too fast to see. From here he couldn't see the action, but he could still hear the steady metronomic *whunnng* sound of the crossbows volleying. Then he couldn't, and a few seconds later there was a long rasping slither, a deep shout, and then a frantic multiple clang and thump and snarling brabble of voices.

"And the din of onset sounded," he quoted to himself. He was coming to have a deeper appreciation of Homer than he'd ever imagined . . . or wanted.

The Fiernan archers standing on the wagon beds were still shooting, but carefully now—picking their targets, holding the shaft, and then loosing. Occasionally one would stop to yell a taunt, or pull up his tunic and slap his buttocks at the enemy.

What do I do now? The answer to that was "nothing"; he couldn't even shout for news, his Fiernan wasn't up to it and it wouldn't really be tactful to use the Sun People tongue right at this moment. Casualties trickled in, not all that many of them; more than half came from the Fiernans fighting along the forward edge of the wagons. *Amazing how important armor is.* The noise grew greater, and there were high-pitched screams, piteous and astonishingly loud. *Wounded horses.* Somehow they sounded even worse than the human beings; their pain was without comprehension or recourse.

"Look out!"

That was the petty officer who'd reminded him to load the shotgun. Ian whipped around. A couple of Zarthani were climbing through the wagons almost directly behind him, trampling Fiernan corpses.

The battle suddenly seemed very close indeed. The noncom and an orderly snatched up their big oval shields, and

Doreen reached for her oak staff. One of the Zarthani made a flying leap and hit a shield feet-first. The sheet metal boomed under the impact of the callused heels and the collision sent them both down. Less burdened, the barbarian was back on his feet first; his spear slammed down, scoring the enameled eagle on the shield. The American had no chance of getting back on her feet, not with the armor on. Instead she curled up under the shield as she'd been trained, keeping it between her and the barbarian with the tip of the *gladius* ready around the edge if his unprotected legs came too close. Screaming frustration, the warrior danced around his prone opponent, his spear darting out like the flickering of a frog's tongue. The fallen noncom's companion was backing up himself, desperately trying to fend off two Zarthani who were edging out to take him in the rear, their axes moving continually in blurring, looping arcs. The edges glinted, razor-sharp. Even if they couldn't cut through steel, they could still break bones under mail.

"Oh, shit," Ian muttered, looking frantically around.

Nobody else here but the doctors and nurses, so frantically busy with the wounded that they didn't even look up. The rest of the stretcher-bearer-cum-orderlies were back along the line, bringing in more wounded. Nobody else in reach.

Doreen had come to the same conclusion a split second earlier. She swallowed, took a firmer grip on the *bo,* and stepped forward.

"Wait!" Ian croaked, hands fumbling on the shotgun.

Goddammit, this isn't my field!

The Zarthani didn't seem to consider any of that important. He caught the movement of Doreen's staff out of the corner of his eye and struck, turning almost as fast as the outflung head of his long tomahawk. The axhead sliced through the upper part of the *bo,* but the staff saved Doreen's life even as a third of its length went flipping end over end. Deflected, it was the flat of the ax rather than its edge that glanced off the side of her head. Blood welled up from a torn scalp, and she dropped like a puppet with its strings cut. The barbarian crowed triumph and swung the bronze ax up again.

Everything seemed to move very slowly after that. He took two steps forward. The Zarthani turned toward him, lips peeled back from his teeth, the ax whirling. For an

instant his finger froze on the trigger. *I'm not a killer.* He
never knew just what it was that released him; perhaps it
was the crooked cross painted on the man's shield. The
barbarian wasn't a Nazi, but he was near enough to an
original-article Aryan as no matter.

Thudump. He'd fired at less than four feet distance, with
the butt of the shotgun clamped between elbow and ribs.
Recoil spun him around and wrenched at his arm, nearly
tearing the weapon away. He turned back with desperate
speed, bringing it up to his shoulder. His finger tightened
even as he saw the chewed red ruin the deershot had made
of the man's chest. *Thudump.* A bruising, hammering blow
to his shoulder, and the muzzles twisted skyward. Momentum had put the barbarian's contorted face less than a yard
from the business end of the shotgun. He flipped backward,
his face *splashing* away from the shattered bones of his
skull. Bits of it struck, spattering on Ian's face and chest, a
lump of something gelatinous slapping into his open mouth.
He dropped to his knees and vomited in uncontrollable
reflex, shuddering and spitting to clear his mouth.

Even then he clutched the shotgun to his chest, and tried
to open the breech to reload it. Fortunately, that wasn't
necessary. The retreating American had stopped when the
odds against him dropped to even. The other Zarthani faltered, shocked by the thunderous sound and the sudden
death beside him. While he goggled the American sheathed
his short sword in the man's belly, ripped it out, and bowled
the dying barbarian over with a slamming blow from his
shield. The petty officer levered herself back erect, and it
was the last Zarthani's turn to retreat helplessly before
numbers. He was far more vulnerable, though. A moment's
clatter and boom, and he was down on his knees, coughing
blood and clutching at his chest. A short hard chop put the
edge of a *gladius* into the back of his neck with a tooth-
grating wet *chunk-crack* sound, like an ax going into
damp wood.

"God bless the Ginsu," the American wheezed, freeing
his blade with a jerk. "Slices, dices, julienne-fries."

Ian wiped his mouth on his sleeve and dropped his weapon,
fumbling at Doreen's head with trembling fingers. "Oh, God,
she can't die," he mumbled, knowing that he lied.

The wound was bleeding freely, leaving his hands red to
the wrist, but he couldn't find any crack in the bone. That

didn't mean there wasn't internal damage, pressure on the brain. He peeled back one eyelid and then the other; the left pupil was larger, and didn't shrink as much.

"Oh, God."

He put an arm under her shoulders and another behind her knees and straightened up, not feeling the strain, and walked over to the aid station.

The doctor there had splashes of blood on his gown. "Head wound?" he said. Ian nodded, afraid to speak. The gloved fingers probed, washed, and probed again.

"Not too bad," the medic said. Ian felt an enormous shuddering sensation of relief, so strong that he had to grip the edge of the table as his knees loosened.

"I think," the medico added. "No fracture . . . concussion . . . probably be sick as a dog for a couple of days. This scalp wound is superficial, doesn't even need a stitch." He looked up to his assistant. "Bandage it. Next!"

He followed while Doreen was laid out on a blanket, with another over her. People bumped into him. At last an orderly spoke:

"Sir, you're in the f . . . goddam way. She's going to be out for hours. Couldn't you move?"

He did, getting a drink of water and trying to force his mind back into action. He found the captain standing with her helmet under one arm, talking with a knot of her officers and a worshipful-looking pair of Fiernan Spear Chosen.

" . . . five dead, and twenty seriously wounded," someone was saying.

"Damn," Alston said sadly. "Well, no worse than I expected—better, actually." She looked around. "We'll make camp over there. Ditch and obstacles, if you please; best we get into the habit. Let's get on with it. As I understand it, we have to wait for permission to approach the Great Wisdom anyway. Ah, Ian."

Her gaze sharpened on him, taking in the spatters and the blood on his hands; there was some drying across the front of her breastplate as well, and up her right armguard. "Not hurt, I hope?"

"No . . . Doreen was." He swallowed. "That is, she got a thump on the head. I had to, that is, use the shotgun. The doctor says she'll be fine."

"Glad you're both all right," she said. "Come take a look at this."

He forced down an irrational spurt of anger. *She's got more than us to think about.* At least the emotion served to break through the glassy, numb feeling he'd had since the ugly scrimmage among the wagons. They walked out into the ghastly remains. The dead were thickly scattered across three hundred yards of beaten ground, singly and in clumps. The ground was actually sticky with blood in places; the broad triple-edged heads of the heavy arrows cut gruesome channels through flesh and internal organs. Some of the barbarians were still moving, missed by the Fiernan pursuers. The ground smelled a little like an old-fashioned butcher's shop where blood and meat had gone slightly off in the sun, and more like an outdoor toilet.

Like a Marrakesh souk, only worse, Ian thought, gagging slightly. "One thing I can tell you," he said. "You probably won't have any trouble from this particular tribe anytime soon."

Alston looked at him, eyebrows raised. "They seemed remarkably stubborn to me," she said. "Zarthani is what this here bunch're called, by the way."

Ian shook his head. "From what we saw of the Iraiina and what Swindapa's said, not many of these tribes are more than four, five thousand people," he said. "You . . . we . . . probably killed something like every third male of military age in the Zarthani tribe's entire population in less than an hour, plus a lot of their leaders. They can't have battles like this very often. Couldn't afford them."

"Good point," she said, musing. "I think they were plenty surprised, all right." A bleak smile: "Remember the night before the fight with the Indians, when I said what we lacked was experienced troops? We're quickly makin' that lack good."

Where the line of battle had stood, the Zarthani dead lay thicker, two deep where the hedge of spears had met them. The smell was riper; spearheads and swords had pierced the abdominal cavity more often than not. Ian tried to avoid looking at the faces. Alston bent and pulled the light frame of a chariot upright, tumbling a corpse off it.

"Notice anythin'?" she said.

Breathing through his mouth, Ian forced himself to look. After a moment he blinked.

"Iron tires!" he said, and bent closer, adjusting his glasses.

"Heat-shrunk on. Iron coulter pins, too, and those spokes were turned on a lathe." His gaze went forward to the dead horses. "Collar harnesses, too, by God. And horseshoes."

"Walker," Alston said, making the name a quiet curse. "That'll increase their military potential quite drastically."

"That's not the half of it, Mar—Captain. That yoke-and-strap harness these people were using chokes a horse when it pulls. With a collar, it's four, five times more efficient—perhaps more. It revolutionized agriculture in the Middle Ages. I suppose he's given them stirrups, too. Faster transportation. I wonder what else he's come up with?"

Working parties of Americans and Fiernans were stripping the bodies of anything useful and hauling them off, and cautiously taking the enemy wounded toward the aid station. A hundred or so were digging a long trench, six feet deep, spadefuls of the light chalky earth flying up. Ian winced a little again. Granted, it was necessary sanitation, but . . .

Alston pointed out another body. "This for starters."

He bent, ignoring the flies walking across the fixed, dry eyes. "Chain mail," he said, a little redundantly, and looked closer. "Machine-drawn wire, I'd say, but the rest looks like handwork."

He stood, eyes absent. "I wonder if he—Dr. Hong, actually, I suppose—has told them about antiseptic childbirth? That'd start a population explosion all by itself . . . He's already done enough to turn this society—this continent—upside down. God alone knows how it'll evolve now."

"God may know, but I hope we'll have some say in the matter," Alston said grimly. "Well, back to work. I don't think our absent friend is going to be wasting his time. I should look in on the wounded."

"Captain. Captain Alston."

She turned, a slightly different expression on her face. "Captain . . . can I ask you a question?"

"Sure, Ian," she said. There was nobody within overhearing distance, if they kept their voices down. Nobody alive, anyway.

"What . . ." He wet his lips, then nearly retched at the memory of what had flown into them. "What do you think about killing people?"

The thin eyebrows went up, and her face changed—out of the commander's mode, and into a friend's face for a moment. She squeezed his arm; then looked around at the aftermath of the fight. "It's disgusting," she said quietly. "Afterward, that is. At the time . . . at the time I'm concentrating too hard to feel much of anythin', mostly."

He nodded. "That's . . . do you find yourself, ah, thinking about it a lot?"

"Dreams, flashbacks, that sort of thing?" He nodded. She went on: "Not so far. Takes people different ways. My daddy, he was in Korea, it still hit him now and then; he'd take a bottle and go out and sit in the woods, but I don't think that's my way. Losing my own people, yes, *that* bothers me . . . but if these men wanted to stay safe, they shouldn't have attacked me. And if that says somethin' unfavorable about me as a human being, I don't give much of a damn."

After a moment she began to murmur. Somewhat to his astonishment, he realized she was reciting poetry:

> "I am afraid to think about my death,
> When it shall be, and whether in great pain
> I shall rise up and fight the air for breath,
> Or calmly wait the bursting of my brain.
>
> "I am no coward who could seek in fear
> A folk-lore solace or sweet Indian tales:
> I know dead men are deaf and cannot hear
> The singing of a thousand nightingales.
>
> "I know dead men are blind and cannot see
> The friend that shuts in horror their big eyes,
> And they are witless—O, I'd rather be
> A living mouse than dead as a man dies."

She looked around again. "Say what you like about killin', it sure beats the alternative."

Ian remembered Doreen falling under the ax. Two Fiernans were picking up a dead Zarthani, lifting by the legs and under the arms, grunting as they swung the limp weight into the grave trench.

"I see what you mean," he said slowly. *And I actually feel better. Unsuspected depths, the captain has.*

"Hooooly shit," one of the Americans said.
"Quiet," Cuddy barked.

He'd seen local war parties often enough, over the past eight months—never from the receiving end, though. The main difference with this lot was that there weren't any chariots; probably too difficult to ship. He could identify the chiefs by their bronze helmets, grouped around a pole with an aurochs skull for a standard. The warriors milled about, a hundred or so of them, working themselves up for a rush, trampling the young grain. Even at two hundred yards or more he could sense their nervousness; this was the dwelling place of the sorcerer Hwalkarz and the Lady of Pain. On the other hand, they also held riches beyond the dreams of avarice, and what was even more important to the locals, a challenge and the prospect of glory.

"Well, come on, there's only eighteen of us," Cuddy yelled. "What're you waiting for, your mommies to tell you it's okay?"

It seemed like the sort of thing the boss would say in a situation like this. Some of the Iraiina at his back laughed, and one or two of the Americans. One of them spoke, licking his lips:

"Hey, ain't you going to see them off, Cuddy?"

He had the butt of the Garand resting on one hip; he'd clicked a modified twenty-round magazine into it. He'd done a hitch in the Crotch, been in the Gulf, but they'd trained him on M-16s. For present purposes he preferred the old battle rifle. These .30-06 rounds had real authority.

With luck, he wouldn't have to use them. "Nah," he said. "Ammo's too expensive. Let's use what we can make."

He turned to the Mule. The catapult lay ready, throwing arm back and a barrel resting in it, double-strapped with thick bands and wire. Within that barrel was another, and between them were scrap iron, rocks, and pieces of hard pottery. A long cord hung from the side. Cuddy stepped over to it and pulled out his lighter.

"Flick of the Bic," he said, grinning at the weapon's crew.

They were looking a little nervous as he touched the flame to the fuse. It sputtered and refused to take for a moment. Then the red dot and trailing blue smoke raced ahead, hung fire again, raced ahead.

"Fire!" he yelled, skipping backward.

The Mule kicked, its rear wheels lifting clear of the mud as the throwing bar slammed into the padded top. The barrel traced an arc across the lowering gray sky, trailing faint smoke. The men around the spot where the barrel was headed simply opened their ranks to let it land, then stopped in puzzlement when it didn't break apart or burst into flame. One stepped forward curiously and prodded it with a spear. Others gathered around him, unwilling to be outdone in courage. Cuddy fought back a giggle as another rocked it with his foot. A stab of fear followed it. It was a damp day; not exactly rainy, but full of that particularly English raw misty chill. What if the fuse had gone—

KRRRAACK!

A red snap in the heart of the Kayaltwar, and bodies flung backward like jointed rag dolls, a spurting pillar of gray-black smoke and pulverized dirt and body parts. His giggle became a full-throated laugh. Probably fifty or sixty of the eastern tribesmen lay dead or writhing around the small crater where ten pounds of gunpowder had gone off. Most of the rest were running, screaming and throwing away their weapons, running or hobbling or limping and crawling.

Their Sky Father showed His wrath by throwing thunderbolts.

A few were running *toward* the Walkerburg men. As the boss liked to say, the locals often made up for their lack of know-how by sheer balls. Cuddy studied them through the telescopic sight, murmuring *bang . . . bang . . .* to himself as he tracked from one to the other. The men with Nantucket-style crossbows were taking careful aim too, and firing. None of the Kayaltwar got closer than fifty yards.

"Well, as the boss says, nobody said to stop working," Cuddy said, when the whoops and back-slapping had died down a little. Some of the Iraiina were looking a little shaky; they were Sky Father's children too. On the other hand, the Big Boss God had just shown his favor to their lord rather unmistakably. "Let's get shackles on the survivors," he finished. "And we'll have to scout down to Daurthunnicar's and get a message to the boss."

He thought Walker would be rather pleased.

Marian Alston woke to the sound of a bugle. It was followed by the familiar bellow: *"Reveille, reveille; heave out, trice up, lash and stow, lash and stow!"*

She blinked, drowsy with sleep and the warmth of Swindapa's back against her chest. No help for it. It was still dark outside the tent, turning to the peculiar gray-black of predawn, cool and raw under scudding cloud. *C'mon, woman, set an example for the crew . . . the troops.* It still felt damned odd, commanding a force ashore.

And today's the day. Crucial to the success or failure of her mission; on a personal note, she was going to meet Swindapa's kindred. The Fiernan's eyes danced as they exchanged a good-morning kiss.

"Water, ma'am."

A bucket outside the door, waiting when they came back from the latrines. She and Swindapa knelt beside it, scrubbing in the cold river water and then brushing their teeth; nudity taboos were going the way of computers and toilet paper, with a mixed force living in the field. She looked at her watch, a self-winding mechanical model, a minor privilege of rank: five in the morning exactly. The square marching camp stirred into a hive of orderly activity as she dressed in the working uniform they'd designed over the winter, tough olive-drab jacket and trousers. They weren't intolerably smelly yet, but the quilted padding for the armor was, rank as a ferret and difficult to wash out here. Swindapa wrinkled her nose, and they switched to the alternate sets; they were going to have to make a good impression today. When they left the tent a squad had it struck down within minutes, well before they reached the head of their mess line. Breakfast was stale bread, butter and cheese, and slices of cold roast pork, with purified water or milk brought to a rolling boil for ten minutes—the doctors had insisted on that, after one look at the way dairy cattle were kept here. It was also one of the reasons she'd kept everyone at the base camp where they'd landed for some days, time for digestions to adapt as much as they were going to.

Amazing how you get used to things, she thought, looking at the others breaking camp in the gradually increasing light. *A year ago . . .* A year ago, TV and takeout Chinese, flush toilets and daily showers and a spray for the pits, riding in cars, taking a 747 and vacationing in the Rockies. A world where smells were flushed away, and everything was so damned easy. No homicidal savages with spears. . . .

"No, just homicidal savages with Tech-9s," Alston muttered to herself. One of the few merits of low technology was that it was difficult to do a drive-by with an ax.

She dusted crumbs off her gorget and then put on her helmet, clipping the cheekpieces together under her chin. Working parties had already packed the coils of barbed wire back on the wagons; others were shoveling the embankment down into the ditch. Little was left of the rest of the encampment, and less every second. Squads were filling their canteens at the water barrels—easier to purify in bulk—and falling in. Alston looked at her watch again and nodded in satisfaction. Quite an improvement since the first night on the march, much less what they'd done back on the island in practice. Cold raindrops began to tinkle on her helmet, not a steady drizzle but occasional bursts from the ragged clouds overhead. She ignored it, as the troops on foot did. The only people traveling dry would be the wounded under the canvas tilts on the wagons.

Amazing how well they adapt to the fighting, too.

That was *extremely* different from things up in the twentieth. Here you got close enough to look into your opponent's eyes, close enough to smell him. Close enough to watch the expression as edged metal slammed home. Of course, it also had the advantage of being close enough to see what they intended for *you.*

The crowd of Fiernans outside the camp was larger, watching silently as the Americans formed up. Some of their Spear Chosen were turning thoughtfully, looking at the ordered ranks before them and then at the clots of followers squatting or sitting or leaning on their spears behind them. *They don't know what we've got, but they* want *it,* she thought.

The scouts were already fanning out ahead. Alston took her horse's reins, put her foot in the stirrup, and swung into the saddle with a slight grunt; the armor rattled, and she could swear she heard a slight *ooof* from the horse as well. It was a pony, really, barely thirteen hands high, but a sturdy, stocky little beast.

"Forward . . . *march.*"

The officers relayed it. Drums beat and the lead company swung off by the left, spears bobbing in unison. More blocks of troops, then wagons—including the well-sprung ones with the wounded. Alston clucked to her horse and trotted down the line to the front, flags rippling and snapping behind her, and fell into position at the head of the line. The track wound off into the downs; not far from the camp it passed six graves on a hillside with a good view of the battlefield, with stout oak crosses marking them until they had time to do proper stone markers. Alston's right hand came up to the brim of her helmet with a *tick*. Behind her orders snapped:

"Eyes . . . *right!*"

The flags dipped, and the formations honored their dead. Even the Fiernans behind made gestures of respect, although they'd suffered far more cruelly than the armored Americans in the brief deadly fight.

"Soon," Swindapa said as they went through the shallow stream and back up onto the downlands. The burned village was already being rebuilt; the Sun People hadn't had enough time to completely wreck it. "A few miles to the southeast, and they'll send someone to meet us. News will have spread everywhere, to the Great Wisdom and as far north as the Goldstone Hills." Or the Cotswolds, to use a terminology three millennia out of phase.

She sounded eager, but not nervous anymore. Alston looked over at her; the Fiernan was riding with her helmet off and held before her on the saddlebow, looking in her armor like the cover of an adventure novel. The fight last week had changed something. For the better, as far as she could tell.

The landscape became flatter, the fields more open, larger, with more cattle and sheep and less cultivation as they rose. Long earthwork banks ran across it—field markers or symbols or something completely strange. Mounds rose above it, turf-green, sometimes with enigmatic shapes drawn across them in chalk. The crowds along the rutted trackway grew denser as the hours passed.

"Graves," Swindapa said, pointing to the mounds. "For great folk."

A scout came back up the trackway at a canter and saluted. "Party approaching on foot," she said.

Alston returned the gesture. "Carry on."

Swindapa fell silent, went pale, bit her lip, and blinked hard again and again. A party was approaching down the rutted, trampled dirt road. They wore woven straw cloaks against the rain, and broad hats. Two women with walking staffs, an older and a younger, and a couple of men with spears and bows. Alston threw her hand up, and the trumpet sounded *halt* and then *stand easy*. The Fiernans ahead flinched a little at the crashing unison as a hundred and fifty feet pounded to a stop, then came on again. Their eyes went wide again in astonishment as Alston removed her helmet and let them see her skin and features. The middle-aged Fiernan woman moistened her lips and began to speak:

"The Grandmothers of the Great Wisdom have sent me," she said slowly and ceremoniously. Alston found she could follow it, more or less. "To tell you that no strangers in arms may approach the holy place. Stop here, then, or we will call the Sacred Truce against you."

"Mother!" Swindapa squeaked, in her own language, throwing herself off the horse.

The woman's eyes went wide, really looking at the yellow-haired rider for the first time. "Swindapa!" she cried, spreading her arms.

The older woman was in her forties and looked a decade or so older, rangy and blond; the family resemblance was obvious. She wore a longer version of the string skirt that seemed to be standard women's dress here, made of interwoven strips of soft wool, each a subtly different color. Her belt had a gold buckle; the shirt above it was the natural gray of the fleece. Gold bands studded with amber were pushed up her bare arms, and the hands below were worn and capable-looking. Her eyes were the same deep blue as her daughter's; they kept going back to the young woman at Alston's side.

"Swindapa?" her mother asked. "I heard . . . I didn't believe . . ." Tears trickled down her cheeks.

Swindapa hugged the two women again and again, then the men. "Marian, my mother—Dhinwarn of the line of Kurlelo—my sister, Telartano, my uncles Grohuxj and Adaanfa."

Fiernan purled and bubbled between them, too swiftly for Alston to follow. The camp was going up faster than usual, with the early start and the troops fresh from a short march. Dhinwarn blinked a little at it, and more at the folding canvas chairs that appeared outside the commander's tent. She sat in one gingerly, as if expecting it to collapse under her. A bundle on the younger woman's back began to cry; she shifted it forward under her rain cloak, revealed a swaddled infant, and began to nurse it. At points in Swindapa's tale her mother and sister wept again, quite openly; the uncles growled curses as well as shedding tears. Later they glanced back and forth between Alston and their kinswoman with awe and wonder. At last the torrent of speech slowed down so that the American could follow some of it, or her ear grew accustomed to the machine-gun rapidity. It was her turn to blink.

She can't be saying what I think she's saying, can she?

"Ah . . . 'dapa, what are you telling them now, exactly?"

A brilliant, proud smile: "I'm telling them what a wonderful lover you are!"

I thought so, Alston thought with a slight wince. Telling them in extensive detail, from the sound of it; she'd learned Fiernan anatomical vocabulary quite thoroughly. *Talk about your culture clashes.* " 'Dapa, no need for blow-by-blow, okay?"

She leaned back, resting her elbows on the arms of the chair and steepling her fingers, marshaling her scanty command of this language. Silence fell, and Swindapa's mother took up her carved staff.

"We come . . . friends," Alston said at last.

The Fiernans rose, came forward, and placed their hands on Alston's shoulder for a moment. "Thank you," Dhinwarn said solemnly. "You have returned my daughter to life." The others repeated it. "My sister." "My sister's daughter who I put on my knee."

Alston cleared her throat, touched; like the Navajo, the Earth Folk spoke thanks only for the very greatest of gifts, taking everyday things for granted.

"Swindapa, speak for me," she said, when they were back in their chairs. "Tell them we'd like—I would, and a few others of us—would like to travel to the Great Wisdom and talk to the Grandmothers."

Dhinwarn frowned, unhappy. "Why would you want to do that?" she said. "You are . . . Spear Chosen of the Eagle People."

Swindapa stopped translating for a moment and began to explain, or tried to. Dhinwarn smiled and shook her head.

"Swindapa says you are much more than that," she went on. "But a young woman in love often thinks more with her warm heart than her star-cool mind."

The Fiernan metaphor came through accurately enough, but from what she grasped of the original the phrasing was much more . . . earthy. Alston suppressed a giggle.

"We also have knowledge of the moon and stars," she said, and glanced up. The sky was clearing and sunset was only an hour off. "If the clouds allow, we'll show you." The Arnsteins and the telescope would, rather. "Also some other things you'd find useful. For instance, you memorize all the knowledge you keep, don't you?"

Swindapa's mother frowned in puzzlement. "Of course we remember it."

"No, that's not what I meant. You use . . . things, your circles of standing stones, knotted cords, tally sticks, songs, to *help* you remember something, don't you?"

A method with severe limitations. From what Swindapa had told her and what Martha and the Arnsteins had figured out, the Fiernan Bohulugi savants had run into a dead end some time ago. There was only so much information you could store orally; eventually it took so much time that new generations couldn't add any more without dropping something. Swindapa had mentioned how fewer and fewer of the younger generations were willing to go through the arduous apprenticeship, particularly with the Sun People pressing on them. This Bronze Age world looked static and unchanging to eyes brought up in the twentieth, but it was a time of upheaval by local standards. The faith of Moon Woman couldn't adapt fast enough; it was rooted in the Neolithic.

Dhinwarn nodded. "We have a way," Alston said, "of . . . marking down in symbols . . . both words and numbers, exactly, so that those who know it may take the record even generations later and understand it, as if the first person were speaking in their ear."

The older woman leaned forward, keenly interested. "How can this be?" she said. "A tally, you can't tell what it's numbers *of*, unless someone remembers what the notches are for. And the relations between numbers, the Wisdom of their ordering, how can this be put in concrete things? Even the Great Wisdom—" they all made a sign with their hands, like drawing a set of geometric shapes—"has meaning only to those brought up to it, learning the Songs."

Alston sighed and settled down to explaining. The sun faded and a trooper hung a lamp from the tentpole. Dhinwarn took longer than Swindapa had to understand what she was driving at, but her eyes lit like blowtorches when she did. Her voice trembled:

"My daughter . . . she says that among your people, there are great Wisdoms where these *books* are kept, and that any who learn the art may journey among the words of the Grandmothers-before?"

"Yes," Alston said, impressed at how rapidly she'd grasped the concept. "We call them *libraries*. And the skill of reading the words is not hard to learn. Swindapa mastered it very quickly. So we can store knowledge like, ah, like grain in a big jar, and draw it out when we need it. Of course, you need to know enough to know what questions to ask."

The others began volleying questions as well; once when Swindapa mentioned that she had seen constellations farther south unknown here her mother and sister rose and did a slow, stately dance around the fire, singing a minor-key chant. Their astronomy had long predicted it, and exact knowledge of stellar movements was the central element of their religion—it was how you read the intentions of Moon Woman. Alston spread a star map of the southern hemisphere and began explaining. Troopers brought their plates of beans and pork and bread; the Fiernans ate with their eyes glued to the paper.

At last Alston sat back, exhausted. "But I'm not what we'd call an expert," she said. "I sail ships and I fight, when I have to. Here's a learned person—Doreen, bring that telescope out—and she can tell you more."

Damned oddest way to negotiate a military alliance I've ever heard of, she thought, watching the astronomer and listening to Dhinwarn's trilling cry of joy when she realized what the telescope could do. *Still, it could be worse.*

If it had been the Middle Ages, they might have been burned as heretics—or found the locals dead-set on enlisting their help in liberating the Holy Sepulcher from the Saracens. In her opinion, defending Stonehenge from a bunch of blond Apaches was very much to be preferred.

I wonder how things are going back on the island? And how exactly *am I going to explain about Walker?*

CHAPTER TWENTY

June – July, Year 2 A.E.

"Here's the title deed," Cofflin said. "Place is yours."

"Thanks, Chief," the Kayles said.

The crowd cheered. *Sixty-four acres of sand and scrub,* Cofflin thought. The young couple looked eager enough, though; and if you were going to do farming work anyway, you might as well do it on your own property. There would be loans from the Town to pay off, of course. The plank-and-beam barn that stood not far from the house had been financed by the vote of the Meeting, along with the pigs and poultry and miniature herd of three yearling calves brought back by the *Eagle*.

There was a patter of applause as he handed over the title deeds, and now he had to make a goddam *speech*. About land titles and banking, of all goddam things.

The mild spring air cuffed at his hair; Martha put a hand up to her broad hat, the baby neatly balanced in the crook of her other arm. Jared Cofflin looked out over the grain-field, still spotted with an occasional haggled brush stump. That might make it awkward for the reapers, come harvest. *So much to do . . .* and so few sets of hands to do it. Harder than ever with so many strong young backs over in Britain. *God damn Walker to hell.* The air smelled intensely fresh, with a tinge of salt and a hint of cooking from the open-pit barbecue that was getting lunch ready.

Martha turned and smiled at him, a wry quirk of the corner of her mouth, and he felt a decision jell in his mind. "All right, people. I was supposed to sit up here and bray some stuff about the state of our economy, forsooth." A rippling laugh went across the people sitting in folding chairs. Joseph Starbuck winced. "And these poor folks would have had to stand and listen while their party was on hold."

The Kayles and their friends clapped enthusiastically. Cofflin went on: "I'll sort of condense it. We're going to be handing out more of these farms, a hundred and twenty or so. No room for more; it isn't a big island, and we can't take too much of the ground cover off or we'll have all sorts of problems with erosion and so on. Angelica tells me we can build up the soil fertility and we'll have more livestock soon. You all know we'll have another four big schooners by the end of summer, and some more tugs. There's more. Tom Ervine has his paper mill working—" another patter of applause; paper was so damned *useful*—"and the First Pacific Bank is reopening."

Boos and hisses at that. "I know, I know. But it's sure convenient to have money again, isn't it?" He put a hand into his pants pocket and held up a crisp ten-dollar note, the island's new issue. "Believe me, it's a big load off *my* shoulders. It's a lot easier to tell someone to go buy their own goddam dinner instead of figuring out rations!"

He threw his jacket across the chair behind him. Nobody, thank God, was wearing a necktie anymore, except a few fossils like Starbuck. "And I could go on and on. Ayup. What it amounts to is we're getting on our feet again, pretty well—better than any of us expected. So I'll move on to what we're all anxious about, how things are going over in England."

A stir and rustle of interest. "News just came through. That piece of . . ." Martha tugged at his leg. ". . . scum Walker has been making himself a kingdom over there. He's already got an army and he's making them iron weapons, and raiding and killing and taking slaves." A growl of anger rose from before him. "What's more, he and his Tartessian friend have built a ship, at least one, that Captain Alston says could easily carry a hundred men to Nantucket. There's some evidence he's made gunpowder; we've just now gotten our first small load of sulfur from the Caribbean, but there are sources in Britain, so he's ahead of us there."

Complete silence now, intent and focused. "If we'd left him another year, he'd have had cannon and a dozen ships ready to attack us. Captain Alston and the expeditionary force have already fought a battle with the savages he's got working for him." He paused, feeling the tension beating on him like heat. "The captain reports that the savages were completely defeated, with over a hundred dead, many more wounded, and the rest fleeing for their lives."

The crowd rose, cheering madly; men thumped each other on the back, women hugged. Cofflin raised a hand. "It wasn't cost-free. Six of our people were killed." The families had received first notification, of course, but otherwise he was ahead of the rumors.

Silence again, broken by a low murmur. Cofflin nodded. "This is serious business. I think we should have a moment of silence."

They waited with bowed heads. "And," he went on when it was over, "Captain Alston asks that we all remember them in our prayers."

Walker looked around the little natural amphitheater with disgust. It was dark now; attendants had lit torches on poles all around, and they still weren't an inch closer to deciding what to do. The ten chiefs and their principal retainers were making enough noise for a Red Sox game all by themselves. The sound died down a little as he stood and stepped forward to stand beside Daurthunnicar's chair—the others were on stools, to mark the Iraiina chief's status as High *Rahax*. Noise sank further when he slammed the iron butt cap of his spear against a rock; the steel sparked on the flint-rich lump of hardened chalk. When he had full silence, he leaned on the spear and spoke:

"Are you chieftains?" he asked rhetorically. "Are you even warriors of Sky Father's people?"

That brought their anger around on him. *Good enough,* he thought, meeting the glares. Most of these men had enough experience to control their tempers at least a little. If he could get them acting together, he could probably turn things around. Not if they went on quarreling with one another, though. Those hatreds were too old and well set.

"You promised us victory!" a chief shouted, the necklace of wolf teeth and gold bouncing on his barrel chest as he waved his fists in the air. "Instead the fighting men of a whole tribe are dead, and enemies raid our steadings!"

"I promised you victory if you followed my redes," he said coldly. "The Zarthani chose to flout them, going off on their own to raid without my—without our High *Rahax*'s word."

Daurthunnicar stirred slightly; Walker cursed the stumble. His father-in-law was no fool; pig-ignorant and superstitious as a horse, but no fool.

"The Zarthani fell on their own deeds. If in battle one of your warriors turned from the fight to lie with a woman or drive off a cow without your let, while the arrows still flew and axes beat on shields, how would you do with him?"

He could feel the anger checked, coiled back. Bearded faces nodded. They'd hang such a man up by the ankle in a sacred grove and run a spear through him, and their whole tribes would cheer.

"And then the Zarthani had no better sense than to charge at the first foe they met, like a bull at a gate—none of you would have been so foolish, I'm sure." *I'm sure most of you would have done exactly the same thing,* he went on silently, watching their solemn nods. "So they let themselves be beaten by *women,*" he concluded.

More nods. Daurthunnicar had been magnificently angry when he was finally convinced that Alston *was* a woman, and the other chiefs were horror-struck at the thought of the shame they'd bear if they were thrashed by one.

"I came here because you of Sky Father's tribes live as men should," he went on. *They'll believe that. Vanity springs eternal.* "But that doesn't mean that the Eagle People don't have strong knowledge of war. You're wearing it right now."

All the chiefs had mail hauberks and swords turned out in Walkerburg or brought as part of the *Yare*'s cargo. Hands tightened on those swords as he spoke.

"And they have strong magic—thunder-death. I have the knowledge and the magic, together with the battle-luck of my *rahax,* to throw these woman-ruled foreigners back into the sea, dead. But you must move in better order, and obedient to the High *Rahax*'s will, if we are to conquer now. As my handfast men threw back the Kayaltwar who raided us while our war host was away, so we will crush the Earth Folk and their allies—if you obey."

"And if we don't?" one chief said truculently, leaning forward. The firelight caught the ruddy bronze of the rings that held his braided hair and a black beard twisted into another braid that fell down his chest.

"Then the Iraiina will leave you to them," Walker said.

Daurthunnicar's hands clenched on the carved oak of his chair. It had taken a long day of argument, wheedling, and blunt threats of desertion to get him to go along with that.

"We came to the White Isle only last year," Walker went on, stretching the "we." "With the weapons and arts we have now, we can push back the Keruthinii on the mainland. Anywhere away from the ocean, the Eagle People can't touch us." *And I hope it doesn't occur to you that they could intercept us crossing the Channel, so my threat is empty.* Aloud, he went on:

"But they can stamp *you* flat. You'll be beaten by women, ruled by them . . . and you'll lose your lands and cattle and homes."

More uproar, gradually dying down. "You can beat these Eagle People?" one said at last.

"I believe we can—with Sky Father's help, and by striking hard and fast and skillfully, before they have a chance to teach the Earth Folk how to fight. It isn't courage the Earth Folk men lack; you know that." A few unwilling nods. "It's skill and leadership they want for. With it, and with their numbers . . ."

The tribal chiefs weren't very foresighted men. By the standards of the twentieth, they were insanely impulsive. They were perfectly capable of grasping a fact thrust under their noses, though; many of them looked as if he'd not only thrust a horse turd of fact under their noses but down their throats.

"The Zarthani threw away our chance for a quick victory. We'll have to keep some men here, skirmishing and raiding, until the harvest. Then we'll muster the full levy again. Yes, it's a delay, but that gives us a chance to . . ."

When the talking was finished, Daurthunnicar rose from his high seat beneath the stars. "Now we will make the Great Sacrifice," he said. Horse, hound, and man, offered in the grove. "Tomorrow you will hearten the warriors. And we shall conquer."

"Jesus," someone said softly.

Doreen Arnstein whistled softly herself. A small part of her mind was glad to be able to do that, to do *anything,* without the top of her head feeling as if it were about to pop off. Getting whacked hard enough to knock you out meant headaches, blurred vision, nausea, dizziness, all serious business and lasting for days.

What she saw ahead of her was serious too. She'd seen pictures of Stonehenge, of course. Those sunken, shattered, diminished remnants had nothing to do with the Great Wisdom, whole and living in the bright spring sunshine. The circle of more than twoscore standing stones loomed complete, each fifty tons in weight and topped by their rectangular lintels, making a perfect unbroken circle. Within stood the taller horseshoe shape, five great double uprights with capstones, and the scores of smaller bluestones. Without were concentric rings of earthwork, ditch and bank, and three circles of tall wooden posts wrapped in cords like maypoles.

Not maypoles, she thought. Although children were dancing around several, weaving in and out and chanting in high sweet voices—almost all of them girls. They were observation poles. They varied in height, from twelve feet to thirty; each one would mark the prime position of a star at a given time—or rather, dozens of stars, for each cord could be used at a different angle to give a tangent to . . .

"My God," she murmured. "Keeping all that *straight*!"

She felt an unfamiliar pain in her chest. *So much knowledge, so many centuries.* The Great Wisdom itself was eight hundred years old, in roughly its present form; as old as the Gothic cathedrals had been to her. More impressive still was the huge structure of knowledge, myth, song, ritual that surrounded it, a feat of memory and persistence almost beyond belief. She lost herself in it, forgetting the movement of the saddle betwen her thighs, the crowd around her, her very self. She'd been an astronomer-in-training all her adult life, and the passion that had raised these stones was close kin to hers.

"So Thom and Hawkins were right after all," Ian murmured beside her, jarring. "And I always thought they were cranks."

"Even a stopped clock is right twice a day," Doreen said, equally quiet. "I did too, but they didn't get the half of it. Swindapa's mother, Dhinwarn, what really won her over was that list of lunar eclipses I ran off the computer back on the island. You know, they have a complete series for more than a *thousand* years back? And predictions for several centuries—that's one thing they use that ring of fifty-six holes for, besides those sighting posts."

Ian grinned. "Remember when you said how useless an astronomer in the Bronze Age was? You're our damned passport to these people!"

"Let's hope I'm as persuasive to all the Grandmothers as I was to Dhinwarn. She had a personal reason to like us. I get the impression that a lot of the others are pretty xenophobic."

The horses turned away from the monument itself, toward one of the big half-timbered roundhouses. Another chorus of girls sang and danced an intricate measure around them. Waiting to meet them were a clump of older women, wrapped in cloaks and silent dignity.

"End-of-semester exams," Doreen muttered, feeling her stomach clench.

"What's that sound?" Miskelefol said, craning his neck.

There was a full moon tonight, but it was hidden by high scudding cloud. Nothing showed on the water, only an occasional gleam of white as an oar stroked the calm surface of the bay. They dared not show lights, and only the loom of the land to his right kept them from being completely lost, that and the instincts of a life spent at sea.

Isketerol cocked his head to one side, lifting the helmet. "Sort of a buzzing sound, isn't it?" he said. "I don't know, some sort of insect?" The life here was still fairly strange to him. "At least it isn't raining much."

"Hurrah, the first time in months," Miskelefol said dolorously.

They shared a quiet chuckle, and then their craft swung apart. There were five of them in all, long low things like miniature galleys, each with ten oars to a side. The *Yare* and *Sea Wolf* had towed them here, but stayed well off to sea now. The night breeze was directly out of the west, and it would pin any ship at anchor into its port. Even with the *Yare*'s ability to beat to windward he wouldn't like to have to claw off this coast right now, particularly with the shallow water and shifting sandbars common through here. He risked a brief flash of lamplight to check the compass strapped to his left wrist. *Marvelous things*, he thought again.

"Take a turn around the canoes," he whispered to the helmsman.

The seaman leaned against the tiller. Rudders were wonderful too, so *fast*. The crew bent to the oars with only a whisper of noise, sculling in perfect unison. Isketerol gripped the lead stay that kept the pole in the bows upright. Not to hold sails; it was topped by a barrel, and a long cord ran back along the pole. Loose *here,* and the pole would fall until the barrel submerged twenty feet ahead of the bows. Pull on this cord, and a flint-and-steel inside the barrel would spark . . . and the load of *gunpowder* would ignite. They'd tested it against rafts; the results were spectacular enough to make hardened sailors soil their loincloths. The effect on a ship's hull, underwater . . . The Tartessian smiled and licked his lips.

He frowned as they approached the canoes and coracles. The Sun tribes weren't seamen at the best of times, and in the dark they blundered in continuous near-panic, just as they had ever since they climbed down the sides of the ships and into these smaller craft. He hissed warnings and threats and shaming insults across the water as his larger boat coasted by, bringing a *little* more quiet. *I wish they weren't along at all.* They might be useful to ram victory home, but they endangered it beforehand.

"This heading," he said quietly to the man at the tiller. "Slow, all, now."

Around a headland and there was the target, backlit by the fires ashore. Tall masts raking for the sky, the *Eagle*. On either side of it were the smaller shapes of the *Tubman* and *Douglass,* all three ships anchored at stern and bow with about a hundred yards in between. *Pinned down and helpless,* he thought. Arucuttag of the Sea had delivered them into his hands, and in the silence of his head he promised the Hungry One good feeding. There were fires and lanterns in the fortified camp a few hundred yards farther upstream, but they could do nothing. Will reported that better than three hundred of the Amurrukan were marching inland, far from their base. That left only a score or so per ship, and as many in the fort ashore.

The five boats with the spar torpedoes swung into line, quick flashes of shuttered lanterns guiding them as they'd practiced. The men at the tiller were all well trained, and they'd worked out a simple code to direct them to their targets.

"Forward!" he shouted.

The oarsmen bent to their work, the ashwood shafts flexing in their hands.

"Take your eyes off the Swedish Bikini Team, will you?" Doreen said. "This is serious."

With something of an effort, Ian Arnstein obeyed. The two girls who'd been washing his feet were both about Swindapa's age and looked a good deal like her. They were also wearing nothing but their string skirts, and he thought he understood the glances and smiles. Unfortunately, so did his wife.

He sighed, belched slightly from an excellent if unfamiliar meal, and put his mind back to business.

These Fiernan houses seemed to be much of a muchness, varying only in style and size. This one was huge, and circular like all the bigger ones. The walls were a framework of oak timbers carefully mortised and pegged together; the intervals were filled with rammed clay, chalk, and flints, covered thickly with lime plaster. Carved pillars made of whole tree trunks stood in three rings inside, and two huge freestanding gateposts like Abstract Expressionist totem poles marked the southeastern door. There were doors at the four quarters of the building, man-tall and made of pegged oak boards, but they were merely fitted into slots, not hung from hinges. When they were opened, as now, the dwellers simply lifted them out and leaned them against the wall. That let in some light, and more of the fresh spring air, along with a little of the fresh British spring drizzle. More of that came down the big central smokehole at the top of the roof, but not too much—there was a little conical cap over it, leaving a rim all around for smoke to escape through. The fire there flickered in a stone-lined depression in the earth that caught the heat and radiated it back out. Such of the smoke as evaded the hole in the roof drifted blue among the rafters and pillars above, joining that from ordinary family hearths spaced around the big building and gradually filtering out through the thatch.

"Not as squalid as I'd have expected," Ian said to his wife.

She nodded. The interior of the greathouse was cut up

by partitions of wicker and split plank, marking out the notional space of family groups smaller than the great inter-related cousinage that shared this dwelling, each with its own fire. The Fiernans didn't suffer from shyness; they stared, chattered, pointed, asked question after question, held children up at the back of the crowd to get a look. They also pressed things on the visitors, bits of honeycomb, cups of mead flavored with flowers and herbs, pieces of dried fruit.

"And there's the Archaeologist's Nightmare," he said, nodding to a pillar.

Doreen raised a brow, and he went on: "See how the post's resting on a stone block?"

"That's bad for archaeology?"

"Very. I asked, and these people used to set their posts right into the ground for big buildings like this. Post holes like that leave traces—you can dig them up thousands of years later, if the conditions are right. Then they switched over to resting the uprights on stone blocks so they wouldn't rot . . . and that *doesn't* leave any trace, if someone takes the block away later. The stones-and-bones crowd were as puzzled as hell, wondering why the locals suddenly stopped building big round houses. . . . Oh-oh, look out."

Silence spread out through the folk like a ripple through water. Like a wave they sank down on their haunches, leaving a path clear. More of the Grandmothers came to sit by the edge of the fire. Two more walked on either side of a still older woman; the helpers were in their sixties, unambiguously *old,* white-haired and wrinkled, but hale. If you ran the gauntlet of childhood diseases and made it to adulthood, you had some hope of seeing the Biblical threescore and ten here, about one chance in five. The Kurlelo were what passed for an upper class among the Earth Folk, too, partly supported by the gifts of the pious, and so not quite as likely to be prematurely aged by a Bronze Age peasant's endless toil.

The woman the junior Grandmothers were helping along was far older than threescore and ten; older than God, from her looks. Thin white hair bound by a headband carrying a silver moon; sunken cheeks, lips fallen in over a mouth where most teeth were gone; back bent forever. The attendants fussed around her as she sank painfully onto cushions and a wicker backrest, tucking her star-embroidered blue cloak around her and putting a closed clay dish full of embers beneath her feet for warmth. She shooed them aside impatiently and leaned forward a little, long gnarled spotted hands leaning on a stick whose end was carved into a bird's head—an owl, here as in later ages the symbol of the moon.

Her pouched and faded eyes traveled across the assembly. Ian Arnstein felt a disinct slight chill as they met his. The mind that rested behind them was not in the least enfeebled. This was the one who'd received the reports of the Grandmothers who interviewed the Americans, day after day.

"Swin . . . dapa," the old woman said, her voice hoarse but feather-soft. It carried clearly; there were no other sounds in the greathouse, save for the crackling of fires and a quickly hushed baby, and the breathing of sixscore.

The young Fiernan came forward and crouched at the ancient woman's feet. *Great-grandmother?* Ian wondered. *Great-great?*

The knotted fingers raised Swindapa's face, and the ancient leaned forward to kiss her on the brow. They exchanged murmurs, too quiet to carry, and Swindapa turned and sat cross-legged at her feet.

"I will give you the Grandmother's words," she said.

The old woman paused for a long moment, lips moving slightly, hands gripped on the owl-headed staff.

"Uhot'na," she said at last. *"InHOja, inyete, abal'na."*

Her hand shaped the air as she spoke; after a moment her age-cracked voice merged with Swindapa's clear soprano, and Ian forgot he was listening to a translation.

"A good star shine on this meeting. Moon Woman gather it to her breast. Long ago—" Swindapa hesitated, translating from her people's lunar calendar. "Thousands of years ago, the Grandmothers of the Grandmothers came here to the White Isle. They came bearing gifts; the gift of planting and sowing, of weaving and the making of pots, the herding of cattle and sheep, many good things. The Old Ones, the hunters, came and learned these things, and their lives became better, and they became us, and we became them."

The old woman's hand rose skyward. *"awHUMna inyetewan dama'uhot'nawakwa—"*

"Best of all, they brought knowledge of Moon Woman

and Her children the stars, Her sisters of the woods and earth—knowledge of foretelling and understanding. In those days Her messengers traveled from the Hot Lands to the Ice-and-Fog Place, and everywhere they brought Her wisdom, and the knowledge of the building of the Wisdoms and the studying of the stars."

Another long pause; her eyelids drifted downward, covering the faded brilliance for a while. *Is she asleep?* Ian wondered. Then they flickered open:

"atTOwak em'dayaus'arsi immiHEyet—"

"Then the Sun People came from the eastlands where the morning is born, fierce and greedy like little boys grown tall without learning a man's manners, and the great—" Swindapa paused, obviously hunting for a word. "—great harmony-in-changing-time-again-and-again was . . . made to not turn as it should, and as we had thought it would through all the changings of the world."

A pause, and the old woman spoke very softly. *"soSHo t'euho'nis kwas dazya'll—"*

"And since then, the Grandmothers have looked into the future and seen only a darkness without stars before the feet of the Earth Folk."

A slight shocked murmur went through the crowd. The old woman sighed, and went on. Swindapa's voice translated:

"Every turning, the Moon Woman grows old and comes again. So too for all things. Our moon is past full, we wane, perhaps these strangers bring a new one."

Swindapa's face lit as she spoke, a grin breaking through her solemnity. "These Eagle People also study the stars, although not in our way. Already they have shown us things of great worth—the three rules that govern the movement of the planets, and the law of squares of distances that explains them."

Ian squeezed Doreen's hand. She'd thrown the cat among the pigeons well and truly, with that dose of Keppler, seasoned with a smidgin of Newton and soupçon of Laplace. For a while they'd been afraid the Grandmothers would start tearing out clumps of each other's hair over the implications.

"ShahShar'it yewehkey'a—"

"They are the only strangers who tread that path, and they have dealt well with us. The Grandmothers will tell the Council of the Sacred Truce to listen to their words, and follow them if they find them good."

Captain Alston bowed where she sat. Ian felt Doreen jab an elbow in his ribs. They looked at each other in the flickering firelight; she was grinning like a cat. Solemnly, they shook hands.

Commander Sandy Rapczewicz smiled as she slipped down the night-sight goggles. Wouldn't the skipper be livid that she wasn't here, although she'd anticipated this might happen. It was the logical move, after all, and Walker had a high opinion of logic. *I hope you're out there tonight, you son of a bitch,* she thought vindictively. *Break my jaw, will you?* It still ached in cold wet weather. Hell of a thing for a sailor.

"Ready," she said aloud, and into the microphone.

"Ready," the earphones answered back.

The goggles turned everything greenish and flat. She could see an occasional whitecap out on the water, and the giant rowboats heading for the Nantucket flotilla, with the canoes following. More than enough to shatter the hulls and swarm over the Nantucketers left behind when the main expeditionary force moved inland, as the enemy's scouts had surely reported to Walker.

"Only we weren't idle over the winter either, Will-me-lad," she muttered. Louder: "Fire!"

The fruits of the ROATS program stood along the rail. Crews made their final adjustments, turning aiming screws. Then the master gunner stepped back from each and jerked the lanyard.

TUNNNGG.

They were compact little engines, the throwing arms powered by a mass of coil springs from heavy trucks caught on the island by the Event. They were also more accurate than any counterweight system like a trebuchet, or catapults powered by twisted sinew. Four balls of fire soared out through the night from the *Eagle,* two from each of the schooners. Where they struck they splashed on the water, burning with a hot red ferocity. Searchlights stabbed out, actinic blue-white through the cloud-dark night.

"Fire at will!" Rapczewicz shouted.

"Reach Out and Touch Someone—*fire!*" a crew chief shouted.

Hands pumped at levers. Back on shore, within the earth walls of the Nantucketer fort, came a heavy *chuff . . . chuff . . .* sound. It built to a faster *chufchufchufchuf* and then into a racketing snarl.

"Demons!" Misklefol screamed.

"Shut up!" Isketerol shouted, clouting him savagely across the side of his helmeted head.

More of the fireballs arched across the night. The whale oil burning on the surface of the water gave a ghastly semblance of daylight. One of them splashed onto the galley next to his. It was close enough to hear the glass shatter and the men scream as oil splashed them. Seconds later it caught with a *whump,* a sound somehow soft and large at the same time, like a giant catching his breath. Or a dragon. Men screamed again, louder, as flame ran down the length of the boat. They cast themselves overboard, diving if they could. Others thrashed in mindless agony, and the oars drooped limp into the water. After an instant, the Tartessian realized what was going to happen when the flames reached the barrel at the prow of the little galley.

"Right!" he screamed to the man at the tiller. "Hard right, Arucuttag eat you, *quickly!*"

The oars kept moving. Isketerol crouched down behind the scant shelter of the tiller and helmsman, counting the seconds and trying to control the pounding of his heart.

"Four . . . five . . ."

CRACK. A hot breath passed over his back, and the helmsman cried out. Isketerol grabbed the helm as the man collapsed, pawing at a wound in his neck. He braced his feet and clamped the timber between arm and ribs, struggling to keep the galley on course as a wave lifted its hull. Bits of burning timber scattered across the waters; a quick glance rearward showed nothing left of the stricken galley but fragments, and another sinking beyond it.

"Over to the canoes," he said, and called to his signaler. "*Sound retreat* and *rally to me,*" he barked.

The man began swinging his lanterns; the signals had been Will's. The tribesmen in the canoes were sitting motionless, staring open-mouthed.

"Cowards!" Isketerol called through a speaking trumpet.

"You flee, southron!" one of them cried in response.

They looked over their shoulders, fearfully conscious of

the fact that nothing waited out there but the River Ocean and ships under the Tartessian's command—unlikely to help them home if they defied him. If they beached their canoes away from the Eagle People fort, they'd still be in the middle of enemy country, and hunted like hares as they tried to run east to their homes.

"These rowing boats are too big—the Eagle People can pick them out." Isketerol said. "Your canoes and hide boats are small and many. Paddle in quickly, and most of you will get through—you can swarm over them, while we follow close behind. Are you warriors, or little girls who weep with fear?"

A few canoes broke away from the pack and headed for the land that bulked dark to the south. The rest stayed, as the men shouted among themselves. Then they fanned out, heading for the firelit shapes of the Eagle People ships.

His own remaining craft gathered around them. "Hang back," he said to them in his own tongue. "Let the savages clear the path for us. If they can put those catapults out of action or occupy their crews, we can attack behind them."

One of the boat captains looked puzzled. "But most of the tribesmen will die, if we attack with our *torpedoes*"— the word was English—"while they are trying to board."

"So?" Isketerol grinned. "Should I weep for them? Are they kindred, townsmen of ours?"

"It'll be dangerous," the man warned.

"A man lives as long as he lives, and not a day more," Isketerol said—a saying Will had told him, and a good one. "If I'd known you were a woman, Dekendol, we could have gotten more use out of you this last winter."

The crews laughed at that; it was a little ragged, but he judged their spirit was still unbroken. "Spread out again," he said. "Lie on your oars just outside of catapult range"— the farthest those balls of fire had gone was about a quarter mile—"and then dash in if the barbarians make headway."

They turned, their formation opening like a fan, and stroked carefully to the edge of safety. "Wait for it!" he called. "Wait, and then put out all your strength!"

"On the word of command," Sandy Rapczewicz said. *Fuck it. Someone got clever out there.*

There were dozens of the canoes, scores of them. Impossible to hit that many, and they were nimble enough to dodge most of the fireballs. Here and there one was struck, but even then the others could dart in and rescue most of their crews from the water. The others came steadily on to a wild pounding chant of voices.

"Here's where we could use a couple of cannon, loaded with grapeshot," she muttered to herself.

That wouldn't be possible for another year or so. Evidently Walker had found the raw materials for gunpowder in greater abundance; those spar-torpedo boats waiting off at the edge of sight showed how he'd used the sulfur and saltpeter and charcoal. They were silent, in contrast to the barbarian warriors in the canoes. Closer, closer . . .

"Now!" she shouted.

A crewman at the rail swung a long thin barrel, crouching behind it with hands on the grips. Behind him two more pumped frantically, a dark glistening stream arching out from it. Another stretched out a burning wad of rags on the end of a long pole, and the stream of whale oil caught. *Whooosh*-WHUMP, and it was a long arch of dripping flame, scything back and forth through the night. Men screamed as they turned to blazing torches and threw themselves into water that had turned to a lake of flame. The edges of it lapped up against *Eagle*'s steel hull, and the canoes that had approached her were billows in the fiery sea. The air filled with the heavy nutty scent of burning whale oil, and the stink of burned flesh as well.

Rapczewicz whipped her head back and forth. The two wooden schooners couldn't use such a weapon, not without destroying themselves; they'd anchored well away, too. They *did* each have hundreds of Fiernan Spear Chosen packed below their decks. As the Sun People warriors scrambled up the sides, the Earth Folk fighters came screaming up the companionways. They boiled to the sides, stabbing with spears, slamming clubs down on Sun People heads and arms and fingers.

A cry behind her. *"Boarders!"*

Some of the canoes had circled around and were approaching from the landward side. The *Eagle*'s skeleton crew dashed to meet them, drawing weapons or snatching javelins from racks along the rail. Wrought-iron grapnels came upward at the ends of knotted ropes, and the warriors behind them. Armored Americans stabbed and shoved and tried to cut the grapnels free, but the ropes were wound with metal wire for several feet down from the loops that held them to the iron hooks.

Rapczewicz drew the radio with her left hand. "Rapczewicz to Pentagon Base," she said. "Report status."

"Base One here. Status is *go*, ma'am."

"Do it. Rapczewicz out."

Her right hand drew the Colt and thumbed back the hammer. A bearded warrior in a kilt tried to force his way through a gap. She fired at two yards' distance, and a round blue hole appeared in the man's forehead. The back of his head blew away, and he toppled backward to land on a canoe and overturn it. She blinked to let the muzzle flash that strobed across her vision die away, then aimed at another point-blank target.

Isketerol of Tartessos flung up a hand to shield his eyes from the glare of the flame, keeping his other braced against the gunwale. The raw wood was rough and splintery under his palm, reminding him unpleasantly of how fast it could burn.

"Dragon's breath!" his cousin said, his voice trembling.

"Dragon's shit," Isketerol said, and spat over the side. "Remember the pump?"

Misklefol turned to him, his eyes wide and tinted red by the light. "The *pump*?" he said incredulously.

Walker had rigged up a piston-style pump for the Tartessian encampment, sucking through a cast-iron pipe from a deep well.

"Well, think, cousin. That's a pump there, only it's spurting out oil—fish oil, whale oil. Then they set it alight."

The terror of the supernatural faded out of the other Tartessian's eyes. "That's clever," he said. "But using it on a *ship*—"

"On a ship of *steel*," Isketerol said, peering through his binoculars. "Wait . . . the savages are heading around to the other side of *Eagle*. And they're closing in on the schooners, by the Crone. More balls than sense."

Misklefol tensed. "If they can carry them—"

"No." Isketerol spat again, peering through the dark. "Too many fighters—more on board than I thought they could have, hidden belowdecks. May the Crone's knife *cut* the fatherless sheep-sucking bitch, she's clever."

As clever as you? Isketerol thought uneasily. *As clever as Will?*

"Still, they're heavily engaged. We may be able to run—"

He was about to raise his voice in a shouted order to close in when the *chuffchuffchuff* sound from the Amurrukan camp rose in pitch and speed. A high shrill whistle clove the air; he recognized it, a steam whistle from one of the hot-water-engines the Amurrukan used on Nantucket. Then it changed to a hard quick rapping sound, as of a stick dragged quickly down a set of iron rods.

The air whistled, a different note. One of the rowers pitched sideways, threshing. Isketerol could see the fletching on the short heavy dart that stood three-quarters buried in the man's temple. Another two quivered in the timbers of the galley, sunk almost as deep. The water whickered to his right as a spray of the same missiles hit it. The full force had struck the galley to his left, and half the rowers were down. His eyes widened. *That's over two thousand paces away!* his mind protested. Then it leaped quickly, to the big spinning wheels the steam engines had . . . flywheels, that was the word. If you could somehow make a flywheel grab and throw arrows—

"Back to the ships! Retreat! Retreat!" he bellowed through the megaphone.

The galley leaped in the water as it turned. Isketerol forced himself not to crouch or cringe. "What *next*?" he screamed, shaking his fist backward at the taunting reach of *Eagle's* masts. It wasn't fair. "You'll pay for this!"

The buzzing noise overhead was back, and louder.

The radio beeped. Swindapa murmured in her sleep and then stirred, waked from her doze as much by her companion slipping out from under the blankets as by the noise. Low words followed, lost before she was fully conscious of them.

Marian was smiling as she came back toward the bed; Swindapa could feel it, if not see it, but the smile was not a happy one. Reeds crackled and rustled under her feet, but she was invisible with only the faint reddish ghost-glow reflected from the beams and thatch above.

"What happened?" Swindapa asked drowsily.

The wicker partitions gave them privacy from sight, but

none from sound. It wasn't *very* noisy; a dog stirring now and then, a baby crying, a couple making love, the low crackle of the central hearth. Swindapa found the noises broke her rest more than she'd expected. *That's strange. This is home. How can it be hard to sleep, when I slept here all my life?* Without the woven walls, either—those were for elders. She was glad of the flea powder Marian had sprinkled on their bedding, too. *I've become fussy.* Her relatives had stared as she ate with a fork and wiped her lips with a cloth.

"What happened?" Marian repeated. Her voice had a growling undertone. "The ships back at Pentagon Base were attacked—the Tartessians, we think, with local allies."

Swindapa stiffened and gripped her as she slid beneath the blankets. "What *happened*?"

Marian gave a whispering wolf-chuckle. "Let's put it this way—the flamethrowers worked."

"Oh." *A bad death,* she thought. *On the shadow side, they deserved it. If they want to live long, let them stay at home.* "Good."

The black woman sighed after a moment. "I was worried," she admitted, her voice soft against Swindapa's shoulder. "Damn worried. Complex plan. Too many things that could have gone wrong. And I couldn't *be* there."

The Fiernan smiled in the darkness, holding her close and stroking her back, feeling the tension in the muscles. *So many worries,* she thought. *Only me to hear them.* Marian bore a weight heavier than the Grandmother of Grandmothers knew. For everyone else she must always be strong.

"It did work," the Fiernan said. Lips met in darkness. "Now forget that, and pay attention to me. And this."

"Sugar, I'm a little tired—*mmmm!*"

"You're not tired, you're tense. And you're pretty . . . so pretty."

Some time later Marian was quivering again. "If you only knew how *fine* that feels," she sighed.

"I know *exactly* how it feels," Swindapa purred. "But maybe this will feel even better."

Marian made a choked sound, turned her head aside and bit into the coarse wool of the blanket, then relaxed with a long sigh.

"You're not tense anymore," Swindapa chuckled, raising

herself on her elbows and peering up toward the other's face.

A hand ran fingers through her hair. "Any less tense and I may just flow away like watah. Why don't you move up here a little?"

Later a cry mounted up from belly to throat, escaping like the swans that bore souls to the moon.

Afterward, a fierce whisper in her ear with unwilling laughter underneath it. "Did you have to *yell* like that, 'dapa?"

Swindapa stretched, blinking and wiggling her toes in pure contentment. "Of course I did, my love," she said. "I had to think of your . . . your reputation, you'd say." She turned and snuggled closer. "Now everyone will think *I'm* selfish, but they'll know you aren't."

CHAPTER TWENTY-ONE

Seahaven Engineering had a sales shop attached to it these days. It was a long wooden structure reaching out from one side near what had been the front entrance, covering a stretch of redundant parking lot. Most of the shop sold metalware to islanders, everything from hardware to eggbeaters, sausage grinders to sheet-steel stoves, but one corner was devoted to the mainland trade. As he came through the door Jared Cofflin suppressed an impulse to hold his breath at the sight of the four Indians there; there was just nothing they could *do* about diseases, except take a few precautions and otherwise let them run their course. Unless they cut the mainland off completely, and that just wasn't practical.

One of the Indians was a man, hook-nosed in a narrow high-cheeked impassive face, looking weathered and ageless and probably in his thirties; his hair was shaved to a strip down the center of his head and a pigtail behind, the bare scalp on either side painted vermilion in a fashion that seemed common to all the New England tribes in this era— at least, they hadn't met any that didn't do it that way, just as the women all wore theirs in braids. His body was naked except for a hide breechclout and an islander blanket over one shoulder; he had a steel-bladed knife on one hip, and a long-hafted island-made trade hatchet thrust through the back of his belt. The women wore a longer wraparound of soft-tanned deerskin like a short skirt, with ornaments of shell beads and bones around their necks and porcupine-quill work on their clothes. One of them was in her twenties, with a bundle-wrapped baby on her hip, the others in their early teens; they all carried heavy basketwork containers on their backs. Cofflin could smell them, a sort of hard summery odor combined with leather and the oil on their hair.

At a gesture from the man they set their burdens down on the single oak plank that served as a counter, four feet broad and four inches thick. Behind it were racks with the goods that held his eye: steel knives, spearheads, axes, hatchets, fishhooks and line, nets with lead sinkers, metal traps. The women were chattering with each other and pointing as well, at metal pots and pans, awls, scissors, cloth, cards of needles—Cofflin knew from reports that they used tailored and sewn clothing of leather in cold weather. One made a soft exclamation as she picked up a necklace of burnished copper pennies and let it run through her hands, then ducked her head obediently as the man spoke sharply and put it down again. A third looked guilty as she put aside a mirror. The islander behind the counter helped unload the sacks; Cofflin whistled silently at the sight of pure-white winter ermine pelts. Fur coats had become extremely popular over the cold winter months without oil for central heating. Besides that, the packs seemed to contain only small quantities of any one item: bark jars of nuts, crystallized maple sugar, dozens of varieties of herbs and plants and patches of deer, elk, moose, and beaver hide.

"Doesn't seem to be much of anything there, Jack," Cofflin said.

Jack Elkins looked up. "Hi, Chief! No, it's samples. Hardcase here—that's as close as I can get to pronouncing his name—"

"At least it wasn't King Phillip," Martha muttered.

"—brings the samples here, we show him what we've got, we agree on quantities, and he brings the actual stuff to Providence Base over on the mainland and picks up his merchandise. Easier that way. I think he's collecting from a lot of his friends and relatives, sort of an entrepreneur."

Cofflin blinked, surprised. "Mighty fancy deal, since you can't talk to him," he said.

"Oh, he's picked up a little English," Elkins said.

The Indian looked up from sorting his goods. "Hardcase very good talk English," he said with an indescribable accent, then inclined his head in an odd gesture and returned to his work.

"And you can do a lot by holding up fingers and such."

"Ayup," Cofflin replied. *Well, they may not have a market economy, but they understand swapping.* "Surprised they can spare the time to find all this stuff."

Martha nodded. "Lot of underemployment in most hunter-gatherer economies," she said. "No point in working to get a surplus, because there's nothing you can do with it. We provide an outlet, and the trade will build up fast. Provided there are any Indians left around here to do business with."

Jared winced. Meanwhile Elkins was demonstrating a metal gadget about the size of his hand. He crumbled tinder into a shallow pan. Above that was a steel wheel with a roughened surface; the islander wound up a spring inside it with a spanner key. Then he clicked a holder with a piece of flint in it against the surface of the wheel and pressed a release stud. The wheel spun against the flint, releasing a shower of sparks into the pan. Elkins blew on the tinder softly, then tipped it out into a clay dish on the counter full of wood shavings. They caught and sent a tendril of smoke upward. The islander waited until flames were crackling, then smothered them with a lid.

The Indian's eyes flared interest as he took the fire-starter up, turning it over and over in his fingers. Cofflin wasn't surprised; he'd seen Martha's Scouts demonstrate using a bow-type fire drill. Fifteen minutes to start a fire, if you were lucky—and everything was bone-dry. Evidently the local Indians hadn't even gotten that far. They were still using the older method of twirling a stick between the palms, and that could take *hours*. This would be a real improvement.

Of course, once they're used to it, they'll be dependent on it, he thought uneasily. The same went for woven cloth and metal tools, even more so. Martha nodded when he voiced the thought aloud, and replied:

"No telling. No telling how that virus epidemic disrupted their society either. . . . Nothing much we can do, dear."

One of the Indian women had looked up with a startled expression at Martha's voice, and she put her hand to her mouth in a gesture of surprise. Cofflin followed her gaze; his daughter was in a stroller in front of his wife, sleeping peacefully. The Indian woman craned her head to see around the hood of the baby carriage, then came over to look down. She unslung her own—*well, papoose, I sup-*

pose—and held it out to Martha, smiling broadly and speaking in her own fast-rising, slow-falling language. Martha smiled back at her and picked up young Marian; the women held their babies side by side, the Indian fascinated by the pink skin and the cloth diaper with its safety pin. She exclaimed and laughed when the American demonstrated that, bringing her own around to nurse as she did so. The Cofflins' child yawned, waved pudgy hands, and went back to sleep.

Well, only fair, Jared thought, smiling. *She didn't do much sleeping last night, and so neither did we.*

The man's voice rose behind them. Then he was at the Indian woman's side, pulling her away with a swift hard tug on one braid. She cried out sharply in pain, then stood half-crouched. He cuffed her across the side of the head, then raised the hand again.

"Hold it, dickweed!"

The guard who'd been sitting unobtrusively on a stool in one corner pushed between them. There was a bolt locked into the firing groove of her crossbow, the edges of the three-bladed head glinting cruel and sharp in the sunlight that came through the window behind her. The Indian froze. One hand moved very slightly toward the knife at his belt.

"Back off, shithead!" the guard barked. "Now. I mean it, fucker. Back off or your liver does the shish kebab thing."

Sweat beaded the Indian's forehead; he knew exactly what one of those crossbows could do. The Nantucketers had demonstrated, and also refused to sell them at any price. Behind him the clerk brought another out from under the counter and laid it on the wood with a small deliberate clatter. The Indian drew himself up, turned, and walked back to his bundles of goods, the woman with the papoose following meekly behind him. The bargaining resumed, slow and stiff.

Cofflin let out a breath he hadn't been conscious of holding. Martha put the baby back in the carriage, tucking her in; there was a small protesting murmur.

"You have much trouble like that?" Cofflin asked the guard. *Amelia Seckel,* his mind prompted him. As far as he knew, she was working for Seahaven's clerical department. "Ms. Seckel," he added.

"Nope, not often, Chief. Just, you know, sometimes with

these guys you have to use, like, visual aids to get things across." She patted her crossbow. "It's the universal language. That's why Ron has one of us out here when they're in to trade, me or John or Fred Carter. Hey, cute kid! You want I should watch her while you're in there? Bit noisy on the workshop floor for a youngster."

"Thanks, Ms. Seckel, I'll take you up on that," he said. "Culture clash," he murmured to his wife as they turned for the main entrance.

Martha nodded, her mouth still drawn thin. "Well, that settles Angelica's notion, I think."

"What—oh."

Angelica Brand had been wondering aloud at Council meetings if they couldn't recruit some temporary harvest labor on the mainland. It *would* be extremely convenient; with enough seed and to spare, they were clearing more land and planting a *lot* more this year, and every other project was crying out for hands as well. Putting everything on hold while they got in the harvest was an absolute pain in the fundament—and the various crops meant that harvest stretched through most of the summer and on into fall.

On the other hand, the locals didn't look like being the best imaginable *braceros,* and anyway, it was a bad precedent to start relying on foreign labor, he supposed.

"I see what you mean."

Martha nodded again, a gesture sharp enough to cut hide. "Well, there's always the Sir Charles Napier method of cultural reconciliation," she said. At his raised eyebrow, she went on: "He was a British governor in India, back— you know what I mean—in the 1830s. A delegation of Brahmins came to him and complained that he was oppressing them by forbidding *suttee,* widow-burning, that it was part of their religion."

"What did he tell them?" Cofflin asked, curious.

"Roughly . . ." She assumed a British accent; it wasn't too different from her native academic New England:

"It is your custom to burn widows. We also have a custom. When men burn a woman alive, we take those men, tie a rope around their necks, and hang them. Build your funeral pyre; beside it my carpenters will build a gallows. You may follow your national custom. And then we will follow ours."

A few people looked up as Cofflin guffawed. *"There's*

British understatement for you," he said. "We're not really in a position to do much crusading, though."

"No, but we'll do what we can where we can." She swallowed. "That's one thing I became quite determined about during the . . . episode . . . down south."

He touched her shoulder, squeezing in reassurance.

"I didn't think Indians were so hard on women," he said, changing the subject. "The Iroquois and all that."

"Depends," Martha said, relaxing. "Lots of variation from time to time and place to place, tribe to tribe—well, Sicily and Sweden weren't exactly alike up in the twentieth, were they? Or New England and south Texas, come to that. Offhand, I'd say it was agriculture that made the difference here. When these woodland Indians took—would have taken—up maize and bean farming, women raised the crops and it probably increased their general say in things."

The inside of the machine shop *was* noisy, also steamy and hot despite the big doors leading to the water being left open. There were four large steam engines going now. Dozens of lathes, grinders, drill presses, and machines more complex whined and growled and screamed. As the Cofflins entered a yell of triumph went up from a crowd at the far end of the building. They walked over, peering at the new machine. It was vaguely shaped like an elongated upright C on a heavy flat base, about twelve feet tall; a cylinder was fixed by wrist-thick bolts to the top, and from it depended a heavy rod with a hammerlike weight at the end. A steel-slab anvil rested below it; Ron Leaton was just placing an egg on that. He stepped back, gripped a lever with a theatrical flourish, and pulled it toward him. The hammer on the end of the piston rod came down on the egg . . . and stopped, barely touching it. The control lever sent it back upward with a hiss and *chunk* sound.

Leaton stepped forward, grinning, and picked up the egg. He peeled it—hard-boiled, evidently—and ate it with ostentatious relish. The crowd dispersed back to their tasks, laughing and back-slapping.

"Another masterpiece of invention?" Cofflin asked dryly.

"Naysmith's steam hammer—pneumatic, actually; we're using compressed air," Leaton said cheerfully, wiping his hands on his inevitable oily rag and stuffing it back into a pocket of his overalls. "He did that bit with the egg to show it had precision as well as a heavy wallop, and I thought, what the hell, it worked for him—" He shrugged. "It'll be really useful, now that we're making progress with that cupola furnace. With that and the hammer, we can start doing some real forging work—crankshafts, propeller shafts even."

"Good work," Cofflin said, sincerely impressed. Leaton was a godsend; without the seed of his little basement shop, the island as a whole would be a lot farther behind than it was. "What was it you wanted to discuss with us, Ron?" He had a couple of things to say himself, but it was easier if Leaton started the conversation.

"Well, a couple of things, Jared, Martha," the proto-industrialist said.

The three of them walked over to his office, a plank box built in a corner. They ducked in and lifted tools, samples, plans, and parts off the board chairs before they sat.

"First thing is, I need more lubricants and more leather for drive belts," he said.

"Talk to the whaling skippers and Delms," Cofflin said immediately. Delms had taken over the contract on the whale rendery down by the Easy Street basin, with a tannery as a sideline. Cofflin approved. Let *Delms* take the continuous flack for the way it smelled. There was a motion afoot to have the whole thing moved farther from town, anyway, and the bonemeal plant and salting works along with it.

His mouth quirked up at one corner. "Government's out of that business, Ron. Thank God."

"And we're getting too much ash built up here," Leaton said. The engines were all wood-fired, and the valuable waste was supposed to go onto the soil immediately.

"Take *that* up with Angelica and the farmers," Cofflin replied promptly. This time he grinned outright. "It's their fertilizer. Government's out of that, too. *Christ,* but it's good to be able to say that!"

Leaton laughed ruefully. "All right, what good *are* you these days?" He shook his head. "The Town still *is* in charge of unused buildings, isn't it? We could use double the space."

Jared and Martha looked at each other. She cleared her throat. "Ronald, the Council *has* been considering that. We were thinking that it might be advisable to have some of your people start their own engineering shops, for the simpler work. Town would help them get started, the way it did you."

"Oh." Leaton blinked, surprised. "Not satisfied with the job I'm doing?" he asked, sounding slightly hurt.

"Hell no," Jared said. "You're doing a wonderful job. It's policy. Better to have competition, ayup? And we want to encourage people to set up on their own, not have too many on wages."

"Oh." Leaton frowned thoughtfully. "You know, that's not a bad idea, now that I come to think of it. Must be a bit annoying, only having me to come to when you need something done."

Glad you see the point, Cofflin thought with an inaudible sigh of relief. These days it seemed that everyone on the island had a wonderful idea that needed a machine built to do it, everything from flax-crushing and ropemaking to pressing hazelnut oil, and only Seahaven to do any of it. It was better to have a lot of little firms, where more people had a chance to become their own boss. *Speaking of which* . . . He glanced over at Martha.

"We were talking with Starbuck about organizing the financial setup here, too," she said. "Now that things are getting less informal. Organizing Seahaven as a company, that is. You put up your experience and the original machine tools, the Town provides the building and all the raw materials we've furnished, and the staff gets a share too that they hold as a block trust, and anyone can cash their share out if they leave. We thought that forty-thirty-thirty would be a proper ratio, organized as a joint-stock company. It won't make all that much practical difference right away, but for the long term . . ."

"Ah." Leaton frowned even harder. "Well, to tell you the truth, I've been thinking about organization myself, this last couple of months. Right now we've got everything jumbled up together—splitting up a bit would help, ah, even out the flows all 'round. Save time and effort. For example, we made up the blowers and hearth and so forth for the glassmaking plant, but there's no earthly reason it should be run as part of Seahaven."

"Exactly," Cofflin said, relieved.

Martha nodded. "Wish that glassworks was more useful than it is," she added. "We've got the glass jars, but you need tight lids for heat canning, though, and it's hard to do that without rubber washer rings."

They all sighed agreement. Everyone had gotten *extremely* sick of salt fish and meat last winter, even if wild greens had kept scurvy and other deficiency diseases at bay. Nobody had wanted to see another piece of dried dulse by spring, either. The icehouses and bigger vegetable crops would help with that this year, and vary the diet, but it would be nice to be able to put up vegetables and fruits in quantity.

"Terri Susman had an idea about that," Leaton said. "She thinks we can reprocess tires to get good-quality sealing rubber. Have to get the steel wire and the cord out, of course, then chop up and reheat the rubber."

"Have her talk to Martha, then," Cofflin said. She was in charge of screening new Town-backed projects. "We should get on to that before summer, when the truck crops start coming in. Plenty of glass jars available now, if we can get the sealing we need."

Martha made a note on a pad she kept with her. "We'll need sulfur to cure raw rubber, won't we?" she said.

Leaton nodded vigorously. "That's getting to be our problem," he said. "Mechanical things, that I and my people can handle. It's *chemistry* that we're running into bottlenecks with. I could use some sulfuric acid for pickling and cleaning steel, God knows I could, but we can't make it in quantity—and what we do make is cruddy, full of impurities, and the quality is variable as hell. Same with nitric acid. Here, let me show you."

He pulled a scrap of crinkly-looking cotton cloth from a drawer of his desk and put it in a metal pan on the top. Then he took out a fire-starter, snapped it, and dumped the tinder. The cloth went up with a *whoosh,* a subdued crackling, and a puff of bitter smoke.

"There's our prospect of nitro powder," he said, exasperation in his tone. "If we *could* do it, we could get blasting explosive and propellants out of sawdust and cloth scraps, anything with cellulose. But we can't. The acid we make's too dirty, and we can't stabilize the results—it goes off if you breathe on it. The chemistry teacher over at the high school, Cynthia Dawes, she's working on it. Probably get it right in a year or two, but it's the old story, not enough people, specialists especially."

"Plus we have to be careful about by-products," Martha said. "No PCBs or dioxin in the groundwater here, and I'd like to keep it that way."

Both men nodded; Nantucket was a small island, and its water supply was completely dependent on the underground aquifer. Keeping that unpolluted had been hard enough up in the twentieth. The island didn't have that much fresh water to spare in the first place—if you overpumped the underground supply it got brackish and then salt—and they couldn't possibly let poisons filter down through the sandy soil into the reservoir below.

"Ontogeny recapitulates phylogeny" Leaton said, and Martha nodded. Jared blinked and shrugged; he got the gist, if not the actual reference. "We're redoing the early Industrial Revolution, only we can't afford to make the mistakes they did. Anyway, smokeless powder's out of the question, for a couple of years at least. Black powder we can do—but there the limiting factor's the raw materials. Charcoal is no problem, but we're just now getting significant amounts of saltpeter from the sewage works. And sulfur, well, the nearest accessible sources are down in the Caribbean."

"Through jungle and up volcanoes," Cofflin added. He'd taken a look at the reports. "It's even less popular than the salt-mining detail. Thanks for that mechanical scoop thing, by the way—it's taken a lot of the heartbreak out of that salt collection."

"Plus it's dangerous," Leaton went on. "Making black gunpowder, that is, no way to avoid occasional frictional explosions, that's why Du Pont got out of the business. Once we're up above the couple-of-pounds-a-batch level, I'm going to move we put the plant out by the old airport."

He sighed. "We're doing the best we can with what we've got . . . I showed you our Hawkeye addition to the ROATS program, didn't I?"

"No, actually," Cofflin said. "With this job and a kid, some details just don't get through. Captain Alston was satisfied, and I took her word for it."

"Ah. Well, come have a look, then."

Cofflin suspected that the machinist just liked an excuse to get out of his office and get his hands on some machinery; but hell, he didn't like sailing a desk much himself. They followed him out into the main shop, and then into the tangle of outdoor projects on the other side of the main building. Leaton dodged into a shed and brought out a weapon, slinging a leather satchel over one shoulder as well.

"Here it is," he said with diffident pride.

"Hmm."

Cofflin hefted the rifle . . . *better check.* Yes, spiral grooves down the barrel. Fully stocked in black walnut, looking a little like a hunting rifle except for the hammer and frizzen pan on the side. He swung it up to his shoulder and looked down the barrel; heavier than an M-16, about nine pounds, but well balanced and with a nice solid feel. Mauser-style adjustable sights.

"Feels sweet," he said. "A flintlock, I see."

"Ayup. We've got another model ready to go into production when we finally get the percussion-cap problem licked. We're going to use a tape primer method, like a kid's cap pistol, only using sheet copper instead of paper."

"How's it work?" Cofflin asked.

"Pull the hammer back to half cock," Leaton said. "Then hold the rifle in your left hand and raise that knob along the back of the stock."

"Ah," Cofflin said.

There was a plunger-shaped brass tube bolted to the underside of the section that had swung up, set so that the head of it would slide into the rear of the chamber when the lever was pushed back down.

"Hmm. Will that give you a tight enough gas seal?"

"Nope," Leaton admitted. "Not by itself. And drawn-brass cartridges are not feasible, right now; too big an operation. Here's what we did instead."

He opened the satchel hung over his shoulder and handed the Chief a round of ammunition. The bullet was shaped much like the rifle rounds he was familar with. Not jacketed, though, and it looked like . . .

"Plain lead?" he said.

"Slightly alloyed with antimony and tin. Ten millimeter, or point-four-inch, if you prefer."

Cofflin snorted, and Martha gave a dry chuckle. The metric-versus-old-style controversy was taking up a lot of time at the more recent Meetings, with the constitution on hold until the expeditionary force in Britain returned. The question of whether or not to hold Daffodil Weekend was a close second.

The rest of the cartridge was paper, and he could feel the black powder crunching within as he rolled it between thumb and forefinger. The rear felt thicker and stiffer.

"Go ahead," Leaton said eagerly. "There's a wad of greased felt at the base of the round. It packs into the gap between the head of the plunger and the chamber under the gas pressure, and seals it—well enough for one use, anyway."

Cofflin slid the cartridge into the chamber with his thumb and snapped the lever back down; an unseen spring held it snugly in its groove atop the rifle's stock. "Ayup, I see," he said admiringly.

"That's really quite clever," Martha said, her tone neutral.

The men both looked at her. She raised a brow and continued: "No, really. I'm just not an enthusiast. Guns are like tractors or can openers to me—tools. It's a gender thing, I think."

"Marian likes weapons," Cofflin said, feeling slightly defensive.

"No, she's *interested* in them. They're part of her work, as filing systems were for-me when I was a librarian," Martha corrected. "And swords are her recreation, like squash rackets. Anyway, dear, I wouldn't deny you the pleasure of firing it."

Jared put a hand over his heart. "Cut to the quick," he said. "Put in m' place. Range is over there, Ron?"

They walked to a shooting gallery that ended in a high sand mound with a wooden target. "Prime it like this," Leaton said. He pushed the pan forward and dropped a measured quantity of powder into it from a spring-loaded flask, then flipped it back.

Cofflin raised the rifle to his shoulder, snuggled it firmly, and thumbed the hammer back to full cock. The target was only a hundred yards away, no need to adjust the sights. Squeeze the trigger gently . . .

Shhssst. Flame and whitish smoke shot out of the pan. *Crack* on the heels of that, the gap almost imperceptible. The rifle thumped his shoulder, harder than he was used to but not intolerably. More dirty-white smoke shot out the muzzle. Almost at once a gray fleck appeared on the bull's-eye, where the bullet had punched through the paper to the wood beneath; it was about an inch up and two to the right of center.

"Not bad," he said admiringly, lowering the rifle and working the lever again. It slid up, releasing more sulfur-smelling smoke. "I'm rusty, I think, to miss that far on a clout shot. How'd you load the next round?"

"Just push," Leaton explained. "The spent wad blasts out ahead of the next bullet, and as a bonus it cleans out some of the black-powder fouling. Insert the next cartridge, prime the pan, and you're ready to go again. It shoots faster than the crossbows with practice, it's less muscular effort, and it's got three times the range. More stopping power, too—that big soft bullet makes some pretty ugly wounds, and the muzzle velocity is up around fourteen hundred feet per second. *And* it'll punch through any practical metal armor."

He paused, pursing his lips. "It's not perfect, of course. Flintlocks are vulnerable to wet weather—we can't help that. You have to watch the fouling buildup in the barrel, clean it regularly, and not let the chamber get too hot between rounds. But it's a hell of a lot better than the crossbows; about as good as 1860s, 1870s weapons, except for the priming."

"Now break my heart," Cofflin said. *Walker can't have anything like this. Not enough precision machining capacity.* "Not enough ammunition?"

"Not enough ammunition," Leaton sighed. "The bullets are no problem. We can stamp them out of sections of drawn lead wire, and half the sailboats here had lead keel weights, so there's plenty of the metal. It's the powder."

Cofflin sighed along with the machinist. A wonderful rifle with no ammunition was just a rather awkward club. And you not only had to have enough to use, you had to have enough for regular practice.

"Keep the miracles coming, Ron. We'd better get back to our baby and the job," Cofflin said.

"What's next on the schedule?" he asked, as they walked back through the factory and picked their daughter up from the cooing guard. The Indians were gone, leaving only a faint woodland smell and a hackle-raising memory.

"Lunch at Angelica's," Martha said. Brand had stayed in her farmhouse; it was the most practical headquarters for overseeing the island's agriculture. "Officially, we're going to discuss who gets the last of the rooted cuttings for the fruit trees. Unofficially, she's going to nag you about that idea of hers, putting in a farming settlement on Long Island."

"Good *God*," he groaned. "Doesn't she ever give up?"

"Rarely," Martha said. "It's a national characteristic."

They came out the end door of the wooden extension. A carriage with a single horse between shafts was waiting for them; it looked rather odd, low-slung, with car wheels and a wooden body, but the seats were comfortable and there were good springs and shock absorbers. They climbed into the open passenger compartment and settled themselves. The teenage driver clucked and flapped the reins, and the vehicle set off; up Washington, to avoid some street repairs, down Stone Alley, past the Unitarian church on Orange, up Cherry to Prospect, then out into open country along Milk until it became Hummock Pond Road. Cofflin shook his head slightly as the countryside slid past. *Not the same island at all,* he thought. Oh, the contours of the land were there, but apart from a strip along the road and some windbreaks, the scrub of bayberry, low oak, hawthorn, rose, and whatever was mostly gone—haggled-off stubs at most. Instead there were open fields divided by board-and-post fences, many with the beginnings of hawthorn hedges planted along them.

"And it looks good," he said aloud; Martha nodded in instant comprehension, looking down at the baby on her lap. Young Marian smiled toothlessly and drooled in response, stuffing a small chubby fist into her own mouth.

"Damn good," Cofflin said.

A tourist might not think so. The fields—wheat and barley and rye planted last fall, corn and oats, potatoes and vegetables put in this spring, an occasional young orchard—were a bit uneven and straggly. The long lines of field workers were just barely keeping ahead of the weeds, too. But that was *life* out there, dearly bought with aching hard work. That waving blue-flowered field of flax wasn't just pretty; it was rope and sails for the fishing boats that brought in the other two-thirds of their food.

"You can lose the habit of taking food for granted really quickly," Martha said. "I *love* the sight of those cucumbers."

"Ayup," Jared said. "But notice how sensitive we've all become to the weather?"

She looked skyward reflexively—clouds, but no rain today—and they shared a laugh. Everyone *did* talk about the weather now, and not just because there wasn't any TV or national newspapers. The weather was *important.*

"I hope Angelica doesn't go on too long about Long Island," he said, as the carriage turned off onto the appropriately named Brand Farm Road.

That was unpaved, and gravel crunched under the wheels. *Gravel we've got plenty of,* he thought, making an automatic note to check on how much asphalt they had left in stock for patching streets.

A piece of gravel bounced off the wooden side of the carriage, flung up by the horse's hooves; there was a faint smell of dust in the air, despite yesterday's rain. Spring flowers starred the sides of the road, daffodils and cosmos and the first tangled roses. There was a fair cluster of livestock this close to Brand Farm, on fields planted to ryegrass and clover; Angelica was keeping most of it under her eye, breeding stock being as precious as it was and the new farmers so inexperienced. Last year's weanling calves brought from Britain were small shaggy surly-looking adolescent cattle now, with budding horns and polls of hair hanging over their eyes; next year they'd be breeding themselves. The young ewes were adults with offspring of their own, tottering beside their mothers on wobbly legs and butting for the udder. A clutch of yearling foals went by, led on halters by young girls; getting them used to the idea of doing what they were told, he supposed. Far too much hauling and pulling was being done with human muscle, and steam engines weren't really suited for field work. More horses would be a godsend.

The baby began to complain, wiggling with little snuffles and *whu-wha* sounds. Martha did a quick check as they passed the brewery, winepress, and small vineyard just before the house; a cleared field off to the right was being planted with grafted rootstocks for more vines. The field was full of people, many of them rising to wave and call greetings as the Cofflins went by; they waved back.

"She's not wet. That's the 'I'm getting a little hungry' one," she said. "I'll leave you to tell Angelica no about Long Island again while I feed her."

Jared nodded; some mothers thought nothing of nursing in public, but Martha didn't work that way. The carriage slowed as it went uphill to the farmhouse proper, amid its cluster of outbuildings and barns and the great greenhouses. The heavy timber frame of a new barn was going up, with people pulling on ropes and shouting.

"You might consider the Long Island idea again," she went on.

"Not you too! We don't have the people to spare, and besides—there are the locals."

"Only a few hundred on the whole island," she said with ruthless practicality. "That's scarcely an impediment. And the climate and soil are a lot better for agriculture. Not this year or next, I grant you, but Dr. Coleman says that with the birthrate the way it is since the Event, our population's going to double in the next thirty-eight years or less. Not counting immigration."

"Immigration?" Jared said, raising his eyebrows. "I wouldn't have thought so, from what we saw this morning."

"Oh, I was thinking of Swindapa's people," Martha said, rocking the infant to try to calm its growing volume of complaint. "They seem compatible enough. Odd, but compatible, and eager to learn."

Now, there's a thought, Jared mused. He made a mental note of it. More people would be *so* useful, but not if they caused too much trouble.

He looked east for a moment. "It all depends," he said.

"And we can talk about the university . . . again. Never too early to start planning."

"Jesus *Christ.*"

"It's the only way the Spear Mark will listen to you. A lot of them, ah, the Grandmothers sort of . . . well, irritate them," Swindapa had said. "They always have. And the Grandmothers treat them like bad little children."

Which leaves me out here in the woods, buck nekkid with mosquitos biting me, Marian Alston thought, gripping her spear. *Well, not quite. I get to wear this knife, too. What was that remark I made last spring, about the bare-assed spear-chuckers of England?*

"Goddam Paleolithic rituals," Alston whispered, barely moving her lips.

Literally Paleolithic. The Arnsteins thought this probably went right back before agriculture, two or three thousand years. She gritted her teeth against the chill that raised goose bumps down her dew-slick ebony skin. She was crouched in a clump of tall ferns, with the crown of a hundred-foot beech tree overhead. Most of the trees about her were oaks, though, huge and gnarled and shaggy. Water dripped down from the fresh green of the leaves and the ferns, splashing on her. *Dammit, hypothermia amd pneumonia are* not *what I need.* She was covered with the juices of crushed plants, too, that were supposed to kill her scent. They certainly itched. The forest was more open than she'd have expected, kept that way by the shading crowns of the big trees and by periodic forest fires that swept away the undergrowth. It was eerily quiet, only a few birdcalls and the buzz of insects.

She breathed deeply, forcing thought out of her mind as Sensei Hishiba had taught. The discomfort did not vanish, but bit by bit it became simply another sensation, cramping and cold and hunger flowing without feedback across the surface of her perceptions. Slowly everything faded but her surroundings, rustle of growth, drip of water on the deep soft layer of rotting leaves, the faint cool scents of decay and growth. Outlines grew sharp, down to the feathery moss that coated the gnarled oak bark.

And . . . a rustle. Faint. A footfall, a small sharp *clomp.* She let her eyes drift closed, focusing. Inch by fractional inch the spear went back and her body shifted balance without moving, feet digging into the softness of the forest floor, pressing until wet clay oozed up between her toes.

The eyelids drifted up again. Alston made no attempt to focus them, let movement and color flow by and through. Her heart sped, not in excitement but in natural preparation for movement. She took a long, slow breath—

—and *lunged.*

The movement was too shocking-sudden for the buck to do more than begin a leap sideways. The long sharp steel thudded into its flank, behind the left shoulder; she followed through, shoving and twisting as the wood jerked in her hands. A moment later the deer pulled free and staggered off sideways, head down. Blood pumped from its flanks and mouth and nostrils, spattered her with thick gobbets; it staggered sideways, tripped, went down by the hindquarters. For an instant its forelegs struggled to lift it, while she waited, panting. Then it laid down its head, kicked, voided, and died.

She leaned on the spear, panting, so exhausted that her knees began to buckle. *Takes it out of you.* When you focused like that, there was nothing held back.

"Time's a-wastin'," she said, laying down the spear and kneeling beside the dead animal. *Sorry*, she thought, touching the soft neck. *It was necessary.*

The sun had fallen, and the air was growing cooler despite the great fire in the ancient pit at their backs and the smaller blazes around the edge of the clearing. "It's a new thing," one of the men grumbled. "A foreigner . . ."

Swindapa glared at him. Pelanatorn hushed him with a gesture. "Not the first," he said. "Let the forest spirits decide. If she brings her deer, well enough."

A younger man's voice called out, cracking with excitement. "It is the hour!"

Swindapa stood with the others beside the high-leaping fire, beating time on the ground with her spear, listening to the thudding rhythm and the slapping of palms on drumheads that matched it. Sweat ran down her face under the overshadowing tanned mask of a deer, down her flanks beneath its hide. Around her stood the ranks of the Spear Mark, their heads bearing the likeness of deer and boar, aurochs and wolf and bear, the bronze or Eagle People steel of their spears glinting reddish. She strained her eyes into the spark-shot darkness, knowing it was useless—the trees came close here, and nothing was visible under their branches. Wind ghosted out of them, cool and green on her hot skin, smelling of green and damp earth.

The chant broke, but the drums continued under it like a giant's heartbeat, echoing back from the forest edge.

"Terge ahwan!" someone shouted.

That was in the Old Tongue; *The hunter comes.* The rest of them took it up, making a new chant in the flame-shot darkness. The crowd parted for Marian. The bloody hide of her kill was draped around her flanks, and the open eyes of the head stared out from above hers. The butchered quarters and organs dragged behind her on a travois of poles bound with sinew.

A man in breechclout and leggings stood forth. Gold bands shone around the tusks of his boar mask and on the haft of the ceremonial mace in his hand. He held it up to bar her way.

"*Shm' u-ahwa?*" he asked. *Who comes?*

"*Na-ahawun t'ngamo sssgama nwn'tu,*" Marian replied, her voice loud and firm. *One who brings meat for the people.* She stood tall and let the travois fall, holding out her spear so that the bloodied head could be seen.

"*Na-terge ahwan!*" the boar-man shouted. *It is a hunter who comes!*

The crowd shouted it out together: "*Na-terge ahwan!*"

Swindapa felt her heart swell. Marian was doing everything perfectly—even the difficult sounds of the Old Tongue, the hunter's language, that nobody really spoke anymore. Helpers came forward to take the meat away for preparation, and to throw buckets of water over the initiate—part of the ceremony, more comfortable, and preparation for what must follow. Sleek wetness glistened in the firelight, like a statue of living onyx.

"Is the hunter weary?" the man with the boar said. "Does the hunter seek to rest?"

"The hunter runs faster than the deer, longer than the wolf," Marian answered. "The hunter runs hotter than the breath of fire."

She turned left and began to walk. The Spear Mark formed a laneway for her, in a spiral that led counterclockwise around the blaze again and again. A tense silence, then a spear lashed out—reversed, the butt low to trip her. Without breaking stride she dove over it, in a forward roll that seemed to bounce her back to her feet as if on cords let down from the moon. *The Art,* Swindapa thought. *Ah, if only I could move like that!*

To the Spear Mark it seemed like magic. A roar of approval went up. More spearshafts darted out, and sling cords swung to tangle and trip. Beneath the mask, Swindapa bit her lip in worry. *She's so hard to see in the dark, someone might slip.* Nobody was supposed to be really hurt in this, but accidents were not unknown—particularly if someone had ill-wishers. She'd collected more than a few bruises herself, on the night of her initiation; a lot of men felt annoyed when a woman took the Spear Mark. None landed on Marian that she could see, and the woman of the Eagle People ran faster and faster as the rite prescribed, dancing, jinking, dodging, throwing herself forward in diving rolls over an outstretched shaft or leg. The hunters yelled, egging her on; the sound rose as she disappeared behind the fire, and Swindapa knew she was sprinting up the ramp. And . . .

She soared over the flames; the Fiernan girl felt the blast of heat as if it were drying her own skin. Landing, standing with legs braced and spear held aloft on widespread arms.

Swindapa grounded her own spear, pulled down the deer mask, and danced out into the cleared space before the fire, taking the part of the prey in the Showing. She was a good enough hunter, and she'd learned warrior's knowledge from Marian—but this was her first skill, the one that had earned her the name Deer Dancer, an adult's name and not a child's. The hard soil was easy as turf beneath the balls of her feet as she sprang, seeming to float in the air as a deer did when it leaped, her long legs flashing in the flamelight. She landed, crouched, stepping light, quivering with the seed of leaps to come, as a deer was, always ready to flash away, turning and darting. She *was* the deer, and Marian was the hunter—stalking closer, her movements just as swift and smooth but harder, more focused. They spiraled about each other, playing the mime of stalk and flight, until the spear flashed below her last leap. She crumpled around it, lay still as the steel was withdrawn from the earth and thrust upward.

"It is accomplished!" Marian shouted.

"It is accomplished!" the hunters roared, and the drums gave a final flourish and went silent.

The tense hieratic stillness of the moment broke in laughter and cheers. Swindapa hurried forward, snatching up a parcel she'd arranged herself. It held a breechclout and leggings of fine white doeskin, and moccasins; she'd have liked it still better if she could have made them with her own hands, but there hadn't been time and her sisters and aunts had done it for her. She grounded her spear near Marian and began to help her on with the clothes.

"Looks like a goddam diaper," the black woman muttered under her breath . . . in English, though, glancing down at the breechclout.

"It looks lovely on you," Swindapa said stoutly. The smell of the other's sweat was so familiar, yet still had that trace of sharp musky strangeness that was uniquely *hers*, alien and exciting. "You did everything perfectly. There's only the Marking, now."

Everyone crouched down on hocks as another man came forward; his mask had boar tusks and wolf fangs and antlers as well, and his helper carried a leather tray with bone needles and little horn cups of pigment. The Fiernan girl squatted on her haunches, confident that Marian would bear the slight pain without flinching. She did, the light of the bonfire running ruddy on her dark skin, the full features motionless as the needles pricked and tiny droplets of blood flowed down between her breasts.

Strange, she thought. Very strange, to be here again—and with Marian; it was like two different worlds meeting. *And I not myself, not as I was.* She shook off the memory; there was enough sadness without raising ghosts from their barrows.

At least it was getting comfortable to squat naturally again; after a year of sitting on chairs, her legs had started going to sleep after a few hours in the old position. With the ceremony over, people sat about the fires and began the feast—Marian's deer had been set to cook, but they didn't have to wait for that. The finest hunters among the Spear Mark had brought in other deer, boar, rabbit, duck, and geese, and a good deal more easily than the candidate, since they were allowed to use the usual bows rather than the spear that ancient custom prescribed for the rite. There were wild fruits, nuts, and roots as well, but no bread or beer; for this ceremony only forest foods could be used. That didn't mean there was no drink, of course. Beakers of honeymead came out, tall bell-shaped clay pots marked with wavy lines. She accepted one and drank a little; it was a fine dry make, seasoned with meadowsweet and powdered hemp seeds.

"How's everyone taking it?" Marian said, as she sipped in her turn.

"Well, I think—most of them," Swindapa said.

Truly. I can feel the goodwill. The Spear Mark were her people's main defense, and they knew better than the Grandmothers how desperate their straits were.

"Good," Marian said. "We can get to work, then."

"Not tonight," Swindapa warned. "That would be . . . bad manners."

Strange, she thought. The Eagle People were always pursuing tomorrow, as if it were a precious quarry and they hungry wolves running it down. It was so hard for them simply to *be,* because they were always thinking of becoming.

A man leaned over. "Your friend Marawaynd is a great hunter," he said, grinning. "She caught a fine deer—both times she came to the White Isle."

Marian raised her brows at the good-natured guffaws, then smiled herself when Swindapa translated. She replied in her slow, accented Fiernan:

"Other way. She"—nudging Swindapa with an elbow—"track, hunt, leap on me like wolf."

Laughter rose into the night, as loud as the cracking of the fires. Men staggered forward with a roast boar and set it down before the chief feasters, and knives flashed in the firelight as they carved. Swindapa watched the sparks rising toward the stars, and felt a bewildering tightness in her throat.

Why should I feel like weeping? she thought, turning her head away from the others. *I only wish this could last forever.*

That was so strange a thought she ran it over and over in her mind, forgetting the pang in her chest in puzzlement. *I too am hunting the future and letting the Now slip past,* she thought with a slight chill. *It's catching.*

Dammit, I'm a sailor, not a diplomat, Alston thought, making her fingers unclench from the rough board table that occupied the center of the HQ hut.

"We've beaten back their raids before," one of the Spear Chosen said.

"When the Sun People come against you, they're going to be coming with every man in their tribes," she replied. "This won't be a war of raids, not after the harvest is in. It'll be a war of—" She switched to English. "Oh, hell, 'dapa, what's the word for *battles*?"

Swindapa frowned. "I don't . . . I don't think there *is* a word, not really," she said at last. "Not if I understand the English properly."

"—of *really big fights,*" Alston went on. "They're going to bring *thousands* of warriors into your land. You have to match them. Then the *armies* . . . the big groups of warrior bands . . . will fight until one flees. We call that a *battle.*"

The command tent had been replaced by a post-and-board structure; she could see it made the Earth Folk leaders a little uneasy, which was all to the good. *All the better to kick them out of their mental ruts.* That was why she was holding this meeting at Fort Pentagon. The garrison and the locals they'd hired had done a great deal in the past month. There was a timber-framed rampart all along the edge now, and towers of squared logs at the corners and over the gates. More logs made a rough pavement for the streets, and plank-and-frame barracks had replaced the tents; the little uniflow steam engine that powered Leaton's dart-throwing machine gun could also pump water, grind grain, and saw timber. There was also a log pier, which meant that the ships—even the *Eagle*—could tie up regardless of the tides and transfer cargo.

"Thousands?" the Fiernan warrior said, scratching at his head. Alston suppressed an impulse to check hers. The locals were a clean enough people, by Bronze Age standards. Those standards weren't anything like twentieth-century America's, and didn't include her horror of resident insect life. He cracked something between finger and thumbnail and continued:

"How can they bring thousands of warriors all together? What would they eat?"

"Your crops," Alston answered. *Maltonr,* she remembered. Redheaded, the one who'd been with her when they ran head-on into that Zarthani warband. *More flexible than most.* He'd undone the multitude of small braids he'd worn before and cropped his hair in an American-style short cut.

"That's why they'll come after the harvest," she said. "They'll live off what you've reaped and threshed. And your livestock, to be sure."

The dozen or so Spear Chosen sitting uneasily around the table looked at each other. "But . . . then we would all starve," he said.

"Exactly. Except the ones the Sun People kept as slaves, of course."

Swindapa winced. Alston restrained an apologetic glance; it was ruthless, but the truth.

Maltonr nodded thoughtfully. "We can't sit behind our walls and wait for them to go away, either," he said.

"Exactly," Alston repeated. *Except that that word means*

something more like running with the same feet, *approximately,* she thought. *Damn, but this is awkward.*

"They've got engines to batter down walls," she went on. "They're heavy and slow, but if the Sun People can move in open country, they can bring them up and smash you to sticks. And if you move out of their way and refuse to . . ." *Damn again, no way to say* give battle *in this language.* ". . . to meet them and have a really, really big fight, they can eat up your settlements one by one."

Maltonr still looked as if he was thinking hard. The others were simply appalled. "What have you Eagle People brought among us?" one whispered.

Alston felt like wincing herself. "Ask your Grandmothers," she said. "The Sun People were eating you a little bit at a time; in the end, they would have destroyed you anyway. Walker the outlaw has taught them how to do it all at once . . . but we can show you how to smash *them* all at once, too. Think of being free of their threat, forever."

That had them nodding. Except the redhead, who cast a thoughtful look around at the solid-looking American base. The very *permanent*-looking American base. *Oho, no flies on Rufus, here. Have to talk to him later.*

"Hmmm." That was Pelanatorn son of Kaddapal, the local magnate. Very much a trader, and very rich, now. "If *we* gather a host of thousands, how will *we* feed them? For that matter, there's always sickness if too many gather in one place for long."

"We can show you ways to stop the sickness," she said. *Boiling water and deep latrines, mostly.* Luckily they'd gotten a lot of prestige with the locals by healing diseases their witch-doctors-and-herbs medicine couldn't, so they'd probably go along with sanitation.

"Also, there are ways to feed large groups of people. With the proper—" She stopped again.

Oh, hell. How do I say organization *or* logistics? She settled down to grind the right meanings out of the Fiernan Bohulugi vocabulary.

After the Spear Chosen had left, Alston slumped in her chair. "Christ, I feel like a wrung-out dishrag," she said.

Swindapa sat looking at her, chin cupped in her hands. "You really have brought a new thing here," she said slowly.

" 'Dapa—"

The girl sighed and closed her eyes. "Oh, I know you—we—must," she said. "But . . . other change, it's like growing old. You don't notice it every day, and when it comes, it comes to someone that Moon Woman has made ready for it. But this is like a great tree growing up between nightfall and morning. There's no . . . no time to get used to it, to change the way the Eagle People bring it."

Alston sighed herself, as she rose and put a hand for a moment on the girl's shoulder. There was nothing much comforting to say. In a couple of generations, the Earth Folk way of life was going to be changed beyond recognition. That was better than being overrun and butchered, but it still wasn't easy to swallow.

Andy Toffler came in, checked for a moment, then continued when she nodded. "Goin' pretty smooth, ma'am," he said. With the air survey, we should be able to estimate the harvest pretty close, and do up proper maps of the whole area with updated terrain features. Ian wants to get together with the both of us on it. They're getting records from the local bigwigs, too—seems they've got a sort of tithe system here."

He grinned. "And God Help Us, it surely does impress hell out of the locals, ma'am."

"They haven't seen people fly before," Swindapa said dryly.

Toffler ducked his head, looking surprisingly boyish for a man in his fifties. "No offense, miss. They're good folks, your people, and I'm happy to be here helpin' them against those murdering scumbags."

He scowled; they'd all seen evidence of the way the Sun People made war, and there certainly wasn't a Geneva Convention in this millennium. *Seems to have hit Toffler harder than most,* she thought. There were hints of a knightly soul under that good-old-boy act . . . and he'd been scrupulously respectful to *her*, whatever his private opinions, which she had to give some credit for.

"Tell Ian I can see you at . . ." She glanced at her watch and read down a mental checklist. *The day would have to be forty hours long to get all that done.* ". . . at about eighteen hundred hours."

"See you later," she went on to Swindapa, answering the Fiernan's mute nod, scooping up her helmet, and leaving.

Sometimes you need to be alone to think. The guard fell in behind her; it was getting so she hardly even noticed that.

Enough space to drill several hundred had been left in the middle of the fort. As she passed along the edge of the field, Alston watched about that number of Fiernans in Nantucket-made armor learning the rudiments of close-order movement.

"*Hay*-foot, *straw*-foot," the Nantucketer noncom screamed, to the pulsing beat of a drum. "*Hay*-foot, *straw*-foot!"

That was strange, too. Most of the locals could do any number of intricate, precise dance steps, but simple left-right-left gave them endless problems. They looked rather silly, each with a piece of hay tied to the left foot and a twist of straw to the right, but it worked. *What really worries me is keeping them in line in a fight.* They were brave enough, but they weren't used to the *concept* of taking massive casualties all at once, the way you did in open-field massed combat.

She exchanged salutes with the guard at the sea gate, walking through the open portals and under the snouts of the flamethrowers that protruded from the bunkerlike slits in the flanking towers. There was a fair bit of traffic; boots and wheels and hooves boomed on the bridge over the ditch. The smell of stale water came up from it, around the bases of the sharpened stakes that bristled forward from the lower bank around the moat. That mixed with other smells—woodsmoke and horse sweat, leather, cooking from the tangle of Fiernan huts that had gone up outside, dung from the corrals. There were as many locals as Americans in the bustle. Spear Chosen war chiefs coming to learn or take council; traders, scores of them, with little oxcarts or pack donkeys or porters, or hauling stuff up from the beach where they'd landed coracles or canoes or whatever; others come to trade labor for the wonderful things the strangers had, or just to gawk. Even a few weirdly tattooed men from across the channel to the west, from what the locals called the Summer Isle.

The pier was even busier. As she came to the end, a sedated, blindfolded, hobbled, and still rather resentful-looking horse swung up into the air and over to the *Eagle*'s deck on a line and a band slung under its belly.

"Let go . . . and *haul*," the line leader barked.

The animal slid down gently, whinnying as its hooves

made contact with the decking. Alston paused for a moment, looking up at the clean lines of rigging and clewed-up sails and masts, feeling the familiar rush of love at the sight of her ship. *Beautiful as . . . as Swindapa, by God,* she thought, smiling with a slight quirk at the corner of her mouth. Right now the *Eagle* was leaving her for a while. Heading back home, with a cargo of horses, firkins of butter, and meat pickled and salted and smoked. Plus several small, heavy little chests full of gold bars and dust and some crude silver ingots.

Tom Hiller came up and saluted. "Captain." The sailing master was looking harassed, his long face like a basset hound's expecting yet another kick. "She trims . . . oh, hell, she trims as well as you'd expect. She wasn't built for carrying horses, Captain."

"She wasn't built for carrying anythin' but people, Mr. Hiller," she replied, returning the courtesy. "Needs must when the devil drives. How are the new hands shaping?"

They'd sworn on two dozen Fiernan deckhands, out of hundreds wild to enlist. *Which is a good sign in itself. They're not afraid we're going to roast and eat them as soon as we're out of sight of land.* Taking on locals also meant that she could get another transatlantic voyage in without putting too many of her precious trained Americans out of reach. For various reasons, she'd seen that more than half of the recruits were young women, and all from the coastal fishing hamlets.

"Pretty well," Hiller said, turning his cap in his hands. "They're all fit—better than your average cadet was to start with, and they're used to living rough. And they pick up stuff like *haul* and *climb* damn quick. That phrasebook was really useful, by the way."

"Thank the Arnsteins. What else is on your mind, Mr. Hiller?"

"Look—" He hesitated. "Look, Captain, I just don't like leaving right now. Couldn't somebody else—"

"No," Alston said bluntly. "You're the best sailor, and you're leaving with the next tide. Everyone else who could command *Eagle* is doing something I can't spare him or her from. And I need those wagons, and all the rest of it."

"Yes, ma'am," he sighed.

CHAPTER TWENTY-TWO

July – September, Year 2 A.E.

"**O**ne of them died, Chief," Hiller said. "I think we over-tranked it in that storm off the Azores. Heart just stopped—or maybe it died of fright. Damn all horses anyway."

"Damned lucky it was only one," Cofflin said.

The *Eagle* was back at her usual berth, the old Steamboat Wharf. The wild-eyed little horses were led down a special ramp rigged with canvas barriers on either side, snorting and balking. It was a bright breezy-cool day in early July, with only a scattering of people watching; today was a working day, and there were enough fishing boats these days to sop up most of the able hands on the island. Even the strong sea breeze couldn't quite hide the odors of drying fish, offal in the giant tubs waiting to be hauled out to the fields. A whale-catcher was coming in between the breakwaters as well, the long dark shapes of its catch towing behind. A cheery *toot-toot* cut through the bustle, sending a white cloud of gulls storming skyward.

Well, we're certainly a seafaring island again, Cofflin thought.

Beside him Angelica Brand was rubbing her hands with glee. "Ninety-seven, ninety-eight," she counted. "All mares. *Marvelous.*"

"It means we can spare Captain Alston the people she wants," Cofflin nodded. "Wasn't sure it was possible."

Hiller looked up sharply. "How so?" he asked.

Cofflin hid his smile; he'd noticed that the Guard people all bristled like that at a suggestion that Alston wasn't infallible. *Sign of a good boss. God, but we were lucky.* They might have gotten a regulation-worshiping martinet . . . or, heaven forbid, someone with political ambitions. A grown-up Walker. He gave a mental shudder at the thought.

"Angelica's arithmetic," he said aloud.

The woman beside him touched her gray-streaked brown hair. "Oh, my, yes. The reapers are ready to go—all we lacked was traction. Two horses to each, so with the ones we've already got, that's over seventy-five reapers we can put into the fields. Fifteen acres a day each, say a thousand acres a day all up, that means we can harvest the whole small-grain acreage in less than a week with only a hundred and fifty people. Granted we still have to shock and stook it by hand, and then there's the threshing, but it's still hundreds of people rather than thousands, the way it was last year. *Plus* we can use horse-drawn cultivators to spare a lot of hoe work done by hand."

"Which frees up people for a *lot* of other work," Cofflin said. "Not that it took that long even with sickles, but the people had to be *here*—sort of tied 'em down." He exchanged grins with Angelica. "We could use a lot more livestock like this."

"Oh, my, yes," she said. "Another hundred horses at least, and a couple of hundred cows, more sheep too. As long as we can feed them on salt-marsh hay and fishmeal, they're a perfect way to put humus and minerals in the soil. Virtuous feedback cycle, little fertilizer machines."

"The captain said we'd be bringing back machinery," Hiller said.

"And specialists to handle and repair it," Cofflin agreed.

One of the crew came down the gangplank, duffelbag over her shoulder. It took a second glance before he realized she was a . . . *local,* he reminded himself. Quite a nice-looking youngster, apart from a few missing teeth that showed as she glanced around with a dazed grin. A Guard cadet came clattering down behind her, and they walked off hand in hand.

Angelica left too, anxious to shepherd her precious horses out to Brand Farms. Cofflin stood looking after her for a moment.

"I'm worried," he said abruptly.

"Why?" Hiller said. "Everything's going according to plan, so far."

"That's what worries me," he said, and shrugged. "Well, let's get to work."

* * *

"Ahhhhhh," the crowd muttered.

Alston nodded and smiled, raising a hand to shade her eyes from the sun. Inwardly she was breathing a long sigh of relief; horses were better, but they were using oxen for this demonstration, because they were so much more common. Evidently they would work, too.

The bright burnished-bronze color of the ripe grain was a pleasure to the eye, she had to admit; field after field of it, across the gently rolling surface of the downs. The reaper rumbled and clanked down the edge of one field, the little red-and-white oxen rolling their eyes and walking at an almost-trot as the driver goaded them. A small girl led the four-ox team, and her mother drove the machine itself—they wanted to show how easy these were to use. The plank-and-wire reel spun like a slow paddle wheel, bending the tall stalks backward. Behind them the serrated edges of the cutting bar hummed, slicing the grain off three inches above the ground; it fell onto the moving canvas platform behind, and the raking attachment let it fall behind in a neat linear row.

A roar went up from the watchers. Two women darted forward and bent over the row, grabbing double handfuls and tying them into sheaves with a twist of the straw. Small children ran back and forth shrieking; crowds of their elders trotted into the field and followed the reaper, making the oxen even more nervous. Alston crossed her fingers behind her back, licking lips salty with sweat and thick with dust— at least the weather had been good, hot cloudless days. Less rare now than up in the twentieth, but still unusual for a warm spell to last so long. A good omen, in its way.

Two older men and a woman, richly dressed, stayed by the clump of Americans and their Fiernan allies; one of the men had a thin-bladed bronze sword like a rapier, and the woman carried a walking staff with a carved owl's head on it.

"You did not lie," the man with the sword said. "One such *machine*"—he used the English word, horribly mangled—"does the work of twenty."

"Yes," Alston said. "And the ones who work the machine need not be strong or fit."

Abe Lincoln's secret weapon, she thought. McCormick's machines had cut the grain of the Midwest while the farmers' sons were away in the blue-clad legions of Sherman and

Grant. Unlike the slaves the Confederates had relied on, a reaping machine wasn't likely to run away.

"And that means"—she switched to English for a moment—"Ian, Doreen, the maps"—then back into Fiernan, with occasional help from Swindapa—"that you can send fighters and grain to the meeting place that the Grandmothers of the Great Wisdom and the Council of the Sacred Truce suggested."

At our strong urging, she added silently. No need to complicate matters, and the Fiernans could be damned touchy if they thought someone was trying to boss them.

The three locals were leaders in this area, or at least as close as the rather anarchic Fiernan Bohulugi got. They looked at each other, and then back at the machine making its way around and around the grainfield, working its way in from the edge. Then the woman looked up at the sky.

"The weather is good," she said. "But you can't count on that."

Everyone there nodded. Bad weather in harvest meant grain that had to be dried over fires, or worse still that went bad in the storage pits. That was why these people nearly killed themselves in harvest time; you had to get the harvest cut as fast as humanly possible.

The man with the sword tugged at his barley-colored mustaches; he had a stubbled chin. The cloth of his tunic was plaid, squares of woad blue and pale yellow.

"I don't . . . will that *machine* keep working? What if it falls sick? If our strongest are away, and it sickens, then we lose the harvest and our children starve."

"If the Sun People burn your houses and steal your crops, you'll all die. And we have skilled craftfolk who can tend any hurts the machine takes," she went on. *The miracle of interchangeable parts.* "They'll show your own people how, too."

The third man rubbed a gold neck ring. "As you say it, these machines need fresh . . . pieces . . . every now and then? They wear down, like a knife that's been sharpened often?" Alston nodded. "Then if we use them to harvest, we'll have to buy the pieces of you in future years, even if you give them freely this season."

Damn, got to remember—primitive doesn't mean stupid. At that, the Fiernan were better traders than the charioteers; they didn't think of all trade in terms of gift exchanges, for starters. That was one reason the Tartessians didn't like them. The easterners were easier to trick.

"You can always go back to using sickles, when there's no war," Swindapa pointed out spontaneously.

The gold-decked man laughed; he had a narrow dark face and black eyes. "Water flows uphill faster than people will give up an easier way of doing," he said. "And it'll be, *Drauntorn, you're the Spear Chosen—go bargain for us with the Eagle People, so we don't have to break our backs or risk untimely rain.* And scowls and black looks and no help for us trading men if we don't, so we'll have to pay even if the price ruins us."

Alston spread her hands. "We're not mean-hearted bargainers," she pointed out. "Ask any of your people who've dealt with us."

"I'm kind to my pigs, too, when I'm fattening them," the man said.

"Would you rather deal with a Sun People war band?"

"Few have come this far west . . . but no, no, there's wisdom in what you say."

"Many of your people think so," Alston said delicately. "Many are gathering."

Swindapa had suggested the strategy. If a Fiernan community got violently unpopular with its neighbors, they'd steal all its herds, plus withdrawing the day-to-day mutual help that was an essential safeguard against misfortune.

The Arnsteins returned and spread the map on the table. The Fiernans' eyes lit as she explained it; they understood the concept, but it took a while to understand the alien pictographic technique.

". . . so this shows your land from above," she said, circling her finger over a map of southwestern England from Hampshire to Cornwall and north to the Cotswolds. "Here is your district. Here is where the host will muster, three days' march. All shown as a bird would see it."

Or it shows things as Andy Toffler sees them on surveying flights with his camera, she added to herself.

Aloud: "From this, and from the . . . ah, memories . . . of the Grandmothers, the number of fields and the number of houses and people can be told. To make sure that everyone bears a fair share of the burden of the levy, you understand."

And so nobody can wiggle out.

"Men can walk," the mustachioed Spear Chosen said.

"Cattle and sheep can walk." Both the men looked pained; those were their capital assets. The woman—priestess, Alston supposed—gave them a sardonic sideways glance. "But grain can't walk, and it's hard to haul any distance."

Alston rested one hand on the map and pointed with the other, to the big Conestoga-style wagons the Americans were using; dozens of them had come back with the *Eagle*, knocked down for reassembly.

"We have better wagons, as well," she said. "Each can haul, ah—" she looked down at a conversion list that translated English measurements into the eight-based local number system and units—"two tons of grain five to eight miles a day." *Even over these miserable tracks you people call roads.* "We have a *machine* to do the threshing, too. So you can move both the fighters and their food."

The discussion went on. So did the work in the fields; the Fiernans there were singing as they bound and stooked the sheaves of grain behind the reapers, happy as children on holiday. Alston remembered what her back had felt like after stooping over a sickle for a few days. *I know* exactly *how they feel.*

"These Eagle People think of everything," the Spear Chosen with the bronze rapier said, his hand on the bone-and-gold hilt.

Swindapa looked after Marian; she was over by the wagons, taking some message. One of the *radios* had come with them; she shivered a little. She could understand a lot of what Marian's people did—even a steam engine made sense, once you made a picture in your head of the hot vapors pushing through pipes. No different from boiling water lifting the lid on a pot over the fire, not really. But radios were too much like talking to ghosts.

"They are . . . forethoughtful, careful, they work very hard to make every small thing happen as they desire," she said. *How do you say* methodical *or* systematic? she wondered. That sort of thing happened all the time these days, and it made her head itch inside. You just couldn't *say* some things she'd learned in her birth tongue.

Swindapa's mother shifted her youngest sister around and began to nurse. The girl fought down a sharp stab of envy, followed by an all-consuming anger. Her own hand clenched on the hilt of her *katana*. The Iraiina would pay for robbing her of that, pay with *pain*. Yet if all of them died, it would not be enough.

"They have more things than these *machines* you've seen," Swindapa's mother went on. "Wonderful things . . . I've seen the hills of the Moon Itself with their *tel-e-sk-opes*." Everyone touched brow and heart and genitals in awe.

"And the tools, the weapons and armor, and the cloth, and the ornaments," the dark-haired Spear Chosen said eagerly. "We must *have* these things! We must find what they want in exchange."

"No," Swindapa said slowly. The others looked at her in surprise. "We must learn how to *make* these things, for ourselves. Or we would become as little children to the Eagle People forever, without their meaning us any harm."

Slow nods went around the circle.

"Another raid so soonly?" Isketerol said, in English. "Soonish? Nowly?"

"So *soon*," Walker said, correcting him absently. *Odd. He's kept getting better at English . . . oh, he must speak it with what's-her-name, Rosita.*

"Political necessity," he went on in Tartessian, unshipping his binoculars. "Got to keep the tribes thinking about the war, if we're to get the levy together again."

Bastard quieted as he dropped the reins on the horn of his saddle. The shade of the trees overhead was welcome—it'd been getting pretty hot for an English summer, and they'd all been out in it as the war of ambush and border skirmish went on relentlessly. Sweat trickled out of the padding of his armor, and out of the helmet lining, stinging his eyes. It mixed with the heavier smell of Bastard's sweat, the oiled-metal scent of armor, going naturally somehow with the creak of leather and the low chinking of war harness from man and horse alike.

Typical enough, he thought, scanning back and forth across the enemy hamlet. They were up on the downs of what would have become Sussex, just on the edge where the open chalklands gave way to the forested clay soils lower down—New Barn Down, the Ordnance Survey maps called it. The Earth Folk settlement was five round thatched huts inside a rough rectangle of earthwork, two of the walls overlapping to make a sort of gate; a palisade of short poles topped it all around. Square fields and pastures of an acre or so each lay about the steading, fading off into forest on the hills to the north. A rutted track led off that way, through a shallow dry valley between two of the downs. There was something odd, though. . . .

Isketerol spotted it. "They've been beforehand with their harvest," the Tartessian said. He looked up. "It's been hot and dry for this sodden marsh of an island, but it's still early for them to have it all in."

Walker lowered the binoculars and nodded thoughtfully. The grainfields were all reaped stubble, not even any sheaves of grain standing in the fields. Usually the locals left those in little three-sheaf tipis in the fields, so the crop would dry better. He looked through the field glasses again. *Yup. Grain stacks inside the wall.* Even so . . . He did a quick mental calculation. Less than there should be, and the harvest had been good this year from all the scout's reports. Maybe they'd rushed it because of the war.

"Yeah, something funny there," he said slowly.

The creaking got a little louder. He looked around; his followers were grinning and sweating with single-minded eagerness. For them it was just another fight, and an easy one with sixty of them in full gear against one little farm hamlet. Plus there were cattle and sheep grazing around the Earth Folk settlement, and he'd found that the Iraiina and their relatives had a peculiar attitude about livestock. Sort of like a yuppie and his Lamborghini, or his car and his bank account put together. Their idea of status was to sit and watch endless herds of their very own cow-beasts driven by: Iraiina used the same word for *big herd of cattle* and wealth in general. Not entirely unlike the Bitterroot ranchers he'd been raised among.

"All right," he said quietly. "Let's do this by the numbers."

Ohotolarix raised his aurochs-horn trumpet to his lips. It dunted *huu-huuu-huuuu* through the beeches and oaks, a harsh droning echo. With a crashing and ripping of branches and underbrush, two parties of a dozen men each spurred their horses out and around on either side, heading upslope to cut the Fiernans off from the north. The rest came out of hiding more carefully, forming into a line and trotting forward. Screams sounded from ahead; Fiernan herders tried to get their charges moving north, then saw they'd be cut off and abandoned the animals to run for the settlement. His followers whooped triumph as they rounded up the bawling, baaing livestock and edged it out of the way, back toward the woods.

No horses, he thought. Not much of a surprise; the Earth Folk didn't keep many of them. He swung down out of the saddle and the rest of the band followed, except for a few scouts; youths not ready for full warrior status came forward to hold reins. *Make more sense to have the men do that, taking turns.* Not possible, though. *Honor forbids.* He sneered a little. That attitude would have to go eventually, but for now it wasn't worth the trouble of offending their superstitions.

"Let's go," he said, drawing his sword. "No male prisoners." Too much trouble to take back; they were a fair way from home. "Forward!"

The men bayed answer: *"Forward with Sky Father! Horned Man with us!"*

Hard dusty ground and ankle-length stubble caught at his feet. Shieldmen formed up before and on either side of him, and his bannerman by his side. His head swiveled as he checked. Front rank with shields up—the Fiernans had some pretty good archers, much better than the eastern tribes—and spears bristling. Crossbowmen behind them, with their shields slung over their backs. He frowned as he looked ahead. Those L-shaped entrances could be tricky; you couldn't just hit the wall on either side and storm the gate. *All right, we'll hit the outer wall, cross the laneway, and* then *turn in.* He gave orders, and the pace picked up to a trot, his plate armor clattering among the musical *chink-chink* of the others' chain hauberks. *Makes it easy to stay in shape, this does. No more steppercizer.*

An arrow wobbled out from the palisade and stood in the dirt. Men barked laughter, and the taut *whung* of crossbows sounded. They were well within range, and the heavy quarrels would probably go right through the rickety stakes that made up the chest-high defenses; those were as much to keep livestock in as enemies out. Screams of pain confirmed the thought.

Walker paused a half-stride to pull the enemy arrow out of the ground. About thirty inches long, ashwood, fletched with gray goose feathers—fairly standard. The head was not— a narrow steel thing like a miniature cold chisel. His teeth skinned back from his lips. Nantucket-made, to an old pattern. Bodkin point, they'd been called in medieval England.

Arrowheads like that had flown in deadly storms at Crecy and Agincourt.

The first wave of Walkerburg men hit the embankment and scrambled up, chopping the edges of their shields into the turf as they toiled to mount the breast-high earthwork; the others stood close behind and shot over their heads—*his* men didn't just bull in regardless, he'd gotten that well drilled into them, that winning was more important than showing how brave you were. He hung back himself, watching the action. Walker had proved himself often enough to make that possible, and besides, he was a wizard—halfway to a god, in fact, which exempted him from the usual standards.

"This is too easy," he muttered.

Sections of the palisade were down, ripped aside. His men stood exchanging spearthrusts through the gaps, then began to push through—and none of them were down, that he could see. The second rank were slinging their crossbows, drawing swords, and setting shields on their arms. He signed abruptly to the men around him, and they trotted toward the gate, holding their shields up to protect him. Few arrows flew as they ran, although there was a sharp *crack* and yelp as a slingstone struck a man on the thigh. He stumbled and limped, but kept walking, which made him lucky—those things could break bone easily enough.

The gate was closed with wattle hurdles, woven stick barriers usually used to pen sheep, reinforced with a two-wheeled cart and some pieces of thorny bush. Walker's eyes narrowed in interest as a thin column of black smoke rose from within the enclosure; that was probably a signal. He noticed something else as someone on the other side of the cart tried to hit him with a flail—a long stick with a short one fastened to it with a leather thong, usually used to beat grain out of the stalk.

Shunngg. The thong parted against the razor-edged *katana,* and the shorter oak batten went pinwheeling off. His downstroke slashed the wielder across the upper arms as she goggled at him, and the Fiernan fell in a spray of blood that caught him across the face.

Too many women, he thought, spitting out the warm salt-copper taste and wiping a hand across his mouth. Even Iraiina women would fight sometimes when their homes were attacked, and the Earth Folk were less hidebound about things like that. But there should still have been more men behind the barricade, a solid majority at least. Those that *were* there were too old, or too young, besides being too few.

Conical iron helmets came up behind the Earth Folk, and red-dripping blades. Combat turned into flight and massacre.

"Prisoners!" Walker shouted. "Get me some prisoners!"

He stalked through the chaos, keeping an eye out to make sure nobody got enthusiastic with torches. The black smoke was coming from a small hot fire that had been half doused with damp straw and old woolen rags; he kicked it apart with a boot and stamped on the embers. Isketerol was already busy with a girl, his buttocks pumping like a fiddler's elbow as she screamed and sobbed and writhed—the Tartessian wasn't as bad as Rodriguez, but he did have a severe case of Spanish Toothache nonetheless—while most of the rest were looting by the numbers, the way he'd taught them. He knocked aside one spearshaft poised to run through a screeching five-year-old.

"Nits make lice, lord," the warrior growled.

"The young ones train easier," Walker replied mildly; the man lowered his eyes and shuffled feet. "Get to work."

Something's wrong, he thought again, standing by the big stack of unthreshed grain.

Ohotolarix and another of his Iraiina came up, pushing a woman ahead of them. "Here's your prisoner, lord," they said, grinning; one shoved her forward. She was naked, a big-breasted brunette staring around in near-hysteria. "We didn't even mount her ourselves," Ohotolarix added virtuously.

"You," Walker said, putting the tip of his reddened sword under her chin. She froze at the touch of the sharp wet steel, eyes going even bigger. "Where men? Where *of-you* men?

She licked her lips and spoke, very carefully. He caught about one word in four; the Earth Folk language was just too damn difficult. The man with Ohotolarix frowned and translated:

"Toward the big . . . the Great Wisdom, she says, lord." The warrior made a warding sign of the horns, with the index and little finger of his right hand. "The Moon-bitch's place. Evil magic."

A gust of fury filled Walker, like a blinding light behind the eyes. Thoughts strung themselves together, dropping into place. He was suddenly conscious of the woman flopping and gurgling on the ground before him with her throat gashed open, and the two Iraiina staring at him goggle-eyed.

"We don't have much time," he forced himself to say, running his sword through a rag and sheathing it. "Ohoto-larix, see to the most portable loot, nothing else—no women, nothing bulky. We leave *now*. Nothing that can't keep up with the horses. Go, go, go!"

They went, running; it was a big perk of having people think you were supernatural. It was on the tip of his tongue to tell them to turn the cattle loose too, but there were things even Hwalkarz the Wizard had to think twice about.

"What's the matter, blood-brother?" Isketerol said, coming up smiling and adjusting his clothing.

"Look at that," Walker grated in English, pulling a sheaf of wheat from the stack.

"It's just . . ." The Tartessian's eyes flicked from Walker's face to the grain. "The straw is too long. Why would anyone bend that low to cut grain?"

"No one did," Walker said, remembering the smooth low cut in the fields outside the settlement. "A machine did it. So the fighting men here didn't need to. And if they're gone even from this pissant little place close to the frontier—"

Isketerol's eyes bulged. "The Fiernans could be mobilizing *all* their fighting men—right now, while we thought they were still working on the harvest!"

Walker turned and walked up to the top of the embankment, facing north, unshipping his binoculars, and looking carefully from horizon in the east to horizon in the west until he caught the *blink . . . blink . . .* from the hilltop two miles away.

"What *is* that?" the Iberian asked.

"Heliograph. Signals by flashing lights off a mirror in code. With good binoculars, it's almost as fast as radio—and harder to detect." He had a continuous radio watch kept on the equipment *Yare* had brought over; a bicycle rig for charging batteries had been part of the cargo. "And we, my friend, have been suckered. Let's torch this shitheap and get going. Time to get the army together."

Isketerol nodded thoughtfully. "Perhaps . . . we should take some, ah, what's the word, *precautions*?"

Walker nodded. "Just in case."

Andy Toffler swore softly under his breath as he stooped, pushing the goggles up on his forehead. *Bad one,* he thought. The buildings and grain were all burning, and the raw harsh scent made him cough as he flew through it. Lower, and he could see bodies lying between the burning huts, and more scattered outside the enclosure. Some of them were moving.

"*GHU* here. Hamlet has definitely been destroyed," he said. "Doesn't look like much is left. Over."

"Central here. Any sign of wheel tracks?"

"That's negative, Central. Ground's too hard anyway. I'm going in."

"Negative on that. Return to base. Over."

"Sorry, transmission breaking up. Over."

He eased the ultralight down, into the stubble field next to the hamlet. The soft balloon wheels touched as he flared the nose up a little, killing speed, and the machine ran itself to a stop in scarcely twelve feet. There was a shotgun in a scabbard on the frame next to his seat. He racked the slide and made his way cautiously toward the fires.

"Damn," he said softly. "Gawd damn."

The first thing he ran into was sheep, savagely hacked and stabbed, as if by someone in a very bad mood. Then people, together as if they'd been herded into a bunch. Women mostly, and some children. A lot of the women lying on their backs naked, with their throats cut, or curled around a spear wound. Toffler swallowed a mouthful of spit and made himself look at the ground. In the stretch about the hamlet's embankment there was sign of horses—dung, and the imprint of a shod hoof where one of them had stepped in it. More bodies just within the wall, these looking as if some of them had gone down fighting. Many of them had Nantucket-style crossbow bolts in them, or the broken stubs, or gaping holes where they'd been cut out for reuse.

"Walker," Toffler said, as if the word made his mouth feel dirty.

The heat within the enclosure was savage, as the wooden frames of the buildings went up. Walls collapsed, and he could hear voices . . . and there was *nothing* he could do.

"God damn me if there isn't," he muttered, and turned on his heel.

The track of the cattle was obvious even on this hard ground, pointing southeast toward the lower wooded ground and the river valley. He ran back toward the ul-

tralight and flung himself into the seat, ignoring the faint
squawking from the headphones of the radio. The run was
downhill and into the wind; the little fabric-and-struts aircraft hurled itself aloft as if angels were pulling on strings
from the cloudless sky. Toffler took it recklessly low, the
tricycle undercarriage virtually brushing the tops of the big
oaks and beeches. He remembered things from his boyhood
in the knob country of Kentucky. *Driving cattle like that,
you'd have to . . . yes!*

A faint track, more like a deer trail than a road—just
barely visible through the lush late-summer leaves. They
couldn't have gone far, even by the plodding standards of
this abortion of an aircraft—oh, God, for his Phantom and
a mixed load of snake and nape! Nothing like white phos-
phorus and napalm for chastising the evildoers. He did have
a helmet with a holder for a pair of binoculars. He used it,
and blurred closeness appeared.

There. Cattle, and men on horseback, glimpsed in flickering instants through the leaves and branches. He throttled
back the engine and pushed up the glasses with a *snick,*
ghosting down through the air as quietly as he could. His
left hand held the yoke while his right was busy with the
racked glass bombs by his seat, unlatching the safety fas-
tener and making ready. They'd put in some improvements
since he flew against the Olmecs, including a friction primer
and fins to guide the fall. Plus he'd practiced.

Ahead, the enemy were coming out into a small almost-
clearing, littered with the trunks of dead trees and briers,
grass, brush—second growth. The herd of small hairy cattle
bawled and churned with panic at being driven so fast from
their accustomed range, and even expert herdsmen were
having their hands full. His eyes flicked back and forth;
forty, fifty men, pehaps a few more. No chariots. They were
all on horseback, riding with regular saddles and stirrups,
leading packhorses as well. All in metal armor . . . *Jesus,
maybe that's Walker himself down there!*

Ease back on the throttle, engine noise sinking to a low
buzzing drone. The ultralight was almost like flying a para-
chute; when you headed into the wind the stall speed was
near zero. *Careful. If the wind dies down you could drop
like a rock.*

Closer, closer, coming down as if he were falling along

an inclined plane. A few of the men had time to look up at the last moment.

Snap. The first bomb soared away in an arc, trailing smoke. It shattered a dozen feet up on the trunk of a sapling and fire sprayed in all directions. Horses went berserk, and men tumbled on the ground screaming as clinging flame ran under their armor.

Toffler rammed the throttle home and hauled the nose of the little arrowhead-shaped craft skyward, banking. *Sorry about the horses,* he thought. This time he came in fast and level, adjusting by eye. *Long way from computerized radar bombsights, aren't we.*

"Eyee-yeeeeee-*haaaa*!" he screamed, a yell his Rebel great-grandfather might have used when he charged behind Nathan Bedford Forrest. "Take that, you motherfuckers!"

Snap. Snap. Snap. More of the bombs tumbled away and slashed knives of flame across the clearing. Cattle scattered into the woods, and horses. Men died, and the brush itself was catching alight. This late in summer it might well turn into a full-fledged forest fire. Then something winked bright at him from the ground.

Pttank!

A hole appeared in the aluminum framing not far from him, with a fleck of sparks that licked his own neck in stinging fire. Hands and feet hit yoke and pedals with automatic skill, and the ultralight jinked from side to side with the agility of a hummingbird. *Crack. Crack. Pttank!* Another hit, and gasoline was leaking from the tank behind him.

"Uh-oh," he muttered, pushing the throttle forward to the stops. *I know what uh-oh means,* he thought. *Uh-oh means "I fucked up."*

Walker fired a last round on the off chance, then lowered the rifle and looked around. A scream died off into a gurgle and then silence as a comrade's knife gave a man burned over half his body the mercy stroke.

"How many?" he called. "Let each man answer his name."

They did, as horses were caught and brought under control. Three dead, five badly wounded, another half-dozen burned to some degree. And the woods around them were going up . . . while the men looked at him. The smell of singed hair and burned flesh was heavy, and heat prickled sweat across his skin under the armor.

"That flying thing can kill you, but no deader than a spear," he said quietly. "I warned you that we would be making war against wizards . . . but my magic drove it off."

"It *flew*, lord. A great bird, with a man in its talons."

"The man ruled it. I've flown so myself, in the past."

Murmurs of awe. He went on: "Are you men and warriors? Do you fear death because it wears a new face?"

Of course you do, he knew. But they couldn't possibly admit or show it, and that put new strength into them. They might have fled screaming a few minutes before if he hadn't fought back, but now they would be all the fiercer for that moment of weakness.

"Ohotolarix," he said. "Rig horse litters for the ones too badly wounded to walk."

The war band grew busy. Isketerol got his horse under control and led it over.

"*That* must have been shadowing me all the time I moved against the *Eagle*," he said bitterly. "That's how they knew my attack was coming. Why haven't they used it to drop death from above before?"

"At a guess, they only have the one. And probably they were saving it for a surprise," Walker said tightly. He clicked the magazine out of the rifle and inserted a fresh one. "It's too low and slow to be a great threat if there's someone with a rifle waiting."

Which means I have to black out Walkerburg against air raids, and keep Cuddy and one of the Garands there. "Oh, but there's payback time coming."

"There he is!"

Swindapa reined in and stood in the stirrups. Beside her Marian lowered her binoculars and passed them across. The Fiernan focused them. Yes, the flying thing had landed, and Toffler lay unmoving in the harness. The air of a summer afternoon enfolded her, warm and sweet with the smells of horse and crushed grass, but she shivered a little.

The party urged their horses into a trot and then a gallop. Even then she enjoyed that a bit; it was like being a bird, flying to the drumbeat of the hooves. The horses blew and stamped as they reined in, and the American physician ran across to the injured man.

"Alive!" he said, and others crowded around to help him

lower the man to a blanket. "Cracked rib, hole in his side—lost a lot of blood."

He looked up, hands busy and red. "Who's Type O?"

Several hands went up, and one of the volunteers dismounted and lay down beside the injured man, baring her arm. Swindapa looked over at Marian, remembering how they'd been joined that way on *Eagle,* after the battle with the Jaguar People. The black woman was frowning at the flying thing, leaning close to examine it.

"Thirty ought six," she said. "Or near enough. One of those Garands Walker had with him. Probably him, then. Smith, Valenz, you take six and stay with the medic and Toffler. Message to forward HQ, we need a wagon, a mechanic, spare parts, and reinforcements. The rest of you, follow me."

She drew the pistol at her side. Swindapa brought up the crossbow that hung at her knee, checking to make sure the quarrel was seated properly, and noticed the others doing the same. They spread out into a line across the fields and cantered slowly forward, examining the ground as they went, checking every hollow and patch of trees. In one small copse they found a body, a woman lying facedown in the litter of oak leaves and acorns, not far from a spring that bubbled slowly out of a moss-lined hollow.

Swindapa dismounted. The body was cool but not stiffened, and there was a wound under the ribs, and blood turning black all down the side and flank. Despite the shade, flies were busy already, walking over drying eyeballs and swarming around the rent flesh. *She would have been very thirsty,* the Fiernan girl thought sadly, with a touch of anger like a bronze gong rung far away. *So she was crawling to the water.*

She closed the staring eyes, then brought her head up sharply at a sound. A *squeaking* sort of sound. . . .

"Wait," she said when Marian motioned impatiently. "Wait."

Casting back and forth, she caught a smell familiar to anyone who'd grown up around infants. She followed it, and another squeaking sound. The baby was swaddled in a pair of wool shawls, hidden in the roots of a half-fallen oak. She opened the bundle, cleaned the infant and her hands with leaves and springwater—it was a girl, she saw—and rewrapped it.

"The mother must have run this far with it," she said to Marian. "It's not hurt, just hungry."

Marian nodded grimly. "You'd better stay here with it, then."

"I will not!" Swindapa said hotly. Then, remembering she was supposed to keep the *discipline:* "Ma'am."

Marian snorted; the Fiernan could see her smile struggling to break free, and wondered again why she kept the lovely thing caged so often. It should fly like a bright bird.

"All right then," she said. "Let's be on the alert, people."

They rode farther. The low smoldering told them the fire had had its way with the hamlet. Swindapa looked down in bewilderment at the dead sheep; somehow they seemed almost as bad as the people. Ravens rose in a protesting storm of black wings as the horses came near, except for a few too busy with their feasting.

"Why . . . why kill like this?" she said.

"Because they were interrupted, at a guess," Marian said, her face like something carved from basalt. "That made them angry. Stevenson, Hamid, Cortelone, scout the enclosure. Everyone else, keep your eyes moving."

They did, but nothing moved. Nothing but the wind drifting scraps of bitter smoke across the sun-faded fields, and the grass, and birds and insects. One of the Americans raised his crossbow and shot a raven perched on a body and trying for an eyeball; it died in a spatter of blood and long glossy feathers, and that made her feel worse. The baby fretted.

"Nobody," the Eagle People soldier called Stevenson said, wiping the back of his hand across his mouth. "Not even the children. They . . . put them all in a hut before they . . ."

Marian nodded. "Let's get going," she said tonelessly. "It's time to put an end to this."

Swindapa let her eyes fall to the wiggling bundle in the crook of her arm. She could scarcely feel the movements, through the armor. *Time and past time,* she thought, as unshed tears burned her eyes. Then: *I'll have to find a nanny goat.*

The baby cried, lonely and hurt and alive.

"Another raid, while we wait here," Maltonr raged.

"How many struck that place?" Alston asked patiently,

looking down over the assembled warriors from her hillside perch. *More than I expected. A good four thousand.*

"Sixty, from the tracks! It was a slaughter!"

"And . . . 'dapa?"

The Fiernan hesitated, looked at them both, and then went on reluctantly: "Five warriors are here, from that place."

"Would five warriors have made a difference against sixty armored fighters of Walker's own band? . . . Well? I asked you a *question*, Maltonr son of Sinsewid."

"No," he said after a long moment, looking aside. "No, they would not."

"They would have *died*, Maltonr, died with the rest to no purpose. But this—" She jerked her head toward the assembly. "This *can* accomplish our purpose and put an end to such things forever. Is that truth?"

"It is truth," he ground out.

"Then let's get on with this."

"Congratulations, Captain," Ian said from her other side. "You've managed to introduce conscription and taxation to the Earth Folk at one fell swoop."

"More like one swell foop," Alston muttered, looking out over the plain. More and more bands of Earth Folk fighters—and would-be fighters—were trickling in. The provisions were coming in, too. "Not really conscription. They're all volunteers."

"Volunteers after you made it plain that the ones who'd joined you would all raid the herds of the ones who hadn't," Ian pointed out. "Thus bankrupting them. All the ones who don't want to go back to farming have to join up."

"Volunteers. And somebody has to feed them. The Grandmothers have always collected this tithe thing."

"For building and maintaining their monuments," he said. "You're handing around the collection plate for the Pentagon. Sorry," he added as she turned to look at him.

The broad-featured black face showed white teeth in a smile. "No offense," she said. Her helmeted head jerked toward the east. "When Walker brings the Sun People at us, they're goin' to come with levies of near every fit man in their tribes. If we don't get some organization into this shambolic crowd, these here'll get ground into hamburger."

"Don't you like my people?" Swindapa said, frowning.

Alston started slightly and turned. " 'Dapa, I like your

people very much. They just need to learn some new things, is all." *She's been saying things like that too often lately.*

Swindapa sighed and looked down from the slight rise. Her expression grew glum. "That is true."

Alston turned again, blinking slightly at the sun that was almost in her eyes. That meant everyone could see *her* clearly, though. The speech ran through her mind, cobbled together in all-night bull sessions with the Arnsteins, Swindapa, a clutch of Fiernan bards and poets who'd provided local symbolism and would spread it far and wide.

"Warriors of the Spear Mark," she began, raising the microphone to her lips. She waited for the gasps to die down as the amplified sound boomed out. "Friends, allies, Earth Folk—this is *your* earth. Eastward lies the enemy, those who burn and destroy, those who come to take all the White Isle from you—this sacred isle, this almost-heaven, this village set about with the palisade of the sea against misfortune and the storms of war . . ."

Half an hour later she licked sweat from her lips, lifting her arms until the rolling cheers died down somewhat, and continued:

"Forward, children of Moon Woman! You fight for your hearths and your families, for the ashes of your ancestors"—luckily the Earth Folk *did* cremate their dead, which meant she didn't have to find a better metaphor than the author of *The Persians*—"and the Wisdoms of your faith. Forward! To the fighting! *Winner takes all!*"

The long slow roar of their voices washed over her like surf. She threw her arms up again in the Fiernan gesture of prayer; and between them was framed the rising moon, just as they'd planned. A growl came from behind the hill, and then Andy Toffler soared over in the repaired ultralight. He'd insisted on flying, and the wound was healing. This time the craft's wings were painted to mimic those of the sacred Owl, messenger and avatar of Moon Woman.

The roar turned to a shuddering mass gasp. "Victory!" she shouted.

CHAPTER TWENTY-THREE

September – October, Year 2 A.E.

"Well, this is it," Alston said.

Christ on a crutch, that's inane, she thought. Her mouth was dry, despite a swig from the canteen, and the morning's bread and meat had settled under her breastbone in a sour lump. *Too much. Too* fuckin' *much depends on this.*

The command group was placed on a slight rise behind the long ridge. All along the reverse slope stood—and squatted and sat and lay—the Fiernans and Americans. *Five thousand four hundred thirty-three as of this morning.* There might be a hundred more or less by now; the locals still had a tendency to come and go as they pleased. About a thousand of the Fiernans in Nantucket-made armor, and the rest in their native linen tunics; at least now everyone had a short sword and knife, the spears all had steel heads, and the archers had steel arrowheads and the slingers lead shot.

Scattered clouds went by above, pushed by a freshening wind out of the west cool enough to make sweat feel a bit chilly. Patches of shade went with it, throwing the host into shadow. When they passed, sunlight glinted on edged metal, on unit banners, on the crouching shapes of catapults and flamethrowers. Her eyes flicked back and forth to make sure; reserves, solid blocks of archers and spearmen, heliographs and mounted messengers ready . . .

Up. Her gaze came up, and fixed on the host of the easterners, bending slightly to look through the eyepieces of the big tripod-mounted binoculars. *About our numbers—probably a little less.* That confirmed what Toffler and the scouts and spies had estimated.

Turning the traversing wheel put blurring jumps between

moments of clear vision. Ordinary herdsmen-warriors in leather kilt and tunic, their hair twisted into braids . . . but most of the spearheads and axes flashed with the cold brightness of steel, not the ruddy warmth of bronze. Here a grizzled patriarch came trotting, ax over his shoulder and six sons around him, from a solid bearded family man down to a fresh-faced youth barely old enough to raise a fuzz. There an iron-armored chief in a chariot bright with paint and bronze and gold, throwing up his spear and kissing it, laughing as his stocky ponies pranced in their bedizened harness. Here, there, thousands upon thousands of them, coming to battle as eagerly as to their bridal nights. A haze of dust marked their coming, stretching from south to north nearly a mile; and all along it light sparkled and broke and glittered on point and edge, rippling like a field of stars as they marched.

Where . . . ah. There in the center of the enemy, four or five hundred men marching in a solid block, every one of them armored in chain mail, with conical helmets and metal-faced shields. Most of the shields bore the same emblem, a fanged wolf's head in red on a black background. One or two figures in Nantucket-made plate suits, beneath the banner with its wolf's-head flag and aurochs horns. A huge man in a chariot following behind; that must be Daurthunnicar himself, accompanying his son-in-law. Spies and prisoner-of-war interrogations had given them a pretty fair assessment of the enemy command structure.

And behind him, two metal shapes on wheeled carts, each pulled by six horses. *The cannon, dammit.*

"Ian, Doreen," she said. "You'd better get back to the aid station. This isn't goin to be so . . . neat and tidy for long. Not with these armies."

The Arnsteins grinned at her; a little stiffly, but they did it. "No, I think we'll hang around for a while," Doreen said.

Ian nodded. "Priceless opportunity for a historian," he said. "Besides, we've got these shotguns, if worse comes to worst."

Alston nodded, and took a cup from Swindapa's offered hand. "A toast then. Ladies, gentlemen—let's kick their butts back to the Channel!"

She knocked back the whiskey. The Americans in the command staff cheered; so did the Fiernans, as the translators gave them the words. The glasses tinkled and crashed on a rock as they all emptied theirs and threw, and then she motioned to the signaler:

"Phase one, *execute.*"

Flags went up all along the line—Old Glory in the center, flanked by the crescent Moon the Fiernans had chosen when they grasped the concept of a national banner. It was silver on green, the same as the traditional flag of Islam; even then she spared a brief instant's cold inner laughter at how the Muslims would have hated that. *Slave-trading, woman-hating bastards. And better still, odds are you'll never even* exist *here.*

There was a massive rumbling sound, thousands of feet pounding the dry short grass. The front ranks of the allied force crested the hill and went a few steps beyond it; she could see the easterners halting in ragged clumps as they saw the ridgeline before them sprout armed men. Meanwhile all along the allied front warriors were at work, pounding short stakes with iron points at either end into the ground; swine feathers, they'd called them in Europe back in the old days. Planted at a forty-five-degree angle, they were just the right height to catch a horse in the chest. The blocks of archers started planting shafts in the dirt at their feet, ready to hand, and moving their quivers from their backs around to their waists. Alston turned and checked; cartloads of bundled shafts were moving up in the low ground behind the line, ready to replenish as needed.

"What are they doing?" Swindapa asked, nodding toward the enemy. Her voice was a little husky, but calm.

"Maneuvering," Alston said. "Their center's hanging back, flanks are moving."

Head and horns formation, she thought. Evidently she wasn't the only one who'd studied the Zulu Wars. *Damn, and here I get to play the British. Life's little ironies.*

"Messenger. Unit commanders are to repeat the standing orders; when the cannon points at you, fall flat. Keep *lookin'* at it, and when the flash is over, get up again."

That wouldn't work if the other side had more guns . . . *hell, it might not work now with only two.*

The thunder of feet from the enemy host grew, and the squealing of ungreased wooden wheels. The sound drew her eyes over to the right, where the barbarians were moving in.

"Here we go." *Here's where I find out if they were* really *listening to what I said.*

Merenthraur felt his heart swell with pride. Fifty chariots! Fifty chariots followed him. He looked upslope toward the Earther host. Many, many . . . but the sons of long-speared Sky Father were many, too, and the gods fought for them. *Not much of a slope. Smooth grass, not enough hill to really slow a team.*

A swift-footed youth ran up, panting. "The *rahax* commands—take your men, smash those of the foe on the end of their line, there," he said, pointing to the southward. "If you prevail, the host follows, and great will be your reward."

"I hear the word of the *rahax*."

Word of Hwalkarz, in truth, but that is as good. Better. Daurthunnicar was a good *rahax* for the tribe in the old way, but Hwalkarz would make the Iraiina lords of all the earth.

If we win this fight, he reminded himself, looking back. The chariots were ready—Iraiina, and allies. The footmen waited behind. He waved his spear, then blew three blasts on the cowhorn war trumpet.

His knees flexed automatically to take the jerk of the chariot starting forward, moving from a walk to a trot. Earth hammered at his feet. "Keep it slow," he commanded. "No more than a trot to just outside bowshot range, then fast as they'll go."

He pushed back his helmet by the nasal; the new headgear gave more protection than his old bone-strapped leather cap, but you couldn't see as well. The Earthers were standing oddly—in a line, the way Hwalkarz taught. In two lines, one just over the crest of the hill, another behind it on the highest ground. More strangeness; on the edge of their line was a clump all with spears, then a larger one only with bows. Foolishness—a man with a spear had *some* chance of stopping a chariot at close quarters. They were counting on those little spears driven into the earth, but he had a cure for that.

"When we get to flung-spear distance, turn right," he barked to the nephew who drove his chariot. "Take their line at a slant, *so*."

He pointed with a javelin, and blew the cowhorn again. That way the breasts of the horses would take the sides of the poles, not the points—and now their breasts were protected by armor too. *We'll lose some to the arrows,* he knew. Perhaps he'd be killed himself. Well, he had sons and nephews enough to carry on his blood, and Sky Father would greet him in the halls of the sun, perhaps grant him rebirth. That was the way for a man to die, at another warrior's hands, not in his sleeping-straw like a woman. He lifted the javelin, ready to cast. *And the sun will be in their eyes, anyway.*

Nearer. Behind him the tribesmen were snarling, roaring into the hollows of their shields, shaking axes and spears and screaming out threats and the savage war cries of their clans. Now the driver shook out the reins, and the horses rocked into a gallop, the other chariots spreading out on either side of him like the wings of a bird—like the wings of a falcon, stooping on its prey! His heart lifted, but he crouched down slightly and brought his shield forward on the left, ready to protect himself and the driver as well. The javelin cocked back.

The front rank of Fiernans were raising their bows, drawing to the ear . . . but none were shooting! *What is this?* The enemy grew nearer, nearer, nearly close enough to cast. Behind him the charge of the chariots was a groaning thunder, the whoops and shrieks of their drivers the howling of a pack.

Then someone shouted on the slope ahead. Arrows rose into the air—first those of the Earthers he could see, then more, impossibly many and *all at once*, swarming up from the hollow behind the ridge. All headed at *him.* A deep-toned thrumming rose and died, and over it a wailing, whistling sound.

Arrows cracked into his shield, half a dozen of them, driving his crouch down into an almost-squat. Points jammed through sheet steel and leather and wood, glittering on the inside of the curve. Another whacked off the side of his helmet and skittered away. Three hit the driver, sinking feather-deep into his unarmored torso. Too many to count struck in the frame of the chariot, and as many more into the horses that drew it. Merenthraur was far too shocked to react consciously, but a lifetime's training curled him for the impact as the war-car went over at speed. Still something wrenched with blinding pain in his leg as he landed, an explosion of stars in his head and the taste of blood and dust in his open mouth. He spat a tooth and dragged the shield over him as arrows sprouted in the ground all around him, driving into the turf with multiple *shink* sounds.

He could see the iron-tipped rain falling on his men. The chariots were mostly down, or wheeling back. Behind them the footmen faltered and stopped, doing precisely the wrong thing—hesitating between courage and fear. Rage filled Merenthraur; what trick was this? Arrows came at you one at a time, as the archer drew and loosed! Not in a single blasting storm, so thick no man could dodge or shield himself.

Above him a man's voice bellowed. He didn't know the Fiernan Bohulugi language. If he had, the words would still have sounded odd, in an accent like that of his sorcererlord. Three words, shouted over and over again: *draw . . . all together . . . shoot!*

The footmen broke and ran, the few surviving chariots among them. Merenthraur pushed himself to his feet with his shield, shouting incoherently against the piteous squealing of wounded horses. The Fiernan spearmen were rushing out into the wreck of the chariots, points busy. He drew his sword and set himself as two attacked him, one a youth and one with a grown man's beard; his blade chopped a shaft aside, but his knee betrayed him when he tried to follow through with a blow of the shield, and he toppled sideways.

He had just enough time to realize the youth was a woman before the point of her spear grated through his face and into his brain. The sound of splintering bone was the last he ever heard.

"Shit, shit, *shit,*" Alston swore under her breath. "Rapczewicz, you're in charge here until I get back. *Shit!*"

She ran down the slope and flung herself into the saddle, barely conscious of how six months' practice had made that possible—not easy, she realized as she groped for a stirrup and the animal squealed and surged sideways, but possible. Then she was galloping southward along the front of the line, ignoring the cheers, barely conscious of Swindapa's form beside her with the banner in one hand and the butt braced on her stirrup iron.

"Back!" she shouted. "Back, damn you all, *back.*"

The milling chaos that had been the right wing of her line

slowed and stopped. "They flee!" one man shouted, pointing back toward the easterners line. "They run in fear!"

Alston stood in the stirrups, the flag beside her and her height on horseback drawing eyes. "Back! It's a trick—" *not now it isn't, but it might be next time*—"and you'll fight when I tell you, not before. So you swore! Is your oath good?"

Swindapa came in on her heels, in a torrent of Fiernan Bohulugi. Slowly, the general rush stopped and then turned back toward their positions. Just then there was a huge flat *whunk* sound, and a rising screech came at her, the horse rearing as something plowed up the turf not twenty feet away. Alston slugged the reins and forced it trembling back to all fours; it tried to turn in a circle and then subsided. A glance over her shoulder showed the plume of dirty-white gunpowder smoke rising from the enemy line.

"Stay in your positions until you're told!" she shouted, and repeated the message as they cantered back to the original position. "Stay! Hold them!"

"That was a fucking fiasco," Walker muttered, tracking with his binoculars. "Refusing the slope—Alston has me pegged as Napoleon, but I'm not that crazy yet."

She must have the archers standing on the opposite side of that rise, just out of sight. The old trick the British had used in the war against Napoleon's marshals, keeping their infantry out of cannon fire until the last moment.

He went on in Iraiina: "It's not the first blow that settles a fight," he said confidently, and moved over to the cannon. "They may—yes, they're giving us a target. Lay her so."

Two men at the end of the first gun's trail heaved, and the muzzle swiveled around. The gunner turned the elevating screw and stepped aside, poising the linstock and its glowing slow match. Walker raised his glasses again. The Fiernans were swarming forward to the attack.

"Yup, can't stand seeing someone run away . . . Oh, *good*, it's the black bitch herself. There's your aiming point, men—that flag. *Now*."

The crew were practiced enough, but he'd only had enough powder for a few live firings. The massive *whump* sound set horses rearing and men starting in fear down the long ragged line of the Iraiina-led host. He watched the fall of shot and swore softly as the streaming Stars and Stripes came galloping out of the plume of dirt plowed up by the roundshot. Cheering ran along the enemy line as the two riders made their way back along it.

"Reload with ball and hold fire," he said to the cannon crew as they ran their weapon forward; recoil jumped it back every time, of course. Louder: "Sky Father fights for us! Hear His thunder!"

That brought cheers for him, too. The crew went through their routine: stick the bundle of rags on the end of the rammer into the leather bucket, then down the barrel with a quick twist to quench any lingering sparks in a long hiss of steam. Then the cartridge, powder in a dusty linen bag, a wooden sabot, and the iron cannonball.

"They're obviously not going to come to us," he muttered to himself. Well, he wouldn't in Alston's position, either. His army needed to get into the Fiernan Bohulugi lands and get at their supplies, or hunger would force them to disperse in a week or less. He had to attack, to *break* them, and do it soon.

"Father and lord," he said, stepping over to Daurthunnicar's chariot. "Summon the chiefs."

"Aren't they going to, ah, try and take us in the flank or something?" Ian asked.

Alston chuckled without lifting her eyes from the big tripod-mounted binoculars. "They just did, Ian, and it didn't work."

Her head came up. "They're havin' a staff conference, looks like . . . You see," she went on to the scholar, "that sort of thing is easier said than done—flank attacks, indirect approach, blitzkrieg, *elegant* ways of fightin'. Usually happens when one army is a *lot* better than the other—better organized, most often. Or the generals are. Or somebody gets dead lucky. But there's not much room for that here; neither of these armies is what you'd call maneuverable. The Sun People are a bit fiercer, but the Fiernans are fightin' for their homes. No real unit structure on either side, not much cavalry except those chariots, and they're awkward. And I'm not a fool, and neither is Walker, damn him. Worst sort of battle, both sides pretty evenly matched."

"What decides who wins, then?"

"Luck and endurance. There *they* are, and here *we* are, and both of us have a pretty good idea of where all the other side's forces are. So we'll probably just pound and pound and pound at each other, till somebody makes a really bad mistake, or breaks under the strain. We've got some advantage, since defending is easier than attacking."

"Oh," Ian said, shivering slightly. *Last man standing wins.* It didn't sound very pleasant.

He switched his attention back to the enemy. They were stirring, a stream of chariots wheeling away from the central location to points along the line. Bright sunlight flickered and glimmered on the war-cars, gold and bronze and plumes on the horses. *Chiefs,* he realized. Probably called in to hear orders; more likely to listen to them that way than to a low-status messenger, from what he knew of Iraiina customs. Horns sounded, dunting and snarling.

Then the enemy formation stretched at the ends, thinning out. The center of it seethed for a while, then began to move forward in a compact mass many ranks deep. The armored elite in the center was moving in a blunt wedge shield to shield, chanting as they came, a deep rolling male chorus, thousands of voices. *Ha*-ba-da, *Ha*-ba-da, *Ha*-ba-da, endlessly. After a moment they began to punctuate it by beating time on their shields with the shafts of their spears: *BOOM-boom-boom, BOOM-boom-boom.* It was shattering to hear, seemed to take control of his heart and make it thunder to escape from the cage of his ribs. In the middle of the swaying, chanting horde men trundled something on wheels, like a small wagon, covered in tarpaulin.

"Well," he heard Alston mutter, "either he's given up on subtle, or he's bein' more subtle than I can grasp."

Then she rapped out an order. "Ready with the darters. Prepare to execute Phase B, part one. Execute."

Closer, and the enemy on the flanks was moving forward as well. He moistened his lips. Two slamming-door sounds, and the bronze cannon behind the enemy jumped back as they vomited plumes of smoke. A rising, whistling sound and a crash; plumes of earth shot up from the slope in front of the Fiernan position. Not ten yards in front of him it struck again, and several Fiernan were down, some of them screaming. The others closed in as the dead and injured were dragged backward into the shelter of the ridge.

"Not too bad," Alston said quietly. "Come on, boys and girls, hold them, hold, *hold* . . .

"Now!" she said.

Bugles and trumpets blew. The crews of the dart-throwing

engines pushed them up over the crest of the hill and spun
the wheels. *Tunk. Tunk.* Six-foot shafts leaped out toward
the easterner phalanx in long arching curves, seeming to
slow as they gained distance. Ian winced as he saw one
strike, slamming through a shield and the man behind it
and the man behind *him*, like lumps of meat on a shish
kebab. The enemy formation was just close enough to begin
to see faces now, still chanting and pounding, their pace
picking up. The cannon firing in support were aiming at
the dart-casters. A cannonball struck one twenty yards
down the line with an enormous crash of splintering wood
and metal. More screaming came from around it, and bodies were carried away.

Oh, God, make it stop, he thought.

To either side and ahead the massed archers were putting
shafts to their bows; only the first two rows could see the
approaching enemy, but the others behind were taking their
alignment from them. A cannonball struck two of the forward rank as he watched, and they *splashed* backward onto
their comrades. He could see staring eyes and clenched
teeth, but the ranks stayed firm, raising their yew bows
skyward. Marian drew her sword and held it over her head,
marking the time for the central blocks. Officers turned
their eyes to it, raising their own hands or blades to repeat
the signal.

"What a fuckin' waste of courage," she said quietly, looking at the approaching host. "Now!" The blade slashed
downward.

A thousand bows released within a second of each other.
The arrows streaked upward, the points winking at the top
of their arches as the sunlight caught the whetted metal,
then poised for a second and fell. Before they struck, two
more volleys were in the air, whistling.

A hundred yards away, the pounding chant of the enemy
gave way to a long, guttural howling roar that made the
small hairs along his spine struggle to rise under the con-
stricting cloth. Their measured advance broke into a crashing trot, and the rear ranks swept their shields up over their
heads. The arrows came down on them like iron hail. Most
stuck quivering in the shields, or bounced aside from the
tough wood and leather, or glanced from helmets and mail
coats. Many went through, and the marching ranks rippled
and eddied around bodies still or writhing on the ground.

Again and again, a volley falling every six seconds, but the warriors of the Sun People kept coming.

"Forward the spears," Alston said. Drums and trumpets signaled.

Columns trotted forward, up and over the rise, spreading out with a deep-chested shout mixed here and there with the hawk-shrieks of female voices. These were the Fiernans who'd received Nantucket plate-armor suits and a modicum of training in the last few months. A cannon round struck one six-deep file as it breasted the rise, and a whole row went down in wreck. The remainder closed up and followed, fanning out to meet the Sun People in a bristling array of spearpoints.

God, I can smell *it,* he thought—like the aid station after the last battle, but here it was in the open air, shit and blood. *Like any slaughterhouse. God, I may become a vegetarian after this.*

"Open fire, catapults," Alston ordered, her hand clenching on the hilt of her sword.

The second set of machines went into action, throwing arms lobbing globes that trailed smoke. There were four of them; one fell short, trailing fire between the forces. Another overshot, and a splash of orange-red streaked the slope behind the attackers, where arrow-wounded men screamed and tried to crawl out of the path of the sticky jellied gasoline. Two more came down squarely on target, shattering on the upraised shields of the attackers. Men dropped to the ground writhing, or ran tearing and beating at their flesh. The whole phalanx wavered, and then steadied as chiefs shouted and waved their standards.

"Forward!" he could hear them screaming. "Forward with Sky Father! Death-shame for all cowards! Will you turn your backs on *women*? Your ancestors will piss on your spirits!"

The Fiernan spears were ready, but their ranks were thinner—had to be, when so many were archers. The shafts kept falling out of the sky, but soon the foremost enemy would be at handgrips, too close to risk blind fire.

Everything seemed to hesitate for a moment, and then the rhythmic shouting gave way to a long roar, and under it the flat unmusical clang and crash and rattle of metal on metal and wood and leather. The Fiernan ranks swayed back a step under the impact, then another . . . and held. Men gasped and struck, and here and there one would sink down; the front ranks were dropping their spears and drawing shorter weapons, while their comrades thrust over their shoulders. Knives were out, and men were rolling under the feet of others locked shield to shield, stabbing upward. He saw one such take a heel in the face, try to crawl back, and then go down under a half-dozen boots as the line swayed over him and men stamped desperately for footing. Flung spears from the rear ranks of the attackers answered the rain of arrows, and dead men stayed upright in the close press.

Alston was standing like an onyxine statue as she tried to keep the whole long thrashing line of battle in sight, through dust and smoke and confusion. Then something wobbled up out of the enemy ranks, slow enough to be clearly seen—a barrel.

"Down!" she shouted, diving for the earth.

Something jerked Ian's feet out from under him; he went down awkwardly, the air battered out of him through his armor. Something went *bwammp* behind him, and something else went *whrit-whrit-whrit* over his head, hitting something with a sound like a buzz saw going into wet wood. Blood splashed his face. Then there was a larger, softer *whump* from behind him, and he felt heat wash over the back of his neck.

Doreen's hands were fumbling at him. "I'm all right," he gasped, kicking in revulsion at the mangled *something* that lay across his legs. "I'm all right." Which was physically true, he realized, but otherwise a lie. "What *happened*?"

"Gunpowder, barrel full of gunpowder—it landed right on top of the flamethrower and its fuel. Why didn't you get *down,* you idiot? I had to pull on your feet—you could have been *killed*. Meshuggah!" Her voice had a touch of shrillness.

"Oh," he grunted, coming half upright. "Thanks."

He looked back that way and then averted his eyes, wishing he could squeeze out the memory as people braver than he felt tried to haul survivors out of the lake of fire. Alston was on her feet again, listening to a messenger.

"Running?" she said sharply.

The Fiernan messenger grinned. "No, but backing up very fast—that way," he said, pointing. "They don't like our arrows, not as many there have armor, either side."

Alston blinked, looked to her left, to the north, and tried to remember exactly how the ridge curved, and her line with it. "They're backing up to the northeast? Not just east?"

The sound from that direction had altered, a different note to it.

"Yes," he said happily. "Northeast—maybe they want to go home."

"Oh, *shit*," she said. "Rapczewicz! Take over! Ortiz, move the second company to face north, refuse the flank, we've got a disaster brewing. I'm taking the first company and doing what I can. Get to it. *Now*."

She turned and ran down the hill—the horses were gone, they'd been too near where that barrel of powder had landed, and thank the *Lord* Walker didn't seem to have more to spare. One of the reserve companies was waiting there, a company of her precious Americans—troops she · could really rely on to do as they were told. As she ran her mind's eye could paint the picture. The Sun People falling back, Maltonr—he was the senior Fiernan on that end—going whooping in for glory and vengeance, real redhead stuff. Then the enemy turning out in the open where the Fiernan archers couldn't mass their fire, turning the fight into a melee, sweeping back up the ridge and into the rear of her line . . .

Just like Senlac. And Harold Godwinsson led an army of militia from Wessex too, and the Norman commander was named William. God, I know You're an ironist, but isn't this going a bit far?

"Enemy breakthrough," she snapped to Hendriksson. "We're going to contain it." *Or so I hope.* "Follow me."

The Americans formed up smoothly, moving off at the double-quick. Ahead of them was a growing roar.

"Ask me for anything but *time*," Walker quoted angrily to himself, then took his temper in an iron grip.

"No, father and lord," he said to Daurthunnicar. "You must stay here with the last of the *reserves*. I and my hand-fast men will strike the enemy from the rear, and then they will give way. You must strike then, to push them into rout—when they start to run, to flee in terror, then we can slaughter until our arms grow tired. But it must be at the right *time*."

Daurthunnicar hesitated, shifting in his chariot. The

framework creaked; he'd put on a good deal of weight over the last six months. "Honor is with the foremost," he protested. "How can men obey me as high *rahax* if my spear is not red and my ax is still bright?"

Oh, fucking Jesus Christ on a skateboard. "Honor is in *victory*, father and lord," he ground out between clenched teeth. "When all men see your banner sweeping the enemy into flight, honor will be yours."

After a long moment the Iraiina chieftain shifted his eyes, not convinced, but giving way to his son-in-law's superior *mana*. "I hear your word. Go and take the victory, chieftain who shares my blood."

"All *right*," Walker muttered, raising a hand in salute. "Let's *go*."

His eyes were fixed to the north. *Right on target. That Shaumsrix is a smart cookie.* Pretend to run away, take 'em when they got scattered in pursuit, then follow up with a nice brisk attack of your own—the Iraiina had caught on to the idea like it was a religious revelation. Just two things were needed to turn it into the battle-winner it deserved to be.

He turned in the saddle to look at his men. They were gripping their weapons and leaning forward, their longing eyes trained on the great heaving scrimmage up along the crest of the ridge.

"Listen up!" The helmeted faces turned to him. "We're going there—" he pointed northwest—"and we're going to kill them all. Limber up those guns, and keep in good order—any man who breaks ranks, dies like a dog. This is the ax blow that will decide this fight, and I mean to hit hard and straight."

They cheered him, roaring out his name. "Cheer after the victory, not before. Let's go!"

He led off, keeping the horse to a fast walk; the men behind him were on foot, and no matter how fit you were, you started puffing and blowing pretty fast if you tried to run in armor. No use at all getting there with the men too exhausted to fight. The field guns rumbled along behind him, and he grinned at the sound, looking down at a map drawn on deerhide with charcoal held across the horn of his saddle. Most of Alston's army was sheltering on or just behind this long ridge, with a broad smooth stretch of open country just beyond. If he could get the cannon set up there at the north end of the Fiernan line, they'd have enfilade fire right down the whole enemy force. Alston wouldn't have any choice—she'd have to come to *him*. All the men would have to do would be to guard the guns, and when the enemy rushed them . . . well, that was why God and William Walker had invented grapeshot.

The ground ahead was littered with wounded, and he was only a couple of hundred yards from the rear of the Sun People's array as he hurried toward the right flank. Most of the injured here had arrows in them; they were lying and crying for water or help or crawling slowly back toward the host's lines. A few of them tried to grab at the boots of Walker's band as they passed, and were kicked aside. Eastward was a long dry valley, filled with scrub and second growth; they'd trampled paths through it that morning, marching to the battleground.

I'll really have to organize some sort of medical corps someday, he thought. It was wasteful to allow useful fighting men to die unnecessarily. His own band had a horse-drawn ambulance to take their wounded back to Hong.

He bent his head again over the leather map. Just as he did so something went through the air where his head had been, with a flat vicious whiplike *crack.*

Walker's men stopped and milled in puzzlement as their leader's uptime reflexes threw him out of the saddle and flat on the ground. He peered through the nervously moving legs of the quarterhorse and saw a puff of smoke from a clump of bushes two hundred yards away.

"There!" he roared, pointing. "Kill him! *There, you fools!*"

He scrambled upright, gripping at the reins to keep the horse between him and the unseen sniper, reaching over the saddle to grope for the Garand in its saddle scabbard. "Keep still, Bastard," he hissed, but the stallion was rolling its eyes and laying back its ears, spooked by the smell of blood and the noise.

A second later there was another *crack,* this time accompanied by a *ptank* and a tremendous sideways leap-surge of the horse; that knocked Walker flat, still gripping the reins as Bastard reared. An ironshod hoof came down on his shoulder, and he shouted at the hard sharp pain as a thousand pounds of weight shifted for a second onto the thin metal protecting muscle and bone . . . and yielding to the weight. He hammered his right fist into the horse's leg and scrambled upright again, sick and dizzy with the wave

of cold agony washing outward from the wound. All he
could do for a moment was cling gasping to the saddle;
when he tried for the weapon again his fingers found a
splash of still-hot lead across the receiver, and crushed parts
below that.

Anxious hands gripped him. "They've caught the evil
one, lord—are you all right?"

He moved his left arm, snarling at the sudden streaking
fire. "You . . . grab my arm. Ohotolarix, hold me steady.
Get ready. *Pull.*"

They were all familiar with putting a dislocated shoulder
back in action. Walker clenched his teeth; you couldn't
show pain with this gang if you wanted to keep their respect, at least not something this minor. *Minor. Jesus
Christ.* By the time he could move the arm again, two of
his troopers were dragging up a third limp figure. One covered in a net cloak, the cloak stuck all over with twigs and
bunches of grass.

"Here, lord," one of the men said. He held up a rifle.
"This evil one had a death-magic, but weak compared to
yours." The little finger of his left hand was missing, the
stump bound with a leather thong. "All it made was a big
noise and this small hurt, and we speared this one like a
salmon in spawning season."

"Let me have it," Walker said tightly, examining the action. *Oh, that's clever. Westley-Richards, but in flintlock.
Good thing you couldn't make more of these.*

He took the satchel of paper cartridges and the horn of
priming powder and slung them over his own shoulder. The
landscape went gray for a second. *God, I'm not that badly
hurt . . . oh.* A glance upward showed thickening cloud
sliding in from the west, and a welcome coolness in the
breeze.

"Let's get going," he said. Ohotolarix made a stirrup of
his hands to help him into the saddle; the left arm was
mobile, but it would be weeks before it was first-rate again.
"Now! Go, go, go!"

"Halt!" Alston shouted. The false retreat had caught the
Fiernan left well and truly, and they looked thoroughly
smashed. "Fall in beside us! You'll just die if you run!"

Swindapa joined in, but it was probably the sight of the
ordered American ranks that stopped the fugitives. Many

fell in on either side of the Americans, readying bows and spears or snatching up rocks from the ground, gasping as they tried to recover their breath.

Alston looked left and right. The ridge was sharper here to the east, the country flat and open to the west. *They'll come straight down, try to hit us in the rear.* The ground to her right was too steep for easy footing, far too steep for a chariot—chances were they'd avoid it.

"Open order," she said, heeling her horse a dozen paces to the left. She looked upward; it was typical English weather, utterly unpredictable. Right now it looked as if it might rain soon. *Just what we need. Damp bowstrings.*

The first chariot came around the east-trending bend of the ridge just behind the hoof-thunder and axle-squeal herald of its passage, horses galloping with their heads down. She was close enough to see the goggle-eyed look of surprise on the driver and warrior-chief, just before Hendriksson snapped an order and a spray of crossbow bolts hit the two horses. They went down as if their forelegs had been cut out from under them, and the pole that ran between them dug into the dirt and flipped the chariot forward like a giant frying pan. Driver and warrior flew screaming through the air to land with bone-shattering thumps. Behind the chariot came panting a group of fighters on foot; they sensibly took one look and pelted back around the curve.

"Here's where it gets hands-on," Alston said grimly, swinging her leg over the horse's neck and sliding to the ground with a clatter of armor.

"I'm glad I'm with you, Marian," Swindapa said, dismounting and handing the banner to the color party.

Alston touched her shoulder for an instant. "Me too, 'dapa." Their eyes met. *But I'd rather we were both back home, lying in front of the fire and making love.* The thought passed without need for words.

She reached over her left shoulder and drew the *katana,* drawing a deep breath and then letting it out slowly, pushing worry and confusion with it, letting the first three-deep file of the reserve company trot past her.

"Runner," she said calmly. "Message to Commander Rapczewicz. I need some archers here, and backup on my left; also a catapult. Lieutenant Commander Hendriksson, we'll advance at marching pace from here. You have tactical command."

The high ground swung away to her right. This time the enemy came in mass, two hundred of them at least. They all seemed to have iron weapons, though; quite a few had helmets, and there was a scattering of the chain-mail suits. The chiefs dismounted from their chariots, sending them to the rear—that was one of their standard tactics, and it meant they were planning on a serious fight. For a moment men milled around their lords, shaking their weapons and shouting. A couple of the iron-suited leaders drew their swords and threw the sheaths away; if that meant what she thought it did . . .

The cowhorn trumpets blatted, and the mass of kilted clansmen howled and began to trot forward, their yelps rising into a screaming chorus as they broke into a headlong rush.

"Company . . . *halt*," Hendriksson barked. "Spears . . . *down*." The points came into line, the crossbows spread out like wings on either side, pointing a little forward as if they were the mouth of a funnel.

"First rank . . . *fire.*"

WHUNG.

"Reload! Second rank . . . *fire.*"

WHUNG.

The steady sleet of bolts shook the easterners' charge, but it couldn't stop it. Alston could see the set contorted faces of the clansmen, a glare of exaltation like the homicidal equivalent of a Holy Roller's trance. She spared a glance for the Nantucket troops; faces set and hard, teeth clenched between the covering cheekguards, tiny shifts as they braced themselves for the impact.

WHUNG. WHUNG. WHUNG.

A sleet of flung spears and axes came in the last second. Americans went down, still or kicking, and their comrades closed ranks over them; metal rattled off metal with a discordant clatter. A long slithering rasp went on either side as the crossbowmen slung their weapons, swung their bucklers around, and drew the short swords at their right hips with a snapping flex of the wrist. *They feel sound,* she thought. Something down in the gut told her; some intangible border had been crossed, in the months of marching and skirmishing and drilling. These were veterans now.

So am I, I suppose, she thought with mild surprise. *Which doesn't mean we can't get wiped out.*

"Fair fights are for suckers," she muttered. Circumstances seemed to have forced her into one. "This way!" she said aloud, moving off to the left where the barbarians might overlap the American line.

That put her and the dozen in the color guard party behind the left-flank crossbows—fighting at close quarters, now. She saw an American sink his *gladius* into a tribesman's belly with the short upward gutting stroke he'd been taught, then stagger back as a tomahawk slammed into the side of his helmet. A relief from the second rank stepped forward into the hole, stooping and slamming the edge of her shield into the axman's foot while he was off-balance and then into the side of his head as he bent in uncontrollable reflex.

"Give 'em the Ginsu!" she shouted, crouching and taking her place in line. The half-stunned American fell into the second rank shaking his head and wobbling a bit as he recovered from the blow.

"Here's our part of the job," Alston said as they came to the end of the line.

A man in a mail hauberk was leading a dozen warriors at the vulnerable end of the ranks, where two Americans were fighting back to back. He yelled frustration as the dozen swords of the color guard swung into place and blocked him.

Beside her Alston heard Swindapa gasp. *"Shaumsrix!"* she screamed.

That's a name—an Iraiina name—wait a minute, wasn't that the one who she said—

"Remember me, Shaumsrix!" the Fiernan girl shrieked.

The Iraiina turned, rattlesnake-swift. His spear lanced out. Swindapa's *katana* was in *jodan no kame,* up and to the right. It snapped downward, slashing through the tough ashwood just behind the iron wire that bound the shaft for a foot behind the head. The metal spun and tinkled away; his shield boomed under her second stroke.

"Remember me, Shaumsrix! Remember the Earther girl!"

"Oh, hell, 'dapa—forward! Forward!"

Shaumsrix was staggering back on his heels as the *katana* blurred at him, backed by a cold, bitter rage. Alston moved by the girl's side, let a knee relax as an ax flashed by to bury itself in the turf, took the wielder's arm off just below the elbow, whipped the long sword up to knock aside a spear. The Iraiina chief had recovered his balance and unshipped his ax, a copy in steel of the old charioteer's weapon. His sworn men closed in on either side, meeting the Americans of the color guard shield to shield.

Alston lunged one-handed, using the *katana* like a saber. The man on the end of the point hadn't been expecting that, and he ran right into it. The blade sank in, then stuck in bone. The warrior folded around it, and someone stabbed at her from behind him. She ignored it, ducking her head, and the spearpoint slid from the helmet as she put a boot on the man's body and *pushed*. The layer-forged steel sliced through a rib and came free; the sprattling corpse tripped the spearman behind.

She ignored him as well, as he struggled to regain his balance. Instead she let her right knee go slack and turned as she went down, striking hard and level and drawing the cut. It slashed through the tough leather binding around the Iraiina chieftain's left calf. *Fair fights are for suckers,* especially *if you're a woman,* she thought, and brought her sword up to guard position just in time to deflect another ax. The impact jarred through her wrists, but beside her Swindapa screamed again:

"Remember!" and lunged two-handed past the chieftain's falling guard. The point jammed into the bone of his face. She ripped it free, and he fell to his hands and knees, helmet rolling free. The next stroke went across his neck.

Wailing, the fallen man's followers cast themselves on the American points, and died, while Alston and her companion stood guarding each other. She saw sanity seep back into the Fiernan's eyes.

Thack. A spearman fell backward, his face a red mass. Alston's head swiveled. Fiernans were running along the ridge to the east, nimble on the steep turf. One of the first was a slinger; he waved his leather thong over his head at her, and then reached into his pouch for another round. More archers and slingers came behind him, moving forward and shooting over the Americans' heads, into the growing mass of easterner warriors jammed against their line. Alston could feel the pressure on that line waver as the shafts and lead bullets whistled into them. Spear-armed Fiernans were trotting up as well, fanning out on the open flank of the Nantucketer force.

Alston spat to clear her mouth of gummy saliva and reached for her canteen. The motion froze as she recognized the banner behind the enemy mass. *Walker.* Walker, and his special goon squad, marching in step and in line. And behind them, the cannon.

"Christ," she whispered. *We can't run. They'd be all over us like flies on cowshit.* And if they stood . . .

Even at a hundred yards' distance, the muzzles of the cannon looked big enough to swallow her head as the crews unhitched them and wheeled them around.

William Walker laughed, despite the nagging ache in his shoulder. "Oh, how *surprised* you must be, Skipper," he chuckled. "What a sad end to the day. How fucking *tragic.* Christ, this feels *even better* than I thought it would!"

He turned to his men, hand around the stock of the rifle, letting it fall across his shoulder. "We'll move off to the right, away from the ridge," he said. "When they break, we'll move in and take a new place for the guns. And get those fools ahead of us out of the way!"

The gun crews were busy, grunting with effort as they rammed the grapeshot down the barrels of the bronze fieldpieces. His men were drawing off to one side with him, except for the ones he'd sent forward to get the tribal levy out of the way—it was tempting to just fire anyway, but that would be *really* bad politics. He chuckled again at the thought.

It was never easy to get the Sun People fighting men to give way, but they'd all acquired a healthy superstitious dread of gunpowder weapons. A minute, and they were backing away from the American line; then they turned and ran, to get out of crossbow range as fast as they could. The Nantucketers didn't fire, although the growing mass of Fiernan archers and whatnot up on the slope to his left did. The retreating warriors halted behind the guns, panting and glaring. Walker called one of the chiefs over.

"Take some of your men and put them right behind the guns," he said. "Men not afraid to hear a loud noise and see their enemies slain. My crews will need help pushing them forward after each few lightning bolts. I and my sworn men will go there"—he pointed to the right—"to attack when the foe runs. When we do, your men will push the guns forward quickly."

That way they could move down the ridge in bounds, and it wouldn't take too many forward leaps before the whole Nantucketer-Fiernan army disintegrated; they were still at it hammer-and-tongs with the Sun People force attacking their front.

He walked over to where Ohotolarix waited. That put him nearly three hundred feet away from the guns, and to their side—a perfect vantage point. He laughed again as the Americans ahead went flat, and the linstock came down on the first cannon's touchhole.

BAMMMMMM. A long plume of off-white smoke, and the gun leaped back.

Screams up ahead, as shot tore into the backs of the prone Americans—fewer hit than if they'd been standing up, but enough, enough. The crew leaped to reload, the second gun waiting until they were halfway through.

"Lord," Ohotolarix said, tugging at his arm—the sound one, fortunately. "Lord, isn't that the fire-dropper?"

Walker's head came up. *The ultralight.* He snarled and unslung the flintlock, thumbing back the hammer, then cursed as his left arm wobbled a little. "You," he said to one of his men. "I'm going to brace this on your shoulder. *Don't* move, or I'll turn you over to Hong."

He smiled a little, to show that it was a joke . . . but the man went pale anyway. *Control your breathing,* he told himself. *This thing's got good sights, and he probably can't hit anything with those bombs anyway—no real bombsight, he'll have to go by fast or I'll get him. God* damn, *I wish I had the Garand. Breathe in. Breathe out.*

He waited. The arrow shape grew, coming in straight and level. *Fool.* He adjusted the Mauser-style sights and led it off, the way he would a flying duck. *Squeeze gently . . .*

Crack. The ultralight wobbled, nearly heeled over into the ridge.

Walker threw his hands into the task, reloading, pushing with his thumb until the wad went forward, slapping down the slide, cocking the hammer, and priming the pan. When he looked up he almost lost the target, because the aircraft *hadn't* pulled up into the shallow arc he'd anticipated.

"What's the crazy bastard—no, you idiot, pull up, pull up—"

Crack. He thought he'd hit this time too, but it didn't matter, the kamikaze fool was going to— *What did I do to deserve this? Why's an American ready to do* this *to me, for Christ's sake?* he thought, helpless resentment paralyzing him for an instant. Then:

"Oh, Jesus, the ammo in the limbers with the cannon, there's better than a hundred rounds. Down, down, everybody *down*."

He threw himself to the earth. It said much for the discipline he'd imposed that more than half obeyed without even pausing to think. Walker felt the earth rise and smash him in the face like an enemy's fist. When he rose, there was nothing left but a crater, and his dulled ears heard the screams of the survivors running or crawling away from its fringes.

"Lord, lord, what shall we do?" someone was asking.

William Walker drew himself up, climbing to his knees and then his feet, spitting blood and ignoring the ringing in his ears. A quick glance showed him the Americans and Fiernans were almost as stunned, but that wouldn't last. And Bastard . . . for a wonder, Bastard wasn't far away. He fumbled his canteen free and croaked:

"Get me the horse." He groped inside for the handset, and clicked it on.

"Walkerburg, come in. Come in, Walkerburg."

"Here, boss."

"Operation Bugout, Cuddy," Walker said into the microphone.

"Ah . . . roger, boss."

Walker grinned mirthlessly at the note he caught. "And remember, Cuddy—I'm the one who knows the rendezvous point."

"Sure, boss. See you on the road. Out."

Walker turned to his native followers: "I mean to leave this land and cross the water, seeking a new kingdom. Who among you comes with me?" he said harshly, his voice hoarse and throat sore.

The men before him were fewer, but they gave a low growl at his words.

"Lord, we are your handfast men," Ohotolarix said, a note of protest in his voice. "We have eaten from your board, taken weapons from your hands, our blood is sworn for yours. Lead us anywhere—even to the Cold Lands beyond the sunset and the grave."

"Right," he replied. *Touching, you fools.* "This battle is

lost. Now those who would follow me, follow. We'll have to fight to do it."

Slowly, wearily, he began to climb aboard the horse. They just *might* make it off the field before the enemy caught them—Daurthunnicar was still there with the reserves, after all.

"Orders? Ma'am, orders?"

Marian Alston shook her head in wonder. "The poor brave bastard," she whispered.

"Orders, ma'am?"

That brought her back to herself. She looked northward; the surviving enemy were running as fast as their feet could take them. "North, and then we do to them what they were going to do to us. Runner! Notify Commander Rapczewicz that the enemy is broken on this flank and I'm swinging in on them. Commit the reserves—general advance, and pursuit when they break."

The Americans were climbing to their feet, gazing in an awe almost as great as their allies'. "Hard pounding, this," Alston murmured under her breath. A chilly feeling of purpose filled her. "We shall see who pounds the hardest."

"I thought . . . I thought vengeance would feel better," Swindapa said quietly, looking at the mound of dead. "But I just feel . . . like it's over."

Rain clouds scudded across the low plain, dimming it even more than the early-autumn twilight. The battle was breaking up into clumps of men who stumbled with fatigue, blundering into each other and hacking in a weary frenzy. Bands of the Earth Folk and their American allies pursued easterners. Some fled in blind panic, wailing; others stood shield to shield and retreated toward the woods to the southeast. The wounded screamed and moaned, calling for their friends; those farther gone toward the waiting darkness called for their mothers, whether they were Sun People, Fuinan, or Nantucketer. Thrashing around the wreckage of chariots, horses added their louder note to the agony that sounded across trampled stubble and muddy pasture. The chill air kept the smell down, a sickly sewer stink under the whetted wind.

"So this is war," Swindapa said, her voice hoarse and

quiet. "O Moon Woman, what have we earth dwellers done, that we deserve each other?"

Alston braced herself erect and reached for the water bottle at her belt. It still held a little; she raised it, then saw how it—and her whole arm, and the front of her armor—were splashed with red. Blood, and bits of . . . matter, and hair. She drank regardless, and handed the bottle to her friend.

"I'm afraid it is," she said gently. *The most disturbing thing about it is how numb I feel,* she thought. Only a faint generalized nausea. . . .

She looked around. A dozen of the reserve were still with her, and the banner. "It isn't over yet," she said. "We have to make sure. If too many get away, we may have to do this all over again."

Swindapa shuddered and closed her eyes for a second. Tears had worn streaks down through the blood and dirt on her cheeks, but the cerulean eyes were steady. She nodded.

They formed up and moved across the muddy plain, collecting stragglers as they went. The ground rolled, hiding one band from the next; in a few minutes they were away from the spindrift of bodies that marked where the opposing hosts had met. "This is about as far—"

Alston stopped. The group that came over the slight rise was unquestionably enemy; several on horseback, many others in leather kilts and jerkins. They were still in fairly good order, and they outnumbered her own band by about three to one; sixty of them, say. A number were in Nantucketer armor; surviving members of Walker's traitors . . . *Thank you, God. That's Walker himself.*

"Saunders," she said to the only one of the command group still leading a horse. "We need some help, and we need it fast. Go."

The cadet threw herself across the back of the shaggy pony and drummed her heels into its flanks. A horseman from the enemy group began to pursue, then turned back at a shouted order. She spared a moment to touch hands with Swindapa as the little group of allied warriors spread out into a line and moved to cut the easterners off from the forest.

"Can we hold them?" Swindapa asked. She leaned her sword against her armored thigh for a moment, clenching and unclenching each hand and shaking out her wrists.

"They outnumber us, but they've been beaten and run once," Alston said. "On the other hand, we're between them and safety. We'll see." She paused. "By the way, I love you."

"Me too," Swindapa said. Her face was radiant for an instant through dirt and weariness. It changed, clenching in. "Here they come."

"Halt!" Alston called, when they came in earshot. "Lay down your weapons and you won't be harmed."

Alston ground her teeth slightly as she saw the familiar boyish grin . . . although it looked more twisted now. Walker himself looked older, a little thinner in the face.

"What, even me, Skipper?" he gibed.

"You get a rope around your neck," Alston replied.

"*Not* interested," he replied jauntily. "How's this—you get out of *our* way, right now, and I'll let you and your squeeze there live."

His hand began to creep toward the rifle at his knee. *Oh, damn,* she thought, taking a closer look. It was the Island-made flintlock. *Androwski must be dead. Dammit to* hell.

She blinked, rigid in shock for a second. How to delay them, how, how—

"I challenge you," she said—in Iraiina. The men behind Walker were mostly locals, all from the Sun People. "If you have the courage, meet me blade to blade and let the gods decide between us."

Her smile was cruel as she saw his face whiten. *Gotcha,* she thought. He had to keep these men with him if he wanted to get out alive—and if he refused a challenge to single combat, they'd turn on him like wolves on a crippled pack leader. *Particularly a challenge from a woman.* There was a certain satisfaction to catching him out this way.

Neither of them wasted time on words after that. Walker swung down, murmured a few orders to the men around his horse, and walked forward drawing his sword. Alston swung hers in a few practice arcs to loosen the arm muscles and came to meet him at the same measured pace. *I'm tired. I'm better with the sword—ought to be, lots more training—he's stronger and younger and has the reach on me. And he's . . . ahhh, favorin' the left arm, by God. Now let's do it, woman. Empty the mind. Don't think, just* do.

The *katana* came up to *chudan no kame,* the middle guard position. Alston let the breath slide out through half-open lips, felt her attention focus down to the man alone, hands and eyes and blade and feet. In a way this was home-like, like a *kenjutsu* match in the dojo back by the Bay, even the style of the armor. *Throat, waist, hips, underarm, inside of the thigh, face,* she remembered. Bad habits had crept in from fighting near-naked opponents.

Now. Walker cut, smooth and very fast . . . but there was a tiny grimace, a tensing, first. She parried, contact on the flat—you never parried edge to edge. A long musical *scring* sound and they were circling again, the tips of their blades almost crossing.

Again. Again. *Hard attacking style,* Alston thought dis-passionately. *He likes overarm strikes.* Safer for him, with his longer reach. A bit of a tremor in her arms, but just as much in his—whatever that injury to his left was, it must be hurting him badly. Good. You took what was offered and used it.

Victory is achieved in the heiho *of conflict by ascertaining the rhythm of each opponent, by attacking with a rhythm not anticipated by the opponent, and by the use of knowledge of the rhythm of the abstract.*

"Very well, Master Musashi," she murmured, trancelike. Just words. You had to *do*.

She lunged forward with a two-handed stab, cutting edge up—very difficult to counter, since you exposed the wrists. He jerked his torso backward from the waist and snapped his blade across and down. She followed with an attack, overarm, the pear-splitter. The response to *that* was automatic . . . but it put the strain of holding the block on your left arm as the swords clashed and slid and locked at the guards.

They stood *corps à corps,* and his arm began to buckle. Another leap back, and she stepped in, the last thing he expected, leaving her vulnerable to his greater weight and strength . . . and able to hammer the pommel of her sword two-handed into his arm, six inches above the elbow.

Walker screamed, as much rage as pain, as his left hand spasmed open on the long hilt of the *katana* Martins had forged for him. Momentum spun him half around, setting the sight path for her stroke. The sword seemed to float along the line of its own volition, angling up and to the right—under the flared brim of his helmet, his first-model helmet without the hinged cheek guards she'd had added

after the Olmec war. The move had a dreamy slow-motion
inevitability, even as her breath came out in a rasping *kia*
to add force to the blow.

So did his response, dropping the sword, punching out
with the bladed fingers of his right hand. Mail coif and
padding took some of it, but the impact threw her off
enough that she felt her blade grate glancingly on bone
instead of sinking into the soft flesh under the jaw. Walker
fell backward as her sword flew free trailing a line of red
droplets. She was down in the dirt, choking, trying to suck
air through her impacted larynx, trying and failing.

A voice, in the Sun People's tongue: *"Save the chief!
Save him, Hwalkarz's men!"*

Vision flickered. Americans driving forward past her. Walker's native guards throwing themselves onto the points, selling
their lives for time with furious gallantry as others of their
band dragged away the man whose salt they had taken. Gray-
ness closing in around her vision as Swindapa knelt above
her, hands scrambling under the coif, thumbs pressing on either side of the dented section of cartilage. A *pop* and a
shooting pain, and unbelievable fainting relief as air flooded
back into her lungs. Then the pain hit, enough to bring a
breathless scream. Blood thundered behind her eyes, turning
the rain-misted landscape reddish.

The power of will could substitute for strength. Her right
hand scrabbled at her hip and pulled the Beretta; Walker
wasn't ten paces away.

A shadow loomed over them both, the bleeding figure
of one of Walker's troopers, his ax raised in both hands
over Swindapa's neck. An instant to alter the point of aim,
and the man's kneecap exploded into ruin. A crushing
weight fell—two bodies on top of hers. She dropped the
pistol and locked her fingers into the man's windpipe. He
drew his knife and stabbed clumsily, wheezing; Swindapa
grabbed the flailing arm.

Alston poured herself into the gripping hand. Fingers
sank in behind the windpipe as awareness faded, and with
the last strength in her she *wrenched*. There was a scream
from very far away, and a warm soft falling.

CHAPTER TWENTY-FOUR

October – November, Year 2 A.E.

"Will the chieftain live?" Ohotolarix said, his voice shaking.

"He'll live," Alice Hong said, completing the bandaging. "Bad scar, and that eye's gone, I'm afraid. Still, it's clean and the stitching was neat if I say so myself," she added, twiddling her fingers before she washed them in the bowl.

The little log surgery-clinic was empty except for the tools she'd just finished using; her assistants were cleaning and packing them as she laid them aside, and she'd been working in her custom-made traveling leathers, black with silver studs. A few more bloodstains wouldn't harm those. She paused to pat Walker's cheek; he was out with the ether, but he'd be awake soon enough. With a nostalgic sigh she looked around the board-and-split-log room, and the cheery little fireplace with its built-in rack for heating irons. *Ah, well, there will be other places,* she thought.

"Take him out to the wagon," she said, picking up her shotgun and slinging it muzzle-down over her back.

It was raining again outside, so she added a hooded cloak as she stepped out the door and watched the warriors carry the litter to the waiting Conestoga. Drops pattered on the veranda above her and on the canvas tilts of the wagons; people were still running around with crates and barrels, loading the last of the stuff they'd stripped out—what hadn't gone with the first caravans, back before that damned battle. *You've got to hand it to Will—he thinks ahead.*

Bill Cuddy came up with the big black ex-cadet. "It's Ygwaina," the young man from Tennessee said. "She's . . . isn't it taking too long? Why doesn't she open her eyes?"

"Bad labor," Hong said absently. "Aneurysm, possibly—it's quite a strain, you know."

"How are we going to move her?" the young man said.

He's actually wringing his hands, *by the Divine Marquis,* Hong thought. She'd never actually seen anyone do that before—but then, she'd been having a *lot* of new experiences lately.

"We aren't, of course," Hong said. "First, it would be too much trouble, and second, it would kill her—if she isn't brain-dead already. I'll leave that local midwife, what's-her-name."

"No—" McAndrews began. Then he heard the soft *snick* of an automatic's slide being pulled back behind him and froze.

Hong brought out the hypodermic from under her cloak and stabbed it through the wool of his jacket, sending the plunger home with her thumb. Two men caught the unconscious form as it slumped; she carefully retrieved the hypodermic and examined it to make sure the needle wasn't bent—no disposables *here*.

"Neat," Cuddy said. "He'll get over it, especially when we're going toward his Egyptians. Dumb bastard."

"Now, now," Hong said. "What about the slaves?"

"The ones we're leaving? Got 'em locked in the *ergastula*, like we have since last week," Cuddy said, beginning to turn away.

Behind him Ekhnonpa was handing her swaddled baby up into the two-wheeled light carriage, and climbing in after it. Martins and his wife were in the one behind; that one was closed, and securely locked. He'd been under guard since the day of the battle, also part of Walker's contingency plan.

"Why not set the *ergastula* on fire as we leave?" Hong said brightly. "It would be sort of . . . appropriate, wouldn't it?"

Cuddy looked at her with wondering distaste; "You just never stop, do you?" he said softly.

"Well, why should I? Live for the moment and enjoy every day, that's my motto, Billy-boy," she said, fluttering her lashes.

"No," he said curtly, and walked toward his horse. Louder, he called: "Let's get going! Now!"

*   *   *

"I . . ." Ian Arnstein swallowed. "Most of them are still alive. Some of them ate . . . well . . ." He spat into the muddy cobblestones of the street.

Oh, God, he thought. He'd been a classical historian, and he'd thought he knew what *latifundium* and *ergastula* meant. *I didn't.* There was no mind left behind their eyes, most of them, as they yammered and cowered away from the light. He met the captain's eyes, and she nodded quietly in perfect understanding.

Marian Alston stood by the neck of her horse, stroking it absently as she looked about the remains of Walkerburg. There was a giant crucifix of whole logs standing in the middle of the square, with iron shackles dangling from the arms.

"You can see the sort of kingdom Walker would have built," she said quietly. "Two days?"

"Two days," Arnstein said. "Nobody knew which way they were going."

"I can guess," she said. "We may be able to catch them at sea." *But Eagle's still halfway across the Atlantic, dammit,* she thought with cold self-reproach. With Isketerol's ships gone, she'd assumed the Tartessian had bugged out for Iberia. *Instead he waited for Walker. He's probably lying up in a marsh somewhere, or the fenland, or the Thames—could be anywhere. Not many places in Britain more than two days' wagon-travel from the sea. Certainly not this one.* Granted she'd been laid up right after the battle, but . . .

Swindapa came out of a hut. There was a squalling bundle in her arms. *Oh, God, not another one . . . why couldn't it be puppies?*

Her smile changed as the Fiernan lifted the baby up close enough to see. That milk-chocolate color was *not* something she'd expected to see in the White Isle. McAndrews's child.

"The mother is dead, in the birthing."

"Well," Alston said after a moment. "There's room on Main Street for the four of us, I suppose."

A chill colder than the rain ran down her spine as Swindapa lowered her eyes silently.

"We've won," Alston rasped into the microphone; her throat still hurt. "The question is, what the hell do I do now?"

"You've done a damn fine job," the chief said, his voice

clear under the crackle of static—very clear, for a transatlantic broadcast with this equipment. "What you should do now is wait a little. From the sound of it, you're not up for much diplomacy."

She leaned back in the canvas chair, conscious mainly of an overwhelming weariness. Fort Pentagon's HQ hut was chilly and drafty in the aftermath of the week's rains, despite the brazier glowing in one corner. *And Swindapa's hardly spoken to me in a week. She turned pale as a ghost when I mentioned going home . . . home, Christ, where is her home. Enough. There's work to do.*

"I got a third of my command killed." She sat silent for a moment. "Christ, Jared, those were kids. They should have been back in the Academy, cramming for exams, with nothing more serious to worry about than zits and their social lives."

"We're none of us where we would have been," the slow Yankee twang said. "Anyway, we've sent some people over on *Eagle* this trip. . . . That conference you arranged still on?"

Well, I said *I was an ass-kicker,* she thought wryly, suppressing a tinge of hurt. *Jared's taking me at my word and sending someone to handle the problems that* aren't *nails. Put the hammer back on the shelf. . . .*

"Right. We've got a lot of *mana* with the Earth Folk now, and the Sun People tribes are too scared not to do what we tell them. They lost a *lot* of their fighting men, especially in the pursuit." She'd tried to keep the Fiernans from slaughtering those who surrendered, but it had cost her a lot of grief and chunks of political prestige.

"All the better," Jared said, a hint of iron in his voice. "If they wanted to stay safe, they shouldn't have started a war. Over."

"Over and out."

She clicked the microphone back onto the radio and sat, silent. It was with a start she saw how much time had gone by, and hauled herself erect. *Eagle* would be arriving with the flood tide; and for appearance's sake, she had to be on hand. Alone. Swindapa was off visiting her relatives again.

"Oh, Christ," she murmured, squeezing her eyes shut for an instant, gripping the edge of the table to the brink of pain. "Get a grip. Now *go*."

*   *   *

Jared Cofflin shook Alston's hand at the bottom of the gangplank.

"Martha and the daughter are along, too," he said, grinning. "Why miss the chance?" He looked around, searching the faces. "Where's Swindapa?"

"Visiting her mother," Alston said neutrally.

Cofflin started to speak and visibly switched gears. "Hope the voice is getting better," he said.

"The medics say it will. Inconvenient as *hell*, let me tell you. If I talk above a whisper for more than a few minutes I'm dumb as a fish. If you'll pardon me, Chief, I have some organizational work. . . ."

He looked after her, then turned to the Arnsteins with raised brows.

Doreen coughed. "Swindapa's people . . . her family . . . they've been after her to stay. She won't talk about it. Marian . . ."

"Damn," he said quietly. "Well, let's get on with it," he said wearily.

He swallowed. The noise from the crowd outside was growing louder, almost a roar until a steady clanging cut through it. He puzzled over that for a second, then realized it was the sound of short swords being slapped against the sheet-steel facings of Nantucketer shields—the American troops reminding the audience of decorum.

"No sense in waiting," he muttered, squaring his shoulders. At least it wasn't raining anymore.

The crowd were standing—some had been sitting, but they stood for him—all around the slopes of the natural bowl. No more than a hundred all told; Spear Chosen of the Fiernans and a clump of Grandmothers to the left, and the Sun Folk chieftains to the right. Most of those were very young or very old, survivors because they'd been noncombatants. They looked at him with sullen, hangdog anger, seeming half naked without their weapons, bright with defiant finery. Along the circular ridge stood the Nantucketer troops, with another two squads on either side of him.

He raised his hand. "Please, sit down," he said. "We have to talk."

The translations echoed him; he forced the distraction from his consciousness, and the feeling of sweat trickling down under his collar. *Christ, the fate of nations, and I have to decide.*

"The war is over," he went on. "Too many have died in it, us"—the translators rendered that as *Eagle People;* he supposed the Americans were stuck with that moniker— "Fiernan Bohulugi, and the eastern tribes. No more."

That got him nods, even from the Sun People. Nobody here had ever experienced war on this scale before.

"We must take council to see that it never happens again, here in the White Isle."

A Spear Chosen shot to his feet, wincing and staggering a little as a bandaged wound on one leg caught him with a spike of pain. "Throw the Sun People back into the sea! They brought nothing but trouble with them. Their tread on the land disturbs its spirits. Let them go, or die if they refuse!"

That brought nods from the left side of the circle, and a sound halfway between a groan and a rising growl from the right. The American pointed to a white-bearded chief.

"My people came here in my father's father's time—" he began.

"Your tribe? One hundred twenty-six years this spring," one of the Grandmothers said dryly. "That is yesterday. Nothing."

The easterner glared at her. "—time out of mind, we have lived here. Here are the graves of our fathers and the holy shaws of our gods, here we plow and sow and herd, here our children are born. This is our home. We will not leave it."

Cofflin nodded. "We *could* expel you all—or kill you all, we and our Earth Folk friends. Do you doubt it?"

The charioteer lords fell silent again, a shuddering stillness. Jared turned to the Americans' allies. "But we will not, unless they force us to it. If you drive these out, others will come—or these again. You can't take away their knowledge of what Walker taught them . . . and Walker himself is still out there, over on the mainland."

Great, now I've got them both *mad at me,* he thought, through the uproar that followed. *And Martha was right.* The Fiernan Bohulugi were lovely people, but they needed what the charioteers had, or some of it.

Eventually the clamor found a voice: "Would you leave them free to attack us again?"

"No," he said. "Not that." He turned to the defeated, raising his hand. "If you are to live in this land, it's by our say-so—our leave," he added, as the translators looked puzzled. "On our terms."

"What terms?"

"First, you must swear by your own gods that you will make no more war on the Earth Folk or on us."

Slow nods; they'd expected that.

"Next, you will make no war on each other, either. Every *teuatha* of Sky Father's children must swear to aid us in punishing any tribe that breaks this pledge. In return, we—the Eagle People—will swear to let nobody"—that was directed at the Fiernan, but tactfully—"attack you, either. You'll be guaranteed safety in the lands you now hold, but no more."

That stunned them. "No war?" one young chief with a peach-fuzz beard said, blinking. There were actual tears in his eyes. "How . . . how will we blood our spears, where will we find honor and bridewealth? Are we to sit in our fathers' houses and never do anything of our own?"

"There are other ways to wealth besides taking it from someone else," Cofflin said. "We'll show you some—new ways of farming, new crafts, and trade. We'll be trading with all of you. And besides that, we're going to be sending more ships out, all over the world. The world is bigger than you can imagine, and a lot of it's dangerous. We'll need marines—guards—more than we can supply. I imagine some of your adventurous young men would find that an acceptable way to gain honor. And wealth."

There were frowns, but the young chief looked interested. So did many of the other younger tribesmen. *No grudges,* Cofflin thought. From what the specialists had gathered, a straight-up fight didn't breed lasting resentment among the Sun People; they considered it the way of nature.

"You ask no tribute?" the older man asked skeptically.

"For ourselves? No," Cofflin said. "But you can't expect to start a fight, lose it, and go scot-free . . . I mean, get away without loss. You attacked the Fiernan Bohulugi without cause. You'll give back any lands you took in the last few years, you'll release all slaves and captives of their people you hold—*with* gifts in compensation—and you'll pay the Earth Folk an indemnity for the harm you caused.

We'll set it; it'll be heavy, but not beyond what you can pay. Consider it a . . . a fee for learning a valuable lesson. Oh, and some of our holy men would like to travel among you and tell you about our beliefs. You don't have to listen, but you won't hinder them, either."

That didn't seem to make much impact compared to the prospect of having to pay indemnity, but it was far more important in the long run. The full-grown warriors might not want to give up their sky-clan of godlets, but he'd bet others in their tribes would—the women, to start with. Nantucket-style Christianity had a lot more to offer them than their own people's faith; and while they might not convert their husbands, they'd certainly have a lot of influence on their sons. He hid his smile. These people weren't sophisticated enough to see through that sort of gambit—hell, he hadn't been either. Martha and Father . . . Prelate Gomez had come up with it between them.

Again, the grumbles came from both sides of the circle. "We've suffered, we've bled at your side! Many of us have lost everything—we've lost homes, fields, flocks, brothers and parents," a voice from the Fiernan ranks called. "What do you have for *us*?"

"You fought and bled for your own land and your families," Cofflin said sharply. Then more gently: "We don't forget our friends.

"You have our word—and everyone in the White Isle knows what the Eagle People's word is, now—that we'll stand by you if you're threatened again. You'll have peace, the first real peace you've had in centuries. Freedom from fear. Isn't that something for the Fiernan Bohulugi?"

"It is a great thing," one of the younger Grandmothers said firmly. "We do not wish to see our sons ever returning on their shields. Moon Woman did not mean mothers to bury their children."

Cofflin nodded. "There's more than that, as well," he said. "You Spear Chosen are great traders—well, there's going to be more trade than you can imagine. As you say, there are many of your people who've lost their homes, lost their kin, in this war. We Eagle People have need of new helpers. We'll welcome them; we'll adopt the orphans, give homes to the displaced. Those who wish can learn our ways and become part of our people. Those who don't will return here with new wealth and new skills, because they'll learn from us. You'll be the first people to learn our arts, and it'll make you rich and strong beyond your dreams."

And Angelica will get that damn settlement on Long Island she's been wanting, he thought. The adults might never fit in really well, but their children would—universal schooling was a wonderful thing.

"Besides that, we'll send skilled folk here to set up new things—mines, forges, water mills." Brand and Leaton thought that with a little technical aid they could just about quadruple the Earth Folk's productivity in a single generation. "Wealth for you, and for us. We'll also send our healers"—*thus ensuring a population explosion, but we can deal with that later*—"and wise folk. Your Grandmothers will learn more of the stars than they ever knew before." *Which will gradually undermine their religion, but sufficient unto the day is the evil or not-so-evil thereof.*

There was a fair bit to recommend the cult of Moon Woman, but it did breed an unhealthily otherworldly attitude, and excessive fatalism—sort of like an astrological Buddhism, as Ian had put it.

The uproar began again; this time it got to the fist-shaking stage and the soldiers had to start thumping their shields again. He sighed. This was going to take a good long while.

He took off his coat and shifted his shoulders, as if settling a load. This was his work, and he was going to by God do it the best he could.

"We're going to need someone to stay here and ride herd on this bunch," he muttered. "Ayup. I can't stay, Martha can't stay, Marian's got too much else to do . . ."

He turned his head and looked at the Arnsteins. Ian raised his hands.

"Now, *wait* a minute, Chief—"

Marian woke to find the bed empty. She ran a hand into the spot where Swindapa had lain; it was still faintly warm. The children were sleeping in the next room, from the sound of it; the wet nurse was with them anyway. She slipped out into the chill and dressed quickly. The sanded log planks were warmer than any tent or the locals' housing, but she'd never felt entirely easy sleeping in the house Walker built. *I'd rather have burned it.* That would be far too wasteful. They'd take what he'd made, and put it to better use.

Or Swindapa will, she thought. *God, God—*

Outside the stars were frosted across the arch of heaven. The full moon was setting, casting a bright glimmer over dew-wet fields past the guards pacing their rounds. She found Swindapa standing in one meadow, her arms raised with palms up, swaying and chanting. The half-song broke down in sobs, and the Fiernan girl covered her face with her hands.

" 'Dapa?" Alston asked softly, touching her shoulder. "Can I help?"

"I want to stay, it's my home, they're my family, my people, they *need* me! I want to stay!"

Alston stood frozen. *I need you too* flashed through her, and her lips clenched on the words. *And I cannot say that, not when you're in pain like this.*

"I want to stay, and I *can't,*" the Fiernan went on, and turned to grip with bruising strength. "You're my life."

Alston wrapped the cloak about both of them; they stood in silence, watching the moon—*the Moon,* she thought—fade below the horizon and the first stars turn pale in the east.

"We'll come back here, again and again," she murmured at last. "Believe me, 'dapa—your people and mine, we'll never be apart, now."

"Yes," the other sighed. Then, later: "I'm cold. Let's go back to bed."

I'm not cold, Alston thought, as they walked hand in hand through the chill wet grass. Birds were piping, fluting greetings to the coming dawn. *Never cold again, I think.* The years stretched ahead, and the work that filled them stoked the glow below her breastbone.

EPILOGUE

March, Year 3 A.E.

Ian Arnstein stepped off the gangway and slung the duffel bag over his shoulder. Nantucket was its chilly, foggy March self this evening, but they'd learned to make a pretty good turtleneck sweater over in the White Isle.

"Home at last," Doreen said. "Praise God, home at last."

They walked up past Easy Street, keeping to the sidewalk—the horses from *Eagle*'s latest shipment were being led up the cobbles, their new horseshoes casting sparks and an iron clangor that echoed back from houses-turned-warehouse, factor's office, chandler's shop. People bustled about as work shut down for the evening; a long blasting steam whistle echoed from one of the new factories.

"Dirty trick, making us ambassadors plenipotentiary," Doreen said.

"Oh, I don't know. The work was sort of fun, actually," Ian answered. Laying the foundations of a country, and who'd have thought he was flying from California into *that* when he left LAX, two years ago almost to the day on his personal world-line.

"Making us stay through the English winter—now *that* was a dirty trick."

Of course, they'd also gotten Walker's mansion as their own in fee simple, and the surviving Iraiina and their new chief had insisted on throwing in a tract of land around it.

"Come on, everyone's waiting—we've got all the gossip since last September to catch up on," Doreen said.

In theory the dinner tonight was supposed to be a surprise anniversary party for them, combined with Event Day and coordinated by radiophone. Doreen wormed it out of Sandy Rapczewicz on the trip back from Fort Pentagon.

He had an uneasy feeling that the chief and Marian had something else in mind, too, like the role he was going to "volunteer" for in this Mediterranean expedition everyone was talking about. *Oh, we're off to see the Pharaoh, the wonderful Pharaoh of . . .*

Ian Arnstein began to laugh as they turned onto Broad, looking around and drawing a deep breath of air pungent with whale oil from the street lanterns, woodsmoke from hearths, the delicious scents of cooking and the not so pleasant but infinitely familiar smells of horses and their by-products.

"What's the joke?"

"That time travel forward can bring you back full circle just as surely as time travel backward," he said, and shook his head at her puzzled frown. "Later. I'm *hungry.*"

They hurried up the street past whalers and fishermen, Indians in blankets and Fiernan Bohulugi Moon Priestesses wrapped in dignity, past kilted Sun People warriors gawking about in wonder, past carts and steam carriages and running whooping children. Some things *didn't* change. They *still* served a mean seafood dinner in the basement restaurant at the John Cofflin House, even in the Bronze Age.